SOCIAL
CREATURE

SOCIAL CREATURE

TARA ISABELLA BURTON

RAVEN BOOKS

LONDON · OXFORD · NEW YORK · NEW DELHI · SYDNEY

RAVEN BOOKS
Bloomsbury Publishing Plc
50 Bedford Square, London, WC1B 3DP, UK

BLOOMSBURY, RAVEN BOOKS and the Raven Books logo are trademarks
of Bloomsbury Publishing Plc

First published in Great Britain 2018

A catalogue record for this book is available from the British Library

ISBN: HB: 978-1-4088-9611-2; TPB: 978-1-4088-9610-5;
eBook: 978-1-4088-9609-9

2 4 6 8 10 9 7 5 3 1

Printed and bound in Great Britain by CPI Group (UK) Ltd, Croydon CR0 4YY

To find out more about our authors and books visit www.bloomsbury.com
and sign up for our newsletters

For Brian—

who has been on this adventure from the beginning

1

THE FIRST PARTY LAVINIA TAKES LOUISE TO, she makes Louise wear one of her dresses.

"I found it on the street," Lavinia says. "It's from the twenties."

Maybe it is.

"Someone just left it there. Can you believe it?"

Louise can't.

"They probably just thought it was trash." She puckers her lips. She puts on lipstick. "And *that* is the problem with people. Nobody understands what things *mean*."

Lavinia fiddles with Louise's collar. Lavinia ties the sash around Louise's waist.

"Anyway, the second I saw it—Christ! I wanted to—oh, I just wanted to *genuflect*, you know? Kiss the ground—do Catholics kiss the ground, or is that just sailors? Anyway, I wanted to put my mouth right there on the sidewalk on somebody's chewed gum and say, like, *thank you, God, for making the world make sense today*."

Lavinia puts powder on Louise's cheeks. Lavinia adds rouge. Lavinia keeps talking.

"Like—it's all so fucking *perfect*, right? Like—somebody's grandmother or whoever, dies in some random brownstone in the East Village nobody's even visited in twenty years and they dump all her shit out into the street and then at sunset—here I am walking across East Ninth Street and I find it. This old woman and I who have never met have these two beautiful, poetic, nights ninety years apart, wearing the exact same dress—oh, Louise, can't you just *smell* it?"

Lavinia shoves the lace in Louise's face.

"You could fall in love," says Lavinia, "wearing a dress like that."

Louise inhales.

"So you know what I did?"

Lavinia gives Louise a beauty mark with her eyebrow pencil.

"I stripped down to my underwear—no, that's a lie; I took my bra off, too. I took off everything and I put on the dress and I left my other one in the street and I walked all night, wearing it, all the way back to the Upper East Side."

Lavinia does Louise's buttons.

Now Lavinia is laughing. "Stick with me long enough," she says, "and I promise—things will just *happen* to you. Like they happen to me."

Lavinia does Louise's hair. At first she tries to do it, like she's done her own: savagely and exuberantly tendriled. But Louise's hair is too flat, and too straight, and so instead Lavinia braids it into a tight, neat bun.

Lavinia puts her hands on Louise's cheeks. She kisses her on the forehead. She roars.

"God," says Lavinia. "You look so beautiful. I can't stand it. I want to kill you. Let's take a picture."

She takes out her phone. She makes it a mirror.

"Let's stand against the peacock feathers," Lavinia says. Louise does.

"Pose."

Louise doesn't know how.

"Oh, please." Lavinia waves the phone. "Everybody knows how to pose. Just, you know: Arch your back a little. Tilt your head. Pretend you're a silent-film star. There. There—no, no, chin down. There."

Lavinia moves Louise's chin. She takes their photo.

"The last one's good," Lavinia says. "We look good. I'm posting it." She turns the phone to Louise. "Which filter do you like?"

Louise doesn't recognize herself.

Her hair is sleek. Her lips are dark. Her cheekbones are high. She's wearing a flapper dress and she has cat's eyes and fake lashes and she looks like she's not even from this century. She looks like she's not even real.

"Let's go with Mayfair. It makes your cheekbones look shiny. Christ—look at you! Look. At. You. You're beautiful."

Lavinia has captioned the photo: alike in indignity.

Louise thinks this is very witty.

Louise thinks: *I am not myself.*

Thank God, Louise thinks. *Thank God.*

They cab it to Chelsea. Lavinia pays.

It's New Year's Eve. Louise has known Lavinia for ten days. They have been the best ten days of her life.

Days don't go like this for Louise.

Louise's days go like this:

She wakes up. She wishes she hasn't.

Chances are: Louise hasn't slept much. She works as a barista at this coffee shop that turns into a wine bar at night, and also writes for this e-commerce site called GlaZam that sells knockoff handbags, and is also an SAT tutor. She sets an alarm for at least three hours before she has to be anywhere, because she lives deep in Sunset Park, a twenty-minute walk from the R, in the same illegal and roach-infested sublet she's been in for almost eight years, and half the time the train breaks down. When they call her, once every couple of months, Louise's parents invariably ask her why she's so stubborn about moving back to New Hampshire, say, where *that nice Virgil Bryce* is a manager at the local bookstore now, and he won't stop asking for her new number. Louise invariably hangs up.

She weighs herself. Louise weighs one hundred fourteen and a half pounds on a period day. She puts on her makeup very carefully. She draws on her brows. She checks her roots. She checks her bank balance (sixty-four dollars, thirty-three cents). She covers up the flaws in her skin.

She looks in the mirror.

Today, she says—out loud (a therapist she had once told her that it's always better to say these things out loud)—*is the first day of the rest of your life.*

She makes herself smile. Her therapist told her to do that, too.

Louise walks the twenty minutes to the subway. She ignores the catcaller who asks her, every morning, how her pussy smells, even though he's probably the only person in the world she interacts with regularly. She spends the ride into Manhattan staring at her reflection in the darkened subway windows. Back when Louise was sure she was going to be a go-down-in-history Great Writer she used to take a notebook and use the commute to write stories, but now she is too tired and also she probably will never be a writer; so she reads trashy *Misandry!* articles on her phone and sometimes watches people (Louise enjoys watching people; she finds it calming; when you spend a lot of time focusing on the things wrong with other people you worry less about everything wrong with you).

Louise goes to work as a barista, or at GlaZam, or to give an SAT lesson.

She likes lessons best. When she speaks with her very carefully cultivated mid-Atlantic accent and puts her very carefully dyed blonde hair into a bun and alludes to the fact that she went to school in Devonshire, New Hampshire, she gets $80 an hour, plus the satisfaction of having fooled somebody. Now if Louise had actually gone to Devonshire Academy, the boarding prep school, and not just the public Devonshire High, she'd get $250, but the kind of parents who can pay $250 are more assiduous in checking these things.

Not that most people ever check these things. When Louise was sixteen, she took to leaving her house early and eating breakfast and dinner at the Academy's dining hall. She made it a whole three months, watching people, before anybody noticed, and even then it was just her mother who found out, and grounded her, and by the time she was allowed out of the house again she'd started AIM-chatting Virgil Bryce, who didn't like it when she went anywhere without him.

Louise finishes work.

She looks in her phone-mirror, a few times, to make sure she's still there. She checks Tinder, even though she hardly responds to anybody she matches with. There was one guy who seemed really feminist online but turned out to practice relationship anarchy; and another who was really into kink in ways that she was never entirely sure were not abusive; and one guy who was really great, actually, but he ghosted her after two months. Sometimes Louise considers going out with somebody new, but this seems like just another thing to potentially fuck up.

Sometimes, if Louise has been paid cash that week, she goes to a really nice bar: on Clinton or Rivington, or on the Upper East Side.

She orders the nicest drink she can afford (Louise can't really afford to be drinking at all, but even Louise deserves nice things, sometimes). She sips her drink very, very slowly. If she doesn't eat dinner (Louise never eats dinner) the alcohol will hit her harder, which is a relief, because when Louise gets drunk she forgets the invariable fact that she is going to fuck everything up one day, if she hasn't already, whether it's because she loses all her jobs at once and gets evicted or because she gains twenty pounds because she is too tired to exercise and then not even the catcaller will want to fuck her or because she'll get throat cancer from all the times she has made herself throw up all her food or because she will get another kind of even rarer and more obscure cancer from all the times she obsessively dyes her hair in a bathroom without ventilation or she will fuck up by unblocking Virgil Bryce on social media or else because she will get into another relationship in which a man who seems nice on Tinder wants to save her, or else to choke her, and she will do whatever he says because the other way to fuck it all up is to die alone.

Louise waits until she sobers up (another very certain way to fuck up is to be a drunk woman alone in New York at night), and then she takes the subway home, and although Louise no longer writes in her notebook, if she is still tipsy enough to feel that the apocalypse is no longer imminent she tells herself that tomorrow, when she is that little bit less tired, she will write a story.

They say if you haven't made it in New York by thirty, you never will.

Louise is twenty-nine.

Lavinia is twenty-three.

This is how they meet:

Lavinia's sister, Cordelia, is sixteen. She's at boarding school in New Hampshire—not Devonshire Academy but one of its rivals. She's home for Christmas break. Their parents live in Paris. Lavinia found one of Louise's SAT TUTOR? AVAILABLE NOW! flyers at The Corner Bookstore on Ninety-third and Madison, which has a free Christmas champagne reception Louise has been crashing for three years, even though she lives so far away, just to drink for free and watch rich, happy families be happy and rich.

"I'm afraid I don't know a damn thing," Lavinia says over the phone. "But Cordy's brilliant. And I know I'll corrupt her—unless somebody else is there to stop me. You know what I mean. A good influence. And anyway she's here for a whole week before she goes to Paris for Christmas and we've watched every single Ingmar Bergman DVD in the house and now I'm all out of ideas to keep her off the streets. I can pay. How much does a person pay for these things? You tell me."

"One fifty an hour," says Louise.

"Done."

"I'll start tonight," Louise says.

Lavinia lives in a floor-through brownstone apartment on Seventy-eighth Street between Park and Lex. When Louise arrives on the stoop, there is opera blaring from an open window, and Lavinia is singing along, off-key, and this is how Louise figures out that Lavinia lives on the second floor without even having to check the buzzer.

Lavinia has flowers in all of her window boxes. All of them are dead.

Lavinia answers the door in a sleeveless black dress made entirely of feathers. Her hair comes down to her waist. It is wild, and coarse, and she has not brushed it in days, but it is the hue of blonde Louise has spent many hours experimenting with drugstore dyes to achieve, only it is natural. She is not tall but she is thin (Louise tries to calculate exactly how thin, but the feathers get in the way), and she fixes her eyes on Louise with such intensity that Louise instinctively takes a step back: half-knocking into a vase filled with dead lilies.

Lavinia doesn't notice.

"Thank God you're here," she says.

Cordelia is sitting at the dining-room table. She is wearing her hair in one long thick braid, coiled and pinned. She doesn't look up from her book.

There are antique hand fans all over the walls. There is a gold-embroidered caftan hanging on a wall, and a powdered wig on the head of a mannequin whose features are drawn in lipstick, and there are several illustrated tarot cards—the High Priestess, the Tower, the Fool—in rusty art nouveau frames on all the surfaces in the room. The walls are all a regal, blinding blue, except for the moldings, which Lavinia has made gold.

Lavinia kisses Louise on both cheeks.

"Make sure she goes to bed by ten," she says, and leaves.

———

"She does that."

Cordelia finally looks up.

"She isn't really that oblivious," she says. "That's just her sense of humor. She thinks it's funny to tease me. And you."

Louise doesn't say anything.

"I'm sorry," says Cordelia. "I started studying already." Her smile twists at the edges.

She makes Louise a pot of tea.

"You can have chocolate-vanilla or you can have hazelnut-cinnamon-pear-cardamom," she says. "Vinny doesn't have any normal tea."

She serves it in an intricately patterned teapot ("It's from Uzbeki-stan," Cordelia says. Louise doesn't know if this is a joke). She sets it down on a tray.

Cordelia forgets a teaspoon, although there is one in the sugar pot, but after the second cup Louise realizes if she stirs the tea it will wet the spoon and then ruin the sugar. If she keeps the spoon dry the sugar will settle in the cup.

Louise sips her tea without any sugar in it. She briefly considers asking for another spoon, but the thought of doing this makes her nervous, and so Louise doesn't say anything at all.

They do SAT words: *What is the difference between* lackluster, laconic, *and* lachrymose? They do math: all the 3-4-5 triangles, sur-face areas of different shapes. Cordelia gets all the questions right.

"I'm going to Yale," Cordelia says, like that's a thing people just decide. "Then I'm going to a pontifical university in Rome for my master's. I'm going to be a nun."

Then: "I'm sorry."

"For what."

"I'm trolling you. I shouldn't. I mean—I do want to be a nun. But even so."

"That's okay," says Louise.

She drinks another cup of sugarless hazelnut-cinnamon-pear-cardamom tea.

"I feel guilty," says Cordelia. "Keeping you here. I don't really need a tutor. Don't feel bad—I mean, you're doing a very good job. Sorry. It's just—I know all this already." She shrugs. "Maybe Vinny really does want you to be my babysitter. Only—she won't be back by ten."

"That's okay," Louise says. "I trust you to make your own bed-time."

"That's not an issue." Cordelia smiles her strange half-smile again. "Vinny's the one with the cash."

Cordelia and Louise sit in silence on the sofa until six in the morning. Cordelia puts on a dressing gown covered in cat hair (there is no cat to be seen) and reads a paperback copy of John Henry Newman's *Apologia Pro Vita Sua*. Louise reads clickbait articles from *Misandry!* on her phone.

She is very tired, but she also needs four hundred fifty dollars more than she needs sleep.

Lavinia comes home at dawn, covered in feathers.

"I'm so terribly, *terribly* sorry," she exclaims. She trips over the threshold. "Of course, I'll pay you for the hours. Every hour. Every one."

She catches her skirt in the door. It rips.

"Christ."

Feathers slice the air as they fall.

"*All my pretty chickens,*" Lavinia cries. She gets on her hands and knees. "*All? What, all my pretty chickens and their dam.*"

"I'll get some water," Cordelia says.

"It's a bad omen." Lavinia has fallen over, now, laughing, with a black feather in her hand. "It means death!"

Louise grabs the trailing feathers from underneath the door.

"No, don't! Let them be!"

Lavinia grabs Louise's wrists; she pulls her in.

"It died a noble death." She hiccups. "This dress—it has been *felled in battle*." Her hair fans out on the floor all the way to the steamer trunk she has made into a coffee table. "And what a battle! Oh— what's your name again?"

"Louise."

"Louise!" Lavinia yanks her wrist again, but joyfully. "Like Lou Salomé. [Louise doesn't know who that is.] Louise! I've had the most wonderful, wonderful night in the world. One of *those* nights. You know?"

Louise smiles politely.

"Don't you?"

Louise hesitates.

"I *believe* in things again, Louise!" Lavinia closes her eyes. "God. And glory. And love and fairy dust—God, I *love* this city."

Cordelia leaves a glass of water on the steamer trunk.

But Lavinia is scrambling to the sofa. She's beatific and dark with glitter, and light with different glitter, and Louise doesn't know what to do or say to make Lavinia like her but she is good at watching people and she knows what they need and so, like she always does, she finds an opening.

"I can fix that, you know."

Lavinia sits up. "Fix what?"

"It's just the hem. I can sew it back on. If you have a needle and thread."

"A needle and thread?" Lavinia looks at Cordelia.

"My room," says Cordelia.

"You can fix it?"

"I mean—unless you don't want me to."

"Don't want you to?" Lavinia gathers up her skirts. "*Lazarus, back from the dead.*" She piles them in her lap. "*I have come to tell thee!*" She flings back her arms. "Oh, I'm so—so!—sorry."

"Don't be," Louise says.

"I know—I know—you must think I'm ridiculous."

"I don't think you're ridiculous."

"Are you sure?"

Louise doesn't know what Lavinia wants her to say.

"I mean—"

Lavinia doesn't even wait.

"You're not judging me?"

"I'm not judging you."

"You're *sure*?"

Louise speaks very slowly. "Yes," she says. "I'm sure."

"It was just—it was only just a few of us. Me and Father Romylos and Gavin—Gavin's a narcissistic sociopath. He told me so, once. One of the nicest people in the world, but technically, a narcissistic sociopath. Anyway, we decided to see if you can break into the Botanic Garden. Apparently you can! Look!"

She shows Louise a photograph. Lavinia and an Orthodox priest and a bald man in a turtleneck are collapsing in a hedgerow.

"Father Romylos is the one in the cassock," she says.

"Are there even any flowers this time of year?" Cordelia has returned with a sewing kit. She hands it to Louise.

"It's my favorite thing in the world, breaking into places! It makes you feel so alive—to be somewhere you're not supposed to be. We got caught, once, had to pay an awful fine at the Central Park Zoo, but other than that! Oh—don't look at me like that."

"Like what?"

Louise is sewing the hem. She hasn't even looked up.

"Like you think I'm horrible!"

"I don't," says Louise.

What she is thinking is this:

Lavinia isn't afraid of anything.

"I'm not drunk, you know," says Lavinia. She sways her hair—her long, coarse, wonderful hair—across Louise's shoulder. "I swear. Do you know what Baudelaire said?"

Louise puts another stitch in the hem.

"Baudelaire said that you should get drunk. On wine. On poetry. On virtue—as you choose. But get drunk."

"Vinny's drunk on virtue," says Cordelia.

Lavinia snorts. "It's only prosecco," she says. "Even Cordy drinks prosecco. Mother makes us."

"I abhor alcohol." Cordelia winks at Louise as she picks stray feathers out of the couch cushions. "It's a vice."

"God, don't you just *hate* her?" Lavinia puts her feet on the steamer trunk. "I bet you don't even believe in God, do you, Cordy? She's kept it up a whole year—can you believe it? Before that she was vegan. And—oh, God, you're *brilliant!*"

She has seen the hem Louise has fixed for her.

"Are you a costumier? I have a friend who's a costumier. She makes eighteenth-century outfits every year for Carnevale in Venice."

"I'm not a costumier."

"But you can sew."

Louise shrugs. "Lots of people can sew."

"Nobody can sew. What else can you do?"

Louise is caught off guard by the question.

"Not a lot."

"Don't lie to me."

"What?"

"You're special. You have the mark of genius on your brow. I could tell—soon as I saw you. And you—you kept vigil with Cordy, didn't you? All night long. *That's* special."

Louise isn't special. She knows this. We know this. She just needs four hundred fifty dollars.

"Are you an actress? You're pretty enough to be an actress."

"I'm not an actress." (Louise is not pretty enough to be an actress.)

"An artist?"

"No."

"Then you're a writer!"

Louise hesitates.

She hesitates because you can't really call yourself a writer when you haven't written anything anyone else likes enough to publish; not when you haven't even written anything you like enough to even ask somebody to publish; not when there are so many failed writers to laugh at in this city. But she hesitates long enough before saying "no" that Lavinia seizes.

"I knew it!" She claps her hands. "I knew it! Of *course* you're a writer. You are a woman of *words*." She scoops up the flash cards: *assuage, assert, assent.* "I shouldn't have doubted you."

"I mean—"

"What have you written?"

"Oh, you know—not a lot. Just a couple of stories and things."

"What are they about?"

Now Louise is fully afraid. "Oh, you know. New York. Girls in New York. The usual stuff. It's dumb."

"Don't be ridiculous!" Lavinia is staring up at her with those bright and blazing eyes. "New York is the greatest city in the world! Of *course* you want to write about it!"

Lavinia's hand is so tight on her wrists and Lavinia is staring at her so intently and blinking so innocently that Louise can't bring herself to let her down.

"You're right," Louise says. "I am a writer."

"I'm *never* wrong!" Lavinia crows. "Cordy says I have a sense about people—I always can sense if a person is going to be interesting. It's like telepathy, but for poetic qualities—it makes things *happen*." She stretches like a cat along the sofa. "I'm a writer, too, you know. I mean—I'm working on a novel, right now. I'm on a sabbatical, actually."

"A sabbatical?"

"From school! That's why I'm here." She shrugs. "Living in squalor, you see. I've taken the year off to finish it. But my problem is I don't have any discipline. I'm not like Cordy. She's so smart." (Cordelia is back at her Newman and doesn't look up.) "Me, I just go to parties." She yawns, long and luxuriant. "Poor Louise," she says, so softly. "I've ruined your night."

The light streams in through the window.

"It's fine," Louise says. "You haven't."

"Your beautiful Friday night. Your beautiful winter Friday—right in the middle of the holiday season, too. You probably had plans. A Christmas party, right? Or a date."

"I didn't have a date."

"What did you plan, then? Before I smashed it all to pieces?"

Louise shrugs.

"I dunno. I was going to go home. Maybe watch some TV."

Truth is, Louise was planning to sleep. Sleep is the most seductive thing she can think of.

"But it's almost *New Year's Eve*!"

"I don't really go out, much."

"But this is *New York*!" Lavinia's eyes are so wide. "And we're in our *twenties*!"

It is expensive to go out. It takes so long to get home. You have to tip for everything. It's too cold. There are puddles in the subway stations. She can't afford a cab.

"Come with me," Lavinia says. "I'll take you to a party!"

"Now?"

"Of course not *now*, silly—what am I, crazy? There's a New Year's Eve party happening at the MacIntyre—it's going to be *wonderful*. It's going to be their best party yet. And I owe you! All those extra hours you stayed—I owe you interest."

"You owe her one-fifty an hour," says Cordelia, from the armchair. "Seven until"—she checks her wristwatch—"seven."

"*Jesus fuck,*" says Lavinia, so violently Louise starts. "I gave all my cash to the busker. He was playing "New York, New York" outside the Bandshell. *We were very tired—we were very merry.*"

She straightens up.

"Now you *have* to come," she says. "If I don't see you again, I won't be able to pay you for tonight."

She smiles so ecstatically.

"I owe you more than money," she says. "I owe you the most beautiful night of your life."

———

This is the first party Lavinia takes Louise to, and the best, and the one Louise will never stop trying to get back to. She goes in Lavinia's dress from the 1920s (it is actually a reproduction from the 1980s, store-bought, but Louise doesn't know this), which she found on the street, because that is the kind of thing that happens to people like Lavinia Williams, all the time.

Now, the MacIntyre Hotel is not a hotel. It's kind of a warehouse and kind of a nightclub, and kind of a performance space, in Chelsea; there are a hundred or so rooms over six floors. Half of them are decorated like a haunted hotel from the Great Depression, but also there's a forest and a whole insane asylum on the top floor where Ophelia goes mad (they also perform *Hamlet,* but they do it without any words), and Louise hears that sometimes actors take you into secret bedrooms or chapels and kiss you on the cheek or on the forehead or on the mouth, but tickets are a hundred dollars each (and that's before you add the coat check, or the ten-dollar ticketing charge), and so Louise has never been herself to verify this.

Some nights, *those nights, one of those nights,* they do special themed costume parties in the space: all-night open-bar kiss-a-stranger-and-see parties where everybody dresses up and lurches through all the labyrinthine interconnected rooms, where every floor has its own sound system and even the bathtubs in the insane asylum are full of people making love.

Louise has never had one of those nights before.

Don't worry. She will.

Here is what's inside the MacIntyre, in the order Louise makes sense of it: red velvet, candles, ostrich feathers, champagne flutes, people with *Happy 2015* glasses, people taking selfies, a woman in a red backless sequined dress singing Peggy Lee's "Is That All There Is?," people taking selfies. Lavinia. A girl in a tuxedo. Marie Antoinette. Someone in a lion tamer uniform. Lavinia.

People in black tie. People who actually own black tie in black tie. People in corsets. People in lingerie. Lavinia.

A man in a cassock ("Don't tell him I told you, but he's actually defrocked"). A woman six feet tall wearing nothing but pasties and feathers with the most grating and New York accent Louise has ever heard ("Her burlesque name is Athena Maidenhead. I don't know her real name"). A bald man in black skinny jeans and a turtleneck who is the only person there not in costume and who doesn't seem to notice ("That's Gavin. He keeps Excel spreadsheets of all the women he dates"). Lavinia.

Lavinia dancing. Lavinia drinking. Lavinia taking so many photographs, pulling Louise in with her, pulling her so close Louise can smell her perfume. It's made for Lavinia, Louise will learn one day soon, at a Chinese hole-in-the-wall over on East Fourth Street, and it smells like lavender and tobacco and fig and pear and everything beautiful in this world.

Peggy Lee sings the line *is that all there is to a fire?* and Louise downs a flute of champagne like it's a pickleback and then she starts to get nervous because when she drinks she stops concentrating as much on not fucking up, and when Louise stops concentrating is when she fucks up most; but Lavinia puts one hand on Louise's waist and uses the other to tilt a bottle of Bombay Sapphire straight into Louise's overflowing mouth, and even though Louise is not stupid and she is so good at watching people and she is so very careful—all the time she is so careful!—the intense pressure of Lavinia's hand on the small of her back makes her think that if the world is going to end, anyway, it might as well end tonight.

"Friends! Romans! Countrymen! Bring me more gin!"

Lavinia. Lavinia. Lavinia.

When Louise lived in New Hampshire, she often imagined that once in New York, she'd go to parties like this.

When she and Virgil Bryce would stand on the railroad bridge, and she would beg him to touch her breasts and he would finally, magnanimously agree, and they would talk about running away together (he wanted to live in Colorado and illustrate manga), and he would remind her how cruel the world was, she would try to explain to him that New York wasn't like anywhere else.

It didn't matter if you weren't that special, she'd say, or even if you weren't pretty, not even by the standards of Devonshire, New Hampshire, as long as you wanted it badly enough. The city would scoop you up and carry you skyward to all your vaulted aspirations; every single party on every single night in that whole, glistening, glaring city would make you feel like you were the only person in the world, and also the most special, and also the most loved.

You and I, of course, we know the truth.

We know how easy it is to fake it. All you need is to keep the lighting low; all you need are a couple of showgirls with cheap feathers superglued to the end of their corsets; all you need is to keep people drinking.

But girls like Louise don't know this. Not yet.

This is the happiest Louise has ever been.

Nine o'clock. Lavinia and Louise and Gavin Mullaney and Father Romylos and Athena Maidenhead and so many other people without names are dancing the Charleston on top of a stage, underneath a chandelier the size of a giraffe. "Are we even allowed to be onstage?" Louise asks, but Lavinia can't hear her over the music. Two aerialists are knotting their bodies together, kicking the crystals in the chandelier, and Athena has abandoned her feathers and there is nothing between her skin and everybody else's sweat except for two pasties and a merkin in the shape of the moon.

"New Year's resolution," Lavinia roars. "Be it resolved: we shall drink life to the lees."

Lavinia's dress has fallen off her shoulder, exposing her breast. She doesn't even care.

Then two hands close over Louise's eyes. Someone kisses her on the neck.

"Guess who," she whispers, into Louise's collarbone.

Louise jerks around so quickly.

The girl is so confused. "But . . ."

"Mimi?" Lavinia has stopped dancing. She isn't smiling.

"Butyourdress." The girl's voice is loud and monotonous and artificial, like she's speaking lines from a high school play. "I thought . . ." She laughs. It is no less artificial, and no less loud. *"Yousee?"* Her smile hangs desperately off her mouth. *"Shetookyourdress!"*

Nobody says anything.

"SorryImlate," she says. *"Therapytookforever. AndthenIcouldntfindmyniceunderwear."*

Nobody reacts to this, either.

"HesaysIhaveneuroticdespair."

The music is so loud. The girl gets closer. She blinks very intently.

"ISAID: HESAYSIHAVENEUROTICDESPAIR."

Nothing. Not even a nod.

"IT'SNOTEVENINTHEDSMYOUKNOW."

Father Romylos lamely nods at her and this is worse, Louise thinks, than if nobody acknowledged her at all.

The worst part is that she's still smiling.

Even when she goes over to Lavinia. Even when Lavinia recoils.

"I've missed you," she says.

The girl gyrates up to Louise.

"I'm me," she says. "Me."

"What?"

"Mimi," she says, like Louise is supposed to know her.

"Oh," says Louise.

Mimi hands her her phone. She knots her arms around Lavinia's neck.

"Take a picture!"

Lavinia isn't smiling.

Mimi snatches the phone back. She scrolls through the photos.

"We look great," she says. "I'm gonna post them all."

Now it's ten. Now the moon is full.

"Promise me something," Lavinia says. They're smoking on the rooftop; they're in a hedgerow or a maze or something full of rose-bushes that are still in bloom despite the frost; Louise has no idea how they got here. "I want to usher 2015 in right. I want things to be as they should be. I want it to be a better year than the last one." She breathes out smoke. "It's got to be." (Nobody else is here, not Mimi nor Gavin nor Father Romylos nor Athena Maidenhead, but Louise doesn't remember saying goodbye to them, either.)

"Of course," Louise says.

"I want to recite poetry with you tonight."

At first Louise thinks Lavinia is joking. But Lavinia is tight-lipped and unsmiling and more serious than Louise has yet seen her.

"Don't let me forget, okay?"

"Okay," Louise says.

"Promise?"

"Yes," Louise says. "I promise."

Louise can't remember any poems.

Lavinia takes a pen out of her purse. She writes it on her arms. MORE POETRY!!! The letters are misshapen. She writes it on Louise's, too.

"There," Lavinia says. "Now we'll remember."

Together they gaze out over the city. There are so many stars, although Louise knows some of them must only be city lights.

"Hey, Louise?" Lavinia's smoke spirals from her lips.

"Yes?"

"What's your New Year's resolution?"

Louise has so many: *eat less lose weight make more money get a better job write a story write that story finally write that fucking story and send it somewhere if you only had the nerve stop reading* Misandry! *at four in the morning when you can't sleep read an actual fucking book sometime maybe maybe write a fucking story.*

"I don't know." (*Be less boring, that's another one.*)

"Come on—you can tell me!"

She says it like she means it. She says it like Louise is safe.

Louise wants to believe her.

"It's stupid," Louise says.

"I bet it isn't! I'll bet you a hundred dollars it isn't." Technically Lavinia owes Louise between four hundred fifty and eighteen hundred dollars, depending on whether or not Louise counts the hours spent with Cordelia waiting for Lavinia to come home, but Louise is no longer counting.

"I want to send one of my stories out. Maybe. If it's good enough."

Louise is so afraid that, having said it, she will have to do it.

"To a magazine?"

"Yes."

"You've never done it before?"

"No. I mean—I have. But not in years."

"I bet they're brilliant," says Lavinia. "I bet they're *genius.* I bet everybody's going to love you."

"Come on, that's not—"

"Don't contradict me. I have a feeling. I *know.*" Lavinia throws back that never-ending hair.

"What's yours?"

Lavinia shakes the last ember out of her cigarette. "Same one I make every year. Same one I'll make every year until I die." She takes a deep and delicious breath. "I want to *live,*" she says. "I mean really, *really,* live. Do you know what Oscar Wilde says?"

Louise doesn't but she knows it was probably witty.

"He says—*I put my talent into my work, but my genius into my life.* That's what I want to do, too. Or maybe you think that's *trite*?" She spits the last word.

"No—no!"

"Probably it is. Fuck it. I don't care. That's what I want."

———

Now it's eleven. Now they're on the dance floor, again; now everybody on the dance floor is kissing everybody else; everybody except Lavinia, who is standing in a spotlight in the center, inviolate, dancing alone.

"Whatawildoutrageousnight."

Mimi's lipstick is smeared. So is her eyeliner.

"Come *on*!" She's tugging at Lavinia's sleeves. She's still speaking in that clipped and amateurish way. "We'll have some champagne!" Mimi cries. "We'll take a selfie!"

Then Louise gets it: what's so uncanny about that strange, pantomime way Mimi is talking.

She's trying to talk like Lavinia.

Lavinia isn't smiling. "We've already taken a selfie."

Mimi is smiling so desperately. "Then we'll take another!"

She pulls herself against Lavinia and holds out the camera. She leaves a sloppy lipstick kiss on her cheek.

"Jesus, Mimi!"

"Shit—my eyes were closed in that one! *Let'stakeanotherokay?*"

She can't keep her hand steady. The photos all come out blurry.

"Okay, we're done here."

"Just one more! One more!"

Mimi keeps pawing at Lavinia, pushing her breasts against her, leaning in to kiss her.

"Just one more, come on!"

She reaches out for Lavinia's sleeve. She tears it.

Louise cannot believe how loud a sound the rip makes.

"For fuck's *sake*, Mimi, don't you know when to fucking leave?"

Lavinia's eyes are terrible.

Mimi's eyes fill with tears. She's still smiling.

"Come on," Mimi keeps whimpering, like a dog. "It's one of those nights. Isn't it? Isn't it?"

"You're drunk, Mimi. Go home."

Mimi does.

An hour later Mimi posts every photo she's taken that night. She tags Lavinia in all of them.

Me and bae, she writes, with a dancing fox emoji and a wiggling Hula-Hoop girl emoji and a cat that rolls over and over doing somersaults, like anybody even says *bae* anymore.

Now the music is so loud you can't hear anybody else unless you're close enough to kiss them; now we are dancing; now we're all standing four abreast on one of the raised columns, seven feet above the crowds, and here Lavinia stands, chin up, shoulders back, like a god.

Now they've lowered the big clock; now everybody's screaming *yes, yes;* now Lavinia's standing and scanning the crowd with those eyes so bright they burn.

"What is it?"

Lavinia doesn't answer her.

"Are you looking for Mimi?"

Lavinia keeps looking, looking, and Louise tries to follow her gaze but she doesn't see anything, just a couple of boys in black tie doing shots she doesn't recognize, and then it is like an electric shock, the way Lavinia digs her nails into Louise's wrist, and Louise asks *what is it* but by now she's so drunk that by the time Lavinia turns back to her Louise forgets what she was asking about in the first place.

Lavinia grabs Louise's shoulders.

"We should jump," Lavinia says.

"What?"

"You. Me. We should do it."

"You want to *crowd-surf*?"

Nobody crowd-surfs. Not in real life.

But this isn't real life.

"What's the worst that can happen?"

It's one minute to midnight.

"Trust me," says Lavinia. "Please."

———

Ten—nine—

Now Louise remembers everything she is afraid of.

She remembers that she doesn't have health insurance and if she breaks a bone she will not be able to afford to fix it and that she has work tomorrow and she can't afford to take off even if she could (*eight*) and she doesn't even know Lavinia that well and shouldn't even trust her because new people generally let you down if they don't do worse and (*seven*) even though Lavinia is looking at her so raptly Lavinia is a stranger and the most surefire way of fucking it up is to open up to another person and (*six*) she cannot afford to be stupid—stupidity, like happiness, is a luxury, but her heart is beating so fast, like it is a hummingbird that will beat out all its breaths (*five*) and die before midnight but for the first time in as long as she can remember Louise is happy, and she will spend all her heartbeats if she has to, if it means feeling like this (*four*) because in the end she only really wants one thing in the world and that is to be loved and (*three, two, one*).

The crowd catches them.

So many people—they bear up her waist and thighs and back and Louise isn't afraid; she knows, *she knows* they will not let her fall; she knows she can trust them, because they are all in this together and they are all so riotously, gloriously drunk and they all want her to stay up as much as she does, because it is a beautiful thing to be up so high, and they all want to be *a part of it.*

Lavinia reaches across the crowd; she is smiling; she is so far away and then she is closer, just a little bit closer, and then she is close enough to grab Louise's hand, and she squeezes it tightly.

Now it's almost dawn.

Everybody has spilled out into the street. They've taken off their heels. Girls walk barefoot on the ice. Taxis are charging a hundred dollars a person just to go to the Upper East Side.

Louise is a little bit sober by now; she can feel the blisters in her shoes, but she is too happy to care. She wraps herself in her coat, which is not elegant enough to justify how flimsy it is, and huddles against the wind, and Lavinia orders an Uber without thinking about it, even though the surge pricing must be insane at this hour.

"Where are we going?"

Lavinia puts a finger to her lips.

"I have a surprise for you."

The cab takes them through the West Village, the Lower East Side, across the Brooklyn Bridge.

"Was it what you wanted?" Lavinia is huddled in an enormous fur coat. She is blinking very intently.

"What?"

"The party. Was it what you wanted?"

"Yes," Louise says. "It was wonderful!"

"Good. I'm glad. I wanted to make you happy."

The cab rolls on past the water.

"Just think," Lavinia says. "You could be home in bed right now."

Louise should be home in bed right now.

"But instead . . ." Lavinia opens the window. The wind whips their faces. "You're going to watch the sun rise. Isn't that wonderful?"

The cab comes to a stop underneath the Ferris wheel: by the bright-painted gates, the freak-show signs, the Cyclone.

The park is closed for the season. But the streetlights illuminate the carousel, the haunted houses, the boardwalk beyond it: beyond that, the waves.

"I wanted to be near water," Lavinia says.

The boardwalk is frozen slick, and so Lavinia uses Louise to steady herself; both of them slip and both of them fall and they skin their knees a little bit, doing it, but there they are.

"At last," Lavinia says.

It is too cold to sit, but they squat, anyway, and huddle together under Lavinia's enormous fur.

Lavinia hands Louise a flask.

"Drink this," she says. "It'll warm you up."

There's whiskey in it—*good* whiskey, that's much too nice to be tippled out of a flask just to keep you warm when you can't feel your hands, but that's Lavinia for you.

"On the *Titanic*, they drank whiskey," Lavinia says. "They were going down with the ship and they saw the end before them and they said *fuck it, we might as well* so they got completely plastered on the finest whiskey, and then once the ship sank it saved them. They were so warm on the inside they didn't feel the cold. They swam all the way to the lifeboats. I think about—all the time—when—oh, your *dress*!"

Lavinia's dress—the one she has been so kind and good and generous enough to entrust to Louise, the one she found on the street in the East Village and which represents beauty and truth and everything good in the world and maybe, even, the existence of God, is in shreds. There are wine stains. There are cigarette holes.

And Louise thinks, *you fucked it up.*

She wasn't careful. She was selfish and thoughtless and she drank too much and she let her guard down—even animals know never to let their guard down—and now Lavinia will turn on her the way she turned on poor, pathetic Mimi, who ripped Lavinia's sleeve. It will be so much worse than before, now that the night has been so good, now that she knows what she's been missing.

Louise tries not to cry, but she is drunk and weak and so of course she can't, and so she starts to sputter tears, and then Lavinia looks at her with astonishment.

"What is it?"

"I'm sorry. God, I'm so sorry—your dress."

"What about it?"

"I ruined it!"

"So?"

Lavinia tosses that long hair of hers. It whips in the wind.

"You had a good night, didn't you?"

"Yes, of course, I—"

"So what's the problem? We can always get another dress."

She says it like it's so easy.

"I told you," Lavinia says. "Things happen around me. The gods will bring us another one."

Louise's tears freeze-dry on her face.

"It's a sacrifice," Lavinia says. "We'll sacrifice to the old gods—we'll put the dress in the water and let the water take it and, oh!"

"What?"

Lavinia shoves her forearm in Louise's face.

MORE POETRY!!! is mostly smudged by now, and really more like MRE PERY!1, but Louise can make it out.

"You almost let me forget! How could you?"

"I—"

"That clinches it."

Lavinia leaps to her feet. She lets the fur fall. She lets her beautiful white dress that makes her look like an angel fall, too. Against the snow she is cold, bitten, naked. Her breasts are blue. Her nipples are purple.

"*Fuck, fuck, fuck!*"

She's hysterical, laughing.

"*Fuckfuckfuckit'ssocold!*"

Louise gapes.

"Come on! Your turn!"

"You want me to—"

Louise is already shaking from the cold, now, under the furs.

"Come on! You have to do it!"

Lavinia's eyes are so wild, so wide. Louise is so cold.

"You *promised*!"

Lavinia extends her trembling, blue-veined hand.

"You *promised*!"

Louise did. So she does.

———

At first she thinks the cold will kill her. It is in the back of her eyes and at the back of her throat and up her nose and all the way down her esophagus, and not even the whiskey can help. If she were on the *Titanic* she would drown. Lavinia takes the dress from the crumpled heap of frost and sand and boardwalk splinterwood at her feet and gathers it up to her breasts and says "Come."

'Tis not too late to seek a newer world.

The thing about Tennyson's "Ulysses" is that everybody knows it. You're not special for knowing it. If you know one poem by Tennyson it's probably that, and if you know one poem, period, there's still a greater-than-fifty-percent chance that it's this one. Lavinia is not special for knowing it (some of it), and Louise is not special either, for having memorized it (all of it) back in Devonshire, nor for whispering it to herself on the railroad bridge, nor for trying so desperately to make Virgil Bryce see that *sail beyond the sunset* were the four most beautiful words in the English language, and if she could not sail then she would, at least, swim. There is no such thing as fate, probably, and it is probably just coincidence. It's probably trite: like Klimt posters, like Mucha, like "The Love Song of J. Alfred Prufrock," like Paris (Louise has never been to Paris).

But Louise has that poem written on her heart, and she is so relieved that Lavinia does, too.

Push off, and sitting well in order smite
The sounding furrows; for my purpose holds
To sail beyond the sunset, and the baths
Of all the western stars, until I die.

Lavinia hurls the dress in the water. It recedes; it comes back: borne up—like a drowned woman—on the waves.

Lavinia and Louise look at each other.

And they're so goddamn cold Louise thinks they will turn into statues, they will turn to ice like Lot's wife (or was that salt? she cannot think) and they will stay there forever, the two of them, hand to hand and breast to breast and foreheads touching and snow on their collarbones, and Louise thinks *thank God, thank God*, because, if they could petrify themselves for all time so that all time was nights like these and never any morning afters, then Louise would gladly give up every other dream she ever had.

They take a selfie of their naked bodies, from the lips down. They use their arms to cover their nipples, because otherwise Instagram will censor it, and so they have two remnants of MORE POETRY!!! across the center of the photo.

"We'll get that tattooed on our arms," Lavinia says.

They are huddled, now, under the fur. Lavinia has put her dress back on. Louise has nothing but a shift, and a useless coat.

"I want to remember this forever," Lavinia says. She can't stop laughing. "Until the day I die."

When somebody says *I will remember this until the day I die,* they usually mean *I had a pretty good time,* or else, just *I want to fuck you.* That poly male feminist Louise dated that time used to say that he'd never forget her; so did the guy who was really into kink (*I'll never forget what you let me do to you, you are so not like other women that way*); so did Virgil Bryce. Even the guy who ghosted her once said, the night he took her for a walk in Prospect Park in summertime, *I'm probably going to leave New York, eventually, but when I do I want to remember nights like this* (that was the night she fucked him).

But Lavinia isn't like other people.

And when, six months from now, Lavinia dies, she will be thinking exactly of this night, and of the stars, and of the sea.

Louise will know this. She will be there.

They walk toward the elevated train.

Lavinia hails a cab.

"Take it," she says. She is smiling. Louise marvels at Lavinia's lipstick, still so dark even after all that champagne. "My coat is warmer than yours."

Louise can't afford a cab.

"It's fine," Louise says. "I'll take the subway."

Lavinia laughs, like this is a joke. "God, you're beautiful," she says. She kisses Louise on both cheeks. "I miss you already."

She throws herself into the cab.

Two minutes later, Louise gets a notification on her phone. Lavinia has posted the photograph of the two of them on Facebook.

She walks ten minutes to the Coney Island Q, because none of the other trains are running, for reasons that passeth all understanding. She doesn't step on the cracks in the sidewalk.

She sits on the subway, shaking in her slip underneath her flimsy coat, with holes in the pockets, that she bought at H&M like four years ago when GlaZam gave her a hundred dollars for a Christmas bonus, tries to avoid eye contact with the man who wanders up and down the subway car in a hospital gown with a medical bracelet on his arm, but everybody else is doing this, too, and you have to watch out for yourself, especially when you're five-foot-five and weigh one hundred fourteen and a half pounds on a period day. She is drunk enough to be sick, and tries not to throw up when two young men get on at Kings Highway with Burger King bags and proceed to noisily chomp on their fries all the way to Atlantic Avenue.

Here Louise has to switch to the R, even though it means doubling back, and some girls who maybe were part of a bachelorette party are screaming and waving their sparklers, and on the R-train platform there's a man standing on a plastic crate prophesying the end of the world.

I hate, I despise your festivals, he is shouting, although nobody is looking at him. He is looking straight at Louise. (*Though ye offer me burnt offerings and your meat offerings, I will not accept them: neither will I regard the peace offerings of your fat beasts.*) At least, Louise thinks he is looking straight at her. (*Take thou away from me the noise of thy songs; for I will not hear the melody of thy viols.*)

Louise gets off the R at Fifty-third Street.

Her heels bleed. There is sand between her toes and it blisters. She keeps her keys between her fingers.

On the corner before her house she sees the man who catcalls her, every day, to and from the subway. He is smoking weed. He is looking at her.

"Hey," he says.

She keeps her head down. She does not look at him.

"Hey, little girl," he says.

Louise does not answer this, either.

"You know it's cold outside?"

She thinks *just keep walking; just keep walking.*

"You know I'd warm you up!"

He is smiling—like this is friendly, like she should be flattered, like this is the nicest thing anybody has ever done for her.

"I'd warm you up, little girl."

He is following her—sauntering, not running, like this is a pleasant stroll, like this is not something that makes her want to scream.

"Don't you want me to warm you up?"

Louise tries so hard not to hear him.

She is so fast, with the key in the door, even though her hands shake. She's had practice.

"Don't flatter yourself," he calls after her, when she has at last made it inside. "I wouldn't fuck a dog like you with a ten-foot dick."

By the time Louise gets to bed it's nine.

She sets her alarm for twelve.

When Louise wakes up she can barely move but she moves anyway, because her shift at the coffee shop starts at two, and the knee-fondling cokehead who runs it will dock her pay if she is even a half-minute late to work.

2

LOUISE DOESN'T HEAR FROM LAVINIA.

She'd think she'd dreamed it, were it not for the MORE POETRY!!! on her arm, that she cannot bring herself to scrub off underneath her sleeves, were it not for the bad cold she gets that week that makes her have to cancel one of her tutoring sessions with Paul, whose parents are so much more annoyed by this than he is. Nights like that, with people who know "Ulysses" and stroke your hair—are not real. People take what they want from you, and tell you what you want to hear, and forget if they meant it.

Louise wonders, from time to time, if it was because she tore the dress.

Louise works. She takes the subway. She fixes her roots, strand by strand by strand.

Lavinia does so many interesting things that week. Louise sees them all on Facebook and Instagram. Lavinia goes to a Russian Orthodox Christmas party and she goes to the season premiere of *Rusalka* at the Met and gets photographed for the opera fashion blog in a floor-length silver-sequined gown and she goes for a snow-capped tea-party picnic with Athena Maidenhead and Father Romylos at the Alice in Wonderland statue in Central Park, and she spends a whole night going back and forth, back and forth, on the Staten

Island Ferry (*we were very very tired,* she captions the Instagram photo, *and we were very very merry*). The official photographs from the MacIntyre hit *Urban Foxes* and also the gossip section of the *Fiddler* blog, which used to only cover literary gossip but now makes an exception every now and then for literary-adjacent party photos, and Lavinia is in every single photo in the gallery.

Louise finds herself in one of them.

It's not actually of her, exactly—she's reflected in a mirror on the hotel lobby floor where the gin bar was, her face half-turned, while Lavinia poses, but it's so beautiful she doesn't even recognize it at first.

She right-clicks it. She saves it. She even goes to the Staples near Union Square before her bar shift, and spends $4.99 to print it out glossy, just in case the whole Internet collapses one day because of nuclear holocaust or war or something and she is never able to look at it again.

After a week, Lavinia texts her:

Just a name—Bemelmans—and a time.

Louise is supposed to work a shift for GlaZam. She does a Google search for Bemelmans and finds out that it's in the Carlyle Hotel and that glasses of wine start at twenty dollars, before tax, before tip.

Lavinia is there first.

She has spread out over two stools. Her skirt is voluminous and she's slung her ratty mink and her purse over one of them, even though the bar is so crowded with hotel guests, tourists, businessmen, all of whom are staring with unacknowledged fury at Lavinia's accessories.

"Sit. I've already ordered us champagne. I'm on my second drink, already—you're late!"

Louise is out of breath. "I'm sorry. The train."

"Have you ever been here before?"

"Not that I can remember."

Lavinia tosses her hair back—it looks like she might have tried to pin it up, this morning, but since then it has come undone and the pins have relented and she doesn't care enough to try to fix it.

"It's my local," she says. "I'm the only person under forty here who isn't a prostitute."

The wood is dark and although the place isn't candlelit this early in the evening, it looks like it might be and that is the beauty of it. There are murals on all the walls. There is a piano in the middle of the room and the piano man is playing "New York, New York." Lavinia hums along.

"They always play that here," Lavinia says. "Everyone always plays it. I don't mind. It's comforting. Like Christmas."

She slides Louise a champagne flute.

"Shall we have a toast?"

Louise's hands are still shaking from the cold. "To what?"

"To our New Year's resolutions, of course!"

"Of course."

"And to us!"

"And to us."

They clink glasses.

Sure, Louise has been in beautiful places before. Sometimes, when she has time between tutoring sessions, she goes to the Met and pays a dollar admission to wander the halls alone, like a ghost, just to be around beautiful things. But she has always been an alien there. For Lavinia this is home. "Have you done it yet?" Lavinia is beaming. "Your story. How many journals have you sent it to?"

"Oh."

Louise hasn't worked on her stories at all.

"None, yet—but I'm almost ready!"

"Will you let me read it? I want to read it. I can't *wait* to read it."

"What about your novel," Louise says. The best way to get somebody to forget they've asked you a question you don't want to answer is to encourage them to talk about themselves. "How's it coming?"

"Oh. It is as it always is. Ever was. Ever shall be. But I won't go back to school until it's finished—I promised myself that—I swore the solemnest of oaths. I will not step foot in New Haven until the final period is on the final sentence. Not that anyone wants to ever step foot in New Haven."

Lavinia knows the bartender, and so they get another round without asking for it.

Across the bar, Louise sees somebody she recognizes. High cheekbones and a plunging neckline, lips that are wine-dark, and she is leaning on the arm of a man who is older, and whose wristwatch blinds Louise.

"She's always here," Lavinia says. "With *someone*."

She raises her glass. The woman winks.

"Mother would be horrified. *What company you keep,* she'd say. *You'd have more luck getting a boyfriend, you know, if you went to dinner parties with your Chapin friends.* But I don't think it matters what a person does for a living, do you? Paris in the nineteenth century had a demimonde. And nobody judged Baudelaire. Anyway, she looks perfectly all right without the feathers."

Now Louise gets it. It's Athena Maidenhead.

"Anyway, she's not *really* a prostitute," Lavinia says. She applies more lipstick. "She's just—you know. A *demimondaine.* She's on Whats YourPrice and everything." She purses her lips. "How do I look?"

"Beautiful."

"Perfect," Lavinia says. "Selfie."

They do.

"I'm sending it to you. I want you to put it up. And tag me. And make it public, okay?"

"Okay."

They have another drink, and then another, and then another still.

An ambassador buys them one, and Timmy the bartender brings them yet another round Louise isn't sure whether or not they've ordered, and they send one over to the piano man, and then—and then, the bill comes.

Lavinia picks it up without even looking at it.

"Come on," she says. "Let's go to my party."

The second party Lavinia takes Louise to is in a bookstore that is not a bookstore. It is a rent-controlled apartment on East Eighty-fourth Street whose tenant, a gap-toothed belly laugh of a man called Matty Rosekranz, used to have a real bookstore, only he lost it after the recession because nobody buys books anymore. So he gutted his apartment and threw out the sink and got rid of the gas stove and now it holds nothing but books—good books but also pulp erotica and science fiction novels from the 1950s that have been out of print almost as long. The people who know the number buzz up and they bring a bottle or a joint. If they're pretty girls they just bring friends, and read their work out loud, and Matty entertains them, and nobody really buys a book but everybody leaves feeling like they've been part of something special.

Nobody has ever seen Matty Rosekranz outside the secret bookstore.

"Gavin says he saw him at the DMV in Harlem once," Lavinia says, as she leans against the buzzer. "But I don't believe him."

"What the fuck are you doing here?" asks Matty Rosekranz, when they come up. At first Louise is afraid he means her, but then he laughs, and lifts Lavinia up by her waist. "I thought we got rid of you."

"You can't get rid of me," Lavinia says. "I'm like a bad habit."

There are so many people here. The air is swamp-like and smells of beer. Everything that isn't full of beer has been turned into a bookshelf, except for a bookshelf that has been turned into a table, and over this Matty Rosekranz presides, with a bottle of Tito's and a six-pack and a bunch of red plastic Solo cups that everybody keeps knocking over and which Louise automatically picks up.

"Identity politics have been decimated," insists a man in a bright turquoise-and-dandelion bow tie, "by the left. The whole basis of truth relies on that fundamental statement—*x* equals *x*. But then you say *oh, I'm a man, but I'm a woman*—sorry, I know it's not politically correct."

He's talking at a very thin, very frail-looking woman with wide eyes and flaxen hair who looks impressed.

Lavinia gets right between them.

"Hello, stranger."

She kisses him on the cheek like she's not even interrupting him.

"Lavinia!" It takes him a second. "How have you been? I haven't seen you since—"

"I'm doing *splendidly!*" Lavinia flings out her arms. "It's been *wonderful*—I've been doing such things lately—Christ—it's a wonder I get anything done, these days, it's just been so busy—thank God I have Louise." She grabs Louise's hand and holds it up in the air. "She's keeping me on the straight and narrow. She's so disciplined— she writes all the time. She's an inspiration."

"You're a writer, too, then?"

"Oh, I'm so sorry! You haven't met. Louise, this is Beowulf Marmont. Beowulf, this is Louise—"

"Wilson."

"Louise Wilson. Oh, you have *so* much to talk about. Louise is the most interesting person you'll ever meet. Christ—there's Gavin!"

She sails away.

This is a test, Louise thinks.

Lavinia is testing her: to see how well Louise gets on with her other friends, now that they're not all piss-drunk, now that they can hear one another speak.

Louise doesn't blame Lavinia—it's a thing you do with an outsider.

"So." She is so chipper. "How did you and Lavinia—"

"Yale."

"Oh. Of course."

"You?"

"Oh." Louise shrugs. "You know. Parties." She keeps smiling.

Beowulf sniffs. "Sure," he says. "Where are you from?"

"I went to school in Devonshire," Louise says. She does that thing she does—almost without meaning to, now—where she sounds so clipped, it might as well be foreign.

"So you know Nick Gallagher."

"Oh. No. I mean—he probably graduated after me."

"When did you graduate?"

She hesitates. She works out his probable age, how young she can get away with being.

"2008."

She hopes she can pass for twenty-five.

"You should know him, then. He was class of 2010. He's a good kid. He's on staff at *The New Yorker* now."

"Sorry. I mean—it was a pretty big place."

"You should look him up. I just had lunch with him—last week. At the *New Yorker* offices. You've been?"

"Not yet!" She is doing such a good job of staying so desperately chipper.

"You should look him up. If you want to, you know, write for *The New Yorker*." He shrugs. "I mean—like, a lot of young women writers don't. Because, you know, the patriarchy. They're really into, like, new media or whatever. Like, *The New Misandrist* or whatever." He snorts. "So where have you written for, then?"

She could lie. But she knows he already knows what she is. Insufficiency is a thing people can smell.

"Sorry," Louise says. "I'm not a writer."

"Oh, great."

Louise knows this look. He's looking over her shoulder for somebody more important to talk to. "Great, great, great."

"Where do you—"

He's already halfway across the room. Lavinia's in a corner, talking to Gavin Mullaney, grabbing books off the shelves, so unafraid, talking to one stranger, and then another, and looking so happy the whole time.

She's not even looking over at Louise.

Louise does her best. She smiles prettily in a half-frozen way so nobody registers how petrified she is, and makes herself look busy, fingering all the books on the shelves, and feigning intense interest. She overhears somebody else talking about how he's the online editor at *The Fiddler* now, which makes him generally speaking the second or third most important person under thirty-five in any given room. She watches people but not too closely, and she both wants and does not want them to approach her, because if they do she does not have anything impressive to say, and Lavinia will see.

The reading begins.

Beowulf Marmont reads his story, publishing soon in *The New Weehawken Review*. It's about a man who drinks too much and loves women with pillowy lips. Beowulf is so confident, the way he strides up, the way he clears his throat and silences even Lavinia, who is whispering to Gavin about Edna St. Vincent Millay, and the logical part of Louise knows that he isn't looking at her—that he doesn't even care about her—and maybe it's just the secondhand pot smoke making her paranoid but the whole time that Beowulf is reading and Lavinia is looking away Louise remembers what happens if you can't pull your own weight at a party. People look over their shoulder; they forget you; they talk about you once you've gone and they do not reinvite you; Louise knows she isn't pulling her own weight—not standing like a lump against the wall, not stammering at strangers (she could say something brilliant and witty to strangers, she thinks, if Lavinia were at her side), but the more conscious she is of this the drier her throat gets, and the more impressive she needs to be the more insufficient she knows she is.

She bolts.

———

There's only one open window in this whole mold-eaten warren of an apartment and that's in the room that was once a kitchen; Louise runs and she grabs a book, any book, one on the top shelf, so that at least she'll look like she's cool enough to leave a reading to focus on a better book and not like she's just too afraid to stand in a room with people who think they're better than she is without Lavinia by her side to guide her through it.

"Are you hiding out, too?"

Louise starts.

He is sitting, half-curled, on a pile of books. He is smiling at her.

He has floppy brown hair and the kind of tortoiseshell glasses nobody wears anymore. He is in tweed, which also nobody wears anymore. He has wide, childlike brown eyes and very thin lips.

"Is it that obvious?"

"I mean—don't we *all* just want to hide out at these things?" He laughs a strange, croaking laugh. "I guess some of us just have weaker constitutions. Or, you know, don't need to network so much."

"Lucky them," Louise says.

"Lucky us," he says.

"Sure," Louise says. "Lucky us."

Then: "So, you're not a writer?"

He snorts. "Oh, no. I make much more sensible career decisions."

"Such as?"

"Grad school." His smile flowers. "Classics."

"I hear it's a lucrative field."

"Oh, yeah." He makes room for her on the bench, which is really just more books. "The margins are huge." He lights a joint, offers her a puff.

"I don't know if I should," she says. "Pot makes me paranoid."

"I mean, so does everything, right?"

"Except *networking*. Obviously."

Louise takes a puff. It makes her cough, and splutter, and so he takes out a handkerchief from his blazer pocket and offers it to her.

"*Really?*"

He starts to stammer, a little, and Louise realizes she's embarrassed him.

"I mean—thank you. I'm sorry. I'm sorry—that was rude. I was just—"

He laughs.

"Well, you know, *someone's* got to keep up standards."

"Of course." She does not understand why he is being so nice to her? "Naturally."

"So, you're not a writer, either?" He takes the joint back.

"Yes. No. Maybe?"

"There is *no such thing* as a writer anymore." The ugliest man Louise has ever seen stumbles into the room. "That's what Henry Upchurch says."

He has a square, simian face. His jaw is too big for his skull, and his skin is stretched too tight over it, and he is pale in an uncomfortably yellow way. He is short, and a bit fat.

"Hal, don't—"

"*America was great once. Not now. Then. Then we had men of letters. Then we had men of action.* Really? Nothing?"

"I'm sorry," Louise says.

"Christ. Where did you go to school? *Did* you go to school?"

"Hal!"

"I'm not being an asshole! Genuinely—I'm curious." He rummages through the books. "Here. Take it. An education."

He holds it out. *A Dying Fall.* Henry Upchurch.

"Only the best opening line in American literature. A literary lion. And a Great Man. Don't you think he's a Great Man, Rex?" He pronounces it *Reksh*, but then again, he is very drunk. "Christ, Rex—*cheer up.* This is pathetic."

"I'm just tired."

Hal claps him on the shoulder, hard.

"Is my friend boring you?"

"No."

"Are you boring him?"

"No!" Rex gets up. "No—we're fine, Hal."

"Come on." He turns to her. "What's your name?"

"Louise."

"I want to do you a favor, young Louise." He presses the book into her hands. "I want to expose you to the great and the good and more dead white men and yet-living white men you can shake a stick at. Where did you say you went to school?"

"In Devonshire."

"Devonshire. Of course. Look. It's Faber. 1998. The thirty-year-anniversary edition." He takes the book. He opens it up. "And would you look at that. *Signed,* too!"

In the other room, Louise can hear Beowulf Marmont's voice drone on.

Hal squints. "*Dear Marcus*—how nice, good old Marcus, probably a fag. *Dear Marcus. I am so delighted to read your very kind letter of March 3rd and to learn all about your fondness for* Folly's Train. *Please do ass-cheept this copy with my very pesh wishes and my hopes that your coursh of study at Harvard will be a prospph-prospsp-profitable one.*" He coughs. "What a generous, generous man. And look—we have a dedication, too! Will you look at that? *With deepest gratitude to my comrade-in-arms and agent, Niall Montgomery, to my longtime editor, Harold Lerner, and, with affection, to my wife, Elaine, and to my son.* Would you look at that?" He slams the book shut. "*And to my son.*" He's grinning, gap-toothed, like Louise is supposed to be in on the joke.

"I'm sorry." Rex stares at the floor. "Hal's drunk."

"I'm not drunk. I just appreciate literature, that's all—not like that cuckold in the other room. Christ! It's true. No great writers. Nothing new under the sun."

"Are you a writer, too?"

"Not for all the tea in China, young Louise. I'm just a humble insurance executive."

He waves the book in Louise's face.

"I'm going to go buy this book for you." He catches sight of what's in Louise's hand. "He didn't give you a handkerchief, did he?"

Louise doesn't say anything.

"You're such a faggot, Rex. Love it. Lawl."

It takes Louise a second to figure out he means *LOL,* like the acronym, and not *loll,* like what he does with his tongue.

Hal grabs the red Solo cups. "I'm getting us all refills. And one more thing. Rex?" His grin gets wider. "She's here."

They stand in silence for a while, once Hal has gone. Then Rex sits. He exhales. He picks up a book. He puts it down. He lights another joint. He drops the lighter.

"Are you okay?"

"I'm sorry," Rex says. "Christ—Hal. I'm sorry."

"No worries."

"He's an asshole. He's—I mean, he's not normally that bad. He just likes to troll. But he's a good person, deep down."

"Is he?" She tries to smile, a little bit, to let him know it's not his fault.

"Very deep down."

They laugh together.

"He just gets weird, you know, when he drinks. About his dad."

"His *dad?*"

"The Great Man of American Letters."

"*No.*"

"I've known him my whole life," Rex says, "and I still can't tell whether he knows we've figured out he means it."

"Darling."

Lavinia is brilliant in the doorway. Her pearls glimmer. Her hair cascades.

"Darling," she says, and it takes Louise another second to figure out that Lavinia means her.

"I've been looking for you *everywhere*!"

She is looking straight and steadfastly at Louise with a steely smile.

"I'm sorry!" Louise isn't even sure why she springs to her feet so quickly. "I needed some air."

"Darling—we'll get you all the air you need. I'm so excited. Don't forget our picnic."

Her smile is plastered on. Her teeth are sharp. Suddenly, without understanding why, Louise is afraid.

"Our picnic?"

"Don't you remember? It's going to be wonderful. I'm getting us champagne. I've been thinking about it—ever since New Year's—I just know you'll love it."

"Right," Louise says—so slowly. "Of course."

Lavinia takes Louise's hand. She pulls her in. She kisses her cheek. She leaves a lipstick mark.

Rex is silent. His cheeks are red. He does not move.

"Oh, Lavinia, I'm sorry, this is—"

"We're late." Lavinia's lips haven't faltered once. "Let's go."

"Who was that?" Louise asks, when they're on the stairs. Lavinia just keeps smiling.

They cab it to the High Line. Lavinia pays. They go to a liquor store and buy two bottles of Moët. Lavinia pays for that, too. They find this place Lavinia and only Lavinia knows, where the gate to the High Line is slightly bent, and then Louise follows Lavinia as they crawl on their stomachs through it.

Now, Louise knows she has another shift at the bar tomorrow, and her rescheduled lesson with Paul, and she'll have to be up at six to make up the work for GlaZam she missed today, and because she knows that getting arrested and having to pay a fine and spend a night in jail is definitely one of the ways a person can *fuck it up,* but Louise is so relieved to be away from the secret bookstore, and the people who see right through her, and she is so relieved to be with Lavinia (who maybe sees through her or maybe doesn't but in any case only sees what she wants to see), that Louise follows Lavinia, anyway, joyfully, by the light of the moon.

"How do I look?" They are standing alone on the High Line, with the snowflakes studding their hair and making flowers that are not flowers on all the branches. Lavinia adjusts her lipstick, the velvet, the pearls.

"You look beautiful," says Louise. She does.

"Will you take a picture of me?"

Lavinia holds out her phone.

"Of course."

Louise takes one of Lavinia making snow angels. She takes one of Lavinia leaning against the bushes. She takes one of her seated with her skirt spread out on the bench.

Louise shows them to her.

"Yes. Yes. No—delete that one. Yes. Post it."

She lights a cigarette. Her hands are shaking.

"Isn't it wonderful?" she says. "To be outside—on a night like this, under the moon and the stars."

Louise wants to laugh with relief.

"You didn't like the party?"

"God no! Did you?"

"God, no!"

"Beowulf Marmont—"

"God, I'm so sorry I left you with him! I was trying to get away—I made you a human sacrifice—oh, Louise, will you *ever* forgive me?"

"I thought you liked him."

"He wears a yellow bow tie. Who could like a man in a yellow bow tie?" She hands Louise a cigarette, and Louise doesn't like to smoke, really, not when she's sober, but she loves the way the smoke looks against the snow. "Back at Yale, he once told me male circumcision was as bad as rape. He wasn't even trolling."

"He was pretty awful."

"Did he hit on you? He hits on *every* girl he sees."

"Oh. No." This stings a little bit.

"Thank God. I think he's dating this awful girl with these huge fucking eyes—she looks like an anime character or something. And his writing is *terrible*."

"It's so terrible!" says Louise, even though she hasn't actually heard much of it.

"God—if only we lived in—in—in nineteenth-century Paris, or somewhere! Somewhere with *real* artists. Real writers. People who were above all this horrible, pretentious—"

"That's what Hal said."

Lavinia's smile freezes.

"Christ—*Hal*!"

"You know him?"

"You talked to him?"

"I mean—a little."

"What did you think?"

"I mean . . . he's a little . . ."

"He's an inbred moron, you mean?"

"Yes. Yes!"

It feels so good to be able to relax at last.

"He's a fucking mental Habsburg, isn't he? Brings up his father every five seconds just to sound like he's done anything of substance with his life!"

"That's all he did!"

"Of course he did! That's all he ever does! That and cocaine—he's such a fucking cliché I'm embarrassed for him. And Rex!"

"What about him?"

Lavinia freezes.

"You liked him?"

"What?"

"I mean—you two were talking."

"Oh. I mean. No. I mean—not really."

"You shouldn't talk to him. He's the worst of all of them." Lavinia lights another cigarette, but this time her hands are shaking too violently and she drops the lighter, and Louise is the one to pick it up. "He's a coward."

"What happened?"

"What do you mean? Nothing happened!" Lavinia laughs.

"You seemed—"

"It was nothing," Lavinia says. "It was stupid. It's in the past. He's nothing to me. I don't care about him."

"Wait, did you two—"

Lavinia doesn't say anything. She tosses her hair, like she always does.

"It doesn't matter. Let's take a selfie. The light's good. Your skin looks great. I wish I had your skin. God, I hate you."

"I'm sorry," Louise said. "I didn't know. If I'd known, I wouldn't have talked to him."

"You can talk to him. I don't care. I don't care about *him*. He's—he's normal and he's boring and he wants an ordinary life with an *ordinary* girlfriend he can, you know, get brunch with or whatever. That's his right."

Lavinia stubs out the cigarette in the snow. It sizzles, and then the fire dies out.

"Do you want to know something funny, Louise?"

"What?"

"He's the only person I've ever really loved."

Lavinia is leaning on the railing, looking out toward the river, and so Louise can't see her face to tell if she means it.

"Isn't that stupid?" Lavinia says.

"I don't think that's stupid."

Lavinia rounds on her. "Because you think he's worth it?"

"No, of course not. I mean . . ." Louise casts about for the right thing to say. "People fall in love for all sorts of reasons."

"He wrote *letters*. That's why. You don't think that's a stupid reason?"

"Depends on the letters, I guess."

"I mean—we were kids. Like—sixteen. I was at Chapin and he was at Collegiate and, you know, we'd go to all the same parties. Whatever."

"Whatever."

"Anyway, we exchanged numbers or whatever it was and he asked if he could write me a letter, sometime. Like—with stamps and everything. I didn't expect him to do it. People never do the things they say they will." She looks up. Her face is white with the cold. "I mean—normal people. Not people like us." She beams, and in the moonlight she is radiant. "You and me, we keep our promises. We say—*we're going to recite poetry by the sea*. We say—*we're going to break into the High Line*. And we do. Anyway, he did. Back then, Rex was a real person."

She has gone through half the cigarette pack.

"He used to hand-deliver them, sometimes. Quill pen. Green ink. A *seal*. Leave them with my doorman. He didn't even have Facebook for the longest time—he had a whole complex about it, too. He wanted to wear a wristwatch. Christ—he still used a *flip phone*. I loved it."

She exhales, slowly. In the distance, the lights are going out, one by one by one, all over the city.

"We were partners in crime—*contra mundum*. We used to hold hands and walk through the Met and talk about running away together. We had the whole itinerary planned out. It was going to be this Grand Tour—you know—just going everywhere beautiful and seeing every beautiful thing and we were going to go to Vienna to see Klimt's *The Kiss* up close at the Belvedere, and to Venice for Carnevale. When we were finally free."

Louise thinks about Virgil Bryce, on the railroad bridge.

"Anyway," Lavinia says. "We never went."

"What happened?"

"Nothing *happened*. He just got boring. That's all."

"When?"

Lavinia snorts. "A couple years ago. Anyway, it doesn't matter. I told you. He's dull. He's even got Facebook now. At least, I think he still has. I wouldn't know. He blocked me."

The snow shines on her cheeks. Her lips are red.

"God, I hope he hates me," Lavinia says, suddenly.

"Why?"

"It means they still think about you." Lavinia exhales smoke.

Lavinia leans out over the railing: "Have you ever been in love?"

Louise has to think about it.

"I don't know. Maybe."

"Don't be ridiculous. When you know, you know."

"I moved to New York with someone," Louise says. "I was in love with him. I think."

Louise does not talk about Virgil Bryce, ever. But then again, nobody has ever asked.

"Was he in love with you?"

"Yes."

"Where is he now?"

"I don't know. I blocked him."

"Did he break your heart?"

"I don't know. I think I broke his."

Lavinia claps. "I knew it. I *knew it*! God—you're such a little femme fatale."

"I'm really not."

"All quiet and haughty and mysterious—God, I *knew it*. The second I saw you—"

"I'm really, *really* not."

"I thought—a man would slit his wrists for a woman like that."

"He didn't," Louise says. "But he did threaten to, once."

Lavinia grabs Louise's wrist.

For a second, Louise thinks she has said too much, that she has shocked Lavinia, that she has done that awful over-sharing thing people so often do that makes the room go quiet, and makes everybody say something sympathetic, and makes everybody feel sorry for you, and makes everybody hate you.

Then Lavinia bursts out laughing.

"Jesus *Christ*, I love you."

There are tears in her eyes. She is shaking. She squeezes Louise's hand so tight.

Louise can't help it. She starts laughing, too.

It has never been funny before.

But with Lavinia, on this bridge, which is so much higher and so much brighter than any bridge in Devonshire ever was, everyone else seems that little bit less real. Everything about that other Louise— the Louise with mousy brown hair and a crooked smile and who was a little fat and whom nobody but the charitable and the insane could ever really love—is fiction.

"Of course he didn't do it, did he?" Lavinia is still racked with laughter.

"No, of course not." Not as far as Louise knows.

"Men."

"Men!"

"They never keep their fucking promises."

Lavinia is laughing so hard that tears seep from her eyes.

Louise offers her a handkerchief.

Lavinia stops laughing.

"Where did you get that?"

"Oh. Oh—Rex."

"He *gave* it to you?"

"I sneezed. I forgot to give it back. I'm sorry."

"Let me see."

Lavinia takes it.

"He probably still has his *wristwatch*, too."

"I'm sorry. I didn't see."

Lavinia is silent.

Then: "Hand me the lighter."

Louise does.

A slow smile spreads across Lavinia's face. She lights the corner of the handkerchief. The fire is slow, at first. Then the whole thing bursts into flame.

"Jesus, *fuck*!" Lavinia drops it.

For a moment the two of them stand there, staring, at the small, persistent fire in the middle of the path.

Lavinia sucks her thumb where she has burned it.

"You see," she says softly. "They don't mean a thing to us, do they?"

She is so beautiful by the firelight.

She is so beautiful, Louise thinks, that you even believe her.

Lavinia takes another step closer to the fire.

"We should be maenads, instead," she says, so softly. "We should abjure all men and tear them apart with our teeth when they come near us. *Fuck you, Rex Eliot! Fuck you, Hal Upchurch! Fuck you, Beowulf Marmont.*" She spins on her heels. "Your one—what's he called?"

"Um—Virgil?"

"What a name!"

"His mom was a history teacher."

"Virgil what?"

"Bryce."

"Fuck you, Virgil Bryce!"

Lavinia turns to her.

"Well, come on! Your turn—what's the point if you don't say it, too?"

"Fuck you, Virgil Bryce," she says quietly.

"Pathetic!" Lavinia grabs her wrist. "Do it again!"

"Fuck you, Virgil Bryce!"

"For God's sake—FUCK YOU, VIRGIL BRYCE!"

"FUCK YOU, VIRGIL BRYCE."
"FUCK ALL MEN EVERYWHERE."
It feels so good to scream.
"FUCK ALL MEN EVERYWHERE!"
The fire goes out.
Lavinia says, "Let's get drunk."

They do.

They go through both bottles of champagne, right there on the High Line, with nothing but the stars over them and the rails extending to convergence in both directions. They drink and Lavinia tells Louise about all the places they will go together, when they finish their stories, when they are both great writers—both of them—to Paris and to Rome and to Trieste, where James Joyce used to live, to Vienna to see the paintings, to Carnevale.

Lavinia will never go.

She is going to die soon. You know this.

They take more photos. Louise in the snow. Lavinia on the railing. Lavinia and Louise: leaning, about to fall.

They post them.

"You should add him on Facebook," Lavinia says.

"Who?"

"Rex. He's on there now, isn't he?"

Louise looks.

"Yes."

"Add him. Hal, too."

Louise does.

They drink until the stars spin. They lean on each other's shoulders. They make more snow angels.

"Hey, Louise?"

"Yeah?"

"Will you read my novel?"

"Of course."

Lavinia sits straight up. "Fantastic. Let us *set off.*"

"Wait, *now?*"

Lavinia's already on her feet. "It's not that far!"

"It's two o'clock in the morning!"

"So there's no point in you going all the way to, like, Bumfuck, Brooklyn, is there? You might as well stay at mine."

She is so charming, pleading.

"Oh, *don't say no,* Louise. Please—*please*—*please* don't say no!"

Louise can't.

They cab it back to Lavinia's. Lavinia pays.

Lavinia gets her enormous skirt caught in the cab doors. Louise pulls it out. Lavinia is drunker than Louise realized and she has to help her into the apartment. She doesn't mind. It's nice, she thinks, to be so necessary.

"Home at last!"

Lavinia tumbles in.

"Christ, it's so *empty.* I hate it when Cordy leaves." She sails to the kettle. "We shall have tea. From the shores of Asia! From the Edgware Road. Do you want chocolate-caramel or lavender-mint? And we should have music, too! Mood music! Atmosphere!" She makes her way to the computer; she blasts Wagner's *Tristan und Isolde* so loud Louise worries that the neighbors will hear, and come down, and start a fight.

"So they'll hear!" Lavinia shrugs. "Fuck 'em! If there's one thing the Upper East Side needs it's more Wagner!"

She turns the volume higher still.

"I love this part." She lets herself fall on the sofa. She closes her eyes.

Louise makes the tea because nobody else will.

"Do you want me to put milk—"

"Shhh!"

Louise puts milk in the tea.

"It's the lovers' duet. They're the only two people in the world, right now. The two of them."

Louise brings the tea over.

"Listen!"

Louise does.

"It never lasts, though, does it? It all falls apart in the end. Doesn't it?"

"Yes," Louise says. She sets the tea down. "It does."

"God, you're so mysterious—I love it! *Fuck*—my dressing gown!" She extends a long white hand into the middle distance. "It's in my bedroom."

Louise gets the dressing gown. It is powder-blue and silk and stained and very impractical, with little flowers on it. She helps Lavinia put it on.

Louise sits next to Lavinia on the sofa. Lavinia strokes her hair. "It's three in the morning."

"I know. I know. But—just one chapter, okay? Please? Then—then you can take Cordy's bed and—and I'll get up early and I'll make us pancakes tomorrow before your shift, okay?"

"Just one chapter?"

"It's just that I care so much what you think! You should be *flattered*!" Lavinia whines, a bit, and puts her shoes up on the steamer trunk. "I'd stay up all night reading yours, you know. If you had it for me."

She takes out her phone.

"Here," she says. "It's all on here."

The light is blinding. The text is so small.

Louise starts to scroll. "How long is it?"

"Just start it. If you don't like it you can stop. I promise."

"I can barely read it."

"I want to see your reactions. That's the best way. If I can see your face. And you don't have to like it, you know. In fact, if you like it too much—I won't respect you. So you should probably hate it, just a little bit."

"Come on—I'm not going to hate it!"

But here's the thing: Louise does.

It's not just that it's bad. It is bad—the prose is too purple and the sentences are too long and the literary allusions are too forced and every other line is a quotation or a character monologuing about the nature of Life and Art; or a character does something intensely symbolic but that doesn't quite come off. But it's worse: it's self-indulgent. There's a character called Larissa who is very beautiful and very blonde and is kind of like a saint because her passions are so much greater and more important and more significant than anyone else's.

Even Louise knows the first rule of good writing is to never assume that your life is more significant than anyone else's just because you say it is. And Larissa wants to live Life as Art, except of course she can't, because nobody around her understands concepts like Beauty and True Love the way she does. So she tries to make a suicide pact with her lover, who of course is undeserving of her, and of course he doesn't go through with it and so she throws herself off a bridge all on her own for no obvious reason.

Also, she uses too many em dashes.

Louise feels so many things. She does not show any of them.

She is embarrassed, like she has walked in on somebody watching porn. She feels that she has looked at something raw and quivering, exposed and unholy.

She is angry, too, because in everything Lavinia has written there is such a perfect confidence: that Lavinia's thoughts and Lavinia's passions and Lavinia's philosophy and Lavinia's heartbreak are worth hours of somebody else's time, and Louise has never had that confidence.

Also, Louise is relieved.

There is something she has that Lavinia doesn't.

———

Louise's eyes glaze over. She is tired; she wants to sleep—she wants to sleep so badly—but Lavinia is looking at her and bouncing on her knees on the sofa, and nodding, and smiling, and if she gives away a hint—a single hint—of all that she is feeling she will never be able to take it back again.

"What do you think?" Lavinia is breathless.

Louise hesitates.

"You think it's bad."

"No! No—I don't think it's bad at all!"

Lavinia lets herself laugh. "I wasn't sure."

"It's good! It's—I mean, it's *good*!"

"But?"

Louise takes a deep breath.

Lavinia takes a deep breath.

"But nothing—"

"Oh come on!" Lavinia pats Louise's hand. "There's always *something.*"

"It's just—"

"Yes?"

"I mean—Larissa is you, of course."

"Why do you say of course?"

Lavinia is blinking so quickly.

"I mean the name."

"Well of course the *name.*"

"I mean—I wonder . . ." Louise has to be so careful, now. "I mean—I wonder if there's just *so much* overlap."

"Too much? You can tell me. I can take it. I can take it. Tell me."

"No. No—not too much. Just—there's not a lot of distance from the protagonist, is there?"

"What's that supposed to mean?"

Louise has seen that face on Lavinia before. She saw it on New Year's Eve, when Mimi tore her dress.

"Nothing."

"You think I let her off easy, or something?"

"I didn't say that!"

"I'm sorry." Lavinia inhales. "I'm sorry." She pulls the throw over her knees. "I'm sorry. You're right. I should—I'm just tired, that's all. I'm tired and I'm in a bad mood. I should let you go home."

She pulls the blanket up to her chin.

And Louise thinks *she cannot mean to do this.*

You are crazy to think this of her, Louise thinks. *You are a bad person to think this of her. She just forgot. That's all. Just ask to stay—just remind her—that's all you have to do. You cannot always think the worst of people.*

Lavinia's eyes are already closed.

And Louise, she knows that all she has to do is say *it's still cool if I stay, right.* But she is so afraid Lavinia will say yes and mean *no,* that Lavinia will make pancakes and then never call her again, because she has fucked it up because of course, *of course,* she's fucked it up. Nobody ever wants to know the truth about themselves, not really, and she—of course—she should know this more than anyone.

It would be so easy, she thinks, just to ask for what she wants.

"I love it," Louise says.

Lavinia's eyes pop open. "You do?"

"That's what I was trying to say. It's so—emotional. It's so—*raw.*"

"Really? You really think that?"

"You're going to be Great, Lavinia. I don't have any doubt. I don't have any doubt in the goddamn world."

That night, for the first time, Louise realizes just how young Lavinia is.

It's so easy to lie to her.

That's the other thing Louise realizes.

Lavinia flings her arms around Louise; she squeezes her so tight Louise can't breathe.

"God, I love you so much," she says. "You really don't know how much it means to me." She draws the blanket over Louise's feet. "I wouldn't trust anyone else to read it, not even Cordy. Nobody but you."

Louise leans her head on Lavinia's shoulder. Lavinia squeezes her hand.

Louise thinks: *we cannot be known and loved at the same time.*

It is very simple, Louise knows. There are two kinds of people in the world: the people you can fool into liking you, and the ones clever enough not to fall for it.

The day Louise dyed her hair, that first time, the month she first moved to Sunset Park, the month she bought a book of mantras and changed her number and blocked Virgil Bryce on social media, she looked into the mirror and found, for the first time in her life, that she was fuckable.

It was like she was getting away with something.

It took her a month or two to get the measure of it. First the cat-callers, and then the older men in bars, and then even the men a little closer to her own age in bars, and on Tinder, back when she used Tinder (the polyamorist, the kinky one, the ghost). Men thought she was special.

They did this, you understand, because they were stupid.

They didn't notice *Louise.*

It was just that Louise *looked* blonde and thin and pretty, and they were dumb enough to think that all these things were true of her, and not just qualities she wore. And so they were dumb enough to think that her other qualities (she was so chill, she was so clever, she was so open-minded in bed) were real, too.

It never lasts, of course. Louise knows this. You can't fool them forever, not even the very stupid ones. They realize every good thing about you is a trick.

Louise has fooled Lavinia, she thinks, and so Lavinia must be stupider than she is. She hates herself for thinking like that about Lavinia, who has been nothing but kind to her, but she thinks it all the same.

Unless Lavinia said *go home* because she knew Louise couldn't— not at this hour, not in this cold—

Louise would hate herself for thinking that, too.

"Hey, Louise?"

Lavinia is half-asleep.

"What is it?"

"You don't think I'm, like—*too much,* do you?"

"Too much?"

"I mean. You know. *Too much.* Too everything."

"No," says Louise. "Of course not. Am *I* too much?"

"Of course not," Lavinia murmurs. "You're—I mean—you're the *opposite* of too much."

Louise doesn't say anything.

"I love you."

Lavinia starts to snore on her shoulder.

Louise tries to sleep on the sofa, because if she moves she will wake Lavinia. She plays with her phone. She reads stupid articles on *Misandry!*

She wants to cry.

She hates herself for wanting to cry, because she has had such a good night—not the assholes at the bookstore, maybe, but after that. They have had such a wonderful night and they broke onto the High Line and they burned Rex's handkerchief in effigy for all men, everywhere, who had ever hurt them, and they took so many cabs Louise didn't even have to pay for, and now Louise is sleeping in such a beautiful apartment surrounded by such beautiful things and there is somebody who has squeezed her hand and said *I love you* and everything they have done tonight is everything that Louise, in Devonshire, would have been so happy—so happy and so proud and so *justified*—to see Louise, in New York, doing now.

You're being dumb, she tells herself. *That's all.*

She keeps looking at the photograph Lavinia has posted of the two of them.

They're on the High Line. They're surrounded by snow and branches and stars that, on this filter, you can't even distinguish from the city lights.

We look happy, Louise thinks. Maybe they were.

Everybody's Liking it. Father Romylos and Gavin Mullaney and even Beowulf, and so many other names that are by now at least a little bit familiar.

Mimi Kaye.

hey lady.

Mimi has added Louise on Facebook.

you look super cute in those pics

Winking smiley cat-eye emoji.

Thanks (Louise says)

(flirty heart-eyed fox, says Mimi)

isn't it fun out there?

(boggle-eyed dancing-footed toad)

yeah it was nice thanks

lavinia and I used to do it alllll the time hahaha

one time we even slept out there

the cops found us but lavinia got us out of it

isn't that so funny

(chicken with clown makeup on)

don't you think that's funny?

(owl wearing a cap and gown and glasses looking inquisitive)

Louise doesn't answer.

She doesn't sleep, either.

3

THE THIRD PARTY LAVINIA TAKES LOUISE TO is a loft party off the Jefferson L at this performance space this guy she knows owns where they've turned the entire mezzanine into a poetry library. The fourth party Lavinia takes Louise to is this cabaret benefit at the Laurie Beechman Theatre over in Hell's Kitchen, where everybody but Louise and Lavinia is ninety and is wearing tattooed eyeliner and sequined shawls. The fifth is the release party in Gramercy for this coffee-table book called *Sexual Secrets of Europe* by this degenerate Australian travel writer called Lydgate who must only be fifty-five but looks eighty, and it is there that Louise does coke for the first time and races Lavinia all the way up First Avenue.

They go to parties neither of them is invited to.

"It's easy," Lavinia says. "You just walk right in."

They get matching tattoos. This is Lavinia's idea.

"I don't ever want to forget our trip to the sea," she says. "I want to think about that night all the time. I want to commemorate it."

They are standing on Saint Mark's Place, which is the most expensive and least hygienic place to get a tattoo in New York City. They are drunk because they've just gone to that speakeasy you can only get to by entering through a telephone booth and putting your name down two hours in advance. Earlier they'd gone to the perfume shop on East Fourth Street, because Lavinia had to get her signature fragrance made, which is called Sehnsucht and which Louise can by now smell on all her clothes, and that night is the night Louise gets her own (because Lavinia pays for this, too), which is made of dandelion and fern and tobacco and heather, but when she smells it now she thinks it smells all wrong, because it smells nothing like Lavinia's.

"Come on!" Lavinia says. She has gone into a shitty shop that even Louise knows only NYU freshmen patronize. "God, Louise, don't you want to *live*?"

Two hours later Louise sobers up in Washington Square Park and realizes that both of them have MORE POETRY!!! tattooed in tiny letters on their forearms, and she isn't as horrified as she should be.

"Worst case scenario"—Lavinia shrugs—"you get it lasered off. It's not that expensive."

She leans her arm against Louise's arm.

They take a picture of the two of them, holding hands.

There are so many wonderful pictures of them on the Internet. There's the one of the two of them in Lincoln Center, between the opera and a costume party at the MacIntyre, taking off their evening gowns to reveal the corsets underneath. There's one of them in drag at something called the Tweed Picnic, which is a flash mob in Bryant Park.

Everybody, everybody Likes them.

"You certainly look like you're taking better care of yourself," Louise's mother tells her on the phone. "Your hair looks nice."

Louise has been dyeing it a slightly more strawberry shade of blonde. It looks so good on Lavinia, she thinks, and the two of them have the same skin tone.

People from Devonshire Like the photos—people who have barely spoken to her. So does Beowulf Marmont. So does the guy that ghosted.

More than once.

Louise starts finishing stories. She even sends them out.

She and Lavinia sit on the divan in Lavinia's apartment that smells like incense and sit together at their laptops and set the timer for an hour and write, and even though half the time Lavinia gets bored and gets up to make a pot of cinnamon-raisin-date tea and then forgets about that, too, Louise sits and types. Lavinia orders dinner for both of them on Seamless and it is so glorious to eat food that somebody else has cooked, and not to have to clean up, after.

"It's the least I can do," Lavinia says. "You're keeping me on the straight and narrow. You inspire me."

She sends an essay about Devonshire to Gavin Mullaney after a *Fiddler* Valentine's Day party. It's not the one she deep down wants to write, which is the one about pretending to go to the Academy for a week, because she doesn't like writing about herself, but she writes a *reportage* kind of thing about this crazy thing that happened to her sophomore year when a couple of Academy kids went nuts and ran away and they had the whole police after them. Gavin likes it.

I'm not a really big fan of narrative, Gavin says, *and I don't also personally really care about things like characterization since personally I don't have a lot of empathy for other people but it's super-readable and people apparently really like stories that are very driven by primal emotions.*

Could you Tweet it when you get a chance?

A few days later he suggests she pitch his second-favorite person of all the people he's dating (he has a spreadsheet), a woman called Michelle-Ann who left *Misandry!* to start a new, more intersectionally aware magazine called *The New Misandrist.* Louise does.

Louise lets herself get stupid.

She stops paying such close attention to money (somehow, even with Lavinia paying for everything, Louise is always broke, and she isn't sure why). She starts missing GlaZam shifts. She starts eating bread (Lavinia loves the croissants from Agata & Valentina, and insists on buying a dozen even though she only ever eats one). She starts trusting people, the way Lavinia trusts people, secure in the knowledge that the world is a well-ordered and reasonable place in which nothing ever goes unsalvageably wrong.

Louise stops waiting for the world to end.

Until the night it almost does.

Louise is so happy, that night. They have gone to this erotic illustrator's art Ballets Russes party at this gay culture museum on the Lower East Side, and they have stayed out so late at this Marie Antoinette–themed cocktail bar, and she is so happy that she has that final glass of champagne that she knows she shouldn't have. She takes the long, slow train ride, and when she gets off she is singing.

Louise never sings.

When she walks home she always hunches over. She puts her hands in her pockets. She always stares straight ahead. She always puts her keys between her fingers.

Always.

But tonight Louise is drunk, and Lavinia has invited her to the opera, in a couple of weeks, and promised to sew her a dress. Of course Louise will do the sewing but Lavinia will buy the raw materials and the vintage base; and they have so many grand plans, so Louise is humming "As Time Goes By," because that's what they played over and over at the Ballets Russes party and she leaves her keys in her purse.

"You've got a voice on you, little girl."

He is always there.

Louise isn't afraid of him tonight. She tosses her long strawberry-blonde hair, and shoots him the kind of world-destroying smile Lavinia shoots bartenders when she doesn't want to pay for something.

"You want to give me singing lessons."

"No, thank you!"

She's almost skipping.

"What's your name?"

"What's it to you?"

God's in his heaven, Louise is thinking, with the part of her brain that can still think, *and all is right with the world.*

"I said—what's your name?"

"Artemesia Gentilleschi!" She flings out her arms.

"You fucking with me?"

He is so close to her. She has not realized how close he is to her.

"Hey! I asked you a question!"

He grabs her arm.

Here's the thing: there's only so much you can lie to yourself. You can blunt instinct, if you want to—you can drink too much, you can laugh and smile and reapply your lipstick and say *let us get drunk, on poetry and virtue,* you can pretend to be a human being, a little while—but in the end, you are what you are.

Somebody comes too close, you run.

He follows you, you run faster.

His steps meld into yours, you stop.

You turn.

He hesitates.

You do what you have to do.

And if you're lazy enough and stupid enough and arrogant enough to forget to put your keys between your fingers—the one time, that *one time,* you're lazy and stupid and arrogant enough to not put your keys between your fingers—you use whatever you have to hand.

Your elbows. Your nails. Your teeth.

You punch a stranger straight in the eye before he can tell you whether he wants to rape you or just tell you he likes your smile.

You keep hitting him, and scratching him, and pulling out his hair, and even kicking him, straight between the legs, until you have made sure he is on the floor.

You kick him once more, in case he still wants to follow you.

You run.

Louise doesn't stop shaking until she's on the stairs.

She doesn't let herself cry until she's inside.

She doesn't let herself scream. Not now. Not ever. She just holds her wrist to her chest, her wrist with the bruise where he has grabbed it and MORE POETRY!!! still healing on her forearm, and she takes very slow, very measured, very deep breaths, that rack and strangle but do not make any sound.

You little fool, she thinks. *You deserve everything bad that ever happens to you.*

Maybe the moon is full. Maybe the stars are bright. Maybe cigarettes smell like incense.

But not for her, she thinks. Never for people like her, who don't live on the Upper East Side, who don't go to Yale, who aren't even naturally blonde.

Everybody who has ever told her this was right.

"That's bollocks," says Lavinia, when Louise tries to return the opera tickets the next day. "It's the season premiere."

Louise has made some vague and unconvincing excuse. Paul needs extra SAT lessons because he smokes too much weed. Something like that.

"The tickets are paid for," Lavinia says, like that's all there is to it.

She catches sight of Louise's bruise.

"Jesus Christ."

Louise explains that it's nothing, that there's just some guy who likes to chat her up, that he got a little handsy because she was too sassy, that this kind of thing happens all the time.

"All the time?"

Lavinia stretches out her legs along the steamer trunk. She fans herself with the peacock feathers. She turns up the music.

"Just move into Cordy's room," she says. "She's going to be in Paris the whole summer, anyway."

It is a stupid thing to do. Louise knows that.

But so is turning down a free room on Seventy-eighth and Lex.

Lavinia hires a moving van a week later. She shows up at Sunset Park in palazzo pants, with a scarf in her hair, like she's some 1930s explorer, like she's off on an adventure to the land of here-be-dragons, even though it's only South Brooklyn (it's not even real South Brooklyn, like Gravesend or Bensonhurst, just Sunset Park). She looks with such bewilderment at the bodegas, at the white plastic chairs, at the Greek man pissing in the lobby.

"I love it," Lavinia says. She taps a cigarette against the lobby walls. "You should write about him. A mad Greek—maybe he's a prophet. I bet *The Fiddler* would love it."

Louise never wants to think about the mad Greek again.

They get in the moving van, which Lavinia apparently can drive ("I learned in Newport one summer. I destroyed a mailbox"), with the single box of useless shit Louise doesn't plan to keep anyway.

There he is, on the corner.

He has a black eye. He has a bruise on his lip.

He sees her. He looks up.

"What's wrong?"

"Nothing," says Louise. "Keep driving."

"You look like you've seen—"

"Let's go!"

A strange, slow smile spreads across Lavinia's face. "That's not—"

"Please, Lavinia."

All she wants is to go. All she wants is to never see this street or this apartment or any of these bodegas with their loose cigarettes and their hanging rosaries and their uniform packs of knockoff microwave meals again.

Lavinia stops the van.

She is a terrible driver, and Louise lurches forward so violently bile rises in her throat.

"How dare he," Lavinia says. "How *fucking* dare he?"

"I just want—"

Lavinia's already out of the van.

"Hey!"

She gets in his face.

"Hey! You!"

"What do you . . ."

"You—you—catastrophic piece of shit!"

Louise can't breathe.

She sits there, strapped in the passenger seat, and she knows she should get up or do something or say something or stop it but her heart is beating so fast that she can't stop it, and Lavinia looks so ridiculous—in her cream-colored palazzo pants that are already gray (for God's sake, it is only April), and the scarf wound around her head, shouting at this man with a black eye and a bruise over his upper lip.

The funny thing is: he looks so confused.

Louise almost feels sorry for him.

"Lady, I don't know what you're . . ."

"You ought to be—drawn and quartered. You ought to be *hanged*!"

He looks up at her.

Of course, Lavinia doesn't mean it like that. Lavinia doesn't live in the real world, which is a world where when a white woman tells a black man he should be hanged it does not mean what it means in Lavinia's world, where men still fight duels with muskets or swords or bow to each other in the morning—Louise knows this. It doesn't even occur to Lavinia—not even now, not even when he's looking at her like she's hit him—what she has done, and all Louise can think is *fuck, fuck,* and then she's running out of the van; then she grabs Lavinia so hard by the arm Lavinia yelps and she screams *let's go* and almost throws her in the passenger seat; she grabs the keys and presses the pedal down because God knows Lavinia can't drive this thing, and the tires screech and they are all the way into Park Slope before anybody says anything.

"What the hell was that?"

Lavinia is rubbing her arm where Louise has grabbed it.

"You shouldn't have done that," Louise says.

She keeps her eyes on the road.

"Done what? Defend you?"

"Said what you said."

"What did I say? He—he *insulted* you!"

"You can't just—" Louise's heart is only just going back to normal. "You can't just—fucking—*say* things without thinking about them."

She doesn't know why she is protecting him. He has done nothing for years but follow her home. He has done nothing but call her names, and tell her he's going to fuck her, or else he wouldn't if his life depended on it. She has given him a black eye.

Maybe he was just trying to be friendly (how can she even think that, now?).

Maybe I should have just asked his name.

And Louise is so angry with herself and angry with Lavinia for being so stupid and angry with Lavinia for meaning so well and angry with Lavinia for not knowing why she is angry and she doesn't say anything.

They drive in silence all the way to the Upper East Side.

"You know," Lavinia says, when Louise stops the truck, "I thought you'd be grateful."

The bed is soft. The bedspread is jacquard, fur-lined. The walls have moldings on them. There's a midcentury modern chandelier. There are Persian carpets, and an art nouveau wardrobe Lavinia bought at the flea market in the Flatiron and there are antique postcards from all the childhood places Lavinia and Cordelia have been to. There is a framed photograph of the sisters on the bedside table.

There is no room for Louise's clothing in the closet. Lavinia has filled it up with formal dresses—ball gowns and vintage taffeta and silks and sequins and feathers and the long velvet trousers Lavinia wears those nights she wants to look like Marlene Dietrich.

"I'm sorry," Lavinia says. She is in her powder-blue gown with the stains on it. Her hair is halfway down her back. "I didn't think. But, I mean—it's not like you have a lot of clothes, anyway. You can always wear mine!" She says this very brightly. "It's so good that we're the same size, isn't it?" She brings Louise a glass of champagne. It's ten o'clock in the morning. "Speaking of which . . ." She sits on the bed, right on top of Louise's sweatshirts. "I was thinking. You should join ClassPass. I'm going to. That way we can work out together, in the mornings. God, I know, I know—but I'm turning over a new leaf. I'm going to get up early—we both are. Apparently your metabolism starts to slow down before your mid-twenties—I'm going to have to be so much more careful."

It takes Louise a second to register that Lavinia has no idea how old she is.

"Here, give me your phone. I'll sign up for you." Lavinia grabs Louise's purse. "Do you have a credit card in there?"

"How much is it?"

"Not a lot. Like—two hundred? One ninety? Something like that." Lavinia grabs the card.

"That's kind of expensive."

"Oh, don't worry!" Lavinia beams. "It's unlimited. You can take as many classes as you want—we can go *twice* a day, even!"

"I don't think . . ."

"It'll be so much *fun*! You know me, Louise—I'll never do anything unless you make me. I'm positively useless. I wouldn't even write—and then this whole sabbatical—it'd be a waste, wouldn't it? If it weren't for you I'd just lie around the house all day and drink—you see, you have a *moral* obligation to me. My life is in your hands!" She lies back on the pillows. "Besides, aren't you saving a bunch of money in rent?"

"I mean, some."

Lavinia sits straight back up. "How much did you pay? You know—in *that place*?"

Louise hesitates.

"Eight hundred."

"Is that *all*?"

"It was rent-stabilized." There were months eight hundred seemed impossible.

"So, that's perfect. Save eight hundred, spend two hundred—you've still got six hundred a month more than you did before, right?" She dangles the card. "And we'll both get so skinny—oh my God! We're going to be like—*sylphs*."

She cocks her head at Louise, like a dog.

"Come on—say yes, *please*."

Louise is so, so grateful.

Isn't she?

She takes her card. She takes the phone.

"Do it now—come on."

Louise does. Two hundred dollars a month.

"Thank you! Thank you! Thank you!" She kisses Louise on the forehead.

Then: "Come on!"

She holds out the phone.

"Photo," she says. "Wait—no." She puts on lipstick. She grabs another dressing gown. "Put this on."

They take a selfie lying on the Karabakh carpet in the living room.

Lavinia titles it en famille. Everybody Likes it.

Even Mimi Kaye.

"What are you going to wear tonight?"

Louise is very tired. She has a lesson with Paul and another with a boy called Miles and a third with a girl called Flora, all the way in Park Slope. She has at least three hours of work to do for GlaZam. She has a barista shift in the morning.

"What's tonight?"

"What do you mean, *what's tonight*?" Lavinia laughs. "God—what's *wrong* with you today?"

"I don't . . ."

"The premiere. *Roméo et Juliette.*"

"Fuck. The opera."

Louise has completely forgotten.

"Christ—Lavinia—I'm so tired!"

"But don't you see—it's perfect! Now you don't have to worry about getting all the way home. We can just take a cab, after. On me." She says it so innocently, like Louise hasn't just spent two hundred dollars on ClassPass just to make her happy. "Come on—we should *celebrate*! We're roomies now—wasn't that the whole point?"

Her smile is frozen on.

"Of course," says Louise. "I'll be back after my shift."

"Right," says Lavinia. "There's just one little thing. The co-op board here, you know. They're really strict about copies."

"Copies of . . ."

"So Cordy has a set and I have a set, but that's it. Not even the maid has a set. So—I mean, you'll have to buzz up for me to let you in." She shrugs. "That's not a problem, right?"

"Of course not," says Louise.

She teaches her lesson with Paul. She teaches her lesson with Miles. She goes to Park Slope to teach Flora, and then comes all the way back.

She buzzes in.

"What took you so long?" Lavinia is in a long red silk dress that shimmers as she walks. She has pinned and gelled her hair into fingerwaves.

She has probably been getting ready since Louise left.

"Subway."

"Well, hurry . . ."

It's only four. Louise wants to get at least a couple hours of work in at GlaZam.

"I've just got some stuff I need to finish."

"Can't you do it tomorrow?"

There will be more work tomorrow.

"But it's a *gala* night," Lavinia says. "Listen—listen, I have the *perfect* dress for you. I want to dress you in white, okay? I have this one I got from this seller on Etsy I know in Paris. It's from the fifties—cost me an absolute fortune but it's so beautiful and I've worn it so much I'm just—I'm just completely sick of it. I've already laid it out for you."

It is taffeta and silk and enormous and princessy. It is not something Louise would ever wear.

"Are you sure?"

"You'll look gorgeous! And I'll do your hair, too—it'll take a while, but I think we should curl it, a little bit. Give it some body! God, I'm so excited! And Rose will be there tonight, too—she'll be taking photos for *Last Night at the Met*."

She has Louise strip. She zips up the dress. It just about fits.

"I'd never wear it again," she says.

"Why not?"

"Tragic memories." Louise can see Lavinia smile in the mirror. "I lost my virginity in this dress."

"Jesus!"

"It's dry-cleaned. Plus I took it off first. Obviously."

Lavinia sits Louise down in front of the vanity. Lavinia plugs in the curler.

"Stay still."

Lavinia yanks Louise's head to the left. She twists her chin up.

"How did you lose your virginity?"

Lavinia takes a chunk of Louise's fine, finely dyed hair, and wraps it around the iron. She burns her ear.

"I mean—the normal way?"

"Was it nice?"

"It was fine."

It was not fine. Louise had to beg for it.

Of course, she wasn't pretty then.

"Was it—what's his name? Victor?"

"Virgil."

Louise is so tired. Louise doesn't want to talk about it. But Lavinia is being so soft with her, now. She is stroking her hair idly.

"What an idiot," Lavinia says. "I mean—I'm assuming. He didn't know what he had with you. I can't imagine a man in the world deserving you—look at you." She tilts Louise's chin up. "You're beautiful."

Even now this makes Louise smile.

"He should have taken you to—to—what's the most romantic place in New Hampshire? The—the nature! He should have taken you to, like, a cabin with a great big roaring fire and animal skins."

As it happens, Louise did lose her virginity in nature. It was in the woods behind the Devonshire Academy tennis courts.

"I lost my virginity after the opera," Lavinia says. She says it so idly. "I was seventeen." She is staring, vaguely, into the mirror, which is the only way Louise can look at her. "Did you know that?"

"No."

"We'd been together about a year—it's a long time, now that I think about it. But we were both, you know. We were very sweet. He was very gentlemanly—I told you. He's old-fashioned. We got student rush tickets to the Met. It was the first time I ever went. We held hands the whole time—it was pathetic, the two of us, both of us, these scared little virgins, holding hands, but—it was *Carmen* and I was seventeen and there's that bit, at the end, when he kills her—and there's a bullfight and there's this great skinned bull on one side of the stage and he's got his hands around her throat on the other and—God, our hands were so sweaty. And it was so perfect. And I remember thinking—I remember exactly what I was thinking. *I want him to remember me.* If he hadn't been a virgin, too—I mean, I was such a little prude. I wouldn't want to be one of a litany."

She exhales slowly.

"Of course we couldn't go to my place and we couldn't go to his place because of our parents—my parents lived here, then; this is back before they fucked off and bought this place—and nobody would give us a hotel room because we were both underage and we went to the Carlyle and the Algonquin and all these places and we swore we had money but they didn't believe us. We had to go all the way to—God, it was so awful—to this horrible place near the Flatiron I found that had bulletproof glass at the check-in desk. We were both so embarrassed. But we closed the curtains and turned the lights down and lit a candle and put on Liszt's *Liebestraum* No. 3 and—well, it was the most beautiful night of my life.

"You know, he's the only man I've ever had sex with? It's stupid—I know. I just—if things can't be *that* perfect, you know, then I don't want them. I don't want an ordinary life. And—*fuck*!"

The fire alarm is blaring.

There's smoke coming from Louise's hair.

The thing is: Louise hadn't noticed, either.

She has been thinking of what it must be like, to go to the Carlyle, or the Algonquin. Or it wouldn't even matter if it were a by-the-hour place with bulletproof glass. Not if somebody loved you that much.

They tuck the singed strand of hair underneath.

"I think you're beautiful however you do your hair," Lavinia says. "But this is precisely why I need you. I'd set my house on fire, telling stories, without you.

"I need you," Lavinia says, and squeezes her hand, and then it all feels perfect.

Except when Mimi texts, while Lavinia is finishing her makeup.

omg did u move in w/ Lavinia?

(shocked-looking lipstick-wearing pig)

(yes, says Louise, today)

```
omfg that apartment is soooo nice
i loved living there.
```
(gingerbread man in a gingerbread house that gets smashed)
```
what are you two up to tonighhht?
```

"Hey, Lavinia?" They are in the cab.

"What?"

"Did Mimi used to live with you?"

"Of course not. Why?"

"It's nothing. She just sent me this weird message—"

"I let her crash for a couple weeks between places." Lavinia is re-applying her lipstick with her cell phone camera. "That's all."

She gets out of the cab.

She lets Louise pay.

Tonight the full moon is smiling on Lincoln Center.

They take so many photos.

Lavinia takes some of Louise, pirouetting on the fountain's edge. Louise takes so many of Lavinia under the archways.

Lavinia posts them with the caption ah, je veux vivre!

They do a line of coke in the bathroom before the curtain.

Lavinia leaves a twenty in the bathroom attendant's tip jar.

They buy a glass and a glass and another glass of champagne, at fifteen dollars a glass, and Lavinia buys most of them but Louise also buys some, and because she is drunk she is not keeping track of how much money she is spending but she knows she has six hundred dollars a month that she did not have before, and that champagne tastes so good, and that they both look so beautiful tonight.

They really, really, do.

Even people they don't know tell them so. Old women and tourists stop them, to tell them so, and Lavinia smiles so magnanimously and says thank you, thank you.

———

On the stairway, Louise sees Athena Maidenhead. Her hair is piled neatly on her head. She's wearing pearls. She is in a long rose-colored dress and is on the arm of a man with no hair.

Also, Anna Wintour is there.

Lavinia takes Louise to the press room, which is half-hidden off the bathroom and which nobody but press (and Lavinia, who is not press but knows things) knows about.

Beowulf Marmont is there already. He is trying very hard to muscle into a conversation between two older men, making booming and staccato pronouncements about the significance of Wagner calling his operas *dramas.*

"That's the problem with Gounod," Beowulf says. "Their emotions are just so straightforward—it's all very expected, isn't it? It's emotive, but at the risk of complexity."

Gavin Mullaney punches Louise on the shoulder.

"I have to say," he says, "I'm impressed by you. And that's off-brand for me. So be proud." He turns to Beowulf. "Of course you know Louise Wilson. She writes for us now."

Beowulf looks appalled.

"Of course," says Beowulf. "What a pleasure."

He's still looking over her shoulder, of course (the two older men, who are married, work for *The New Yorker* and *The New York Times,* respectively), but this time he stays perfectly still.

"Wellhellothere!"

Somebody pushes in.

"You'reBeowulfMarmont."

Mimi thrusts out her hand.

She's wearing a sequined dress with a neckline that goes all the way down to her navel, and a hem that goes all the way up to her ass.

"I am," says Beowulf, who doesn't know who the fuck she is.

"You're Lavinia's friend."

"Sure."

"You write for *The Fiddler* and *The Egret* and you're doing your PhD at Columbia."

"Okay."

"*IreadwhatyouwroteaboutJoanDidionfor*The Egret*Ithinkyou'retotally rightandshe'sabsolutelyresponsibleforthepervasivefeminizationofnarrative nonfictionwillyoupleasetellmemoreaboutit?*"

Then, and only then, does Beowulf Marmont smile.

He puts his hand on her back.

"Let's get you a drink," he says.

"Let's go," says Lavinia, grabbing Louise's hand. She doesn't even look at Mimi.

"What's her deal?" Louise tries again, as they make their way up the stairs toward their box seats.

Lavinia doesn't answer. She leans against the statue at the top of the stairs and scans the crowd.

"Who are you looking for?"

"Nobody," Lavinia says. "The only person in the world I care about seeing is you, and you're right here." She keeps her eye on the stairway.

"Let's take a selfie," Lavinia says. They do.

"God, I love opera," Lavinia says, as they shrug off their furs and take their seats, as Lavinia scans the horizon, once again. "It's so nice to close your eyes for three hours and really *feel* things.

"And—look!"

She has brought her flask, even though they are already so drunk.

"Take. Drink."

She raises the flask to Louise's lips and tilts it so Louise's mouth overflows and she chokes a little.

Lavinia laughs. "Don't worry," she says, so suddenly.

"What?"

"You're nothing like Mimi."

Louise hates how happy this makes her.

"You're smart. And you're strong. And you're not fucking *desperate*. You're like me. You get shit done."

She squeezes Louise's hand.

"I'm sorry I made you come tonight—I shouldn't have—I know how tired you were."

"Don't worry about it," Louise says.

"But you're glad you're here, now, right?"

"Yes," Louise says.

"You're not mad at me?"

"No."

"I'm so glad you moved in," Lavinia says. "I hate being alone!" She takes another swig from the flask. "We're going to be—you and me. *Contra mundum!*" She takes Louise's hand. She raises it, so slowly, to her lips. She kisses her knuckles. She pulls Louise's arm in. She kisses where it says MORE POETRY!!!

"We're going to have the most wonderful night," she whispers, as the curtain parts.

The music is baleful and wonderful and the sopranos are beautiful and Vittorio Grigolo is so handsome and so passionate and you really believe how much Romeo loves her. And Juliette sings *ah, je veux vivre* and the waltz is a trill and Louise's heart is beating fast. She thinks *yes, yes, I want to live, too* and then she thinks maybe it is not so bad that she has spent two hundred dollars today (maybe three hundred if you count the champagne, the cab) and maybe sometimes you can be a little late with your work for GlaZam and sometimes (if you are with Lavinia at the opera) you don't have to worry, so much, about the men who follow you home in Sunset Park, and maybe it isn't so bad that she doesn't have the key to Lavinia's apartment; maybe it isn't so bad that she doesn't sleep sometimes because she is reading Lavinia's novel over and over again; maybe it isn't so bad that she has no space in the house for her clothes; none of it is so bad, when Lavinia is with her.

Especially when Lavinia is holding her so close.

Especially when they smell like whiskey, and champagne, and they've done a couple of lines in the bathroom, and Louise can smell Lavinia's perfume which is like fig and pear and lavender and which smells so much nicer than her own.

Especially when the music is swelling.

Especially when Lavinia kisses her neck.

Louise freezes.

This is one of Lavinia's affectations, she thinks—just like kissing her hand, or her knuckles, or her tattoo, like falling asleep on her shoulder, like curling up next to her in the same bed. Lavinia is exuberant and she shows love too boldly. Lavinia has never had sex with anyone but Rex (*was it—any man; was that a hint?*). This is just a thing Lavinia does to let you know you matter to her.

Just kiss your neck. With tongue.

Just bite, a little bit.

Just put a hand on your knee.

Louise looks over at her, but Lavinia is smiling like nothing is different, like nothing is wrong or weird or strange about it, like there's definitely nothing, nothing gay about it, not Lavinia sliding her hand up Louise's thigh, not her squeezing the skin between her fingertips, not her leaning in, again, and kissing the back of Louise's ear.

And Louise is so confused, because in all the times they've been together and looked at one another's breasts and compared cup sizes or changed in the same room or peed in the same stall, has Lavinia ever stopped to stare at her (she has stopped to stare at Lavinia, but mostly to think *she is so perfect-looking* and *she is so thin* and Louise does not think there was anything sexual in that, exactly, but now she isn't sure), but Lavinia is kissing her so delicately and so expertly—that's the other thing; like she knows exactly what she's doing.

Here's the thing: Louise doesn't know if she wants to.

She knew she wanted to the time she begged Virgil Bryce to take her virginity, because even though she was fat then and she was not pretty he was dating her all the same and that must mean he wanted her on some level. He had so often said he loved her despite all her unlovable qualities (silence, ugliness, anxiety, unceasing need) that made her unlovable. But even then, she thinks, she wasn't sure if she wanted to fuck him, or just wanted him to want to fuck her.

So then. So now.

There isn't, exactly, a single moment when Louise goes from *is she . . . ?* to *she is.* Or it was always: *she is.* Lavinia's hand on her knee. Lavinia's hand up her thigh. Lavinia's fingers moving her underwear. Lavinia's fingers inside her.

It feels good. That's the other thing. There's sexual orientation but there's also biology and when somebody is lightly biting your neck and also fingering you under this rose-colored taffeta dress with so many petticoats (thank God, thank God, she wore this ridiculous thing with all the petticoats; *was that why Lavinia asked her to wear this dress with all the petticoats?*) that feels objectively good no matter who is doing it as long as they know what they're doing, and also a little strange (and also cold?).

And Louise thinks *how can she want this?*

And Louise thinks *I cannot say no.*

She's just spent half of her rent money; she has a free apartment on East Seventy-eighth Street; Lavinia paid for the cab; Lavinia paid for the tickets; Lavinia paid for most of the champagne (*so what? So what? Does it matter? It matters*) and she wonders *is that what Mimi didn't do* except she can't imagine Mimi *not* letting Lavinia finger her (she *can* imagine Mimi begging Lavinia to finger her).

But also, this means Lavinia thinks Louise is hot enough to fuck.

But also *of course we're not fucking,* not that Louise is sure what counts as fucking with girls. Maybe Lavinia is just drunk or maybe Lavinia has been in love with her the whole time (*I love you; you're beautiful; I need you*—how many times has Lavinia said those things?

Has Louise really been so stupid?). Louise can't say no and this makes her angry but also, also, she doesn't really want to.

And the music, the music, the music. And the velvet. And the lights. And the champagne.

Lavinia pulls back. Her eyes are shining.

"I told you," she whispers. "I told you—what an *epic night*."

And her fingers are still inside Louise and she's kissing Louise right on the mouth and she's using tongue which of all the unreal elements of what is happening to Louise right now is the one thing, the *one thing*, that makes Louise think *oh God oh God* and maybe this, this, is what it feels like to be wanted, and maybe this is what it feels like to be loved.

And Louise thinks: *maybe it is not so important, to be able to say no.*

"I love you," Lavinia keeps whispering, into her mouth. "I love you; I love you; I love you so fucking much."

Here's the stupid thing: Louise believes it.

For a whole minute (a whole aria; Mercutio thinks Queen Mab has been with everybody; maybe she has), Louise thinks that this is where it has all been leading (the night but also this whole year; this year but also her life); that every stupid thing she has ever been or said or done and every time she has ever fucked up has been in the service of being known, like this, and also loved.

Until she sees Rex.

He is in a box across the way.

He is with Hal.

He is watching them.

Louise yanks herself away so quickly she almost falls over.

"I have to pee."

She bolts.

———

You can lose weight. You can dye your hair. You can learn to speak with a very charming mid-Atlantic accent. You can stay up until four in the morning, missing your own deadlines, just to read somebody's novel and tell them how great it is.

But nothing, nothing you do will ever be enough.

Even if somebody loves you (or they think they do, or they say they do), it'll just be because you remind them of someone else, or because you make them feel a little less bad about having lost somebody else, or because somebody else is watching, across the auditorium, in an opera box, and they just want to make them jealous, and you were just an accessory to this.

I am almost thirty, Louise thinks, *how did I not know this by now?*

She runs out onto the balcony. It's so cold—she's shivering, even though it's April—but she'd rather be here, shivering, looking out over Lincoln Center and that moon-infused fountain and that empty, geometric square than be inside for another second anywhere, anywhere Lavinia's perfume still hangs in the air.

She can't even get her cigarette to light.

"Need some help?"

She rounds on him.

"Here," Rex says. "Let me."

She still can't talk.

She gets her shit together long enough to offer him one, too.

"I'd offer you a handkerchief," he says. "But I think you stole mine last time."

"Oh," she says. "Sorry."

"It's fine," he says. "You can keep it."

"Lavinia burned it."

She puffs on her cigarette. She doesn't look at him.

"Oh." He puffs on his. "Really?"

"Yep."

"Okay." He exhales. "I probably deserve it," he says.

Then: "I'm sorry."

"Why? You didn't do anything."

"I didn't know. At the bookstore—when we met. I didn't know the two of you were . . ."

"We're not." Another, furious, puff. "She's straight."

"Oh." Again: "Really?"

She shrugs.

"We both are." She doesn't care, anymore. "But, you know. I hear men really like it when straight girls hook up."

"So I hear." He swallows. "How have you been, Louise?"

She is being so rude to him. He is being so kind to her. She can't stop.

"We've been having so much fun." She flicks out some ash onto the railing. "All these parties—haven't you seen the photos?"

"Can't miss them."

"Of course you can't. That's the idea."

"What?"

"Nothing. I'm sorry."

Finally, finally, Louise breathes. "I'm sorry. I'm—I'm in a mood."

"What's wrong?"

She turns to him. "Why does she hate you so much?"

He leans out on the railing. He sighs. "It's not my place," he says, at last. "Look—she deserves to be happy. God knows—I don't want to fuck it up."

"Did you cheat on her or something?"

"No—no!"

"Hurt her?"

"No—I mean—not like that."

"What, then?"

"It's not my story to tell."

"It's hers, you mean?"

"Isn't it always?" He is smiling, just a little bit.

"I won't tell her you told me," she says. "If that's what you're worried about. I don't have to do everything she says."

"It's stupid," he says. "Even now. I feel responsible for her."

"Well, you're not. She's not your problem. She's mine. And I want to know."

"Look," he says, finally. "I loved her—I really did. For a long time. And I still care about her—a lot." He sighs. "Look—she's a *lot.*"

Too much, Louise thinks.

"When we were, you know—when we were growing up, it was just kind of, like, the two of us, you know? I mean, there was Hal, sometimes, but he was at school, and, I don't know—we found each other. And when you're with her—God! It's like a drug—you know that."

"Yes," Louise says. "I know."

"And you're, I don't know, breaking into places and you're writing each other secret letters and—I mean—it's the most wonderful thing in the world, but we were in *college,* and I wanted to do—you know, normal, college-kid things."

"Beer pong?"

"I mean, sure."

"A *frat!*"

"I mean, frats aren't really a Yale thing, but . . ."

"Football?"

He lets himself laugh.

"Yes. Exactly."

The wind has gotten chillier.

"We shouldn't have gone to the same school. I mean—I told her it was a bad idea—or, I don't know, maybe she talked me into it, you know. And the first year, whatever, even the second, we did it her way. Then—look, it's not a bad thing to want to grow up."

"Careful," says Louise. "You might regret it."

"I waited until Christmas break. We talked about it. And she seemed, I mean—she took it well. She didn't freak out or anything. She was calm. Then two days later she calls me at two in the morning and tells me she's in Central Park, that she's taken a bunch of pills and stolen a paddleboat and that she wants me to come find her."

"A boat? Really?"

"I'm just reporting," he says. "Look—maybe it sounds funny, now—but it wasn't. I mean—she was off her face and she'd taken a fistful of her mother's Xanax and a bottle of gin and she kept trying to tell me that I should do it, too."

"Did she mean it?"

He hesitates.

"Yes," he says, finally. "She meant it. She told me that—that I'd promised to love her forever and she didn't want to live in a world where people didn't keep their promises and I shouldn't want to, either. A world of—God, I don't know."

"Football."

"Football," he says, and they both smile because this is almost fair. "Anyway, that's when she took medical leave. And—there she will remain. Until her parents stop paying tuition. Or, you know, she goes back. Her *sabbatical*. And, until then, I'll just, you know, run into her everywhere I go." He sighs. "It's my own fault. I should have known she'd be here tonight. I wasn't even going to come—but Hal insisted. Mustn't waste *Henry Upchurch's season tickets.*"

"God forbid."

There is a busker by the Lincoln Center fountain. Louise knows him. He plays every night, after the opera, and every night he plays something from the opera that people will recognize; that's how he gets his tips. He is practicing, now: *ah, je veux vivre dans ce rêve.*

"You know what's funny?" Rex says.

"What?"

"Sometimes I think she's right." He laughs. "Like—obviously, I don't *wish* I'd done it or anything. I'm not *crazy*."

"Of course not."

"I like my life. Only—" He takes a deep breath. "What can I say? She made a pretty fucking compelling case."

"She's a pretty fucking compelling person."

He laughs. "I mean—people *should* keep their promises. Probably. In a perfect world—we all would."

"It's not a perfect world," says Louise.

"Hers is," says Rex. "That's the problem."

"It isn't," Louise says, so softly he doesn't hear her. "Trust me."

Rex leans on the railing. "It's nice to talk to someone who gets it. Maybe that's selfish."

"You're not selfish," Louise says. Rex shrugs.

"You should tell her."

"What?"

"That I told you. I mean—I don't want to be the cause of any secrets." He sighs one last deep and expansive sigh. "I've done enough damage. I don't want to ruin her for you too."

You don't understand, Louise thinks, *it's too late, now.*

"Spoiler alert." Hal is behind them. "They both die."

"Jesus—Hal!"

"How long were you going to be out here? You missed the whole second half!"

Rex doesn't say anything.

"Philistines. You ran out on me, young Louise. I never got to give you your book!"

"I'm sorry," says Louise. "We left in a rush."

"Women." Hal rolls his eyes. "Educate yourself, sometime."

Everybody is spilling out into Lincoln Center: in their black tie, their silk dresses, their velvet trousers, their heels.

Mimi is falling over.

She's half-lurching, half-kissing Beowulf Marmont.

He hails a taxi. He hauls her in.

"Someone's getting raped tonight," says Hal.

"Jesus, Hal!"

"Christ, Rex, I'm not making a rape joke."

He puts his arms around both of them.

"I take rape very seriously," he says. "I'm a very, very good feminist."

Nobody says anything.

"Now, if I said he was taking her home to make love to her in a very gentle and assured and consensual manner," Hal says, "now *that* would be a rape joke."

Louise and Rex exchange looks.

"Besides, all men are rapists. Just read *Rolling Stone*." Hal straightens his dinner jacket. "Poor Michelle. Lol."

"Michelle?"

It has never occurred to Louise that Mimi has a real name.

"She was fun," Hal says. "I miss her putting on a show at parties. Remember New Year's 2014, Rex? Wasn't that great? We walked in on Lavinia and Mimi making out in the bathtub at the MacIntyre, didn't we, Rex?"

"Stop it, Hal!"

"What was the theme, Rex? Do you remember? Was it *The Great Gatsby*? It's always *The* fucking *Great Gatsby*. But it was a good party—not like this year, don't you think so, Rex—they're getting worse and worse."

And Louise thinks *this, too, was for them; this, this, too.*

"I have to go."

Rex pushes past them both.

"Oops," says Hal. He looks at his watch.

"By the way, young Louise," he says. "Lavinia's looking for you. And she's not happy."

"Shit."

"I told her you were hanging out with Rex."

"Shit—*shit!*"

The square is full. The party's over. The busker's playing *ah, je veux vivre* at full forte.

There are so many people in sequins and not a single one of them is Lavinia.

"Chop chop, Cinderella," says Hal.

Louise runs.

Between waves of champagne and whiskey and the coke comedown Louise thinks all the thoughts she always thinks, except this time they're louder and clearer and more true.

This, *this* is how she's fucked it up; Lavinia hates her, now—Lavinia will be so angry—and now she has no money for rent and she doesn't have the keys and her subletter has moved in, already, because an empty rent-stabilized place doesn't even linger five minutes in this city, and Louise thinks *oh God oh God* and she thinks *just let her not be mad* and she thinks *I will even let her fuck me, just please God don't let her be mad.*

She doesn't even have the fucking keys.

Lavinia isn't anywhere. She's not on the landing and she's not on the Grand Tier and she's not on the balcony or in the box or anywhere in the orchestra, and Louise tries to call four or five times but Lavinia has turned off her phone, but somehow that just makes Louise try to call more times, even though it goes straight to voicemail, because if there is a definition of insanity it's trying the same thing over and over, expecting a different result.

And Louise tries so hard not to panic or to cry or to scream and she tries to focus on the next steps she can take: she can go back to the apartment and wait by the buzzer (what if Lavinia never comes home? What if Lavinia is already home and won't let her in? What if the neighbors who come in and out see her and think she is loitering like a criminal and call the police?).

She could call a friend (she has no friends). She could get on Tinder and hook up with someone, but then she would have to explain to her supervisor on her shift at the bar (oh God, her shift) why she has shown up to bartend brunch in a taffeta dress that makes her look like Shirley Temple, because everything she owns (her clothes, her clean underwear, her laptop which she needs for her GlaZam job; fuck, *fuck,* her GlaZam job) is all with Lavinia, who now is furious with her.

Then she sees her.

Lavinia is passed out on the side of the fountain.

"Christ, Lavinia—"

Louise runs so fast she loses a shoe and has to carry it, limping, across the square.

"Jesus Christ!"

Her eyes are open.

She reaches down to help her.

Lavinia grabs her so violently she drags her down, instead.

"Where were you?"

It's a snarl.

"I'm sorry."

"Where. The Fuck. Were you?"

"I'm sorry—I had to pee."

"You left me *alone.*"

"I know. I'm sorry."

"I needed you."

"I'm sorry."

"I do everything for you—fucking *everything.* And you left me alone!"

She's sobbing so hard she chokes.

"Were you with *him*?"

"No! I mean—I had a cigarette—I gave him a—"

"Did you fuck him?"

"No! Of course not."

"You fucked him! You fucked him and you laughed about it, the two of you, you laughed behind my back!"

"I would *never!*"

And even as she's saying it she thinks *almost, almost.* Even as she's saying it she thinks *maybe.*

"You're so fucking ungrateful!"

Lavinia sits straight up.

"After everything, what more do you want from me?"

"You're tired." Louise is so calm. "You're drunk. You're tired. That's all. You want to go home."

"I let you live in my house."

"Please!"

"Give you—give you a fucking *gorgeous* dress to wear, buy you booze, give you—give you a fucking *free room* and you can't even sit through a whole fucking opera with me?"

"It's not like that."

She does not know if Lavinia has forgotten fucking her, or only wants to forget, pretend it didn't happen.

"What more do you want from me?"

"Lavinia, I—"

"What—you want *cash*, too?"

Lavinia throws her purse.

It hits Louise square in the chest.

She doesn't even think to catch it.

She lets it fall, clattering, to the ground.

Wordlessly, Louise kneels and picks it up.

Lavinia is sobbing; she tucks her knees under her and bites her own palm, just to stop from screaming.

Louise just watches her.

Louise can't get upset. Louise can't get angry.

Louise doesn't have the keys.

"It's okay," Louise says. "You're fine. You're fine. You're okay. I'm here. It's okay."

Here's the thing: she's lying.

You'd never know it. Louise is so good, wrapping Lavinia's coat around Lavinia's shoulders, smoothing Lavinia's hair out of the way of Lavinia's collar, whispering Lavinia's name. She is efficient, in the way that she holds Lavinia's hair back, when Lavinia throws up, when Lavinia wipes her mouth on the beautiful, unsullied taffeta. It is like Lavinia never fingered her in an opera box to make Rex jealous. It is like Lavinia never called her a whore.

The busker has started playing "New York, New York" on his violin.

Lavinia tries to sing along, but she's too drunk, and her voice cracks, and all she can manage is *I want to be apart.*

I want to be apart.

"We should tip him," murmurs Lavinia. She lies back down on the ground. "Do you have any money?"

"No," says Louise. She's lying now, too.

"We should give him some money! He's so good!"

"We should get you home."

"No!" She drops her purse again. She picks up the credit card and drops this, too.

"You can't stand."

"Please, Lou—*please.* Get some cash out, okay?" She's smiling so helplessly now. "My PIN number is 1-6-1-9. Just—give him a hundred, okay?"

Louise starts to say *we have to get you home,* but then Lavinia starts screaming and Louise realizes she doesn't have a choice now, either.

So she gives the busker a look, a significant, pleading, humiliated look that she hopes to God conveys *I'm getting you your hundred dollars, okay? So just make sure she doesn't choke on her own vomit until I get back,* and then she goes to the Duane Reade across the street.

It's not that she means to hit the *balance* button. But it's not that she doesn't mean to, either.

Lavinia has 103,462 dollars and forty-six cents.

Lavinia lives in an apartment her parents own, and she has 103,462 dollars and forty-six cents.

Lavinia lives in an apartment her parents own, and has 103,462 dollars and forty-six cents, and fingered Louise in an opera box just because she could.

Also, she made Louise pay for the cab.

Louise takes two hundred dollars out of Lavinia's account.

Lavinia has jumped into the fountain. She's standing with her arms outstretched, with her hair dripping and the violinist watching her and still playing "New York, New York" on his violin, over and over. Louise puts six twenties into his case.

The final twenty is from her.

"Look at me!" Lavinia cries. "I'm Anita Ekberg."

"Of course you are," says Louise.

"Take a video of me." Lavinia makes such a big splash. "But make it black-and-white."

Louise does.

"I'm the worst," Lavinia murmurs, when at last Louise gets her into bed. She held back her hair for an hour or two or three while Lavinia sweated out all the coke and Louise apologized, not for the first or last time, to Mrs. Winters who lives next door, who is a friend of Lavinia's parents and has had it up to here with the loud music and the banging at all hours and has half a mind to write the Williamses herself and tell them to come home and take care of the problem. "I'm the worst; I'm the worst; I'm sorry."

"Don't worry about it."

"I shouldn't have—I know, I *know* you really like me."

"Good," says Louise.

"And I'm sorry we—you know."

"It's fine. It happens."

"It didn't mean anything, you know. It was just—you know, the opera."

"Of course."

"Like—I'm *straight*."

"I know."

"I'm sorry. I'm sorry. I'm too much. I know—I know I'm too much."

"You're not too much."

"I *am*."

"You're not."

"Don't leave me, Lulu," Lavinia says. "Please—*please*."

"I won't leave you."

"I love you, Lulu."

"I love you too, Lavinia."

Here's the most painful part: she still does.

Louise waits until Lavinia falls asleep. She extricates herself so gingerly, so that she won't wake Lavinia, and then goes into the other room, the one that is nominally hers, with Lavinia's closet overflowing with Lavinia's dresses and Lavinia's jewelry and makeup overflowing all over Lavinia's vanity, in this apartment where she isn't on a lease, where she doesn't even have a key.

She goes to the dining-room table.

She opens up her purse.

She counts them: the four crisp, inalienable twenty-dollar bills.

Not even half a ClassPass membership.

She opens up her laptop. The light is so bright it hurts and she has to close her eyes, just for a second, which only reminds her how tired she is.

She has two more hours of work to do for GlaZam tonight. She has a shift tomorrow at noon. She has a lesson with Paul right after.

Louise goes to Lavinia's drinks cabinet, which is so full of good booze. Louise never noticed how good it was, before, but she notices it now—the Talisker and the Laphroaig and Hendrick's and Rémy Martin and she fingers the labels on all of them and thinks *this, this is where you live now.*

She pours herself a glass of whiskey.

She gets to work.

4

"QUEEN MAB HATH BEEN WITH ME."

That's all Lavinia ever says about that night.

She says it once, in the morning, clicking through all the photos Louise has taken of her. She changes her profile picture to the one that made *Last Night at the Met*. She sits at the dining-room table with her feet up on either side of the stale croissant she's photographing atop turquoise china she had shipped all the way from Uzbekistan.

"You know, Lulu?"

Louise clears the table. Louise pours the tea. Louise sets down the eggs that she has made.

"Yes, Lavinia?"

"I think I saw the fairies last night."

Lavinia leaves it there.

So Louise does, too.

"It's a good video," Lavinia says, of the one in the fountain. "I'm going to send it to Cordy—just to annoy her. She's always telling me I go out too much."

Louise gets dressed in silence.

"Where the hell are you going?"

"Work."

"*Work?*" Lavinia gives a little laugh. "Jesus, how are you *up?*"

"It's eleven."

"Exactly! Just call in sick!"

"I can't."

"You shouldn't go out. You look like hell." She stretches out on the table. "Come on—let's pull a sickie. It'll be great—we can watch every single episode of *Brideshead Revisited*—we'll do tea and scones and—like, I think I have a teddy bear somewhere we can carry around."

"I'm sorry."

"I don't want to do it alone."

"I'm sorry," Louise says. "It's work. I can't miss it."

"Of course," Lavinia says. "Of course—you're right. I'm being selfish. I'm selfish. You're right. Don't let me stop you."

Louise buttons up her top button. She pins up her hair.

"Hey, Lulu?"

"Yes?"

"Can you pick up dinner on the way home? I don't want to cook. Just, you know, whatever they have at Agata's. Like—a roast chicken, maybe? And, like, a few—fuck it, I'll text you a list. I'll pay you back."

Lavinia's grocery list at Agata & Valentina comes to $61.80.

Louise pays for it with the money she has taken out of Lavinia's bank account. Lavinia doesn't pay her back.

Louise does such a good job, being Lavinia's best friend.

She sews Lavinia's dresses. She mends their hems because Lavinia is always tearing them. She cleans the house. She buys the groceries. She does the laundry. She irons. She sweeps crumbs off the steamer trunk.

She apologizes to Mrs. Winters, again, when she sees her in the hall.

She is very careful to emphasize—Lavinia has made this explicit—that of course she doesn't *live* there (the co-op board, Lavinia says and says and says again, is very strict). She's visiting.

She reads Lavinia's novel (it is always the same novel; there are only twenty thousand words of it and Lavinia never writes any more) over and over, and tells her every time how great it is, and when Lavinia starts to cry and say that she is *too much* and the book is trite and that nobody could ever like a trite book written by such a terrible person as her Louise says *no, you're beautiful* and holds her hand.

They don't do their cowriting sessions anymore. Lavinia has stopped asking for them.

It's just as well. Louise doesn't really have the time.

Louise saves three thousand dollars a month, being Lavinia's best friend.

She works it out, one time, on the back of a napkin.

Lavinia buys Louise at least two drinks a night (*$20 each, including tax, including tip*) (*$40 x 30 = $1,200 a month: entertainment*).

Louise saves eight hundred dollars a month (*nine with utilities*) (*more if you take into account location, location, location, but Louise is being conservative, here*).

(*$900 a month, rent*)

Lavinia also gets all their Ubers (*$900 a month, transport*).

That's before you count the clothes, which are castoffs so don't cost money, exactly, but are still more beautiful than anything Louise has ever worn before, even if Lavinia slams a car door on her hem, even if Lavinia spills something on it, even if Lavinia insists they break into Central Park after a black-tie function and so the skirt becomes covered in grass stains and Louise can never wear it again. That's before you count the Seamless meals (Lavinia doesn't really cook, so most of the groceries she has Louise buy she throws out). That's before you count the enormous oil portrait of a naked courtesan Lavinia buys at the Flatiron flea market one day, and puts above Louise's bed as a gift without asking her.

That's before you count the Adderall.

Of course, there's also the question of expenditures.

There's ClassPass. Lavinia is always too hungover to work out, and usually Louise is too tired, but she insists they enroll for another month, anyway, and this time, she says, it's Louise's responsibility to make her do it.

Also, the time Lavinia sent her in the middle of the rain-soaked night to a sketchy street corner in East Harlem to buy some shrooms that weren't even hallucinogenic, anyway. Also the cash tips for the bathroom attendants at the Met, at Trattoria dell'Arte, at Shun Lee, at all the places that Lavinia and Louise either surreptitiously snort coke or throw up.

Also the shifts that Louise misses, because sometimes not even the Adderall works, when Lavinia swoops in last-minute and says she has tickets for an aerialist performance that Athena Maidenhead's friends are doing at this multipurpose space full of mirrors called House of Yes. The GlaZam work, because that's so easy to say *I'll do later,* and then the shifts she's too sick for, sometimes, and then sometimes she even misses a lesson with Paul, even though he's just a couple of blocks away.

So the second time Louise takes money from Lavinia's bank account, when Lavinia is passed-out drunk on the sofa (because she's been sobbing because they saw Rex and Hal, again, at the Mr. Morgan Spring Gala at the Morgan Library and neither of them looked at her but Rex raised his glass to Louise and smiled, and she is so angry that he has done this, and yet so glad), Louise doesn't even think of it as stealing. She's just balancing the books. Just a hundred here, a hundred there. Then another fifty. Then another hundred.

Somehow, she's still always broke.

Here's the other, funny, horrible thing: Louise has never looked better. She loses six and a half pounds. Mostly this is the Adderall, and the coke, although she and Lavinia actually make it to FlyBarre exactly twice before Lavinia loses interest and declares working out a Calvinist abomination. Lavinia does her makeup. She gets her hair done by professionals. This is at Lavinia's insistence.

Lavinia knocks on her door, one night. Louise doesn't answer, at first, because by now she's learned that the only way to avoid dealing with Lavinia is to pretend to be asleep, but Lavinia knocks again.

"You've dyed the bathroom grout," she says.

She sits on the bed.

"I *what*?"

"The tub. It's yellow."

Louise has been so careful. She has spent hours scrubbing.

"I'm sorry," she says. She turns over like she's falling back asleep.

"And the bathroom smells like bleach."

"I'm sorry," Louise says again.

"Look—*I* don't care," says Lavinia. "You could dye the house purple, for all I care. But my parents—you know—I'm not *really* supposed to have guests. And they're very particular about making sure the place is, you know. In case they decide to retire back here. Or sell it. And, you know, it's not ordinary grout." She tightens her stained dressing gown around her shoulders. "It's Italian or something. I don't know. You're not even really supposed to get it wet."

She lies down next to Louise in the bed.

"You know what? I think you should go to Licari. That's where I go."

Louise is very, very good at sussing out people's natural hair color. It's one of the things she used to do on the train. It has never occurred to her that Lavinia's hair is anything but perfectly natural.

"I've already made an appointment for us both," Lavinia says. "Besides, I get a discount for bringing in a new client."

She curls up against Louise. She leans her cheek against Louise's back.

"I wish my hair were straight like yours," she says. "It's so shiny. God, I hate you."

Lavinia falls asleep next to her in the bed, with her arm flung over Louise's breast.

The color costs four hundred dollars.

She takes half of it out of the ATM the next day.

———

Other people *notice* how much better Louise looks. Her mother, of course, who for the first time in five years doesn't bring up Virgil Bryce, but instead makes a comment about how all those nice young available men in their early thirties in New York must be lining up around the block. Paul actually checks her out during their sessions, which would feel violating if he didn't start to stammer and blush and look so astoundingly ashamed of it that Louise almost pities him. Beowulf Marmont Facebook messages her at three in the morning to tell her he really liked her piece for *The Fiddler* and maybe they could have a coffee to talk about it sometime.

Also: that guy who ghosted her.

In May, he sends her a Facebook message.

Looks like you've been having fun!

Winking face.

Maybe we should take another stroll through Prospect Park,

sometime.

I feel so bad we never got to do that again.

He doesn't even apologize. He doesn't have to.

Sure, Louise says.

Blushing face.

She carries this knowledge all day in her heart. She scrubs Lavinia's countertops and she beats Lavinia's carpet and she sews Lavinia's fur collar onto Lavinia's vintage opera cape and she spends the whole day smiling.

She doesn't tell Lavinia.

Not until Lavinia has them go, one morning, to the King Cole Bar, at the St. Regis, which might be the most expensive bar in New York. But they're famous because of their murals, and also because they apparently invented the Bloody Mary, and they charge like twenty-five dollars for them (before tax, before tip). Even though Louise doesn't like Bloody Marys, Lavinia does, so there they are, hogging a table.

"You know what, Lulu?" Lavinia says. "I've just had the most incredible idea." They've had two drinks each. Louise feels sick.

"What?"

"Tomorrow," Lavinia says, "we're going to go on a *pèlerinage*."

"A what?"

"A pilgrimage. It's French."

"No, I know—" Louise hasn't slept in three days. "But—"

"To the *sea*, silly! Let's get up really early tomorrow morning and watch the sun rise from the Cloisters and then walk all the way to Coney Island."

"Why?"

"To prove our mettle! To prove we can! Like—like the medieval pilgrims, you know—have you ever listened to Liszt's *Années de pèlerinage*? We can recite 'Ulysses' again, can't we?!" She points at the tattoo. "MORE POETRY!!!" She says it just like that.

Tomorrow Louise and the guy who ghosted her are going to Prospect Park to take a walk. She has suggested an afternoon date, especially, for a Sunday afternoon, because she knows Lavinia never gets out of bed before dusk on a Sunday afternoon.

"I'm sorry," Louise says. "I have work."

"What work?"

"I have a shift."

"Why don't I come by, then? I'll come by the bar—I'll sit and be very quiet, just like a mouse, and then when you're done . . ."

"No," Louise says—too quickly. "Not a shift. A lesson. Um—Flora, in Park Slope."

"I thought you have Flora on Tuesdays and Thursdays."

"It's a makeup session. She's—she's going on holiday next week."

"Where?" Lavinia signals the waiter. She orders a bottle of Chablis without asking Louise.

"I don't know—why?"

"She didn't say? I mean"—Lavinia laughs—"It's the middle of

the school year. Believe me—Cordy won't shut up about her mid-terms; she's been blowing up my phone . . . who'd let a student go on *holiday*?" She shrugs. "Well it's fine. I can meet you in Park Slope."

"Actually," Louise tries again—she tries so hard. "I have plans."

"It's not a *full* walk, but it's still a few miles from Prospect Park to the sea. We can go through Midwood—look at all the Hasidic men with their, you know, hair-things."

"I have *plans*," Louise says again.

"With who?"

"I have a date."

"A *date*?" Lavinia's laugh is sharp. "With who?"

"This—this guy I used to go out with. Nobody important."

"Why didn't you just say?"

"You're right," Louise says. "I'm sorry. I should have. I was embarrassed."

"*Why*? It's *wonderful*." Lavinia pours herself a glass.

"I know I should have checked with you, I'm sorry."

"Checked with me? Don't be ridiculous, Lulu—you're not my *prisoner*! You can go anywhere you want to!" She downs her glass. "It's probably good for us to, you know, have a little time apart. I mean, I know I can be a bit much sometimes."

"It isn't that!" Louise starts, and then stops, and then tries again. "I mean, it's just a date. That's all."

"Wait," Lavinia looks up. Her eyes are shining. "This is The Ghost, isn't it?"

"No," says Louise, automatically, before saying "Yes."

"What does he want?"

"No—we just started, you know, talking again."

"Did he explain why he ghosted?"

"I'm sure he will," Louise tries. "In person. We'll talk about it tomorrow."

"You're very forgiving, Louise," says Lavinia. "If somebody did that to me—I'd never speak to them again." She pours Louise a glass.

"You really shouldn't let people treat you like that." She smiles a sad and sympathetic smile. "He probably just wants sex."

"We're going to the *park!*"

"Where?"

"Brooklyn."

"He's making you come all the way to him?"

"I mean—we just wanted to go to Prospect Park, that's all."

"I'm just saying, be careful. Men like that, you know. They like to see how far you'll jump. Don't be surprised if he just wants to sleep with you. Only—"

"What?"

"You'll probably have to go through with it."

"*What?*"

"I mean—don't come back, like, late or anything. I want an early night's sleep. I don't want to wake up to buzz you in. So, you know, if you're coming all the way from Brooklyn, you might as well spend the night." Lavinia is editing a photo on her phone.

She doesn't look up when the bill comes.

$220. Four Bloody Marys. A bottle of wine Louise has barely touched.

Lavinia keeps playing on her phone.

And Louise thinks *say something, say something, say something.*

Louise doesn't say anything. She puts down her credit card. She signs.

"I think you should sleep with him," says Lavinia. She's still looking at her phone. "You really need to get laid."

Louise doesn't: not really.

She used to (all the time: she used to). Virgil (when Virgil would), and then when she finally (for once, for once) changed her number she'd have so many one-night stands and she fucked the male feminist, the night they met, in a bar bathroom in Crown Heights. She used to crave it (the touch; mostly the touch, but also the laughing and the biting and the *God, you're beautifuls*).

Louise hasn't had sex in four years.

Not unless you count what happened at the opera, but it's hard to put a label on what happens between two straight girls when they're drunk and neither of them comes.

Sex, Louise thinks, is probably a waste of time, anyway.

Louise tells Lavinia her date bailed.

"Men." Lavinia shrugs. "I told you. Fuck them all."

Louise skips her work for GlaZam. *I am a little bit Concerned that you R Not taking this Project seriously?* writes the woman in Wisconsin who runs the business. *We need to Step things up OK??*

"You're just too good for everybody," Lavinia says. "There's nobody in the world who deserves you."

That evening, Louise takes three hundred dollars out of Lavinia's bank account at the bodega on the corner of Seventy-sixth and Lex, while she's supposed to be at Agata & Valentina at Seventy-ninth and First, buying expensive cheeses Lavinia will never eat.

She takes a walk.

It is late, she knows, and she should be getting sleep (she has so much to catch up on; she has so much left to do), but she is afraid if she goes back to the house she will wake up Lavinia. If Lavinia wakes up she'll want to talk to her, or do her hair, or take photos, and Louise can't deal with that again, not right now.

She goes to the park (everything is in bloom; everything is pink), not Prospect Park but Carl Schurz, which is that little sliver of green by Gracie Mansion where you can see the East River and also there's a statue of Peter Pan. Because everything is in bloom and in pink everybody is out, at sunset, and the people who love each other are holding hands, and leaning in. Every single person in New York City except Louise is out there kissing and being in love. And Lavinia is asleep or watching *Fortunes of War* in bed for the umpteenth time and all of a sudden Louise feels so lonely, so goddamn lonely, even though she shouldn't, even though to be lonely is ungrateful, because Lavinia has given her so much (*the room, the booze, the drugs, the parties, oh God the parties*). And to steal money (*it's not stealing; it's insurance; it's reparations; she's still flat broke anyway*) is ungrateful. Maybe that's just who she is, maybe, just the most ungrateful person in the world, that she could have all this and still wish she were in Prospect Park, holding hands with some guy who didn't care enough about her to break up with her by text.

Louise isn't angry. She can't get angry.

She Facebook messages Rex.

Nice to see you at the Morgan Gala.

Nothing loaded. Nothing treacherous. Just pleasantries.

Haha, you too.

I hope I didn't cause any problems?

To which Louise responds: No more than usual.

Good.

How are you doing?

You holding up okay?

To which Louise responds: The usual.

Is that a yes or a no?

I'm not sure, she says. It's been a long day.

I saw.

Of course he saw. All the photos Louise posts are for him.

You two looked like you had fun. Very glamorous.

They were in vintage bathing suits. They had perfect flapper makeup on.

It's the makeup, Louise says.

I don't believe that.

I swear.

Prove it, says Rex.

How?

Take the ugliest photo of yourself you can manage.

She does.

She is afraid, but she scrunches up her face and sticks out her tongue and bugs out her eyes and takes a selfie.

Hm, Rex says.

The little box that shows he's typing stops, and starts, and stops again.

It's not the makeup, he says.

Then: I'm sorry.

Am I allowed to say that?

You're allowed to do whatever you want, says Louise. Makes one of us.

Laughing face.

It is dark by the time Louise comes home.

She puts the groceries down on the table.

"What took you so long?"

Lavinia is sitting in the dark, staring into space.

"Nothing," Louise says.

Then: "I picked up some flowers for you."

Lavinia looks so happy.

"I went all the way to Jerome—I thought you'd like them."

"They're beautiful," Lavinia says. She puts her arms around Louise.

Louise has gotten so, so good at this.

It's easy, so long as Louise thinks of it as a game.

She takes a couple hundred dollars out, every couple of days.

She takes ten milligrams of Adderall a day.

She takes so many photos.

She sleeps in Lavinia's bed.

She stops sleeping.

She keeps it together.

In June, Louise gets fired.

It is not from GlaZam, although her work has suffered. It's not from the bar, although she's always late there, too, and out of it.

It's Paul.

She arrives to do one of their thrice-weekly sessions, which at eighty dollars an hour and three hours a session and three sessions a week (Paul really wants to go to Dartmouth) is her best-paying gig by far. She is late, but not by much. She and Paul go over the difference between *assent* and *assuage*. Nothing is wrong.

Then Paul looks up.

"So," he says. "It turns out I don't need you anymore."

He's been quietly assured by somebody at Dartmouth that he will be able to go as a squash recruit.

"I mean, I've probably gotten everything I'm going to get out of these sessions, anyway."

He gives her an extra fifty.

He's on his phone before Louise even leaves the room.

Louise is fine. Louise can work with this.

Louise just has to take out a little more money from Lavinia's account (Lavinia won't miss it, anyway). Louise just has to make sure she doesn't lose any of her other jobs.

She just has to be out of the house at the same time, every day, so that Lavinia won't know (nine hours a week, there are only nine hours a week where she can be out of the house and Lavinia knows not to ask after her).

She can take walks.

She can get work done at cafés.

She can see Rex.

Not that Louise sees Rex regularly, or anything like that.

It's just that they had one text message conversation, then another, and he asked her about the stories she was writing and told her he thought the one about those runaways from Devonshire Academy was pretty moving, and she asked him how the second year of grad school was going and he told her it was a lot of work, especially Classics where there's a lot of language classes, but that it was rewarding to do something you really loved. Louise said sure, and said something about wanting to go to the Met to see the Greek and Roman sculptures and he said it's a shame, I'd love to go with you some-time, I haven't been for ages and she said haha that would cause WWIII and he said haha and she said I'm going Wednesday at like four wouldn't it be funny if we ran into each other haha and he said well that would be a coincidence and then they do.

"It's nice," he says, as they walk from hall to hall, and from statue to statue. "I always feel peaceful in museums."

Louise has three whole hours to feel peaceful.

"I used to come here all the time as a kid." Collegiate was just across the park. "Whenever, like, I needed to get away."

"Not exactly the Devonshire Mall," she says.

"Was it weird?" he asks her.

"What?"

"Growing up in a campus town."

It strikes Louise, suddenly, that Lavinia has never asked her any-thing like this.

She shrugs. "I guess it's a bit like growing up next to a museum," she says. "It's nice to have it there—but, you know, it's not, like, *real*."

She tells him the story about the time she was sixteen, and spent a whole week in the dining hall before anybody noticed, and when he hesitates she's afraid she sounds crazy, but then he laughs.

"Did you go to any classes?"

"No!"

"Why not? You should have!"

"They'd have noticed."

He shrugs. "I don't know," he says. "People are pretty oblivious."

They stare awhile at an armless Aphrodite.

"It's a good story," says Rex. "Even so."

"No it's not," says Louise. "If it were a *really* good story, I'd have gone for the whole year."

Rex sighs. "I think being in a really good story is overrated," he says.

They both focus very hard on Aphrodite.

"I just want a quiet life," Rex says.

They say goodbye on Eighty-sixth and Lex, because Rex is taking the subway home to the East Village, and they stand for a little too long by the station stairs.

"I had fun," says Rex, and Louise says *yes, so did I.*

"I hope—you know." He takes a breath. "Is she *okay?*"

She doesn't know why it stings that he cares.

"She's fine," Louise says.

"Don't let me—"

"Of course not," Louise says.

They shake hands awkwardly and then he vanishes underground.

"Lulu!"

Louise's head snaps up.

"Lulu!"

Lavinia is across the crosswalk.

It's the only time Louise has seen Lavinia out of the house on her own.

For a second Louise thinks *she has seen everything;* her gut plummets. She did not know it was possible to be so afraid. She can taste her own heartbeat.

"I thought you were teaching!"

Lavinia's arms are laden with shopping bags.

"Christ, I was so *bored,* all afternoon!"

She is smiling, Louise thinks. *Thank God, thank God, she is smiling. She doesn't know.*

"Why aren't you at your lesson?"

"It ended early."

And Louise thinks *how close will you come to fucking it all up.*

"I've got a present for you," Lavinia says. "I was so bored I went to Michael's—it would look *perfect* on you."

She hands it to Louise in the middle of the street.

It's the most beautiful dress Louise has ever seen.

It's bias-cut. It has a halter. It has sequins all the way to the hem.

"I told Mimi, *this dress would look perfect on Lulu.* I just had to buy it for you! Don't you love it?"

"You went with *Mimi*?"

Lavinia shrugs. "You were out! And she was available. Come on, Lulu, don't be mad."

"I thought you hated her."

"Anyway—let's go home and change. I want you to wear this tonight."

"Tonight?"

"It's *The Fiddler*'s spring fling—didn't I tell you?"

Lavinia is already half a block ahead of her.

"You might want to take an Adderall now," Lavinia calls out. "It's going to be a late one. Ugh—it's going to be a shit-show. Beowulf Marmont has an interview with Henry Upchurch in the next print issue and he's telling everyone who will listen he's going to be one of their Five Under Thirty. God, I fucking hate these people."

They go to the party.

They do lines with Gavin Mullaney's quasi-feminist girlfriend. They do shots with Gavin, who tells Louise she should pitch another story to them, maybe for print this time, and Louise says *yes, of course, when I have time.*

They dance until dawn, because Lavinia has the keys, even though Louise is in heels.

The next morning, Louise sleeps through her shift at the bar, and then she's fired from there, too.

"Just as well," Lavinia says, when Louise tells her. She is painting her nails and doesn't even look up. "That job was beneath you. You're supposed to be a Great Writer. Besides, it's not like you have rent to worry about."

Louise stops texting Rex after that.

She figures it's probably for the best.

He just wanted information about Lavinia, anyway.

Louise is fine. She is still fine. Everything is fine.

Louise is so fucking good at keeping it together.

Even without half her SAT income. Even without the bar shifts. Even without Rex.

She just has to take out a little more money, that's all, just a little more often.

It's not like she has to pay rent.

It's not like she'll ever need a deposit for a new place.

I can do this, Louise tells herself. *I can do this.*

Until the night Louise comes home from teaching Flora in Park Slope, and nobody lets her in.

She stands for a while in front of the door—idly, stupidly—like maybe Lavinia's just in the shower.

Nobody answers Lavinia's phone.

Louise stands like that for almost an hour, even though it's raining, because her bag is heavy with SAT prep books and her laptop and her charger and she has no idea what else to do, and it's only when she sees Mrs. Winters coming down the stairs through the glass in the door that she bolts, because—of course—she does not live there.

I can do this, she tells herself.

So Louise goes to the Carlyle.

She walks so slowly. She walks with her head high. She walks in like she belongs; maybe she does.

Her dress—it is Lavinia's dress—is beautiful. Her hair is impeccable. She has Lavinia's cash in her wallet.

She sits at the bar. She keeps her hands in her lap.

She orders a drink—just like Lavinia would—without betraying the slightest sense that her world is falling apart.

She sips her champagne very, very slowly.

"Thank *Gawd, hunny.*"

It is Athena Maidenhead.

It is the first time Louise has seen Athena here alone.

"I got stood up—*can you believe it?*"

She always talks with an exaggerated New York accent, like she's chewing gum.

"That's the last time I *evah* make a date on OKStupid—that's what I call it, yannow? *Okaystupid.* Get it?" She laughs a mannish, throaty laugh and smacks Louise on the arm.

Louise smiles, like Lavinia isn't missing, like her world isn't about to end.

"From now on," Athena says. "I'm sticking with What'sYourPrice."

She orders herself a glass of champagne, too.

"You looked cute the other day. At the opera. *Whaddya* see?"

"*Roméo et Juliette.*"

"The opera. *Gawd,* I would die!"

She leans in real, real close. "I would *love* to go to the opera, *yannow.* You should get Lavinia to get *me* a ticket, sometime."

She laughs like this is a very funny joke.

"You think, maybe, sometime, you can get a plus-one?" There's lipstick on her teeth.

"Maybe," Louise says.

"Smart girl," says Athena. "Keep your cards close." She gives Louise another playful shove. "Girls like us," she says, "we gotta stick together. You ride it out while you can. Just—you know—be smart."

"What do you mean?"

"How long you known her?"

"Six months. Give or take."

"Yup." Athena taps her wrist. "Thought so. Right on time, too."

"What do you mean?"

"I mean, I wouldn't panic, yet. You probably have another coupla months." She raises one painted eyebrow. "But if I were you—I'd have a backup plan." She gestures for another round of drinks, even though Louise hasn't finished the first one. "When she kicked Mimi out, she had to move back home for, like, two months just to get a deposit together—it was so sad. And the one before her—Lisabetta, God, I think she just packed up and left—"

"Before Mimi?"

Athena shrugs.

"I'm just saying. Sell up while you can." She brays a laugh. "The meek don't inherit shit." She downs her glass. "Get me an opera ticket, sometime."

She leaves Louise with the bill.

It is midnight by the time Louise gets home. It is still raining. Lavinia is still not there. She doesn't answer her phone.

Louise waits across the street, on the stoop of one of the brownstones, so that if Mrs. Winters comes, she will not see, even though there is no awning there and it's still raining.

Louise does numbers in her head to keep herself calm:

First and last month's rent: sixteen hundred dollars—no, that's a lie, she won't find a studio for eight hundred—that one was rent-stabilized—she'll have to find another roommate—*oh God, one with a second set of keys*—somewhere so much further out; *oh, God, the commute.*

She has sixty-four dollars in her bank account.

She has three hundred dollars of Lavinia's cash in her pillowcase.

She barely even has a job.

I can do this, she thinks—she makes herself think—*I can do this.*

Here's the thing: Louise can't.

Lavinia gets home at two.

She stumbles out of a taxi.

She falls over in front of the building.

Her stockings are torn. Her dress is inside out. She's bleeding from the lip.

"Jesus!"

Louise is there, so fast, to help her up.

"Where the fuck did you come from?"

Lavinia's eyes aren't focusing.

"I've been waiting for you (*don't get angry; don't let yourself get angry*). I don't have keys."

"Oh." Lavinia drops them. Louise picks them up. "Okay."

"Where were you?"

"Nowhere. Out."

They go into the lobby. They go up the stairs.

"Your dress is inside out."

Lavinia doesn't say anything. She climbs up the stairs on her hands, on her knees.

"I was worried about you."

"No, you weren't!"

Lavinia tries to pull herself up on the railing, but she falls over again.

"You were glad—weren't you? You were glad—you had the *whole night* to yourself, didn't you?"

There are tears in Lavinia's eyes. There are tears streaming down Lavinia's face.

"I mean, I was locked out of my house, so—"

"*Fuck you,*" Lavinia screams. "Fuck you—it's *my* house! My house—mine and Cordy's!"

A door opens at the end of the hall.

"*Really.*"

Mrs. Winters is standing in the doorway.

Louise mouths another apology.

Lavinia just starts laughing.

"Can you believe it?" she says, right in Mrs. Winters's face. "This bitch thinks it's her house, now."

"I'm just putting her to bed," Louise says. "I'm just taking her home—that's all. Then I'm going."

"I should hope so," says Mrs. Winters.

She raises her eyebrow. She closes the door.

Lavinia keeps laughing when Louise forces the door open, pushes her inside.

"Christ—don't *touch* me! What's wrong with you?"

"Just get inside," Louise says. She's so tired. "Please."

"Don't fucking touch me!"

"Just tell me what happened!"

Louise sits her down. Louise gets some ice for the lip.

"Did—did someone do something to you?"

"What, you *jealous*?"

Lavinia tosses that long, unnatural hair.

"What—you want to make another pass at me, is that it?"

"I'm going to bed."

"Fine! Go to bed! I don't care—I don't fucking care *what* you do."

Louise can't sleep.

She stares at the ceiling, for a while; at Lavinia's chandelier, at Lavinia's painted gold moldings, at Lavinia's ten-foot oil painting of a naked Parisian courtesan that's probably fake, anyway.

She gets up.

She goes into the living room.

She opens the door to Lavinia's bedroom.

Lavinia is lying there, with the light from the moon falling on her in slanting rays. Her hair is golden and billowing and haloed all around her, like a Rossetti angel, like Ophelia drowned. She's wearing a nightgown.

She still sleeps with a teddy bear.

And Louise thinks *oh, God, don't let it be true.*

She goes to the bed. She sits on the edge. She is so careful. Lavinia is clutching the teddy bear so tightly.

Maybe there was a Lisabetta, she thinks, maybe there was a Mimi.

She'll do anything, whatever it takes. She'll lie about the novel.

She'll stay up late no matter how many shifts she misses. She'll stop taking out money. She'll never speak to Rex again. She'll take photos for Lavinia, however many photos Lavinia wants, of Lavinia looking beautiful and glamorous and maenad-ish and world-destroying, whatever Lavinia needs. Just as long as she is not like the others. She won't even ask for love; she doesn't even know if Lavinia can love. Just as long as Lavinia needs her.

Louise gets into the bed and Lavinia's back is still to her.

She is so careful, putting her hand on Lavinia's shoulder. She is so careful, sliding her arm against Lavinia's arm.

Lavinia doesn't move.

Louise lies, so stiffly, against her.

"I love you," she whispers. "I love you; I love you; I love you."

Lavinia doesn't say anything.

They lie there a little longer, in silence, and then Louise gets up and goes back to the other bedroom, and then the next day this is just another thing that never happened, and also Louise sleeps so late she misses her last GlaZam deadline and she's fired from there, too.

The next morning, Lavinia sends Louise out for croissants from Agata's, and it's like nothing ever happened.

The last party Lavinia ever goes to is at a sex club that's not a sex club.

It's called the P.M., which is supposedly short for *petit mort*, and it's bottle service only. It's housed in an old theater that looks like a bordello and it's impossible to get in unless you know somebody (even if you pay six hundred dollars for prosecco; even if you pay eighteen hundred for champagne). One of the sideshow acts is a little person taking a dildo up the ass, and another is a woman who covers herself in shit, and someone who can whistle show tunes with her cunt.

Lavinia isn't even supposed to be there.

It happens like this:

There is a special party that night. Athena Maidenhead is performing her fan dance except with a cat-o'-nine-tails, but they're short-staffed and they need more girls and so she does Louise a solid and hooks her up.

"How wonderful!" says Lavinia, when she hears. "I've always wanted to go. I heard they have orgies onstage—do they have orgies onstage?"

"I mean—I'll be *working*!"

"But you're a bottle girl! All you have to do is stand around and look pretty and hold a tray, right?"

"It's *work*." Louise tries again.

"I see." Lavinia's smile turns sharp.

"I just don't want you to feel obligated," Louise says. She is so careful. "I don't want you to come to keep me company and be miserable because I'm stuck, like, pouring some finance bro champagne—I'm not going to be much fun for you."

"Don't be stupid, Lulu," says Lavinia. "You're always fun for me."

"We can do something else that day." Louise's smile is so much wider. "The Chelsea Flea Market, maybe? Or jazz brunch at Hotel Chantelle—you love jazz brunch."

Lavinia doesn't say anything.

She rises, goes to the dining-room table.

"Hey, Lulu?"

"Yeah?"

"I left a couple of rolls of cash on here. Not a lot—just a few hundred dollars, or so. I could have sworn there were five, but . . ." She looks very evenly at Louise. "You haven't seen them, have you?"

Louise's heart is beating so quickly again.

"No, of course not."

"I figured." Lavinia gathers up the rest. "I just wanted to check."

"I'll keep an eye out."

"Maybe there were four," Lavinia says. "God knows I never remember these things."

And Louise casts about so desperately for that thing, the one thing, that she can do—that she can *always* do—that will make Lavinia happy again.

"You know, the light's really good right now."

"Is it?"

"Let me take a picture of you. Just—you, on the couch, with the dressing gown, and the light on your hair."

"No, thank you," says Lavinia.

Now is the part you've been waiting for.

You and I both know what happens now: Lavinia doesn't make it.

But the thing you have to understand is: why.

Now you and I, we've been to parties before. We've done this a few times before already.

But here's the thing: you've never been to a party like this.

That's the whole point.

When they hire the fire-eaters, the midget who takes the dildo up his ass, the guy who rolls around in buttercream, the conjoined twins, the glitter-eater, the woman who queefs show tunes, they do it because the most important thing in a party like this is that it should be unlike any party you've ever been to before, and if you throw up or cry or run screaming then so much the better, because at least you've felt something.

The bouncer is short and the drinks are watered-down and the only people who pay for them are assholes, anyway, but the line goes all the way to the end of Chrystie Street, some nights, even though none of those people will ever get in (except Lavinia; always, always, except Lavinia), because it is the sort of place that finally, finally surprises you.

Here is a girl who was the villain on *Survivor* one time.

Here are some bros drinking frozen rosé.

Here is the guy who invented this app that's like Uber, except it's for helicopters, except it goes to the Hamptons, except it's five hundred dollars a person.

Here is a former child star who does stand-up now (that's the joke).

Here is a guy who is getting married tomorrow, and doesn't want to be.

Here is Louise in a miniskirt, serving shrimp.

It is hot. It is sweaty. Everything sticks to everything else. Two guys, already, have felt Louise's ass (she isn't allowed to object). Another guy has gone straight between her legs. Athena Maidenhead is completely naked except for these little pasties in the shape of Greek columns, jiggling the tassels in perfect figure-eights. The dwarf is in makeup.

"Spoiler alert." It's Hal, in black tie. "The fire-eaters fuck."

Louise puts on her most docile and most flattering smile.

"Shrimp, Hal?"

"You know, they do horrible things to girls like you in places like this."

"I hadn't noticed."

"It's not a bad thing. You should go for it. Some illustrious Great Men around the place." He considers. "Who knows, you could make a decent wife for somebody, one day. You seem like a nice enough girl."

"Another shrimp?"

"What, you embarrassed to be here? You shouldn't be. Nobody gives a fuck about you. You're a complete nonentity."

She's still smiling.

"I'm not being an asshole, by the way. That's a good thing."

"Tell me more."

She grits her teeth so hard she thinks they'll break.

"It's freeing. Nobody expects anything from you." His tongue lolls, like it always does, and he goes on nodding long after he's finished talking. "I bet nobody cares whether you're a Great Man in New Hampshire."

She starts making eyes at strangers, hoping someone will signal her.

"Are you a Great Man, Hal?"

"Fuck, no. I'm just a humble insurance executive. Just give me a classic six and a Filipina woman to iron my shirts and Wagner on my sound system and I'll happily be first up against the wall when the revolution comes. *Me ne frego.*"

"Sounds lovely."

She's craning her neck now, looking so desperately at the guy who five minutes earlier grabbed her ass and wanted to know if she'd gotten butt implants.

"You know Rex is crazy about you, right?"

"What?"

"It's really fucking pathetic. I told him so. He's a pussy."

"I'm Lavinia's best friend."

"Sure you are," he says. His teeth are yellow but they glint with the strobe lights. "You're such a good friend."

"Is—he here?"

"You think Rex would watch some girl get fucked by a robot?" He snorts. "He'd probably rush the stage and leap to her defense." He takes the last shrimp off her plate. "If it makes you feel better, he feels super-guilty about it."

"It doesn't."

"He's got a hair shirt on, under all that tweed."

"Don't tell me," says Louise. "I don't want to know."

"All property is theft," says Hal.

He tips her a fifty and pats her on the ass.

Louise keeps smiling at strangers. Louise does whatever Louise has to do to keep the wolves from the door.

She smells Lavinia before she sees her. That same, familiar perfume: even here where it smells like bodies and sick. That cloying, heady smell of lavender and fig somehow gets through. Then she sees Lavinia's hair.

She's worn it long and down tonight, and she's in a dark velvet dress; she's leaning back on the banquette and laughing and flashing her teeth.

Mimi is with her.

"Lavinia?"

Lavinia looks up so idly. "Oh, hello, Lulu." She leans back on the banquette. "You're out of shrimp."

Mimi is smiling her dog-like smile.

"Isn't this place *insane*? There was one act—I swear to God—if that dildo thing was a trick . . ."

"Mimi, darling?"

"Mhm?"

"Can you get me another glass of prosecco?"

Mimi trots off happily.

"God, this place!" Lavinia fingers the cocktail toothpick like it's a cigarette. "God, Lulu, everything's so *filthy*. It's disgusting. Don't you love it?" She laughs. "Isn't it, like—what you imagine Pigalle was like, during the fin de siècle. Like, the *real* Moulin Rouge—was it shocking, do you think? Come sit."

"I'm working," says Louise.

Lavinia shrugs. She sips the remnants of her prosecco.

"So," Louise says. "Mimi's here."

Lavinia smiles, too, like nothing's wrong. "Oh, I *know* you don't like her," she says. "But she's all right in *small* doses."

"I never said I didn't—"

"She's just intense, that's all. But then again, so am I—don't you think?"

Louise doesn't say anything.

"Don't you think so, Lulu?"

"I mean," Louise has already lost, "a little, I guess . . ."

"God, you must be so *bored*—"

The woman who rolls in her own shit is rolling in her own shit onstage.

"Poor Lulu. It must be a very great burden on you, putting up with me."

"Don't be silly," says Louise. "I love every minute of it."

"So—how's Hal?"

Louise freezes. "What?"

"I saw you over there—chatting."

"He wanted shrimp."

"You like him, don't you?"

"God—Hal!" Louise doesn't even think Rex likes Hal. "Of course not."

"I mean, it's fine if you do. You should fuck him. I mean—he's an idiot. But he's a rich idiot. And he's, you know, funny."

"I don't want to fuck Hal, Lavinia."

"You should fuck *someone*, Lulu. It'd be good for you! You need a boyfriend. It's not good for us, you know—spending, like, *all* our time together."

Out of the corner of her eye, Louise can see Mimi, raptly applauding the woman rolling in her own shit.

"I want to spend all my time with you, Lavinia," she says.

She keeps her eyes down. She is so good at this part.

"We're best friends, Lavinia."

She has always been so good at this part.

"You were so good to come tonight, Lavinia. You knew—you knew I really wanted you here, deep down."

"I know."

"I wish I could be watching the show with you."

"I know."

"I know—I was stupid—I shouldn't have taken this gig."

Lavinia just looks at her phone.

"No," she says. "You really shouldn't have."

At ten-thirty, Mimi falls asleep on the banquette. She snores.

Lavinia keeps dancing alone, under the neon lights that bathe her in red, blue, green.

"Lulu," she murmurs. Two more men have felt up Louise's ass, by now, and it hurts so much to stand in heels. "My Lulu."

Louise hates how relieved she is.

Lavinia sidles up to the bar.

"You're my favorite, Lulu. You know that."

"I know."

"We should get a picture. Just the two of us."

The aerialists are so high above them.

"When I'm off shift," Louise says. "We'll take a photo. I get off at four."

"We should break into the green room! See if the dildo-fucking is real!"

"When I'm off shift," Louise says again, in exactly the same tone of voice, like it's going to do any good.

"We should break in and take photos with the robot!"

"Please," Louise whispers, "please, Lavinia, don't—"

But Lavinia is so certain and determined. "Mimi promised she'd do it with me. But she's—well, you know Mimi—she can't hold her drink; she isn't like you; she's not like *us,* Lulu."

"I don't want to get fired," Louise says. *"Please."*

"Christ, Lulu." Lavinia rolls her eyes. "You used to be so *fun!*"

She gets up.

"I am fun!"

Lavinia picks up her arm, points to it. "More poetry, remember? More fucking poetry—what the *fuck* did I get this tattoo for?"

Louise can't stay like this. She can't talk to a customer (worse: a female customer); there's the guy who tapped her ass already looking pissed, and Hal enjoying himself with one of the other waitresses in the corner, and if this job goes well they said there would be others, and sure she gets her ass squeezed but the tips are so great, and she doesn't have time for this—*fuck,* she doesn't have time for this—and if she could only explain—

"Fuck it," says Lavinia. "I'm going. Come or don't come. I don't give a shit."

She spits out a cocktail toothpick.

"You can't rely on anybody."

She turns.

———

Things always turn.

You pack up, push off; you get in a beat-up Chevy or a moving van; it doesn't matter. You read poetry on the water or smoke a joint on a railroad bridge; you say *I love you* on the top of the High Line or in the middle of the Devonshire woods.

It's the same, either way.

There's the day you pick up the keys to this railroad one-bedroom in Bushwick and you think *today, today is the day everything changes.* You think you will never see Devonshire and its fading strip malls and its railroad tracks and its squat unhappy houses ever again. You swing the door wide-open and stretch out your arms and dance through the emptiness of every new inch of the space, with your hair short and dark and your eyes closed. When you open them Virgil Bryce is standing there, on his spindly legs, with his arms crossed, and he is telling you: *don't get too excited, dearest, who knows how long you'll be able to make it work here,* and even though you've argued on the way over, even though you've spent the whole six-hour drive arguing, you think *no, no, this time is different, this time I've outrun it; this time I've won.*

Even when he comes so close to you. Even when he runs his fingers through your hair.

Even when he says *I just don't want you to be disappointed when the world doesn't see what I see.*

There're the days you don't believe him, not deep down. There're days you do.

"Lavinia!"

Louise catches up to Lavinia in the green room.

She's out of breath. She's covered in other people's sweat. There's a drag queen putting on fake lashes who doesn't even look at them.

"Lavinia—*please.*"

"Go back to work, Lulu. I don't want to put you out."

"That's not what this is!"

"I get it. You know what? I get it. I'm a *lot*. I'm a lot to fucking deal with—" She strides past a ballerina with pierced nipples. "You—Louise—you must be a fucking *saint*."

She is all the way to the backstage area, now, and Louise keeps thinking somebody is going to notice them, or stop them, but everyone is so drunk and the performers are looking in the mirror and the bouncers are dealing with a brawl, and so nobody does.

"Jesus, Lulu, quit following me!"

They pass ropes and red velvet curtains and lights and sandbags and everything smells like grease paint and cigarette smoke.

Louise doesn't even know why she's following her anymore.

"Christ—leave me alone."

Lavinia presses through a dark red door.

Louise follows her.

"Jesus—you want to watch me pee, now?"

They're in a mirrored bathroom, just between the stage and the dance floor. They are the only ones there. There are art nouveau naked ladies painted onto the ceiling. There's a red velvet chaise. There's a chandelier. Of course there's a chandelier.

Louise locks the door.

"Can you just listen to me for a second?"

A different Lavinia laughs in every mirror.

"Fine," Lavinia says.

She hikes up her skirt.

She takes a piss right in front of Louise.

"I'm listening. Are you happy?"

She bursts out laughing.

"Are you fucking happy now?"

She wipes, flushes.

"Go ahead."

"Please." Louise is doing such a good job. "Can we just talk about this?"

"Go back to work, Lulu." Lavinia has gone to the mirror. She is reapplying her lipstick. "God knows, you need the money."

Louise takes a very deep breath.

Louise is very calm.

"I'm sorry," she says, in such a small, clear voice. "I miss you. Things have been weird, I know, I'm sorry."

"You want a raise?" Lavinia spins around, and all the mirrored Lavinias spin, too. "You want overtime?"

She grins. She's got lipstick on her teeth.

"One card not enough for you? You want the Amex, too? God—how stupid do you think I *am*?"

Louise's heart is in her throat and her stomach is in her feet and nothing in her body is where it is ever supposed to be and she cannot think except to think *it is all over, now*. She tries to focus on just the practical things (*a place to sleep, a place oh God to sleep, don't let me go back home please that's all I want don't make me go back home*).

"I'd have just *given* it to you," Lavinia says. "If you'd asked."

I will go anywhere, Louise thinks, *I will never go back home*.

"Am I really that awful—that it's so hard just to *pretend* you like me?"

"I do like you."

"You hate me!"

"I love you."

"Don't lie to me!" Lavinia's voice goes so high. "Like I don't know—like I don't know how much I fucking *disgust you*. I remember—I fucking remember the opera, okay? God, you couldn't *wait* to get out of there—it's not like we even *did* anything!"

Louise can't even breathe; Louise thinks *make this better fix this do anything say anything make her happy calm her down make it right make it right* and so she blurts it out, among the no's:

"I'm in love with you."

She doesn't mean it. She doesn't know if she means it.

It is the only thing that will make Lavinia stop shouting at her.

"What?"

"I—the opera. I—*like* you, okay? I freaked out because I liked you. I'm sorry. I'm sorry—I know you're straight—I *know*."

God, listen to yourself, Louise thinks. *Not even Lavinia can be this dumb.*

But Lavinia is smiling.

"Poor Lulu," she whispers. She puts her hand on Louise's cheek—so magnanimously, now—*God, this makes her so happy*—"Poor, poor Lulu"—*of course everybody dies of love for Lavinia; she is just that beautiful; that is how it goes.*

She laughs a little bit.

"It's not your fault," Lavinia says.

She takes a deep breath.

"Come on," she says. "The light is beautiful in here. Let's take a selfie."

Louise can breathe again.

It's worth it, she thinks. *It has to be worth it.*

Louise has been this desperate before.

She has wandered the streets of Bushwick at three in the morning, covered in blood, with a credit card and a driver's license and a sweater and a bus ticket back to New Hampshire on her phone with four percent battery life, and nothing else. She made it work then.

Just go to an all-night diner. Just go to a nightclub where the lights are real low. Just go to a shitty bar and wash your face in the bathroom. Fuck a stranger, just to have a place to stay that is not a night bus to New Hampshire.

It's not pretty, but it works.

She'll make it work now, too.

Lavinia puts Louise's lipstick on. Lavinia wipes the mascara off Louise's face. Lavinia smooths back Louise's hair.

"Give me your phone," Lavinia says.

She moves the candles from the toilet tank to the sink to give them better light.

She turns the camera inward.

That's when Rex texts Louise.

I miss our Met outings.

Another one soon?

Is it weird that I miss you?

Lavinia doesn't even get mad. That's the worst part.

She doesn't rage. She doesn't throw things.

"You're moving out," she says. She shrugs. "You're moving out—*now*."

"Lavinia, let me explain—"

"I don't care." Lavinia is carefully, very carefully, putting her lipstick back in her purse. "Whatever it is—I don't care. Here—take the keys. Get your shit. By the time I come home I don't want to see you."

"I don't have anywhere to—"

"All that cash," Lavinia says. "And you don't have enough for a hotel room?" She shrugs. "Stay with Rex. I don't give a shit."

She throws the keys on the floor.

Louise bends down to get them.

She's already on her phone.

"What are you doing?" Louise can't even think *please, please* anymore. Everything is so still. Movement in the room stops with the finality of it all.

"I'm telling everyone," Lavinia says. She closes the toilet, sits down. She types with both fingers. "I . . . had . . . the . . . most . . . *ridiculous* night." She looks up. Just for a second. "Period. I found out that my crazy roommate stole my money and fucked my ex and tried to fuck me in a nightclub bathroom."

"That's not what happened."

Lavinia keeps typing.

"*My crazy dyke roommate stole a shit-ton of money from my bank account while she was hooking up with my ex-boyfriend and trying to convince me she was in love with me*—how do you spell *deceitful*—is it *i* and then *e*—come on, Louise, you're a fucking SAT tutor, you should know!"

"Don't," says Louise. "Please—please—I'll go, just—"

"It's fine. I have AutoCorrect. My *deceitful psycho dyke roommate I felt fucking sorry for stole four thousand dollars out of my bank account while I was letting her live rent-free in my sister's bedroom.*" She raises the camera. "Come on—fucking *smile*, Lulu!"

Louise grabs the phone.

"Jesus Christ, what the *fuck* is your problem!"

Lavinia yanks it back.

And Louise, all she can think, all she has left, is *let them not know; let them not know;* and she doesn't know who it is that she cares about knowing, because she doesn't care about Beowulf Marmont and she doesn't care about Gavin or Father Romylos or Athena or Mimi or Hal and she doesn't even like them, anyway, but in the moment she isn't considering that. All she's thinking is that nobody can know what she has done, and so she pulls harder, so much harder than she means to, and then she and Lavinia are on the floor, grabbing for it, and the stupid thing, the really stupid thing, is that the phone clatters under the sink, anyway, so that by the time Louise is pulling out Lavinia's hair, by the time Lavinia is scratching at her shoulders, by the time she is yanking her up against the mirrored and the mirrored and the mirrored walls, by the time she hits her head on the sink, the phone isn't even there, not the first time she hits her head, nor the second, nor even the third.

This is how Lavinia dies:

Putting a hand to her head. Looking down at her forearm: at the MORE POETRY!!! that is covered with droplets of blood.

Looking up at Louise.

Falling, with all the other Lavinias: against the mirror, against Louise, onto the floor.

This, this, is how Louise fucks everything up.

5

LOUISE IS ALWAYS RIGHT.

She has known, for years, that you can fool some of the people all of the time, and all of the people some of the time, but you can't fool everybody forever, no matter how good you are at this, no matter how hard you work at it. If you are a deceitful psycho dyke who steals money and also your best friend's ex-boyfriend, no matter how thin you are, or how pretty, or how good that one piece you wrote for *The Fiddler* blog was, the truth is that everybody, sooner or later, will know.

Anyway, it's over now.

Lavinia's dead.

The bass is thumping. People are screaming applause. Somebody's knocking at the bathroom door.

Lavinia's phone rings.

Whatever Louise does, she can't scream.

She puts her hand over her mouth.

There are three hundred people in this club, right outside the door.

Louise tries to breathe in that very calm and mindful way she practiced once, during therapy, that's supposed to put things in perspective.

It doesn't work.

Lavinia's phone keeps ringing.

———

Somebody keeps knocking on the bathroom door.

Mimi's face is glowing on Lavinia's phone.

Just breathe, Louise thinks. *Just breathe.*

The phone goes to voicemail.

Mimi sends so many texts.

where r u???

i woke up all alone

Sad kitten emoji.

Crying fox emoji.

Weeping deer emoji.

r u still here?

Louise breathes.

Louise wipes the blood off the floor. Louise washes blood off Lavinia's forehead. She uses a hand towel and very expensive basil-smelling liquid soap. Louise hides this in the bottom of the trash.

Louise pushes Lavinia's long, loose hair over her shoulders. Lavinia's hair is so long and luxurious that it covers her face. She takes off Lavinia's necklace, which is enormous and glittering and bloodstained, and pins it to her hair so that the medallion falls over Lavinia's forehead, like she's wearing a crown, so that you cannot even see the blood.

The banging on the bathroom gets louder.

"You *cunt,*" cries somebody. "You fucking *cunt!*"

There is nothing Louise can do.

She opens the door.

Twenty people are in line for the bathroom.

There is no way, she thinks, *that this is not the end.*

———

Lavinia is propped up in Louise's arms.

Lavinia is dead, and her eyes are open, and she is propped up in Louise's arms, and a very skinny girl with fried blonde hair and a 1980s dress is staring straight at them both.

She takes them in.

She stumbles to the floor.

She starts throwing up in the toilet.

People swarm in around her—the girl's even skinnier friend, who is holding back her hair, and some guy shouting *gross, Jesus Christ, I've got to take a piss* and then the drunk girl who is holding back the other drunk girl's hair is getting in a fight with the drunk guy who just wants to take a piss and at some point he unzips his fly and gets his cock out and starts pissing on the wall and because everyone is watching him nobody notices Louise haul Lavinia, like she's stumbling, like she just needs her hair held back, back toward the dank and narrow corridors that lead toward the stage.

And still it is only a matter of time, and maybe, *maybe* Lavinia is not dead but only stunned (Louise has watched a lot of *Law & Order* but even so she's not sure how much effort it takes to kill somebody because murder doesn't really feel like a thing that actually happens in the real world), and it is so loud and so crowded and so dark that Louise just hauls Lavinia against the wall (which is sticky, and provides friction) and hides her body with her own, pushing her up, like it's just the two of them, like they've gone in seclusion to some corner so they can make out, so Lavinia can finger her again, so that Louise can kiss her neck.

"Get a room!" somebody is shouting, and Louise doesn't even know if it's at her, because there's a guy getting a blow job out of the corner of her eye.

There is an aerialist's globe abandoned in one corner of the corridor. The fire-eaters have used it, already, and it smells like gasoline still.

Louise lays Lavinia down there, under the skeleton of the globe, under the lights, under the fake chandelier jewels, which shine every time the house lights strobe.

She feels Lavinia's face. She kisses it. She feels her throat and her neck and her heart and nothing, nothing is beating, but still this cannot be real, because people do not die like this, because she is not a person who kills people, she is not a person who does anything wrong, ever, and killing a person is about the worst thing you can do, and also there is a God and He sends down lightning bolts at this sort of thing, and so if Lavinia were dead a judgment would be made and Louise would turn to ash.

Except that the guy who smears himself in buttercream is up for an encore.

This time, he's making balloon animals, except they're not made of balloons.

Lavinia is so beautiful, under the aerialist's globe.

Louise leans over her. She tries to arrange Lavinia's hair, again, so the blood stops showing, and she thinks that Lavinia would love this because Lavinia looks just, just like Ophelia right now and then she starts to feel sick because what kind of sick person justifies killing someone on the grounds that they have always wanted to be Ophelia, a little bit, or at the very least the Lady of Shalott.

Then everyone starts screaming and the lights are blaring and some guy she has never seen before says "CROWD SURF" right in her face and the skinny girl (one of them) screams like this is the first time in her life she's ever heard of crowd-surfing and then everybody is looking at them, *straight at them,* at this beautiful dead blonde white woman and this slightly less beautiful blonde white woman who is still alive and breathing and on top of her and everybody is screaming, screaming, like they are gods, and then they start rolling the globe with the two of them inside and everything is spinning and Louise thinks she is going to be sick—she is sick, and she thinks *now, now is the moment they realize* but they don't, because the lights are pulsing and the sound is blaring and they're crossing the orchestra pit, crossing the main hall, and then glitter falls from the ceiling, in a big grand-finale burst, and it falls thicker and harder than any blizzard Louise has ever seen and in this thickness it sticks to both of them: to the sweat and whatever that clammy thing is called that makes you a little bit wet after you die, and then they are both so covered in silver you cannot even see the blood, you cannot see (how is it that everybody cannot see?) that there is a dead girl with long blonde hair and open, confetti-sliced eyes.

Louise pukes.

Everybody cheers at that, too.

As they roll the globe toward the wings of the stage, Louise catches a glimpse of Hal. He's sitting with the ballerina with the pierced nipples.

He raises a glass at them both.

Now they are in the shadows.

Now Louise is pushing, so desperately, against the wall.

Now Louise finds the service door.

She hauls Lavinia into the service alley. It smells like rotting fish, and sweet wine, and cooking fat.

Lavinia isn't even the only girl prostrate in that alley.

She hauls Lavinia into a splintering wooden trolley. She pushes the crates out of the way. She avoids the rats.

She cuts herself on one of the screws holding the wheels on. She looks down to see if she is bleeding, but Lavinia's blood has stained her calves, too, and so Louise can't even tell.

———

Mimi is still fucking texting.

Where are u? I'm upstairs? Are u here??

And Louise thinks: *I am not myself.*

This is not real life, Louise thinks. Police sirens are blaring, and they aren't even for her.

Louise decides.

Louise grabs Lavinia's phone. She calls an Uber.

She pulls Lavinia's arm over the back of her neck.

"Come on," she says, loud enough for everybody on the street to hear. "Come on, sweetie! Let's get you home."

She is so chipper.

She is just another overworked waitress, helping just another drunk girl to a cab.

They are both covered in glitter. They're both covered in puke.

It's one of those nights: in the city.

It's a Friday night and everybody's screaming, and no matter how late it is it's like daylight out; and it's so uncanny but also it's a relief, because it means you're not alone.

You can walk past so many nightclubs with blood on your face and nobody will even notice.

You can walk down a city street, on the Lower East Side, in Bushwick, with blood on your face and nothing but a driver's license and a credit card and a phone with almost no battery life, and your knuckles bruised from when you have hit a man (you are not even the kind of girl who would lose control and hit a man) (you have always been that girl) (he always told you you were that girl), and nobody will even notice, or care.

Louise has done this before. It didn't feel real then, either.

Louise waits for the Uber in the alley outside the club.

There are so many people out there.

A lot of people are drunk-crying, and so Louise gets on her knees and holds Lavinia real close, and real tight, and murmurs into Lavinia's stiffening neck *I know, honey, I know, I'm sorry, I'm sorry, I love you* and she doesn't even know if she means it.

Another text from Mimi.

Questing exploring fox emoji.

I'm all alone.

did u go off w/ luis?

are u ok????!!111

Louise did not want to hurt Lavinia, when she hurt Lavinia. (She wanted to hurt Lavinia.)

She did not want to hurt Virgil Bryce.

(She is not that kind of girl.)

It's just that when you've had the same conversation over and over for a year, in a tiny little railroad apartment in Bushwick, and once again a man you love is saying *I love you* but also *this is a benediction and a mercy, because I know you better than you know yourself and I have made the choice to love you anyway, and nobody else who knows you will,* and he is both kissing you and also telling you you'd be hotter if you just lost a little weight. He is both fucking you and also telling you it'd be better if you both moved somewhere a little quieter, where you'd have a better chance at *making it,* because then you wouldn't be disappointed, maybe, just maybe one time—instead of nodding, instead of sighing, instead of saying *yes, yes, you're right,* you hit him so hard he falls backward, the way men hit women in films, the way men aren't supposed to hit women in life.

(Maybe you do this, once, and then you know he is right about everything he has always said about you.)

That is when you see that he sees that you are the crazy bitch he always knew you were, and that, that is the only way you can leave.

You are the crazy one, now. You always were.

"I was right about you," he says, in this priggish way that almost,

almost, sounds like he's glad to be able to say it, and mops the blood from his cheek, "you're a fucking psycho, Louise" and he grabs her by the back of her neck, like a dog, and pushes her out the door, and he is right, and it is the last thing he ever says to her.

It's so easy, hauling Lavinia into the Uber. (*Thank God, thank God she's so thin.*) It's the only time Louise hasn't hated how thin Lavinia is.

"Your friend okay?"

"She's seen the fairies," Louise says. She holds Lavinia on her lap. Lavinia's eyes are still open. There's blood on Louise's miniskirt, on her legs (*thank God, thank God I'm wearing black*).

"What?"

"Nothing."

"She smells like shit."

"I know."

"It's a hundred-dollar fine, you know, if she does it again."

"She won't," says Louise.

Lavinia's nipple is showing, where the dress has slipped down. The driver is staring at her in the mirror.

Louise lets him.

There's a joke Louise has always liked, about these two men who find a bear in the woods. This is the joke: You don't have to be faster than the bear. You just have to be faster than the other guy.

She's thinking about that joke now.

Louise has done the next part before.

Getting Lavinia out of a cab. Getting Lavinia onto the stairs. Getting Lavinia into the bathtub. Putting the water on.

Washing that long, tangled, glorious golden hair.

Washing the blood off.

———

should i just go home?

This is Mimi's twentieth text.

lol I'm so drunk I'm getting blackout.

And Louise thinks: *this cannot be real.*

Nothing is real.

Lavinia's eyes are still open.

This cannot, cannot be real.

Lavinia's phone won't stop ringing.

Louise will get through this, too.

I just need time, she thinks. *I just need a little more time.*

"Darling!"

Louise can sound so much like Lavinia, when she wants to. She knows her voice so well. "Darling—Mimi—I'm so terribly sorry!"

"Where are you?"

"Are you still at the P.M.?"

"Hal said you left. He said you got sick."

"Just for a second—darling. Needed a moment's respite, that's all."

"Where are you?"

And Louise thinks *fuck, fuck, fuck.*

And Louise thinks *just let the world stop, just for one second, just long enough for things to start making sense.*

"I'm so drunk!" Mimi wails. "I can't even see straight. Come *party* with me!"

Louise taking an inert Lavinia across the dance floor.

That cannot be the last thing Hal sees. That cannot be the last thing anyone sees.

She just has to keep Lavinia alive a few hours longer.

———

"Just meet me at the Bulgarian Bar," says Lavinia. Lavinia is always, always up for another adventure. "I'm in an Uber right now. I'm on my way, darling, I *swear.*"

"You'll come?"

"Yes, of course, I'll come."

"Is Louise coming?"

It's such a sour, pathetic little sneer.

"God no," says Lavinia. "To tell you the truth, I'm a little sick of her, anyway."

It is not as hard as you'd think, getting Lavinia's dress off. It is not as hard as you'd think, rinsing it off, putting it on, covering the back with a fox-fur stole. Lavinia is so stiff, but she resists so little.

The hair is trickier—for now she can back-comb it, then put it up, so it looks like Lavinia's tried to pin it up nicely and failed (Lavinia never pins her hair neatly, not once).

She puts on Lavinia's lipstick.

She puts on Lavinia's perfume.

She closes the shower curtain.

Lavinia posts their selfie in the cab. Best friends.

It gets fifteen Likes in four minutes.

Lavinia introduces herself by name to the Uber driver. She chatters so splendidly about art and life and how if you want it badly enough, you can make yourself into a work of art. You can create yourself.

"I don't think people realize the freedom they have," she says as they pull up on the corner of Rivington and Essex. She tips in cash, even though you don't normally tip your Uber driver, so that he will remember her, and fondly.

Lavinia uploads another photo to Facebook: of Rivington Street, of the sky, of the stars, of the lights. Forget it, Jake, she captions it; it's Chinatown. Technically, it's the Lower East Side, but Lavinia wouldn't let that stop her, because Lavinia believes that Art is nobler and more important than truth. She checks in at the Bulgarian Bar.

Mimi has sent her so many emojis: Lions. Tigers. Bears.

Be there in a sec, Lavinia says.

You should go in the ice cage.

Here's how the Bulgarian Bar works:

Take off your clothes, get a free shot. Have sex on the bar, get a free bottle. Thirty bucks and you can enter the Soviet ice cage, put on the real vintage Soviet military uniform they give you, and also the Soviet fur hat, and then a bartender will take your phone and take pictures through the glass while you drink as much vodka as you can from a shot glass made of ice before it melts.

Now Mimi is in the Soviet ice cage. Now she's naked, except for her underpants, and a Soviet military jacket. Also: the hat.

She's pressed up against the glass, and a man Louise has never seen before and will never see again is kissing the back of Mimi's neck and sliding his fingers through the triangle of her underwear.

Lavinia puts Lavinia's card behind the bar.

She explains that she wants all of that drunk girl's drinks on her tab, too.

She takes a photo of Mimi. She posts it. She tags it. Beowulf Marmont Likes it.

When Mimi stumbles out, Lavinia catches her.

"Darling!"

"Lavinia?"

Lavinia is whispering in her ear, with her hair falling on Mimi's shoulder, with her perfume, standing right behind her. "I'm so sorry I made you wait."

"WherewereyouImissedyouImissyousomuch."

Mimi can't even stand.

"I brought you another drink."

She presses it into Mimi's hands.

"Down it!"

Mimi does. Mimi sways.

Mimi puts a hand over her mouth, like she's going to throw up.

"IwassoscaredLavinia."

There are so many people. It's dark. They're dancing.

"Iwassoscaredyouweremadatme."

"I could never be mad at you," says Lavinia. "I love you!"

"I missed you," Mimi is murmuring. Her eyes are unfocused. Lavinia is always just out of her field of vision. "You have no idea."

"Selfie!" Lavinia says.

They do.

Lavinia is leaning in, kissing Mimi's cheek, features obscured by the flaps of her Soviet fur hat, so you can't really see her face.

Lavinia posts this, too.

"We're going to have a good night tonight, right?"

"The best," says Lavinia.

She sails them both into the crowd.

She leaves Mimi in the arms of the man who was fingerbanging her earlier.

It's four in the morning. Lavinia is still alive.

Whatever happens to her, next, tonight, is not Louise's problem.

Not so long as she, too, has an alibi.

That is the logical next step, Louise thinks, once you've killed somebody. At least, she supposes it is.

Louise texts Mimi from her own phone.

Where are you guys?

Is Lavinia with you?

I need the keys.

Mimi doesn't answer. She's probably in bed with the stranger by now. But in the morning, wherever she wakes up, you will never get her to admit—not for a second—that she and Lavinia Williams didn't have one of those gorgeous, epic, once-in-a-lifetime nights, or that they did not stay out until dawn.

At four in the morning, Louise calls Rex.

"I'm sorry," she says. "I'm so sorry. I didn't know who else to call."

"Are you okay?"

He sounds so awake, for four in the morning.

"It's just—I don't have the keys."

"What?

"Lavinia—she went out with Mimi, after this burlesque thing we— it doesn't matter."

"She has your keys?"

"There's only one set," Louise says. "I don't have it. She's not picking up her phone."

"You didn't go with her?"

"She didn't invite me."

She can hear Rex exhale on the line.

"Come have a coffee with me," he says.

Lavinia goes into a bathroom at a twenty-four-hour diner. Louise comes out.

She has her hair up in a ponytail. She's wearing a miniskirt similar enough to the ridiculous miniskirt they made her wear at the P.M. (there's no use thinking about that job, now; she's lost that one, too), a sweater over the top, which is slutty and sequined and makes her feel like Athena Maidenhead, but she needs to be able to argue that she never made it home.

She packs Lavinia's dress so neatly, in a plastic bag, in case she ever needs it again.

Louise astonishes herself, sometimes.

Louise meets Rex near his place, in the East Village. They go to a 24/7 pierogi place called Veselka, with murals of people doing old New York things, and they sit by the window under the halogen light and watch the darkness fade, moment by moment.

Rex has bags under his eyes. He's wearing a blazer.

"You didn't have to get dressed up for me," Louise says.

They've been sitting in silence for ten minutes, eating greasy pierogis, drinking burnt coffee, staring at each other.

"I didn't," Rex says. "I mean—I mean, I didn't *not*. I mean—" He takes another sip of his coffee.

He sighs. Louise doesn't say anything.

"Look," says Rex. "I'm sure she'll be home soon. Has she done this before?"

"Sometimes." She looks up at him. "Not this late." She swallows. She has to be so careful, now. "I mean—you don't think something's happened to her?"

Maybe Lavinia will get mugged in an alley. Maybe she'll trip and fall in the park stumbling home. Louise can't think about that right now.

All Louise can focus on is not screaming.

"Have you heard back from Mimi?"

Louise shrugs. "Not yet."

"You don't have the keys," Rex says. He says it like he feels so sorry for her.

"It's some co-op board rule."

"Sure it is," he says.

"Sure," says Louise. "I'm sorry—I'm sorry—I shouldn't have woken you up. Not for this. It's just—I didn't know who else to call."

"I'm glad you did," says Rex. "I like talking to you."

"If she finds out—"

"We're dead," Rex says, and Louise has to work so hard not to flinch.

The light is just starting, outside, and rosy fingers claw shadows out of the diner floor.

"I hate that I'm getting you into trouble," Rex says.

"You're not," says Louise. "No—it's my fault. Believe me."

"I know it's wrong," says Rex. "I know that." He exhales. "She's a good person—deep down. Isn't she?"

Louise doesn't even know, anymore.

"Maybe."

"It's just—she's so—"

"Much?"

"Yes," Rex says. "Just—too much." He sighs. "It's not fair of her—to ask so much from you."

"It's fine," Louise says.

Just a couple more hours. Just until morning. You can do this.

She'll find a way to kill Lavinia in the morning.

"You're smart, and you're funny, and you're *nice*."

"Stop it," she says quietly.

"And you're a good friend—you *are*—and, I'm sorry, but you shouldn't *have* to be here at five o'clock in the fucking morning—I'm sorry."

"Stop," she says again, "please stop," but he doesn't hear her.

"You deserve so much better," he says. He takes her hand.

Here's the thing: Louise doesn't.

Louise has promised herself she wouldn't cry. She has been so good at not crying. She hasn't cried picking Lavinia's body off the floor, and she hasn't cried dragging Lavinia out of the theater, and she didn't cry in the Uber or putting Lavinia in the bathtub or posting that photo of the two of them and so Louise doesn't know why she is crying, now, but Rex is looking at her with such kind and magnanimous eyes. All Louise can think is that every terrible thing everyone has ever seen in her is true, has always been true, that there was no universe in which she would not end up doing this.

"I'm sorry," Rex keeps saying, like this has anything to do with him, looking at her like nobody should ever look at her again, and if he keeps looking at her like that another second she will not be able to stop herself from telling him everything, "God, I'm sorry, I shouldn't have— it's not my place."

"It's *fine*."

She throws down a twenty on the table.

"I have to go."

Here's one way this night can end: Louise turns herself in.

Rex keeps looking at her—with those wide unblinking eyes, with his perfect faith—and Louise thinks *in a perfect world people do the right thing,* and although it is not a perfect world Louise decides it should be, and so she goes to the police and tells them, unstinting, everything that she has done.

For a moment, at dawn, Louise is sure she will.

Rex follows Louise onto Second Avenue.

"Louise, wait!"

He's out of breath. He's forgotten his blazer.

Louise waves for a cab—frantically, wildly, tries to work out where you're supposed to go, exactly, when you've killed somebody: if there's a head office or if you Google your local precinct or just go up to the first cop you see and say *there's a dead girl in my bathroom, sorry?*

Rex sprints the crosswalk so fast a cyclist nearly hits him.

"What do you want from me?" she asks him, and then he kisses her.

Rex isn't kissing her.

He is kissing a girl with fine, blonde hair and docile eyes who is as good as he is. She is shy, clever and witty and kind, and she suffers so terribly and she means so well. He is kissing a girl who does not complain when her friend locks her out at four o'clock in the morning, and who goes to the Met when she is lonely. He is kissing a girl who never killed anybody.

She kisses him back, anyway.

They take that cab back to Rex's place, even though it isn't even ten blocks away, because they can't keep their hands off each other, and Louise pays with all the cash in her wallet and leaves a ridiculous tip because it is Lavinia's cash, and now she can't even stand to touch it.

They climb on top of each other. They annihilate each other. Rex gets his scarf tangled in Louise's tacky, ridiculous sequins and although she doesn't even realize that she's crying at first her tears stain his face. He keeps kissing her despite this and he keeps whispering *it's not your fault; it's not your fault; I'm sorry*. They kiss in front of his apartment building and they kiss again in the lobby and they kiss again on the stairs and on every landing, which is a lot of landings, as it happens, because it's a walk-up and he lives on the fifth floor, and they kiss again by his front door and Louise hasn't even been drinking but she feels drunk. Or maybe it's Lavinia that is drunk—Lavinia who is still alive, Lavinia who is having the greatest night of her life with Mimi, Lavinia whom Mimi only just now has tagged in another incoherent status with every word misspelled about Baudelaire and wine and virtue, Lavinia who is going to get mugged tonight, Lavinia who is going to die—and maybe they are still tethered together because of that one night by the sea and Louise feels everything Lavinia feels and so she is drunk, too, or maybe it's just that somebody is warm and kind and kissing her and whispering her name, *her name*, into her ear, and telling her just how good she is.

"I'm ruining everything for you," Rex whispers, "I'm ruining everything; I know; I'm sorry; please make me stop." But they just cling to each other harder, and he takes off her sequined top and that ridiculous cunt-high miniskirt and then her bra (she realizes, too late, that it is one of Lavinia's, but he doesn't seem to notice). He runs his hands up and down her body and looks at her, I mean really looks at her, and says *Jesus Christ you're so beautiful* like he means it.

"Tell me to stop," Rex says. Louise doesn't. Not even when he kisses her neck; not even when he goes down on her; not even when he asks if she has a condom and she says "don't bother" because the risk seems so insignificant now.

She closes her legs around him and her arms around him and he's on her and around her and against her and inside her. But here's the thing: all Louise can think about is this one time in January that Lavinia decided they hadn't had one of *those nights* in a while, so Lavinia locked all the doors, turned off all the lights, and lit all the candles in the house. She put on Liszt's third *Liebestraum,* which Louise had never even heard before, and in the candlelight explained that the song was all about love in death, how *der stunde kommt, der stunde kommt* where everybody dies. Lavinia was leaning back on the divan with the moonlight on her breasts. But maybe Rex is the only reason Lavinia listens to that song in the first place, Louise thinks *yes, that part was real,* and she doesn't know, now, kissing him back, whether anything will ever be real again. Louise doesn't know whether she's terrified or terrible or triumphant, whether she is in love or just surviving. All she knows is that the world has ended but that it is also still turning.

All Louise needs to know right now is this: Rex is inside her, and she needs him to stay inside her; she clings to him, too, tightly, so tightly, still breathing, because if she does not hold on, if she stops holding on for a single second, Lavinia will sweep her out to sea.

6

LOUISE WAKES UP HAPPY.

This surprises her.

She can't remember the last time she's woken up like this: with somebody's arms around her; with somebody pressing his chest against her, or stroking her hair, or brushing her forearms softly with his fingertips. She's not sure she ever has.

Not with somebody kissing her neck. Not with somebody's lips on her shoulder. Not with this much light streaming in.

It streams through the shutters. It makes a lattice on the wall. She marvels at it, and although she's seen a thousand shadows in her life just like it this one is the one she presses her fingertips to, because she is half-asleep enough to think she can catch it.

"Morning, beautiful," he says.

It astounds Louise that he has spent the night with her—the whole night—and never once suspected the kind of person that she is.

"Want to know a secret?"

He's kissing her shoulders quickly, now, it tickles and Louise laughs without meaning to.

"What is it?"

"I don't want to get out of bed."

He blinks a lot without his glasses.

"Don't tell anyone."

"I won't," she whispers.

———

The phone rings.

Then Louise remembers.

"Shit—shit!"

"What's wrong?"

He smooths her hair back from her face. He is so sweet with her.

It's Lavinia's phone. It blasts the prelude from Wagner's *Tristan und Isolde* all through Rex's apartment.

She is afraid he will recognize it but he reaches into her purse for her and hands it over.

It's Mimi calling. Five missed calls.

Louise sends it to voicemail.

"Is everything okay?"

Lavinia has fifty-six Facebook notifications.

"Nothing." Louise turns the phone off. Louise has just killed somebody. "It's fine. Everything's fine."

"Was it . . ."

"No."

She takes a deep breath.

"Just Mimi," she says.

"Have you heard from her?"

"No."

Now he exhales.

"It's probably fine," he says. "She's probably at Mimi's. Or—you know—dancing on a table. Or in Paris. You never know."

"You never know," says Louise.

He gets up and goes to the window.

He is thinner than she expected, now that she sees him without clothes on. His chest is waxy, and a little concave. She can see his ribs. He is so handsome to her, anyway.

"So," he says. He rubs his eyes. "What do you want to do?"

"About what?"

"About Lavinia."

"What about Lavinia?"

"Do you want to talk to her, or should I?"

"About what?"

"About us."

Maybe Louise is still dreaming.

"What about us?"

You've fucked me, she thinks. *What more is there to say?*

He sits at the edge of the bed. "I mean—if we're going to keep doing this—we can't keep it a secret."

It has never occurred to Louise that Rex would want to do this more than once.

People want to fuck you, sometimes. This is natural, if you're pretty; or if you're not pretty, then at least if you're blonde. People want to fuck you once. Then they leave early for work, and tell you they'll text you in a few days, and they don't.

"You want to do this again?"

(This is not the relevant point, maybe, with a body in a bathtub uptown, but Louise can't think about that right now.)

"Don't you?"

"Of course I do," Louise says, before she can even think about what she's saying. "But—I mean—we—we *can't.*"

"Because of Lavinia?"

"Yes," Louise says. "Of course because of Lavinia."

He sighs. "Maybe, you know—maybe it won't be so bad. I mean—maybe, you know, it'll be hard, at first, but—"

She marvels at how stupid he is.

"She burned your handkerchief."

"Christ," he says. He laughs—just a little. "Of course she did."

He says it with something like admiration, and Louise hates that even now, even now, this gnaws at her.

"Look—Louise." It has been so long since someone has called her by her actual name. "I know it's selfish." He is so quiet. "How much I like you. I know that."

Instinctively, she reaches out. She puts her fingertips on the back of his neck.

"It's not selfish," she says, "to want to be happy."

It is automatic: how she does it. Touching his shoulders. Massaging them.

"I should do it," says Rex. "I'll talk to her. This is on me. I'll explain that you said no, at first, that I pursued you. I'll be the bad guy. I don't mind . . ."

"No!"

She is so loud.

"No—no, I'll talk to her. When she comes home."

"Are you sure?"

"I'm sure."

"I can wait outside?"

"I'll be fine," she says.

"Look—if you need somewhere to stay for a couple days . . ."

"What?"

"Like, if you need some space. I mean—it's a studio, you know. It isn't much. But I *do* have two sets of keys."

He kisses her knuckles, like she is precious.

That's when it hits Louise.

This part would have been true no matter what.

If she'd called him at the P.M.—in tears, hysterical—it all would have happened the exact same way. He'd have kissed her. He'd have taken her home. He'd have let her stay.

Lavinia has died for nothing.

"What is it?" Rex asks her.

Louise can't stop laughing.

The tears run down her face and still she can't stop laughing.

Louise takes the bus home from Rex's place. She wears his Columbia sweatshirt over her sequined top, her skirt. It's a long, slow route up First Avenue, but Louise doesn't mind. When Louise gets home, there will be a body in the bathtub, and, she will have to decide *how to kill Lavinia.*

It is summer. The sun is out and the sky is a deep and inimitable shade of blue and were it not for the body in the bathtub, Louise could almost be happy.

This cannot last forever.

Louise knows this.

She will have to find a way to kill Lavinia. She will have to get out of town before they realize that whatever a mugger uses to brain you isn't a sink at a Chrystie Street nightclub; she has no money, anyway—once they cancel Lavinia's cards she will have nothing, because she doesn't have Paul or GlaZam or the bar and she definitely doesn't have bottle-girl shifts at the P.M. any longer, but how much is a one-way bus ticket back to Devonshire, anyway?

She turns on Lavinia's phone.

Forty-three new Facebook Likes on the selfie of her and Mimi.

Twelve texts from Mimi. A Facebook message from Beowulf Marmont, asking her for a drink (it is, Louise notices, uncannily similar to the Facebook messages he sent *her*, asking for a drink).

An email from Cordelia about an upcoming history test at summer school.

She checks her own phone. Nothing.

Then, when the bus passes Seventy-second Street, a text from Rex:

I'll be thinking about you today, he says. Good luck. Whatever happens.

And Louise thinks: *if only, if only, if only.*

And just a small part of her thinks: *what if?*

The smell is so much worse than she expects.

She is sure that she remembered to close Lavinia's eyes, before leaving, but she is here and they are open and glassy and they stare straight up.

Louise sits on the toilet for a while, staring at the body.

She has never seen a dead body before, but she imagined it would look more like a dead body than it does. It just looks like Lavinia, only less so, like somebody has made a prop of Lavinia for a play.

She opens a private browser (she knows *Law & Order*; she knows your search history is the first thing they check).

She Googles *what do I do with a dead body*.

She doesn't really expect a useful answer, but she scrolls through the results anyway, because she can't think of what else to do.

Turns out, *Urban Foxes* did a listicle on it, once, as a joke. Turns out, there are a lot of bodies in the Gowanus Canal.

This doesn't surprise Louise, thinking about it.

Louise continues to stay very, very calm.

She runs through her options.

She has sixty-four dollars. She has a set of keys. She has a driver's license.

She has an ATM card with the PIN 1-6-1-4 and a hundred thousand dollars in it. But she cannot think about that right now.

She can leave Lavinia in a park, somewhere, late at night (she is never home; she never finds Lavinia; somebody finds Lavinia in Sheep Meadow; she comes back to Rex worried, so worried, she hasn't found her). Maybe it is a mugging. Maybe, maybe it is a suicide (maybe she is found in a paddleboat on the Lake in Central Park, like Ophelia, like she always wanted). She can leave Lavinia in an alley.

On TV, they can always tell the time of death.

Louise isn't sure how that works in real life. She Googles this, too. Apparently there's a window of a couple of hours, which means she is probably safe, but then again, you are never, ever safe.

Maybe it is better, she thinks, if they never find the body.

Another text from Mimi.

`I had the best night with you last night.`

Let's do it again soon!

Two capybaras holding hands.

And Louise thinks *you can't fool all the people all of the time.*

And Louise thinks *maybe you can.*

It wouldn't have to be for very long, she thinks. Just long enough for her to get a little more money together out of Lavinia's account. Just long enough for her to come up with a plan.

There is a plausible story, now: Lavinia is brokenhearted over Rex. Lavinia doesn't want to live, knowing Rex is dating somebody else. Lavinia takes too many pills. Lavinia writes a brilliant suicide note. She posts it.

Everybody misses her. Nobody is surprised.

Maybe, Louise thinks, this is exactly what Lavinia would have done, anyway. Maybe Lavinia was always supposed to die, and Louise has done nothing but help Fate along.

I had the most wonderful night with you too, darling!

Lavinia writes texts in very long and elaborate and letter-like sentences. Louise knows this.

Sorry to do an Irish goodbye I got mesmerized by the music and then instantly collapsed.

Did you have fun?

It is so easy.

Louise puts Lavinia's body into the steamer trunk.

That's the hard part.

It turns out you can't just make a person smaller by arranging them. You have to break their bones. You have to take a hammer or an axe, or if you're in an apartment like Lavinia's, an antique nineteenth-century neo-Gothic mallet that's lying over the plastered-up mantelpiece, and crush a person's elbows and their kneecaps until they fit. The sound is a little bit like a cantaloupe. The smell is like nothing Louise has ever smelled before.

When you are done breaking their femur, their forearm, in two or three different places, they look even less like a person than they did before.

Louise will never forget the sound of snapping bones.

She spends thirty minutes with a curling iron, curling and recurling and recurling her hair.

Lavinia rents a moving van.

She wears the exact same thing she wore last time she rented a moving van, the same halter top and palazzo pants, the same scarf in her hair, the same sunglasses. She goes to the same place. She shows her ID.

Lavinia says lots of very memorable things about how she's going on a *very great adventure,* a *pèlerinage,* even, and the woman behind the counter rolls her eyes and slams down the keys, just to get Lavinia to shut up.

Lavinia posts a photograph of First Avenue, of the summer sky, of the Fifty-ninth Street Bridge. She quotes that song by Simon & Garfunkel, which is all anybody thinks about when they see that bridge, anyway. She checks in there.

Lavinia is having such a peaceful Sunday in New York.

Any news? Rex texts.
We're talking tonight, says Louise.
She heaves up the steamer trunk by one handle. She scratches those gorgeous hardwood floors, sliding it out the door.

It is almost midnight. The trunk makes so much noise on the landing, down the corridor. Louise does not understand. Lavinia is so skinny—she's paid so much attention to how skinny Lavinia is. How does a person that skinny weigh so much? The trunk scrapes the walls.

Louise almost pulls her arms out of her sockets, moving the trunk into the elevator.

Down the hall, the apartment door opens.

Mrs. Winters watches as the elevator doors close, and Louise and Lavinia descend to the ground floor.

It takes Louise thirty minutes to get Lavinia into the back of the van.

There are moments, in those thirty minutes, when Louise doesn't think she will be able to get Lavinia into the back of the van, when Louise heaves and gasps and strains. Her muscles ache and her tendons scream and still Lavinia's weight is too much for her, and Louise thinks *it is not worth it.*

She thinks *I will sit here until the police come.*

When they come I will tell them there is a body in the trunk.

They will not believe me. I will show them.

They will take me away and then at last, at last, I will sleep.

Lavinia will win, she thinks.

So what? Let Lavinia win.

She sits like this on the steamer trunk for three, four, five minutes, hugging her knees to her chest.

Lavinia's phone is buzzing in her pocket. Lavinia's perfume is all over her hands.

Lavinia cannot win.

So Louise takes a deep, deep breath.

She practices that breathing: one more time.

She heaves.

She turns herself inside out, heaving. She vomits up acid and it burns her throat and her tongue and even her lips but that doesn't make her stomach untwist.

She does not think she has ever been in so much pain before.

She gets the body into the back of the van.

————

Louise drives all the way up the FDR, along the flank of Manhattan, to where the East River meets the Harlem. She has Googled all of this. She doesn't really know what she's doing but she assumes that most people who are trying to hide a body don't really know what they are doing, either.

She drives all the way up to Swindler Cove, hedging the projects over at 201st Street, in the shadow of the Con Ed station.

Louise has not been up so high, she thinks, since she and Lavinia went to Harlem that one time because Lavinia decided she liked gospel music, but she cannot think about that right now.

They have renovated much of the park, here; but so much is still undone. There are abandoned slats of wood over the marsh, forgotten Coke cans, rotting piers that collapse into the river, one by one.

Louise waits in the van until three. Just in case.

She drives as close as she can to the water.

The funny part is that there *are* people out—one or two—men smoking joints, or on their phones. She has always been so afraid of being alone, at night, with men. Not now.

She pulls her sweatshirt over her head. She has a cigarette. She waits.

They don't even look at her.

When they go, Louise drags the trunk out of the back. It's easier, going down than up; except for the sound it makes when it hits the cement (*is that what it sounds like,* Louise wonders, *the rattling of bones?*).

She drags it by the handle all the way to the waterside. It hurts, but by now Louise has gotten used to the pain.

Then Louise does a very stupid thing.

She opens the trunk.

Lavinia's eyes are still open. They are still glassy. They are still blue.

Her hair winds all around her face, her neck, her broken limbs, like snakes. Her hair, which is long and loose and Pre-Raphaelite, and looked when Lavinia was alive like it, too, was alive, of its own will, that it would grow unfettered and strangle you if you got too close.

They say hair keeps growing after you die. Louise read that once. She doesn't know if it's true.

Louise slams the trunk shut.

She lifts the trunk, one final time, against the railing.

She lets it fall in the water. She lets the water carry it away.

By the time the current has closed over it, it's like it never even happened at all. Maybe it didn't.

It is dawn when Lavinia takes a picture of the sunrise over the East River.

To sail beyond the sunset, and the baths

Of all the western stars until I die.

Lavinia takes out four hundred dollars from an Inwood bodega on her way home.

Louise leaves the van parked in Inwood. She takes the subway home.

Louise makes piles of *things*. Lavinia's clothes. Hers. Lavinia's. Lavinia's. Hers. She makes piles of jewelry. She counts up all the cash in the house. Lavinia has left $450.42, in twenties and tens and crumpled dollar bills lying around and coins in the couch cushions.

She charges Lavinia's phone. Lavinia has so many more messages. She sits at Lavinia's desk. She opens Lavinia's laptop. Lavinia is signed into everything.

She checks Lavinia's email.

An invitation from Lydgate to the launch party of his new coffee table book *Sex Toys: An Illustrated Secret History.* Some links from Gavin to gossip-party stories in *The Fiddler* and a request to contribute a diary piece (*you just have the kind of narrative voice that pisses peo-*

ple off and that's great when it comes to engagement numbers). An email from her parents.

> Dear Lavinia,
> We are saddened to learn from your Dean that you would like to delay your return to Yale another semester. We believe that this will be detrimental to your future in the long term, and have jointly decided to cease paying to reserve your spot at the end of this academic year (2014–15). If you wish to complete your degree you will have to return in September at the very latest.
>   We have discussed our decision with the Dean and believe it is for the best.
>   Your sister is doing very well here and enjoying her summer school. I am sure you have heard she got a 2400 on her SATs–very proud. I think it important that you set a good example as she prepares her college applications as she is still insisting on applying to exclusively Catholic schools . . .

Louise slams the laptop closed.

Louise tries to think of where she will go, when she runs. *Anywhere but Devonshire,* she thinks.

The phone rings.
    It's Rex again.
    "It's good to hear your voice," he says.

Louise downloads a picture from Google Images of a sunset over a beautiful lake upstate. It's the sort of place a person would go to—say, if they'd just found out their best friend was fucking their ex, and they had the money to just pick up and go upstate.

Lavinia checks in at Beacon, New York. She posts the photo.
Rebirth, she writes.

Rex meets Louise for afternoon tea at the Hungarian Pastry Shop,
near the Columbia campus. His satchel is full of various Loeb editions. He has bags under his eyes.

"I fell asleep in a seminar today," he says. He's holding her hand.
"Isn't that something?"

Louise stirs the whipped cream into her coffee without drinking it.

"How did it go?" he asks, at last.

She shrugs.

"Lavinia, you know."

"Did she set anything on fire?" He's smiling. A little.

"No. She was calm."

"Really?" he asks. "I can't imagine that—somehow."

"I mean—quiet. Not calm. Quiet."

"You think she's okay?"

Louise holds up the keys.

Like Lavinia would ever be that magnanimous.

"She said she needed space. She's gone away for the week. Upstate."

"And then what?"

"And then . . ." Louise tries not to think about it. "And then she
comes back."

He sighs. He looks up. "Hey, Louise?"

She stirs her coffee. She smiles her slow, kind, sweet smile.

"We're not bad people, are we?"

She pats his hand. She twines her fingers in his.

"Of course not," Louise says.

"You're right," he says. "Of course you're right. I'm being stupid.
Let's do something fun. It's a beautiful day—I don't have class until
Wednesday. Let's go to a museum."

"There's always the Met." Louise thinks of places she knows a
boy who always wears tweed blazers will like. "Or the Neue Galerie—

they've got this whole Ferdinand Hodler exhibition on . . ." It costs twenty dollars to get in.

Rex doesn't say anything.

"They do good Sacher torte at the museum café." (*There is not a body underwater; there is not a trunk at the bottom of the river; there is not blood in the shower drain.*)

"Maybe—"

"What?"

She sees his face. His ears are red.

"Is it—her?"

How, she thinks, *can one person matter so much?*

"It's stupid," Rex says. "We should go—of course we can go."

"But—"

He sighs. "I've been there before."

"Okay?"

"I mean—*we've* been there before."

"What?"

"Like—it was our first date."

"Oh. *Oh.*"

"I'm sorry—that's weird—I'm being weird."

"No, *I'm* sorry. I should have—"

"It's not like you could *know*!"

Louise can't stop picturing them, the two of them, with Lavinia's long and unbrushed hair, with her rapt smile, Lavinia so radiant on his arm, Lavinia in a steamer trunk with her ankle next to her ears.

"Let's just go home," Louise says.

They cab it to Rex's place. Rex pays.

They have sex on the bed, and then again on the sofa, and then they cuddle and order Thai food and watch *The Jewel in the Crown* on Netflix. The weather is so nice outside and there is so much to do on a night like this one in New York but Lavinia has done all of those things, already, and so they just drink beer out of his fridge, because that, at least, Louise is sure that Lavinia has never done.

He is so careful when he has sex with her. He buries his face in her neck, and murmurs things between and underneath her breasts, and rests his head in the crook of her hips, and against her inner thigh.

"God," he keeps saying, "you're so beautiful."

And Louise knows she doesn't deserve it, but she thinks *just one more day like this. Just give me one more day.*

"Hey, Louise?"

He says it to her shoulder blade.

"Yes?"

"How much—on a scale of, say, one to ten—do you hate Hal?"

"Eight? Why?"

"He's having a birthday party this Saturday. Like—a hybrid birthday–Fourth of July type thing, and it's at his father's house, and there will be, you know, people there. And drinks. And food." He's leaning on one elbow. "And if it wouldn't be strange . . ." He exhales. "I told him about you. I hope that's all right."

"It's fine," says Louise. "It won't surprise him." She leans back on the pillow. "He's been giving me shit about it long enough."

"He doesn't mean it. Any of it. When you get to know him . . ."

"He's an angel?"

"You know how it is," says Rex. "He's my best friend."

"Yes," Louise says. "I know how it is."

Louise goes back to the apartment (it feels so good, so strangely good, to unlock it, to fling open the door, to switch on the light). She puts all of Lavinia's clothes back in the closet. She puts all her clothes on the shelf.

She puts on Lavinia's powder-blue dressing gown.

It smells of Lavinia's perfume.

She stares at the hole in the living room where the steamer trunk used to be.

Lavinia posts another photo from upstate.

Everybody Likes it.

Lavinia texts Mimi.

Been having a Crisis of Faith. Long story. Gone upstate to clear my head. But I miss you! LET US GO TO THE ICE CAGE AGAIN SOON yes yes yes?

Mimi responds with an emoji of a spider trying to hug you with all its arms.

Rex texts Louise a photo of the view from his window.

I miss you already, he says.

And Louise thinks *he does, he does.*

She tries not to think about his face when she asked to go to the Neue Galerie (she should have known—it was one of those places Lavinia insisted they go all the time, in Lavinia's opera cloaks, in Lavinia's furs).

She thinks: *there are so many things I should have known.*

She goes through Lavinia's drawers. She throws all of Lavinia's clothes (her lingerie, her thigh-high stockings, her silk blouses, her handkerchiefs) on the floor. She looks through Lavinia's bookshelves. She throws volume after volume on the floor. She looks under the bed, under the Persian carpet; in the little jewelry boxes on the vanity. She strips the sheets.

She claws out the desk drawers. She throws staplers and glue sticks and pens and gets ink on the duvet.

Then she finds it. A stained wood box at the back of Lavinia's bookshelf.

An envelope.

A pack of letters.

There are things it is better for a person not to know. The day and the manner of your own death, that's one, or whether or not you're going to fuck your mother and kill your father. What people say behind your back. The names somebody you love has called somebody else. There's a reason people are able to function, in this world, as social creatures, and a good part of that reason is that there are a lot of questions intelligent people don't ask.

Rex wrote Lavinia two hundred letters in four years.

Most of them are from when they were sixteen, seventeen, eighteen—before they went off to school. He wrote them with quill pens, green ink. He sealed them—the wax is still there, if broken, on some of the edges.

They are awkward. They are pretentious. They are filled with literary allusions Louise already knows, many misquoted. He doesn't even write well.

They are the most beautiful letters Louise has ever read.

She tells herself she will only read one: *My dear Lavinia, what a pleasure it was to see the Klimt exhibit at the Neue Galerie this afternoon*—she doesn't know why she's not laughing, but all she can think about is walking through the Devonshire woods with Virgil Bryce, holding his hand, smoking American Spirits, staring blankly ahead, until he turns to her and says *well if you want it so goddamn badly . . .*

I didn't know, Rex wrote to Lavinia, the night after they lost their virginities to each other in a Flatiron fleabag, *that people could feel as strongly as this.*

I'm scared, Rex tells Lavinia, the night before he went off to college, *that the real world is going to destroy us.*

I'm scared nothing in the world will ever mean as much to me as this.

Louise stays up all night, reading them.

He wrote her about the places they will go, that they will never go to, and Louise cannot see Lavinia's answers but she can imagine them—they are written on her heart, and in the lines on the palms of her hands.

I want to really live, Lavinia says, in every letter that Louise cannot read. *All I want is to live.*

She falls asleep at dawn, on Lavinia's floor, with the letters spread out in all directions: like a mandala, like a halo.

Lavinia posts a Facebook status about how much she loves the countryside.

Lavinia withdraws another five hundred dollars from her bank account, at a sketchy bodega in Inwood, near the van.

She's wearing sunglasses.

Louise gets through the week.

Lavinia is having the most wonderful time upstate. Lavinia is doing yoga. Lavinia is going to the contemporary art museum in Beacon and posting all about Louise Bourgeois's spider and how it made her think about anger in a new way. Lavinia is learning to embrace what she cannot change. Lavinia is discovering inner peace.

Louise sits in the apartment, reading letters, trying not to throw them across the room.

The night of Hal's Fourth of July party, Rex texts Louise to tell her that the party is black-tie.

Sorry, he says, Hal only just decided.

All Louise has are Lavinia's clothes.

Lavinia has so many dresses. Louise knew this already, of course, but she has never quite appreciated how many. She has never gone into Lavinia's closet and rubbed her face into the silk and the damask and the velvet of every single one. There's vintage and there's black-tie and there are elegant conservative cocktail dresses. Louise has never, ever seen Lavinia wear, short and well-tailored dresses, the kind you wear with pearls.

Louise buries herself in all of them.

Louise lays one dress out on the bed.

It still smells just like her.

She puts on Lavinia's earrings. She puts on Lavinia's shoes.

It frightens her, she thinks, looking at herself in the mirror, how much she looks like Lavinia. She has to touch her face, just to be sure.

She puts on Lavinia's foundation, and it is so strange to be the one putting it on herself, and not to have Lavinia's fingers against her skin, and not to have Lavinia wipe the pouf against her cheekbones, or over her lips, or on her chin.

She puts on the blush, and the mascara, and the eyeliner, and all these things she is so unused to doing on her own.

She puts on Lavinia's wine-dark lipstick. She puckers up. She blows a kiss to the mirror, like Lavinia is on the other side of the glass, like this is the only way to get to her.

Louise's fingers are shaking, but she gets the lipstick perfectly inside the lines, anyway.

Lavinia is reading Thoreau.

She is quoting Whitman.

She is sitting by a fireplace, somewhere.

Henry Upchurch lives in the Dakota. He is in Amagansett, now, and even though Hal has his own place in Tribeca, with this friend of his from Deerfield who works at Goldman, when Hal entertains it's always at the Dakota.

Louise has never been in a home this nice before.

The windows look straight onto the park. The ceilings are so high Louise has to crane her neck to see the chandeliers. There are crown moldings and hardwood floors and a room that is so indulgently full of nothing but books, and there is *space*—so much space to move around in, and Louise has not realized before what a luxury *space* is.

Hal has put American flags everywhere.

He has draped them on the sofas. He has hung them off the portrait frames. He has put tacky paper bunting in every doorframe. They cover every surface in the house except the three portraits along the fireplace wall.

"Jeremiah Upchurch. Henry Upchurch—the third, as it happens. Prince Hal."

Hal on the hall is wearing a bow tie. He is almost handsome.

Hal in the living room is wearing an Uncle Sam hat on top of his pink shirt, his bright-blue trousers. His bow tie has little red elephants on it, which clash violently with everything else he's wearing, his blazer with pink elbow patches. He's holding an unlit sparkler and a red-white-and-blue kazoo.

"Look at you." Hal considers her. "You almost look like you fit in."

Louise smiles.

"So, Rex finally gave in." Hal gulps from a red Solo cup. "What? It's an American tradition!"

He hands her a cup, takes a flask from his blazer pocket. "The swill's on the sideboard," he says. "Henry Upchurch's liquor cabinet is open to a very select few."

"I feel special, then."

She toasts.

"Good," he says. "You should."

"Happy birthday, Hal."

He grins. There is a gap in his two front teeth. "A quarter century," he says, "and I have accomplished exactly nothing with it. Just as God intended. The blood in the race starts to thin." He raises his glass to the portraits. "Or so they say. Can you see the resemblance?"

"I can't say I do," says Louise.

His mouth twists. He smiles. He pours more whiskey into her cup.

The sound system is playing "Dixie" on repeat.

"How about now? Wait—let's ask your boyfriend!"

Rex is in a summer suit.

"Young Louise here questions my paternity! What is it?"

Rex is looking at her so strangely and Louise wonders if this is something Lavinia has worn with him.

"Nothing," Rex says. "You look beautiful, that's all."

He takes her hand. He kisses her on the forehead in front of everybody, like he's proud to be here with her, like he wants everybody to know.

Beowulf Marmont is here; so is Gavin Mullaney; so are so many people Louise hasn't met but whom she has seen, if not at the secret bookstore then at the opera, or the MacIntyre, or the P.M., or so many other places that Lavinia's people—dispersed though they are—seem to go.

"Always a very great pleasure, Louise," says Beowulf. He kisses her on the cheek. A girl with fragile eyes sits very quietly on the couch with her hands folded, watching them. "I didn't realize you knew Hal!" He says it like she's been holding out on him.

Louise just smiles.

"How's your work for *The Fiddler* going? I did enjoy those online pieces you did, earlier this year."

"Thank you. I enjoyed writing them."

"You're not bad, you know. I mean—compared to all the tripe that's out there."

Gavin comes to greet her, too.

"You owe me a pitch, motherfucker," he says. He gives her a high five.

Everybody acts like she belongs.

Hal smokes a cigarette out the window. "Here's the thing I love about house parties," Hal says. "I hate new people. Henry Upchurch always used to say that meeting anybody new after the age of twenty-five is a waste of time." He says it winking, in case anybody thinks he means it. "I guess I'm all out of time. There's only ten people in New York—and I know you all. Everyone else is a garbage fire."

"Only five more years to make Five Under Thirty," Beowulf calls out.

"Please," Hal says. "I'm just a humble insurance executive."

Everybody laughs (and laughs. And laughs).

———

"I've never been inside the Dakota before," whispers an anorexically thin girl with very clearly defined brows to the girl with the fragile eyes.

Louise fakes it.

She chats with Beowulf Marmont about the opera, about all the productions that Louise has definitely, definitely, not fallen asleep through (that she definitely, definitely, has not spent getting fingered by Lavinia in a private box); about the time the donkey they use for *The Barber of Seville,* who is called Sir Gabriel, took a shit onstage, and this other time that Diana Damrau coughed.

She chats with Gavin Mullaney and the anorexic girl (who is called India) about people they know from Collegiate and St. Bernard's and Chapin and Exeter and Devonshire, of course Devonshire, which Louise knows so very well (she tells the story of the two kids who ran away like she knew them, and Gavin backs her up on what a good piece it was for *The Fiddler*), and then Louise tells a story that Lavinia told her once about this girl at Chapin who masturbated with a lacrosse stick and sent the video to her boyfriend, and how it went viral and she had to withdraw, and everybody laughs because they haven't thought about that story in years, and they're so glad to have a chance to tell it again.

"Aren't you lucky?" Hal's voice is low in her ear. "I told you—so much better to be a nonentity. You could have fucked the entire football team at Devonshire, and nobody would have any idea."

"I *wish*," says Louise, and everybody laughs, even though, come to think of it, it's probably true.

Louise tells a story about the time the whole campus was snowed in and she (and Virgil Bryce, but she doesn't mention that part) got cross-country skis and made a couple hundred dollars selling hot coffee (and Virgil's weed, but she doesn't mention that part either) dorm door to dorm door.

Everyone laughs.

"She's amazing," Rex says. "She even got away with pretending to be a boarding-school student, once. For a whole year! Before somebody finally figured it out."

Louise rounds on him.

For a second, a horrible sickening second, she thinks he is making fun of her.

But Rex is smiling at her with such affection, and such pride, even the story as he tells it is total bullshit (it was only a couple of weeks, and only in the dining hall, and the only person to ever figure it out was her mother, because she was too afraid to talk to anybody, and her mother had been so ashamed), but everybody is laughing and acting like this is the funniest thing in the world, and even Hal is grinning between his gap teeth, so what can Louise do but cough and swallow her fear and tell the story, the most wonderful story, about the fantastic prank she pulled, and how she even attended Greek classes for a year, and how she even handed in a paper, once, and everybody thinks this is the funniest thing in the world, and also that she is very brave.

Rex puts his arm around her, and kisses her on the cheek, and nobody seems to acknowledge that this means that she hadn't gone to the academy, after all.

Louise goes to the bathroom.

She reapplies her lipstick. She puts on more powder.

She checks Lavinia's phone.

Eleven Facebook messages. Most from Mimi. Thirteen Likes.

A text from Cordelia: where have you been?

Sorry darling! Been having an existential crisis. Things mad. Will write soon!

Lavinia posts a photo of an American flag, flying from a very beautiful colonial house one could very easily think was a charming country inn, where a girl whose best friend fucked her ex might go to get away, for a little while.

She writes: All the past we leave behind;

We debouch upon a newer, mightier world, varied world,
Fresh and strong the world we seize, world of labor and the
march,
Pioneers! O pioneers!
Within a minute, Beowulf Marmont Likes it.

Everyone inside is drunk on sideboard wine, except for Hal, who has
been refilling his flask all evening.

"Christ," Hal says. "How cliché."

"What is it?" India was telling everybody how much better barre is
for your ass than spinning.

"*Fresh and strong the world we seize!*" Hal rolls his eyes. "*World of
labor and the march.* Wow. Such labor." He snorts. "Try coal mining."
He flashes the phone to everybody, so everybody can see.

"Don't," says Rex. He says it very quietly.

"*Pioneers—o, pioneers,* did you dodge a bullet or what?"

Rex doesn't say anything. He has gone very pale. He chews on his
lower lip.

"How'd she take it?" Hal's looking right at Louise now. "When
you told her. Was there a catfight? Did you get naked?"

"She's out of town right now," Louise says. "She's taking a break."

Hal laughs. "Exile. How precious. Diddums. I'd watch your back,
young Louise—she might stick a knife in your ribs while you sleep."

Louise laughs like she can still see straight.

"I mean—you might get lucky. Maybe she'll swallow a fistful of
Mommy Williams's Xanax again!" He blows into his kazoo. "Lock
up all the razor blades. Don't let her near water."

Louise's gorge rises, and she thinks she is going to be sick—she *will*
be sick; she thinks she's going to get hysterical—she will, she *will*—
except Rex is the one to jump to his feet.

Rex is the one to bolt.

That, at least, gives Louise an excuse to go after him.

She finds him in one of the bedrooms—a single Spartan bed in the middle of an enormous floor, a frayed rocking horse, boarding-school flags from Devonshire and Andover and Deerfield on a corkboard on the wall.

He's smoking a joint out the window.

"You know." Rex stares so blankly out the window. "I think we really *are* bad people."

"No—no!"

"I shouldn't have kissed you. I'm the worst—I shouldn't have done that."

"It's fine! You're fine!"

"If something happens to her," he says, "if she—Christ—*whatever happens to her,* it's my fault."

"It's not," Louise tries. "I promise you—"

"You don't understand!" It is the first time Rex has ever raised his voice to her. "You don't get it—how long have you known her, what? Half a year?" He exhales so slowly. "She's not your problem—she's mine! You can't just—make that go away because you want to." He puts out the joint on Hal's desk. "I'm sorry," he says. "I'm sorry—this isn't fair to you. None of it is."

"She'll be fine!" Louise puts her hands on his shoulders. She buries her lips in the back of his neck. She takes a deep breath. "I promise—I *promise.* She'll be fine." She forces herself to smile. She forces her heart to stop beating the way it beats. "Things will go back to normal," she says.

He clings to her hand so tightly. He presses it to his shoulder. He looks up at her so gratefully, like she's made this true, just by saying it.

They go back inside. They smile. They toast.

Beowulf Marmont's big-eyed girlfriend breaks a champagne glass, and immediately Rex says "I'll fix it" while Hal just stands there, and then Hal starts laughing.

"That's what they're going to call your biography when you die," Hal says. *"I'll Fix It: The Rex Eliot Story."*

"Nobody's going to write my biography," says Rex, from the floor.

"Probably not," says Hal. "Nor mine, either. Or maybe they will. *Being the life and opinions of a humble insurance executive.*" He shrugs. "Oh well. When the revolution comes, nobody will be reading books, anyway."

He clears his throat.

"We'll burn them all for firewood," he says. "Won't we, young Louise?"

Louise holds his gaze. "Of course," she says, and raises a glass.

Now they're drinking more champagne. Now they're turning up the music. Now they're playing *pin the tail on the donkey* with a novelty set where the donkey is a Democrat and all the pins are flags. Now they're doing lines off the coffee table, and drinking punch Hal tells everybody has molly in it although Louise isn't sure.

"What do you want for your birthday, Hal?" asks India.

"A blow job."

Everybody laughs along with him.

"You're disgusting," says India, but she's smiling.

"As it happens," says Hal, "I want absolutely nothing. A true man severs all attachments."

"Is that what Henry Upchurch says?"

Louise doesn't mean to be cruel. But Hal's mouth twitches, and he makes a strange little grimace, and then he smiles and he laughs, which gives everybody else permission to laugh, too, and he says "That's exactly what Henry Upchurch says" and then he says "Christ, you're a bitch," but he says it so affectionately, and Gavin Mullaney claps her on the shoulder and India mimes the dropping of the microphone and even Rex shrugs helplessly as if to say *is she wrong?* and everybody is laughing and taking photographs and telling Louise that she's *won the evening* and, in a sense, she has.

———

Now they drink even more. Now Hal proposes a toast that begins "and let us now praise famous men." Now they put on old-school swing-dance music because Hal thinks they should all listen to "Brother, Can You Spare a Dime?" and meditate on its significance for the American manufacturing industry, and Rex lifts Louise high into the air, and Hal catches her legs, and everybody thinks it's hilarious to carry Louise aloft between the drawing room and the library and the kitchen, so she can grab a bottle of Henry Upchurch's hidden, very nice whiskey from the kitchen and pour a whole bunch of it down her throat.

Now Beowulf Marmont is posting a picture of Louise to Facebook.

In it, she sits with Rex on the sofa, under portraits of all the Upchurch men. Rex is kissing her cheek.

Everybody Likes it.

Rex Likes it, too, even though he's sitting right next to her, and when he does Louise looks up at him and he smiles at her and Louise smiles back.

By dawn, everybody except Louise has fallen asleep on Henry Upchurch's couches, even Hal, even though he took a bunch of his modafinil that night, just to stay awake.

Louise flips through the photos on her phone.

She doesn't recognize herself in that dress, that lipstick, happy in the arms of a man who loves her. Borne aloft without Lavinia even there to hold her hand.

Like she belongs.

You cannot do this forever, she thinks.

But when Rex is asleep, and Hal is asleep with India nuzzled up to him and facing into his chest, and Beowulf Marmont is asleep with the fragile-eyed girl's arms slung over his waist, and everyone else is on the floor, Louise slips on her shoes. She goes downstairs, she nods at the doorman, and she walks outside into the barely breaking dawn.

She calls Rex from Lavinia's phone.

It goes to voicemail, just as she knew it would.

"Darling," Lavinia says, in that light, affected way of hers. Her voice is shaking. "It's—it's been grand, hasn't it?" She swallows. "You're probably asleep right now—maybe—maybe *she's* there. I suppose she's there. That's fine. I mean—" A deep, sincere breath. "I mean: I wanted you to know. I'm fine. Lulu told me everything. And—well, I suppose I raged a bit and set a fire or two but I want you to know—I've decided. I—I've got no interest in doing that, now. So—well. I want you to be happy. I've decided that. You and Lulu—both of you. I love you—don't think I don't. I love you both. And I want the best for both of you. Only—you'll understand, won't you? If I prefer not to see you for some time. Anyway. Anyway. Goodbye. I love you. Goodbye."

It's the happiest ending, Louise tells herself, *that she ever would have had.*

7

LAVINIA TURNS HER LIFE AROUND.

She posts photographs of sunrises over the East River, of morning skies, of birds in Central Park. She uses ClassPass every single day (you can tell this because the app uploads it to Facebook, when she goes), mostly to go to different iterations of yoga class, and from time to time she uploads a picture of her ever-leaner body—always with her tattoo visible—although you generally cannot see her face. She posts pictures of healthy meals (they are mostly green; many of them are juice). She posts one status about how she's going to give up drinking for a month or two, just to get healthy, just to prove to herself that she can. She updates her friends on her progress every day with an inspirational quote or two.

Nearly everybody Lavinia knows Likes it.

"I'm really proud of her," Louise says, when people ask, which is not as often as you might think, given how many people Liked it. "Of course, I miss her at parties. But I think she's doing the right thing, don't you?"

There are lots of places that Lavinia goes that you'd know about: if you look at Facebook (if you follow the paper trail). She takes out cash two or three times a week, always her max. If you were ever to go look at the camera footage, for whatever reason, you would always see a very beautiful girl in vintage clothes and sunglasses and wine-dark lips get cash out at the ATM. She goes every morning to her ClassPass classes, like every other rich blonde white girl in New York City nobody ever scrutinizes too closely, and the record of this attendance, too, is synchronized with the app and goes on Facebook. She goes to brunch, sometimes, and to bars where she orders seltzer (you cannot be too careful) and always, always, pays with a credit card, and always, always, leaves a memorable tip. She texts Mimi, from time to time, to say I miss you let's hang out soon, and Mimi always says—immediately!—yes, when? but there's always a scheduling conflict, and they say next week and then never make concrete plans.

If you found her on Facebook, too, you'd know she made so many new, wonderful friends, many of whose profiles are locked or whose photographs are blurry, but who frequently check in with her at vegan bars or health-food spas or meditation centers on Jefferson Avenue in Bushwick and post long, thoughtful comments on her wall about how good it was to see her the other night, and how they can't wait to hang out again soon!

There are the photos of her on Facebook, too.

These are, admittedly, not as frequent as they once were (Photoshop, it turns out, is actually very difficult to learn), and a lot of photos are blurry or vague, or involve her turned away from the camera at a distance while in a very elaborate costume (you can ascribe that to a natural flair for drama; even sober Lavinia wears the same clothes drunk Lavinia always did). But they come at intervals, and when they come everybody Likes them, and comments on how great she's been looking lately.

Lavinia tells her parents she is doing very well, too.

Dear Mother and Father (she writes),

I hope you're well. You're right. I think I'll be ready to go back to school, soon. My novel is almost finished. If there's any way I could have just a little more time, I'd love to be able to complete it and submit it to agents and I'm happy to supply pages of a sample chapter to show you to give you confidence in my abilities and dedication (Louise hopes Lavinia won't have to do this, but she's prepared to make it happen if she does).

Lavinia points out very cleverly that a large gap on her collegiate CV will be much better explained by a sold novel than by nothing at all.

This seems to mollify them. They tell her she can have one more semester, but that's all.

They tell her Paris is very pleasant, this time of year.

They remind her, vaguely but firmly, not to embarrass them at parties. They hope she's not wearing any of her ridiculous clothes again. They remind her how beautiful she is—too beautiful, they say, to waste *that* body and *that* hair and *that* face on outlandish and grotesque creations that will only have other people mocking her.

They remind her how important it is for her to be a good influence on Cordelia.

After all, they do not say directly, but heavily imply, Cordelia still has a future.

Sure, there are challenges.

Like the fact that Louise can only leave the house very early in the morning, or very late at night—times Mrs. Winters, or any other less-perspicacious neighbors would be less likely to open the door, or look down the hall. Lavinia has taken to ordering from Seamless with her credit card—a different restaurant every time—and opening her door just a crack for the delivery guy when he comes. Like the fact that a few times a week Louise has to take selfies where her face isn't visible, and that means spending several hours with the curling iron, wrapping her hair into tiny strands around her fingertips and setting them so that they look long and savage and untamed. Like the texts Louise has to keep sending—to Mimi, to Cordelia—keeping things so wonderfully vague, coming up with such bohemian and adventurous reasons why she doesn't want to come to Paris for the tail end of summer, or to Cordelia's starring role in *Antigone* up at Exeter in September, or to this amazing taxidermy-and-wax museum hidden in a Brooklyn cinema that Mimi wants to go to in October. Or the time the pipe bursts, and Louise stays up all night to fix it herself, with instructions she has found on Google, so that Lavinia will not have to call the super.

But Louise meets every single challenge.

She tells herself, at first, that this arrangement is only temporary. She saves almost all of the money she takes out of Lavinia's account. She buys a fake ID from a bodega near NYU that gives her name as Elizabeth Glass (*twenty-three*) and has a photo of a middling-pretty white girl with red hair she could almost look like, and keeps it, along with a duffel bag and a change of clothes, at the foot of her bed, for the day that everything goes wrong. But here's the thing: that day doesn't come.

In fact, Louise has never been better.

She is writing for *The Fiddler* again (she has so much free time to write, now that she does not have to worry about teaching, or ghostwriting, or tending bar, now that she takes so much of Lavinia's money). She writes book reviews and essays about Devonshire. Gavin talks her into writing about the time she faked being a student, because it was such a hit at Hal's birthday, and she does, and everybody on the Internet thinks it's hilarious, too. And then she starts writing for print because after Hal's party Louise goes with Gavin to India's birthday at Soho House and that's where she meets the print editor who is actually India's father, as it happens, and he gives her his card and says "email me, sometime." She is writing for both *The New Misandrist* and *Misandry!*, even though the editors don't speak. She writes a short story about an art thief who steals a painting but becomes convinced it's a forgery, which is an idea she and Lavinia talked about, one time, while blasting Wagner, and Louise can't remember whether it was she or Lavinia who came up with the idea, or maybe both of them, but she supposes it doesn't really matter now. She sends this short story to a literary magazine called *The Egret*, where Beowulf Marmont interns.

She tries not to think of the nights she and Lavinia decided to cowrite on the divan; the nights Lavinia grabbed her wrist and said "we will be *great*, Louise, *both of us*" and Louise said *yes, yes,* and believed it.

Louise starts reviewing opera for *The Fiddler*, because she asks Gavin if she can, and so she gets free press tickets.

Sometimes, it's like Lavinia isn't even dead.

Sometimes, Louise forgets.

Sometimes, in Rex's arms, with Rex kissing her and inventing new, sweet names for her, Louise lets herself believe that everything Lavinia posts is true.

Now Lavinia is reading Edna St. Vincent Millay, she thinks.

Now she is making chocolate-hazelnut-coconut-saffron tea and spilling it.

Now she is out with her wonderful friends, not-drinking at a wonderful party.

Now she is smiling: that beautiful and world-destroying smile.

Louise can see it when she closes her eyes.

In the mornings, if Rex doesn't have class, they go to Mud down the street for breakfast and eat enormous plates of eggs and hold hands and talk about their plans for the day. Louise invents some SAT clients and they walk through Tompkins Square Park and point out all the dogs they think are adorable and Rex talks about what he's studying. She spends at least four nights a week at his place (of course, he can never come to hers), and she frames it as *giving Lavinia space* but the funny thing, or maybe not the funny thing but the thing that shakes her most, is that he believes her.

There's just one little thing.

Rex never mentions the voicemail.

In fact, he never brings up Lavinia again.

Louise goes to great syntactical lengths to avoid saying her name, and often says things like *oh, you know* when describing her day. Rex never asks.

She thinks that it is so strange he would *not* mention it, after how guilty he has felt, even though sometimes she tries to bring up the subject without bringing up Lavinia. "Getting closure is so *good,* don't you think," she says, after she tells the actually-very-funny story of this guy who ghosted her, once, only for her to stand him up at Prospect Park two years later, and he smiles and nods and squeezes her hand but doesn't say what she wants him to.

Come to think of it: the only time Lavinia comes up at all is when Louise is riffling through her purse, one night, and the keys fall out.

"She let you have them?"

The way he says *she* frightens her, a little, because it's so reverential. Even now.

"She finally copied me a set," Louise says, like it's nothing, like Lavinia is just an ordinary normal slightly flawed somewhat-neurotic human being who has gone to a lot of therapy, lately, and who cannot hurt them.

There's another thing, too. Also very small.

Rex has unblocked Lavinia on Facebook.

He hasn't friended her, but he shows up on the People You May Know sidebar, which means he's taken her off his banned list, so she could see him, and add him, if she wants to.

She doesn't want to.

Louise isn't jealous. She doesn't need to be. She and Rex are so happy. She is the perfect girlfriend. She knows because she has read every single letter Rex has ever written Lavinia that Rex loves picnics, and they have gone on so many picnics that summer, and in September, too. She knows that he loves jazz and so they have gone to the Jazz Age Lawn Party, and to Zinc Bar in the West Village every couple of weeks. She knows he loves Korean food and she surprises him for his birthday in October by taking him to this wonderful high-end place in Hell's Kitchen. She even pays, even though the place is very expensive—she *insists* on paying—in cash, as it happens, because it has been so long and Louise thinks probably she will not have to run tomorrow, or this week, or the next.

She tries not to think too much about the expression on his face when she asked him to go to the Neue Galerie with her, or the way he looked at her when she came to Hal's party, wearing Lavinia's dress.

It's just that sometimes—not often, just sometimes—Rex will do something or say something that makes Louise wonder if he is still thinking about her. He'll say something idle—like at the Chelsea Market, one time, he mentioned he liked peach jam—and then Louise will get to thinking (because she has read every letter he has ever written) that he and Lavinia once had peach jam at a French café called Bergamot in Chelsea, sometime, and Louise will wonder whether right now, with his hand in hers and his mouth on her cheek or forehead or shoulder, he is thinking about her.

Like this one time, in early autumn.

It's a beautiful Sunday in October and Rex has just started the second year of his degree. They are sitting in Rex's apartment, and they are being boring (they have already had sex, and drank beer, and watched *The Third Man* on Netflix), and Rex is looking out the window and half-working on a seminar essay, and Louise is flipping idly through records for something to put on.

They listen to classical music, because Rex likes classical music, and Louise has started to appreciate it, too.

They listen to *La Traviata* and Berlioz and Chopin. Louise does the dishes in Rex's sink. Louise wipes their take-out kimchi off his kitchenette counter.

She isn't even thinking about Lavinia. If she lets herself think she lets herself think only of Lavinia the way everyone else thinks of Lavinia (into her fourth month of sobriety, now, getting really into the mystical writings of Simone Weil). She is so good at not thinking about what she has done.

So when the music comes on, and it is slow and dark and mournful and romantic, and there are those sustained three notes which sound a little like a wail, Louise thinks at first that the song sounds familiar without remembering what song it is, and even when she realizes, slowly, more certain with each bar, that it is Liszt's third *Liebestraum,* she does not panic. The piano stumbles higher, and lower, and softer, and darker, and Louise does not think *Rex and Lavinia lost their virginity to each other in a Flatiron motel, thinking about this song* (or maybe, maybe, maybe she does), but she doesn't think it out loud until she sees Rex's face.

He is very, very pale. He is biting his lip.

He looks, Louise thinks, like he has seen a ghost.

"Hey, Louise?"

He does such a good job pretending it doesn't bother him. Louise can see right through him.

"Do you mind turning that off?"

"Sure," says Louise.

She stands in the kitchen doorway. She watches his face. She watches him fidget and stare down at his laptop and his Loeb copy of *Medea* and then look up again at the speaker and turn paler, and even though Louise feels the adrenaline so sharp in her she thinks she may never sleep again, she doesn't move.

She feels a strange, sick power in not moving. She feels like she's proving something to him.

"For Christ's sake!"

It is the only time Rex has ever been annoyed with her.

"What is it?"

"Nothing. Nothing. It's just—I'm trying to work, okay?"

Louise is impeccably swift, sailing to the speakers.

"Okay," she says. She kills the music.

Of course, Rex does not love Lavinia. Rex has spent so much time not loving Lavinia, escaping Lavinia, moving on from Lavinia.

That is precisely why he has chosen Lavinia's roommate, who has nothing to do with Lavinia, to love.

"Thank you," says Rex, when the music stops.

He kisses her forehead.

"You're wonderful," he says, and she says, "You too."

You'd be surprised how easy it is for time to go by: just like this. When you don't work, except for your pieces for *The Fiddler* and *The Egret* and the various iterations of *Misandry!* When you spend your nights holding someone. When you take early morning fitness classes in the name of the girl you've killed.

Except that you know, you know the thing about Louise. It's this: she always, always, fucks it up.

Here is how:

Louise uses Lavinia's credit card, sometimes. You know that part. She goes to the places Lavinia goes and makes her presence known, there, in Lavinia's clothes (just in case), in makeup, in sunglasses.

But one night in December Louise gets lazy. She is tired and she wants a drink and she is upset because Rex has asked her to watch *Brideshead Revisited* even though he must know Lavinia well enough to know how much she loved it, and so instead of going to a vegan bar or a place that does very expensive tea Louise goes to Bemelmans, again, to wait until it's late enough that she doesn't have to worry about Mrs. Winters seeing her come in, and slides Lavinia's credit card to Timmy (it has been four months, remember, and nobody has even noticed that Lavinia is dead, so maybe, maybe, nobody cares at all).

Louise sits alone at Bemelmans. She drinks a glass of prosecco, and then another. She wears Lavinia's 1940s dress, the little black crepe one, the one she wears with a little '40s velvet bolero with gold embroidery on it and angular shoulder pads, and a black wicker fascinator with a daffodil on it, and Lavinia's burgundy lipstick, which looks so beautiful on her, and also Lavinia's perfume—even though there isn't an alibi in the world that necessitates smelling like a dead person, even though the bottle is running out. She drinks until she's drunk enough to face going home.

"Well, *hunny.*" Athena flings a white fur coat over a barstool. "Fancy seeing *yew* here."

She sidles in next to her without even asking.

"It's been a *million fucking years.*" She leaves a smear of foundation on Louise's cheek where she kisses her.

Louise stammers something vague.

"You here with *her*?"

"I wish!" Louise shrugs, like shrugging is an easy thing to do (to be fair, it has gotten so much easier, with time). "Now she says she's not drinking until the New Year."

"Jesus Christ—I'd *die*! I hope you told her to drink at the MacIntyre party."

"Maybe she'll make an exception," Louise says.

"Jesus, look at you—fuck—you look so skinny I'm worried about you!"

"Thank you," says Louise.

"My life's shit," says Athena. She orders them a round. "I dated this guy a couple months. Turns out—he's shorter than me! Can you believe that?"

"I mean—"

"Men," announces Athena. "They're all the same. Every last one."

Then the bartender brings the bill back.

"Williams?" he says, as he slides the card back across the table.

Now, Louise thinks. *The world is ending now.*

Athena and Louise look at each other. They look down at the card, which is black and has LAVINIA WILLIAMS branded on it.

Athena is smirking.

"Well," she says.

"I can explain—"

"Aren't *you* clever?"

Stay calm, Louise tells herself. *You can get through this, too.* She always, always does.

"Actually," Louise says, cocking her head at Timmy (she doesn't look at Athena). "Why don't we have two more?"

She slides the card back across the table.

"Let's make it Taittinger," she says.

Athena smiles so broadly she gets lipstick on her teeth.

"Look at *you,*" she says.

"Hey." Louise downs her glass, the way Athena downs hers, without grimacing. "Lavinia's not using it." She toasts when the champagne comes. "I told you. She's off the sauce. She goes to bed at eight."

Athena snorts.

"You know," she says. "You'd better be careful. She'll notice—sooner or later."

"You think she checks her statements?"

"Her parents might."

"It's not my fault," says Louise, very calmly. "She keeps losing her wallet. If I didn't hold on to her cards she'd leave them at every bar in town. Just the other night, she left her Amex at Apotheke."

"Even sober?" Athena raises an eyebrow.

"Exactly," Louise says. "Even sober." She raises her glass. "To the girls who hustle," she says to Athena. "Enjoy."

Athena tilts the entire glass right into her mouth.

"To the girls who hustle," she says.

"Which reminds me," Louise says. "You wanted to go to the opera, didn't you?"

Athena's smile spreads across her face.

"I'm going with Rex and Hal tomorrow. We have an extra ticket" (they don't, but Louise has a credit card). "Hal needs a date."

"Of course he does," says Athena. "His mouth is weird. And he's retarded."

"You don't want to go?"

"I'll be there," says Athena.

Louise swallows as she asks for the bill.

Louise pays.

She thinks *now is the time for you to run.* There is no way, she thinks, she can keep this up any longer (if they start to worry they will trace the cards; Athena will talk; she will *always* talk). But her print piece in *The Fiddler* is coming out so soon, and Gavin has been talking about inviting her to the Five Under Thirty benefit that's every winter, and there's a Halloween party happening at the MacIntyre Louise wants to go to and also Rex has gotten them a reservation at Babbo and also has texted her to tell her he misses her because he hates not spending every single night by her side.

Just a few more days, Louise thinks. *That's all.*

A last-minute orchestra seat to *Carmen* costs $260. Louise pays it, anyway.

Lavinia posts an extended meditation on her yoga poses: just in case.

Rex and Louise and Athena and Hal go to the opera.

They meet at Boulud Sud, an hour before curtain. Athena sticks her hand straight out when she meets Hal and shakes his hand so hard he grimaces.

"I'm Nathalie," she says, and grins.

She doesn't even speak with her New York accent, when she says it.

Louise doesn't think she's ever heard Athena's real name before.

"Pleasure," says Hal. He does a double take. "Have we met before?"

(They have, actually; she was performing at the P.M., but Athena is wearing so much less makeup, now, and so many more clothes.)

"So, Hal?" Athena orders a bottle of champagne before anyone can say anything.

"You got any phobias?"

"What?"

"Like—heights or snakes or something?"

She leans her chin on her hand. She stares straight at Hal.

Hal shrugs. "I don't like the Eurostar," says Hal. "Going underground for too long dehumanizes a man. It makes us into animals."

"What do you think of the subway?"

"I don't take the subway."

Athena brays.

"All I'm afraid of is the two *D*s," she says. "Death and death."

"You're a charmer," says Hal.

It's almost nice, Louise thinks, to exchange the kind of looks she exchanges with Rex, that night. Like the two of them are in on a secret.

Rose photographs the four of them that night for *Last Night at the Met.*

In the photo, they're standing together, four abreast, on the grand stairs, and all four of them look beautiful.

Louise knows the mezzo now. She has seen this Leonora do Rosina in *The Barber of Seville.* She knows when to say *bravo,* and *brava,* and *bravi.*

Her hand is in Rex's hand. Her hair tumbles over his shoulder. The music is so beautiful, and so dark, and so sad, and every time it swells Louise wonders whether he is thinking of the time he has heard it before.

Afterward they go back to Henry Upchurch's apartment in the Dakota, because Hal wants them all to try this very special whiskey

Henry Upchurch bought once, which Louise is reasonably certain Henry Upchurch wouldn't want them to drink.

"You really should meet him, sometime," Hal says to Louise, as they all gather under the portraits. "He'd love you. He loves bootstrap stories. He was the great chronicler of bootstrap stories. I mean—other *people's* bootstraps, but still." He grins. "It'd be good for you, young Louise—if you're going to stick to this whole writing thing."

Athena gives Louise a significant look.

"Well, look at *you*," she murmurs.

She downs the whiskey like it's meant for a shot glass. "Nice place you have here, Hal."

"I know," says Hal.

The four of them drink so much. They drink Hal's whiskey and Henry's whiskey and also scotch and also gin because the drunker they get, the sloppier they are, and even though they're not celebrating anything in particular and even though they're not drinking to forget anything in particular, somehow they get so drunk that Athena lets on that she performs onstage, sometimes, and then Hal leaps to his feet.

"That's where I know you." He grins. "Fuck it—I knew I recognized you. I've seen your tits."

Louise gasps.

"The P.M., right?"

"Fuck, no," says Athena. "I don't work there anymore. Fuckers tried to stiff me on tips."

She pours herself another drink.

Hal just laughs.

Rex and Louise laugh, too.

Hal brings out the modafinil at three, so that they can stay up late. Hal shows them all photographs he's taken on his phone of dinner parties he's attended, the labels on the bottles of wine.

No people. Just wine.

"I'm going to ask out India," he says, to nobody in particular. "I'm going to invite her to Miami, next week." He puts his feet up on the coffee table.

"Look at you," says Rex. "Getting serious."

"Please," Hal says. "I never want to get married." He crushes another pill and snorts it.

There is snot dripping out of his nose where he has snorted. He doesn't wipe it.

"Do you know what I want in a wife?"

He turns to Athena. He puts his arm around her.

"We will discuss the morning paper and the children's education and absolutely nothing else. How does that sound?"

Snot is still trickling so slowly out of his nose.

Rex takes a handkerchief out of his breast pocket. Hal ignores it. He lights an enormous Cuban cigar and blows smoke in Louise's face.

"Also, she should have a patrician nose. The Upchurches are very big on patrician noses. Jeremiah Upchurch's wife—a fine woman, a Havemeyer—had the most delicate, upturned nose—look!" He waves the cigar at another, smaller portrait. "The age of eugenics is upon us." He goes to the stereo. He puts on Wagner. It's *Tristan*.

"I love this part," he says, and maybe it's the wine or maybe it's the whiskey or maybe it's the modafinil they've been snorting but Louise thinks *everything we do we have done before.*

For the first time, Louise is almost bored.

There is nothing, nothing, Louise thinks, *that does not belong to her.*

Then it is four.

"Fuck," Hal says. "*Fuck!* Everybody needs to shut the fuck up!"

"What ate your ass?" Athena is puffing on Hal's cigar.

"It's three in Beijing."

"What?"

"In the afternoon—Christ." Hal clears his throat very ostentatiously. "I have a work call." He plugs in his cell phone. "My boss is a Very Great Man. His name is Octavius Idyllwild."

Athena snorts.

"Maybe you've heard of him."

"Sure," says Athena.

"He lives between New York and the Cotswolds. He has a classic car collection. He and his wife are the same age—can you imagine that?" He starts dialing. "Listen."

Louise and Rex sit, and Athena sits, and they listen to Hal talk to Octavius Idyllwild about spreadsheets, and at first Louise thinks this is whatever Hal's sense of humor is, and they're all supposed to laugh at Hal performing Hal, but it's only when ten minutes have gone by and they're all still listening in silence to an elderly and very posh British man talking about compliance regulations on speaker, and Hal has shown no signs of stopping, that Louise realizes he isn't in on the joke.

"Don't trust Alex Elias with the numbers," Hal says. "He's fucking incompetent, and he should know better than to think he isn't."

Hal's grinning at them, and winking, and pointing at the phone like they're all supposed to applaud him.

They all stare right back at him.

"Henry," says Octavius Idyllwild. "Language."

"There's nothing worse than an incompetent fucking underling," Hal says. "Nothing at all."

He winks at Louise again.

"Language, Henry."

Hal hangs up the phone.

"Will you look at that," Hal says. Dawn is breaking out the window. "Men like that—I swear." He snorts. "Don't mind me. I'm just your ordinary bro."

He turns to Athena.

"I want nothing in this life," he says. "Isn't that wonderful?" He puts his hand on her knee. "Just a beautiful woman and a nice glass of whiskey and some Nazis on the radio. That's all."

Rex and Louise exchange looks.

"I'm not like Rex," Hal says. "Rex is a romantic. Women *love* Rex. Just look at those big brown eyes—aren't they adorable? Don't you just adore him?"

Athena shrugs. She shows all her teeth.

Hal goes on: "Not me. I know what I am. I'm . . . a Stoic. I don't feel anything." He thumps his chest, just to make this clearer. "What do you think, sweetheart? Which would you prefer?"

He leans in real close to Athena.

"You're not the woman I'm going to marry," he says. "But you're better than a blow job on Tinder."

Athena slaps him.

It's such a forceful, astounding blow that Hal staggers back; he drops the whiskey and the tumbler spills all over Henry Upchurch's perfectly upholstered cream-colored sofa, all over Henry Upchurch's Oriental rug.

"Fuck," Hal says.

"Fuck—fuck—fuck!"

He has gone white.

"Mother*fuckers!*" He throws the empty glass clear across the room. It hits the fireplace and shatters.

"What the fuck is wrong with you?"

He gets in Athena's face. For a second, Louise thinks he is going to hit her.

"What the absolute fucking *fuck* is wrong with you?"

"Hal!"

Rex is already on it. Rex is touching Hal's shoulder so lightly, like he knows what to do, like he has done this all already.

"Didn't your *pimp* ever fucking teach you anything?"

When Athena stands up, she's taller than he is.

"Don't you know how to behave in *other people's houses*?"

The snot is still dripping from his nose.

Also, he's crying.

"I'm out of here," says Athena. She says it very quietly.

She says it *out of,* without her accent, and it is the first time Louise has ever clocked that the accent is not real.

She turns to Louise. She kisses her on the cheek.

"Next time," she whispers. "Just give me cash."

She takes the rest of the bottle when she goes.

Hal is on his hands and knees on the floor, rubbing so hard the suede flakes.

Rex is helping him.

"Don't touch it," Hal keeps saying. "Fuck you, Rex—don't touch it—you're making it worse."

Louise knows what to do.

Louise gets the white wine from Henry Upchurch's sideboard. She gets salt.

"For fuck's sake—she *was* a whore, wasn't she?"

Louise doesn't say anything. Louise scrubs.

"I'm not the asshole here!"

Louise gets the stain out.

When she does, Hal smiles like nothing has even happened.

"See?" he says. "That's why you need a woman. They know things. You're so lucky, Rex, to have a woman like this."

He sits back down on the sofa. He puts his feet back up on the coffee table.

"I wasn't *really* angry," Hal says. "Actually—I was *performing* anger."

Nobody says anything.

"It's important for a man to perform anger, sometimes. So people know they can't get away with things."

Louise puts the dirty paper towels in the sink.

"You know, I did her a favor," Hal says. "Next time—she's going to spill something on something *actually* priceless. If she's not care-

ful. Now she knows better. Now she can bag herself a rich husband."
He chuckles to himself. "I call it *broblesse oblige*." He nods at Louise.
"You know how it works, don't you, young Lulu?" He pats the stain
where she has cleaned it.

Louise flushes.

She looks over at Rex—waiting for him to say something, to
object, to defend her. But Rex only smiles a sad, soft smile.

"You're going to make a very good wife one day," says Hal.

"Thank you," says Louise.

Louise and Rex take the elevator down, together. It is morning.

She does not know why she is so angry at him.

"What is it?"

He puts his arm around her. He kisses her head. She recoils without meaning to.

"What's wrong?"

She exhales so slowly.

"He shouldn't have said that to her," Louise says, as they walk
down Central Park West.

She doesn't even know why she's defending Athena. She doesn't
even like Athena. Athena has just blackmailed her.

She is angry, anyway.

"It's Hal," says Rex. "What can you do?"

"He called her a whore!"

"He was joking—you know how he is."

"I do know! He's an asshole!"

"You have to get to know him." Then: "You don't just go around
slapping people."

"Why not?"

"I—" Rex sighs. "People just don't do such things."

"Lavinia would!"

Louise doesn't mean to say that, either.

She hasn't said Lavinia's name out loud in so long.

It feels good, strangely, to say it.

Rex looks like she's hit him.

"I'm sorry," Louise says. "I'm sorry, I didn't mean—"

How stupid are you, she thinks, *to make him think of her right now.*

"You're right," Rex says. He says it like it chokes him. "She would."

He hails a cab. He doesn't invite her in it.

"When you get home, tell her." He swallows. "Tell her I say hi."

He leaves her alone on the street as the cab drives away.

Louise walks home through Central Park.

And Louise thinks: *if Lavinia were here, we would laugh at everybody*—at Rex and his cowardice, at Athena with the lipstick on her teeth and her disappearing accent and her *two Ds, death and death,* at Hal ("a mental Habsburg!" Lavinia had called him), just like the night at the High Line, where they set everything on fire, where they shouted names, when they were gods.

Louise hates how much she misses her, sometimes.

Louise and Rex make up, via text, but it's one of those stopgap let's not fight about this texts that nobody feels good about sending *or* receiving, and Rex has finals for this semester so he's pretty booked up that week, and Louise is almost relieved.

She doesn't do a lot that week.

She gets up early to go to 6 a.m. ClassPass classes—yoga, strength training, barre. She peers down the hall. She avoids Mrs. Winters.

Or she doesn't get up at all and stays in bed, answering Lavinia's emails, telling Cordelia not to worry about AP Latin because she's so clever she'll pass with flying colors, anyway, and that she's sorry she won't make it to Paris for Christmas break, either, but she hopes Cordelia has a wonderful time and enjoys the stained glass in all the Gothic churches on the Left Bank, around St.-Germain.

Or she reads and rereads Rex's letters, in bed, in Lavinia's powder-blue dressing gown (Rex writes about this, too; one time, he tells Lavinia how beautiful she looks in it).

Or she answers the calls of her own parents. They're proud of how beautiful she looks, and how thin. They tell her they photocopied the *Fiddler* piece that ran in print and Louise's mother took it to book club, and Louise's mother grunts and says, "Everybody's real surprised."

Still, Louise's mother reminds her, she can't do this forever. At some point she should probably come home, before it's too late to start over.

"You're almost thirty," Louise's mother says, and reminds her that her fertility will soon decline.

Athena sends her a text that week.

Hey hunny, she says.

Turns out I'm a little short on rent this month.

I know you've got such a good thing going maybe you can Venmo me like $200 maybe?

Just to help a friend out!

Xxx

Louise does.

A few days later Louise runs out of Lavinia's perfume.

She tells herself that she needs it. She can't leave anything to chance.

So she goes down to the East Village, one night, to East Fourth Street (she thinks about calling Rex, asking to come over, but that is a thing desperate, clingy girlfriends do and Louise is neither of those things), to the little fragrance shop where Lavinia keeps her recipe, which she has named Sehnsucht, on file.

The woman behind the counter shuffles through a stack of index cards, down to the Ws.

"Wilson?"

"Williams."

She takes out the card. She gathers up the oils: lavender, tobacco, fig, pear. She mixes them.

They are so much stronger, here, than they are at the bottom of Lavinia's vial—aged, distilled. Every jar is overpowering.

"Give me your hand," the woman says, because the whole point of the fragrance shop is that you're supposed to mix them on your skin. She dabs droplets of oils against Louise's wrist, shakes the mixture and then rolls it against Louise's palm, and then her neck, and when she does this the smell is so overpowering that for a second Louise thinks that this has all been a trick, that Lavinia must be behind her, with her hand on Louise's hand and the MORE POETRY!!! tattoo against hers. She has not realized until now how strongly it smells, and how she must have been smelling it all the time. Maybe now she is just inventing it, but Louise bursts into tears in the middle of the store. The woman puts down the beakers and the eyedroppers and asks if she should call a doctor, and it is all Louise can do to shake her head, and close her eyes, and sob.

She doesn't call Rex that night.

She is afraid to go home until she is sure Mrs. Winters is asleep, so instead she walks all the way home up First Avenue, and tries not to think about the fact that this, too, is something she and Lavinia used to do.

She doesn't leave the house the next day. She locks the doors. She starts drinking at noon. She has worked her way through most of Lavinia's liquor cabinets, by now, but there is some cheap gin left, and Louise drinks that, straight. She is hungry but she doesn't even order in because now she is afraid to open the door. She is drunk and loses track of what time it is (she was supposed to write a piece for *The Egret* today, but she hasn't done that, either).

It's dark. That's all Louise knows. It's dark outside and she hasn't even bothered to turn the house lights on. She hasn't even bothered to turn Lavinia's phone on. It's easier to pretend it doesn't exist.

It's dark outside and then the buzzer goes off.

Louise ignores it.

If it's someone else's delivery guy, or a package guy, a Con Ed guy, or any other kind of guy, really, he'll go away eventually.

The buzzer sounds again.

"Jesus Christ."

Again. Again. Again.

She goes to the video screen.

It's Mimi.

Her hair is unbrushed. Her lipstick's smudged. She's sobbing.

"Lavinia!" she's shouting into the intercom. "Lavinia—please, please, *let me in*!"

It's eight o'clock at night. Prime time for neighbors to come and go.

"*Lavinia!*" Mimi screams.

"*Fuck.*"

Louise lets her in.

Mimi is even worse up close.

Her mascara is all over her face.

"I'm sorry," she sniffles. "I've been calling for hours—I can't get through."

"Lavinia's not here," says Louise. "I'm sorry."

"Out with her cool new friends, huh?"

"Yes," says Louise.

"Can—" Mimi swallows. "Can I come in anyway?"

She hops from one foot to the other. Her fishnets are torn.

She makes too much of a spectacle in the hallway.

"Sure," Louise says.

It's Beowulf Marmont.

Mimi has been sleeping with him since the night of the *Roméo et Juliette* premiere, when he took her home, even though she was passed out, and had sex with her ("I mean," she says, so brightly, "if I *were* conscious I would have had sex with him, anyway, so it's not like I didn't consent!"). He'd write her the sweetest texts. At Burning Man, Mimi explains, they even gave him the playa name "Hemingway," that's how good a writer people thought he was. He's dating the girl with the fragile eyes, and he'd been up-front with her about that, which was so good of him all things considered, but, he'd said, it's like that Fitzgerald quote, what was it, *he climbs highest who climbs alone,* and Beowulf Marmont had an Alpine peak to scale. If anyone was at his side, he'd said, it should be someone like Mimi—someone smart, who was beautiful in that rare, feminine way.

"It was stupid," Mimi says. "I'm stupid."

"You're not stupid," Louise says.

Mimi is getting mascara all over the couch cushions.

Louise has poured her ginger-turmeric-pineapple-champagne tea. Mimi drinks it with shaking hands.

"He didn't mean it."

Louise doesn't know whether Mimi means *he did not mean I was special* or *he did not mean to fuck me while I was unconscious* but she nods, anyway, and rubs Mimi's back while she cries.

"I don't know why I keep doing this," says Mimi.

Louise sighs.

"You don't have to," Louise says. "You don't have to put up with it—from anyone."

"Why not?" Mimi says, and Louise doesn't really have an answer for her.

Mimi swallows. Hard.

"I know what everybody thinks of me." She wipes her eyes with the back of her hand. "But what's the alternative? *Not* loving the people you love?" She laughs a little. "Is that really what we're supposed to do?"

"I don't know," says Louise.

"I thought, you know, that there was something beautiful in

being the one left behind. Isn't that how the poem goes? *Let the more loving one be me?* That's not how it works here, is it? Whoever cares least, wins." Mimi gulps. "*Does* she care about me?"

Her eyes are so wide, and they are glassy with tears.

Louise has the strangest compulsion to hold her.

"No," Louise says. "Probably not."

Mimi blinks.

"What?"

"Lavinia doesn't care about anybody," says Louise. "That's why everybody who loves her, loves her."

"She cares about *you.*"

"Lavinia cares about Lavinia," Louise says. "That's all." She tries to find some kindness in that. "You deserve somebody who cares about you," she says. "You deserve somebody who treats you like you treat them."

"So does everybody," says Mimi. She shrugs. "I'm not, you know, *added value.* I don't *optimize anyone's experience*—Gavin told me that, once. That I wasn't optimizing Lavinia's experience, and that's why she didn't want me around. I'm sure he thought he was being help-ful. Gavin usually thinks he's being helpful." She takes another sip of tea and laughs. "I'm not like you, Lulu" (nobody has called her Lulu in so long). "I'm not smart. I'm not a brilliant writer."

"*I'm* not a brilliant writer."

"But you are!" Mimi spills a little bit of tea into the saucer. "Believe me—I *wanted* you not to be. I remember when your first piece for *The Fiddler* came out I bookmarked it just so I could hate-read it. I thought I could at least enjoy you being bad at something. But that piece about the runaways—it was beautiful! And the one you wrote for *The New Misandrist* about polyamorous men—I loved that one."

"You read it?"

Louise cannot remember Lavinia reading a single one of her stories.

"I read everything you write."

Mimi is beaming.

"I even put a Google Alert on your name," Mimi says, "so I can read them as soon as they go up. Sorry. That probably makes me a stalker."

It probably does, but Louise doesn't mind.

"Do you think you'd ever write a novel?"

"I don't know."

"Because I'd read it. If you ever did. I bet it would get published, too."

"I don't know about that."

"Oh, it would!"

And the way Mimi's looking at Louise, with such wild surety, with such dog-like love, is exactly like Louise once looked at Lavinia, and Louise doesn't know whether or not this means that Mimi is lying, now, or whether Louise was telling the truth, then, but didn't know it.

"You're a better writer than Beowulf Marmont," says Mimi. She finishes her tea. "I'm not saying that because he raped me. It's true, either way."

"Come on," says Louise. She slams the cup down on the saucer. "Let me buy you a drink."

"Really?"

"Really. Let's have one of *those nights.* Okay?"

Mimi's smile spreads like honey. "Okay."

Louise suggests that they go to this swing-dance night over in Hell's Kitchen, because she remembers how much Mimi loves to dance and truth be told she hasn't danced in ages, not since Lavinia, and *Urban Foxes* has an article in this week's edition about a bar themed after the London Underground during the Blitz where they serve cocktails in repurposed pea cans, but Mimi doesn't want to go near Times Square, not so soon after the Paris attacks, and so Louise takes Mimi down the block, to a boxy little gay piano saloon called

Brandy's halfway down a Yorkville side street, where they have wood paneling and ten-dollar well drinks and the guy at the piano plays Frank Sinatra. A stark and lonely sadness has branched into Louise's spine tonight and she wants to be somewhere where there are other people singing.

They sneak out of the apartment.

"It's like we're secret agents," Mimi whispers, when Louise explains about the co-op board, and then: "I remember. We used to have to sneak me all the time."

They take a selfie outside the bar.

Out with my girl, Mimi captions it.

Two dancing bears dancing with each other.

Brandy's isn't really a Lavinia place. It's not elegant or exciting. The only interesting thing that happens to them is that when the waiter pours Mimi and Louise two glasses of house wine there's a little left over in the bottle, and the waiter tells them they can have it for free if they drink it straight from the neck, and everybody applauds them when Mimi does.

"Do you miss her?" Mimi asks. "I mean—with her new friends. Her sober friends." Mimi laughs. "Her *successful,* sober friends."

"All the time," Louise says.

"So do I," says Mimi. She downs a little more wine. "Only—"

"What?"

"Sometimes, like—it's like a *relief,* sometimes, you know, I miss her so much. But at least, you know, I don't have to try so fucking hard anymore." She orders another glass of wine. "I remember, when we were friends, I was so scared she'd figure out I was just, like, this nobody. That she might as well have, like, drawn my name out of a hat. If we hadn't been at the same audition . . ."

"Audition?"

"She was an actress, when we met." Mimi grins. "She didn't tell you that, did she? Before she was a writer. She'd taken time off from Yale to pursue her *stage career."*

In the corner the pianist is singing "A Nightingale Sang in Berkeley Square."

"Who was I to her? A fat failed actress? Every time we went out, we had an adventure, I thought: *tonight's going to be the night she gets sick of me.* And now I have nothing left to be afraid of, I guess."

Another round. Another toast.

"I didn't care about the money. She made you feel so *special.* Until she didn't. I mean—as long as you played the *game,* right?"

"Right," says Louise.

"It's stupid. Sometimes I still feel that way—I mean, no offense. But I feel, sometimes, if I'd just, like, done better, been *better,* she'd have let me stay. If I'd just—played the game."

She starts to giggle.

"Of course, the funny thing," Mimi says. "Is she's the one who fucked it up."

"What do you mean?"

"No!" Mimi clasps a hand over her mouth. "I can't."

"What is it."

"She'd *kill* me."

"I promise you," says Louise. "I'll never, *ever,* tell another living soul."

"It's awful." Mimi's laugh sounds like little hummingbird noises in her mouth. "God—it's so embarrassing. I can't even."

"*Say it.*"

Mimi takes a deep breath. "Okay. So you know—you know Lavinia's big thing about Rex?"

Louise just stares at her a second.

"Of course—of course you do. But I mean, before. Lavinia's whole thing—*I've never had sex with another man.*"

"I remember."

"I mean—there's a lot of loopholes, there. If you think it through."

"You mean—"

"I think that's why she liked us—sometimes. Maybe that's mean. I mean—I think that's an awful thing to say. But—I did wonder, some-times. If she just uses us to, you know—fill a need, so that she never had to be, like, the person who wasn't so special and so wonderful and so magical and *so in love* that she *never let another man fuck her,* again."

"The two of you—"

"I don't know," says Mimi. "I don't know what you call it. Maybe it was sex. For me, it was sex. But—I mean—I haven't been *straight* since I was twelve. For her—maybe it wasn't."

Louise hates that she's a little bit jealous, even now.

"But—that's not it. I mean—that's not the reason she threw me out. God—she'd have done it indefinitely, I think. As long as I gave her what she wanted. I shouldn't be telling you this, Lulu; I'm *such a bad friend.*" She says it like she relishes it.

"No, you're not," Louise says.

Louise pours Mimi more wine.

"I was working at this bar in Alphabet City. And I had the same shifts, all the time. And Lavinia—she knew them. And one night, I drank too much with this bachelor party that came in and made me do shots, and I started feeling really sick to my stomach and so the bartender sent me home early. You promise you won't tell her I told you?"

"Cross my heart."

"I walked in on her," says Mimi. "On—both of them."

"Who?"

"It's really gross."

"*Tell me who,* Mimi."

"Hal Upchurch."

Louise spits out her drink.

Louise tries to imagine him—his sweat and the snot dripping down his nose and the gaps in his teeth and the smile so much wider than his face—on top of Lavinia, and can't.

"But that's not it," says Mimi. "I mean—that wasn't the worst part." She buries her face in her hands. "Jesus—I'm the worst friend in the world."

"Believe me," says Louise. "You're not."

Mimi takes a deep breath.

"He was . . ." She bursts into hysterical, tearful giggles. "He was . . ." She swallows a glass of red wine in one gulp.

"He was fucking her in the ass."

She devolves into a series of helpless giggles, which somewhere along the line turn into sobs.

Louise was not expecting that.

"Wow," says Louise, because really there is nothing else to say.

"I know . . ." Mimi can barely breathe she's cry-laughing so hard. *"I know."* She swallows her phlegm. "So I guess, like, *technically,* she's only had *vaginal* sex with one man!"

Louise can't help it.

She starts laughing, too.

"I didn't even *care,*" Mimi hiccups, when at last they can breathe again. "I mean—I was jealous, of course I was jealous, but I *knew* she was straight, deep down. I knew—I'm not dumb. And he was single and she was single and, I mean—*what does it matter?* I didn't care how he fucked her. I just loved her."

And Mimi starts to cry again, and laugh some more, and also hiccup, and tell the whole horrible story about opening the door and walking in and then pretending she hadn't, slamming the door and running to her room and turning up her headphones as high as they would go, and never mentioning it again. Never asking *why* even though of course she had so many questions: like *really* and *do you love him* and *is this to piss off Rex* and *this is probably to piss off Rex, isn't it.* Mimi was so good, *so good,* for a whole week after even though Lavinia shouted at her so much more than normal, and made her go to so many more parties than normal, and got angry at Mimi for having gained five pounds and not being able to fit into that taffeta-princess dress Louise wore at *Roméo et Juliette* one time. This gets Mimi to thinking about Beowulf Marmont again and this, too, makes her cry, and anyway, anyway, Mimi got a little drunk one night and felt a little too free, and a little too safe, and a little too loved, and she asked Lavinia, point blank, what the hell was up with Hal Upchurch, anyway. Lavinia didn't even look up—*she didn't even look at me*—but everything warm and fecund and flickering inside her crumpled into ash and she told Mimi to get her things and get out and never come back.

The pianist passes around the tip jar and Louise puts a twenty in, just another one of Lavinia's twenties she's supposed to be saving for when she finally runs.

Then the pianist tells everybody it's open mic night and asks for volunteers.

"You know," Mimi murmurs. "I came to New York to go onto Broadway. Isn't that so funny?"

The world is so full of so many desperate, unhappy, guilty people. All Louise wants is for one person to have something good happen to them tonight and so she says *Mimi you should volunteer* and Mimi laughs and sighs and blushes and says *no I can't I lost my voice years ago.* Louise grabs her hand and holds it up and waves and cries out *over here over here,* and even though Mimi's blushing and cringing she is so delighted. The crowd collectively drags Mimi up onto the little platform that constitutes a stage.

They play "New York, New York." (They always play "New York, New York," Lavinia used to say, but Lavinia loved the song so much and the city so much that she never got sick of it, not even once.) Nothing in this city changes, and every party is the same, and every bar is the same and every Friday night is just like the Friday night that came before it, and the same photographers take the same pictures of the same people at the opera and the same passwords open the same speakeasies like skeleton keys and every single fucking piano bar in the whole fucking city plays "New York, New York" at the end of the night.

Mimi sings it, anyway.

Here's the thing you never knew about Mimi:

She's good.

Mimi's not *good-for-an-amateur,* or *good-for-New-Hampshire,* or even *good-enough-to-make-the-chorus-maybe.* Mimi is the kind of good that makes every single person who is laughing and drinking and taking photos stop and put down their phones and stare.

If I can make it there, she sings, and when she sings it's raw and when she sings her mascara runs with her sweat and for the first time Louise realizes that Mimi is beautiful.

When she sings *I'll make it anywhere* it's like she's tearing her throat apart, and everybody is clapping their hands and screaming her name because *that* is how good she is.

When she finishes, she gets a standing ovation. Even the waiters whoop her.

She looks over at Louise, across the bar, her eyes shining with tears, and even though nobody is done cheering her on Mimi tears across the bar and throws her arms around Louise and says, over and over, *thank you, thank you* and then *I'm sorry, I sniffled on your shirt* and Louise keeps saying *you're okay, you're okay, I got you.*

"This is the best night of my life!" Mimi breathes, and she is so happy and right now all Louise wants is to say *come home with me;* all Louise wants is to make Mimi cardamom-cranberry-cinnamon-elderflower tea and sit with her on the divan and play classical music so loud Mrs. Winters knocks on the door to complain, or fall asleep with her in Lavinia's oversized bed, under that enormous, fur-lined jacquard bedspread, or just *talk,* in that endless up-all-night nobody-will-judge-you way. But of course Louise can't, because Lavinia is *at home* (she has checked in on Facebook at this goddess consciousness group in the East Village but it is past midnight and she is probably home by now) and also because Louise can never be truly honest with anybody ever again.

"You're so *nice,*" Mimi says. "You're so *nice,* Lulu. Why weren't we friends?" She grins. "We should hang out sometime."

"That'd be nice."

Mimi stumbles onto Second Avenue.

"I love you, Lulu."

Louise hails her a cab.

She gives her sixty dollars in cash for the fare, because Mimi lives all the way out in Flatbush, because Mimi never has any money.

"I can't—"

Louise closes the car door before Mimi can give it back.

The cab rolls on toward Flatbush.

Louise can't do this anymore.

Anything would be better than faking pictures on Lavinia's phone or Googling motivational quotes just vaguely literary enough for Lavinia to use; anything would be better than sending cryptic, cheery texts to Beowulf Marmont and Gavin Mullaney and chipper, studious emails to Cordelia and Lavinia's parents and hiding from Mrs. Winters and humoring Hal Upchurch and sending Venmo payments to Athena and trying not to make Rex remember her and panicking every time the newspapers report somebody found a body in the East River and pretending to Mimi's face that Lavinia is still alive.

Louise calls Rex, even though it's after midnight, even though he's probably asleep, even though she's not one of those clingy girlfriends who calls her boyfriend after midnight. She lets the phone ring through.

"I need you," she says. "I need to talk to you—*please!*"

"Are you okay?" (She wonders if he is hesitating.)

"I need you," she says again. "Come over."

"But—"

"She's not there."

And Rex says, "*Of course; of course; don't worry; I'll be there.*"

She wants him so badly with her. She wants him in her. She wants him to hold her and stop her shaking and listen to her sobs and her sins, and understand all that she has done and left undone, and maybe then somebody will know her and love her at the same time.

Louise fumbles with her keys in the lobby. She doesn't even remember to look out for Mrs. Winters on the stairs.

The stairs have never seemed so tall before.

She clomps up the stairs—she makes so much noise (*let that old bitch open her door,* she thinks; *just let them come*).

The light is already on.

The door is already open.

Lavinia is sitting on the divan.

Her hair is long and savage. Her feet are tucked under her thighs. She is wearing her dressing gown.

Louise drops her keys in the doorway.

Of course, she thinks, through the wine, through the adrenaline, through all her sleepless nights, *nobody ever really dies.*

Lavinia turns toward her slowly.

They have the same cheekbones. They have the same brilliant blue eyes.

"I've come to see my sister," Cordelia says.

8

LOUISE PICKS UP HER KEYS. She walks inside. She sits down next to Cordelia on the divan.

"I'm sorry," she says. Her voice is not her own. "Lavinia isn't here."

"Where is she?" Cordelia lifts her chin.

"She went away," Louise says. "With some friends."

"Away where?"

"She didn't give me details. Like—a road trip." She thinks so quickly. "A kind of, like, meditation thing. They were going to drive out west."

"When did she leave?"

Louise tries to remember the last thing Lavinia posted on Instagram.

"Just today," she says.

"What friends?"

"Nerissa. Jade—Jade Wasserman. Holly Hornbach." They all have Facebook accounts, too.

"Did you meet them?"

"When?"

"Before she left?"

Cordelia doesn't move.

"A couple of times. Why?"

"Has she been taking her meds?"

"What?"

"Her meds—has she been taking them?"

"How should I know?"

"I went into the bathroom cabinet," says Cordelia. "I'm sorry. I don't mean to be rude—coming in like this. But you see—she hasn't been taking my calls."

"You know Lavinia," Louise says, so lightly. "She can be—"

"Of course I know Lavinia." Cordelia is very calm. "She's my sister."

Cordelia gets up. She goes to the liquor cabinet.

Louise is so numb.

"You've gone through a lot of booze," Cordelia says. She turns around. "I thought Vinny wasn't drinking."

"Oh—she's not. That's all me." That part, at least, is true.

"You shouldn't drink around her," says Cordelia. "Not if she's trying to quit."

"I mean that was from before."

"Why did she quit drinking?"

"She—" Louise decides this is not the best time to bring up the fact that she's fucking Rex. "I think she wanted to make, you know, a clean break. With her past."

"The bottle in the medicine cabinet's still full," she says. "I thought you should know. The prescription's old. She hasn't been taking them. You didn't notice?"

"She seems fine. She's doing a lot of yoga."

"With Nerissa? And Holly? And Jade?"

"Yes."

Cordelia looks up.

"Don't lie to me," Cordelia says.

Louise can't move.

"You think I can't tell when you're lying to me?"

They even have the same glare.

"I was there—remember? The first time this happened."

"The—what?"

"Thanksgiving. 2012. She was—you know—*fine,* then, too. Told everyone she was absolutely at peace with what had happened. She got into astrology—spells, Wicca, tarot cards, that was the big thing. Said the cards had predicted Rex would leave her but that one day when they'd done all the growing up they were going to do they'd get back together. She used to insist on telling my fortune, too. She got into painting. She'd post all sorts of her art online—tell me she was *fine,* back at school, excited to start dating again—she even told me there was someone she thought she might like to date, some TA of hers." Cordelia lifts her chin. "Then she swallowed a bunch of pills over Christmas and tried to kill herself in a boat. So if you're protecting her," Cordelia says. "You're doing a very stupid thing."

"Do your parents know you're here?"

"I'm supposed to be on a flight from Boston to Paris, tomorrow for Christmas. Mother's *very excited* to have at least one of us back." Cordelia's mouth twists into a smile. "Instead I got on a bus from South Station and came here. A homeless man showed me his Johnson outside Port Authority. It was disgusting." She shrugs. "Vinny needs me."

"You need to call your parents," says Louise.

"It wouldn't be fair to them. They've already got one fuckup. That's bad luck. But two looks like carelessness." She kicks off her shoes. "When's Vinny getting back?"

"I don't know," says Louise. "She didn't say."

"Then I'll wait here until she does."

"You really need to call your parents."

"Why?"

Louise gets up, goes to the phone.

"I told them I was invited to Aspen last-minute with some friends from Exeter. They'll like that. You won't tell them I'm here, will you?" She smiles again. "And I won't tell them *you're* here." She cocks her head. "And what happened to Granny's steamer trunk?"

"Lavinia took it to use for some photo shoot she was doing."

"Did she?" Cordelia looks up.

She swings her legs around. She stands.

"You're sure you don't know when she'll be back!"

"I told you—she didn't say. She just said she was going on a road trip—that's all!"

"And you *let* her go!"

Louise doesn't understand.

"Christ—how stupid are you?" Cordelia spins around so quickly the bottles on the sideboard rattle where her dressing gown has whipped them. "Don't you get it? She can't be left alone."

Louise doesn't say anything.

Cordelia draws in breath so sharply.

"I'm sorry," Cordelia says. "I'm sorry—that wasn't fair of me." She sits down on the divan again. She folds her hands in her lap. "She's not your problem," she says. "She's mine. But if she's drinking—I mean, if she's *lying*—I want you to tell me."

"I understand," says Louise.

"*Is* she drinking?"

"No," Louise says. "Not that I've seen."

Cordelia exhales. She closes her eyes.

"Good," she says.

Then: "But she *could* be?"

"All she ever tells me," Louise says. "Is that she wants to stop that kind of life. That she wants to be different."

"But you don't know these *new* friends?"

"Only in passing."

Cordelia nods.

"You know," Louise says, "how Lavinia is—when she's found new people."

Cordelia has softened, just a little bit. "She collects people. Like stray cats." She laughs. "She used to say I was the only one who ever stuck with her."

She goes to the kitchenette. She starts making tea.

"Do you want some?"

"No, thank you," says Louise.

She is so tired, all of a sudden.

"You should have water," Cordelia says.

"I'm fine."

"You've been drinking. You should have some water."

Louise sighs.

"Look," she says. "Lavinia's all right, okay? She's doing well. I know—I've seen her. She's happy. She's—getting over her issues. So—you don't have to stay. She'll—she'll be gone a couple weeks, anyway; there'd be no point."

"But I'm *here*."

"Look, I can rent a car tomorrow. What time's your flight? I can drive you to Logan."

"That's very kind," Cordelia says. "But I don't want you to. I'm going to stay here." She sits down. "I don't want to go to Paris. After all," she says, "this *is* my house."

That's when the buzzer rings.

That's when Louise remembers.

Cordelia goes to the intercom before Louise can think of a good lie.

They watch Rex pacing on the video screen. He is out of breath, disheveled. His blazer is wrinkled, like he's picked it off the floor.

"Bloody hell," says Cordelia.

Then she starts to grin. "I *knew* it."

"What?"

"I knew it!"

She starts to laugh, and it sounds so much like Lavinia's laugh that Louise starts to shiver, just a little. "Of *course* he's come back—I always knew he would—of course he loved her. It was just—it was just—*cowardice*!" She spits the word.

Louise doesn't think she's ever seen someone so happy. She doesn't think even Lavinia could be this happy.

"I can't wait to see the look on his face—"

"Wait!"

It's too late. Cordelia has already buzzed him in.

"If I were a man." Cordelia is pacing. "*Gosh*, if I were a man. I'd—I'd sock him in the jaw for what he did to her."

"It's not like—"

"He ruined her life! He's a miserable, cowardly, sniveling *black-guard*!" She draws herself up to her full height.

"Please," she says. "Vinny's honor is at stake."

She opens the door.

Here's what happens next:

Rex sees Cordelia.

Louise sees him start, because she sees him thinking the exact same thing she thought, seeing that long hair and those wild eyes and those dark, heart-shaped lips—and he goes so pale, for a second, the way people go pale in books when they have seen a ghost, and Louise hates that a person (not a ghost, not a femme fatale, just an ordinary twenty-three-year-old girl) can have that effect on somebody.

Then he gets it.

"Cordelia?"

"You're too late."

Cordelia is enjoying this so much.

"What?"

Louise catches his eye, behind Cordelia's back, and she shoots him such a desperate, plaintive look, and mouths *please, please.*

"Vinny. She's gone. She's run away. You can't see her."

"I . . . *what?*"

"She's on a road trip. She's gone out west. On an adventure."

"Okay . . ."

"I'm so sorry," Louise says, in such a burlesque of sincerity she thinks Cordelia must be able to see through it, *"I know you're here to see Lavinia. She's out of town."*

"You should be ashamed of yourself." Cordelia crosses her arms. "Showing up here—after all this time."

Rex just blinks.

"She's moved on. She's over you. She'd never stoop to *lower* herself to your kind again!"

Rex looks over to Louise, who keeps just mouthing *please, please.*

"I'm sorry." He speaks very, very slowly. "You're—you're right, Cordelia."

"Vinny's not interested in your bourgeois, boring, Biedermeier little life." Cordelia spits it. "She's doing *far* more interesting things, now. She's on—she's on Route Sixty-one, right now!"

"Right." Rex's ears have turned red. He's staring straight at Louise. "Right—I can go . . ."

"Don't you *dare* ever come back!"

"You're right," says Rex. "I won't."

He turns and leaves without even looking at Louise.

When they at last see him storm out on the intercom screen, Cordelia bursts into laughter.

"Did you *see* that?"

"I saw it."

"The look on his face!"

Cordelia locks the door. She rounds on Louise. She is radiant.

"God—I can't *wait* to tell Vinny!" She claps a hand over her mouth. "Promise—promise you'll let me tell her, okay?"

"I promise."

Louise's head is spinning.

"I knew it—I *knew it*! Nobody—nobody could ever forget Vinny!" Cordelia kicks up her feet where the steamer trunk used to be. "Nobody!" She lies down on the divan. "Ordinary people—you know! People like Rex. They can't handle her." She sits up on her heels again. "I know my sister's a lot, sometimes. She's silly and frivolous and vain and she thinks about herself too much. But she's not *selfish,* not really."

"Oh?"

"If Vinny was really selfish she'd make herself happy. And—Vinny's never happy. Not really. She can't be—not so long as the world is the way it is." She hugs her knees to her chest. "It's original sin, you know?"

"I don't understand."

"You're like Vinny." Cordelia smiles a little bit. "She hates when I say things like that to her. They give her the creeps, she says. But I think it's the only way to explain everything. Everything's our own fault—and also nothing is." She sighs. "Of *course* he couldn't be enough for her. And still—*what if he had been?*" She absentmindedly starts to braid her hair. "Anyway," she says. "That's why I'm Catholic. That—and Mother hates it."

Louise texts Rex while Cordelia is in the bathroom.

`I'm so so so so so sorry.`

`I'll explain tomorrow.`

She'll come up with something tomorrow. Louise always comes up with something.

`Can I come over so we can talk about it?`

Rex Reads it.

He doesn't answer.

It's three o'clock in the morning before Cordelia at last yawns.

"You're right," she says, so suddenly. "I'm sure I'm worrying for nothing. Vinny's—fine, right?"

"Of course she's fine," says Louise.

"She'd tell us—if things were getting bad again."

"Of course she would."

"The last time . . ." Cordelia puts her chin on her knees. "I *knew*—before. She started getting manic. She'd do card readings for herself and stay up all night trying to work them out and call home from Yale predicting her own death."

"I promise you," Louise says. "Lavinia's getting better. She's—" She tries so hard. "She's even over the Rex thing."

"She'll *never* get over the *Rex thing*. She'll cling to that until the day she dies. Vinny wants to be the sort of person who only loves once." She drinks the tea she has made. "Even if it makes her very unhappy." She rises. "I should let you sleep. I suppose she's not coming back tonight, so there's no point worrying."

"Text her in the morning," Louise says. "I'm sure she'll be so sorry to miss you."

By then, Lavinia will have posted so many photos of her road trip. She will have posted so many, splendid photos. Louise will have worked out the whole itinerary. She'll have Googled the relevant literary quotes.

"Hey, Louise?"

Cordelia stands in the doorway.

"Yes?"

"You'd tell me—if you were worried. Right?"

She looks on Louise with such a pure and unblinking gaze. Like she trusts her.

"Of course," says Louise.

"I suppose you've been sleeping in my room," says Cordelia. "Would it be easier if I just slept in Vinny's bed?"

Louise has slept in Lavinia's bed every night she has not slept with Rex.

"No—please," says Louise. "Take your own room. I insist."

"But won't you have to move all your stuff?"

"You're right," says Louise. "It's just—Lavinia left it a bit of a wreck."

Cordelia giggles.

"She is a bit messy, isn't she?"

"Let me just clean it up a little for you," Louise says.

Louise goes into Lavinia's room. She makes the bed. She takes everything incriminating—the fake ID, the cash, the jewelry Louise has been selling, bit by bit, Rex's letters—and shoves it all into a messenger bag.

Louise checks her phone. Rex still hasn't texted her.

She checks Lavinia's phone.

The missed calls from Mimi, from Cordelia.

That photo she posted of the High Line, yesterday, has gotten twenty-six Likes.

"All yours," Louise says.

Louise goes back into her old room, which is so much smaller than she remembered.

Lavinia posts some photos from her road trip. A car (the license plates are not displayed). Some more Whitman. A sunset over a forest that could be anywhere (some Thoreau). A woman doing yoga from a distance who could be Holly, or Nerissa, or Jade (Louise finally decides that this is Nerissa and tags her accordingly). Lavinia posts a long and rambling meditation about *sitting well in order* and *striking the sounding furrows* and *all the western stars until she dies,* and maybe it is in keeping with who Lavinia is that she has posted that quote so many times before.

Lavinia texts her sister.

DARLING.

Lulu told me you're in town.

I'm so sorry I wish I'd known but you see we're having the most marvelous time out here and we want to see if we can make it all the way to California by hitchhiking (I have long relied on the kindness of strangers).

GO TO PARIS and bring me back some Mariages Freres tea please.

I like the Marco Polo best.

Xxx

Cordelia Reads it.

She doesn't respond, either.

Rex finally texts Louise the next morning.

Come over after class, he says; she does.

She explains how Lavinia went off on this hitchhiking-Bob-Dylandiamonds-and-rust road trip without telling her beforehand, and left her alone in the apartment that's not even hers, and how Louise was so angry and so foolish—*I don't even know why I was upset*—that she freaked out and called Rex and won't he forgive her for that?

"Girl stuff," Louise says. "That's all."

Also, Lavinia hasn't told Cordelia about the two of them.

Cordelia is so fragile, Louise says, and so ferociously protective of her sister. She has no idea why Lavinia hasn't just told Cordelia the truth but she feels like it's not her place to do it, because she doesn't want to come between the two of them, either. The important thing is that they convince Cordelia to go see her parents in Paris because they can't have a seventeen-year-old girl just wandering around the apartment pretending to be in Aspen because if Louise gets her upset she can just tell her parents that Louise is living there, which, of course, she's not supposed to be doing.

"So you see," Louise says—so desperately.

"That's insane," says Rex. He's right.

"It's complicated."

"I don't see why you don't just move out," he says, like there's a person in this city who wouldn't live with Goebbels if it meant free rent.

"It's *complicated*," Louise says again.

"Look," he says. "I know—the two of you—have your shit. And I don't want to know what it is. It's between the two of you. But don't make me part of this."

He says it like Lavinia isn't dead because of him.

"I just don't want to cause any more drama," says Louise.

"Well, you've done a great fucking job of that!"

Louise hates it when he raises his voice at her.

She puts her hands on his shoulders. She kisses him.

"It's just for a little while," she says. "Just—to keep the peace."

"So, what? I pretend I'm still in love with her to keep some *kid* happy?"

"You don't have to pretend anything," she says. "We just lay low.

Until we can convince her to go home. So I don't have to live with somebody who hates me."

She waits for him to say *stay with me.* He doesn't.

"And what happens when Cordelia tells *her* I've been *pining.*" He doesn't even say her name. Not even now. "Do I keep the peace then, too?"

She tries so hard to come up with a way this can sound less bad than it is.

"But you're not." Louise can't stop herself. "Are you?"

He rolls his eyes.

"It's always about her, isn't it?" he says.

He doesn't say *no,* though.

Lavinia roasts marshmallows over a campfire in Louisiana.

Cordelia sits at the dining-room table making notes in the margins of the writings of Julian of Norwich.

Louise pays Athena Maidenhead another two hundred dollars.

They never discuss outright *why* Louise is doing it. It's just that one day Athena sends her a text to say hey hunny do you have any leads I'm pretty broke right now haha and the guy who usually pays my rent turned out to be an asshole.

Maybe you could ask Lavinia if she knows any way a girl could make like $500 fast?

She's always so generous. (Haha)

Louise pays.

Athena thanks her, and then mentions so casually she'd also like to buy a new dress.

Turns out, she met a guy the night they all went to the opera. He asked her out during the intermission. She wants to dress real classy for him.

Athena sends her the Net-a-Porter link and Louise buys this, too.

Lavinia's parents start to put pressure on her to come home for Christmas.

We understand Cordelia has impulsively decided not to return home, they say. We can't help but wonder if this is in part due to your example? Now that Cordelia is getting older we feel it's more important than ever that you be a role model for her, and your current way of living is—your father and I agree—hardly an appropriate one for her to emulate.

We feel it would be prudent for you to come home for the remainder of the holiday season. We can discuss your imminent return to Yale then.

Lavinia writes a very earnest letter explaining that her novel is almost done, and that this road trip she's doing—completely sober, she adds!—is of utmost import for her physical as well as emotional well-being.

Be that as it may, Lavinia's mother says, we cannot support you in this endeavor. We may not be able to alter your course of action at this stage, but we can, at least, play a role in setting an example for your sister.

With that in mind: we'll be cutting off your cards until you return. You have until December 19th to decide.

If you would like to return to Paris we would more than happily purchase a one-way plane ticket for you.

But your father and I are in agreement: we're both unable to justify our bankrolling of your lifestyle choices any longer.

Please contact us with your passport details and details of your proposed flight.

I hope you realize that this is the kindest thing you could possibly do for your sister at this stage, Lavinia's mother adds.

Lavinia doesn't answer them.

Louise starts running out of money again.

She'd planned to save every cent she took from Lavinia. But Louise hasn't worked in so long, and the payments from Athena have started to add up, and also the times she takes Rex to dinner, because it makes her feel like she's capable of giving him some kind of happiness, and also the times they go Dutch, because Louise never wants to admit she can't afford the kinds of things Rex can afford, because Louise can never say *no* to him.

Lavinia doesn't take Cordelia's calls.

Sorry darling! she says. The signal's terrible out here! Last night we went bathing naked underneath the stars and nearly froze to death and it was BEAUTIFUL.

Every day, Louise thinks *today.*

Today will be the day everything ends.

She will run away; she will take Lavinia's passport or the fake ID belonging to the redhead from Iowa called Elizabeth Glass; she will take whatever money she has left and she will walk out the door and she will vanish into the city, but then Gavin Mullaney tells her that he wants her to do another piece for *The Fiddler* in print, and gives her a heads-up that they're considering naming her one of their Five Under Thirty of that year, if she can impress the rest of their editorial board with her upcoming piece. And then Rex texts her a picture of Central Park in the snow, even though they've been fighting so much, lately, and Louise thinks *just one more day; that's all I need; just one more day,* but then another day comes and she needs that one, too.

Truth is, Louise has nowhere else to go.

The twentieth of December is Louise's thirtieth birthday.

Rex knows it's her birthday, because he sees it on Facebook (she tells him she's twenty-six).

I'm sorry things have been stressful lately, he says. *Let's do something special, okay?*

Louise tells Cordelia she has a date with a guy she met online.

"He's probably a serial killer," says Cordelia, without looking up from her work.

———

Louise dresses up in the only dress she has that Cordelia will not notice belongs to Lavinia, which is too big for her now and also made of cheap polyester and which she bought at Housing Works for twenty dollars two years ago, and which at the time was the nicest thing she had ever owned.

Rex has texted her: an address, a time.

It's a surprise, he says, with a smiley face so she knows he is not angry at her, this time.

It's a secret cocktail bar in Williamsburg with only three chairs, one of which is for the bartender.

He has dressed up for her—his blazer is darker than usual, and less creased. He leaps up when she comes in (even though she is wearing such a frumpy dress, such an ugly and oversized dress) and when his eyes rest on her she wonders if it is because he thinks she is beautiful, tonight, or because he has finally figured out that this is just what she looks like when she is not being Lavinia.

"You look nice," he says, which doesn't clarify anything.

Louise has spent an hour looking in the mirror this evening.

I look thirty, she thinks, and it baffles her that he does not know this.

They don't talk about Lavinia. They don't talk about Cordelia. They talk about the weather and Rex's seminar papers and some of the qualifying exams he'll have to take, soon, and what he thinks of his professors and this amazing living-Latin program he wants to do in Rome next summer. They talk about Hal and how he's dating India, now, and how he's decided already that she is the girl he's going to marry, without asking her what she thinks of it. They talk about Louise's pieces for *The Fiddler* and how Gavin thinks she has a real shot at being one of *The Fiddler*'s Five Under Thirty, which Rex seems to find impressive.

They talk, Louise thinks, like any other boring couple in this city who only have sex two or three times a week.

They talk like Rex has never dated the kind of woman who sets shit on fire, or stands naked at the water's edge at the dawn of the New Year.

They have Korean-Mexican fusion. They have red wine. Rex pays.

After, he asks her to take a walk with him. They do.

It is all very sweet. It is all very ordinary. They walk, hand in hand, through the snow, down Bleecker, then through Washington Square Park, then back down to Chinatown. The stars stud the sky and Rex's ears get red when they are cold, as they do when he is nervous or embarrassed. All of a sudden Louise starts to feel intensely sure that the only reason they're walking so romantically in the moonlight is because he doesn't want to fuck her (not in that dress; maybe not ever).

He hums softly as they pass Doyers Street.

She takes his hand. She pulls him down the alley, which is unlit and dark and cobblestoned and where mobsters used to commit murder, once upon a time (Lavinia once said), because nobody could see you there.

He laughs. He follows her.

She pushes him up against the wall. She kisses him so hard she bites his lip.

She kisses him so hard he gasps.

He looks so confused when she pulls away.

He should not be so surprised, Louise thinks; *he should be used to this by now. This is exactly what Lavinia would have done.*

She kisses him again, harder this time, and slides her hand up the inside of his thigh, feels his cock (it is not yet hard; this is on her).

She draws away. She looks at him.

"What are you doing?" He's laughing as he asks her, but he means it.

"Come on," she says. "Nobody will see" (*everybody wants to fuck the crazy ones, that's the whole point*).

"I want you," she says.

And he's still laughing, a little, like this part is ridiculous. Is it the dress? Is it because she's thirty? Is it because Cordelia has said *nobody will ever forget Lavinia* and because she is right? Louise kisses him harder, so hard, she thinks, that she even means to hurt him, because if she can't make him want her she can at least make him afraid of her, just a little, and because if she cannot be Lavinia she might as well be a whore (*you're not the woman I'm going to marry*, Hal had said to Athena, so easily, like she'd ever fuck him if it weren't for the Dakota), and she kisses him harder and harder and says *I want you to fuck me* in his ear. Finally, he gets hard, and it's only when he grabs her wrist, when his breath gets ragged, that he moans in that sharp and desperate way that means she has power over him, when he gets rough with her in that way that means that she has power over him, that she pulls away.

He pulls her back.

She wants to savor him wanting her like this forever.

He pushes her up against a wall, hikes up her skirt and pulls aside her panties, and now Louise isn't sure which of them is initiating it, whether she has tricked him into wanting her (she has gotten so good, now, at that part) or whether all along this is just what he wants because he's a man. He feels her up underneath the skirt of her dress (*this I have done before;* Louise thinks; *all this, all this I have done before*) and Louise starts to whisper to him all the things that a woman you'd want to fuck would say, and she doesn't know if she means them or she just wants to be the woman who makes men hear them but she tells him, right in his ear, that she wants him, that she needs him, that she is wet and needs him to take her home right now, and he is hers, now, hearing it; he gets rougher, hearing it, and then without thinking she tells him she wants him to fuck her in the ass.

"What?"

He says it like this isn't something every single straight man dreams of.

He pulls away to look at her.

"Nothing," Louise says, "never mind."

"But—"

"Keep going," she says, and they start to stumble over each other and get in each other's way and their bodies don't fit, and then Rex says "Fuck it, let's get a cab" and they cab it back to Rex's place (Louise pays) and Rex fucks her, just like every other time he's fucked her. He burrows into her shoulder and buries his face into her hair like he's hiding from something, like the crook of her arm is his harbor. She clings to him, too, and thinks *this has to be enough,* and he starts getting so rough with her that she thinks *I have driven him mad* and she half-wants him to get rougher, still, just to prove that this is a thing she is capable of doing to a person, but he's not even looking at her—he's thrusting so hard it hurts but he's not even looking at her—and maybe because she means it or maybe to shock him or maybe to make him notice her Louise says *I love you, I love you,* just as he comes.

He kisses her forehead.

He rolls off her.

"I need you," he whispers. He kisses her shoulder.

Louise doesn't sleep that night, either.

"Did you have sex with him?" says Cordelia, when Louise gets home the next day. "Your serial killer?" She's fully dressed at nine in the morning, in a dowdy little skirt and a turtleneck. She's reading.

"That's none of your business," says Louise.

"Why?"

"Because you're seventeen."

"The age of consent in plenty of places is sixteen," says Cordelia. "Anyway, I waited up for you."

"Why?"

"I was worried. In case he *was* a serial killer and he'd chained you up in a basement."

"How would you know?"

"Well, you wouldn't have come home." She raises her chin. "Was that the first time you met him?"

"I'm taking a shower," says Louise.

"I'm not trying to intrude," says Cordelia. "I'm just curious. Can you really have sex with somebody you've just met?"

She follows Louise to the bathroom door.

Louise closes the door. She takes off her clothes.

"Aren't you afraid?" Cordelia's voice is muffled through the door.

"Of what?"

"I don't know. Diseases? Getting hurt?"

Louise steps into the shower. She turns up the heat so it scalds.

Cordelia spends her days studying, and texting Lavinia, who rarely responds.

"You don't have to worry," Cordelia says, three days before Christmas. "I mean—about leaving me alone. I don't drink and I don't do drugs and I don't do anything, really. So you can go home, if you want to. I'll just stay and wait for Vinny. I'm not going home."

"Why not?"

There is such a great space in the living room, where the steamer trunk once was.

"Why aren't you going home?"

"I don't like my parents very much," says Cordelia, so simply.

"Well, I don't like my parents very much, either," says Louise.

"Why not?"

Louise shrugs. "I don't think they really like me."

She says it like it's a joke.

"Why don't your parents like you?"

Back when Louise went to therapy (she ran out of money for therapy, and also didn't really trust her therapist), she spent a lot of time developing mantras like *people express love in different ways* and *concern can sometimes translate into criticism* and *letting your children go out in the world is a difficult process,* but now that she thinks about it that's probably bullshit.

"I don't make enough of an effort," Louise says.

"That's what Mother always says about me, too. But she likes me." She swings her legs up onto the divan. "That's why I don't like her.

She likes me better than Vinny—and that isn't fair. You should love all people equally." She winks. "It's really the only Christian thing to do."

"Are you really religious?"

Cordelia plays with the tassels on the throw pillow. "At the beginning," she said. "Maybe I just liked to annoy Vinny. When she was a very terrible pagan I used to tell her I'd pray for her soul." She considers. "But I think I believe it, now." She leans her hand on her cheek. "The more I read," Cordelia says, "the more it's the only thing that makes sense to me. If God doesn't exist—this world would be too terrible for words."

"Look at this!"

She shows Louise her phone.

Lavinia is at the Grand Canyon. Her shadow fades into the rock.

"Have you ever been to the Grand Canyon, Lulu?"

"No."

"Me neither." Cordelia blows up the photo to make it bigger. "I'm not really very adventurous. Do you know—I've never even disobeyed my parents, before this week? I'm the good daughter, you see. Look—isn't it beautiful?"

"Lovely."

"I tell Vinny all the time—it's not good to be so frivolous. She should go back to school. She'll regret it when she's older, if she doesn't. Only, Lulu?" She takes a deep breath. "How long does it take to drive to the Grand Canyon?"

"Five days" (Louise has Googled this). "Why?"

"You don't think . . ."

"No."

"We could rent a car! And we could go and surprise her! Or we could fly—if we flew, we could be there by Christmas!"

Louise keeps her eyes on the photo, so she doesn't have to look at Cordelia's face.

"We can't do that," she says.

"Why not? Vinny's always doing crazy, impulsive things—why can't we? And look—it's *beautiful* out there!"

"Because she's with her friends, Cordelia."

"So? Vinny likes me better than any friend she's ever had—I'm sorry, Louise, but it's true—there's no *way* she wouldn't want me there! She'd be *thrilled* to see us both!"

Louise closes her eyes.

"We can't."

"Why not?"

"Because."

"Because why!"

"Because she doesn't want you there!"

Cordelia looks like Louise has just slapped her.

Cordelia doesn't say anything.

She puts her hands in her lap. She folds them. She is very quiet for a while.

"Hey, Lulu?"

"What?"

"Do you want to get a Christmas tree?"

Their first and only Christmas in New York, Virgil and Louise bought one of those potted-plant firs they could keep on the kitchen counter, which was the apartment's only real surface, because they didn't have space for anything bigger, except they kept arguing over who would take care of it and the thing died without either of them noticing even though they're supposed to be evergreen and that, Virgil said, was proof that Louise should never be a mother.

Cordelia and Louise go to the guy on Seventy-ninth and Third.

They jack up the prices, so close to Christmas Eve, but Louise pays, anyway, with one hundred of the eight hundred or so dollars she has left.

Louise offers to pay for the guy to deliver it, but Cordelia insists that you haven't earned a tree if you haven't at least dragged it with your own two hands and so the two of them lug it all the way back to Lavinia's house.

They spend the afternoon decorating it. They don't have ornaments so they decorate it with detritus of Lavinia's: tarot cards, crystals, peacock feathers, erotic statuettes.

"I suppose it's not *really sacrilegious*," Cordelia says. "Christmas trees are pagan, anyhow."

Cordelia puts Lavinia's present under the tree.

"I want it to be waiting for her when she gets back," Cordelia says.

That night, after they go to bed, Cordelia calls Lavinia.

She calls her four or five times, and Louise huddles up in bed and watches the phone go off, and go to voicemail, and lets it go, and doesn't say anything either.

Cordelia leaves so many voicemails: *pleasepickuppleasepickuppleasepickup.*

Louise can hear them through the bedroom wall.

On the sixth call, Lavinia answers.

Louise has gone out the fire escape. She's gone all the way up to the roof.

"What is it, darling? Is it *catastrophe*?"

Louise is shaking, doing it, even though she's been doing it so long.

"Vinny!"

Cordelia's voice trembles.

"Vinny—I've been trying to call for days!"

"Darling, *tell* me you're not still in New York. I'm so sorry, Cordy—you should be furious with me; really, you should; it's just that Nerissa wants to make it *all the way* to Big Sur and I really, truly, think we could—"

"I need you!"

Louise can hear Cordelia three flights up.

"Cordy, please, be reasonable—"

"Just come *home,* okay?"

"I'm sorry, darling, you know I'd love to, but—"

"Please!"

"I'm so sorry. Look, Cordy—the others are all here—"

"Please!"

"I have to go."

Louise hangs up the phone.

She tiptoes so quietly downstairs. She sneaks so quietly in back through the window.

She gets so quietly back into bed.

She can hear Cordelia in the other room, quietly sobbing.

Cordelia doesn't mention it to Louise.

She is impeccable, the next morning, which is Christmas Eve. It's like she hasn't even been crying at all. She gets up before Louise does, cleans the house, makes breakfast.

"I'll probably go back to Paris soon," Cordelia says. "You must be quite sick of me."

"Not at all," says Louise.

She forces down some coffee.

"I suppose we should do something for Christmas. Maybe Midnight Mass? There's one I want to go to at St. John the Divine—I know it's Protestant, but I really like the music there . . ."

"I'm sorry," Louise says. "I have plans."

She and Rex planned it weeks ago. Henry Upchurch is throwing his annual Christmas Eve party. He's rented a room at the Yale Club, like he does every year. She and Rex have not gone to a party in so long. They're getting so dull.

"Oh," says Cordelia. "Of course you do. You probably have a lot of friends."

She shrugs. "That's fine. I don't mind going by myself. It's a religious holiday, anyhow. It's good to focus on, you know, God and things."

"I'm sorry," says Louise. "I said I'd go before you even got here."

"Of course," says Cordelia. "I mean—you don't owe me anything." She swallows. "You hardly even know me. It's Vinny who—" She stops herself. She turns back to her book. It's Hildegard of Bingen, this time.

Louise can't stand this.

"Look," she says. "Why don't you come?"

"Where?"

"It's a party. At the Yale Club. It's—it's Henry Upchurch's Christmas party."

"Oh," says Cordelia. "I don't think his books are very good."

Louise has actually never bothered to read any of Henry Upchurch's books.

"Well, don't tell Hal that."

"I don't like him, either. He's got no social skills and he's friends with Rex."

"He's not that bad," says Louise. "I mean—neither of them is. And, I mean, there's going to be a lot of people there. We might not even see them."

"Vinny would be furious if I even spoke to them," Cordelia says. "Anyway, I haven't got anything to wear to that sort of thing."

"You could borrow something of Lavinia's? I'm sure she wouldn't mind."

"She hates it when I borrow her clothes without asking." Cordelia considers. "What were you going to wear?"

Louise hesitates.

"If we *both* borrowed something, she couldn't very well stay mad at us both." Cordelia breathes in. "Besides, if she wanted us not to borrow her things she should have come back and worn them herself—right?"

"Right," says Louise. "Exactly."

"It serves her right." Cordelia smiles. "Rex coming all the way here—and she'll never even know! You kept your promise, right? You didn't tell her?"

"I didn't tell her."

"Good. Don't."

Cordelia goes to the closet. She fingers Lavinia's things.

"I'm going to be *very polite* to them both," she says.

I'm sorry, Louise texts Rex.

I couldn't just leave her alone.

Rex Reads it. No answer.

We can still have fun! We just have to be discreet, that's all.

Blushing Przewalski's horse emoticon.

She sees the ellipses on the screen that mean he's typing. They go on for five minutes.

ok.

That's all he says.

Louise does Cordelia's makeup.

She shows Cordelia how to straighten her hair, to transform the wilderness of her curls into something neat and smooth. She shows her how to put on lip liner, so that the lipstick will stay within the bounds of her mouth. She highlights Cordelia's eyes with mascara (*how blue they are,* she thinks). She puts Lavinia's lipstick on Cordelia's lips.

She helps Cordelia choose a dress.

Cordelia fingers a red one, silk, cut along the bias.

"This one, do you think?" She stops herself. "No, I can't."

"Why not?"

"My breasts are too small. And I'll look ridiculous." She sits on the bed. "*This* is silly—you should just go without me."

"No—no, you should come!"

Louise doesn't even know why it matters.

"I'll look stupid!" Cordelia says. "I don't—I don't even know how to stand."

"I'll show you," says Louise. "Just—put it on."

Cordelia does.

It hangs long and loose on her.

"It looks like a tent."

"You're not standing right," says Louise. "You have to, you know, *pose.* Arch your back a little—right there, good."

"I feel like a cobra."

"That means you're doing it right. And put your tongue behind your teeth when you smile."

"Why?"

"It makes you smile with your eyes."

Cordelia looks dubious.

"It comes out better in photos."

"So?"

"Just—trust me, okay?"

Cordelia's lashes are so dark when they flutter, now.

"Will you take a picture of me? I mean—I don't want to post it, or anything. Just—just for me to have?"

Louise does. She shows it to Cordelia.

"I look ridiculous," Cordelia says.

Actually, Cordelia looks beautiful.

"Will you send it to me?" Cordelia asks.

They take a cab to the Yale Club. Louise pays.

She has $402.63 in her checking account.

When they pull up, Hal is already there. He is smoking a cigar on the steps. Beowulf and Gavin are with him.

Hal does a double take when he sees them.

"I heard you were in town." He looks Cordelia over. "You've sure been causing trouble, haven't you?"

"It's nice to see you again, Henry," Cordelia says. "It's been a while."

She shakes his hand.

"Last time I saw you, you had braces."

"Last time I saw you, you were thin."

Hal grins.

"Are you even legal?"

"Only in New Hampshire."

"Shame."

"No," says Cordelia. Her mouth twists a little. "Not really."

Then: "You're Henry Upchurch's son."

"For my sins."

"What's that like?"

"Go read his books." Hal puffs on his cigar. "That'll tell you everything."

"I've read his books," says Cordelia. "I thought *Folly's Train* was cliché and every character in *A Dying Fall* was too easily redeemed."

Louise bites her lip so Hal won't see her smile.

"I'll have you know, little girl," says Hal, "that Henry Upchurch is the greatest American writer of the past fifty years."

"Don't worry," Hal says to Louise, as Cordelia checks her coat. "I've been briefed. I'll be good." He hands her a drink. "It seems like a whole lot of fucking trouble, if you ask me."

"I didn't," says Louise.

Hal reaches out to grab Rex by the arm.

"Now, do you two *know each other*?" Hal's tongue lolls a little to one side. "Or do I have to introduce you."

"Hal, don't—"

Louise squeezes Rex's elbow, just a little, and feels so pathetic for doing it. Rex smiles—or maybe grimaces.

Cordelia sees them.

She walks over. She's measured and unsteady in Lavinia's heels.

"Hello, Rex," she says. Her voice is low.

They shake hands.

"I'm prepared to be civil," Cordelia announces, "if you are."

Hal bursts out laughing.

"However you like it," says Rex.

Hal raises his glass.

"To your sister," says Hal. "Who has brought us all together."

Everybody clinks glasses.

Nobody drinks, except Cordelia, who closes her eyes and drinks her champagne in one gulp, and then makes a face.

The Yale Club is like a wedding cake—white, gold-shot, confectionary: with its curved windows, its white, whipped curtains that seem to flutter up to the sky. There are so many people here who know Henry Upchurch, or don't and want people to think they do, or who have never heard of Henry Upchurch but who want to drink for free.

Louise drinks. Hal drinks. Rex drinks. Cordelia drinks.

She drinks more than anybody else.

"It's not so bad," she says, on her third glass. She hiccups.

She claps Rex on the shoulder.

"You're not so bad, either," she says. "I've decided."

Rex doesn't say anything.

"You're a fool," she says. "But I forgive you. If Vinny weren't my sister, I wouldn't be able to stand her, either." She smiles. "Cheer up, Rex—maybe she'll take you back, after all. If she ever comes back. Who knows, with Vinny? You never know *what* she'll do!"

Rex forces his drink down.

"No," he says. "You're right. You never know."

"Come on," says Hal. He puts his hand on the small of Louise's back. "I want you to meet my father."

———

Henry Upchurch is old.

Also, he's fat.

He looks like a little sphere glued to a bigger one. He has a flap in his neck, like a turkey's. He sits because he is both too old and too fat to stand. He doesn't speak.

Beowulf is stuck to his side, his fragile girlfriend hovering over them both like a mosquito. Beowulf is midway through his discourse on *A Dying Fall,* which Louise has already heard. He's talking about that famous scene where the protagonists get into a fistfight over Latin conjugations, and he is making the point that in today's world, with today's sensitivities, you could never write a scene like that and have it be understood by *hoi polloi* (he is very careful not to use the article) because the *you-know-what* brigade is always turning over rocks to look for homosexuality and there's no time for discussing what it means to be a *man,* in the Classical sense.

Rex stands close by but doesn't touch Louise.

This is what the two of them agreed. It hurts anyway.

"I bet," Hal says into Cordelia's ear, close enough for Louise to hear, "that Beowulf Marmont gets off picturing his girlfriend fucking black men."

"What?"

"Exactly."

"You're disgusting."

"I'm honest," says Hal. "Some men are like that, young Cordelia. Better you learn now the ways of the world."

"I know the ways of the world just fine!" She pronounces it *wheyze.*

Hal pours some whiskey from his flask into his champagne flute. "Henry Upchurch just *loves* Rex. Doesn't he?"

Louise isn't sure whether Hal is trolling Rex, or trolling Cordelia, or trolling her.

"It's a good story, actually," says Hal. "Rex has never even read *A Dying Fall,* have you, Rex? But Rex is a good little Classicist. He went on some tangent about Greek verbs when he came over for tea—Christ, ten years ago, now? About how *substantia* and *hypostasis* mean the same thing, etymologically speaking, but are totally opposite theologically speaking."

"It's true," says Cordelia, suddenly. "There's one *substantia* and three *hypostases* in the Trinity." She hiccups. "Or is it one *hypostasis* and three *ousia*? I forgot."

Hal ignores her.

"They're nouns," says Rex, under his breath.

"Henry Upchurch was *so* impressed—he wrote one of your Yale references, didn't he, Rex? Weren't you impressive?"

Rex is looking down at the carpets.

"There's a stain on this carpet," he says, without looking up.

"He always asks about you," Hal says. "Every single fucking time he and my mother come in from Amagansett. *How's your clever friend Rex doing? Isn't he clever?*"

"You would think," Rex says, "that in a place this expensive, they'd clean their fucking carpets."

He jerks his head up.

"I'm going for a smoke," he says.

Louise can't follow him.

"I'm getting another," Cordelia says.

She glides off.

Now Louise meets Henry Upchurch.

Hal steers her to him once Beowulf has been dismissed.

"Louise Wilson," Hal says, in that half-whine whose sincerity Louise still cannot ascertain, "is going to be one of the great writers of our generation."

Henry Upchurch lifts his head with very great effort.

"My name is Louise Wilson," Louise says.

She sticks out her hand. He looks so confused and so she grabs his hand, which is flabby and unsteady, and shakes it firmly. She looks him straight in the eye. "I write for *The New Misandrist* and *The Egret* and *The Fiddler.*"

"Ah," says Henry Upchurch.

His head bobbles, just a little bit. He drools. Louise thinks, at first, that he is nodding, but it's only a tremor.

"Louise is looking for representation," says Hal. He's still smiling, like he doesn't even notice that his father's snot has pooled on his tie.

"Ah," says Henry Upchurch.

His eyes are glassy. He doesn't look at either one of them.

"I'm going to send her to have lunch with Niall Montgomery, okay?"

"Ah," Henry Upchurch says.

He dribbles into his tie.

"That's just his trick," Hal says. "Everybody knows really powerful men don't *talk*. It just means everybody has to work harder to engage *him*. Niall Montgomery is his agent. A friend of the family. We're going over there, tomorrow, for Christmas lunch. I'll mention you."

"Why are you being so nice to me?"

"Because," he says. "You're in on the joke."

"What joke?"

Hal grins. "*The* joke." He wiggles his eyebrows at her. "You get it. And I get it. And none of these other poor fuckers gets it. Least of all Rex. Poor, poor Rex."

"I don't know what you're talking about," says Louise.

"There are some benefits," Hal says, "to being the ugly friend. Don't you think?"

Then Louise sees Cordelia.

She's standing in a corridor, talking to Beowulf Marmont, who is leaning in so intently. She is swaying, just a little bit.

They're standing under mistletoe.

"I am nothing," Beowulf Marmont is leaning into Cordelia's ear, "if not a man of tradition."

That's when he leans in to kiss her.

Cordelia starts to put her hands up, but she's too late, or else Beowulf pretends not to notice that she's doing it, and he grabs her by the back of the neck and pulls her in and jams his tongue so confidently down her throat, and it takes Louise yanking him off her and shouting *she's seventeen* straight in his face before he stumbles away.

To his credit, he looks horrified.

Cordelia stands very still.

She doesn't look at Louise.

"Do you have a tissue?" she asks.

Louise hands her one.

Cordelia rubs her mouth raw.

She lets it fall.

"That," she says very slowly, "was my first kiss."

She hiccups again.

"I'm going to be sick."

Cordelia doesn't even make it to the bathroom.

She throws up in a wastepaper basket in the corridor outside the function room.

Louise holds her hair back and strokes her shoulders.

"It's fine," Louise says. She has done this so many times before. "Don't force it. You'll feel better once you've thrown it up."

"I shouldn't have drunk so much."

"It's my fault," says Louise. "I should have been watching you—I didn't realize—" And then she stops herself, because it should be obvious that most people can't drink a bottle of champagne on an empty stomach without vomiting.

"I'm not your fucking problem!" Cordelia says. She chokes out more phlegm into the bin.

It's the first time Louise has ever heard Cordelia curse.

"It's my fault," Cordelia says again. Louise can't tell if she's convulsing because she's sick, or because she's sobbing. "It's my fault—I betrayed her."

"How?"

"I spoke to Rex! And Hal! *I shook his hand*—oh, God! God! She'll never forgive me!"

"She will!"

"I *shook his hand*! I want to burn it off!"

Cordelia starts rubbing it on the carpet, like she can blister off her sin.

Louise tries, so vainly, to shush her.

"I'm awful!" Cordelia cries.

"You're not."

She begins to sob, so brokenly, in Louise's lap.

"It's all right," Louise says, like she knows what to do, like she knows how to handle any of this. "It'll be all right."

"She hates me."

"She *won't*. I promise." Like that, too, is a thing she can assure.

"How do you *know*?"

"Because," Louise says, at last, "she was fucking Hal!"

That's when Cordelia finally, finally looks up, to see Rex and Hal behind them.

Rex doesn't even bother to first ask if it's true.

He punches Hal anyway.

They fight like dogs do.

They roll on the carpet. They smash each other's faces into the wall. Hal forces his fist into Rex's mouth. Rex kicks Hal in the stomach. They roll on top of one another. Rex grabs a fistful of skin from the back of Hal's neck. Hal grabs Rex by the hair. Rex slams Hal's head into the ground.

It takes Gavin and Beowulf (*really, Henry, at your own father's fête!*) to separate them.

When they separate them, Hal is laughing.

"And they say," he wheezes, "that men aren't men anymore."

Louise watches Rex go.

She wants so badly to follow him. For a second she thinks she will.

But Cordelia is sobbing, again, in her arms, and blowing her nose on Louise's skirt which is really Lavinia's skirt, and getting makeup all over her red silk dress which is Lavinia's dress. The only thing Louise can do is take her home, in a cab, which costs thirty of the three hundred eighty dollars Louise has left in the world, and whisper *it's okay, it's okay,* and haul Cordelia up the stairs, and take off her clothes, and put one of Lavinia's crisp nightgowns over her head, and tuck her in.

"I hate them," Cordelia whispers. "I hate them *all.*"

"I know."

"They're all *awful.*"

"I know."

"I hate *her!*"

"I know," Louise whispers.

"I hate her *so much!*" she hiccups. *"I hate her! I hate her! I hate her!"*

"I know."

"Rex should have let her jump."

Louise's breath catches in her throat.

"Don't say that."

"Why not? It's true—isn't it?"

"I don't know." Louise's heart is beating so quickly. "No! Of course not!"

"What has she ever done but lie to anyone who's ever loved her?"

Louise doesn't have an answer for her.

They lie together, in Lavinia's bed, and Cordelia sobs so brokenly, and she curls into herself and there is nothing for Louise to do but hold her so tightly, and so close, tight enough that she shakes when Cordelia shakes, and is racked with Cordelia's sobs.

They lie there together until Cordelia falls asleep in Louise's arms.

Louise goes into Cordelia's room. She sits at the desk, in silence. She texts Rex—she's texted him so many times tonight—telling him she can explain, begging him to let her explain, begging him to let her fix everything she's fucked up, in the service of fixing things.

He's Read every message. He hasn't responded.

Please.

Louise is so clingy, now. She disgusts herself.

She plugs in her phone on Cordelia's desk. She stares at the photographs, awhile, at Cordelia's books: Julian of Norwich, Thomas Merton, Teilhard de Chardin, John Henry Newman, St. Augustine. She stares into the darkness, awhile more.

She goes to bed.

At one, her phone pings.

She can see Rex's name, flashing on the nightstand.

I miss you.

Can we talk?

Thank God, Louise thinks. *Thank God.*

She can taste how relieved she is; she is so relieved, as she grabs the phone, that she starts to laugh out loud, and she starts typing yes, of course, you can call me right now, I don't care what time it is, we can talk as long as you need even though her phone is right there, charging, on Cordelia's desk.

I'm sorry, Rex tells Lavinia.

I hate that I still love you.

9

CORDELIA IS SNORING IN THE OTHER ROOM.

Louise can't feel anything, anymore.

Lavinia Reads Rex's text, so he will know she's read it. She doesn't answer.

Now he will know exactly how Louise feels.

It's Christmas.

Louise goes for a walk. She smokes five or six cigarettes, even though she hasn't smoked since taking up Lavinia's workout regimen (the only good part of Lavinia's being away, she thinks, is that her thighs don't ache so much anymore).

Rex keeps texting Lavinia.

Please.

Just talk to me.

I'm sorry.

I'm the worst.

I know.

I know how selfish I am.

Lavinia posts a public Instagram picture of the Rocky Mountains, just to hurt him.

Can't sleep, Lavinia says. The whole world is just too beautiful to stand.

Rex Eliot Likes it.

When it's late enough Louise calls her parents in Devonshire to wish them a merry Christmas. It's a very formal conversation. They ask how she's doing and she tells them about *The Fiddler*'s Five Under Thirty, which is the closest thing you can get to a big break when you've only written personal essays on the Internet.

"Most people who get on it get agents soon after," says Louise, like this is a thing that still matters. "One girl got a book deal for a memoir within a week."

"Oh," says Louise's mother.

"But you're not under thirty."

"December counts," says Louise, even though that isn't true.

"Does it pay? If you win?"

"No," says Louise. "It's just prestige. And it's not a prize—it's a list."

"Oh," says Louise's mother. "That's a shame."

"Yes," says Louise. "It is."

"You know," says Louise's mother. "You'll never believe who I saw on the street, the other day."

Louise already knows.

"He's gotten very handsome—now that he's cut his hair. He's left the bookstore. He's actually got a job managing the Devonshire Inn. Pretty good, huh?"

"Sure," says Louise.

"Now I don't *presume* to know what happened," says Louise's mother. "But he is a *very* nice boy. It's not like there's a line around the block for you."

Louise opens her mouth to say something about how she has a boyfriend now, actually, and he's very handsome and he goes to Columbia and he loves her, but then she closes it again.

"Anyway," says Louise's mother. "I *know, I know* you'll be mad at me—but he asked for your number, and, well—*I know* what you always say, but it's been *so* long since you mentioned anybody else, and he—he's done so well for himself, lately, and he still always asks after you, and he cares about you *so much* . . ."

Louise hangs up the phone.

When Louise comes back to the apartment, Cordelia is already up. Her hair is pinned in a braid. She's washed all the makeup off her face. She's in pajamas.

She looks, Louise thinks, so young.

"I've been waiting for you," she says. "I wanted to give you your present!"

She hands a wrapped package to Louise.

"I bought it for Vinny," she says. "But I think you'll appreciate it more."

It's an antique miniature booklet of Tennyson's "Ulysses." The binding is split. It's beautiful.

"Vinny told me about your adventure," Cordelia says. "It sounded beautiful."

"It was," says Louise.

"Nobody does that at Exeter," Cordelia says.

"I bet."

"They only do things that look good on their college apps."

Cordelia takes out her phone.

"Do you have plans?"

"No," Louise says.

"Want to order Chinese?"

"Sure."

"I booked my flight," Cordelia says. "I'm heading to Paris New Year's Eve. Mother's very happy. I told her my friend in Aspen had a mental breakdown because she didn't get in early to Brown. I'll be out of your hair, soon enough. I'm sure you'll be relieved."

Louise doesn't know why she isn't.

"I bet she's bathing naked in the Pacific right now," Cordelia says.

"Probably."

"Fuck her," says Cordelia. "I'm getting fried rice."

———

Louise pays for these, too. The order comes to $32.41. Louise even tips.

Rex finally texts Louise that evening, because Lavinia hasn't texted him back.

I'm sorry, he says.

I needed some time.

Do you want to come over tonight?

They sit in silence on Rex's bed, because his apartment is too small for a sofa.

She waits for him to break up with her. He doesn't.

"I'm sorry," he says. "I shouldn't have left you, last night."

He has a split lip.

Then: "How long did you know?"

"Not long," Louise says. "I only found out before she left."

"She told you."

"I saw her phone. I should have told you. I'm sorry. She made me promise not to."

"No," he says. "No—you shouldn't have." He swallows. "It's— you're in the middle." He sighs. "I never should have come between you two," he says.

"Don't say that."

"I put you in an impossible position—I'm sorry. I never should have."

"Don't *say* that."

Like she's begging him.

"It's stupid," says Rex. "I don't even know why I was mad. It's just—Hal being Hal. And her being—"

He can't even say her name.

"Lavinia," Louise says, so quietly. "Lavinia being Lavinia."

"Right."

He keeps checking his phone—right in front of her.

"Cordelia's leaving," Louise says. "She's going to Paris. She's realized that Lavinia's not coming back, anytime soon."

Rex exhales.

"Of course," he says. "Good."

He squeezes her hand.

"Then everything will go back to normal," he says.

Gavin emails Louise that night to let her know she's been selected as one of *The Fiddler*'s Five Under Thirty. They'll be announcing it on New Year's Day, he says. There will be a party. He wants her to read that piece she wrote about pretending to be a Devonshire Academy student. *It was the third-most-read piece this year,* he says.

Louise dyes her hair again. It leaves stains all over Lavinia's bathtub.

Rex keeps texting Lavinia.

Please, he says. Just talk to me.

Lavinia doesn't.

The day after Christmas, Hal texts Louise.

Let me buy you a drink, he says. Bemelmans? 8?

"I talked to Niall Montgomery about you," says Hal. "He likes your work. I told him you'd been selected as one of the Five Under Thirty. He's going to the launch party."

His black eye makes him look more misshapen than ever.

"Really," Hal says. "You should be buying *me* a drink."

Louise can't afford to do that, but she smiles anyway.

"Don't worry." Hal puts his card down. "Henry Upchurch always keeps his word. And you're an Under Thirty. You actually matter, now."

"I'm grateful," says Louise. "Really."

"Good. You should be."

Then: "How's Rex?"

"He's fine."

"He still mad at me?"

Louise shrugs. "I don't know."

"He didn't say?"

"We're trying not to talk about it."

"Good girl," he says. "Poor Louise."

"Why?"

"Don't forget—I've known Rex longer than anybody. Including her." He toasts to her. "I'm his best friend. I know what he was like—about her."

"So why did you do it?"

"She was hot and desperate and I wanted to fuck her. That's all."

"You know that's not true," says Louise.

He looks affronted, but Louise doesn't even care anymore.

"You want to play the bad friend game?"

"No," says Louise. "Not really."

"What do you want me to say?"

"Nothing."

"Rex didn't deserve her," says Hal. "Is that what you want to hear?"

"Not really."

"She didn't deserve anything, either. She wasn't anything special. She wasn't even good in bed. But—she loved him. And he doesn't deserve to be loved like that." Hal drinks. "She wasn't like you," he says. "She never got the joke."

Under the bar, Lavinia's phone pings. Louise doesn't even have to look at it.

"He shouldn't complain," says Hal. "He got *years*. He got love poems and love songs and long walks along the beach and classical music. What did I get? A couple of filthy weekends and some light kink." He stretches out along the bar. "Anyway, she put a stop to it. She was terrified you'd find out."

"I wouldn't have cared," Louise says.

She remembers the night that Lavinia stumbled home, with her dress inside out, and blood in her mouth.

"Oh, you would have. You'd never let yourself be bossed around by a girl who liked to get fucked in the ass."

He wipes his face with a cocktail napkin.

"Fuck it," he says. "I'm getting out of New York. I'm going to quit my job. I'm going to buy a vintage air-cooled Porsche and I'm going to drive it to Big Sur. Maybe I'll see her there. Maybe I'll see you."

"Maybe," says Louise.

"I'm going to become a writer, young Louise. Just like you. I've still got five years to make Five Under Thirty. And I *do* have, as it happens, the first fifty pages of the novel I'm going to write."

"Good luck with that," says Louise.

"Maybe I'll send it to you. Maybe you'll tell me if it's good?"

She can't tell if he means it.

"I'm sure it's fine, Hal."

"It's a piece of shit," says Hal. "I haven't even written it. And I'm never going to quit my job." He pays the bill.

"And *that*, young Louise." He grins at her. "Is the joke."

Please, Rex has texted Lavinia.

I understand if you need more time.

Just tell me if I should wait for you.

Lavinia texts him only one word: Don't.

Rex is so good to Louise, that week. He gets her a Christmas present, a beautiful art nouveau brooch he found for her at an antique market on the Hudson and Louise tries not to think, as she admires it in the mirror, whether she was the one he bought it for.

Rex is so good at not letting Louise know. He takes her to Mud, to Veselka for pierogis just like he did the night he first kissed her; he takes her back to the secret bookstore to celebrate her making Five Under Thirty with Gavin and Matty Rosekranz, even though it hasn't even been announced yet, not formally ("I can't wait to see the look on Beowulf Marmont's face," says Matty, who doesn't like him, either).

He goes down on her every single time they have sex.

Guilt's such a useful mechanism, Louise thinks. It makes you a much better person than you otherwise would be.

Lavinia has made it all the way to California.

She posts Instagram photos all the way up Route 1.

She's doing the last phase of her pilgrimage alone.

She posts a photo of her tattoo, against a blue body of water that might be the Pacific but also might be Photoshop.

MORE POETRY!!!

Always, Lavinia says.

Only: Rex has blocked her again.

On New Year's Eve, Cordelia packs her suitcase.

"Big plans?" she asks.

Louise is going to the MacIntyre again. She's meeting Rex there. Mimi is coming over to the house beforehand: officially, to get ready, but really because neither of them can stand to be alone.

Louise shrugs. "Just the same thing as last year," she says.

"I suppose I'll be midair when it happens," says Cordelia. "I don't know which one counts—midnight in Paris or midnight in New York. I don't suppose it matters."

"No," says Louise. "I don't suppose it does."

"I'm sorry to miss your reading," Cordelia says.

"It's fine," Louise says. "There will be people there."

"You know—it wasn't such a bad Christmas," Cordelia says. "I learned a lot. And a first kiss—that's a milestone, isn't it?"

"I mean—sure."

"It's better than Christmas in Paris, that's for sure." Cordelia lifts her chin. "You don't have to worry. I won't tell our parents Vinny's been letting you live here. I didn't tell about Mimi, either—and I didn't even like her."

"Thank you," says Louise. "I think."

"And you won't tell Vinny—I mean, when she gets back. I was drunk, when I said those things."

"I won't tell," says Louise. "I swear."

The house feels so empty, once she's gone.

Mimi comes over a couple of hours later. She's wearing false lashes and a Louise Brooks wig.

"OhmyGod!" she exclaims. *"Ihaventseenyouinforever!"*

She's brought a case of those little Sofia Coppola cans of champagne you're supposed to drink through a straw.

They get dressed for the MacIntyre.

This year's theme is Weimar Berlin. Louise wears a tuxedo jacket she's borrowed from Rex and nothing else, because the idea of wearing Lavinia's clothes one more time has made her nauseous.

She paints her face white. She draws kohl over her eyes.

Mimi is flipping through Lavinia's pictures on her phone.

"I'm so jealous," she murmurs. "I wish I could drive." She looks up. "Maybe I'll give up drinking, too," she says.

"You—I mean—that might not be such a bad idea."

"I'd get so skinny, that way. God, did you *see* the picture she posted of her abs?"

Louise was so proud of that one.

"I saw."

Mimi applies glitter to her cheeks.

"Starting January First," she says. "New Year's Resolution. Don't let me drink. Wait—" She swallows. "I forgot. Five Under Thirty. Okay, *January Second,* don't let me drink. Promise?"

"I trust you," says Louise. "If you say you won't drink, then you won't."

Louise puts on Lavinia's lipstick.

She considers herself in the mirror.

She wipes it off.

She doesn't even want to taste it.

They cab it to the MacIntyre. Louise pays. *January First*, she thinks, *I will reach out to Flora and to Miles. I'll find more clients. I'll get a job. I'll go on SeekingArrangement and find a rich boyfriend, just like Athena Maidenhead*—she can't let herself think about Athena Maidenhead, right now. She can't afford it, but there's a blizzard on, outside.

It's so cold, in the line, and even though it's freezing half the people there are dressed in club dresses and stilettos or jeans, and not in costume, and Louise doesn't know if that was true last year, or whether it's just that the parties aren't as good as they used to be.

The bouncer's rude and everybody's so busy taking photos that they shove Louise clear into the wall, and this one girl steps on Mimi's toe.

At ten-thirty they let them in.

This is what Louise sees:

Red velvet, electric lights, plastic bags, a taxidermied deer, torn upholstery, a spread of tarot cards, speaker cables, a woman in a backless sequined dress singing Peggy Lee's "Is That All There Is?," drunk bros in baseball caps, chandeliers, watered-down champagne.

This is all Louise sees:

Nothing she hasn't seen before.

Louise drinks.

She drinks just like Lavinia used to, getting a whole bottle all at once and pouring it down her throat, and Mimi thinks this is so hilarious that she takes different pictures, all from different angles.

"It's just like Weimar Berlin," Mimi chirps. "It really is."

She starts dancing on the tables.

Louise starts doing shots.

Just one more, she thinks. *Just one more.*

Then you'll start to have fun.

Mimi is kissing strangers.

Mimi is taking photos (she's in one of the asylum bathtubs, pretending to be a suicide; she's straddling the taxidermied deer; she's wrapped around Louise's neck like a mink; she's Liza Minnelli with her legs backward on a chair).

Mimi is having the best night of her life.

You'd know if you checked her Facebook.

Louise sees Rex across the ballroom.

He's wearing black tie. That's the closest thing he's made to an effort.

He smiles when she goes to him.

"Look." She tries so hard. "We match!"

He holds her hand. He kisses it. He looks out into the crowd, like Lavinia might be there.

The lights flash. The music is so loud. Louise can't hear a single word Mimi says.

Father Romylos is there and Gavin Mullaney is there and reminding her *tomorrow is your big day, isn't it?; aren't you so fucking excited you actually leveled up in this life?* and so is Athena Maidenhead, in the dress Louise has bought her, on the arm of Mike from the opera; Rose the photographer from *Last Night at the Met* is there, and so is the girl who was on *Survivor,* so is Laurie the erotic illustrator who drew Lavinia's tarot cards, and so is the Egyptologist Lavinia knows who got kicked off the faculty at Yale for leaving his wife for a student.

Mimi takes a picture of Louise and Rex, holding hands, and they look so goddamn happy in that one.

The lights are so bright. Neon blinds them. Smoke gets in Louise's eyes and makes her sneeze. Some drunk girl spills a rum and Coke all over Louise's nice borrowed jacket and even her collarbones get sticky.

Somebody who isn't Peggy Lee keeps singing Peggy Lee.

"Wasn't she here last year?"

Mimi shrugs. "Of course not!"

She is singing it on a loop, and maybe Louise was just that drunk last year or maybe she's just that drunk this year but in any case it turns out the woman isn't even singing, just lip-synching to the actual Peggy Lee, and she's doing it over and over again.

If that's all there is, my friends (turns out, it's blasted from every single boom box in the place). *Then let's keep dancing.*

"It's even better than last year!" Mimi grins.

She grabs Louise's hand. She makes her dance, and Mimi pulls in Rex to dance with them, too, because Mimi is so extravagant with her love that it has never occurred to her to want to win more than she wants to love somebody.

Louise has to pee.

Rex and Mimi and Gavin and Athena and Father Romylos and Laurie and Rose and the Egyptologist and the girl who was on *Survivor* all promise to wait for her by the downstairs bar, the one that looks like an art deco podium.

When Louise comes out, everybody's gone.

It's eleven-forty-five.

"Tick tock!"

Hal is marching toward her.

He's dressed like a Nazi. Nobody will look at him.

"Get it?" he says, when he sees her. "Because of the theme."

"I got it."

"You know, it's actually real Hugo Boss."

"Jesus Christ."

"I mean, it's not like I'm wearing a mustache or anything."

"Small mercies," says Louise.

Hal's black eye is almost gone. Now he just looks like he hasn't slept in a couple of days.

"Do you know what I gave Henry for Christmas?"

"I don't really care," says Louise.

"A copy of 'The Social and Political Doctrine of Fascism.' One for my mother, too. Plus an Hermès scarf, obviously. I'm not a monster."

"Are you done?"

"We all are. The world's ending. The revolution is imminent."

"Why are you even here, Hal?"

Hal shrugs. "All my friends are here."

He leans against the wall of the corridor.

"Come on, Lulu," he says. "Just be a fucking person, okay?"

"What does that mean?"

"Dance with me!"

The bass is turned up so high the walls shake.

"I should go find Rex."

"Don't."

"It's almost midnight."

He grabs her by the waist.

"Hal, don't!"

"It's almost midnight. I'll come with you!"

"Hal," Louise says, because the last thing in the world she needs right now is for Rex to have another reason to hate her. "Don't."

"Please!" he says.

The light strobes and that's the first time Louise really sees him.

He's been crying.

"Please don't go," he says.

"I have to."

"I want to talk to Rex!"

"You can talk to Rex tomorrow."

"I want to talk to Rex now!"

"Well, you can't."

"Tell him—" Something strangles in his throat. It's like a cat, dying.

It's five minutes to midnight.

Louise doesn't let him finish.

———

Louise stumbles in the crowd. She sees doubles, everywhere.

She sees Athena swaying with Mike (or maybe it is a stranger) and there is Beowulf Marmont, or someone who looks just like him, swaying with a girl who is definitely not his fragile-eyed girlfriend, and she sees Gavin Mullaney with his second-favorite girlfriend and she sees Mimi, Mimi dancing alone, Mimi moon-bathed in some spotlight, Mimi dancing for the first time like she's not desperate for somebody to come dance with her, and this huge deco clock in the shape of the numbers 2-0-1-6 has descended like a chandelier from the ceiling and it's thumping with the bass so Louise can't even tell what part's music and what part's the march of time.

It's one minute to midnight.

All Louise wants to do is sleep.

But that's not the world Louise lives in, now.

At a minute to midnight Louise sees Rex.

He's standing all alone, at the bar, with a martini in his hand.

Louise runs to him.

He looks so happy to see her.

They're counting down, everybody's counting down from sixty, and slurring the numbers wrong, and Louise is so lonely and Rex looks so happy to see her, even though she knows, she *knows*, that there is no way he can be, that he can't possibly be, not if Lavinia is somewhere in the world just beyond his field of vision, but remember Louise is drunk, and Rex is drunk, and both of them have had their hearts broken beyond repair this week, and more than anything in the world Louise just wants to be a person who is held in someone's arms.

Rex takes her in his.

He falls to his knees.

He kisses her stomach, like she's pregnant, or like she's a god.

His eyes are so full of tears.

"I'm sorry," he says. He keeps kissing her, like he knows she knows.

He kisses her hands. He kisses the insides of her wrists. He kisses her palms. "I'm so sorry, I'm sorry; I've been so stupid; I'm so stupid."

She's crying, too. She shakes her head.

Ten—nine—eight

She kisses and kisses him with a hungry mouth.

Seven—six—five

His tears are tributaries into hers.

"I miss you," Rex says; "I need you—*I need you,*" and Louise is standing on a precipice, and the world is vanishing and spinning and flickering all around her and Louise is falling, Louise is falling, and there is nobody else in the world who can catch her.

Four—three—two

"I love you," Rex says.

Maybe he does.

They cab it back to Lavinia's place. They kiss all the way uptown. Rex says *I love you* on every block; Rex puts his hand up Louise's shirt and feels her breasts like the cabbie isn't even listening to every sound they make; it's snowing so hard Louise can't even see the black of the sky; it's snowing so hard the cab radio keeps repeating *haven't seen snow this bad in sixty years* so maybe Hal is right, maybe the world really is ending, but right now it doesn't matter because they are so lonely but they have each other, both of them, because Lavinia is never coming back and this is the next best thing.

Her makeup smears his face. Their jackets crumple on the floor. Their clothes tear when they take them off.

I love you; I love you; I love you.

The door opens.

Cordelia just stands there.

She lets her suitcase drop in the doorway.

They're scrambling so fast—they're rushing—to cover their nakedness, their shame; Rex grabs a couch cushion and Louise grabs Lavinia's dressing gown and they're stammering out excuses and they're saying *this isn't what it looks like* even though it so manifestly is.

"It's—snowing, you know." Cordelia's voice is so calm. "There's a blizzard. Haven't you heard? All flights are grounded."

She walks into the living room. She goes to the kitchen. She puts the kettle on. Rex is so hasty, zipping up his trousers.

"I'm sorry," Cordelia says. She doesn't look at them. "I've intruded."

Cordelia picks up the teapot.

She throws it at Louise's face.

"*Damn* you!"

It shatters just behind Louise's head.

"God*damn* you."

It cuts Louise, a little, grazing her. She doesn't even feel it.

"Wait!" Rex is trying, so manfully, to put his shirt on. "I know this looks bad."

"You sniveling little *coward*!"

"She knows, okay? She knows!" Rex is out of breath. "She's fine with it—she's known the whole time—I swear!"

Cordelia is so pale.

"Don't you *fucking presume* to know my sister. She is *not* fine!"

"She told me! I swear to God—I swear to God—she called me up! She gave me her blessing! Both of us."

Cordelia laughs in his face.

"She didn't!"

"She did—Christ, Louise, tell her!"

Cordelia looks straight at her.

Her eyes are so clear, and so blue.

She looks at Louise, standing in the space where the steamer trunk once was.

"You want me to believe Vinny knows?"

Louise hesitates just a second. "She knows."

Cordelia exhales. Just once. "No," she says. "She doesn't."

"She *knows*."

Cordelia looks so slowly, from the door to the space in the floor, from the space in the floor to Louise.

"Then where is she?"

"I told you. She's in California."

"No she's not. Where is she?"

"You know as much as I do."

"Where is she?"

"I swear," Rex says, again, but Cordelia isn't even looking at him.

"Let's call her, shall we?" Cordelia begins, and Louise says *no,* so quickly, and that's when Cordelia starts to scream.

"Where is she?"

"I don't—"

Cordelia slaps her clear across the face.

"I said—where the *fuck* is she?"

"Cordelia!" Rex tries, but she's grabbing at Louise, she's pulling at Louise's hair; she's trying to claw out her eyes.

"I know you know where she is!"

She is so small, and Rex is so much larger than she is, and still it takes all his strength for him to pull Cordelia off her.

The two of them crash to the floor.

Louise is bleeding.

Cordelia gets up, staggering. She's out of breath. She's bleeding, too.

"You're a fool," she says, to Rex. "God—what a fool you are."

She doesn't take her eyes off Louise.

"God—you *idiot*!"

Rex is helping Louise to her feet. He's scrambling for their coats.

"We should go," he says.

Cordelia is panting. Her gaze is so, so blue.

"Look, I'm sorry," Rex says, like that's even what matters, now.

"Just get out," Cordelia says.

———

"We'll fix it." That's all Rex can repeat, all the way down to the lobby, all the way in the cab. "Look—she's upset. She's just upset."

Louise is shaking.

"You can stay at my place tonight," he says, because now, now he can save her, now this is a thing for him to do. "In the morning we'll go back, we'll explain. We can explain!"

It's stopped snowing. The world is frozen and stark and dead. Even the trees look like bones.

"We're not bad people!" Rex says.

Louise can't stop laughing.

Then she is so hot.

She is so achingly, boilingly, paralyzingly hot that she thinks she's going to die.

"Stop," she tells the driver.

"Louise, what are you—"

"Take us to Coney Island," she says.

"Louise, it's two o'clock in the . . ."

"I said." Louise has never been more sure of anything in her life. "Take us to Coney fucking Island."

The driver does.

Louise pays with the last of her hundred-dollar bills.

They sit in silence.

"Lou—" Rex tries—just once—but Louise kisses him, so hungrily, and does not let him speak.

When they arrive it is so cold, and so dark, and so empty.

Louise opens the car door. She bolts toward the water. She lets her purse fall on the sand.

Rex trails after her.

"Are you going to tell me *what the hell is going on?*"

Louise is just so fucking hot.

She walks so much faster, on her way to the water. She runs.

The water is so cold. She washes her face with it. She washes her face and her neck and her hands and she is still so fucking hot she thinks she will burn up completely.

"You're going to kill yourself, doing that."

Rex is standing with his hands in his pockets, away from the water.

Louise doesn't care.

She rubs her skin until it's raw.

"Look—we'll just *call Lavinia*," Rex says. "It's not hard. It's not complicated. We just—we call Lavinia and we ask her to explain to her own fucking sister—"

"That's not going to happen," Louise says.

She is knee-deep in the water. She doesn't understand why she is still so fucking hot.

"Of course it will," says Rex. "Lavinia's not a bad person, she's not going to try to fuck with us; she'll tell Cordelia—"

"Lavinia's dead," Louise says.

Here's another funny thing: Rex doesn't believe her.

He just stands there, so stupidly, gaping at her, opening and closing his mouth, like a fish.

"Don't be ridiculous," he says. "Of course she's not dead."

"Believe me." Louise gets deeper and deeper into the water. "She's dead."

"She's in California."

"No, she's not."

"I just talked to her!"

"No, you didn't."

"We just—"

She turns around to face him. Her pantyhose are drenched. Her lipstick has smeared halfway down her chin.

"No," she says. "You really, really didn't."

———

Rex still doesn't get it.

Louise marvels—she can't stop marveling—at just how stupid he is.

"Lavinia's been dead since July," she says.

"That's crazy," Rex says. He says it a few times, as if repeating it will make it true. "Jesus—Lou—are you *on* something?"

"We had a fight at the P.M. I killed her."

"What did you take?" It's like he hasn't even heard her. "Jesus Christ, Lou—tell me what you took! I'm—Christ—I'm calling an ambulance, okay?"

It feels so good, how cold the water is.

"We had a fight. Put your phone away."

It astonishes her how confusing he finds this.

"What happened?"

"I told you. We had a fight. She hit her head. I dumped her body in the East River."

"No, you didn't."

"Why not?"

He's stammering. "People don't *do* things like that."

It's almost funny, Louise thinks, how she could love someone so stupid.

"It's very simple," Louise says. "I dumped her body in the East River. I've been posting on her Facebook every day for six months." It gets easier and easier to say these things. "I get money from her ATM every week. I left you that voicemail. I can do her voice."

"Jesus!"

Rex finally puts his phone down.

Rex finally, finally believes her.

"Jesus."

"Christ," Louise says. "It's freezing out here."

———

Louise is up to her hips in the water.

She lets herself sob.

She lets herself scream.

Here's, no *here's,* the thing:

All Rex has to do is understand her.

All he has to do is say *yes, I love you, I know why you have done this, you are not a bad person; you tried; what matters is that you tried.*

I love you. It's so easy. That's all he has to say. He's said it before.

"Fuck," Rex says. It's the first thing he says in a minute. *"Fuck!"* He looks at her so helplessly. "What do we *do*?"

Louise doesn't say anything.

"For Christ's sake—tell me what to do, Lou!"

"Nothing," Louise says. "There's nothing *to* do. It's done."

Rex takes so many deep breaths.

Rex can't speak. Rex can't deal.

"Look," he stammers, when he can finally get out words. "We'll go to the police, okay? Both of us. We'll go and tell them it was an accident—*Jesus*—it was an accident, right?"

"Does it matter?"

"It wasn't an accident?"

Louise isn't even sure anymore.

"Christ, Lou, tell me it was an accident!"

His eyes are so goddamn wide.

Louise doesn't.

Rex is hyperventilating.

He can't even look at her.

"You need to turn yourself in."

"There's no point," Louise says. "It won't change anything. Lavinia's dead."

"It's the right thing to do!"

"So?"

He's looking at her with such horror.

He's looking at her like he really, really knows her.

Louise keeps her eyes on the horizon, on the point where the water is black and it meets the blackness of the sky. She has not noticed, before, how much salt water stings where somebody has clawed you, or slapped you, or yanked out your hair, how it feels like you are being flayed alive.

It's just nice to feel something.

"I'm sorry," Louise says. "I know you loved her."

Louise doesn't know when she started crying. Maybe she's been crying this whole time.

"Come out of the water," Rex says.

He takes off his jacket. He takes off his watch, his phone. He puts them on the sand.

"You loved her so fucking much."

"Please," he says. "Please—just come out."

"Didn't you?"

"No—Christ, Lou."

"Don't fucking lie to me! Please—please—don't lie to me."

"I love you," Rex says.

It feels so fucking good to hear it.

He goes into the water. He goes up to his waist. He takes her by the shoulders.

"I love you—just please—come out of the water."

Here's the thing: he doesn't.

Rex tries—God, he tries—he tries to pull her out; he grabs her by the forearm, harder, maybe, than he means to, or should—it's forgivable, maybe, if you're trying to bring a murderer to justice; it's the right thing to do, maybe, if you're a hero, or playing a hero, or need to be a hero no matter fucking what; it's not a terrible thing—even if you are playing justice, it isn't the sort of thing you kill a person over.

But it is so stupid of him, to grab her like that, when she is sobbing, when she is screaming; it is so stupid of him to lie to her, when
all she has asked of him is to stop lying to her.

He wraps his arms around her, and he bales her up, but here's another
thing: Louise is so much stronger than he is, or at least, she's been
in the water longer, and she's been in the cold before, and she's used
to being cold or wet or just plain in pain, and she can stand pain so
much better than he can, so when Rex goes numb he goes weak, and
that is enough for her to get her hands around his neck, and that is
enough, too, for her to get her legs on his back, and that is enough
for Louise to hold him under the water which is so cold that it stuns
him and Louise is not sure—she never will be sure—if it is the water,
or the cold, that gets him.

He goes under.

He bursts back up.

He screams and his lungs fill with salt water and he kicks and
Louise has to push him down again, and deeper, with a strength that
sickens and thrills her at the same time.

He goes under.

He bursts back up.

He flails and he writhes and he elbows Louise in the face so violently her nose breaks; he cries out half of her name and Louise has
to shove her hand over his mouth until he bites.

He goes under.

He doesn't come up.

Then it is just Louise, in the water, shaking, by the light of a full
moon.

10

LOUISE KNOWS WHAT TO DO NEXT. Louise has done it all before.

Louise has Rex's phone.

Once, a girl, by a full moon, took a fistful of pills and said *if the world is not what it should be I want to die,* and Rex did not die with her. Not now. Then.

Now there is a man who has had too much to drink facedown in the water; this happens all the time.

Louise knows how to create an alibi (there's a whole trick to it: getting the right combination of check-ins and time stamps and specificity because that's what people respond to most and if they respond to you that means they think you're alive but also leaving things vague enough that you never have to explain a discrepancy). She knows how to move a body. She knows how to write a frenetic, late-night text from one phone to another, that says *please don't make me live without you.*

Louise gets through things. She always gets through things.

She can take a cab back to the MacIntyre with the cash in Rex's wallet. She knows, she *knows* Mimi will still be dancing there, and she can say that she and Rex had a fight after Cordelia found them; he stormed off (how likely is it that they will ever find that same cab driver again; she paid in cash—she hadn't meant to pay in cash but she has gotten so used to paying in cash when she is not Lavinia, just in case); they might not find his body for days.

Everyone will feel so sorry for her at the funeral.

Rex has killed himself over Lavinia (everyone will hate Lavinia, more), and maybe if Lavinia vanishes somewhere in Big Sur, everyone will think they know why.

Louise can probably move in with Mimi.

Louise sits on the sand, alone, soaked, so cold she can't breathe, and she stares at Rex's body bobbing up and down where the shore meets the sea and thinks *I can do this.*

I can do this.

She can get another tutoring job, or two. Tomorrow (*today, oh God, today*) is the Five Under Thirty party at this loft space in Bushwick that is constructed entirely with reclaimed wood from shipwrecks. Niall Montgomery will be there and so will so many other people she could potentially impress, by telling the story of the time she pretended to go to Devonshire Academy when she didn't, which is a great story but by this point it's barely true.

She can convince everybody that she is the injured one (Hal likes her; Mimi likes her; everybody, everybody likes her); she can be a martyr; she can write a really moving personal essay about the time her boyfriend and her best friend killed themselves, over each other, and about what it feels like to always, always be the one left behind. Gavin Mullaney would probably publish it.

The stars are like nails hammered in the sky.

The sea is just so unrelentingly black.

Once, Louise stood naked, facing it, with the sand in between her toes, screaming *that which we are, we are*, but that is not now, either.

You can do this, Louise keeps thinking. *You can do this.*

She can borrow money from Mimi. She can make five hundred dollars, writing a good *Fiddler* online piece, more for print. She can find a way to get Athena Maidenhead off her back (she has only to *think*). She has the keys to Rex's apartment (she never wants to go to Rex's apartment again). She can fix everything (Louise can always fix everything).

Except, of course, there's Cordelia.

She can make it so Cordelia is crazy. Everybody already knows Lavinia is crazy; maybe it runs in the family. She can make such a big deal about how poor Cordelia, poor *troubled* Cordelia attacked Rex in the apartment—if it ever comes to that—how this sweet well-meaning kid with a narcissist for a sister is growing up just like her, because if the Greeks taught us anything it's that we can't control Fate. She can make it so nobody believes whatever Cordelia says about her sister and the steamer trunk and Rex and Big Sur and the phone calls; people don't do such things; they don't even believe you when you tell them straight-out you've done such things.

She can't make Cordelia believe her.

She doesn't want to.

A ping on Rex's phone, on the sand. Hal. I need to talk to you.
Please.
Please.

Louise has such pity for everyone.

She has such pity for everyone in the whole, wide world.

A ping on Louise's phone. Gavin.
Get ready to ACE tonight!

A ping on Lavinia's phone. Cordelia. Twenty missed calls.

They all sound so fucking loud.

Louise thinks the stars will fall from the sky, shook loose by that sound.

So here, *here,* is what Louise does next:

She dyes her hair.

She leaves Rex's body on the beach. Mimi posts a photo of Rex and Louise at the MacIntyre, kissing, and it must be the moment he told her he loved her because the confetti is streaming down all around them.

She leaves Rex's phone there (*drunk, lonely Hal, won't stop calling him*).

She gets on the subway. (*Gavin is posting a lot of promotional material about Five Under Thirty and reminding everyone on Facebook it's the closest thing to an anointing you can possibly have and if you're important enough to edit for* The Fiddler *you can get away with saying shit like that and nobody will roll their eyes at you in public and he tags all of the five people who are Under Thirty and announces the winners formally on all social media channels but he writes something extra nice about Louise Wilson and calls her "the one to watch."*) She takes the Q from Coney Island. (*Beowulf Marmont is drunkenly ranting about how some people think that they're the shit because they're Five Under Thirty but actually it's just like a giant racket meant to appease a certain kind of emotive, feminine aesthetic and has nothing to do with real literature, anyway.*)

She takes it all the way to Forty-second Street. (*Athena Maidenhead has just gotten engaged to Mike from the opera and she is showing everybody her ring, and she posts the video and it sparkles so gorgeously in the MacIntyre lights.*)

Everybody is drunk. Everybody is loud. There is vomit and confetti everywhere, and glitter and tassels and discarded 2016 glasses and street preachers with signs. (*Now Cordelia is posting a long public Facebook post that begins "When you read this, you will think I have gone insane. I am not insane. My sister is dead. Louise Wilson has killed her."*)

The police horses are being loaded, one by one, into their vans. Australian tourists are singing "Auld Lang Syne."

(*Now Hal is messaging Louise and Lavinia, both, to tell them that Cordelia's had a typical Williams breakdown and probably swallowed a fistful of Mommy Williams's Xanax, too, and maybe everyone in that whole fucking family should deal with their shit, already, okay?*

And if Lavinia says "okay," it will buy Louise more time.)

Hey? Mimi hasn't even noticed Louise isn't still dancing. Where did you go?

Are u still here?

Dancing flapper emu.

Louise goes to a 24/7 Duane Reade near Bryant Park.

She gets hair dye, whatever clothes they sell—black leggings, a plain white T-shirt, the sort of anonymous things nobody notices anybody wears.

She doesn't have any money left, so she just shoplifts.

Nobody even notices this, either.

Louise walks right into the public bathrooms at Bryant Park, the nice ones, the ones that there are even flowers in. She locks the door.

She takes off her wet clothes.

She washes off the salt, the blood.

She washes her hair in the sink.

She opens the box. She puts on the gloves.

The water is so red, through her hands.

People are knocking (of course they're knocking; it's New Year's Day, and she's in midtown, and people who have been standing in line all night need to pee) and their knocking is so loud but Louise ignores them; Louise doesn't care; Louise keeps her gaze focused on the mirror, and thirty minutes go by and Louise just stands there, naked, staring at herself, and at the fake ID of some twenty-three-year-old redhead called Elizabeth Glass who probably never existed in the first place.

Louise looks so different with red hair.

She looks paler. Her cheekbones look higher. She is not as beautiful as she was, when she had Lavinia's hair. She is no longer the kind of girl you'd stop, when you saw her. You wouldn't check her out, or turn around, or stare.

You might see her on the street, and not even know her.

Louise should be horrified. Maybe she is horrified, because Lavinia is dead and Rex is dead and Rex's body is bobbing up and down on the water and Lavinia is rotting in a steamer trunk at the bottom of the East River but there is no justice on earth that can make this right, any longer, so the only thing to do now is not be who you are, and that is the best and the worst thing in the world, and also all Louise has ever wanted.

Today, Louise tells herself, *is the first day of the rest of your life.*

"Hey! Fuck you! We all have to pee."
She elbows past them.
Lavinia's phone, smashed, is in the trash.

It is morning. Times Square is still so full of people.

Louise walks faster, now, and then faster still, and Cordelia has posted I am not insane. My sister is dead. and all her Exeter friends keep telling her to calm down, that she can call them if she needs to, and there will be a moment for Cordelia, when Cordelia checks her phone and among all these expressions of placating sympathy she sees that Louise Wilson, too, has Liked this status, but when she goes to click on it she will see that Louise Wilson does not exist.

There is no way in which Louise can fuck up because she has already done all of the worst things, and maybe nobody will ever love her again and maybe that's okay, too, because why else do you set things on fire except to burn them, and maybe they will find her or maybe they will never find her but Louise hopes if somebody finds her it is somebody who deserves to.

Louise hopes Cordelia will.

Now Louise has one dollar and forty-six cents in change. She has a fake ID. She has one set of clean clothes and auburn hair so dark it's almost violet.

She doesn't even have a phone.

Louise keeps walking, into Times Square. She walks so quickly. She walks into the crowd, and then we have to crane our necks to keep her in our field of vision, because there are so many people in this city and so many of them have violet or auburn hair, many, many white women, about five-foot-five, who are reasonably thin, who walk very quickly, or who are wearing black leggings, with white T-shirts, under dark but flimsy coats, and then Louise, or someone who is not Louise, turns a corner, or crosses the street, and then we do not see her.

Acknowledgments

With immense gratitude to everyone who has made this book a reality: to my agents, Emma Parry and Rebecca Carter at Janklow and Nesbit, for their faith, their patience, and their work in shaping the first draft of *Social Creature,* and reminding me to tell a good story, first and foremost, and worry about the rest later.

And to my wonderful editor, Margaux Weisman, whose sharp eye and editorial acumen helped me see the manuscript with a fresh eye, and make it so much better, and to the entire fantastic editorial, marketing, and design teams at Penguin Random House and Doubleday, who have made this book look and feel so beautiful I'm almost afraid to touch it.

Thank you to Simon Worrall, my mentor, who set me on the right path early on!

And a special thank you to Brian McMahon, who has been reading drafts (and drafts and more drafts) of this story since 2009, and who has been putting up with my chaotic tendencies nearly as long, whose faith and guidance alike have made telling this story possible. I owe this book to you—and I'm so glad I do.

About the Author

Tara Isabella Burton is a writer of fiction and nonfiction. Winner of the Shiva Naipaul Memorial Prize for travel writing, she completed her doctorate in nineteenth-century French literature and in theology at the University of Oxford. Her essays have appeared in *National Geographic, The Wall Street Journal,* and *The Economist*'s *1843,* among other publications. She currently works for *Vox* as their religion correspondent, and divides her time between the Upper East Side of New York and Tbilisi, Georgia.

THE KINDNESS
OF STRANGERS

THE KINDNESS
OF STRANGERS

The Life of Tennessee Williams

BY

DONALD SPOTO

THE BODLEY HEAD
LONDON

British Library Cataloguing
in Publication Data
Spoto, Donald
The kindness of strangers: the life of
Tennessee Williams.
1. Williams, Tennessee—Biography
2. Dramatists, American—20th century—Biography
I. Title
812'.54   PS3545.I5365Z/
ISBN 0-370-30847-6
© Donald Spoto 1985

Printed in Great Britain
by Redwood Burn Ltd, Trowbridge

Designed by Robert G. Lowe

for Irene

Look, here is some water!
What is to stop me being baptized?

The Acts of the Apostles

Fame is a bee.
It has a song —
It has a sting —
Ah, too, it has a wing.

Emily Dickinson

Contents

Acknowledgments

M Y LITANY of saints includes many whose kindness and generous assistance facilitated the various stages of my research.

At the University of Texas at Austin, where very large portions of the Tennessee Williams papers and the files of Audrey Wood are catalogued at the Humanities Research Center, I was given gracious help over a considerable period of time by the endlessly cheerful efficiency of Ken Craven. Cathy Henderson, Ellen Dunlap, Pat Fox and Barbara McCandless also came to my aid during various visits to the University.

Gary L. Smith, director of admissions and registrar at the University of Missouri–Columbia, enabled me to find important material and the record of Williams's attendance there. His colleagues, Julie Still in the Rare Books Room and Larry D. Clark in the drama department, were equally helpful in locating relevant data.

At the University of Iowa, Julia Mears arranged for me to obtain Williams's records.

Daniel C. Patri, at the Billy Rose Theatre Collection of the Lincoln Center Library for the Performing Arts, New York, directed me to important materials — among them, the Cheryl Crawford papers and the correspondence between Williams and Brooks Atkinson.

The director of personnel at the International Shoe Company, St. Louis, is Paul E. Nagel; he helped me to untangle employment records and to fix important times in Tennessee Williams's life in the 1930s.

Robert Knutsen, in Special Collections at the University of Southern California's Doheny Library, made it easy for me to work in the Warner Brothers files on films based on Williams plays. And at Metro-Goldwyn-Mayer, Herbert Nusbaum offered his usual friendly welcome and cleared time and space for me to study Williams's period at M-G-M.

Walter Kerr kindly allowed me to quote from his letters to Tennessee Williams and made several perceptive additional remarks.

At New Directions Books, James Laughlin directed me to Griselda

Ohannesian, who opened the Williams files and enabled me to follow the history of the plays' published versions.

Harry Rasky and Patrice Brun, at the Canadian Broadcasting Corporation, made it possible for me to see Mr. Rasky's documentary film celebrating Williams's life and career.

The Goodman Theatre, Chicago, was important to Williams in his late career. I am grateful to Gregory Mosher, Steve Scott, Ann Cusack and Susan Padveen for welcoming me to their offices, for providing a complete record of their Williams productions and correspondence, and for an extremely cordial encouragement.

At Florida Keys Community College, I was warmly received by William Seeker, president; Hal Massey, provost; Maria J. Soule, librarian; and Linda Jones, director of public relations.

Pat Castro and Jody Rodriguez, at the Monroe County Court House, Key West, helped me to locate important files and records.

Personal interviews provided an incalculably rich field of material. First and most important in this regard was Dakin Williams, my subject's brother, who shared important family memories, facts, anecdotes and impressions, and who generously assigned me permission to quote from the letters, journals and other writings of his mother, Edwina Dakin Williams.

Meade Roberts, who collaborated on two major screenplays based on works by Tennessee Williams, and who knew him and his social and professional circle during very important years, was an incomparably generous guide all through the preparation of this book. His memory is as keen as his literary sensibility, and he not only gave me firsthand accounts of important events and dates — he also guided me to other people and places I might otherwise have missed. I owe him my gratitude for much that is special material here.

Jill Krementz, one of the artists who has raised photography from a craft to an art, generously opened her collection of Tennessee Williams photographs to me. Her generosity, her enthusiasm, and her creative contributions grace the cover and the inserts of this book.

Invaluable information, reminiscences and reflections were offered by these generous people who knew and worked with Tennessee Williams, and to them I am very grateful indeed: Eve Adamson, Richard Alfieri, Craig Anderson and Elena Azuola, Robert Anderson, Eloise Sheldon Armen, Bonnie Sue Arp, Don Bachardy, Hermione Baddeley, Marji Bank, Bill Barnes, Barbara Baxley, Paul Bigelow, Fritz Bultman, Sandy

Campbell, Jay Leo Colt, Elsworth and Virginia Conkle, Ellis Conkle, Frank Corsaro, Cheryl Crawford, Olive Deering, Anthony Dexter, Mitch Douglas, Mildred Dunnock, Margaret Foresman, Robert Fox, Muriel Bultman Francis, Lucy Freeman, Mary Garrett, Bill Glavin, David Greg- gory, Thomas Griffin, Chuck Ingebritsen, Christopher Isherwood, Burl Ives, Scott Jaeck, Elia Kazan, Steven Kunes, the Rev. Joseph LeRoy, S.J., Tony Lincoln, Joseph Losey, Elmer Lower, Charles McDaniel, Joseph L. Mankiewicz, Theodore Mann, Anne Meacham, Taylor Mead, Sylvia Miles, Paul Morrissey, Gregory Mosher, Johnny Nicholson, Frederick Nicklaus, Carlo and Mirella Panarello, Lester Persky, Gene Persson, Wendell Phillips, Les Podewell, Sheldon Posnock, Irving Rapper, Dono- van Rhynsburger, Pancho Rodriguez, Ned Rorem, Alfred Ryder, Marian Seldes, Gloria Hope Sher, Edwin Sherin, Sylvia Sidney, Stephen Sil- verman, Jane Smith, Maureen Stapleton, Rachel Stephens, Vassilis Voglis, George Whitmore and Donald Windham.

A variety of assistances, information and cooperation was also forth- coming from Catherine Arnott, Victoria Bacon, Lansing Bailey, John Baisi and Norman Schneider and the staff at Copy-Line, Inc., Stephen Banker, Eric Bentley, David Blum, Andreas Brown, Hume Cronyn, Jo- seph H. Fulton, Harold Gefsky, Richard A. Holmes, Judith Katz, Rich- ard L. Kennedy, Ernest Lehman, Lyle Leverich, Elaine Lorillard, David and Helen Loth, Robert M. Luck, Michael Mattil, Patrick Merla, Colleen Mohyde, Julie Haydon Nathan, Gerald Pinciss, Sidney Porcelain, Cynthia Reed, A. L. Rowse, Murray Sargent, Renee Schwartz, Alan Sha- piro, Sam Staggs, Mike Steen, Jane Sylvester, Piero Taverna, Samuel Tay- lor, Adrian and Andrea Turner and Gore Vidal.

In New Orleans, I was welcomed to Loyola University by the Rev. Er- nest Ferlita, S.J., who helped me find several important contacts. In the same city, W. Kenneth Holditch and Cynthia Ratcliffe guided me, with their superb knowledge as scholarly guides, through the French Quarter. Kate Schweppe Moldawer was helpful in Key West. And in St. Louis Greg Young offered considerable assistance on several occasions.

Tennessee Williams's first New York production was offered by the legendary Drama Workshop at the New School for Social Research. By a happy coincidence, that has been my academic home-base since 1975, and the encouragement and affectionate collegiality I receive there is a great boon in my life. Dean Allen Austill redeems the pristine meaning of his title: he is a perceptive administrator, a patient colleague and a good friend. Lewis Falb, who guides the humanities division at the New

School, displayed constant, cheerful interest in the day-to-day growth of the manuscript. And among my students, a number helped me to track down arcane materials, rare books and articles and miscellanea: Sylvia Brown, Diane Churchill, Jane Conlon, Leonard Feigenblatt, Chris Fleetwood, Louise Fox, John Freitas, Arthur Green, Emily Harrow, Wendy Kafka, Elizabeth Kenney, Abby Kessler, Sheila Knapp, Richard Longmore, Raul Martinez, Renee McMichael, Diane Outeiral, Margot E. Quinn, Anthony Sacramone, Kelley Shields, John Sirabella, Vicki Stamm, Lauren Stevens, Allen Thompson, Patricia Weber and Patricia Wilkes.

My literary agent, Elaine Markson, is not only a devoted representative — she is also a loyal friend. To her and to her associates, Geri Thoma, Raymond Bongiovanni and Elizabeth Kohen, I owe thanks for as much warm support as professional expertise. And in London, there is Deborah Rogers, who looks after my professional interests in Great Britain with similar acuity and affection. Just as I am grateful to Elaine for my happy union with Little, Brown and Company, so much I acknowledge Deborah for introducing me to The Bodley Head and editor Maureen Rissik.

James T. Caroscio, M.D., who is a gifted physician and an attentive friend, supplied important information on the history and chemistry of drugs and drug therapy. Jerry Bradley has helped me, all through my writing, to keep in order many practical aspects of daily life. And John Darretta again showed his loyal and devoted friendship — not least of all in his discussions with me about some fine points of literary history.

Irene Mahoney (to whom I dedicate this book) is a cherished friend for over thirty-five years, and Ned Mullaney for over twenty-five. No words can express my gratitude for their constancy and their love; they do my life more good than they know.

And how to thank William Phillips? I am of all writers the most fortunate in having so fine an editor at Little, Brown and Company. There are important points in this book that owe their sharper focus to his counsel and their final shaping to his intelligence, sensitivity and perception. As if that were not enough to be grateful for, I am also blessed with his friendship and confidence. As that fact and these pages of acknowledgments disclose, life is very rich indeed.

D.S.

New York
June 28, 1984

Preface

TENNESSEE WILLIAMS first entered my life in the spring of 1956, when I was a high school student in New Rochelle, New York. Our drama club had just finished a boisterous production of George M. Cohan's comic mystery *Seven Keys to Baldpate*, and my performance as a politician of questionable morality had sealed my decision to become an actor. The director then held auditions for the coming autumn production. He had settled on *The Glass Menagerie,* and I won the role of Tom — who, we were told, was really Tennessee Williams himself. With all the passionate eagerness of a fifteen-year-old, I enrolled in Saturday morning acting classes at the American Academy of Dramatic Arts in New York.

By the time school resumed in September, I had memorized the role, only to learn that the drama coach had departed to pursue a career in politics and the production of *The Glass Menagerie* was canceled by the principal. But also by this time, I had discovered the strange and tender world of Tennessee Williams and his work, and I was following news of the theatre religiously.

During the next several years, Williams was discussed more and more as a shocking writer of difficult and severe plays: *Cat on a Hot Tin Roof* had been controversial enough (with its implications of homosexuality and impotence), but it was followed by *Orpheus Descending* (which dealt with sexual exploitation and ended in violence), *Suddenly Last Summer* (which added cannibalism to all those earlier motifs) and then *Sweet Bird of Youth* (which seemed to continue the horrors, with the characters' drug and sex addictions, venereal disease and castration). Tennessee Williams and his work were always newsworthy, and it seemed that not a month passed without an article or interview in magazines and papers about the playwright and his social and professional world. We heard a great deal about Williams, but we learned very little, for interviews were

restricted to safe topics and always subject to the heavy censorship requirements and the prevalent fractious moralism of the 1950s.

All that changed in the following years, by which time I had prudently
become more realistic about my theatrical ambitions and had developed
other interests. In the 1960s and 1970s, my enthusiasm for his work persisted, even as his career was in an odd, dark eclipse. But he was still a
news item; indeed, if his plays were no longer considered to have the
same wild alchemy of the sordid and the sensitive, he now did. He replaced his work as the talk of the town, or at least of the television talk
show. When his *Memoirs* were published in 1975 (and a selection of his
letters to his old friend Donald Windham soon after), the trend of attention to sensational aspects of his life continued. What had been un-
mentionable in the 1950s — that Williams was homosexual — was by
1970 all that many people (and sometimes even he) considered interesting. This corresponded to a new climate of curiosity and tolerance (if not
exactly a warm acceptance) about the varieties of sexual preference in
America.

But the basic problem persisted. Whereas earlier we read a great deal
about Williams but learned little partly because of *silence* on private matters, in the 1970s we read and heard a great deal about Williams but
learned little because of *emphasis* on private matters. *Memoirs* provided a
neat smoke screen, for the details of social and sexual life were really not
intimate: they did not disclose the person. To state that one is heterosexual (or not) provides no information on the depth or quality of life, after
all — we know nothing, from such an admission, about whether one
kicks the cat, is loyal to friends, pays taxes, is concerned for the poor, is
capable of fidelity and devotion, or reflects on the wonder and mystery of
the human condition. *Memoirs,* I had discovered at once, told us very little indeed about Tennessee Williams's deepest life, the logic of his work,
and the place of that work in his hierarchy of values.

By the time of his death, in February 1983, I had gathered substantial
material. Those supervising the disposition of his estate told me that
there would be no decision on an authorized biography — news which
neither disappointed nor deterred me, since the freedom available to an
unrestricted writer had already become clear during my writing of Alfred
Hitchcock's life. And so I undertook this book.

My research took me from the places he lived to the people he knew,
from the theatres and studios where he worked to the vast depositories of
his letters and papers at the University of Texas at Austin. I soon learned

the astonishing inaccuracies of fact, the misrepresentations Williams was responsible for, the egregious omissions of important events and people in his public statements and published disclosures. Great dramatist that he was, he seemed unable to resist the temptation to alter the facts, the chronology, the characters in his own life — to give them, in the recounting, more color or a neater structure than reality provided.

Scores of interviews and months of study in private and public collections of journals, letters and collections of theatre material began to reveal clearer contours of the man's life and character. Elia Kazan, who directed four of his plays, was on the mark when he said to me, "Tennessee's life is in his work." That is not too schematic a summary of the remarkable cross-hatching of art and life which emerges in a consideration of Williams, and it helps to explain the lack of congruence between *his* accounts of his life and the dimensions of reality. What Williams wrote of his friend and fellow playwright William Inge can be said of himself: his life and career and search comprised "a drama as fine and admirable as any of the ones he has given, one after another."

Tennessee Williams's creative legacy is perhaps far vaster than many of his admirers realize: a complete catalog would have to include more than twenty-five full-length plays, more than forty short plays, a dozen produced (and unproduced) screenplays and an opera libretto. These have been translated into at least twenty-seven languages, including Tamil, Welsh, Marathi and Hindi. In addition, there are two novels, a novella, more than sixty short stories, more than one hundred poems, an autobiography, a published volume of letters, introductions to plays and books by others, and occasional pieces and reviews. He gave new meaning to the word prolific.

He also provided scholars, students and journalists with a rich field to explore. In his bibliographical handbook (*The Critical Reputation of Tennessee Williams: a reference guide,* Boston: G. K. Hall, 1983), John S. McCann lists more than 2500 articles on Williams published (mostly in the United States) between 1939 and 1981. And Drewey Wayne Gunn (in *Tennessee Williams: A Bibliography,* Metuchen: The Scarecrow Press, 1980) catalogs over fifty theses and dissertations, four hundred critical articles and books, eighty interviews and thirty-three volumes of collected reviews of Williams's work. I have consulted most of this material; little of it deals with his life, but anything that suggests leads or correspondences had to be pursued.

* * *

The story of Tennessee Williams's life, I think, reveals him as a man more disturbing, more dramatic, richer and more wonderful than any character he ever created. His sensitivities and sympathies were broad, his experience of loneliness and loss made him responsive to others' lives. And he succeeded, remarkably often, in translating those sympathies and cries of emotional solidarity with the wounded into the stuff of great art — *The Glass Menagerie, Summer and Smoke, A Streetcar Named Desire, Cat on a Hot Tin Roof, Suddenly Last Summer, The Night of the Iguana.*

There is something mysterious about the chemistry of that creativity. He was subject to periods of clinical depression but not to philosophical or spiritual inquiry. He was capable of extreme acts of generosity to friends and lovers, and then he could suddenly retreat from everyone into a private, self-absorbed world, from which he might emerge asking others to respond to his various needs. His life was a sine curve of actions and attitudes that at their worst inevitably hurt him more than anyone, and that at their best delighted and enriched others more than himself. He depended not only on the loyalty and commitment of others in order to pass his days with some order and affection, and to enable him to work; he also seemed to rely on frequent excursions to the frontiers of illness, madness and what (in *The Night of the Iguana*) he called "the unlighted sides" of human nature.

His connections with his art, with his life, and with other people were both loving and selfish, involved and coolly detached, tender and brutal; in other words, he was a human being. The paradox resulted in a body of writing that often succeeded better than he did. His work is a series of variations on the great emotional cycles of his own tortured life. The biographer cannot judge the final truth in his subject's soul, he can only assess the meanings that subject seems to have discerned in life. "I hope that I have been able to contribute an understanding about people," Tennessee Williams said not long before his death. No teller of his difficult life could aim higher.

A Note on the Published Plays of Tennessee Williams:

There are substantial differences between variant versions of plays by Tennessee Williams. The so-called acting versions, published mostly by Dramatists Play Service, often contain major alterations from the original play *as performed,* and from the versions he wished to represent him in bound book form — published by New Directions. For the sake of consistency, my citations are drawn from *The Theatre of Tennessee Williams,* the seven-volume New Directions set (1971–1981) which the playwright intended to represent a more or less final record of his plays, at least until he might, later, have another look and make some emendations on notepaper at home. As recently as four months before his death, he was rewriting scenes from twenty-year-old plays.

Chapter One

IN THE SHADOW
OF THE CHURCH
(1911–1928)

I've literally grown up right in the very
shadow of the Episcopal church. At Pass
Christian and Natchez, Biloxi, Gulfport, Port
Gibson, Columbus and Glorious Hill!

— Miss Collins, in *Portrait of a Madonna*

COLUMBUS, a town in eastern Mississippi and the seat of Lowndes County, lies on the Tombigbee River. Originally settled with the unlikely name of Possum Town in 1817, it was noted chiefly for cotton trading, and boats heavy with bales crowded its dock for decades. During the Civil War it was a fiercely Confederate stronghold, and in fact the first observance of Confederate Decoration Day was held in Columbus in 1866. Much of the town was spared the destruction of the war and its aftermath, and by the turn of the twentieth century many antebellum homes stood unchanged. In 1884, Mississippi State College for Women — the first state-supported university for women in America — enrolled its first students on a former Columbus estate.

In the early 1900s, life in the town conformed to the characteristics, principles and practices of Southern social philosophy. Although the majority of the population was black and legally free from slavery, the tradition of white supremacy prevailed: the country-gentry ideal flourished under families of mostly English, Irish and northern European ancestry. Town life still seemed more rural than urban; the pace was unhurried; the belief in a fixed, divinely ordained social order was taken for granted, as were stability, a complex system of manners and etiquette, the art of hospitality and a highly developed sense of the genteel life — to these may be added all the quaint customs of refinement and delicacy familiar to readers and moviegoers over the last several decades. Jealous of its traditions and deeply nostalgic for the values of the Christian home, Southern towns like Columbus distrusted Northern intellectuals and politicians, and the people were proud of the Confederate tradition of bravery and independence. The Northern ideals of progress, material advancement, the mingling of diverse cultures, freedom and mobility — these were held suspect in a way of life that invested considerable energy and talent in sustaining the values of a cherished and (it was thought) gentler era.

Just as the extreme forms of politeness and courtesy were the daily, external signs of moral righteousness, so was local social life arranged round the front parlor, the school, the church hall. Neighbors and even friends regularly prefixed "Miss" or "Master" to others' first names in ordinary conversation. Training in manners and the social graces, in the proper gestures, the correct posture and gait, the way a lady held a wrist-fan, the way a gentleman bowed at the waist, the colors of everyday dress: all were measurements of life. Crudeness was reason for social ostracism, and the imitation of Victorian manners paralleled the importation of Victorian furniture. Georgian mansions also reflected the South's luxuriant, sometimes opulent idolization of Old World gentility and the veneration of style and charm. And although the permanence of this life was questioned by a few before World War I, the enduring power of the Southern-Victorian morality was considered as fixed as the stars. Not sternly ascetical (like the New England Puritan), this ethic nevertheless encouraged an almost impossible and highly theatrical prudery. In the North there had been a tradition of simplicity, industriousness, sensual denial; but in the South (as far back as the time of the great New England orators and long afterward) manner *was* morality. To the description of that moral code — its history and influence, its shifts and its upheavals — Mississippi writers as different as William Faulkner, Eudora Welty and Tennessee Williams often dedicated themselves. Great artists that they became — as their talents transcended parochialism — they nevertheless mixed the colors of their literary vision from the same social palette. And the life they described, like the life they first knew, was one of a strange paradox: prudery and delicacy coexisted with a languid, florid indulgence in the sweetness of detail.

In 1905, Reverend Walter Edwin Dakin became pastor of St. Paul's Episcopal Church in Columbus. That year, the town listed no more than four thousand in its census (virtually none of them Jewish or Roman Catholic), and the minister's social charm, his elegant manner and his serious, hardworking wife and lovely twenty-one-year-old daughter favorably impressed the parish and the entire community. Reverend Dakin (born in Ohio in 1857) came from a family that had left Wales in the 1600s and settled in the Midwest. He had been a Quaker and a teacher before deciding to study for the Episcopalian ministry. This branch of American Protestantism he apparently selected because the bishopric — to which he always aspired but which eluded him — held a promise of glamour and grandeur. From the time of his ordination, in 1895, to his appointment at St. Paul's, Columbus, ten years later, Reverend Dakin — restless, always eager for a pleasanter town and a more comfortable rectory — had moved with his family more than half a dozen times. His taste for luxury remained unsatisfied.

His wife, the former Rosina Otte (called Rose from childhood), had a very different personality. The daughter of German immigrants, she had been born in Buffalo, New York. Her parents then moved west, where, like her future husband, she too had been raised in the simplicity of rural Ohio towns. Her strict upbringing had been reinforced by several years at a Catholic boarding school in Youngstown, where the Ursuline nuns confirmed her in the virtues of thrift, self-denial, piety and humility. She almost became a Catholic herself before the irresistible and handsome Walter Dakin sealed several years of friendship with a wedding ring. In 1884, after they had been married several years, their only child, Edwina Estelle, was born at the Otte home in Marysville, Ohio.

While her husband completed his education and won a teacher's license in the late 1880s, Rose Dakin kept their home, helped with his research and sustained with remarkable grace his compulsive moves. Pampered and indulged by her father, Edwina flourished in the towns of Ohio and Tennessee and Mississippi to which they moved, while her mother worked harder than ever to supplement the family income. Eventually Mrs. Dakin took in laundry and sewing and gave piano lessons so that her husband could complete his studies for the ministry and so that her daughter would not be denied treats.

By the time Edwina was ready for high school, in 1897, the Dakins had returned for a time to Ohio, and she attended the Harcourt Place Seminary, Gambier, a school for wealthier young ladies to which she was admitted on scholarship. The studies were not burdensome, the social life was busy, and the minister's attractive daughter sang in the school chorus, danced at musicales and local parties, and enjoyed every advantage her father's status, her mother's hard work and her own winsome charm bestowed. She had a score of male admirers from Kenyon College — they were termed "gentlemen callers" in the early 1900s — and from the local military academy and the theological school. "I was rarely required," she later admitted about her early life, "to do anything I did not want to do."

With Reverend Dakin's constant uprooting of his wife and daughter to accept one improved position after another, it was natural that Edwina's social life also lacked stability. Between 1901 and 1905, while they went from Ohio to Tennessee to various towns in Mississippi (Port Gibson, Natchez, Vicksburg), she recorded in her diaries no less than forty-five young men for whom she harbored some romantic feelings. At Gambier, she was all aflutter over Richard Lodge before shifting her attention to H. G. Fitzgerald, then to Louis Simon, Arthur Aubrey, Rowland Balfour and John McKim. "I danced with a lot of men," she noted plainly after one party.

In Tennessee, there were many more whose names she recorded along with brief commentaries ("Mr. Frederick Statt has grown to be *very* good-looking!"); and in Mississippi she wrote of her special attraction to Messrs. Huston, Gorman, Martin, Devoe, Henry, Billie, Waller, Morrison, Davidson, Connor and Bagby. Two young men (memorialized simply as Warren and Harry) outdid themselves in sending her little lyrics. She knew them only casually, it seems, but their poems were pasted in her scrapbooks and bordered with brief notations about their suitability as gentlemen callers. By the time she was twenty, she was expert in all the social arts and none of the domestic, and her beauty and a fine singing voice might have enabled her to fulfill what she wrote in her diary was her "secret ambition, to become an actress, a musical comedy star." But for a respectable young lady in the early years of this century that was not a reasonable hope; her participation always remained on the level of amateur theatricals. Her greatest performance was perhaps that of the archetypal "Southern belle," a role the Ohio-born Edwina played so well that it finally became her life; with a convert's fervor, she more than adapted to her Southern homes and habits — she virtually erased from her speech and manner anything that was not appropriate to the Southern Victorian maiden.

By autumn of 1905 the Dakins were involved in all the church and civic activities of Columbus, and at once Edwina — now an eligible twenty-one — attracted attention. "I remember watching her," a neighbor wrote years later, "as her skirts flounced about her ankles, thinking to myself that as soon as I was eighteen I would have long skirts too. She never knew me, but she was the minister's daughter and known to many that she did not know." The local newspaper recorded that "Miss Dakin will be quite an acquisition to our younger social set." Just so, for at once a tornado of attention swept round her:

"Mr. Lide called in the afternoon," she wrote in her diary. "We went to the ice cream parlour, returning in time to see Mr. Harris, Mr. Peyton and Mr. Hardy, who made an engagement to take me to the dance. After

they all left, Mr. Carr and myself went for a drive." Her mother, meanwhile, worked twenty-hour days, giving herself to every parish, school
and community club that sought her time and energy. She continued to
offer music lessons as well, for her husband's compensation was only one
hundred dollars a month. He had social prestige, influence, respect —
even admiration from the people of Columbus, who appreciated that this
Northerner had studied theology at the University of the South, at
Sewanee, Tennessee, and the hint of a drawl modified his accent.

In early 1906, when she was appearing in an amateur production of
The Mikado in Columbus, a friend introduced Edwina Dakin to Cornelius Coffin Williams. Known to friends and co-workers as "C.C.," he had
come to town from Memphis, where he worked for the telephone company in what might later be termed a paralegal capacity. She called him
Cornelius from that day forward.

Cornelius Williams had attended for one year the University of Tennessee's law school, but voluntary service in the Spanish-American War
intervened. Demobilized as an officer, he did not resume his former plans
but took a position with the Cumberland Telephone Company, and
when he met Miss Edwina he had come to Columbus to plead a case. The
evening he saw *The Mikado* began an eighteen-month courtship, sometimes interrupted for many weeks. At such times, Edwina entertained
other young men in the rectory parlor. Unwilling to curtail her social life
and well aware that most of her friends were already married (if not also
mothers) by the age of twenty-one, she continued the kind of acceptable
social behavior that coexisted with intense sexual prudery. Relations between the sexes were rarely more than innocent flirtations; sensual indulgence meant an extra lemonade after a late dance, or ice cream on a warm
evening, or strolling without white gloves in August. Each era finds its
own pleasures.

Although the Dakins saw little of Cornelius Williams at first, he
seemed to be an acceptable serious suitor for their daughter, for he was
from a Tennessee family with a first-rate pedigree. Five years older than
Edwina (and therefore, they presumed, more mature), he had been born
in 1879 in Knoxville. His father, Thomas Lanier Williams, traced his ancestry back to French Huguenots, to musicians at the English courts, and
to politicians and soldiers in North Carolina and Tennessee. His mother,
Isabel Coffin, was descended from Virginia settlers, Tennessee statesmen,
and at least one poet: her uncle was Tristram Coffin, who is linked to the

development of Nantucket Island. While her husband's family listed Tennessee senators, hers boasted at least three governors. Before Cornelius's birth, Isabel and Thomas Lanier Williams had two daughters, Ella and Isabel. Then, in 1884, when the boy was five, his mother died. Cornelius and Isabel (always called Belle) were raised in the quietly rigid Rogersville Synodical College, a Tennessee seminary the boy found overwhelmingly oppressive. After attending a series of boarding schools where he earned a reputation as a hell-raiser, given to card-playing, fighting, boisterous high spirits and (from a remarkably early age) drinking home brew he and buddies filched from neighbors. The pedigree was still there but — perhaps because his youth lacked precisely the decencies of family life — the polish was not.

Nevertheless, Cornelius at twenty-seven — after military service and responsible employment — presented a handsome, courtly air when he called in 1906 and 1907 in Columbus, and when he asked for Edwina's hand, the Reverend nodded approval. "Many men have said I love you," Edwina wrote in her diary on June 1, 1907, "but only three said Will you marry me. I will marry one next Monday. Finis. Goodbye." And with this curious adieu to her maidenhood, she exchanged vows with the Tennessee telephone man in a quiet ceremony in her father's church on June 2. They departed at once for Gulfport.

The details of the early married life of Cornelius and Edwina Dakin Williams, to 1909, may perhaps never be entirely clear, but this much is certain: pregnant with their first child, Edwina fled her husband and returned to the rectory in Columbus. Apparently it was not only work that kept Cornelius in the southern part of Mississippi: the memories of the Tennessee seminary he had lived in as a boy were so unpleasant that he refused to live in another clerical shadow. He visited regularly, however — a few days each month — and when Edwina gave birth to a girl on November 17, 1909, they agreed on a name: she was called Rose Isabel, after both their mothers. Soon afterward, he returned to his job with the telephone company, traveling up and down the state on their behalf, and Edwina remained — permanently, it seemed — with her parents. To no one's surprise, Grandmother Dakin added nursemaid duties to her busy schedule, and Edwina quickly resumed an active social life. When an imminent visit by Cornelius was announced, she was indifferent. The marriage between the rowdy traveler and the pampered Southern belle had clearly been a terrible mistake.

After one of his longer visits to Columbus, however, Edwina received two pieces of news: a letter from her husband, that he was now selling men's shoes and clothing along the Delta; and a note from her physician, confirming her suspicions that she was expecting another child. During the late fall of 1910, Cornelius's visits to Columbus became markedly less pleasant, for he returned to the rectory several evenings drunk and incoherent, and there was talk of card games in bawdy houses at the edge of town. The Dakins pretended to take no notice. Their daughter was embarrassed, angry and sometimes frightened.

On Palm Sunday — March 26, 1911 — Edwina Dakin Williams was preparing to attend services in her father's church when she collapsed in her bedroom and was rushed to a little clinic nearby. A few hours later, she gave birth to a boy, whom the Reverend soon christened Thomas Lanier Williams (after the child's paternal grandfather, who had died in 1908). Tommy Williams insisted on "Tom" by the time he was ten. A few old friends (or new ones, under special circumstances) called him Tom even after 1939, when the first story published under the name Tennessee Williams appeared.

Almost immediately after her return to the rectory on South Second Street in Columbus, Edwina engaged a black servant to help care for her two children and to see to the shopping and cooking. The young woman's name was Ozzie, and for several years she went wherever the Dakins, their daughter and grandchildren went. Ozzie tried, unsuccessfully, to teach Miss Edwina to cook, but the only item her aristocratic mistress learned was angel food cake. By this time, the Dakins noticed, their daughter — perhaps to offset the rumors of her husband's misconduct — began to affect a somewhat grand, slightly imperious manner. She was also a nonstop talker who allowed no more than a second of silence in any gathering.

By the end of 1913, Reverend Dakin — eager to be on the move again, anxious for a slightly better position in a more prestigious community — had secured a pastorate in Nashville, Tennessee, at the Church of the Advent. They remained there almost two years, when they moved to a church in Canton, Mississippi. That was the Reverend's shortest tenure, however, and by Christmas 1915 they settled in western Mississippi — in Clarksdale, a pleasant town where the family thrived and even Cornelius's swaggering visits seemed tolerable. In the heart of the Delta, on the Sunflower River, Clarksdale was an agricultural processing and distribution center near the spot where, tradition has it, De Soto discovered the Mississippi River. Life here was a stencil of gracious living in the Old South.

In early 1916, Rose was six and Tommy almost five, and they had known few companions except for one another. "She was an ideal play-mate," Tennessee Williams said many years later. "She was very charming, very beautiful. She had an incredible imagination. We were so close to each other, we had no need of others." The psychological affinity between brother and sister became so intense, in fact, that when Rose had a cold, or tonsillitis, or mumps, Tommy was convinced he, too, was ill. The two were called "the couple" by Ozzie, as they caught lightning bugs during summer evenings and wandered through the neighborhood and the town's parks alone for hours. "I was a gentle little boy who liked to play with girls," Williams said, and no girl was ever more important to him, then or later, than his sister, Rose.

Their mother, meanwhile, enjoyed the privileges to which Reverend Dakin's status entitled her: deference, prestige, social invitations. Because of Ozzie, Edwina was released from most household duties, and although she was committed to parish club activities, she devoted part of each day to Rose and Tommy. She noticed, from his earliest years, that her son had unusual powers of concentration: "Other children would pick a flower, then carelessly throw it away," she wrote later, "but Tom would stand peering into the heart of the flower as though trying to discover the secret of its life." He paid attention, too, when she read stories and plays, when she sang hymns, recited English and Scottish ballads she had learned in school, and acted out tall tales, the wild adventures of folk heroes like Paul Bunyan, Davy Crockett, Annie Oakley, and Johnny Appleseed.

There were other stories for the children, too. Reverend and Mrs. Dakin knew the Bible stories, and the children heard them at church and at home. The holy men of antiquity, from Moses to Paul, were presented as crusading message-bearers; Jesus was a refuge and a healer; angels guarded sleeping children. Dogma was minimized, comfort maximized. Again unlike the New England Puritans, religion was not so much a challenge as it was a caress. It was a nice thing for nice people, but it had its place and was not permitted too wide a field of activity. God and Country were the enduring realities, to be sure, but President Wilson they could see.

If the Dakins provided uplifting stories, Ozzie was a dramatic competitor. She not only sang spirituals, hymns and African lullabies to Rose and Tommy, she also regaled them with the rich store of black and Indian folklore — much of it free invention at every telling, all of it color-ful, some of it violent. Ghosts and gremlins were summoned up before them, and she was convinced there was the same degree of "de debbil" in everyone as there was of salt in sweat. Ozzie's warnings about demons and damnation were a neat counterpoint to the majestic sweep of the hymnal and the Book of Common Prayer. Along with chicken pies and cornbread, Ozzie fed the children wonderfully spun tales about this world and the other. Edwina, puzzled when Tommy remained digging in the backyard for several hours one day, laughed when he said that he was "diggin' to de debbil."

Life in Clarksdale was not unrealistically happy, however, and there were the usual childhood ailments. Measles, chicken pox, a slight case of fever, a skin infection alternately kept Rose out of school. Then, by 1917, when she was ready to attend, Tom fell prey to a round of illnesses that kept him out of first grade. Most frightening was a bout of diphtheria that was followed by a severe kidney infection. He was confined to bed for so long that his muscles were weakened, and by the time he seemed well enough to go out he was unable to walk more than a few steps. As late as his seventh birthday, in 1918, he could not sustain the pace of other, more active, children. His earlier term at a nursery school had been disastrous in any case: when his mother left the schoolroom he threw a tantrum that was very nearly a fit, and the teacher, alarmed, insisted that Edwina remain for several weeks.

But other children's chatter, and the teacher's stories, could not engage Tommy Williams's attention for very long. His grandparents' Bible stories, Ozzie's fables and folklore, even Edwina's ballads, were far more dramatic. At night, when his mother came to his room, she often heard bits and pieces of stories he was making up, alone and aloud, in the room he shared with his sister.

"It was around this time that I began to invent private, solitary amuse-ments," he told an interviewer years later. The games and the stories lengthened during his illnesses, and during the long period of recupera-tion when he could not walk. Edwina then ministered to him night and day. "She never let him forget that she saved his life," according to Lucy Freeman, a writer who worked with Edwina on her memoirs later. "It was probably the first great dramatic performance he saw, her rendition of his childhood illnesses and her nursing duties." By this time — late 1917 — Ozzie had departed, leaving a legacy of folklore and an unwit-ting endorsement of the prevailing class system.

Even when he recovered from his long confinement, Tom found that the fundamentally happy life of the minister's family occasionally knew the dreadful as well as the delicate. The cloistered atmosphere of the rectory was balanced by a wave of terrible viruses that took the lives of dozens of parishioners. "I got a more intimate view of human problems that year," Tennessee Williams said later. "I remember my grandfather's visits to deathbeds."

"Grandfather was quite a character in Mississippi during those early years," according to the Williams's third child, Walter Dakin, who was born in 1919. "He was a very selfish person, very self-important and very much a social snob. He wouldn't associate with Baptists, for example, or with Methodists, or with people who came from a denomination that didn't have bishops. He was so lordly that when people got to know him they often called him the Bish — 'here comes the Bish!' But he was wonderful to have around in a social situation, because he was such an extrovert. His taste for life's luxuries was checked by Grandmother's frugality. She was more reserved, more serious — maybe because of her German upbringing. And she was a natural aristocrat. Mother told me that whenever Tom thought he was misbehaving as a child, he would ask, 'What would Grand think of this?' The possibility of her displeasure would haunt him. She was his conscience and his angel, and she sewed up money in letters and gift packages for him all his life."*

There was not a great deal of money for the household in Clarksdale, but there was a fine rectory with spacious rooms, a bright, friendly town full of flowers and parks and polite, deferential neighbors. "They had more than money," as Tennessee Williams's younger brother said later. "They had the status of being the minister's family. Tom's life was gentle and genteel, and Rose was the little princess, the minister's granddaughter, the apple of everyone's eye. They were like a royal family, even though they weren't obviously rich."

On young Tommy Williams, however, no influence was stronger than his mother's. She was a beautiful, strong-willed, socially ambitious woman who observed every prescription of Southern etiquette and charm. Aristocratic manners were equated with profound virtue; delicacy of diction and a studied poise had almost religious significance; hard work was a man's solemn duty. And sex (when it was mentioned at all, which was about as often as a July snowfall in Mississippi) was a man's

* Rose Dakin (always called "Grand" by the Williams family) is celebrated in two of Tennessee Williams's most deeply felt short stories, "The Angel in the Alcove" and "Grand."

mysterious reward and a woman's grim obligation: such was God's inscrutable plan for filling the earth.

In early summer 1918, Edwina Williams returned to the rectory in Clarksdale one evening and quietly told her mother that she was pregnant a third time. The news might have been received more happily if it had not coincided with another imminent change in her life. Cornelius had won a managerial position with the Friedman-Shelby branch of the International Shoe Company, based in St. Louis. They were to move at once, for now he anticipated a more stable family life, and he intended to be a father to the new baby in the day-to-day routines that he had missed when Rose and Tom were toddlers. The Dakins encouraged the move, although Edwina doubted the depth of Cornelius's abilities to live up to his promises. She knew he was a private drinker, an open gambler, and a covert womanizer.

And so in July the rector's daughter and her husband and their two children took a frightfully hot train journey north to St. Louis. From the moment of their arrival, the relocation had a devastating effect on the children, whose gentle, ordered parochial life was at once replaced by a cruder, noisier industrial atmosphere ill-suited both to Miss Edwina's social aspirations and to her children's physical frailty. Where Mississippi life had been colorful and close to nature, St. Louis seemed at first merely crowded and coarse; where the warmer attitudes of the Delta softened life and speech, St. Louis seemed all hectic business.

"The changes must have been shocking for them," reflected the biographer and social historian David Loth, who was born and raised in St. Louis during the same years. "Although it was originally a French fur-trading post and a major trading port before the development of Kansas City, it had a busy factory life, a rapidly expanding intellectual life, and a cosmopolitan spirit that the more insulated Southerner would have found disorienting. There was a pronounced German spirit to St. Louis, also — there were at least two German-language daily newspapers for the benefit of the German immigrant population, and Joseph Pulitzer began as a reporter for one of them.

"But it was also, by the time of World War I, the fourth largest city in America, after New York, Chicago and Philadelphia, and it had a population of about 600,000 people — many of whom worked in factories. Cornelius Williams undoubtedly found a managerial position here because of the sudden expansion of St. Louis as a great shoemaking center. Most of us knew someone who worked in the shoe factories or warehouses."

But the industrial importance of St. Louis and its urban mix and sprawl did not make much difference to nine-year-old Rose and seven-year-old Tom. All they remembered was that they were mocked because of their Southern accents and refined manners, although Loth doubts this could have been a virulent or even frequent mockery. "If they were social outcasts because of their accent, it might have been because of the part of town they inhabited. Most St. Louisans were cosmopolitan enough not to take exception to a deep Southern drawl. In certain fringe areas there may have been less tolerance, of course — and children can be inordinately cruel about these things; it's a way of forming their little exclusive groups. Downtown, however, everyone mingled easily."

In one important way, of course, St. Louis resembled Mississippi: there was total segregation between whites and blacks, and that segregation had its focus and its emphasis in the school system. "Half of Missouri had fought for the Confederacy," Loth added, "and the grandchildren of Confederate soldiers weren't allowed to forget it."

The mixture of modernity with ancient prejudice and ethnic diversity was oddly juxtaposed with a first-rate educational system. "We had the best city school system in the midwest," according to Loth, "and by several years of national ratings it was considered one of the best school systems in all America. High school teachers quite regularly had doctorate degrees from the best universities in the country."

In addition, the increase of recreational facilities in the 1920s owed a great deal to Dwight Davis, the commissioner of public works. He is most remembered for his place in the history of tennis, for it was he who gave his name to the famous Cup. It was his civic-mindedness that developed the parks and recreational areas and public baths serving rich and poor alike. Soon Tom Williams would escape to Forest Park or Creve Coeur Lake for a quiet refuge; like famous natives of St. Louis — Sally Benson, Emily Hahn, T. S. Eliot, Sara Teasdale — he later remembered whole days in the delicious greenery of Forest Park.

Edwina Williams set to the task of adjusting as best she could, despite the children's evident misery during the first months. Their first address was a crowded boardinghouse on Lindell Boulevard, a busy thoroughfare that could not have provided a sharper contrast to the quiet streets of Clarksdale. "At the boardinghouse, Mother had to do no cooking — which was fortunate, since she still couldn't make anything except her old standard, angel food cake. In Mississippi, the cooking and chores and

child-care were largely taken care of by Ozzie, or by Grand. Now everything was different," as Tennessee Williams's younger brother recalled.
But the boardinghouse was soon abandoned for slightly larger quarters,
at 3 South Taylor. As her pregnancy advanced, and as the summer heat
lengthened into a torrid autumn, Edwina appreciated the proximity to
Forest Park, and to Barnes Hospital.

In September 1918, Tom was enrolled at the Eugene Field elementary
school, where he soon suffered verbal and physical abuse from the other
children because of a squeamishness and delicacy that had surrounded
him at home. Forbidden by his mother to engage in any sport because of
his diphtheria-weakened heart (a diagnosis never substantiated by a doctor then or later), he relied more and more on himself, his story-spinning
with Rose, his fabrication of short, sometimes grotesque tales, and his
refuge of solitary reading.

"I preferred to play by myself," he said of those early years in St. Louis.
"I had already stopped making connections with other boys." By the
time he was nine, he had put some of that solitude to good use: he had
read at least two novels by Dickens, some of the Waverley novels of
Walter Scott, and generous selections from Shakespeare. At the same
time, Rose absented herself more from classes, often on the pretext of
helping at home. She often sat quietly alone, in the dark, waiting for Edwina knew not what — perhaps just for Tom to return from school.

On February 21, 1919, the third and last child was born to Cornelius
and Edwina, and his mother insisted on the names Walter Dakin; the
first name was ignored almost from the first day. Immediately following
her release from St. Anthony's hospital, Edwina fell ill, and not long after
she contracted the Spanish influenza that ravaged much of America. Cornelius took her farther west for treatment in a warmer climate, and
Grandmother Dakin came from Clarksdale to care for Rose, Tom and
Dakin.

Her arrival was the happiest moment Rose and Tom had known since
the previous July. Grand was a benediction in their lives: "Her coming,"
Tennessee Williams wrote later, "meant nickels for ice cream, quarters
for movies, picnics in Forest Park ... 'Grand' was all that we knew of
God in our lives!" Her sweetness, her generosity and her unselfishness
embraced them for all the years until her death. "Grand cared for us in
every crisis," Dakin remembered, "from Mother's Spanish influenza
through a series of operations she had in the 1920s and 1930s. Even my

father had a great respect for her and was polite and courtly around her. He recognized quality in ladies, after all."

After about two weeks near the West Coast, Edwina and Cornelius returned to St. Louis. She was not entirely recovered, however, and her features were pinched and drawn. But there was something else that struck Rose and Tom about their parents. The cool politeness that characterized Cornelius's visits to his family in the South, the enigmatic distance that seemed to separate him emotionally from his wife and children, and Edwina's resentment of his drinking and gambling and carousing — these now seemed to have frozen the couple in a mutual hostility. Grand returned to Clarksdale, the Williams family moved to a dark apartment at 4633 Westminster Place, and life at home turned chillingly sour.

The new apartment had only two small windows, in the front and rear rooms, and a fire escape blocked the smoky light from a back alley. Edwina, nevertheless, did what she could to make it habitable.* She told the children that better days were ahead, that this was only a temporary stopping-place. Again, she tried to learn to cook, and again the results were not happy: her neighbor Mrs. Katzenstein could succeed only in helping her to perfect a variation on her standard cake.

As if life had not darkened enough, in 1921 Edwina miscarried her fourth child and had a long and difficult recovery. From this she returned to her children with amazing energy and determination, and it is easy to admire the courage and cheer — most of which was carefully and generously manufactured for the benefit of her children — that this small woman brought to an increasingly unhappy life. The rector's daughter, accustomed to a gentler society, a more elegant atmosphere, a servant and well-bred, courteous neighbors and the thousand details of life among the Southern gentry, was sustaining a terrible demotion.

Over the next several years, the family moved almost a dozen times; there were more moves, in fact, than there had been in Mississippi. By the time Thomas Williams was fifteen, he and his mother and sister had lived in more than sixteen different homes. This certainly contributed to the pattern of geographical instability in his later life, when a kind of gypsylike impermanence and wandering characterized even his most successful years.

---

* The rooms at 4633 Westminster Place are the setting for Tennessee Williams's first professional success, and the building was later named "The Glass Menagerie Apartments." The situation and time of the play, however, and the ages of its characters, are based on the life of the Williams household about a dozen years later, and at a different address.

There was, of course, a severe housing shortage at the end of World War I. In addition, more than once Cornelius gambled away his salary, or spent household money on liquor, resulting in the family's inability to pay back rent. Yet another reason was that Edwina was obsessed with the idea that somehow they would be able to live, even in St. Louis, in the more elegant manner they had once known — the manner befitting what she thought was their aristocratic station.

"The many moves we made," Dakin said years later, "were motivated by mother's desire to find something a little bigger and better than what we'd had. And somehow we always seemed to be following in the foot-steps of the Jameson family. Paul Jameson was my father's boss at Inter-national Shoe, and he showered my family with attention. Much of the furniture in our apartment came from the Jameson house, or was a gift from Paul. He paid for mother's recuperation trip when she had in-fluenza. I inherited some of his son's clothes and his bicycle, and even, before that, his baby-carriage. Paul Jameson became something of a pro-tector and a provider to my family — especially when my father became less and less responsible — and this was certainly due to his very warm feelings toward mother. The Jamesons went for picnics with us to Forest Park almost every Sunday. This was one way for mother to get away from Cornelius, and there was no way he could prevent it."

Nothing more than warmth of feeling should be assumed about this friendship, however, regardless of what other desires may have been pres-ent. Edwina Dakin Williams was too much the Victorian belle to have permitted the emergence or release of anything but the most innocent affection, and Paul Jameson, according to Dakin, "was a very moral man, too, with a family he cared deeply about." Years later, Edwina often spoke openly about the friendship, about the attentive generosity that meant so much to her when her own marriage ceased to have any mean-ing and when she found it difficult to provide necessities — much less luxuries — for her children. She spoke to her own mother about it, and she spoke to her daughter-in-law, Joyce Croft Williams (Dakin's wife), about it. She hid nothing because there was nothing to hide. But there is no doubt that Paul Jameson was, in the strictest sense of the term, Ed-wina's gentleman caller.

This relationship was the only light in the dark years of the early 1920s, when life became increasingly dismal. Over the period of the next dozen years, after her miscarriage, Edwina suffered at least eight illnesses requiring surgery, one of them life-threatening and resulting in a total hysterectomy. Each time her mother went to the hospital — and eventually each time a doctor's visit was announced — Rose was almost paralyzed with terror. If her mother died, she would be at the mercy of a father whose airy unconcern and drunken moods kept her in a constant state of anxiety. For a long while, Rose identified with her mother to the point that she would develop simultaneous aches and pains, and suffer identical symptoms. She claimed, with increasing agitation and unreason, that the food was poisoned, that she was dying, that strangers were going to kill them all, and her unhappy state often effected an upset stomach, a sick headache or a fainting spell. And Tom, from age ten, could do nothing but watch, confused and fearful, as the family that had known such genteel peace in Mississippi was thrown into a bitter destiny from which rescue seemed impossible.

Cornelius was a shrewd businessman, popular with his peers and respected by his superiors, and the records of the International Shoe Company reveal that by January 1922 he had been promoted to a managerial position at the warehouse on Washington Avenue. But he was also increasingly alcoholic, a passionate poker player and something of a wildcat. Had he not squandered so much of his money, his family would not have had to live so frugally.

Cornelius was not only volatile and unpredictable and frightening to Rose and Tom, he was also positively intimidating. "He took no joy in the children," Edwina wrote, "seeming to consider them just a nuisance, as though he wished they had never been born. All but Dakin; he and Dakin would listen for hours to the ball game on the radio. Because Rose and Tom did not care for baseball, they were a total loss. . . . Because Tom preferred to read, or write, or go to the movies rather than play baseball, his father contemptuously called him 'Miss Nancy.' Cornelius proved little better than the boys at school who taunted him with cries of 'sissy.' " Of this time in his life, Thomas Lanier Williams said later about his father, "I hated him."

"Life at home was terrible," according to Dakin, "just terrible. By the late 1920s, mother and father were in open warfare, and both were good combattants. He came home drunk and picked up a bill — perhaps for Tom's clothing or schoolbooks — and he'd fly into a rage. 'How dare you spend money on Tom — books! a coat!' and he'd scream something terrific and there'd be a vicious row and finally mother would do her famous fainting act — always managing to fall on the couch, of course, so that she wouldn't hurt herself. Once, however, it was so terrible that she ran into the bedroom and locked herself in. He broke down the door, and in doing so the door hit her and broke her nose. That time she really fainted."

One brief time of calm intervened. "There had been a sex party of some kind among some employees of International Shoe," Dakin continued, "and my father and another employee had contracted gonorrhea from a prostitute. That was a big deal, and it was only because Dad told the truth that he was allowed to keep his job once the word got out at the office. The other fellow lied and was fired." For weeks, Cornelius crept in and out of the apartment in silence — and nearly on his knees, for sheer embarrassment and contrition.

This unhappy scenario took a greater toll on Rose than on either of the two boys. "In her transition to St. Louis, removed from security and thrown into a world of alarm and despair, Rose had hideous inner turmoil in trying to cope with life. She was fragile and sensitive, and she couldn't cope." So Tom remembered his sister's gradual entrance into an inner world of darkness and unreality and, eventually, complete psychotic breakdown.

"Rose was caught in the middle of all this," Dakin agreed. "Her first ten years of life were more peaceful, in Mississippi. Then here they were in St. Louis, and everything conspired for the poor girl's illness. We had very little money and no status, and people in the neighborhood had nothing but contempt for people like us 'poor whites.' The change was a great shock for Rose."

There were some fruitless attempts to bring some pleasure or peace to the girl during her teens, but everything seemed doomed. For a time Edwina took her parents' advice — and some of the savings her mother offered — and arranged for Rose to have violin lessons. On a December evening in 1922, the Elise Aehle School of Music offered a "Costume Violin Recital" at the North Side YMCA Hall. The second item on the program was Rose Williams's rendition of Papini's "Romance," which turned out to be a musical and emotional disaster. She froze in terror, repeated several passages, and finally stopped abruptly in the middle of playing. Her family took her away shaking and in tears.*

Finally, the only refuge seemed escape.

After a brief time at Hosmer Hall — a private junior high school for which Grandmother Dakin once again contributed tuition money — Rose was sent to All Saints, an Episcopal junior college in Vicksburg.

* The events surrounding this are fictionalized in Tennessee's short story, "The Resemblance Between a Violin Case and a Coffin."

The Reverend had been offered a pastorate there for a year, and Rose, at about the age of seventeen, was sent for a formal introduction to society.

"She was doing fine there," Dakin remembered, "but father and Aunt Belle insisted that she be sent to Knoxville for her debut, and it was a catastrophe. She was from out of town, and so no one came. Then, as she was returning, she was delayed at a train station because of floods. Apparently she was approached by a drifter, who made a pass at her or said something vulgar, and by the time she got back to St. Louis she was almost hysterical."

Her mother, soon after, enrolled her at the Rubicam Business College, hoping she would learn to be a stenographer, but that did not turn out well either — she could sustain neither the pressure nor the group contact — and after being hired as receptionist for a dentist she was very quickly dismissed. At home, she soon developed a chronic sick stomach, but none of the tests at Barnes Hospital revealed a physical cause. "It was just the trauma of living in that warring household," according to Dakin. "Things were much worse for her and for Tom than for me. I was Dad's favorite, he took me out and ignored them. Also, I had been raised in St. Louis, in that unfortunate environment, from the start. There was no abrupt change for me — I had been toughened for it. But it shattered Rose's mind, and it affected Tom deeply too."

At the same time, however, there was for Tom the beginning of a more creative refuge. Again with contributions from her mother to the household pocketbook (from which Cornelius took generously for his card games and illegal liquor), Edwina bought Tom a used portable typewriter, thinking it would aid in schoolwork. "It immediately became my place of retreat, my cave, my refuge," he wrote later. At the typewriter he transformed the confusion, the bitterness, the longings into poems, and for a time he clacked out a diary in which he recorded little anecdotes about St. Louis street life. The poems became reflections of his acute observances of everything from a stranger's funny hat to the folds of a flower.

Soon the first writings by Thomas Lanier Williams were published — in the newspaper *Junior Life,* at Ben Blewett Junior High School, which he attended from 1923 to 1926. In October 1924, his short ghost story "A Great Tale Told at Katrina's Party" was considered suitable for the Halloween issue. Not long after, two poems appeared, the first probably inspired by a brief summer visit to his grandfather (then almost seventy), the second an example of the nature ode that every aspiring adolescent poet in every generation seems compelled to try.

"Old Things"

In the silence of the garret,
   'Midst rusted things of long ago,
Aloft from the clamor of life below,
   Old things — sallowed and hallowed,
   Grayed in the gloom;
Things from the old life
   In the dusk of their tomb.
This is the place for him and his dreams,
His old gray head bowed over the remnants
   Of days that are dead.
The silver candelabrum blazes anew,
And the tapestry blooms to a brighter hue.
   The melodeon chimes
   A faint caprice,
And the whole world dims to a softened peace.
Eyes gently shine through
The dusk of years
Old faces he sees
Old voices he hears
Amidst the rusted things of long ago.

"Nature's Thanksgiving"

The Bob-White is whirring
And beating, and throbbing;
The wood-brook is singing
And happily sobbing;
The carnival leaves
In resplendent descent,
Fall in a glory o'er merry content.
The wood has all colored,
And flaunting in pride,
Is swaying and laughing
Before they subside
To the sleep —
And the dark —
Of the winter.

When the fledgling, thirteen-year-old poet brought the school newspaper home, his mother thought his contributions were charming, and his grandparents' reply to a copy he sent was a hearty encouragement, and a dollar. In June 1925, the Ben Blewett yearbook printed Thomas Williams's essay "Demon Smoke," which addressed the problem of factory fumes in downtown St. Louis (not the dangers of cigarettes).*

That summer, Edwina — again with help from her mother's purse — took her three children to Elkmont, Tennessee, a mountaintop resort, and they detoured on their return to visit the Dakins. During those weeks, Rose seemed more calm than at any time since they had moved to St. Louis. This respite would not last long.

From 1926 to 1928, while life at home alternated between merely tense and openly awful, Tom wore out generous supplies of typewriter ribbons. When he transferred to Soldan High School (after still another family move), he at once began contributing to both the newspaper and yearbook, and his review of the film *Stella Dallas,* which he saw with a girlfriend, became the English class topic for several days.† Bored with school, he preferred his poetry, his movie reviews and his brief essays on St. Louis life. The only other activity that engaged his enthusiasm was swimming, which Aunt Belle taught him in Memphis during the summer of 1926.

Edwina, meanwhile, was convinced that Rose's "trouble" would yield to prayer and hymn-singing, and she marched her children to church every Sunday while Cornelius slept off the effects of the previous night. "Mother," Dakin recalled, "became something of a fanatic about Protestant religious things, even though the only church nearby was Presbyterian and she had been raised 'high church' Episcopalian. Her voice floated loudly above the others, and of course Tom and I had to join the choir, which we weren't very keen on." The church-going had no apparent effects on Rose's turmoil, however. She was a delicately pretty young woman with a sweet, slightly vacant expression, but the men who came to the Williams apartment to visit or date her rarely returned or called a second time, for they were greeted either with a scowl and a sarcastic remark from Cornelius, or by a teary-eyed Rose, who had just been through some mysterious, unpleasant ordeal.

By the last years of high school, Tom and his family were living at

---

* Three years later, he won a five-dollar prize in the essay contest sponsored by a group called the Citizens' Smoke Abatement League. St. Louis was apparently having serious industrial pollution problems, and concerned residents were publicizing the dangers.
† His review treated the 1925 silent version of *Stella Dallas,* which was directed by Henry King and starred Belle Bennett and Ronald Colman.

6254 Enright, in five small rooms of a three-story, depressing red brick apartment. At University City High School, to which he had transferred, a great deal soon became clear about him.

First, it was apparent that he was not interested in formal education or the ordinary St. Louis adolescent social life. "Tommy Williams was not socially inclined toward the group," one of his teachers remembered. "He had too many thoughts of his own. His grades were average. There was no evidence of brilliance in his work. I fear he was not well-adjusted. In the period I knew him [1927–1929] he was never clear about tomorrow's lesson."

But he was clear about his writing, and where he wanted it to take him. He had won a five-dollar third prize for a letter that answered the intriguing question, "Can a Good Wife Be a Good Sport?" His reply, published in the national magazine *Smart Set* in May 1927, was a resounding negative; he wrote in the style of a young man who finds that his wife, bored with home life, is dating other men. If being a good sport means "drinking, smoking, and petting . . . I don't think that a wife can be that kind of a 'good sport.'" The editors could not have known that the letter was an ingenious fabrication.

A more innocent, real-life "good sport" was the girlfriend he had taken to see *Stella Dallas*. Hazel Kramer, the daughter of a man who reported to Cornelius at International Shoe, was a tall, slightly plump but pretty classmate who became Tom's constant companion. She was, he insisted for the rest of his life, his one great female love — but the love was strictly Platonic. "Tom and Hazel were extremely close all through the last years of high school," Dakin said. "They were always in each other's company — running around together, dating, laughing, going to the Tivoli and Variety movie theatres near by, or to the museum or the library. With her he was open, he had fun. But Father felt that if they went away to college together, as they planned, they'd get married. This, he said, would ruin Tom's chances for financial independence. So he determined to put a stop to that friendship."

Tom wrote later that Edwina was opposed to Hazel, too, but on other grounds:

"My mother did not approve of my attachment to Hazel . . . nor for that matter had Miss Edwina ever seemed to want me to have any friends. The boys were too rough for her delicate son, Tom, and the girls were, of course, too 'common.' . . . [And she] disapproved more of Hazel's mother."

He claimed that their friendship ripened into romantic but sexually unconsummated love, and that it lasted eleven years. In fact — in this as in so many memories that were freighted with feeling — he exaggerated, turning the pleasantly unexceptional into the melodramatic. He and Hazel knew each other well for about three and a half years. Then, not only because his parents disapproved but also because they were both changing rapidly and developing other interests, they drifted apart. Something of her remained in his heart forever, nonetheless — something perhaps more fraternal than romantic. He could enjoy with Hazel the pastimes and diversions that had become impossible with Rose.

"She married another man," Williams reported later, "but killed herself when she was still very young." His memory of her is represented, however, in the reference to a woman named Rose Kramer — in his one-act play *Hello from Bertha,* written shortly after Hazel's death — whose name and fate combine the physical and mental conditions of both his sister and his friend.

In 1928, however, two happy events brightened Tom's life.

He had submitted to the editor of a "pulp" magazine called *Weird Tales* a short story, "The Vengeance of Nitocris." It was a surprisingly lurid account of an Egyptian queen who avenges the execution of her brother, who had been guilty of sacrilege, by inviting those responsible for his death to a dinner. She floods the banquet hall, drowning all the hapless guests and thoroughly enjoying herself in the deed. The idea had come to him from class readings (there is a similar story in Herodotus's *History*), and the style mimics the worst kind of schoolboy translation. ("Hushed were the streets of many-peopled Thebes," he began. "Weird, high-noted incantations of a wailing sound were audible through the barred doors.") But the story has a sure sense of horror, and the final scene is worthy of the magazine's name, as the wickedly loyal Nitocris watches the death agonies of her victims ("Much pleasure might she derive by recalling that picture . . ."). He later thought that the story "set the keynote for most of [my] work that has followed," a reference no doubt to its shocking finale rather than to its patent lack of poetic diction.

By the time the readers of *Weird Tales* received the issue with his story, in August, Tom had joyfully departed St. Louis for a long summer holiday. Up to that time, his only excursions had been with his mother, or to visit the Dakins, or to summer camp with his brother. But for the summer of 1928, Reverend Dakin had coordinated a European tour for members of his parish, and Tom was invited to come along without cost. It would be one of the great experiences of his life, for at seventeen he had seen only small parts of three states.

"His great affection for his grandfather was sealed with this trip," according to a later friend. "The Reverend opened the world to him, and somehow all his later returns to Europe were associated with this earlier, brief journey. And windows were opened — perhaps the only windows during those early, formative years."

Tom traveled to Clarksdale to meet the tour group, and a lavish party was given for their farewell by the Dakins' neighbor Mrs. Wingfield — a name Tom would later borrow for one of his most famous characters. The *Clarksdale Daily Register* reported that "the hospitalities [were] marked with charm and distinction, and sustained Mrs. Wingfield's well-known reputation as a most gracious hostess."

From there the group went by train to New York for four days. Grandfather took him to see *Show Boat* on Broadway, and Tom was bedazzled by the staging and deeply moved by Helen Morgan's plaintive singing of "Bill." On July 6, they all departed the Biltmore Hotel and boarded the *Homeric*. For the first two days at sea, Tom was violently ill. Then he recovered, in time for the glamour of shipboard life to which Grandfather gaily introduced him.

Chapter Two

GHOSTS
(1928–1937)

There's freedom, Joe, and freedom's the big
thing in life. It's funny that some of us don't
even get it until we're dead.

—Mother, in *The Long Good-bye*

ON FRIDAY, July 13, 1928, the *Homeric* docked at Southampton. Tom wrote home that in spite of Grandfather's permission to have a Manhattan cocktail, he preferred ginger ale. But two days later they were in Paris, and at once he was captivated by the City of Lights: he drank a whole glass of champagne, he said in another letter to his mother, and he found it very refreshing indeed after a day trip from the Hotel Rochambeau to the Louvre and Versailles. Next day, Grandfather took him and a few selected members of their group to the Folies Bergère and to Moulin Rouge. Tom assured Edwina that the spectacles noted for scantily clad dancing girls were more artistic than immodest and that, after all, conventions learned at home had best be forgotten when in Paris. Then he described a lavish production of Gounod's *Roméo et Juliette* at the Paris Opera, which had a powerful effect on him. Shakespeare's lovers came alive, the composer's melodies echoed in him for days, and — though he thought the acting wooden — the romantic atmosphere corresponded to something deep but untapped within him.

Marseilles was their next stopping-place, and soon they were in Monte Carlo for a day's swimming in the transparent blue waters of the Mediterranean. By August 4 they had not only toured the doge's palace in Venice but had also shopped for souvenirs with money saved by skipping an occasional meal. Then they reversed their journey, visiting Milan and then proceeding to Montreux and to the castle of Chillon, where the signatures of Byron, Shelley, Dickens and Harriet Beecher Stowe were scratched on the walls. Almost two weeks were spent making excursions from Interlaken, and at last they traveled by steamer along the Rhine to Cologne, where Tom was stunned by the beauty of northern Europe's largest Gothic cathedral.

By late August he was back in St. Louis, and Edwina greeted him with an envelope containing a check for thirty-five dollars from the Popular Fiction Publishing Company, representing payment for "The Vengeance of Nitocris." But Tom did not need remuneration to go on with his writing. As he began his last year of high school — and when he should have been devoting time to mathematics and history — he set to the task of transforming his "Trip Diary" into a series of travel articles. From October through April, the University City High School newspaper regularly featured the colorful, detailed accounts of his European holiday.

The records for the school commencement that year indicate Thomas Williams's rank was fifty-third in a class of eighty-three — hardly a foretoken of collegiate success. At his father's insistence, he enrolled even before graduation in two additional correspondence courses in typing and shorthand; neither the money nor the talent for more education was in sight. His mother preserved an exercise page on which he had typed five times: "There is a difference between talent and genius. Talent does what it can. Genius what it must. But it is the little more that makes the difference." This she thought an extraordinary insight. It is doubtful, however, that she recognized it as an excerpt from Bulwer-Lytton's "Last Words of a Sensitive Second-Rate Poet."

For it was in fact poetry and poets that claimed his attention that first half-year of 1929, and that certainly accounted for his disappointing record in French and civics (his fourth year of Latin yielded surprisingly good results).

During the summer, there were happy and painful moments. Grandmother sent money for the incidental expenses of a year at college, Cornelius agreed to his attendance, and Tom saw a move to the University of Missouri at Columbia, one hundred fifty miles west, as a great leap toward his goal of becoming a poet. The excitement enabled him to endure a gruesome accident. He slipped on a diving board at the Bellerive Country Club (where his father had a guest membership), hit the cement, and opened his eyes to see a puddle of blood and all his front teeth on the grass before him.* A bridge was hastily fitted before his departure for Columbia, but several readjustments were necessary over the years before permanent dentures were inserted.

Less than a three-hour automobile ride from St. Louis in later years, Columbia was in 1929 difficult to reach from the eastern part of Missouri.

---

* The country club, with a slight orthographic change, gave its name to the DuBois estate (Belle Reve) in *A Streetcar Named Desire*, years later.

"One had to go by a sort of Toonerville Trolley, through Centralia, or by hitchhiking, or by another branch line through McBaine," recalled David Loth, who had graduated a few years earlier. "The townspeople there were mostly very poor black people who worked in its enormous shoe factory, and of course the university was restricted to whites — it was as quietly prejudiced as mainstream St. Louis society."

The academic reputation, however, was something for alumni and students to celebrate. The University of Missouri at Columbia has America's oldest school of journalism, founded in 1908 by the country printer Walter Williams, a man of astonishing vision. Soon it began issuing the daily campus newspaper, the *Columbia Missourian,* and thereafter the major urban newspapers of America always numbered a percent of their staffs as Columbia alumni.

For the first two years, students enrolled in general liberal arts courses prior to the concentration in journalism, and every young man was obliged to enroll in the Reserve Officers Training Corps (ROTC) military training program. Tom may have wanted to be a poet, but Cornelius rightly predicted that would be a short route to poverty, and insisted on journalism. And even before Tom had arrived on campus, his father had also decided that his son should apply for admission to Alpha Tau Omega house, a new fraternity whose enthusiasm for sports and healthy male competitiveness in school and social life Cornelius believed would correct his son's shyness and sensitivity.

"There were no Jews in any fraternities, of course," Loth remembered, "since all the Greek fraternities were restricted. Men there, who paid seventy-five dollars a month for room, board and dues, lived somewhat better than those in the dormitories, where life was very Spartan for the rest of us. There were gradations in the fraternities, too — Beta Theta Pi was considered the most prestigious, and was comprised mostly of society men from St. Louis, those with old money." He remembered that school life was strict and serious, and students were expected to formulate clear professional plans quite early. Loth, for one, was already on his way by 1929 to writing a long and distinguished series of historical biographies — *The Brownings, Lorenzo the Magnificent* and *Royal Charles* among the most noted.

There was at Columbia a nominal academic fee of forty dollars a term (to cover library, health clinic and incidental fees), and over the next three years Rosina Dakin provided this sum. When Tom was a month into his first year, the great stock market crash was announced, and school life for some of the 3300 students and 250 journalism majors terminated abruptly. But the Dakins' generosity enabled Tom to remain and, to his father's satisfaction, to accept the pledge to Alpha Tau Omega, whose new residence was just completed and ready for the forty men who prepared to move in. In a happy letter to his parents in October, Tom wrote that fraternity life looked exciting. The only unhappy note is his expression of concern for Rose's "long trouble," which had by this time necessitated confinement in a private sanatorium.

In addition to his courses that first term — English composition, citizenship, intermediate French, geology and ROTC — there was a great emphasis on social life. Nearby were two two-year women's colleges, Christian College for Girls (staffed by members of the Church of Christ) and Stevens College (founded by Baptists).

"Campus life was free and easy," according to David Loth, "but there was very little sexual license. Women's dormitory rules were very strict, at the two women's colleges and at Columbia, and there was no such thing as parietal hours or visiting women's rooms. Social life consisted mostly of going to one of the two movie theatres in town, or to campus dances, or to a concert or sports event — usually in foursomes or sixsomes. Relations between the sexes were very formal, virtually no one had a car, no one had liquor, and drugs were of course unknown. There were occasional rumors of sexual activity among a few notorious students, but it would have been extremely clandestine, and certainly not generally acceptable conduct."

By the end of the year, Tom's small circle of friends included two fraternity brothers who took the same classes, and a girl who lived at the Alpha Chi Omega sorority. Her name was Esmeralda Mayes, and their friendship — based on a shared poetic sensitivity — continued for the next two years. They read aloud together, took picnic lunches off campus, discussed art and literature and love and the future. Tom's few brief surviving entries about her in notebooks are simple records of meetings, readings, talks about school.

Cornelius was unimpressed with the report for the 1929–1930 academic year, however. Although there were B's in composition and citizenship both terms, a B and a C in French, and C's in geology and literature, the performance in the area his father considered most important was poor — the record showed a D in ROTC the first term, and F the second. Tom was warned about this, and about the eighteen absences that had earned him an additional negative credit that year. Cornelius acted as if the modest sums for Tom's education were coming exclusively from his own pocket — but worse, his son, the son of a Spanish-American War veteran, was not on his way to a military commission.

Tom was, on the other hand, on his way to being a serious writer, and his poems occupied the greater part of his time. In the spring of 1930 he had also submitted to the Dramatic Arts Club a one-act play, *Beauty Is the Word,* which was soon staged in competition.

"We went through the plays and found that Thomas Lanier Williams's was not submitted in the correct format," remembered Professor Donovan Rhynsburger, who was one of the contest judges. "But I thought it showed promise and was worthy of honorable mention." And so it was reported, in the *Missourian* dated April 12, 1930, that *Beauty Is the Word* was the first freshman play to be selected for citation. The paper added that it was "a play with an original and constructive idea, but the handling is too didactic and the dialog often too moralistic." Preserved in the library of the university, the original twelve-page typescript of the first play by Williams contains a simple hand-drawn stage diagram, character descriptions, and the short text.

The story concerns a South Pacific missionary and his wife (improbably and perhaps satirically named Abelard and Mabel); their servant and the wife's niece and her husband. The play both endorses the minister's life and corrects his tendency to Victorian prudery: after the missionary refers to the "shameless nakedness of the natives," the young niece insists that "fear and God are the most utterly incompatible things under the sun. Fear is ugliness. God — at least *my* God — is Beauty."

In May, his name was again in print — this time for a less controversial product, the short story "The Lady's Beaded Bag," which appeared in the campus literary magazine. At the same time, another one-act play was ready for production — an eight-page family melodrama he called *Hot Milk at Three in the Morning,* in which a young married couple argue about their poverty, their infant and their feeling of entrapment. "I thought, when I read it," said Donovan Rhynsburger years later, "that it was quite consciously modeled on [Eugene] O'Neill's [one-act play] *Before Breakfast*" — in which a hero is driven to suicide by his nagging wife.* Whatever the source, the text is strident and expresses the motif of emotional confinement that would emerge in all his great full-length

---

* It is equally possible that Williams's play was inspired by Strindberg's *The Stronger* (a two-character play in which only one speaks), which was almost certainly the model for O'Neill's *Before Breakfast. Cf.* Louis Sheaffer, *O'Neill: Son and Playwright* (Boston: Little, Brown, 1968, pp. 351–352 *et alibi*).

plays. Production of *Hot Milk* was, however, postponed until the spring of 1932.

Back in St. Louis for the summer of 1930, Tom renewed his friendship with Hazel Kramer, in spite of his parents' clear disapproval. Cornelius still resented the attachment on purely professional grounds — love and school, he insisted, were incompatible. Edwina, on the other hand, resented the relationship for a more subtle reason. "The fact is that she was jealous of any woman to whom Tom was friendly," according to a writer who knew her well.

He was glad, therefore, to return to Columbia in September, although the gap separating his academic performance from his personal preference continued to widen. That year, one of his fraternity brothers and house-mates came to know him probably better than anyone at the university. Elmer Lower had just joined the Alpha Tau Omega house, and for two years he saw Williams daily on campus. (After receiving his degree in 1933, Lower began a remarkable career in journalism and broadcasting; from 1963 to 1974 he was president of ABC News, and continued, even afterward, to teach and write as a visiting professor at his alma mater.)

"There were forty of us in the house that year," Lower recalled, "and we considered ourselves very lucky indeed. We ate well, thanks to Ola Crews, our affable and skilled cook, and our house-mother, Blanche Eckard, was a kindly widow who was very good to us all. In addition to the house-mother and house cook, there were two waiters who worked for the free meals that came with their job, and two houseboys who did all the chores — even to making our beds."

Tom Williams, according to Lower, was certainly not an exceptional student or fraternity brother, and could not be called gregarious. "Our friendship was based on a mutual enthusiasm for journalism, which we also shared with a third student, Harold Mitchell, a happy, smiling country boy from the small town of Lancaster, Missouri." This boy gave his name, some years later, to a major character in *A Streetcar Named Desire.*

In classes, however, the enthusiasm of Tom Williams was not so evident. That year, he accumulated thirty-six absences, which certainly contributed to a dismal record at end of term — two F's in military science, C's in zoology, history, composition, journalism and logic, D's in Greek history and French, and one B, in literature. Prudently, he avoided a visit home.

"His father visited him once, however," according to Lower, "either deliberately, because of the terrible record Tom was compiling, or because he had to go to the shoe factory nearby. ROTC was required of everyone only during the first two years on campus, but Tom's father announced that *his* son would have two additional years of it. That meant two days a week of class in military science, and a Wednesday afternoon parade on the quadrangle. For this, all ROTC men had to dress in the prescribed uniform of white trousers and a blue coat. But Tom, who was known for being absentminded, constantly forgot his white trousers, and bystanders would look over the parade to see one pair of blue trousers among eight hundred white. He looked a little ludicrous, which is how he often looked when something derived from his absentmindedness."

That absentmindedness, in fact, typified his schooldays, and fraternity brothers took advantage of him when he forgot his books in the common living room, or left a sweater in the dining hall. "Everybody thought he had two left feet, and he was gently picked on — but he took it all in good humor and without anger, and he never fought back. He kept very much to himself apart from some socializing with me and Harold Mitchell."

Socially, Lower remembers Williams as being almost unbearably shy. "He was too shy to ask a girl for a date, so Mitch and I had to find someone for him so we could have a triple-date for a dance or sports event. Tom wasn't a typical frat man or buddy, and he seemed awkward in groups, even during the simple and brief socializing that was permitted when we brought girls back to the frat house living room for a while. They had a ten o'clock curfew and were only allowed into the house if Mrs. Eckard were there in the parlor as chaperone."

But anyone who spent even an afternoon with Tom Williams discovered that his shyness did not mean a lack of humor. Everything and everyone seemed to amuse him, and he entertained his fraternity brothers with brief, spontaneous scenes of Southern life, his voice rising and falling as he enacted two or three roles in an impromptu skit. "He had a quietly ironic wit," as Lower recalled. "His small monthly allowance came in a letter from his father,* and at mail call Tom held up the check and announced, 'Ah, the Red Goose [the name of his father's branch at International Shoe]! The Red Goose flies again!' "

* Lower is correct: although the Dakins were paying for college fees, Cornelius supplied small sums for monthly expense, ROTC uniforms, etc.

The demands of school and his quiet preoccupation with his writing did not, however, diminish his concern for his sister's health. Tom wrote thanking Rose for a gift package of soap, oranges and a tie she sent in January 1931 and asking if she would visit him before May. But travel was beyond her endurance, and both brother and sister were disappointed.

So was Cornelius, who reacted to his son's poor grades by putting him to work at International Shoe in St. Louis for the summer of 1931; the employment files at 1509 Washington show that he was a temporary office clerk in the Continental Shoe Division from June 23 to September 15. Tom hated it — he had hoped to spend the summer with Hazel Kramer and with his poetry notebooks, but he felt he could put up with the warehouse those few months. What he found even more tiresome than the clerical work, however, was the time he had to spend with his father:

"It's true that Dad never seemed greatly concerned about Rose and me," he reflected later, "but in my case, I can't help feeling it wasn't all his fault. If Mother hadn't held me so fiercely close to her, the situation might not have got so bad between us that I *froze* when he entered the house. I might even have got to know him as a man — and I sometimes feel he *wanted* to know me, but the trouble lay in the fact that, knowing I *was* afraid of him, he resented that knowledge so much he turned against me."

Living with his parents that summer was made even more awkward, in addition, by the rides with Cornelius to Washington Street each day. "We used to drive into work every day.... I used to try to think of something to say to him. I would compose three sentences in my mind ... something like, 'The smog is heavy today,' or 'The traffic is bad,' and to each one he would grunt in some disparaging way [as if to say], 'What's this son-of-a-bitch trying to talk to me for?' ... We were just so tongue-tied with each other." The admixture of fear, resentment and muted longing that prevailed between father and son was soon satirized in Tom's writing, for within a few years he had written the first draft of a one-act play about a shoe salesman with his own father's first two initials: Charlie Colton, in *The Last of My Solid Gold Watches,* is a pathetic man, out of step with time and himself.

Back at Columbia in September, he was admitted into the school of journalism, and there occurred what Elmer Lower called "one of the most amazing and amusing things of the year." Never a participant in sports, Tom was urged to help maintain the honor of Alpha Tau Omega by competing in a wrestling match; the prize would be a silver cup for the house. "At 115 pounds, and with his natural timidity, this augured disaster. The event pitted him against two wiry farm-boys, and Tom — after lots were drawn — was chosen for the finals. A few days before the match, a new aspect of his character and humor emerged, however. He attached a sign on the house bulletin board — 'WILLIAMS ULTIMA-TUM: LIQUOR! LIQUOR! MUST HAVE LIQUOR TO FORTIFY MYSELF AGAINST THE AGGRESSIVE AGRARIANS!' So we got hold of some bathtub gin or some moonshine from the gin-runners up-state. Tom lost, in two falls, but he tried hard, and his efforts helped the total house score." ("I attacked my adversary with great fury," Williams said years later. "I used activity to conceal my lack of skill. I lost the match, but afterward I was known in the house as Tiger Williams.")

That autumn things happened quickly. Although his grades for the term never rose higher than C's, he was writing feverishly and was one of eleven to receive honorable mention out of fifty-five entrants in the Mahan Story Contest. And the writing was accompanied — and per-haps even precipitated at this point — by what must have been a strange and terrifying possibility for him, as it would have been for any Missouri student in 1931. "I was deeply in love with my roommate," he said long afterward, "but neither of us knew what to do about it." According to his very different account in *Memoirs*, the roommate knew very well what to do about it — and offered more than indirect hints — but Tom shiv-ered with anxiety and aborted any sexual contact.

"None of us ever had any inkling of homosexual tendencies in him or his roommate during those years," according to Elmer Lower, "and it would have been certainly difficult to cover it up. Any such activity would have had to be very discreet, and very private, and there simply wasn't very much privacy. Heterosexual sex was rare enough, and mys-terious enough, and alternatives weren't even a topic for conversation." The account in *Memoirs*, while perhaps not a deliberate distortion of the truth, probably represents Williams's confusion, at the time of writing, between 1931 and a crucial period in his sexual development that oc-curred later in the decade.

Oddly coincidental with this time of his life was an artistic experience that he found overwhelming. Just when his literature professor was lec-turing on the plays of Henrik Ibsen, a touring production of *Ghosts*, star-ring the legendary Alla Nazimova, came to campus. "It was so moving that I had to go and walk in the lobby during the last act," he remembered. "I'd stand in the [doorway] and look in, then I'd rush back to the lobby again. I suppose that play was one of the things that made me want to write for the theatre."

Up to this time, Ibsen had been a fascinating and vaguely frightening playwright to Tom, but with *Ghosts* his interest became more personal and emotional than academic. From this time forward, the professional and artistic and personal links between himself and several major writers seemed very clear to him, and he quite consciously identified with those writers — not only in patterns of work, but also in the histories and destinies of their respective lives.

Ibsen was the first of these writers with whom he felt a special, deep bond. He learned that the Norwegian poet and dramatist, who lived from 1828 to 1906, had a youth very like his own: an early dislocation from the comfortable and the familiar to inhospitable new residences; the familiarity with a church and an asylum; undistinguished academic performance and an attempt at journalism. Shy in personality, withdrawn and embarrassed with peers, the outline of Ibsen's life up through his twenties resembled the contours of Tom's, and what appealed to him about Ibsen's *Emperor and Galilean* and *Ghosts* was the attempt to bridge the gap between flesh and spirit, and the obsession, through the stylistic convention of the "guilty secret," to disclose moral truth.*

For a paper that term, he wrote that the central theme of *Ghosts* concerned much more than a simple social problem. Through the use of inherited venereal disease as a symbol, Ibsen established a drama of ideas in which he could reflect on the tragedy of those who cannot liberate themselves from a dead past. Thus Tom came to an understanding that the title referred not only to the spirit of the once profligate, now dead Captain Alving, but to a psychologically bankrupt world in which there is no truth or freedom, a world in which moral diseases inherited from the past affect the living. He did not have to reflect long on his father (almost a duplicate of Captain Alving, with the drinking and the venereal disease), and on the condition of his sister Rose, to find the repetition of Ibsen's characters, his life and his spirit in himself and his own family.

---

* The disclosure of moral truth by unmasking a "guilty secret" is the major motif of a number of plays by Tennessee Williams: *A Streetcar Named Desire, Cat on a Hot Tin Roof, Suddenly Last Summer, Sweet Bird of Youth, The Night of the Iguana.* It also appears in a number of his short plays and stories.

At the same time, he was discovering the work of the Swedish play-wright August Strindberg (1849–1912); Williams's examination books and class notes reveal more than just poetic empathies with Strind-berg — they demonstrate an almost mystical feeling of spiritual brother-hood. In Strindberg he found, too, a tortured life, particularly with regard to his relations with women. From Strindberg he learned the dra-matic potential of a harsh family background, and one passage in *The Link* struck him as astonishingly relevant to his own situation with his parents: "There is room in me," says the baron to the baroness, "for both love and hatred, and while I love you one minute, I hate you the next." Very soon, it would be from Strindberg that he would take (as did Eu-gene O'Neill) the dramatic sense of those whom Louis Sheaffer has called "bound by the closest of ties as both victims and torturers of one another."

In Strindberg's life, however, Williams found additional dramatic ma-terial that suggested to him links between art and daily reality: the emo-tional insecurity of a poor childhood, and a connection with organized religion in his family; the attempt at journalism — and then a public re-jection for blasphemy. Strindberg's mental crisis almost led to madness, and his revolt against social conventions was accompanied by a deeply personal, mystic vision, periods of alcoholism, and mental instability. That season Williams read Strindberg's *Miss Julie,* whose tone of sexual antagonism and class conflict, brutal action and terse dialogue certainly influenced everything he wrote thereafter, especially *A Streetcar Named Desire.* As his life progressed, Williams noted, in conversations with friends and frequently in letters, that he and Strindberg had an unusual kinship.

But his absorption in the lives and writings of the two great Scandina-vian dramatists that year, while it had a profound effect on his inner life and the development of his art, had a more concrete and less constructive effect. In the spring semester of 1932, his pleasure at seeing *Hot Milk at Three in the Morning* was dampened by his D's in journalism courses and political science, C's in English and another journalism course and — the last straw for Cornelius — his fourth F in ROTC. In the last weeks of the term, perhaps knowing full well that the grades to be sent home would be dreadful, he cheerfully wrote to his father about Journalism Week and his place on the Greet and Guide Committee. The letter, dated May 9, 1932, is signed, "Lovingly, Tom." But within weeks he was out of school for good.

"Father used the excuse of poor grades to pull Tom out of Columbia," according to Dakin, "but the real reason was money. In 1932 our family was in a very bad way. Of course Tom's low grades in military education were especially repellent to Cornelius, since he had been in the Spanish-American War."

And so Tom had to leave the sanctuary of Columbia, his camaraderie with fraternity brothers and the intellectual routine of campus life. It was not, to be sure, the classes that ever held his interest; it was the freedom that he began to explore here, the reading and writing, and the first tentative steps toward an understanding of his own complex personality.

"There was absolutely no indication that Tom would become America's greatest playwright," according to Elmer Lower. "He was unremarkable in every way, and when he left he was simply doing what many had to do in the Depression. At the same time, Harold Mitchell left — and, like Tom, he later turned up to finish his degree at the University of Iowa. We remembered Tom Williams as a not especially colorful chap with his head always somewhere up in the clouds. He failed more than one examination because he forgot to appear at the right time and place, and his constant state of disorientation was finally fatal to his career at Columbia."

He had also to see Esmeralda Mayes for the last time. "He had been writing poems to her all along," Donovan Rhynsburger recalled. "In some way they were very devoted to each other. They read one another their poems and it was clear there was some kind of deep sharing, and then he was gone." But like Hazel Kramer she, too, is celebrated in his work — the simple, sensual character Esmeralda in *Camino Real* is given one of his loveliest speeches, and Esmeralda Mayes is also transformed into the odd, marginal Flora, the student poet's girlfriend in his short story "The Important Thing."

What followed was an arid, bleak time in the life of young Tom Williams — and so rudderless that in the telling over the years he exaggerated its most frustrating aspect. To the end of his life he insisted that immediately after the spring 1932 term at Columbia, his father put him to work in an odious, menial capacity at International Shoe, and that this job lasted for two years or three or four years (his dating of the period, and of events in general, was always at best an approximation). And virtually everyone who ever read about him or knew him had the idea of a three-year period in servitude to the warehouse, a time of such anxiety, such creative repression, that he was worn to total physical and mental collapse.

Although there is no doubt about the final toll the period of work took on him, the fact is that he did not work as a manual laborer, carrying huge, heavy boxes of shoes, nor was he employed for three years. The employment records show that he did not actually begin work there until June 24, 1934 and left on April 30, 1935 ("Ill Health" is marked on his card in the personnel office). Apart from the summer of 1931, then, his total period of employment at the warehouse was actually ten months. The remainder of the time, he read, wrote poetry, and endured the insufferably confining atmosphere of family life.*

There was good reason why steady, full-time employment could not begin in 1932. International Shoe was not hiring in that year, which was the lowest ebb of the Great Depression and the year in which one in four American workers was unemployed. Cornelius's position as a sales manager could not, as he had hoped, win his son a job, even if (as was not the case) Tom had had marketable skills to offer the company. Instead, he sent his son for almost a year to night classes in typing and shorthand, against the day when a clerical post might again become available. As late as October 1933, Tom was writing to the Dakins — who had retired to Memphis — that his father assured that a stenographic position would open if he passed the secretarial courses.

His writing, however, continued uninterrupted. Several months after he had resumed life in St. Louis, the alumni magazine of Columbia awarded him honorable mention in the second Mahan Story Contest. And by this time the English department there realized the talent they had lost. On December 10, 1932, Robert L. Ramsey, chairman of English, wrote: "Your absence from the University this year has been a matter of real regret to all of us who knew the excellent work you did here the last few years, especially in the field of creative writing. I hope very much you will be able to return and finish your course." He concluded by offering to submit Tom's story "Big Black: A Mississippi Idyll" to a St. Louis or Kansas City newspaper. It is hard to know who that perceptive group might have been "who knew the excellent work"

* The employment files suggest, however, that he may have been engaged on a *per diem* basis, paid perhaps by his father from petty cash or department budgets, but not as a full-time contracted employee for a three-year period. In addition, he seems to have performed what the factory called "piece-work," for which the company paid even anonymous workers in those days on a daily cash basis.

he had done, but universities and their spokesmen often have an astonishing hindsight in appreciating an outstanding former student.

An extraordinary fertile time then occurred, right in the middle of the
national and familial Depression, in spite of — and perhaps, again, to
some extent because of — Tom's unhappiness at home, boredom at business classes, anxiety for the declining health of Rose, and chafing under
his mother's formality and his father's tyranny. "Mother was an extremely difficult and demanding person during those years," according
to Dakin, who was working hard in high school. "She was so overly
attentive to us, and was clearly the model for Amanda in *The Glass
Menagerie.*"

Tom wrote poems, by the score, often on the streetcar by day and at
the kitchen table or on the front steps or in his room at night. For the
two-year period from early 1933 to early 1935, he received word that his
poems were accepted by publications around the country: *Neophyte* published "October Song" in its Christmas/New Year 1932–33 issue; *Inspiration* gave him first prize in the spring of 1933 for two poems, "Under
the April Rains" and "Her Heart Was a Delicate Silver Lyre"; his lyric
"Modus Vivendi" appeared in *Counterpoint* for July 1933; *L'Alouette* accepted his poem "Ave atque Vale" for its October 1933 number; *Voices,*
in New York, bought rights to "Cacti" and "After a Visit" and ran them
in the summer of 1934; and several other magazines and journals, suddenly aware of the new St. Louis poet who was being compared to Sara
Teasdale, wrote actively soliciting the right to publish his work. This
leavened the long months at Enright Avenue, and also enabled him to
turn over some money to Cornelius and Edwina. The poems themselves
are of doubtful merit and give little indication of the gifts that would
flourish later in his plays. Most of them seem written under the influence
of Teasdale, the St. Louis poet whose short, personal lyrics were extremely popular. Her suicide in January 1933, at the age of forty-eight,
shocked her student-admirers especially deeply.

During the summer of 1934 he worked at fever pitch on a short story
he called "Stella for Star"; it was the twenty-third submission he made
to the editors of *Story* magazine, and since he had at last been given a
position as temporary office clerk at International Shoe, he had to
polish the story at night. His mother remembered finding him in the
morning as she had left him hours before, slumped at a table in a haze of
cigarette smoke, a large, empty coffee pot at his side. There were many
weeks when he somehow survived on only an hour or two of sleep
nightly.

While the editors at *Story* were considering the latest submission, however, he was told that the St. Louis Writers Guild — to which he had also (and imprudently) sent "Stella for Star" — had awarded it first prize among seventy-six submitted in the Winifred Irwin short story contest, and the ten-dollar check was given to him in a brief ceremony in early 1935. Edwina was delighted, Cornelius made no comment, and Rose for once did not share her brother's joy — for she knew that Winifred Irwin had committed suicide after receiving what she thought was one too many rejection slips in her efforts to become a published writer.

At the same time that Tom was drifting into a black mood over his job at the warehouse, Rose was inhabiting almost exclusively a darker and more frightening inner world, for her two confinements in a private sanatorium had effected only slight, temporary respite from sudden attacks of hysteria and unreason. Tom tried to alleviate her misery, but his efforts were futile. He took her to a dance on Halloween of 1933, but the costumes and gaiety upset rather than lifted her spirits. That same season, a series of gentlemen callers Edwina had lined up for Rose caused emotional trauma, too. Elmer Lower recalled that "the very handsome Jim O'Connor, who was with us at Columbia, had met the Williams family, and apparently Tom's mother tried to set him up with Rose." Of this proposed match nothing is known except that there was only one, brief social call — and it may well have been just as it was later described in *The Glass Menagerie,* when the gentleman caller named Jim O'Connor is brought home to meet the lame, shy sister of the poet Tom.

Rose's phobias and obsessions multiplied throughout late 1934 and early 1935. For a time, she would eat only Campbell's tomato soup, saving the labels as if they were coupons for future discounts. (This example of her inexorable descent into unreason is exactly recalled in the case of Miss Collins in *Portrait of a Madonna.*) Edwina still hoped Rose's erratic behavior would pass if she met the right man. Cornelius seemed to have neither the time nor the interest to consider what was happening to his daughter, but it must also be remembered that Edwina denied him virtually every opportunity to share the family's problems.

"Rose became increasingly unhappy and threatened and depressed," according to Dakin, "and even Paul Jameson [Cornelius's superior and the generous provider for the Williams household] no longer interfered. We were at a real time of crisis. The fighting still continued at home, Dad's scandalous behavior wasn't stopped, and he had reached a halt in his upward mobility, professionally and socially. Tom and Rose became terribly fragile at the same time."

But in the unpredictable nature of such things, it was not Rose but Tom who first alarmed the family so severely that they knew a dramatic change was at once necessary.

He had, first of all, become increasingly absentminded, both at home and at the warehouse. It was only several months after a customer repeatedly complained about nondelivery of a $50,000 shipment that the staff traced the error to Tom; he had been given the data, put it in his pocket before lunch, and there it remained. In addition, there was a dramatic weight loss noticed by his mother. Insufficient sleep, high intake of caffeine, excessive smoking and a terrible inner turmoil — not only about his work, but about homosexual feelings and inclinations he only dimly understood (or refused to acknowledge) — conspired to put him on the verge of complete collapse.

A friendly co-worker and an evening at the movies figure as elements in the final weeks before Tom was sent away.

At International Shoe, there was a dark, burly, amiable worker assigned to a job near Tom. He was everything the young poet was not — at ease in crowds and with strangers, sure of his strength and confident of his ability to charm the ladies. He became Tom's closest companion at the warehouse, and with him Tom apparently felt accepted, even protected from some of the harshness that otherwise surrounded his life. Soon, however, the man married, and about ten years later he died. His name was Stanley Kowalski, and his family survived in St. Louis for many years after. It is perhaps hard to know how much of his character and personality are represented by the character with that name in *A Streetcar Named Desire,* but the attraction to him by Blanche DuBois is certainly something that the playwright himself first knew. There is no evidence of a realized homosexual affair between Williams and Kowalski, but according to Dakin it was clear that Tom had a powerful erotic and romantic attachment to Kowalski: Kowalski's name was often mentioned by Tom, and to see them together was to see a love-struck hero-worshipper and the idol of his dreams.

Very soon after Stanley's departure, which depressed him even further, he took Rose to see the film *The Scarlet Pimpernel* — on March 24, 1935, two days before his twenty-fourth birthday. Because they both became nervous in crowded streetcars, they returned by service-car (a kind of taxi-van). But during the ride, as if someone had thrown a switch inside him, Tom's heartbeat increased dramatically, he broke into a sweat, and he thought he was going to die of a stroke or a heart attack. "It was a

Edwina Estelle Dakin,
about the time of her marriage

Cornelius Coffin Williams

St. Paul's Rectory, Columbus, Mississippi

Thomas Lanier Williams

Rose Isabel Williams,
at Westminster Place

In Europe, summer 1928

Edwina Dakin Williams, 1936

Cornelius Williams, 1937

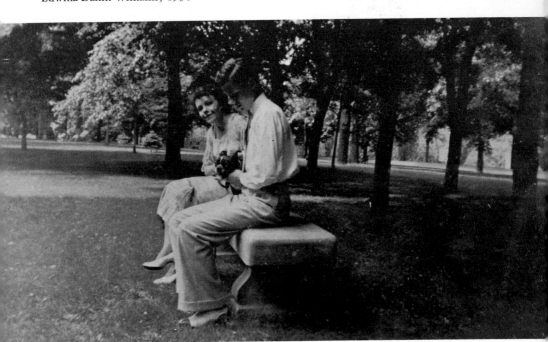

Rose and Dakin Williams,
in Forest Park, St. Louis, 1935

Rose, with a friend and Tom

Rose, just before surgery

terrible crisis of nerves," Dakin remembered, "a fierce anxiety attack which he thought forever after was a real heart seizure. That was the onset of his breakdown."

He was taken at once to a hospital, where tests determined that there was no cardiac incident, no sign of dangerous hypertension — in fact, nothing remarkable beyond evident exhaustion and underweight. During the next month he stayed home from the warehouse several days, and Dr. O. P. J. Falk made house calls to Enright Avenue at Edwina's urgent summons. But if Tom's physical condition was not so alarming, it was clear to doctor and family that he was in an acute state of emotional distress, and two unstable adults in one small apartment was certainly too much for them. Tom's resignation from International Shoe was accepted at the end of April, and in May he began a four-month recuperation in the warmth of the Dakin home at 1917 Snowden Avenue in Memphis.

His grandparents welcomed him with their usual generosity, without asking questions. Tom passed the first weeks lazily, enjoying Grandmother's rich meals, taking long walks through the streets of Memphis in the full bloom of springtime, and indulging himself in afternoon naps. But as he had scribbled in a notebook the previous season, "Words are a net to catch beauty," and he could not for long avoid working at his nets.* His rapid recovery is a testimony to his extraordinary resilience — a trait that characterized his entire life — and at this time it was given great forward momentum by a renowned writer and by a forgotten one.

Before the end of May 1935, Tom had visited the local branch library, and then the central and school libraries of Memphis, where he was enthralled by the life and writings of Anton Chekhov. From then on Chekhov, like Ibsen and Strindberg, was a spiritual mentor — and Chekhov's life he later saw as yet another model for his own. (Asked which playwrights he thought most influenced his work, he usually replied Strindberg and Chekhov.)

After reading at last *The Cherry Orchard* and *The Sea Gull* (which had been on a Columbia reading list he took with him to Memphis), he was soon engrossed in the three volumes of letters that had been translated by Constance Garnett and Louis Friedland. Although no full biography was yet available, these letters and Oliver Elton's *Chekhov* gave him a sense of kinship with the great Russian fabulist and playwright. Perhaps it is not

* The aphorism is put on the lips of Myra in "The Field of Blue Children," a short story he soon began and which was published in 1939.

too strong to say that in time Chekhov's life and destiny were in a deep, interior way assumed by Tom Williams.

After a mediocre school record, Chekhov had discovered the delight of private reading, theatregoing and the pleasures and rewards of writing comic sketches. He took a medical degree, but his writing always dominated, and as he developed the short story form he devoted himself more to serious tales of human struggle and physical illness. "A Dreary Story" and "The Steppe" and *Ivanov,* all written in 1888–1889, were certainly inspired by his experiences as a doctor. The failure of his play *The Sea Gull* in 1894 wounded him deeply, and he claimed at that time he would abandon the stage altogether — a promise which, fortunately, was broken two years later. Tom responded at once to the painful tone of the letters about Chekhov's childhood, seeing perhaps in the Russian writer's hated town of Taganog everything he resented about St. Louis. But it was Chekhov's gentle, elegiac explorations of the secret motives of characters that impressed him, and the tragic vision even within the comic sense that satirized the lack of human sharing. University professors were beginning to speak about Chekhov and a new psychological realism; in May 1935 Tom not only discovered the terms of that for himself, he found a dramatic mood that gripped his imagination and challenged his powers.

He admired most deeply *The Sea Gull,* for this was just the right time in his own life to appreciate its feeling for the sad extinction of youth and talent in an oppressive environment. Its sensitive characters moved him, and at the same time, without the pressure of college papers and examinations, he absorbed the technique of using real objects symbolically in a play: the sea gull, after all, represents not only the triumph of the spirit over adversity, but even the commoner fact of life then known to him — the killing of beauty by those ignorant of it. (In 1981 he wrote a free adaptation of *The Sea Gull,* called "The Notebooks of Trigorin," which was staged in Vancouver and later in Los Angeles. *The Sea Gull,* he thought, showed Chekhov as "the most moving writer." The young New Orleans writer in Williams's short play *The Lady of Larkspur Lotion,* when asked his name, cries out "Chekhov! Anton Pavlovitch Chekhov!")

The theme of beauty threatened or destroyed — already introduced in his college plays and in sheafs of unevenly written poems — he also found in *The Cherry Orchard,* whose title had the same symbolic resonances. And in that play's character of Peter Trofimov, Williams met himself: the university outcast; the threadbare, comic idealist; the eternal student and eternal adolescent; the marginal dreamer who works toward the realization of his dreams.

By June his outlook and energy had greatly improved, and in an affectionate letter to Dakin dated June 25 he congratulates his brother on good high-school grades and then explains an additional reason for his own cheerfulness: a neighbor's daughter, Bernice Dorothy Shapiro, had asked Tom to collaborate on a one-act play for her amateur theatre group. As it turned out, Bernice wrote only the prologue and epilogue, and Tom contributed the rest, a four-scene comedy about the troubled love affairs of two sailors. The play — called *Cairo, Shanghai, Bombay* — took the characters on an imaginary trip around the world in an effort to untangle their romantic anguish. With Miss Shapiro's name preceding Tom's, the play was performed by the Memphis Garden Players in the yard of its organizer, Alice Rosebrough. It was the first nonschool production, however modest, of any play by Thomas Lanier Williams, and its somewhat naïve romanticism does not eclipse its simple and credible descriptions, or the touching sweetness of the two young women characters. The leading lady, Tom added in the letter to Dakin, shouted so loudly that she sounded more like a fishmonger than an actress, but the production was great fun, it was turning his life around, and he was even making a brief, silent cameo in it.

It was perhaps, then, Chekhov and this play and the gentle encouragement of his grandparents in Memphis that summer that sealed his decision to write words for actors, and to create funny and dramatic scenes that could move an audience. From these months he could date himself as a working playwright, and it is actually at this time — long before he took steps to use a new name — that he thought of himself no longer as Thomas Lanier Williams, the quite ordinary son of a mismatched Southern couple, but as a new branch on the Williams tree, one that first flourished in Tennessee.

In September he was ready to return to St. Louis, and to enroll at Washington University — but at first only as an auditor, in a noncredit, less demanding situation. "By this time," according to Dakin, "Dad was making $7500 a year, which was a good salary, and we could afford to rent larger houses in better neighborhoods. And so we moved — first to 6634 Pershing Avenue, then to 42 Aberdeen Place, a comfortable, spacious red-brick colonial house not far from Washington University."

The fall of 1935 was on several counts a time of continuing growth, of intellectual stimulation, and of high-speed creative energy. He read the required books for courses in general literature and philosophy — William James's *Will to Believe* and *Varieties of Religious Experience,* Chesterton's *Heretics* and *Orthodoxy,* Santayana's *Last Puritan,* Russell's *Sceptical Essays,* Walter Lippmann's *Preface to Morals,* John Dewey's *Common Faith;* then he went through the works on literary theory and criticism by Clive Bell, I. A. Richards, Max Eastman and T. S. Eliot. In a notebook at that time he reflected at length on the situation of the poetic, intuitive, subjective side of the artist, of intuition drawing largely from the unconscious. Even after constant rewriting of his poems, he thought, a work continued to expand in his unconscious mind and new ideas and feelings forced revaluations and revisions. This self-imposed demand of aesthetic refinement would become a habit as the years passed; until his death, Williams continually revised his produced and unproduced plays, and in some cases (*Sweet Bird of Youth,* for example) there are as many important variations in the text as there are printed editions.

But his school notebooks and theses and examination books never indicate anything other than passing interest in textbook literary theory — Williams was interested in what he could *experience,* what he could *feel* within himself and then enable his readers or audiences to experience and feel. From the start — and most forcefully this season, when he knew more clearly the acuteness of his own sensitivity — he was excited by the enterprise of transforming that inner experience into controlled poetic emotion. His sympathies were with the Romantics, not with modern realists like Sinclair Lewis. And in a paper on Goethe that he submitted in the spring term of 1936, he embarked on a passionate (if tangential) plea for the preservation of human dignity in a mechanical age. Goethe's study of practical anatomy, he wrote, was but a prelude to the German poet's plea for the moral improvement of the human race. (The original draft of his play *Summer and Smoke,* just a decade later, bore the title *Chart of Anatomy,* and its conflicts are very close to a revision of this early student enthusiasm for Goethe. The possibility of salvation and damnation was, for Williams, as for the German poet, largely a question of a terrestrial battle with the demands of both flesh and spirit, of inner light and inner darkness.)

That year his energies as a working poet were encouraged by friendship with another student who was already an established poet and translator — Clark Mills McBurney, who omitted, professionally, his family name. Soon they were joined by a younger undergraduate, William Jay

Smith, and the trio formed an informal circle they called a "literary factory."

"Tom had fanatical and inexhaustible energy in his writing," Clark Mills recalled. "His persistence was almost grotesque. It was Dionysian, demoniac. He wasn't aiming basically at material success. He wrote because it was a fatal need."

Mills's impression of Williams was on the mark. Although he often referred to himself as a rebellious Puritan, Williams actually was a living example of the creative personality who shared the Dionysian or Bacchic impulse. This term, which derives from the ancient orgiastic rituals connected with the worship of Dionysus or Bacchus (the god of wine, revelry and fertility), refers to the unfettered, passionate abandonment of the senses. The cult of Dionysus was a manic explosion celebrating life, sex, the abundance of food and intoxicating drink; it aimed for an ecstatic loss of control. As the classical scholar H. D. F. Kitto tersely wrote, "the worship of Dionysus stimulated . . . the lively dramatic sense of the Greeks," and it is generally believed that these ancient seasonal festivals in honor of the inebriate god were in fact the beginning of theatre. Dionysus — and his cult-followers — were committed to sensual intoxication, sexual frenzy, and the sudden manifestation of passionate art deriving from unbounded irrationality.

During the 1930s, his fierce attachment to writing — this "fatal need," as Mills called it — had as yet no counterpart in his physical or sexual life. Soon, however, there would be the same intensity, the same apparent helplessness in other areas of his life: Tennessee Williams's passion for writing was soon matched by wildly promiscuous sex. In both activities there was always something obsessive, indiscriminate. Writing was never a Puritanic duty — any more than sex was. In a sense he was a possessed man, overwhelmed by instincts and impulses he never sorted out. The most dangerous result of this part of his nature would finally involve him in the twilight world of drug addiction.

Again that season, as his appreciation of artists widened, so did his interior association with their lives. The stories, poems and essays of Rainer Maria Rilke, the German writer who died only a decade earlier at fifty, were being circulated in translation, and that year the *Sonnets to Orpheus* were snatched up by campus poets and professors everywhere. Rilke's *Notebook of Malte Laurids Brigge* startled him with its account of the personal anguish of a Danish expatriate. Tom now felt another association — with Rilke, whose frustrated, unhappy father was ill-suited to his pretentious, aristocratic mother. Both poets suffered the demands of fathers who wanted them to be military officers; both had frail health in childhood; both had emotional collapses in young adulthood. The similarities in their lives struck him as astonishing — forced to enroll in business courses, each was helped by the quiet kindness of relatives. Tom then read Rilke's *Auguste Rodin,* which reinforced his own sense of incompletion about his art: the creative individual must be committed to the ideal of unremitting work — *toujours travailler,* as Rodin called it and Rilke and Williams learned it. The connections between Rilke and Williams would become even clearer in the years ahead; Rilke's guiding spirit, he thought, followed him right up to the end.

But if his creative life was thriving and the material circumstances at home were comfortable, life with Rose was increasingly sad. For a brief time Edwina put her to teaching Sunday school at St. Michael's and St. George's. Rose, who learned that Reverend Carl Morgan Block, the pastor, was half Jewish, mentioned this innocently to friends and parishioners, and the unwelcome news made the rounds of parish gossip in no time. Dr. Block, perhaps because in a strange way he shared the anti-Semitism of the shocked parishioners, dismissed Rose at once. This exacerbated her already fragile condition.

"She then became increasingly sick with imaginary ills," according to Dakin, "and shortly after we had moved into Pershing Avenue a terrible thing happened. Across the street was Roger Moore, whose sister Virginia was a noted local poet. Roger was a brilliant young man who wanted to get into politics, and he was, as it turned out, the last possibility of someone like a beau or boyfriend for Rose. But Roger had some kind of psychological illness, too, and he was put by his family into a private sanatorium in Kirkwood. One night he broke out, ran into the street and was killed by a truck. This was crushing for Rose. Then, about the same time, Tom uttered a thoughtless remark to her. There'd been a party at the house, while our parents were away for a weekend business trip, and Tom had a few beers. Rose, who was obsessive about alcohol because of Dad, said she was going to tell mother about the beer, and Tom lashed out at her, 'I never want to see your ugly old face again!' Of course he regretted that at once, but Rose was shattered, and from this point on she virtually separated herself from the rest of us."

William Jay Smith recalled Rose's eerie isolation, too. "[She] was rarely mentioned when we came to the house, but we knew that she was up in her room, perhaps listening at the top of the stairs. She was very withdrawn, on the edge of complete breakdown."

On Tom's twenty-fifth birthday, the St. Louis newspapers ran the story of another laurel: he had won first prize (twenty-five dollars) in a verse contest sponsored by the Wednesday Club. His three "Sonnets for the Spring" were selected over more than four hundred other submissions.

This, of course, was marvelously encouraging for Tom and William Jay Smith and their little circle.

"The amount of work that Tom turned out at the time was truly amazing," according to Smith. Many of these poems appeared in *The Eliot*, the Washington University literary magazine, and in *College Verse*, the journal of the College Poetry Society. "Even at parties we always talked about writing," Smith added. "That's what we had decided we definitely wanted to do in life, and that is what we were doing." And they continued to do it by forming the St. Louis Poets Workshop, from which they sent their writings to magazines all across the country. In 1936 and 1937, seven poems by Thomas L. Williams were published in *College Verse*, four in *Poetry* and nine in *The Eliot*. "We have been looking for poetry like this for some time," wrote *The Eliot*'s editor. Another member of the staff remembered Williams as "the model contributor: reliable, neat, careful and literate, [but] I regretted his shyness — he usually slipped his poems under *The Eliot* office door."

Thriving on his success as a university poet and apprentice playwright, Tom was still, according to Smith, "the shyest, quietest person I had ever met. His stony-faced silence often put people off: he appeared disdainful of what was going on around him, never joining in the quick give-and-take of a conversation, but rather listening carefully and taking it all in. He would sit quietly in a gathering for long periods of time until suddenly like a volcano erupting he would burst out with a high cackle and then with resounding and uncontrollable laughter. Those who knew him well found this trait delightful, but to others it seemed rude and disconcerting."

His shyness was at least briefly overcome, however, when the university's French department staged Molière's *Scapin* in April 1936; Tom was persuaded to take the part of Argante, and his performance demonstrated another side to his complex personality. "He read his French lines," Smith said, "with a kind of hound-dog ferocity and deliberation, as if he were chewing on a large section of the Mississippi delta. When he moved woodenly across the stage with absolute seriousness, pounding the floor with his cane, small and square in his satin suit, an enormous blond wig flopping about on his shoulders, he gave a performance that a more sophisticated audience would have taken as deliberate high camp. As it was, our local audience had not the remotest idea of when to laugh since [they] had not a clue as to what was going on."

At the end of that month, the Webster Groves Theatre Guild announced that a one-act play called *The Magic Tower,* submitted by Williams, had won first prize (a sterling silver cake plate Edwina cherished forever after) and would be produced by them later that year. At once he summoned his colleagues in the poets' workshop, and insisted that playwriting be included in their efforts and submissions. When they met at the Williams home, however, both work and socializing were made difficult by Edwina's presence.

"She never stopped talking," Smith recalled, "although there was little inflection or warmth in the steady flow of her speech. One topic, no matter how trivial, received the same emphasis as the next, which might be utterly tragic. I had the impression listening to her that the words she produced were like the red balls in a game of Chinese checkers, all suddenly released and clicking quickly and aimlessly about the board."

The summer of 1936 was a busy time for the entire family. Edwina had been accepted into the local chapter of the Daughters of the American Revolution, and she was occupied with social events and, as secretary, with national correspondence. Dakin and Cornelius were frequently off to ball games. Rose made a few final, frail attempts at attending luncheons for neighborhood ladies. And Tom, in his cramped "studio" in the basement, wrote as if this were his last chance. In August, *Manuscript* magazine published his short story "27 Wagons Full of Cotton," which over the next twenty years would be several times revised as a story, two separate plays and a film — each version progressively more shocking for his audiences. In this early telling, it was the story of a woman lounging indolently on the verandah of her Southern plantation, talking to the foreman who flicks a riding whip and suggests they go into the house where it is dark, cool and private. "I don't know what you'll do to me inside," she says coyly, but adds, "Well, all right, but you must promise not to hurt me."

Even for 1936, the sexy tone and the hint of sadomasochism were a bold step by that magazine; "but Mother and Rose are not used to modern writing," Tom wrote to his grandparents, "and they were very displeased with the subject ... and so Mother forbids me to send the magazine to anybody. She thinks it is too shocking. It is supposed to be humorous but she and Rose don't take it that way."

During the academic year 1936–1937, which Tom began that autumn at Washington University, he studied — for credit now — Greek, French, drama, government, philosophy and literature. But his notebooks reveal where his interests were: there are lines of poetry scrawled round the edges of pages, reflections on nature and dreams and young love. Nature and dreams he had come to know, but young love was entirely a matter of theory to him at this point. His sexual preference was perhaps becoming clearer in his mind, but as Smith noted, "There was not the kind of sexual freedom that there is today. Sex was not the subject of intense campus conversation. And there was little tolerance of sexual deviation. One of the editors of the campus magazine had returned from New York and had openly declared himself a homosexual. We all found this quite shocking."

Tom very likely did not share their shock, but at the same time he discovered an American poet whose life and work and destiny would haunt him for the rest of his life, and with whom — as with Rilke and Chekhov and Strindberg and Ibsen — he saw himself as spiritually linked. Hart Crane's *White Buildings* (1926) and *The Bridge* (1930) were controversial manifestos in the form of radically personal poems. Tom stole these two volumes from the university library, protesting later that they had hardly been borrowed at all. Henceforth, Crane became his most powerful American literary mentor, and a photo of Crane (with one of Chekhov) went wherever Tom Williams lived and traveled.

Crane's poetry and poetic theory — virtually a foreign language for most students of poetry in the 1930s and still enormously difficult for readers — depended on nonrational, hallucinatory associations and connotations to join words. His rich imagery found an intense, sustained explosion in *The Bridge,* which he intended as a reply to T. S. Eliot's "The Waste Land." (Eliot was much studied that year in St. Louis, where he had been born in 1888. His grandfather was a founder and chancellor of Washington University and had given his name to the campus literary magazine.) Williams was at once taken by Crane's idea of art as itself an alternate way of life; his poetic and sexual sensibility, like Whitman's earlier, marked a cry of difference from his fellows and a plea for a fresh vision in a new age. Most fascinating was Crane's affirmation of the Romantic era — and of his own personal history — as a "usable past." It is this aesthetic, this insistence on transmuting the raw material of one's own life into the stuff of poetry and drama, that stung Tom Williams as perhaps the single great challenge he was facing, then or thereafter.

By 1936, Crane had been dead for four years. A mad alcoholic, he had committed suicide at the age of thirty-two by throwing himself from a ship en route from Mexico, and Tom Williams, then twenty-five, was awed by his fiery, profligate life and tragic end. The more he read, the more parallels he found to himself: both endured a miserable home life, both rebelled against fathers for whom they were forced to work. While young, Crane made a break, and began a life of wandering in Cuba, Paris, New York, Ohio and Mexico, until his uncontrollable dependence on drink, and his obsessively promiscuous homosexuality, led him to madness. Everything about Crane's life struck Tom, perhaps precisely because it was a life that consistently defied family, social, sexual and artistic taboos, and that, with its own crazy integrity, rearranged all the accepted icons of American poetry.

In October 1936, the Webster Groves Theatre Guild was ready to stage his one-act play, called *The Magic Tower*. The *News-Times* gave him his first enthusiastic review as a playwright, calling the work "a poignant little tragedy with a touch of warm fantasy. It treats the love of a very young, not too talented, artist and his ex-actress wife, a love which their youthful idealism has translated into a thing of exquisite white beauty. They call the garret in which they live their 'magic tower' and are happy there until the artist's belief in his star fails. Then the magic tower becomes a drab garret once more, and tragedy like a gray woman glides in to remain. [The play] was exquisitely written by its poet author."

A month later, The Mummers of St. Louis, an earnest and polished group of amateur performers, presented Irwin Shaw's graphic antiwar play, *Bury the Dead,* which was preceded by Williams's news dramatization called "Headlines" (for which he was not credited). "I needed a curtain-raiser for the Shaw play," director Willard Holland said years later. "I called Tom and said, 'Could you take some of the headlines and statements by people against war and give us about twelve minutes of stuff to get the audience into the mood for *Bury the Dead?*' "

In a matter of days, Tom turned out four very brief and funny episodes using the short blackout-scene technique: there were an Armistice Day address by a local senator (apt for the day of the play's premiere); two satires on local school and social life; and a sendup of a mythic St. Louis politician. Standing at the rear of the Wednesday Club auditorium, he heard the appreciative laughter of the audience at the three performances. This was a new reaction his words could arouse, and he liked it.

His successes continued. In the middle of March 1937, the Mummers produced his first full-length play. The months in Memphis had given him the idea for *Candles to the Sun,* with its socially alert theme of group and individual welfare against the background of the plight of mine workers in a depressed economy. In the play, the sun represents a group consciousness, the candles that of individuals. The action ends tragically, for individuals come to realize that they cannot succeed and find happiness without the group, which demands some sacrifice of their own small lights. Full of 1930s work-and-union consciousness, but badly structured and overwritten, the play was a local success. (It suggests that Williams may have read John Galsworthy's play *Strife.*)

"They were the disorderly theater group of St. Louis," Williams reflected nine years later, "standing socially, if not also artistically, opposite to the usual Little Theater group.... Dynamism was what The Mummers had.... [Willard] Holland [their organizer] was a great director. Everything that he touched he charged with electricity."

Pleased with these premieres of his work, he set aside the school notebooks and Greek homework and plunged into writing another play, to be submitted in a senior playwriting contest at the university. *Me, Vashya* was about a World War I munitions worker and his eccentric wife (Vashya) — the first of the author's wild ladies. Although years later the judging professor, William G. B. Carson, said that Tom "showed much more ability than the usual student," he did not, that spring of 1937, select the play for presentation. And Tom, who had expected to win at school the way he had been winning with the Mummers and at Webster Groves, was furious.

"It was a terrible shock and humiliation to me. It was a cruel blow. I had always thought I was shy, but I discarded all humility. I stormed into Carson's office. He was a good professor. I screamed at him. I surprised myself." (Dakin added that Carson was "very jealous of Tom's talents, and very unhelpful that year. Tom deserved to win the contest — his play was clearly the best of those submitted — but Carson sabotaged his chances.")*

Tom must have surprised everyone else, too, for the perception about him was identical to that elsewhere. "He wore conservative clothes, tweeds and ties and looked like a young bank teller," Holland recalled.

* If the play was indeed "the best of those submitted," the competition cannot have been impressive: *Me, Vashya* has some crackling dialogue between husband and wife, but dramatically it is not much of an improvement on *Candles to the Sun.*

"Writing always came easier to Tom than it does to most people — it just poured out of him. His original manuscripts were the length of three full plays.... He was enthusiastic and easy to work with and an easy person to talk to. He had no temperament about his plays. Right from the beginning, I thought of him as a professional.... There was an immersion in his work that was staggering ... [and] he had the most inane laugh I ever heard, a high squeaky cackle, a shriek."

Later, Williams always insisted that it was the rejection of *Me, Vashya* that caused his withdrawal from Washington University and his transfer to the State University of Iowa in the fall of 1937. But there was another reason: he had failed Greek that year, and so he was denied the right to graduate. The disappointment was perhaps greater for his mother, who had hoped the commencement exercises might unite them all for at least one happy family occasion, for it would have coincided with Dakin's graduation from high school.

All during this time, Rose's precarious mental health worsened. In November 1936, Edwina had written to her mother that Rose was "very pitiful. I try to excuse all in her, but she *is* a trial.... If I could just get Rose into her right senses we would be 'sitting pretty.'" Moody and withdrawn, then suddenly hysterically angry or weeping at an imagined slight, Rose visited several psychologists at Barnes Hospital, but the counseling seemed not to help her rapid decline. "She still says crazy things," Edwina wrote to Mrs. Dakin in December. "The only thing I can see that the doctor has done for her is to start her to smoking."*

In early 1937, the doctors at Barnes urged Mr. and Mrs. Williams to take Rose to the state asylum at Farmington, for consultation and for out-patient treatments. But after two visits, Edwina saw no improvement: "I can't take her back to those doctors," she wrote her mother on January 26. "The last time she went, the doctor told her that what was the matter with her was 'that she needed to get married.' She has been raving on the subject of 'sex' ever since and I was ashamed for Dakin and Tom to hear her the other night."

During the spring, there was a period of calm, after Rose stayed briefly at St. Vincent's, a mental hospital nearer St. Louis. This was, however, followed by even more outbursts — wild hallucinations, uncontrollable

---

* Some of the poor girl's nervousness at home is easy to understand. In December 1936, Cornelius was engaged in a drunken brawl at a drinking party, and his opponent bit off a generous portion of one ear. When the bandages and stitches were removed, according to Dakin and Tom, something resembling a small cauliflower seemed to have replaced the ear.

rages and outbursts of sexual fantasies — and by threats of physical violence against her father.

The final trauma seems to have been yet another alcoholic rage by
Cornelius, in which Edwina was cruelly beaten. Rose, horror-stricken and
panicky, raved hysterically, and her father, in his attempt to calm her,
made some gesture that was (or that she saw as) too intimate, almost
sexual. Her hysteria persisted undiminished for several days, and doctors
said that she was now a patient beyond their ability to control with medi-
cines or hot baths or temporary confinements in rest homes. Thoughout
the summer of 1937, she was admitted and (inexplicably) discharged at
least twice from the state hospital at Farmington.

Concurrent with this tragic development, however, was Tom's decision to leave St. Louis for Iowa City — the expenses for which would
again be borne by his adored grandmother. "It wasn't only Washington
University that finally disappointed him," according to his brother. "St.
Louis represented everything he hated — everything was materialistic,
everything was valued in terms of money and social status." As Tom told
an interviewer twenty years later, "For all the family, life in St. Louis was
dismal," and as late as 1975 he was still calling St. Louis "that dreaded
city."

The State University of Iowa promised escape, and perhaps even the
success away from home that he so much desired. "It was a great drama
school," he told an audience years later, "and had a great reputation for
training writers. I went there to study with professors like the great E. C.
Mabie and E. P. Conkle."*

At Iowa City, there were at once many important developments in
his life. After a brief residence at the local chapter house of the Alpha
Tau Omega fraternity, he moved to a two-room apartment with his
own kitchen, at 325 South Dubuque, and from there he kept the Dakins
informed of his progress and enthusiasm and newly cherished independence. Here he had the privacy he needed to tackle the serious
business of his heavy first-term schedule, which included courses in
Shakespeare, experimental dramatic production, modern drama, speech
(which he failed) and English literature. But he continued his own

* Mabie later taught playwriting at the New School for Social Research, New York City,
where Erwin Piscator ran the famous Drama Workshop from 1939 to 1951. Conkle's play
200 *Were Chosen* had been staged on Broadway in November 1936, and his play *Prologue to
Glory* was a successful offering sponsored by the WPA Federal Theatre Project.

writing as well, for the Mummers were eager for a new play for their tenth season.

His first decision was to send them one of the plays he was writing for the dramatic production course — *Spring Storm,* a Southern love story that drew from Professor Mabie the cool criticism, "Well, I guess we all have to paint our nudes!" The play was awash in obvious melodramatic sentiment, lacking in narrative subtlety and devoid of an original touch. Instead, Tom sent Willard Holland another effort, *Not About Nightingales,* a violent play based on an incident in which many men died hideously in a Pennsylvania county prison; the event had been a national scandal and provoked a federal investigation. *Not About Nightingales* was postponed and remained unproduced — not because of its unpleasant subject matter, but because later the Mummers disbanded.

But while he was writing papers, attending classes (with unaccustomed regularity and punctuality), directing and appearing in a campus production of *Hedda Gabler* and writing poems, he completed his revisions for a full-length play called *Fugitive Kind,* which the Mummers at once accepted, believing that it justified their conviction that "Mr. Williams has an important contribution to make to the American stage."

Fugitive Kind* — which was performed at the Wednesday Club on November 30 and December 4, 1937 — is the drama of drifters trying to shake off the repressions and restraints of a bourgeois society. Terry Grady, a criminal on the run, finds in Glory, the adopted daughter of a flophouse keeper, the embodiment of his youthful idealism. Set (obviously, though it is unstated) in St. Louis, its action takes place from Christmas Eve to New Year's Eve, and the *St. Louis Star-Times* published a major review, calling it "a vital and absorbing play ... several cuts above ordinary amateur efforts.... Thomas Lanier Williams is a playwright to watch, [a writer] with first-rate theatrical craftsmanship ... [who,] like [Sidney] Howard and Ben Hecht and Maxwell Anderson, wants to say something forceful and true about the chaos of modern life."

But Williams was not only advancing his own playwriting career and moving closer to his college degree. He also had his first (and last) affair with a woman — a classmate at Iowa named Bette Reitz, to whose passionately aggressive advances he briefly yielded. "I was a terrible puritan ... and I remained a puritan until my late 20s," he said later. "I was a

---

* The play has no relation to the film *The Fugitive Kind,* made in 1959; that is based on Williams's play *Battle of Angels* and its later revision, *Orpheus Descending.*

virgin with either sex until the age of 26." After the coed 'ended their brief encounters, a period of chastity was followed by his admission, to himself, at least, that his erotic desires were really homosexual. At ease in the most creative, open and experimental academic setting he had known, and alert to the shifts in a personality he was coming to know and accept as different from most of his peers, he was ready to assert himself, and to do so sexually.

But this awareness remained secret and dormant, and not because of social or psychological pressure. Grief entered his life in a catastrophic way that season, and it overwhelmed every personal or private consideration.

By autumn 1937, the Williamses had been told that Rose's illness was so advanced that she was capable not only of doing herself physical harm, but also of instigating tragedy — perhaps murder, one doctor said. Her fits had become even more violently schizophrenic, and the doctors insisted that a new neurosurgical procedure — called a leucotomy, or prefrontal lobotomy — was the only cure. It was, they said, safe and sure, and since Rose would be one of the first patients to undergo it, the operation could be performed without charge.

Edwina cringed when the procedure was described: her daughter's skull would be opened, and the nerve fibers connecting the thalamus to the frontal lobes of the brain would be severed. This would result in an immediate and total calming of the patient, and a cessation of the fits and hysterics and dreadful fantasies to which she was subject — some of which, Tom said for years, were simple exclamations of sexual desire deriving from the repressions of a sick woman who was almost thirty years old.

But one of Rose's claims was more upsetting, first because there was no way to assess its truthfulness, but also because it was a terrible possibility. One evening, just before Rose's last hospitalization, Edwina had returned home to be met by Rose, who shouted hysterically that her father had come to her room drunk and had spoken and acted in a lewd, provocative way: she insisted, wildly, that Cornelius wanted her, his own daughter, to go to bed with him. This was something unthinkable, unutterable for Edwina. When Rose could not be calmed after two more nights, she was returned to Farmington.

"I was a freshman at Washington University that autumn, when the operation was performed," Dakin remembered. "My father was too involved with his drinking and golf-playing and poker parties to be interested in Rose, so on weekends I drove mother to the state hospital at Farmington to see her. It was of course dreadful, going to that public institution to see your own sister so sad and forlorn, with wild patients screaming all around. It was a real snake pit."

Tom was not told of the operation until he came home for the Mummers' production of *Fugitive Kind* in November. For years he openly blamed his mother: "She gave permission to have it done while I was away. I think she was frightened most of all by Rose's sexual fantasies. But that's all they were — fantasies. . . . She is the one who approved the lobotomy. . . . My sister was such a vital person. She could have become quite well by now if they hadn't performed that goddam operation on her; she would have come back up to the surface. My mother panicked because she said my sister had begun using four-letter words. 'Do anything! Don't let her talk like that!' "

In *Remember Me to Tom,* Edwina wrote that the final decision was made by her husband. She also said that the operation, she later realized, was a grave mistake that might have been substituted for by therapy and medication. The lobotomy soon became virtually an unknown operation.

From then on, the spirit of his sister haunted his life, her personality trapped in a childish permanence like a pinned butterfly. From his earliest one-act plays in 1938 to the end of his life, the name and image of Rose and her beloved roses pursued him.*

In a calm, reflective mood, he could speak with an almost stoic resignation about this irreversible tragedy: "I don't think I would have been the poet I am without that anguished familial situation. . . . I've yet to meet a writer of consequence who did not have a difficult familial background if you explored it."

But his deepest feelings were more anguished, less academic. "She was the best of us all, do you understand?" he wept to a friend years later. "More beautiful, more intelligent, sweeter and warmer than anyone. Not one of us was fit to stoop and tie her shoes."

* A few select examples: the proliferation of rose imagery in *The Rose Tattoo;* Aunt Rose of *The Unsatisfactory Supper,* and her roses; the roses "of yesterday, of death and of time" in *The Milk Train Doesn't Stop Here Anymore, Camino Real, The Last of My Solid Gold Watches* and *Something Unspoken;* the wild roses of *The Case of the Crushed Petunias;* the roses of Picardy in *Moony's Kid Don't Cry;* the mystic rose of *Now the Cats with Jewelled Claws;* the smell of roses in *The Mutilated,* the wild roses of *Will Mr. Merriwether Return from Memphis?* and the roses in *Small Craft Warnings, The Two-Character Play,* etc. He also painted images of roses in astonishing profusion — both quick sketches and carefully rendered representations.

* * *

And so Rose Isabel Williams survived from 1937 to the end of her long life, which outdistanced her brother's. She inhabited a timeless twilight, in which — when she was asked her age or the date or the events of the time — she would always reply that she was twenty-eight, that her brother Tom was twenty-six, and that her world revolved around visits from "that man, Cornelius Williams." She was free of physical pain and fear and emotional distress at last, but no human communion was possible. For years she was treated with exceptional gentleness and generosity by her only friend, her brother Tom, who had collapsed once and lived in terror of collapsing again. For the rest of his life, he saw in her the tragic figure that he, too, could have become, and might yet. And twenty years later, he wrote one of his great plays, *Suddenly Last Summer,* which includes so many of the real-life details of 1936 and 1937.

The deepest poignancy of her life was never known to her, for ever after she was never quite sure just who she, or her brother, was; worse still, she seemed, in her detachment, never to care very much. Little of Thomas Lanier Williams's life after 1937 is comprehensible without appreciating the awfulness of that Christmas season, when the open warfare in family life was stilled forever, along with the last possibility of life as a complete family.

Chapter Three

IN TRANSIT
(1938–1944)

People enter this world without instructions
of where to go, what to do, so they wander a
little. . . .

— Silva Vaccaro, in *Baby Doll*

H E HAD a charming personality, a consistently gentlemanly de-
meanor, and he was full of traditional Southern charm." So was
Tom Williams, in the spring of 1938, described years later by a
classmate at Iowa, Anthony Dexter.

"Tom was in a small clique of people studying under E. C. Mabie, one
of the great directors of all time, in my estimation. He was known to everyone as The Boss, and one day Tom said to me, after a playwriting
class, 'The Boss says my work needs a touch more humor. What do you
think?' And I said, 'Well, that might not hurt it.' "

The other mentor under whose guidance Williams flourished was the
playwright and theorist Elsworth P. Conkle. "I have only one really good
student this year," he recalled telling his wife. "He's poor and shy and
very talented." Mrs. Conkle's interest in young Williams was at once
very keen, for her husband did not often bring home praise for aspiring
writers. "Go and see if you can get him to talk to you," he urged her.
Virginia Conkle attended a rehearsal of one of Tom's short plays, then in
studio production for class.

"Tom Williams was in the front row and I sat down near him. When
the curtain came down and the lights went up he took one look at me,
recognized me as the professor's wife, and quickly ran away. My husband
wasn't there to introduce me, and he was simply too shy to greet me
himself. That was my only chance to meet Tom Williams."

"The course also required the students to work only with dialogue, to
write radio scripts for reading over the Iowa station," E. P. Conkle added.
"I always selected Williams's for broadcast, and for a simple reason: they
were the best. At the end of the school year, I recommended to Mabie
that Tom be kept on as a graduate student on scholarship, but Mabie's
enthusiasm for his work had cooled. 'I've read his new stuff and I don't
like it,' he said." This, it turned out, was a minority report, for Conkle

and other teachers — especially Edwin Ford Piper, who directed the creative writing seminar — realized they had a unique talent with them that year. Conkle and Piper worked with him, briefly, on a manuscript about the most troubled period in the life of Vincent van Gogh, which Williams wanted to call *The Holy Family;* the project, about artistic aspirations and the danger of madness, was abandoned after several weeks.

During the spring term of 1938, it was clear to Williams that playwriting, and not poetry, would dominate. *L'Alouette* published two final poems that season, as did *The Eliot.* On February 22, the *Daily Iowan,* listing Thomas Williams as a charter member of Pi Tau, the honorary writers' fraternity, mentioned only his plays, for that is what he and his department were emphasizing. Word had got around the campus that he had sent *Candles to the Sun* for consideration in a contest sponsored by the Dramatists Guild in New York, and while the Guild's evaluation was not wildly enthusiastic, a summary report praised the author's pronounced individual style.

In April, he also made another stage appearance — as a footman in the first part of *Henry IV,* a performance that did not help him either in the Shakespeare or the stagecraft course.* His report at Iowa — although he had B's in literature, experimental drama and creative writing — was lowered by D's in classical and modern drama and in zoology, and he had to enroll in the summer session to graduate at last, at the age of twenty-seven, on August 5, 1938. The degree conferred was a bachelor of arts with a major in English. The expenses connected with the extra term were diminished by a work plan: the university had a cooperative program with the state hospital whereby needy students could receive compensation for services. That summer, Tom worked as a dishwasher in the doctors' cafeteria. In a letter to his mother, dated June 4, he thanked her for a wristwatch needed for the job, reported that he got three free meals daily at the cafeteria, and said the new attic apartment he had taken (at 126 North Clinton) at least included clean sheets every week.

A time of poverty, nevertheless, was beginning. The Dakins could no longer afford to help support Tom, and Cornelius had no interest in subsidizing what he considered laziness. Tom departed Iowa shortly after the summer graduation, with very little pocket money and a change of name to mark what he felt was a dramatic new time of his new dramatic life.

For the next forty-five years, Tennessee Williams told interviewers that

---

* In *Memoirs,* Williams claimed he played a page-boy in *Richard of Bordeaux;* university records, however, are more accurate.

Thomas Lanier Williams "sounds like it might belong to the sort of writer who turns out sonnet sequences to spring" (which of course is just what he had done). The transformation to "Tennessee," he sometimes said, was suggested because the Williams clan had fought the Indians for Tennessee, and the idea of the defense of a stockade against a band of savages was consistent with a writer's hard life.

On other occasions, he said he got the name from classmates, that it was not his own choice at all: "the fellows in my class could only remember that I was from a Southern state with a long name. And when they couldn't think of Mississippi, they settled on Tennessee. That was all right with me, so when it stuck I changed it permanently."

The truth of the matter lies, as so often with Williams, on a level of feeling — not on a logical, academic-ancestral decision, nor on the accident of others' confusion. From the summer of 1935, when his health, his outlook and his confidence were given healing encouragement in Memphis, he had associated everything that followed with that time and place. And so it was not basically from his *father's* family that he took the name, but from the cherished summer he linked with a turning from emotional collapse to an emergence as a creator of character and dialogue. In the state of Tennessee, with his beloved grandparents, he had become well enough to write his first play produced outside school, and that memory, to which he would often return as to an epiphany, was most deeply responsible for the name some, at time time of its adoption, considered whimsical, ludicrous or hopelessly fey.

Conkle urged Williams to travel first that autumn to Chicago, where the Works Progress Administration's Federal Writers' Project still survived. Aimed at providing employment for writers, editors and researchers, the project at its peak helped over 6,500 young writers, most of whom had assisted in the preparation of the famous *American Guide* series for every state and major cities, as well as ethnic and folklore studies, nature guides and more than a thousand books and pamphlets celebrating history, art and culture in America. At various times, Conrad Aiken, Richard Wright, Ralph Ellison, Nelson Algren, Frank Yerby and Loren Eiseley were among those who benefited from this employment. (Federal sponsorship ended, by an act of Congress, in 1939, but states were free to extend individual programs through 1943.)

When he arrived in Chicago in September, however, Williams was told that there were fewer positions available than he or Conkle had hoped — and in addition, his family was not on the welfare rolls. He argued that he was as close to destitution as anyone could get, but the administrators saw his family's address — a private home in a St. Louis suburb — and he was sent away.

They recommended, however, that he travel to New Orleans, where the Writers' Project apparently needed a larger staff and was not so demanding about family status. He took the long bus ride south, stopping briefly at home when he was told the Dakins were visiting. The autumn chill had settled in Chicago and St. Louis early that year, and he was soon eager to move on. The WPA had bad news for him in New Orleans, however, and even after six weeks there was no chance of anything like a writer's job for him.

But with his usual optimism and endurance — and because he at once had fallen in love with New Orleans — he stayed on, waiting tables in the French Quarter, distributing handbills for jazz clubs, accepting day jobs. The city itself, he felt, was providing incomparably rich ingredients for his writing, and also a heavy counterweight to whatever Victorian shyness about sex may still have lingered in him.

"It was a period of accumulation," he reflected years later. "I found the kind of freedom I had always needed, and the shock of it, against the Puritanism of my nature, has given me a subject, a theme, which I have never ceased exploiting."

From a room at 431 Royal Street for which he paid three dollars a week late that autumn (and for which "modest" would be too gentle a word to describe its cell-like squalor), he went forth each day and evening to absorb the spirit of what is for many people America's most colorful city — especially in its old Vieux Carré, the French sector that has become synonymous with the birth of the blues, the consumption of catfish and bourbon, and the death of virtually every social and sexual taboo.

At first sight, he loved the heterogeneous, unplanned coexistence of architectural styles, the wrought-iron balconies, the interior and exterior spiral staircases, shuttered doors and windows, the verandahs and quiet courtyards with fountains and exotic plants, and the ethnic diversity of the Gallic streets (Dauphine, Burgundy, Bourbon, Dumaine, Chartres, Toulouse) and those named for saints (Ann, Philip, Peter, Claude) and for the order of nuns who founded the first schools in French Canada and French New Orleans (Ursulines).

The French quarter was, for the man who registered in boardinghouses as "Tennessee Williams, Writer," everything that St. Louis was not. It had something of the South he knew as a child, where the climate was hospitable and there was an air of faded gentility, and where his accent aroused no startled reaction. But there was also a vague tincture of decadence, and this was a marked contrast to the Victorian prudery that was taken for granted in his youth — and which, as if she were overreacting to years with Cornelius's rudeness and indignities, Edwina had in the last several years been exaggerating in her own manners.

In the haphazard mixture of cultures in the French Quarter, there were the mobility and eclecticism of a port town, and the cultivation of a kind of creative indolence. Whitman had been fascinated by the city, and in their turn Mark Twain and Sherwood Anderson, William Faulkner and John Dos Passos. And the marginal society there was, in 1938, not quite so self-conscious as later, when it would wear a carefully tended garland of eccentricity for the benefit of tourists. For the first time in his life, Williams lived among those whom his family and neighbors in Columbus and Clarksdale and Clayton would have rejected: pimps and their prostitutes, gamblers, alcoholics, drug addicts — as well as good-natured, indigent musicians, the wandering minstrels who had survived the Depression, sailors just passing through and ready for a day of relaxation and a night of whatever pleasures were offered, working girls of uneven virtue, and — as easily as if the rest of America did not care — a significant population of homosexuals.

For all the excitement, the novelty and the sensuality of New Orleans, he continued to write daily — mostly short stories and one-act plays based on those he met, the lost and abused, the forgotten and the emotionally maimed; they would all, sooner or later, find their counterparts in the characters of his plays.

In addition, the easy juxtaposition of charm and sensuality soon affected him, and as 1939 was rung in — at an impromptu party at the Royal Street boardinghouse — his sexual inhibitions were abandoned and there was a rush of erotic energy.

His first homosexual experience, he claimed, was unforeseen, and with a stranger for whom he at once developed a tender affection. When the stranger vanished before dawn, Williams was confused and a little sad — but only for a few hours. It was a new year, after all, and he was at an important new stage of self-awareness.

Before the week ended, he had moved to an attic apartment at 722 Toulouse Street that he considered wonderfully bohemian. At a rent of ten dollars a month he could afford to take an occasional brandy

Alexander at Victor's Bar nearby. And he could, he wrote to his mother, find a satisfying ten-cent breakfast, and dinner at a good cafeteria near Canal Street for fifty cents. Oysters, at twenty cents a dozen, were often a filling meal. But every morning — sometimes as early as four o'clock, if he had not dallied late the previous evening — he wrote, and from those private times came the scenes of New Orleans life that would later be polished as one-act plays (*The Lady of Larkspur Lotion, Auto-Da-Fé, Lord Byron's Love Letter, Suddenly Last Summer, The Mutilated*), as short stories ("One Arm" and "Desire and the Black Masseur" and "The Angel in the Alcove") and full-length plays (the great *A Streetcar Named Desire* and, near the end, his memory-play *Vieux Carré*). If he had had a particularly tiring day working at the small table in his room, he would treat himself to a hot supper at Alpine's La Bohème Restaurant, which Sherwood Anderson and William Faulkner had frequented.

For a very short time, he worked at a typical eatery, where he conceived the idea of advertising "Meals in the Quarter for a Quarter," which pleased the cook, Mrs. Nesbit, until she decided that the restaurant business was not worth its headaches. She went to Florida at the end of January, and Tennessee was, only by default, a full-time writer again.

During those warm winter weeks he continued to hope that the WPA would be sufficiently impressed with his revisions on *Fugitive Kind* to see that his social conscience was a delicate one and that they could well use his talents either in New Orleans or in Florida; and now, in addition, he could demonstrate authentic indigence and not a penny of family support. While he waited for a reply, he continued to enjoy the heady sexual freedom the Quarter permitted. Sometimes, too, there were parties in the ground-floor apartment of the artist-photographer at 722 Toulouse; one of these revels went on so loudly and so late that the impatient landlady, Mrs. Anderson, poured a bucket of scalding water through the floor-cracks, thereby scattering the guests. (The incident is recalled in his play *Vieux Carré*.)

In February, however, it became clear that the WPA would be of no help to him, and as soon as he heard that the Group Theatre in New York was sponsoring a play contest, he sent them four one-act dramas, as well as *Not About Nightingales* and *Fugitive Kind*.

The Group Theatre had been throughout the 1930s a vital force in American culture, and from its early guidance under Harold Clurman, Cheryl Crawford and Lee Strasberg it had produced vivid and timely plays — among them John Howard Lawson's *Success Story*, Sidney Kingsley's *Men in White,* several plays by Clifford Odets, including *Waiting for Lefty, Awake and Sing!* and *Golden Boy,* plays by William Saroyan and Kurt Weill, and Irwin Shaw's *Bury the Dead.* Everyone who followed serious theatre knew the importance of the Group, which encouraged the talents of these writers, developed the skills of actors and directors like Strasberg, Clurman, Stella Adler, Elia Kazan, Ruth Nelson, Luther Adler, Morris Carnovsky, John Garfield, Sylvia Sidney, Karl Malden and Lee J. Cobb, and evolved a unique style of production and performance that continued to influence Broadway and Hollywood long after the Group's dissolution in 1941.

There was one impossible stipulation for Williams in the contest rules, however: the entrants must be under twenty-five. And so on his application he wrote "Tennessee Williams — Born March.26, 1914." This made him twenty-four instead of twenty-seven and started a little fiction that persisted twenty years, until a scrupulous press unearthed the truth.

While he awaited a reply, even the minimal rent and daily meals became problems. When another boarder offered him a free ride to California, he thought he might be able to find a scriptwriting job in the movies. And so he and Jim Parrott (a young clarinetist who wanted to work with a jazz band in Los Angeles) set out in a battered jalopy. "I was desperately poor," he told an interviewer in better times, "and I had to hock everything but my typewriter to get by."

On February 18 they began their long trek, and three days later Tennessee wrote (always as "Tom") to his mother that after the New Orleans Mardi Gras they found San Antonio, Texas, as quiet as a tomb. They were sleeping under the stars at night, in an army tent, and were cooking on open fires at roadside. Fifty cents a day was keeping him alive. Edwina was horrified at the thought that her son was becoming a drifter, and she fired off a note to *her* mother, which of course resulted in a ten-dollar bill to be forwarded to the travelers. From El Paso they made two short trips across the Mexican border, to Villa Acuna and Juárez, and by March 1 a blinding dust storm had pushed them on to Phoenix.

Williams was now fully aware of, and enjoying the sight of, the "able-bodied and attractive young men" (as he commented to Jim Parrott) he noticed in Mexico and the Southwest, and to whom they sometimes gave rides through desert country. But he was touched by their predicament — they were almost invariably poor wanderers, family men with exhausted wives and hungry children, begging for work. His sympathies and his admiration for their courage, reflected in letters home, were as deep as his appreciation for their physical appeal. Jim Parrott, unregenerately heterosexual, felt that his sidekick had an unusually empathetic and delicate conscience, and he was impressed when Williams shared their rations with the pathetic children they so often met.*

Cornelius, of course, approved of none of this traveling — least of all with no job prospect. He contacted Sam Webb, a colleague at the West Coast branch of International Shoe, and asked for help in finding employment for his son.

For Parrott, things were easier as soon as they arrived in Los Angeles on March 7. Although the jazz band mysteriously disappeared, he found temporary work in an airplane factory. In southern California, Tom wrote to his grandparents, the talk was only of war, and planes were being built in great quantity. He, however, could not pass the physical examination for such a job — a cataract was forming in his left eye, the result of a childhood injury and the gradual scarring after diphtheria. Instead, he took a job as a ranch-hand just outside the city, where he plucked and killed pigeons and squabs and shoveled manure — a task, he told Parrott, that would prove a good preparation for writing movies.

This unglamorous outdoor work occupied him almost eighteen hours a day for a month; he usually spent the nights in a nearby cabin. A temporary suspension in his writing thus occurred, and perhaps because his artistic sensibility had to have some release, he accepted an offer of free painting lessons from Parrott's mother, who gave them a room and a hot meal once a week when they bicycled down to visit her in the part of Los Angeles known as Hawthorne. He might, he wrote home, return wearing a beret.

Back in New York, the decision of the Group Theatre had been announced. A reader and member of their administrative staff, Molly Day Thacher, recognized at once that the gifts of this oddly named Tennessee Williams were rare and deep. "There's a wonderful young playwright riding around southern California on a bicycle," she told her husband, the actor and director Elia Kazan, who recalled years later that this was the first time he ever heard of Tennessee Williams. "Molly was charged with the task of finding plays for the Group Theatre, and she asked [Harold] Clurman if she could offer a special prize of one hundred dollars to Williams. She had an extraordinary gift for discovering new talent; she had

---

* Williams's memories and attitudes about the poor "drifters" are reflected in a story outline he eventually gave playwright Lanford Wilson in 1973. In February 1974, "The Migrants" was presented as a television drama, "teleplay by Lanford Wilson, suggested by a story by Tennessee Williams."

done the same for Irwin Shaw, she was doing it then for Williams, and there would be others later, like Robert Anderson."

On March 20, 1939, Molly Day Thacher wrote to Williams that although the five-hundred-dollar first prize was awarded to another writer (Ramon Naya, for *Mexican Mural*), the one-act plays he had sent under the collective title *American Blues* were "so outstanding that [they] deserved special recognition," and she enclosed a check for one hundred dollars.

By this time, Cornelius and his friends had made the appropriate shoestore contact, and before the end of the month the playwright of whom everyone spoke at the Group Theatre was busy working at Clark's Bootery in Culver City, where he was paid $12.50 weekly for a sixty-hour stint as a clerk-salesman. However, his bicycle died of exhaustion after long hours on the Los Angeles roads, and, after replacing it with a younger and stronger substitute, he tendered his resignation from Clark's (after only two weeks), and he and Jim headed south for Tijuana.

The money from New York and Culver City was quickly spent for beer, chili and tire patches, and by mid-May they had taken a vacation cabin back in Laguna Beach, south of Los Angeles, where for $7.50 a month they each had a room, and shared a shower, cooking gas and a small garden from which Williams tried to coax tomatoes. He set himself as rigorous a schedule as he would ever have, writing each morning (among other stories "The Mysteries of the Joy Rio" and "The Vine" were first drafted here); afternoons, he swam in the Pacific; and in the evenings he worked at a bowling alley, where he replaced pins. It was, he said afterward, one of the most carefree times of his life, and least complicated by any excesses — there simply was no time for pursuing anything remotely resembling the life of the sensualist.

But the vigilant Molly Day Thacher was pursuing a more serious career development for him. She sent the one-act plays to an agent she liked and respected. "And that," as Kazan remembered, "is how Tennessee Williams came to the legendary Audrey Wood."

Thus began one of the most lengthy, remarkable, loving and finally tragic creative relationships in American theatre history. Audrey Wood, six years older than Williams, was one of the few artists' representatives who did more than negotiate contracts and process fees; she assumed many practical responsibilities for some of her clients. In 1939, she and her husband, William Liebling, managed the Liebling-Wood Agency, at Rockefeller Center.

Almost at once, Audrey sent agency contracts, formally defining the relationship between Williams and herself. Weeks passed, and finally Williams wrote that several New York agents had leaped to the mails after the Group Theatre's special award. He was considering her offer. This amused Audrey: "After all, we were an established agency — even in California people knew who Liebling-Wood, Inc., was — and here was a struggling author with no credits whatsoever!"

But Williams did not want to appear too eager, and he was just hesitant enough to play for time to read the contract — an enterprise which, with one eye now unusable, took weeks. On June 20, Audrey wrote again, asking for the countersigned agreement and adding the good news that *Story* magazine had accepted a piece of short fiction Molly had sent along, called "The Field of Blue Children." It would, she wrote, appear in the September–October issue that year — and, as he insisted, under the name "Tennessee Williams." The story was a delicately written account of a college girl who, after once sexually consummating her friendship with an awkward young poet of average gifts but guileless personality, marries a solid provider. It was also one of the clearest examples of the author reflecting on his own college experience, for he is at once the passionate and pragmatic Myra and the shy poet Homer. Audrey loved the story, ignoring Williams's curious reply (on July 30) that he was pleased with the news of publication but that it did not banish his terror of madness. He enclosed the countersigned agency contract.

Toward summer's end, Williams had grown weary of Los Angeles, and he was eager to be part of the New York theatre world. But cross-country travel was out of the question, since he had but a few dollars left to his name. Audrey came to his rescue (for the first of many times) and advanced him, against *Story*'s autumn payment, the price of a bus ticket.

On August 25, he stopped in Taos, New Mexico, to visit D. H. Lawrence's widow, Frieda, to introduce himself as an admirer of her husband, and to pay homage to the place Lawrence had visited in 1922. "Tom's great god," according to William Jay Smith, "was D. H. Lawrence." This is perhaps an inflated assessment of Williams's hierarchy of favorites, but there can be no doubt of Lawrence's influence on Williams's early prose and poetry — particularly regarding the mystic confluence of sex, nature and power. Audrey, aware of the controversy over Lawrence at that time, at once discouraged Williams from writing (as he had promised) a play about him; she suggested instead a play about Vachel Lindsay (as he had originally planned).

But the visit to the widow Lawrence had a different effect. A few days later, stopping to see his family in St. Louis, he was writing first drafts of two one-act plays reflecting Lawrence's life and thematic iconoclasm. *I Rise in Flame, Cried the Phoenix* dramatized the English writer's death, and *The Purification,* a verse play suggesting also the influence of García Lorca, reveals Williams not only adopting a Lawrentian boldness, but also turning it into autobiography.

The central concern of *The Purification* is a confession of incest as direct cause of a woman's death: while a sister and brother slept together, her husband killed her (the play occurs as a trial after the fact). Written hastily and in tense confusion during another visit to St. Louis since Rose's operation, it concerns a man's guilt over his sister's fate: he drove his sister "beyond all fences"; the girl was subject to parental misunderstanding, and "Not even . . . knocking down walls with two blue brutal bare fists . . . could ever . . . enclose such longing as was my sister's!" The mother cries, "I, his mother, must share in this public censure."

The play is a shout of outrage about the Williams family madness, a cry of hatred against his parents for what they had done to Rose; a plaintive wondering about the terrible final battle between Cornelius and his daughter that may, as she claimed, have ended in a gesture too intimate; and it is suffused with guilt for what might have been his own feelings toward his sister. Greek in its conventions but completely personal in its story, *The Purification* is full of anguished longing. (According to Dakin, his brother did not visit Rose in Farmington on this visit — and not, in fact, until several years later.) "Weave back my sister's image," the son cries. "She's lost, snared as she rose. . . . Irretrievably lost . . . too far to pursue. . . . For nothing contains you now, no, nothing contains you, lost little girl, my sister."

Before the end of September, Williams arrived in New York, where he first took a room in an apartment hotel on West 108th Street; at $4.50 weekly, it was one of a block of studios rented to aspiring artists and theatre people who have always flocked into Manhattan. The first week, he wrote to his grandparents on October 2, he was almost paralyzed with loneliness, and when he heard that a Kentucky woman he had met at Iowa was near by on Morningside Drive, he moved in with her. (This was Marion Galloway, for whose book *Constructing a Play* he would, ten years later, write a brief foreword.)

Finally, on October 11, he presented himself at the Liebling-Wood offices. Asking to see his agent, Audrey, he was told to wait with the small crowd who gathered daily, hoping for acting jobs from Liebling, who was a casting agent. Shyly, he took a seat, and when Liebling told him that there was no part for a young man that day, he finally spoke up and announced himself. At that moment Audrey was passing from the outer to the inner office, and heard his name.

The problem they discussed that day was not the acceptance of a story or the production of a play. "His primary need was survival," according to her. "It was unending struggle to stay alive and fed until we could find a producer who would give his work a production. Tennessee needed every penny of the sustenance we could find him." That sustenance included not only trying to sell poems and stories, but also convincing backers or actors to pay option money on his one-act plays. Hume Cronyn recognized the talent behind the short plays, and he advanced money and tried to interest others.*

"I was just beginning to become interested in production and direction," Cronyn recalled. "I peddled these plays around without any success, [but it was] difficult to persuade people to invest in a bill of one-act plays. . . . And there was no such thing as off-Broadway. There was really nowhere else except the commercial theatre to do those plays. . . . I was going to give them up, but Audrey asked me if I could manage to hold them under option for an added six months," because of Williams's financial hardship.

"That was truly an act of faith on Hume's part," Audrey wrote later; "the money came out of his own pocket, not from backers." (Almost eight years later, after a few brief, intermittent meetings, Cronyn and Williams would visit under more auspicious circumstances, after Cronyn had married Jessica Tandy.)

The doling of option money, the small fees from poems and stories and an occasional addition of a few dollars from her own purse — these were managed by Audrey, as well as constant attempts to get him work even outside the theatre. She arranged for him to attend Broadway rehearsals meantime, and she persuaded friends like the wife of theatrical lawyer John Wharton to pass along used warm clothing from her family as autumn turned colder.

---

* Cronyn paid an option fee of fifty dollars a month, which gave him production rights for nine one-act plays. "These plays were extremely poetic and they were very different from the theatre of the time," he said years later, "— the realism, the naturalism. They were plays that haunted me."

In Santa Monica, 1943

The Reverend Walter Edwin Dakin

About the time of *The Glass Menagerie*

Audrey Wood and clients: Williams, William Inge,
Maurice Valency and Carson McCullers

With Frank Merlo, Elia Kazan and Charles Feldman,
during filming of *A Streetcar Named Desire,* 1950

1431 Duncan Street, Key West, about 1952

With Donald Windham, Tanaquil LeClercq (dotted dress), Gore Vidal
and Buffie Johnson, in the garden of Café Nicholson, about 1951

"Audrey came to act as a surrogate mother, or perhaps an older sister, to Tennessee," according to playwright Robert Anderson, who a few years later became another of her most successful clients. "I was shocked, for example, to learn that by the mid-1940s she had already, for a long time, been taking care of his personal finances, paying his bills, answering his mail — sometimes even getting him out of trouble. He frequently called her at strange hours and she rushed to his aid when he was in some difficulty. Now this was not entirely exceptional in those days, when an agent's function was more personal — but Audrey was certainly an extreme example of personal care in the case of Tennessee Williams. I think she liked it, actually — after all, she and her husband had no children, and there may have been something in his dependency that she liked."

In spite of her tireless efforts as guardian angel that fall of 1939, however, the money to survive in New York was not forthcoming, and after a brief stay at the Men's Residence Club on West 56th Street — where the five-dollar-a-week room fee included use of a pool — he had no choice but to return to St. Louis. It was a visit he made with considerable reluctance, for it seemed to justify his father's disapproval. His only contact with the writer's life, from November to January, was his correspondence with Audrey, and his completion of a new long play that had been taking shape for several months within him. By year's end, he complained to Audrey in several letters, he was exhausted from alternate moods of rapture and despair from work on the play; he added that it might be his last, for his nerves could not sustain the creative agony.

But just as he was sending these poignant cries, she was sending happier news: the Dramatists Guild, through a grant from the Rockefeller Foundation, had awarded him a writing fellowship of one thousand dollars — which, she added, she would parcel out to him in monthly payments of one hundred dollars.

Once again, his fortunes and his journey were reversed, and early in January 1940 he was back in New York, where Molly Day Thacher joined Audrey in taking the cause of his new play to the Theatre Guild. The noted critic and theatre historian John Gassner was then an administrator at the Guild, and at once he offered Williams the opportunity to attend, without charge, his playwriting seminar at the New School for Social Research. By this time, E. C. Mabie had emigrated there from Iowa — with the recent arrival of Erwin Piscator's Drama Workshop — and the New School's writing and performing classes were regarded as among the most prestigious in America. (The New School's bulletins from the late 1930s through the late 1940s list among the faculty Robert Frost and W. H. Auden, teaching poetry; Hannah Arendt, philosophy; Paul Tillich, theology; Erich Leinsdorf, directing an opera workshop — a long, impressive list of artists and scholars in all fields.)

The New York theatre season was then also at its peak, and through the help of Gassner and Theresa Helburn at the Guild, Williams was able to see Guild productions of *The Philadelphia Story,* with Katharine Hepburn, Saroyan's *Time of Your Life,* Odets's *Night Music,* and rehearsals for Hemingway's *Fifth Column.* In class with Gassner, he polished revisions on a one-act play, *The Long Good-bye,* and on his new full-length play begun in St. Louis — whose title he had changed from *Something Wild in the Country* to *Battle of Angels.* Gassner, who liked the passion and poetry in the latter play, at once took it to the Guild again for consideration as a production later that year.

In his tenth-floor room at the West 63rd Street YMCA, Williams continued to write; from it he went forth to swim, to attend Guild plays and rehearsals, and to wander through Central Park and midtown. From these excursions there very quickly came a substantial number of acquaintances and of casual sexual contacts (often with men he met at the YMCA pool or steam room); he also found a small number of friends. First among them, and one whose camaraderie he would enjoy for some time to come, was an aspiring Southern writer ten years younger named Donald Windham. Their friendship became a creative collaboration within a few years and was sustained by a remarkably fecund and frank correspondence.

"He put writing before knowing where he was going to sleep or where his next meal was coming from," Windham said of Williams in the early 1940s. In spite of late nights in the cheaper bars of Times Square, Williams managed to produce a constant outpouring of manuscript pages. At the same time, Gassner, Piscator and a cast of nine were ready to present *The Long Good-bye,* and the first New York production of a play by Tennessee Williams was staged at the New School on Friday and Saturday, February 9 and 10; it was so well received that an additional performance was set for the following Wednesday.

The Long Good-bye, almost certainly modeled on Thornton Wilder's *Long Christmas Dinner,* was an experiment for Williams. It is his first memory-play, stretching time and space as a struggling young writer relives crucial moments in his past with his irresponsible father, dead mother and wandering sister. No one — not Gassner, not Audrey nor

Theresa Helburn nor Donald Windham — knew very much about his family at this time, and so no one could have known how personal the play was, how lightly veiled a psychological and emotional family and self-portrait. The brother's alter ego is his sister (named Myra, as in "The Field of Blue Children" and in the play to come next), who makes sexual contacts at a swimming pool, and who both attracts and repels him. The mother constantly moves from house to house and urges her son to stop writing and care for the sister. A friend tells him that his state of mind is abnormal, "starin' off into space like something's come loose in your head." The young poet, however, is more realistic — almost fatalistic: "You're saying good-bye all the time, every minute you live. Because that's what life is, just a long, long good-bye — to one thing after another!"

But the New School's endorsement and the Theatre Guild's evident interest in *Battle of Angels* did not send him back to his portable typewriter with increased confidence in his future; in fact, as he wrote to his mother, he fell into a frighteningly arid period. Through the spring, he took refuge in an increasingly depressing series of distractions that were mostly sexual (about which of course he did not write to his mother).

While he awaited news from the Guild on *Battle of Angels,* he left — for Mexico, he hoped, but he got only as far as Memphis and his grandparents: in early May the Guild sent Audrey a one-hundred-dollar option on the play, and the prospect of immediate casting and an early production drew him back to Manhattan. But at once there was difficulty finding actors for this strange and curious play full of ideas, myths and social-sexual decadence, ostensibly a story of the psychological interplay between a drifter in a Southern town, a dying storekeeper, his frustrated wife, a local seer and a religious fanatic. While Gassner, Audrey and Guild executive Lawrence Langner tried to smooth the way to a production, Williams, in disgust, left for a week of swimming at Lake George.

On his return, he deepened another important friendship which, like that with Donald Windham, never had to finesse the complications of romance. Paul Bigelow, one of the most trusted men in the theatre and a creative adviser on the Guild staff, supported Williams with his compassion and prudence and amity for forty years.

"I had an apartment on East 73rd Street at that time," Bigelow remembered. "We had met through the Guild, and since according to the drift of his fortunes he often had no place to live, I offered him a sofa, or he would curl up in the corner of the living room when he needed lodging. Often enough, he had a knack for finding stranger places to stay, but he stayed with me, irregularly, for considerable periods in the early 1940s. I recognized his talent — his needs no one could ignore — and as we became friends I was pleased to welcome him when I could."

For one weekend in June, Williams was the houseguest of Langner and his wife, actress-producer-director Armina Marshall, at their farm in Weston, Connecticut. "He was a charming guest," Langner wrote in his memoirs, "[who] rapidly completed his work [revising *Battle of Angels*], using a little summer house to write in." His return to New York was almost as brief, for he was restless about the Guild's inability to find a cast and fix a date.

"And so," according to Bigelow, "I put him on a train to Provincetown almost at once. It seemed the best thing for him — to get away to a place he could write and swim, and that welcomed serious writers. He was very rootless in New York, and never happy there. He had to come back, of course, because of Broadway, but it was never his city. At this time in his life, he had what I can only call an unformed emotional persona, and he did not deal very well with the pressures of city life." None of the pressures — urban or professional or personal — were alleviated by the worsening of the cataract that month. Bigelow thought the beauty and the creative life at Provincetown would help Williams's nervous spirit, his often alarming restlessness.

Not yet the overcrowded summer tourist haven of later years, Provincetown was a lively community at the extreme end of Cape Cod, a port of great natural charm and a place — like New Orleans — where Williams could find artists, writers, musicians and those whose sexual preference usually made them unwelcome elsewhere. And of course from 1916 it had been the locale for the famous and important Playhouse, from which Eugene O'Neill was presenting a series of dramatic works that altered the contours and possibilities of the American stage.

Williams took a room, for twenty dollars a week, at Captain Jack's Wharf, Commercial Street, an unpretentious array of small cottages on a pier overlooking Provincetown Harbor, facing east and the Long Point lighthouse. There he wrote, swam and went to the Provincetown Players' summer offerings — Molnar's *Liliom,* Shaw's *Heartbreak House,* Wilder's *Our Town,* O'Neill's *Diff'rent,* and Paul Vincent Carroll's *Shadow and Substance.*

* * *

One of the first in Provincetown to befriend Williams was the artist Fritz Bultman, a painter and sculptor from New Orleans who was studying with the legendary Hans Hofmann. Bultman, who described himself as "one of the irascibles among the founding fathers of abstract expressionism and of its manifesto," remembered Williams that summer of 1940 as "very hopeful and eager, but at the same time knowing and sophisticated about the theatre world and about people. At the same time, he was not a professional person of the stage, and he was a bohemian in his way of living. Up to that time, and often later, he lived from hand to mouth, by doing odd jobs. He was very amusing and witty, and he could be absolutely charming. But there was an undercurrent of self-absorption."

Ruth Hiebert, whose family managed Captain Jack's Wharf and who was there at the time, remembered Williams as earnest about his craft, "just like the other writers and artists who came to Provincetown to work in peace." But she also had "some unpleasant memories," and those no doubt concerned the key element of summer 1940 in his life. It was, in short, a time of considerable sexual activity.

"My left eye was cloudy then because it was developing a cataract," he said later. "But my right eye was clear. It was like the two sides of my nature. The side that was obsessively homosexual, compulsively interested in sexuality. And the side that in those days was gentle and understanding and contemplative."

The "compulsive" interest in sexuality was not only manifested in a quick succession of partners in the first several days. In addition, there was a steady companion during those weeks — a young Canadian dancer who had assumed the name Kip Kiernan. He had been born in Toronto to a family of devout Russian Jews, and he derived his new first name from his uncle, the Ukrainian opera singer Alexander Kipnis. Williams could never remember Kip's family name; in fact, Kip was slow to reveal it to anyone, for he was an illegal alien who earned money that summer modeling at the Hans Hofmann art school in Provincetown. By his own admission, Williams's sexual demands on Kip were relentless.*

"Kip was a very solid, straightforward young man," according to Fritz Bultman, "and he became quite devoted to Tennessee." But although

---

* At the end of July, Williams wrote to Donald Windham a detailed account of a typical night with Kip, who (he told Windham) sometimes had to sleep on the beach to get an hour away from the sexually insatiable Williams. "It was an intense, strange kind of relationship," according to Paul Bigelow, in whom Williams confided later in New York, "but then all Tenn's sexual relationships were intense and strange."

the relationship was intensely physical, Williams was not interested in permanence or exclusivity. Later, he claimed that the end of the affair was "shattering" for him, and that it was precipitated by Kip's fear that his dance career would be jeopardized and his status as an alien draft-dodger would mean deportation if it became known that he was a practicing homosexual. But the truth of the matter is that Williams was as avid in his search for other partners as he was in his need to write intensively, daily. Work and sex were feverish, necessary.

By mid-September he had taken the remaining Rockefeller Foundation money and traveled to Mexico City — and then on to Acapulco, where he met Jane and Paul Bowles, both writers (and he also a composer) whose collegiality and friendship he would enjoy for many years. From there he went on to the Costa Verde, a hillside hotel over the stillwater beach called Caleta.

Until late September he enjoyed the steamy languor of the place and its motley crew of guests, who ranged from a party of German guests (exultant over early Nazi victories) to a few wandering writers and artists, like himself. That summer he later called "a desperate period. . . . I expected to be dead before [it] was over" — not because he had fallen ill, but because he was convinced that the Guild had dropped its option on *Battle of Angels* and because the wound left by the dancer was still fresh in his heart.

"But it's during such times that we are most alive," he added, and indeed, he felt enough vitality to write the first draft of a full-length comedy, *Stairs to the Roof,* and of a short story, "The Night of the Iguana." The story (incomplete until 1946 and bearing the merest hint of a resemblance to his great play of 1961) incarnates, in the character of the spinster Miss Jelkes and her unlikely experiences with a homosexual couple, the summer's tensions, from whose grip the writing was refuge.

By early October he had retraced his journey as far as St. Louis, and he visited for the first time the new family home at 53 Arundel Place, a comfortable, eight-room brick colonial with garden. Here he learned that screen actress Miriam Hopkins had agreed to return to the stage in *Battle of Angels* (a part he had actually written with Tallulah Bankhead in mind); the Guild was ready to proceed. For ten days, this kept him in a panic of inactivity, and he remained with his family — a dubious sanctuary at the best of times. He had regarded the manuscript as only a first draft, on which he would have time to work on substantial revisions with a director and cast; according to the director, in fact, "he had been secretly appalled when . . . he had read in *The New York Times* that the Guild was about to put it into rehearsal. He knew he lacked the technical expertise to make alterations on demand, as the Guild so often required, and he was dazed by all the haste."

On October 24, he was back in a room at the 63rd Street YMCA, New York, going to meetings at Audrey's office and at the Guild offices with Langner and his assistant Theresa Helburn, and with director Margaret Webster.

"Why they should have thought of engaging a young, English woman director who had never been farther south than Washington to direct this work, I cannot imagine," Webster admitted. "[Rather,] the local color and the poetic prose in which it was written called for a director who was at ease in the medium of poetry.* . . . I read the play, and thought that it wasn't, and never would be, a very good one, but that there was power in it and some splendid, multicolored words, and I believed the author would one day live up to his obvious potential talent and write a real dazzler. I also thought the Theatre Guild was very brave to do it. So did they."

There was not, after his trip to Mexico, money left for his living expenses from the option on the play, and Williams had to await box-office receipts for any profit on the work. He took a job at the Gotham Book Mart, a favorite stop for bibliophiles on West 47th Street, but he proved himself so inept at wrapping packages that he was dismissed after one day.

But rehearsals were beginning in New York in November, prior to a scheduled opening on Monday, December 30, at the Wilbur Theatre in Boston; after two weeks there they hoped to proceed to New York. Williams was summoned to the first rehearsal, and Margaret Webster recalled "a short, sturdy young man with crew-cut hair, pebble-thick glasses and an even thicker Southern accent, dressed in a shabby corduroy jacket and muddy riding boots. He greeted us amiably; Miriam [Hopkins] said she hoped he had enjoyed his ride; he replied that he never went riding but that he liked the boots. He then sat down on the spotless yellow satin chaise-longue [in Webster's hotel suite] and put them up on it. We started to talk about the play; he didn't seem much interested; once, when Miriam became a little vehement, he prefaced his reply with 'As far

---

* It was precisely because she was "at ease in the medium of poetry" that the Guild selected Margaret Webster, a noted director of Shakespeare and, in 1939, supervisor of Shakespeare productions at the New York World's Fair.

as I can gather from all this hysteria . . .' This is what is known in the language of *Variety* as 'stoperoo.' . . . [Williams] was, in fact, stupefied by the maelstrom of the Broadway theatre into which he had been flung quite suddenly and unexpectedly," and he responded by withdrawing into himself, by lying down and closing his eyes. This was often mistaken for haughtiness and incivility — in fact it was sheer terror.

Williams himself described *Battle of Angels* as "a mixture of super religiosity and hysterical sexuality co-existing in a central character," and that is true enough.

The action describes several complex relationships. Myra, in her midthirties, is trapped in a loveless marriage to Jabe Torrance, an older man who is dying of cancer. Into her life comes the young, virile, itinerant poet Val Xavier, who is hired to work in the Torrances' shop and who stirs up the town. Besides Myra's attraction to him, Val has to cope with the blandishments of the sexually obsessed Cassandra Whiteside, and the repressed sexual hysteria of Vee Talbot, a painter and a religious eccentric who is also wife of the local sheriff. Val becomes Myra's lover, she learns that she is pregnant, Jabe discovers this and announces that it was he who had killed Myra's father years earlier, and the play ends in multiple acts of violence: Jabe shoots Myra, and Val is hung and burnt by the sheriff's posse. Passionate and symbol-congested, it is clearly the work of a novice (if serious) craftsman, intrigued with Christian symbolism, Dionysian myth, Freudian motifs and D. H. Lawrence (to whose memory it is dedicated). In spite of a dense structural tangle, *Battle* nevertheless introduced all the major concerns of Williams — the urge for life, expressed in the desire for freedom and constant flight ("You and me," says the prophetic Cassandra to the hapless drifter Val Xavier,* "belong to the fugitive kind. We live on motion. . . . Nothing but motion, motion, mile after mile, keeping up with the wind."); the inevitability of sexual tension and jealousy, and the desire to be both immersed in sex and free of its demands; the interweaving of Lawrentian body-mysticism and the Christian yearning for transcendence; the necessity of sacrifice and atonement; the eternal struggle between truth and mendacity. At the same time, the play contains the basic theatrical methods through which these concerns will be more maturely treated in the later plays: material

* Val Xavier's name was derived from that of a distant ancestor in Williams's paternal grandmother's family, whose name was changed to Sevier in England. If, as some have claimed, there is a connection to the Spanish-French Xavier lineage, then it is possible (as Williams sometimes liked to think) that an earlier branch of the family tree was grafted onto the same family from which came the famous Spanish Jesuit missionary, St. Francis Xavier. See p. 164.

experimentation and technical innovation; the counterpoise of supporting characters; naturalistic dialogue that is somehow penetrated with poetic diction.

But of immediate concern to the producers, director and cast were the
mammoth technical demands Williams's script made: sound effects,
lightning and thunder, guitar music and songs, and a great fire at the
end, which is to burn up the entire setting. Smoke pots were called for,
but the effect at rehearsal was weak. By December 30, everyone was in a
barely suppressed panic.

They had, it turned out, good reason to fear. Many at the opening
night, unaccustomed to plays that dealt so bluntly with connections between religious hysteria and unacknowledged lust, and with the unsubtle
innuendoes in the dialogue, abandoned the theatre long before the final
moments. And those who remained were very nearly subjected to as-
phyxiation, for the smoke pots worked all too well, and both cast and
audience were enveloped in a thick, choking smoke.

For years after, the impression was given by Williams and others that
Boston critics and the staid Boston censors at once closed the play as
morally objectionable. But the critics were, in fact, genuinely (if cautiously) in favor of it. Alexander Williams, writing in *The Boston Herald*
the day after the opening, called the play "astonishing. . . . [It was] our
privilege to see it. . . . The scene where the religious fanatic discovers that
she has painted Valentine Xavier as Christ is uncomfortable, but that is
due to our own scruples and the playwright's uncompromising realism at
this point." And Elliot Norton, in *The Boston Post,* called the author's talent "most interesting," the characters "credible," and the playwright
"compassionate, [with] a gift for vividness." (The New York-based
critic from *Variety,* on the other hand, called the play "sordid and amateurish," and farther south, the *Clarksdale Register,* whose critic did not
see the last act, attacked it as a dirty drama about the author's home.)

Battle of Angels did, however, run for its scheduled two weeks, by
which time a member of the Boston City Council, responding to a few
complaints from irate theatregoers, decided to become involved. "Then it
was," Williams wrote soon after, "that censors sat out front and demanded excision from the script of practically all that made it intelligi-
ble, let alone moving."

Williams was overreacting as sharply as the few severe critics, however,
and it was, at last, much ado about not very much: one council member
did indeed denounce it as "putrid. . . . This show is a crime to be

permitted to run in the city of Boston," but his exact objections will never be known. He did not see the play, and later he refused quite rightly to elaborate. Then a minor politician took up the cause, and his tirade forced the police commissioner to call in the city censor himself, but he was out of town at the Sugar Bowl football game. Finally, an assistant from his office attended the January 7 performance and reported to the police commissioner that yes, there were a few offensive lines. The Guild ordered them dropped from the next evening's performance. And so it could be in the more stringent conditions of 1941.

But the real damage, done mostly by society's word-of-mouth, was fatal. Miriam Hopkins, exhausted but not dispirited, called a press conference, defended her appearance in a serious drama, and suggested that the City Council be flung into the harbor with the historic tea.

There was no question of bringing the play to New York, and the Guild drafted a letter to its subscribers, explaining its original enthusiasm for the play, praising its experimental style and its psychological honesty, as well as the author's real poetic gifts. But they admitted that it was not, in the final analysis, dramatically successful.

William Jay Smith was in Boston for that opening, and he thought the play, although terribly uneven, had tremendous power. And Audrey Wood never for a moment lost faith in her client's future success, even after the next morning, when a meeting was held at the Ritz-Carlton and the decision not to move to New York was announced. "Tom asked me to stay on with him for a while," Smith remembered long after the depressing meeting, "and indeed he appeared so depressed that I hesitated to leave him. He said nothing about *Battle of Angels* but went to his suitcase and took out an anthology of poetry and asked me to read aloud to him the poems of John Donne, which I did for the next few hours."

The months that followed were as rootless and displaced a time as he would ever feel. "Wherever he went, even then, as he has done all his life, he worked long and hard, totally dedicated to his craft," Audrey Wood said of those early years. "To say that he struggled is an understatement." And Donald Windham, with whom Williams spent long evenings in 1940 and 1941 touring Manhattan bars, affirmed that "although *Battle of Angels* had failed and he could not get his stories or poems published, his devotion to his writing remained. He was penniless, borrowing when he could, no longer living in the comparative affluence of option money and grants."

The business of survival — not to say the maintenance of creative energy — was further complicated by an extraordinary unworldliness.
Companions from the early 1940s remember retrieving from laundry
sacks the small checks from Audrey. Appointments would be forgotten,
conversations unattended and meetings blithely dispatched to oblivion.
Paul Bigelow described him as "just not being with you during most of
his visits with you"; he counted on the alertness, the alacrity and the care
of those he knew to see him through the practical and the emotional
hurdles of life — both when his fortunes were grim and when they were
glorious.

Continuing his efforts to help a career in which he very much believed,
John Gassner reported to the Guild that producer Cheryl Crawford had
taken a lively interest in a trio of one-act plays Williams had left with
him in January: *At Liberty* dramatized the situation of a once successful
actress who has returned to her Mississippi home as a consumptive profligate, deluding herself that she can return to the stage. *This Property Is
Condemned,* a variant of the first, was the portrait of a lonely girl whose
promiscuous sister died of tuberculosis and who deludes herself into
thinking she has acquired the sister's boyfriends. And *Port Mad,* or *The
Leafless Block,* told of a deranged spinster living in poverty and with her
memories of a former lover. "All three possess sensitive writing," Gassner
wrote to the Guild, "and the last is deeply affecting. . . . From all this productivity an evening of one-acters could be made." (Eventually, *At Liberty* and *This Property Is Condemned* were combined into a double bill,
called *Landscape With Figures — Two Mississippi Plays,* published later in
1941 in William Kozlenko's collection *American Scenes. Port Mad* was revised three years later as *Portrait of a Madonna.*)

At the same time, Williams planned to work in another warm, beach-
front, tolerant refuge — this time Key West, which had been a refuge at
a time of dejection for his beloved Hart Crane. (Crane's *Key West: An Island Sheaf* had been published posthumously in *College Verse,* at the same
time as Williams's own poems were appearing in it.)

Stopping in New York en route from Boston to Key West, Williams
received his selective service classification card; even had he been younger
he would not have been a fit candidate, for his wretched vision at once
demanded a medical exemption. ("His eyesight," as Margaret Webster
wrote, "was such that he could not distinguish an enemy soldier from a
friendly tank.") The cataract in his left eye was so advanced that an operation was performed in New York that month. It was only partly suc-

cessful, and even after several later submissions to surgery he would never have good vision in the damaged left eye.

"I had a small apartment on Morton Street, in Greenwich Village," Fritz Bultman recalled, "and since Tennessee had nowhere to stay when he was recovering from his eye surgery, I put him up for a while. He made a quick recovery, and began working on the revisions of *Battle of Angels,* which Erwin Piscator and Herbert Berghof wanted to produce at the New School. As it happened, Piscator wanted the play reworked as a social drama about life in the South, and Tennessee saw at once that they could never see eye-to-eye and that his play would never be done by Piscator.

"That winter," Bultman continued, "I saw that there was another side to Williams. He had this great sweetness and charm and humor, and then he could be cold and abusive as ice. Very soon it was a nuisance to have him in the apartment. He would drag home a stranger during the night and then expect me to get rid of the fellow later. This went on when he visited again the following winter, but then I had to ask Tennessee to leave." Beside any other consideration, of course, the nightly wandering through the streets near New York's West Side piers was more than unhealthy in midwinter; it was just plain dangerous. But the daily work on his play and the nightly search for sexual excitement continued throughout January and into early the following month.

By February 12, with help from a five-hundred-dollar grant from the Rockefeller Foundation, he had checked into the Trade Winds, a century-old Key West house with separate, small guest cottages. The compound was owned by the widow of an Episcopal minister, Mrs. Cora Black, who had trotted from rectory to rectory as long as her husband was alive and had now settled into a more relaxed life. With her were her son George and her daughter Marion, who at once became Williams's friend and confidante. Five years older than he, she had been in the 1920s a governess to the daughter of Florenz Ziegfeld and Billie Burke; now, she was a delicate, soft-spoken, gentle, alcoholic nymphomaniac. During his intervals from working on the revisions of his play, he shared with Marion glasses of bourbon and stories of sexual escapades. (She became the model for the character named Cora, in the short story "Two on a Party," in which the homosexual Billy is a clear surrogate for Williams; and in 1957, when a new draft of *Battle of Angels* was finally staged as *Orpheus Descending,* it was dedicated to Marion.)

The life of the Black family was financially improved by Marion's wedding, not long after, to Regis Vaccaro; after his death in the late 1950s, he left her a fortune from his investments with a fruit-trading company. Eventually, she built a lavish mansion in Coconut Grove, on Biscayne Bay, and to the end of Marion's comfortably pathetic life she was known to Williams and his friends as "The Banana Queen of Coconut Grove," a double entendre she much relished.

But the genial Cora and Marion and George could not provide Williams with escape that season from a terrible storm of failure that raged inside him. Nor was his unhappy mood alleviated by Key West and Miami parties, where he met Max Eastman, John Dewey, James Farrell, Elizabeth Bishop and the former Mrs. Ernest Hemingway. His shyness and poor vision mostly kept him confined to the corner of a room. Again, his alternations of mood were as severe as his alternations of hope and finances. Physical and creative vision were failing him, and he wrote to Audrey Wood that he was continually harassed by "blue devils" that made him almost suicidal. Alarmed, his agent prevailed on him to take some of the Rockefeller money for a vacation, or to return to New York with the revisions of the play. He chose New York, but the Guild admitted they had by now lost interest, and *Battle of Angels* was quietly shelved.

The return to New York was not by a direct route. He stopped in Miami again, in St. Augustine and in Georgia, where he visited wandering theatre people like himself, those he had known in New York. He then paid another visit to St. Louis, where his father thought at first that he was now ready to settle down at last with a serious job, and to haul firewood to the backyard. After a few days he fled to Manhattan and to its (comparative) acceptance of him.*

Partly because Paul Bigelow and other New York friends found him almost unbearably depressed throughout the early summer of 1941, Williams was encouraged to revisit New England. In July he wandered along the coast of Massachusetts, at last settling into a Harvard dormitory with a brilliant twenty-year-old law student named Bill Cannastra. Extraordinarily handsome and manically bisexual, Cannastra was an addition to Williams's growing list of unusual contacts: alcoholic from an early age,

---

* Early in the spring of 1941 his first published play appeared, in Margaret Mayorga's *Best One Act Plays of 1940* (this was also his first appearance in a book rather than a magazine). The play was *Moony's Kid Don't Cry*, a revision of *Hot Milk at Three in the Morning*, to which he had added some dialogue about a man's psychotic breakdown and confinement to an asylum. The Kozlenko book, containing *Landscape with Figures*, appeared later that year. Total payment for the two was under fifty dollars.

his looks and talent and sexual availability provided access to circles that
included W. H. Auden and Chester Kallman and Jack Kerouac. His preferred form of erotic activity was, it seems, a strange mixture of voy-
eurism and exhibitionism, which Williams found amusing.

Half the summer of 1941 Williams spent in a haze of sexual and al-
cholic confusion that he finally realized was decreative and dangerous. He
returned to Bigelow's East 73rd Street apartment at the end of July,
avoided liquor long enough to converse sensibly with Audrey and a few
magazine editors, and again left for the South. One of the poems he left
with his agent was written the night before the meeting, at Bigelow's
kitchen table, and it included a description of his obsessive nightly wanderings through New York's streets:

> Then I must that night go in search of one
> unknown before but recognized on sight
> whose touch, expedient or miracle,
> stays panic in me and arrests my flight.

New Orleans could, he hoped, provide freshness once again. From late
September through late October he stayed at no less than four boardinghouses, either alone or with those he had met casually at bars or at the
New Orleans Athletic Club. The renovation of the French Quarter was
continuing in the early 1940s, under the inspired supervision of Lyle
Saxon and Elizabeth Werlein, with whom Williams often took breakfast
at the famous Morning Call Coffee Shop; they were sometimes joined by
writer Roark Bradford, to whom Williams first told the story of his
meeting with two bizarre people at the Athletic Club — a sadistic black
masseur who had found a willing partner in a frail white masochist. He
was already beginning a transformation, into short fiction, of this curious
pair. Later he completed his gruesome tale "Desire and the Black Masseur," which concludes with the literal devouring of the masochist by the
sadistic masseur.

Letters to Audrey Wood from New Orleans paralleled his production
of poems and stories that autumn. He asked for cash, and for some hope:
Did she think Hume Cronyn would renew the option on his one-act
plays? Would Cronyn be interested in a long drama about D. H.
Lawrence, or one based on Lawrence's fiction? What about the Guild, or
another fellowship?

He interrupted the New Orleans sojourn once, in early November,
when word reached him about his grandmother's illness. She had gone to

her daughter in St. Louis to consult specialists about terrifying symptoms
that would begin two years of suffering before her death.

Literally penniless and needing a second eye operation, he returned to
New York at the beginning of March 1942, and after a harrowing day on
a surgeon's table he recovered enough to take a job: he recited his poems
and served patrons at the Beggar's Bar in Greenwich Village. There he
sported a patch with an eye brightly painted on it, and Valesca Gert, the
Polish-German refugee proprietor, welcomed this new addition to her
crew of eccentrics. "The Beggar's Bar was a mess of a place," according to
Fritz Bultman, "but there Tennessee stayed. Valesca was just wild and
eccentric enough for him, and she even provided him with a young playwright he had an affair with. The writer went back home to Germany
after the war." As for Valesca Gert, she turned up in Federico Fellini's
1965 film *Juliet of the Spirits,* as the hermaphrodite prophetess of sex-as-
wisdom.

Tennessee's acquaintance with the demimonde of wartime Greenwich
Village was also highlighted by meetings with artist Olive Leonard ("a
pathetic lady who therefore was psychologically attractive to Tenn," according to Bigelow); she later became the model for the mad female artist in his 1975 novel, *Moise and the World of Reason.*

Partly because of his growing obsession with the life and spirit of
D. H. Lawrence, and also because he was at this time often in the company of (more or less) serious artists, Williams began to sketch (as
Lawrence had done). Almost all his artwork, then and later, celebrates
the primitive and the sensual, and reflects the daily and nightly experiences of that winter.

The insistence that dedication to the private life of the senses is itself
an art antedated Lawrence, he knew (and in this regard Williams did not
read Lawrence quite accurately). But in early 1942, he seems to have considered the life of the senses as if it were a new religion. That year, as he
told Donald Windham, was a period of selfish, blind hedonism he could
interrupt only by the hours he was traveling from city to city. And in a
poem written in February he confirmed the association between sensuality and religion:

> ... our blood is sacred; to the mouth
> the tongue of the beloved is holy bread ...
> as earth divides, our bodies meet and burn
> and in our mouths we take the holy bread.

It was at this time that Fritz Bultman had to ask Williams to find other lodgings.

Williams's connection with Lawrence was concrete as well as psychological by the spring of 1942. Windham had completed an outline and several scenes of a projected play based on Lawrence's short story "You Touched Me," and after reading it Williams suggested they collaborate on a full-length comedy.

By the end of May, however, Williams had not even the price of a room at the YMCA, and there was no option money in sight for the first draft of *You Touched Me*. Bigelow was about to leave New York for a visit with friends in Macon, Georgia, "and just a few days after I left him alone at 73rd Street," Bigelow recalled, "he wrote, saying he could not bear to be alone and that if we would have him he would join us in Georgia. Of course I replied at once, and by mid-June he arrived, tired and nervous." He had not been encouraged even by a first-rate production, on June 2 at the New School, of *This Property Is Condemned*, which shared a bill with one-act plays by Synge, Strindberg and Molière.

Board was free that summer in Macon, and Williams used the small attic room to write. He was beginning the short story "Kingdom of Earth"; he completed revisions for the autobiographical comedy he had begun in Mexico (*Stairs to the Roof*, about a young writer in a shoe factory); he dramatized his short story "The Malediction" into a one-act play, *The Strangest Kind of Romance* (which concerns a man and his cat); and he completed more poems. With this impressive productivity, as Bigelow was pleased to see, his nerves calmed, his humor again grew keen.

"He was a real wit — not just that summer, but for most of the years I knew him. He had a constant, quick humor, not just an occasional joke or remark. He was always amused by life, and at the same time he was saddened by it."

The combination of warmth and humor with a kind of wry acceptance of the vagaries of life was maturing in his personality that summer; it would often be reflected in his great plays, and in any case he was always, as Bigelow said, "enormously good fun to be with, no matter what he was working on."

By the end of August, he had earned a small amount of cash by cleaning tables at a Macon restaurant, and so he decided to return to Key West and to the Black family. But he reached only Jacksonville, where he found work operating a teletype machine for the United States Department of Engineers, a division of the War Department. This he held until the middle of November, working mostly nights and writing and swimming by day. (Audrey Wood and John Gassner had suggested major revisions on *You Touched Me,* and he worked on those while writing almost daily to Windham.)

But just as his moods had swung during the previous months, so it was that season. He wrote to Audrey Wood and to friends in New York and Georgia and Massachusetts that since 1938 he had really not known a day of complete serenity, that he lived in continual fear of the world and almost everyone in it, and that the great psychological trauma of his life was the tragedy of his sister. How he would transform these fears and this personal history into his art he did not know. But as he made clear in a ten-page, pencil-written letter to Audrey dated September 15, 1942, the single great threat to his integrity as a writer was the temptation to take the easy way out by not dealing with the things he knew best — family pain, mental instability, emotional obsessions, the conflict between the love of solitude and the desire for human comfort. Better than any woman in his life during the 1940s, Audrey Wood heard his written and spoken laments; better than anyone, she showed him how it was precisely by perseverance in the struggle that the purification he so desired might be effected.

By year's end he was back in New York, pouring out his feelings in person to her, to Bigelow and to Windham, and working (again, for only a few weeks at each job) as an elevator operator at the San Jacinto Hotel, and as an usher in a midtown movie theatre — not the happiest situations for a man of bad eyesight who was also constantly discomposed by his own reveries. One evening Audrey took him to a Chekhov play, thinking this would cheer him; it was the production of *Three Sisters* with Katharine Cornell, Judith Anderson and Ruth Gordon, and with them was his classmate from Iowa, Anthony Dexter.

"It was a depressing night," Dexter recalled. "Tom had his cataract problem, he had not yet had the success he had expected, and he was a most unhappy sight to see. But he showed no sign of self-pity. He was his usual half-laughing self. I believe none of us realized his great potential."

By Easter 1943, boredom and poverty again forced him out of New York — but not before he met the man who would for the rest of his life be his primary publisher. His poems had been passed along from Donald

Windham to Lincoln Kirstein (for whom Windham worked as a temporary secretary at *Dance Index* magazine), and Kirstein gave them to James Laughlin, the publisher of New Directions books. When Laughlin included a selection of Williams's poems in an anthology the following year, it would be the start of an author-publisher relationship that ripened into cordial permanence.

Returning to St. Louis, he found only emotional turmoil and heartache. His beloved grandmother was slowly dying of cancer, but so uncomplainingly and courageously that she brought tears to his eyes as he sat by her bedside or helped her with the small household tasks she insisted on doing. The combination of her valor with the horror of her illness reminded him of Hart Crane, and as he endured the unpleasantness of his father's temper he thought all the more of that poet, driven to suicide. These reflections he put into letters to Audrey, and to Donald Windham.

"He hated being in St. Louis in the 1940s," Paul Bigelow said. "He resented everything about it, and now he worried about his grandmother's dying, and about the future of his eighty-six-year-old grandfather, who found life in St. Louis very painful. He had in some mysterious way lost every cent several years before, and he depended on Cornelius and Edwina, who resented him precisely because of this loss. All this made Tenn's visits home quite painful."

The final and most poignant sadness of those weeks at Arundel Place was a series of letters from Rose, still confined at the state hospital in Farmington. Calm she was, but utterly without clarity or reason. She wrote to her brother that he was lucky to be in prison, like herself, because screaming crowds of hungry people were clamoring at the city gates.

It was precisely the short series of letters from his sister that made him plunge into the first draft of a new play whose title was *The Gentleman Caller*. He was fully aware of its autobiographical nature from the start, for he wrote to Windham that it was taking shape as a personal history of his family. The play would be a tribute to Rose, and a cry from his heart about the serenity they had all gradually lost over the years and were never able to regain.

Then, at the end of April, a telephone call from Audrey Wood altered things dramatically. She had negotiated with executives at Metro-Goldwyn-Mayer, in Hollywood, and had got him a six-month contract as a screenwriter, at the incredible sum of $250 a week. This was so shocking for him that at first he thought that figure represented a monthly salary. But never mind, Audrey exclaimed happily, he should simply come to New York to sign the contracts and to gather whatever manuscripts he wanted to take with him, and then proceed at once by train — by train! — to Los Angeles. He had taken, she assured him, his last bus ride. At the same time, she prudently sent to M-G-M a detailed list of "properties owned by Tennessee Williams" prior to this contract, so that he would always retain rights to what he had written before May 1943. The list included ten long plays, twelve "long short" plays, seventeen one-act plays, nineteen short stories and over two hundred fifty poems.

Film studios were engaging novelists and playwrights in great numbers in those busier days of multiple productions. At various times William Faulkner was part of the group of American writers Hollywood contracted, as were F. Scott Fitzgerald, John Steinbeck, Clifford Odets, Thornton Wilder, Maxwell Anderson, Robert E. Sherwood, Sidney Howard, John O'Hara and Katherine Anne Porter, as well as Lillian Hellman, Nathanael West and Samson Raphaelson. When he went to the Liebling-Wood offices on May 4 to sign the contract with M-G-M, he felt in good company and in high spirits. Three days later he was on his way to Los Angeles, under very different circumstances from the 1939 trek that ended at a pigeon ranch.

The contract specified that his first assignment was the screenplay of *Marriage Is a Private Affair,* which was to star Lana Turner. By May 17, he realized that there was no route by which he could appreciate the story or the requirements for what he bitterly called a "celluloid brassiere" for Miss Turner, but he had no choice except to give his superiors the impression he was hard at work on it.*

Nothing could have been farther from the truth. During the days before he reported to the M-G-M offices in Culver City, he had contacted David Greggory, a friend from the earlier days in New York. Greggory had gone to Hollywood to work in films and now gave him a hearty welcome, helping him get a driving license and a used car. Together they rented rooms in a boardinghouse at 1647 Ocean Avenue, Santa Monica, with a spectacular view of the Pacific and less than a minute's walk for swimming.

But Williams had no typewriter, and since Greggory was about to em-

* Years later, in his play *Small Craft Warnings,* Williams has the elderly writer Quentin say that Hollywood found him "too literate for my first assignment, converting an epic into a vehicle for the producer's doxy, a grammar school dropout."

bark on a cross-country motor trip, he asked him to return by way of St. Louis and bring the old one he had left behind.

"I went to Clayton and met Miss Edwina," Greggory recalled, "and it was a very formal and Victorian interview. I remember that she questioned me about his behavior and his health — in that order. She gave me a letter to deliver to him, and when I got back to Santa Monica he showed it to me. 'It is my opinion,' she had written, 'that anyone who wishes to make a living as a writer should be able to provide his own materials.' And she had enclosed with it a clipping about Edgar Allan Poe, and how he had died a gutter alcoholic. She wasn't thrilled about his occupation as a writer."

The resumption of the camaraderie with Greggory was important to Williams. "We found the apartment quite by accident," Greggory added, "an old frame building with several apartments for boarders. Ours was a large L-shaped studio. The landlady was a remarkable, well-preserved woman, and very freewheeling. She always had a couple of young male admirers courting her." Within days of meeting this formidable landlady — who was partly, Williams told Greggory later, the basis for the character of Maxine Faulk in *The Night of the Iguana* — he had begun a short story she inspired. This became "The Mattress by the Tomato Patch." Simultaneously (as he was always able to do) he began or polished a number of other stories — "The Coming of Something to the Widow Holly," "Chronicle of a Demise," "The Angel in the Alcove," a verse play based on Robert Browning's "My Last Duchess" (which he called "The Balcony in Ferrara") and poems that reflected his nostalgia for New Orleans and his anguish over his grandmother's imminent death.

Life at Ocean Avenue was relaxed and this Williams needed, for he was soon chafing under the M-G-M servitude. "I visited his office there," Greggory said, "and he simply couldn't lick the problems of the Lana Turner film. There in his office was a picture of Chekhov, so it wasn't hard to see how different his intentions were from writing a 'celluloid brassiere' for her." Instead, Williams began to draft film treatments, proposals, outlines and sample scenes for films he wanted to submit to Pandro Berman, a producer of major films at M-G-M; most of them were, of course, based on Williams's own short stories or plays.

On May 31, Audrey Wood received by mail a nine-sequence outline for a film to be based on his short story "Portrait of a Girl in Glass," and the play he had begun which was based on it, *The Gentleman Caller*. With its indication of dissolves and image-overlays, its insertion of musical motifs and its plastic, dreamlike construction, it was conceived as a film of memory. "This is what he most wanted to see realized on the screen," according to Greggory, "and he hoped M-G-M would take it in lieu of *Marriage Is a Private Affair*." Throughout May and June he continued to work on it (while the studio expected him to be occupying himself with the Turner film), and by late July he had prepared a detailed scenario. He also had selected the right actress to play Laura, the surrogate for his sister Rose: it was written expressly, he told Audrey, for Teresa Wright, the Oscar-winning star (for *Mrs. Miniver*, in 1942) and one of the busiest and most popular players in Hollywood.

The reaction to *The Gentleman Caller* was instantly negative, however; M-G-M was not interested in a story about Southern women — *Gone With the Wind* had served up enough of them for a decade, he was told. And so it was that the studio lost the opportunity to buy all rights for what would soon be called *The Glass Menagerie*.

"This really hurt him at the time," Greggory said. "He asked me if I thought he'd be paid each week even if he didn't show up at the office, and I said it was worth a try — things at studios were generally rather loose, and writers simply had to say they were working at home. Sure enough, for a few weeks he got paid even though he didn't go in at all." The paychecks of course were forwarded to Audrey, who, at Williams's request, doled him an allowance and sent most of the rest to St. Louis — for his grandmother's medical care, and for Rose, who was permitted the summer at a North Carolina rest home. He kept little cash on hand for his own amusements.

But for diversions only very little cash was needed. He was making new friends; he swam and wrote daily — these were always his two scheduled activities — and he also pursued the easy life he said had been denied when he had lived in Los Angeles in 1939.

The first of the friendships was with the writer Christopher Isherwood. "He just showed up one day at my house in Santa Monica," Isherwood said, "and we very quickly became good friends. He was very outgoing with me. There was no veneer of a false manner. It was only after we met socially that he mentioned that he wrote poetry, and when he showed me a selection I must admit that I wasn't exactly knocked senseless by them. But after all, a lot of inferior work is produced by great artists, and his poems are nothing like his great plays. Then he told me he was writing a play and a screenplay about his sister, and he confided some of the family history to me. About that history he was incredibly creative."

Isherwood, then deeply committed to exploring the history and practice of Eastern religions, was one of the first to learn something of Williams's private life in Santa Monica. He visited Ocean Avenue and found him "sitting typing a film story in a yachting cap, amidst a litter of dirty coffee cups, crumpled bed linen, and old newspapers. . . . Tennessee is the most relaxed creature imaginable: he works till he's tired, eats when he feels like it, sleeps when he can't stay awake. . . . Since the coastal area had been put under a wartime blackout, the park at the top of the cliffs had become a sex jungle at night, full of servicemen and their hunters. Tennessee was in his element there. I walked with him a little way into the thrilling darkness but didn't join him in the hunt."

David Greggory elaborated life along the Pacific Palisades in those days. "It was wartime, and all bets were off. Everybody who had any money at all was spending it. There was an attitude that was partly desperation and partly the feeling that life had better be enjoyed right now. You couldn't walk a block in Santa Monica without meeting people who wanted to be 'friends,' and quite often many of them were sailors in port. People made friends and short-time lovers all over; the spirit was 'Eat, drink and be merry, for tomorrow —' and this was especially the attitude of the sailors and those who were attracted to them." And according to Isherwood, "In his private life he was very bold, very spontaneous, whereas I was very British and complicated. He made contacts with people very easily."

"He always had strong and governing sex urges and impulses," Paul Bigelow said. "It was a burden, his sexual drive. He once said to me, rather pathetically, that he hoped with the passing of time it would lessen in intensity. He saw his libido as a painful burden, and he discovered later that in his case it did not in fact lessen with time. With Tenn it was a persistent, driving urge that accompanied him through life."

What Isherwood, Greggory and Bigelow (among others) witnessed over the years was in fact a deep, poignant disconnection in the life of Tennessee Williams — a vast space between his artistic vision and his personal reality. From his late twenties to the end of his life, whether he had a stable relationship or not, he sought sexual partners incessantly.

In this regard, the Dionysian side of him — manic, wild and ecstatic — revealed a Byronic romanticism. Rejecting order, clarity and serenity, such a romantic typically abandons logic and revels in chaos. He takes flight in excess — and sometimes in flight itself, constant travel. And often, especially in the case of the romantic who is sexually uninhibited, he seeks his satisfaction in the body of another. But such satisfaction is doomed precisely because no other human can perpetually appease an infinite need and an endless yearning, as any reflective romantic can attest. The search, then, becomes endless, the disappointment inevitable. And because he insists on the possibility of satisfaction in sensuality, there occurs a cycle of futility. He moves on, forever restless, betrayed by himself.

To observe this pattern in one's own life or the life of another is not to pass judgment. It is to assess a derailment that neither precludes great artistic achievement nor forecloses the possibility of great spiritual achievement. Such an assessment does, however, help to identify a real threat to emotional stability and to happiness — a threat that had dire consequences in the life of Tennessee Williams.

By the end of July, it was clear to M-G-M that Williams was not going to produce a screenplay for Lana Turner. Accordingly, he was first given a story about Billy the Kid, and when nothing came of this he was asked if he would write something for child star Margaret O'Brien. He replied that the "something" he had in mind for Margaret O'Brien was unprintable, which did not endear him to the studio after several months of uncooperation. On August 9, M-G-M suspended him without pay for six weeks because of his consistent refusal to work on assigned material.

But another reason for his lack of interest in studio work was the arrival in Los Angeles of the producer to whom Audrey Wood had sent *You Touched Me,* on the final emendations of which Williams and Windham had at last agreed. Margo Jones was an energetic woman from Dallas who had already directed Chekhov's *Uncle Vanya* in Texas, and who was therefore already virtually acceptable to Williams as producer. Strong-willed, magnetic and fiery with enthusiasm for the play, and for the reams of Williams manuscripts Audrey had also sent, she blew in "like a tornado," Williams reported to friends. Henceforth, she was called "the Texas tornado" by his entire circle.

It was Jones's plan to stage *You Touched Me* first at the Cleveland Playhouse in October, then to move west to the famous Pasadena Playhouse (or even to its more intimate performing space, the Playbox). By this time, she felt sure, they would have raised sufficient interest and money to bring it to Broadway.

During the layoff period from M-G-M, Williams and Jones (without the benefit of Windham's collaboration) revised, polished and restructured the play. This was almost certainly the first breach in the friendship with Windham, who felt left out of the final deliberations over a work on which they were to share not only equal credit but also equal compensation. (He was shocked to learn later that he was expected to sign an agreement forfeiting a percentage of his royalties in favor of Williams, who claimed that *You Touched Me* was more his than Windham's.)

While Windham awaited word from Santa Monica, Williams felt a new rush of optimism for the future. "From the day Margo arrived, he had a strong feeling that his success would lie in New York, with the theatre there," according to Greggory. "Much to the credit of Audrey Wood, whose communications to him were not only monetary but also full of affectionate encouragement, he saw hope for his future. Audrey and Margo made it absolutely clear to him that Broadway was in the cards."

By the end of September, Jones had been to New York for casting and had proceeded to Cleveland for rehearsals. Williams had hoped to accompany her, but by this time M-G-M was ready to give him another chance, and he needed the salary after six payless weeks. Windham instead went on to the first performances.

You Touched Me, although originally suggested by Windham, gave Williams an opportunity to formalize his affinity for Lawrence, and to endorse Lawrence's celebration of the flesh's triumph over Puritanism. The story follows Lawrence's with some embellishment: the arrival of a young man wins a repressed young woman away from her prudish aunt. To a rather straightforward romantic comedy Williams added the clear references to Lawrence's *Fox,* with its hen-house attacker. The play — even after its 1943 and 1945 alterations — has a dated quaintness about it, but it is perhaps too innocent for its own good. The overthrow of everything the aunt represents, and the sudden (and not entirely consistent) liberation of the girl, comprise thesis material more than compelling seriocomic action. Williams was prudent to write it in collaboration, so it would not bear his name alone. He seems, despite his somewhat disingenuous protest of devotion to it, to have known that it was a minor exercise — essentially a valentine to D. H. Lawrence.

As his M-G-M contract was about to expire, he added to his list of friends two whose fidelity and affection would remain precious in all the years to come, despite the occasional absences forced by professional obligations. The architectural designer and artist Tony Smith, whom he had met in Greenwich Village and who, working in Los Angeles, had also taken a room at Ocean Avenue, asked Williams to be best man at his wedding to the actress and singer Jane Lawrence, and on September 25, with a taxi-driver as the only other witness, the ceremony was held. Jane Smith remembered Williams's humor and candor and compassion, and his marvelous capacity for life.

It was only a few friends like the Smiths who buoyed him through the last days in Hollywood and the nervous anticipation of the opening of *You Touched Me.* On October 21 he was off the M-G-M payroll, and the same week the *New York Times* reported that the Cleveland press had liked the play, but had suggested a "tidying up" of loose ends before a Pasadena opening. From early November until the opening night, that suggestion was taken up, and Williams worked as if his life depended on it.

By the time of the play's opening at the Pasadena Playbox, however, there was a new wrinkle in his relationship with Margo Jones; quite simply, he suspected that she intended to become his wife.

"Tenn was in absolute terror that Margo would somehow bring about a marriage against his will," said Paul Bigelow, with whom Williams was in constant contact. "Just how this might occur he never specified, but it was clear that she certainly had her eye on him, even at this early stage. She had a remarkable vitality and a toughness of character, and her desire to become Mrs. Williams persisted through later years of their professional association." She was not the last woman to hope that Tennessee Williams's sexual preference could be altered on her account, and in this she shared a belief more widely endorsed years ago as a theory of homosexuality — namely, that by a simple act of will one might change one's orientation. In any case, Margo Jones's intention was particularly problematic, since she not only knew of Williams's preference but was herself quite openly lesbian.

The opening night, November 29, was a gala event, with Ruth Ford in the leading role, and her husband Peter van Eyck and the Smiths among Williams's friends there. This group contrasted sharply with the only guest Williams escorted to closing night, December 5: his father, who happened to be in Los Angeles on business. Afterward Cornelius joined playwright and producer for dinner. "Son," he said when they were alone, "there are two things we've never had in our family — a sober man and a drunken woman." He was afraid that his son (whose sexual preference he may have surmised but never acknowledged) was going to yield to Miss Jones's iron-willed, boozy blandishments.

Next day, the two Williamses and Margo Jones drove to Santa Monica, with a friend of the producer's who came along for the ride: Burl Ives, the singer and archivist of American folk music, was appearing in the touring company of Irving Berlin's *This Is the Army*. "Tennessee was very quiet during the ride from Pasadena to Santa Monica," Ives remembered, "but his father went on and on about Jews and finally said, 'That Irving Berlin must be a *good* Jew — he didn't take a cent for that show!' And Tennessee was mortified — he just shrank back in the seat and said nothing the whole ride."

Before Christmas, Williams went on to St. Louis, but alone, since he wanted to stop near Taos for a visit with Frieda Lawrence at her ranch in the Lobo Mountains. There he stayed two days, alternating vivid conversation with almost religious periods of veneration at the little chapel nearby where Frieda kept her husband's ashes. A few hundred yards from the house, on a small knoll, a white temple had been built, surmounted by a golden phoenix, which was Lawrence's own symbol.

He arrived at his parents' home for the holiday, and in time to see Dakin, who had been called to war duty in the Orient. The holidays were full of boredom, tension and finally grief, for his grandmother was clearly in a protracted death agony; the atmosphere in the house was Chekhovian, he wrote to Windham.

Finally, on January 6, 1944, death came to the woman he loved more than anyone in the world after his sister; the courageous, tireless woman who had sacrificed so he could have money for school and holidays and treats was at last too weary to fight. She was, he wrote, "a living poem . . . all that we knew of God in our lives," and her final hours were a bitter and bloody struggle for breath.

He could not endure the services that were planned, and he quickly arranged to have another eye operation in St. Louis on the day of the funeral. It was the most successful of the procedures to correct his cataract, and with thick lenses he could soon work well and long. The period of recovery and an improved ability to read and write would perhaps distract him from the weight of death. Like most escape routes through which we attempt to flee an inner landscape of sorrow, however, his writing under these circumstances led him nowhere. He could not concentrate. Family once again meant loss and pain and a deep, incurable wound.

At last one night in late January, alone in his room, he allowed a beginning of the healing process. For all of them — for Grand; for his forlorn grandfather and confused mother; for his father, drunk and isolated; for his brother, who was now somewhere in the war; for Rose, who knew nothing of any of them; and for himself and his last six years of wandering — he wept.

Chapter Four

FAMILY AFFAIRS
(1944–1947)

In these trying times we live in, all that we
have to cling to is each other.

— Amanda Wingfield, in *The Glass Menagerie*

HE REMAINED in St. Louis almost until spring 1944, but his work there reflected the continuing antipathies about home, family and that city. "Oriflamme," a short story he completed (which was a revision of an earlier one called "The Red Part of a Flag") accurately described his own feelings that winter, in terms of a disoriented woman who selects a rose-patterned dress to mark and move forward her liberation from a confining tradition. ("The city had never pleased her. . . . Her hope had died in a basement of this city. Her faith had died in one of its smug churches.") Not a fully drawn portrait, the story is a sketch for a later short work ("The Yellow Bird") and for a major play (*Summer and Smoke*). After reading Chekhov's short novel "My Life," he completed another story, "The Vine," whose psychological texture combines the Russian writer's mood and his own that winter. In it, Williams stated as clearly as he ever would his abhorrence of being alone:

"When you really thought about it, when you got down to it, what was there to live for outside the all-encompassing and protecting intimacy of marriage? And yet a great many women like Jane Austin [*sic*] got on without it. There were also men who got on without it. But he, he could not think of it! Going to bed alone, the wall on one side of you, empty space on the other, no warmth but your own, no flesh in contact with yours! Such loneliness was indecent! No wonder people who lived those obscenely solitary lives did things while sober that *you* only did when drunk. . . ."

But enough was, apparently, too much, and by mid-March he was back in New York, staying in single rooms and men's residences and forgetting to keep Audrey Wood quite aware of just how he could be contacted from day to day. New Directions presented him with an advance copy of *Five Young American Poets,* marking his first book appearance as a

poet, and this was heartening enough to send him back to his verse notebooks — but not before death again claimed a loved one.

A message came for him at Audrey Wood's office, the same day in late
March that he kept an appointment with her. Kip Kiernan, the ballet
dancer from Canada and Provincetown, who had regularized his status by
marrying an American, had no sooner begun a career in New York than
there was a diagnosis of inoperable brain cancer. Then about twenty-five,
he was blind and near death in a Manhattan hospital, sending out calls
for "Tenny Williams." And so Williams, who had undergone eye surgery rather than attend his grandmother's funeral, now sat by Kip's bedside, scarcely recognizing him. Kip's hands reached out for his, clasping
and gripping as if to keep from slipping out of this world. But within
days of Tennessee's arrival, Kip was gone. The event of a former lover's
death would be repeated, with startling and chilling congruence, twenty
years later.

The visit to Kip found a place in his poetry that spring, however:

> . . . Beneath me your breathing face
> cried out, Return, return . . .
> Return, you called while you slept.
> And desperately back I crept
> against the ascending fall . . .
> . . ̇ and only your voice calling, Stay!
> But my longing was great
> to be comforted and warmed
> once more by your sleeping form,
> to be, for a while, no higher
> than where you are,
> little room, warm love, humble star!

It was a season of violent shifts in New York, and not only in surprising alternations of temperature, of warm sunny days with sudden
midspring blizzards. For Williams, the pleasure over publication of his
poems was muted by the awfulness of Kip's final hours, followed by yet
another radically different motion of his life. On April 27, he was told
that a grant of one thousand dollars was awarded to him by the American Academy of Arts and Letters, "in recognition of his dramatic works,
which reveal a poetic imagination and a gift for characterization that are
rare in the contemporary theatre."

Rejecting an offer to come to Pasadena, where Margo Jones was staging *The Purification,* he then withdrew for the summer to Provincetown to complete *The Gentleman Caller.**

After weeks of concentrated effort — and, he wrote to Margo, a strange combination of fear and pain — the play was ready for Audrey Wood and, he hoped, a Broadway producer. On October 17, it was announced that actor-producer-director Eddie Dowling's new project would be a play by Tennessee Williams; he was the first to read the manuscript, and, after an afternoon conference with the quietly persuasive Audrey, he convinced businessman Louis Singer to join him in financing a production.

That month, the details moved together swiftly. Dowling, who had directed actress Julie Haydon in *The Time of Your Life,* convinced her that (although she was thirty-four) she would be credible as the lame, fragile Laura, a character at least a decade younger. She, in turn, took the play to her friend and mentor (later her husband), the formidable critic George Jean Nathan, whose approval she felt obligatory. At the same time, the forty-nine-year-old Dowling announced — without a smile — that he would play young (twentyish) Tom, the shoe-warehouse clerk and aspiring poet; for the role of the gentleman caller, Anthony Ross was hired. The remaining role to be cast was Amanda Wingfield — the "little woman of great but confused vitality," as Williams described her in the play, "clinging frantically to another time and place." The role demanded not mere competence, but the nuances of dramatic greatness. Nathan suggested Laurette Taylor. Dowling and Wood and Williams saw his wisdom; they also panicked.

Laurette Taylor, then sixty, had been up to the 1930s one of the great ladies of the American stage. Those who had seen her in *Peg O' My Heart* (in 1912) or *The Furies* (in 1928) or *Outward Bound* (in 1938) knew her gifts. But for almost ten years she had herself become a woman of great but confused vitality, and a confirmed alcoholic.

At that time, Taylor was living in sad withdrawal from the theatre, at a hotel on East 60th Street, where she was daily attended by a drama student named Eloise Sheldon. In return for acting lessons, the young woman cared for the practical details of Taylor's life and offered devoted companionship. The play reached Taylor by the circuitous route of

---

* In his original draft of *Memoirs,* Williams wrote that it was during the summer of 1944 that he met and caroused with Bill Cannastra, the alcoholic and voyeurist Harvard law student. But by this time Cannastra had apparently moved to New York, and the evidence suggests that in fact their meeting took place, as described above, in 1941.

Wood to Dowling to Haydon to Nathan to Sheldon to Taylor. It also bore a new title — *The Glass Menagerie.*

"Of course her first reaction was to turn it down," Eloise Sheldon Armen recalled years later; "she thought her career was over. But we prevailed on her to see that no one could bring this character to life the way she could." At last, with the loving encouragement of Eloise — "a small flame," as Laurette Taylor's daughter appreciatively wrote of the young student, "guiding [Taylor] back to the paths of everyday life" — she accepted the part. She did not, however, stop drinking, nor did she seem to give much attention to memorizing lines before or during rehearsals.

In November, Dowling (with, Williams insisted, Margo Jones as co-director) began rehearsals in New York prior to a scheduled Chicago try-out at the end of December. Terrified that something like the history of *Battle of Angels* would be repeated — not because of the new play's content (which could not have been more different) but because he no longer believed the play was anything but "rather dull, too nice" — Williams fled New York for St. Louis. There he was interviewed on his life and work and hopes by the drama critic of the *Star-Times,* a man named William Inge. The resulting article was full of inaccuracies, half-truths and Williams's typical alterations of personal history; the resulting friendship was much more intense and dramatic.

But Audrey and Dowling would not allow Williams to be an absentee author, and in December he was summoned to Chicago. The situation, he quickly realized, was as bleak as the fierce winter that had already descended.

First of all, Laurette Taylor — with only a week remaining before the December 26 premiere — attended the final rehearsals in what can only be called an alcoholic stupor, barely summarizing the dialogue and so broadly defining the woman's Southern accent and character that, as Williams wrote to Windham, she made the play sound like the Aunt Jemima Pancake Hour. In addition, Jo Mielziner's stage designs were being followed with great difficulty, and the music Williams had commissioned from his old acquaintance Paul Bowles sounded harsh through the theatre's crude sound system. Luggage had not arrived; a winter storm raged; the Civic Theatre was inconvenient to Chicago's main theatre district; there was no budget for advertising or publicity; and everyone in the company (except Eddie Dowling and Julie Haydon) — cast, crew, author — submerged the fear of failure in strong drink. Margo Jones, Williams wrote to Windham, was like a scoutmaster leading a wayward and desperate troop to their doom.

As late as Christmas Eve, the lines of the play had been neither "frozen" (fixed by the producer and playwright to be performed as written) nor completely memorized. Laurette Taylor managed only a martini mumble, Dowling was demanding rewrites, and the cast was stumbling into props and one another. "Mr. Dowling," Williams said quietly that night, "art is experience remembered in tranquillity. And I find no tranquillity in Chicago."

The night after Christmas, *The Glass Menagerie* was somehow performed for a small, diffident audience. By the afternoon of the twenty-seventh, the box office had taken in only four hundred dollars, and the producers prepared a closing notice. But then Audrey telephoned them to read two brief reviews: critic Claudia Cassidy, writing in the *Chicago Daily Tribune,* said the play had "the stamina of success ... [it] knows people and how they tick. ... If it is your play, as it is mine, it reaches out ... and you are caught in its spell." And Ashton Stevens, in the *Herald American,* said *The Glass Menagerie* "has the courage of true poetry couched in colloquial prose."

Before the end of that day, the mayor of Chicago, at the urging of the Civic Theatre's management, authorized a fifty-percent ticket subsidy for municipal employees. On the third night, Laurette Taylor was not simply discharging a half-formed role, she was creating a legend; she had begun to draw a more wonderful portrait than anyone could have imagined — not Eddie Dowling (who resented the critics' subsequent raves about her), not Tennessee Williams nor Audrey Wood, not anyone connected with the play.

"Actually," according to the playwright, "she directed many of the scenes, particularly the ones between mother and daughter, and she did a top-notch job. She was continually working on her part, putting in little things and taking them out — almost every night in Chicago there was something new, but she never disturbed the central characterization. Everything she did was absolutely in character."

The closing notice was removed — not, however, because box-office business dramatically improved, but because Claudia Cassidy and Ashton Stevens had been championing the play, returning almost nightly and telling and writing about it almost daily. "It gripped players and audiences alike," Cassidy wrote on January 7, 1945, "and created one of those rare evenings in the theatre that make 'stage struck' an honorable word." By the middle of the month, no tickets were available. In an unusual example of journalistic salvation, a play was for once not lost but kept alive because of critical support.

The author's spirits were raised also by the admiration and attention of William Inge, who came to Chicago to spread the good news back to St. Louis. What he did not share with the folks back home, however, was the fact that during his short visit to Williams the two men had an impromptu and intense sexual affair, never resumed in their later friendship.

The search for a New York theatre continued even as Williams and Dowling and the cast refined the play, perfected the lighting and music and mood, and tried to keep Taylor away from liquor. They succeeded in everything but the last. But when the curtain rose, something other than alcohol dominated the woman. A grace and gravity changed her, and through her the other actors.

No one was more happily surprised by the sudden turn of fortune than the author, who had tried to prepare himself for another failure. On March 2, he wrote to his mother from the Hotel Sherman that his income from the play was a thousand dollars a week; soon afterward, he wrote again, he had arranged for half the royalties to be assigned to her. For the rest of her life, Edwina Dakin Williams would never lack material support. The play she had unwittingly inspired would give her considerable financial rewards and finally enable her to have the one thing she had so long desired — her independence from Cornelius.

But sudden affluence and increasing fame did not alter the basic texture of Williams's life — yet. In Chicago he began scenes for a new play about a younger, faded Southern belle he named Blanche, who (like Amanda Wingfield) was lost in memories of the old South, and who survived brutality by her own illusions. *The Glass Menagerie* was a gentle lament for missed opportunities; the new play would be more violent, beginning in a character's loss of home and respect and family fidelity, and moving through sexual decadence to lunacy. Writing disjointed scenes for a projected play he then called *The Moth,* with Tallulah Bankhead again in his mind as the doomed heroine, he found the subject sufficiently frightening that he stopped work on the manuscript after a week.

Instead, he tried to relax into Chicago life — mostly campus life, as it turned out, since there were one-night stands with attractive, admiring undergraduates at the University of Chicago, young men to whom he read Hart Crane and who offered the passion typical of students — eager, sexually dynamic, emotionally petulant and less dependable than Chicago weather. The fickleness of young men, he wrote in his poetry notebooks, was like fox's teeth in the heart — a phrase he employed with increasing frequency in poems of the following years.

* * *

By his thirty-fourth birthday (not, as everyone thought, his thirty-first), on March 26, the company had moved to New York. Five nights later, on Easter eve, the curtain rose at the Playhouse Theatre; when it finally descended, after the twenty-fifth appearance of the cast for bows, "the reluctant Mr. Williams," as Laurette Taylor's daughter noted, "was persuaded to show himself at the side of the proscenium arch and bowed low to Dowling and Laurette, presenting a modest behind to the cheering audience." But during the performance, which moved many to tears, Eloise Sheldon (who was appearing that season in *Harvey* and had arranged to have her role taken by an understudy that night) stood just in the wings, holding a bucket for the terrified Laurette Taylor, who took advantage of every moment offstage to vomit. No one in the theatre suspected anything other than what turned out to be the actress's great triumph. But she was not simply suffering the effects of drink; she had contracted cancer. Nevertheless, every performance, for those who saw her, was an experience of great art, of theatre history.

One of the few autobiographical plays in American theatre to reach a common depth of understanding and compassion for the human condition, *The Glass Menagerie* transforms the Williams family of St. Louis into the Wingfield family of St. Louis. The narrator, who bears the author's own name Tom, informs the audience at the outset that "the play is memory," and he leads a series of scenes in family life. He lives with his mother, Amanda, and his sister, Laura. Amanda, a doting, manipulative woman full of good, strong will, is also caught in a net of memories: she reminds her son and her daughter that in her youth she was the quintessential Southern belle, always attended by scores of gentlemen callers. Laura, whose slight limp is both a cause of her shyness and an excuse to capitalize on her fragile emotional state, is unable to sustain the pressures of the outside world and (like her prototype, Rose Williams) has taken refuge in old gramophone records and in tending her collection of glass animals — her glass menagerie, which is a symbol of her difference and her delicacy. The father is absent from the family: he is described by Tom as "a telephone man who fell in love with long distances."

Forced to help support his family by working in a shoe factory, Tom longs to break the ties and become a wandering poet. Before he can try, however, his mother prevails on him to bring one of his co-workers from the factory home to dinner; she is desperate to re-create her own past — and to help her daughter graduate to adulthood — by finding a gentleman caller, a suitor for Laura. When they entertain a young man named

Jim O'Connor, however, it turns out that Laura had been attracted to him in high school earlier, and that now, in fact, he is engaged to be married. With his departure, any lingering hope for Laura's future seems broken, just as her beloved glass unicorn was broken after an impromptu parlor-dance with Jim. At the conclusion, it is clear that Tom will make his own way through life, but that he will always be haunted by the memory of his sister, who will very likely be excluded from any emotional fulfillment.

"The events of *The Glass Menagerie*," according to Dakin Williams, "are a virtually literal rendering of our family life at 6254 Enright Avenue, St. Louis, even though the physical setting is that of an earlier apartment, at Westminster Place. There was a real Jim O'Connor, who was brought home for my sister. The Tom of the play is my brother Tom, and Amanda Wingfield is certainly Mother." Indeed, the portrait of the woman in whom, as Williams wrote, there was "much to admire ... and as much to love and pity as there is to laugh at" is inspired by Edwina from the first moment. ("Honey, don't *push* with your fingers. If you have to push with something, the thing to push with is a crust of bread. And chew — chew! ... Eat food leisurely, son, and really enjoy it. . . ."*)

"We all knew that this play had some correspondence with his own life," according to Randy Echols, one of the key members of the play's technical staff. "Tennessee — and only Tennessee — laughed aloud at lines every time he came to a performance, lines that didn't seem to amuse anybody else." And although Edwina admitted in her memoirs that she had an obsession with proper eating habits, Williams thought she "never understood how much of her was in Amanda."

The correspondence goes deeper than mere details, however. The prevailing tragicomic tone of the play — with a poignancy reminiscent of Chekhov's *Cherry Orchard* — projects the unreconciled ironies of family life far beyond the contours of the Wingfield/Williams group.

"All work is autobiographical if it's serious," he reflected some years later. "Everything a writer produces is his inner history, transposed into another time. I am more personal in my writing than other people, and it may have gone against me." *The Glass Menagerie* so permanently established his fame and fortune that it could not be said to have "gone against" him. But he knew that it never represented the real network of

* There is an identical moment between mother and son in *Auto-Da-Fé*.

feelings, the deepest pain, about Rose, and it was this that he had hoped to exorcise in the play. "It's human valor that moves me," he told an interviewer after opening night. "The one dominant theme in most of my writings, the most magnificent thing in all human nature, is valor — and endurance." A requiem for unhappy lives, this first great success for Tennessee Williams was in a sense an ending as well as a beginning. "I may not have any more nice things to say. I must have known unconsciously that I would never write that kind of tender play again."

Because of its simple structure, *The Glass Menagerie* is often produced by professionals and amateurs on the stage; it has also been filmed and adapted several times for television. Precisely because of its directness and emotional accessibility, it can be misconceived and misrepresented. Compassionate for the misguided devotion of an unrealistic mother and for the unworldliness of a sister who is somehow forever marred, the play is as appealing to read as to see enacted, and its final moments are a summary of the honesty and dignity with which the author met his own memories:

"Tom's closing speech," he wrote in the stage directions, "is timed with what is happening inside the house. We see ... that Amanda appears to be making a comforting speech to Laura, who is huddled upon the sofa. Now that we cannot hear the mother's speech, her silliness is gone and she has dignity and tragic beauty. Laura's hair hides her face until, at the end of the speech, she lifts her head to smile at her mother. Amanda's gestures are slow and graceful, almost dancelike, as she comforts her daughter. At the end of her speech she glances a moment at the father's picture. ..."

And Tom's final words are the clearest memoir Tennessee Williams left to the American theatre:

> Not long after that [evening of the disappointing dinner with the gentleman caller Jim O'Connor] I was fired for writing a poem on the lid of a shoe-box. I left St. Louis. I descended the steps of this fire escape for a last time and followed, from then on, in my father's footsteps, attempting to find in motion what was lost in space. I traveled around a great deal. The cities swept around me like dead leaves. ... I would have stopped, but I was pursued by something. It always came upon me unawares, taking me altogether by surprise. Perhaps it was a familiar bit of music. Perhaps it was only a piece of transparent glass. Perhaps I am walking along a

street at night, in some strange city, before I have found companions. I pass the lighted window of a shop where perfume is sold. The window is filled with pieces of colored glass, tiny transparent bottles in delicate colors, like bits of a shattered rainbow. Then all at once my sister touches my shoulder. I turn around and look into her eyes. Oh Laura, Laura, I tried to leave you behind me, but I am more faithful than I intended to be! I reach for a cigarette, I cross the street, I run into the movies or a bar, I buy a drink, I speak to the nearest stranger — anything that can blow your candles out!

[*Laura bends over the candles.*]

For nowadays the world is lit by lightning! Blow out your candles, Laura — and so goodbye.

[*She blows the candles out.*]

The play is, then, what its author knew at the time of its first production — his tenderest delineation of his feelings about the Williams family and their collective past. Transmuted through his memories of Rose's own glass collection is the purest poetic light — an arc of forgiveness (of fate and of his mother), a ray of apologetic celebration of his sister's tragedy, a beam of understanding for himself and his own painful needs. Stronger plays would follow, works considered by many to be more successful in dramatic content and structure and richness of character. But nothing Tennessee Williams ever wrote after *The Glass Menagerie* has its wholeness of sentiment, its breadth of spirit and its unangry, quiet voice about the great reach of small lives.

The New York critics followed their Midwest colleagues. Even George Jean Nathan, who considered it "less a play than a palette of sub-Chekhovian pastels brushed up into a charming resemblance of one," admitted that *The Glass Menagerie* "provides by long odds the most imaginative evening that the stage has offered in this season." Some reviewers (John Mason Brown, George Freedley, the writers for *Time* and *Life* and *Newsweek*) attributed the success of this fragile play to the genius of Laurette Taylor, but there was unanimity on the value of the whole — the writing, according to Brooks Atkinson, had "pity for people, coolness of perspective, poetic grace." And playwright Arthur Miller, years later said, "It is usually forgotten what a revolution his first great success meant to the New York theatre. *The Glass Menagerie* in one stroke lifted lyricism to its highest level in our theatre's history, but it broke new ground in another way. What was new in Tennessee Williams was his rhapsodic insistence that form serve his utterance rather than dominating and cramping it. In him the American theatre found, perhaps for the first time, an eloquence and an amplitude of feeling. And driving on this newly discovered lyrical line was a kind of emotional heroism; he wanted not to approve or disapprove but to touch the germ of life and to celebrate it with verbal beauty."

With the block-long lines at the theatre on Monday morning, life began to change in a way that it had not in Chicago; "and new problems developed with success," as Williams was the first to admit. The following week, the New York Drama Critics Circle voted *The Glass Menagerie* the best play of the year on its first ballot. Late in April, Edwina and Dakin came to New York, were brought in great style to suites at the Royalton Hotel, and were honored at a reception. (Cornelius had seen the play while in Chicago on business, the resemblance to his family entirely eluding him.) Interview followed interview, and party followed reception that spring; the last of several awards was announced in June by the Playwrights Company (the creative consortium of Maxwell Anderson, S. N. Behrman, Elmer Rice, Robert E. Sherwood and John Wharton), who awarded Williams the Sidney Howard Memorial Prize of fifteen hundred dollars. By this time — after another operation on his left eye — the socially beleaguered playwright had departed for Mexico. With a weekly income almost equal to the prize money, he could afford a private berth on the train, and to book at a first-class hotel. From his impecunious past, only the old portable typewriter on which he had worked on the final draft of *The Glass Menagerie* remained among his new, well-stocked luggage.

At a guest-house about thirty miles southeast of Guadalajara, he settled into the pleasant rhythms of life at the popular fishing resort of Lake Chapala. Strolling the borders of Mexico's largest inland body of water (over four hundred square miles), swimming, drinking rum-cocos with native boys, he decided to extend his visit through early August. Never a man to rest idly, however, he wrote compulsively each day for at least three hours.

The visit, he found, released a flood of more memories. Even as his fame was now established, and other American guests stopped to introduce themselves to the celebrated young playwright, he was still gazing backward to the two Roses in his life, his sister and his grandmother. In

"Recuerdo," a poem written one cool morning at Lake Chapala, the two women joined hands with him over an arch of painful years:

> And he remembered the death of his grandmother . . .
> In childhood's spectrum of violence, she remained pale . . .
> My sister . . . vanished completely —
> for love's explosion, defined as early madness,
> consumingly shone in her transparent heart for a season
> and burned it out, a tissue-paper lantern!

In "The Jockeys at Hialeah," however (which he had begun in Chicago), memory collides with the bluntness of sensory pleasure — and this poem, he knew, failed precisely because of coyness and imprecision.

But the sojourn at Lake Chapala was extended for a more serious project. He returned to work on *The Moth,* which he now called *Blanche's Chair in the Moon.* The image-basis, he said later, was simply that of a woman, sitting with folded hands near a window, while moonlight streamed in and she awaited in vain the arrival of her boyfriend. During the warm, dry Mexican summer so high above sea level, he relived many personal and family memories, and they clashed with the satisfaction of purely physical desires (which were being readily satisfied by cheerful native boys). The new play, in such circumstances, took on a fusion of sensuality and nostalgia and violence new to his writing. The first indication of this violence was in scenes involving men at a poker table.

"During the New York run of *The Glass Menagerie,*" according to Randy Echols, "Tennessee wanted to learn how to play poker. He invited some of the crew from the play to his hotel room, provided cards and chips and liquor and foods, and then he went from player to player taking notes. We found out only later what he was doing and why he needed to learn." Following the method of Chekhov, Williams wanted to learn more background detail than he would use. During the summer, the play — its title soon changed to *The Poker Night* — took shape as a contest between the crude sensibilities of working-class poker players and the delicacies of two Southern women. After several weeks, however, he had only card scenes; there was considerable atmosphere and dramatic tension, but the narrative was undeveloped.

By mid-August he had traveled north to Dallas, for a visit with Margo Jones. Her single-minded loyalty and outspoken confidence not only encouraged him; she virtually demanded that he complete a short story that had remained unattended for three years. And so in one intense afternoon he wrote the final sections of "One Arm," the grotesque but oddly touching story of a young, cynical male hustler in New Orleans, homeless and mutilated, who just before his execution for murder realizes that he needs to respond — once, with wholeness of feeling — to the emotions so long buried in an avalanche of ill fortune. The story affirms a communion between those whom accident and desire have made marginal people. And for perhaps the first time, Williams wrote compellingly of the fight between the aphorisms of sectarian religion and simple, ordinary human needs — and his empathy is at last not with the poor, confused minister, afraid of his own sexual storm, but with the doomed and drained Oliver Winemiller, the boy whose youth was lost long before an arm.

Late in August he arrived in Boston for the rehearsals and pre-Broadway tour of *You Touched Me!* — to which the producer, in Williams's absence, had insisted on adding the provocative exclamation point — and which was having some problems in the playing. The success of *The Glass Menagerie* had encouraged director Guthrie McClintic and his cast — Edmund Gwenn, Catherine Willard and Montgomery Clift — and the late arrival of the tanned and cheerful author, with several final additions to his text, gave them even more enthusiasm. (Among Williams's last-minute personal addenda were a character's dedication of a poem to Hart Crane; the fact that the wife of the Reverend Melton — named for Windham's former roommate Fred Melton — was born and died on the same dates as Williams's grandmother; and the physical ailments of the Reverend, which represent several of Williams's own.)

In the role of the dark and handsome young wartime flier was the dark and handsome young actor Montgomery Clift, who at twenty-five was at the start of a promising career. There was a mutual assessment by actor and author, which Williams later reflected on: "I never knew him well because I wasn't sexually attracted to him" — a statement of a strange logic indeed, or an ambiguity (which he never clarified) as to which of the two men associated depth of acquaintance with sexual activity.

At the end of September, *You Touched Me!* opened at the Booth Theatre in New York; the critics found it genial, pleasant and clearly inferior to its neighbor, *The Glass Menagerie,* three blocks to the north. The comedy seemed too calm and pale in a Broadway season that thrived on *Carousel, Oklahoma!, Bloomer Girl, On the Town, Song of Norway, A Bell for Adano, The Late George Apley, Dear Ruth, Harvey, I Remember Mama, Life with Father* and *The Voice of the Turtle*. From his room at the Hotel Shelton, Williams read the reviews of his and Windham's efforts, and began work on a more serious treatment of sexual liberation, which *You Touched Me!* had introduced perhaps too gently for his increasingly confident voice.

The first pages of a new play had, for a time, the title *Chart of Anatomy*, and were a loose development of his story "Oriflamme" and another story in progress, "The Yellow Bird." After a week, he abandoned the play as hopeless: all he had was the thesis of a woman's erotic awakening to the raucous charm of a doctor she had known from their childhood; the characters, however, were ciphers. And so, as he had done with the inchoate life of *The Poker Night,* he put it aside in favor of short fiction and poems.

In November, *Story* magazine published "The Important Thing," his fictionalized account of the college friendship with Esmeralda Mayes. In the first draft, the marginal, rejected, poet Flora of the story had been named Laura, revealing perhaps a connection between Williams's feelings about his girlfriend and about his sister (who would become Laura in *The Glass Menagerie*); in any case, the tender story is an elegy to the marginal world that author, friend and sister inhabited.

Audrey Wood, meantime, was having her usual difficulty keeping track of her wandering client; on a few hours' decision, he left the Shelton, sending a cable next day that he was back in Boston, or in Washington, or Chicago, or Atlantic City, or simply "in transit." He was reading his poems to a gathering at Harvard; he was meeting a group of students at Northwestern University; he could be contacted at the 92nd Street YMHA in New York, en route to St. Louis; he was off to New Orleans.

Paul Bowles, who saw Williams frequently during these active years, thought that "he was more eager to get away from where he was than he was to get to another place.... I think very much it [was] an eagerness to leave the people ... he [was] suddenly fed up with a place and the people in it and [felt] that somehow any other place, or nearly any other place, [was] more acceptable at that moment than the place he [was] in. So he [left and went] — it doesn't matter so much where, because he always [changed] his mind at the last minute anyway ... he [was] inherently extremely restless." And William Inge, who had at first followed him from St. Louis to Chicago, agreed that Williams was "a restless person, physically restless.... I think he [did] need the diversion that travel [gave] him."

For a time he settled down to serious work — and to the always equally pursued serious life of the senses. And once again he found that the right place to pursue both needs was New Orleans. By December 18 he had taken a suite at the Hotel Pontchartrain, where he wrote to Donald Windham that New York and Broadway were dangerous for the ego — the way the Hotel Shelton was coming dangerously close to being his bordello, he admitted — and that New Orleans felt less intense, and he more relaxed in pursuing both his writing and his private life. "If I can be said to have a home," he wrote for a Liebling-Wood press release, "it is in New Orleans, which has provided me with more material than any other part of the country."

On New Year's 1946, he took a short-term lease on an apartment at 710 Orleans Street — three small rooms on the second floor, where he wrote a long one-act play called *Ten Blocks on the Camino Real* (a fantasy in the style of Strindberg's haunting *Dream Play*) with Kilroy as the archetypal American, a vagrant whose voice is that of the peripatetic Williams. In a comic rearrangement of characters historical and fictional, Kilroy meets Camille and Casanova, Don Quixote and Sancho Panza, a weird assortment of street people, and Esmeralda, the daughter of a Gypsy. Formless and experimental, it was clearly a vehicle for the extreme feelings about the visit to Mexico — the relish of freedom one moment, the retreat to a more rigorous life the next. Audrey Wood counseled him to wait with this one.

Before the end of January, upsetting letters were reaching him from St. Louis. Cornelius had officially retired from International Shoe, and, with nothing to occupy him other than drink and cards, he was making life miserable for his wife and father-in-law. Reverend Dakin, then almost ninety, was virtually blind and found little comfort with a daughter who continued to harbor a strange resentment against him. Edwina, Williams wrote to Audrey on January 15, was a monument to all the psychological hazards of her time, a woman whose endurance and once fine qualities continued to flourish alongside a narrowness of perception and only the dimmest awareness of human feeling. But her self-styled martyrdom to her husband's callousness was about to end with the economic freedom provided by *The Glass Menagerie;* now, Williams hoped, he had only to deal with the misery of his grandfather.

This consideration could not be managed at once, however, for his own living situation had at the same time become more complicated, if happier, simultaneously more satisfying and more raucous. During his last visit to New Mexico, he had met a desk clerk at La Fonda de Taos Hotel, a dazzlingly handsome young man named Pancho Rodriguez y Gonzalez. By the middle of February, Pancho had visited Williams in New Orleans twice and had then moved into the new Williams apartment on Orleans Street. From Williams's more or less protracted affairs and from his array of sexual partners, one had elicited an emotional response deep enough to warrant risking the complexities of a shared life. Thus began a relationship full of warm passion and emotional fire. Pancho was strong and helpful, adoring and enthusiastic — and these qualities Williams needed in a partner. But Pancho was also emotionally insecure, capable of sudden bursts of temper, and afraid of losing Williams to the charms of fame — and Williams could be both impatient and manipulative of those fears. Pancho wanted a sexually exclusive, one-to-one relationship; Williams, as he admitted in letters to friends like Donald Windham, insisted on keeping his own counsel with a variety of bedtime partners.

"Pancho was a terribly nice man," according to Fritz Bultman, who saw a good deal of the couple in New Orleans that season, "but he was a primitive and I'm afraid Tennessee wasn't very good to him. He was too promiscuous for Pancho, who really wanted a stable life. But Tenn insisted on going out cruising almost every night. His life had not changed very much, in that way, from what it had been in [Greenwich] Village several years before. Pancho was a very simple young man who really loved Tennessee and he couldn't get used to the idea that his love wasn't reciprocated, or that their relationship might come to an end. He was a remarkably sweet man, and a religious man. And I think he had a terrible time explaining Tennessee to his family."

At the outset, there was reason for celebration with their New Orleans friends, a circle that now included the poet and teacher Oliver Evans as well as some city administrators who found congenial the often wild and anonymous parties at the Williams apartment. In February, champagne was poured to mark the publication of Williams's collection 27 *Wagons Full of Cotton;* * the distance from New York perhaps enabled him to read with detachment the generally unenthusiastic reviews by Joseph Wood

---

* In 1946 this anthology contained the one-act plays 27 *Wagons Full of Cotton, The Purification, The Lady of Larkspur Lotion, The Last of My Solid Gold Watches, Portrait of a Madonna, Auto-Da-Fé, Lord Byron's Love Letter, The Strangest Kind of Romance, The Long Good-bye, Hello from Bertha* and *This Property is Condemned.* Others would be added in later reissues of the volume.

Krutch (who decried the "romantic pessimism") and of the *New York Times Book Review* (whose reviewer found the plays full of "sentimental . . . disembodied emotionalism").

That same month, he and Pancho and Fritz Bultman were invited to visit Bultman's sister at her home on Louisiana Avenue, a great residence built in 1852. To this house in the legendary Garden District of New Orleans was now added a three-story enclosed greenhouse. With its giant ferns and ficus trees and exotic vines, the "Green Room" at once impressed Williams with its potential as a dramatic setting. Within the decade, it became the model for Violet Venable's terrifying garden in *Suddenly Last Summer* (the second play of *Garden District*), his brilliantly harrowing play that united family history and personal confession. "Tennessee was such a restless soul in those days," Muriel Bultman Francis recalled. "He was always on the move. But he was a gentle man and not one of those writers who felt that he always had to spice a conversation with witticisms or profundities."

The wit and depth were poured, that season, into his work. By April, *Ten Blocks on the Camino Real* was complete, along with the short story "Desire and the Black Masseur." This remains one of his bitterest allegories about what people do to each other, and was in fact a thematic sketch for *Suddenly Last Summer*. There is a fierce guilt about sadistic homosexuality in it. As a celebration of pain and the mute inevitability of self-sacrifice, it has a calmness about universal horror unparalleled until the later *Suddenly Last Summer,* in fact. (The fact that Williams began this story at the height of World War II and completed it just after may explain the theme of universal horror.)

He then began the short story "The Night of the Iguana," which derived from his visits to Mexico, and which introduced the character of Miss Jelkes. Unsatisfying in its early stages as at its completion, it has none of the narrative consistency, character logic or breadth of vision that he would give to a play with the same name in 1960.

Meantime, life with Pancho was becoming more problematic. Pancho could not understand the writer's need for solitude; Williams could not always understand (much less respond to) the young lover's need for reinforcement and attention. The one was passionate and devoted, with the eager conceit of youth; the other was more than a decade older, serious, established, but unwilling to offer emotional stability. He needed Pancho's need; he resented Pancho's neediness.

"Tennessee behaved very badly toward Pancho," Fritz Bultman remembered, "and he did so by using Pancho for real-life scenes which he created — and then transformed them into moments in *A Streetcar Named Desire.*"

By the end of April, it was clear that some brief separation was necessary, and so Williams bought a car and drove from New Orleans to St. Louis. Pancho was sent ahead to Taos, where they were to meet for a holiday in early May. The situation at Arundel Place was more painful than ever: Cornelius spent the daytime in bars, the nights in rages or stupors at home; Edwina was gloomy, if not taciturn; her father was a virtual recluse in his room. This unhappy arrangement Tennessee endured as long as he could, and then, although he felt ill, he resumed his auto trip to New Mexico.

But the sickness he had in St. Louis was not, it turned out, simply psychosomatic. Abdominal pain increased, a fever would not subside, and he had to go to a hospital in Wichita, Kansas, where after a cystoscopic examination doctors found neither a kidney stone nor any acute infection. Diverticulitis was diagnosed, and the likelihood of appendicitis. Williams, however, refused to accept treatment in a strange setting, with only strangers around him; he insisted on proceeding to Pancho in Taos. On May 16 he finally arrived and was brought in acute distress to Holy Cross Hospital where two surgeons, Ashley Pond, Sr., and Albert M. Rosen, correctly interpreted the problem.

Williams was in fact suffering from an intestinal anomaly found congenitally in less than two percent of the general population. Called Meckel's diverticulum (after the eighteenth-century German anatomist), it is a residual sac like the vermiform appendix, whose inflamed and infected state it mimics; impacted, it causes obstruction and requires surgical removal. The procedure is neither complicated nor life-threatening once properly diagnosed. "It wasn't a particularly long operation, and the patient was not near death," Dr. Pond recalled years later. Within a week, Williams's abdominal stitches were removed and he was discharged from the hospital, into Pancho's attentive and tireless care.

But the episode provided Williams with a marvelous bit of melodrama after the initial fear had been dispelled. He wrote at once to Audrey, he wired his family, he telephoned friends near and far, that he was at death's door, and that he had made a will naming Pancho as sole heir. None of this was true, but it did insure the attention and manifest alarm from everyone he contacted. And it coincided perfectly with his tendency to hypochondria and exaggeration; he knew how dramatic emotions are necessary for the artist, and no one but he could manufacture — physically, if necessary — the small scenarios that elicited from those around him the reactions he could transmute into drama.

There was perhaps an additional reason for Williams's little construction of melodrama at this time of his life. He had just finished rereading selections from Chekhov, and letters which recounted how, at the age of thirty-five, he accepted the fact that he was dying; and how, for what would be his last five years, the acceptance of terminal disease colored his work. Tennessee Williams, also thirty-five, saw another link between himself and the Russian writer, and although the doctors in Taos pronounced him entirely healed, he refused to believe that he was anything other than a dying man. It took almost two years for him to see that the parallel was not to be realized; even after that, however, he protested that he was harboring a fatal disease no surgeon was alert enough to diagnose. He was, according to the poet Gilbert Maxwell, who knew him then, a "hypochondriacal being who lived in dread of physical and mental illness," and who was always "morbidly, pathologically frightened" of death. At the same time, however, he realized fully that it was the possibility of death, and the omnipresent danger of accident, that gave life and art — in both content and style — an urgency of feeling.

From New Mexico, he and Pancho passed through New York to visit friends before proceeding for a summer on the island of Nantucket. He met briefly with Audrey Wood, stopped in at the Playhouse Theatre to see the first act of *The Glass Menagerie,* and bought some books for summer reading. One of them he read while in New York: *The Member of the Wedding,* by the Georgia-born Carson McCullers, touched him with its gentle compassion and offbeat family ironies. Eager to meet the twenty-nine-year-old author, he wrote a letter praising her book. And the next day he expressed this admiration to Paul Bigelow and Bigelow's friend and companion, Jordan Massee. As it happened, Massee was McCullers's cousin, and they offered to arrange a meeting between the two writers after Pancho and Williams had reached Nantucket. They had rented for the summer a wind-battered, gray two-story house with an extra bedroom, they told Bigelow and Massee. There would be room for a weekend guest.

"The meeting between Tenn and McCullers happened this way," according to Bigelow. "Alfred Kazin [the literary critic, whom McCullers had met when she was a student at Columbia University] and his daughter had planned to take Carson on a motor trip with them through New England. Tennessee genuinely admired her work, so it was arranged that the Kazins would leave Carson at the ferry on Cape Cod, whence she would proceed on to Tennessee in Nantucket. I had the impression that she always planned to stay on with him, and that she didn't have quite the spontaneity that the more innocent have supposed."

And so began one of the most affecting and strange friendships in American literary history. Williams and Pancho, one Saturday afternoon in mid-June, went to the Nantucket harbor to meet their guest, "a tall, slim figure wearing faded blue dungarees, white moccasins, a man's shirt, and a wide-brimmed straw hat," as her biographer described her appearance that day. At once the two men recognized a member of the group of people with whom they felt at ease. McCullers — married but sexually ambivalent, shy but demanding — was eager to ingratiate herself with the playwright who had achieved the kind of fame she coveted.

From mid-June, she was welcomed, with Williams's easy generosity. He was fascinated with her crooked grin, her ability to spin weird anecdotes for projected novels and stories, her swift infatuation for women visitors, her taste for liquor and for the poems of Hart Crane. They swam together, toured the island on bicycles, had long candlelit dinners preceded by long cocktail hours, and sang at the battered upright piano in the parlor.

"Pancho was of course crazed with jealousy," Paul Bigelow recalled. "Tenn told us later how difficult things got that summer." Without reason, Pancho feared that Carson was out to capture Tennessee as a husband, or at least as a temporary lover. He need not have feared her effusiveness; it was part of her "Southern guff," as Bigelow called it — and in any case, Carson moved from emotional turmoil over one woman visitor to near hysteria over another: "Carson went wild and raved about [a woman visitor's] beauty, poise and elegance," Pancho remembered years later; at the time, however, he feared most of all that she would alienate Williams's affection.

As for Williams, he wrote each day — and in so doing set an example for McCullers, who at once set herself the task of transforming *The Member of the Wedding* into a play. In this, he encouraged her, and daily they sat at opposite ends of the dining room table working, she taking as a model *The Glass Menagerie* (which she had not seen but had read) and he busy on the first full draft of *Chart of Anatomy*. Still convinced that he was under a death sentence, he complained of chest pains and heart palpitations, of rapid pulse and erratic breathing. All this, however, was actually being experienced not by him, but by the heroine of his play — Alma Winemiller, the repressed daughter of a Mississippi minister, the "singing nightingale of the Delta" whose unrequited love is for the wild young doctor to whom she complains of her "palpitations." But she is finally rejected by him, and this leads her to cast off the fetters of her strict background and to go off — for one evening, at least — with a young traveling salesman.

Chart of Anatomy took final shape quickly, with an increased appetite for life on Williams's part that summer that was no doubt due in part to the even zanier attitudes of Carson McCullers, and precisely because of her veneration of him. There are, after all, few stimulants like worshipful praise.

At the end of June, she left for her home in Nyack, New York, returning several days later with her husband, Reeves McCullers, an equally anguished soul given to bouts of alcoholic schizophrenia and a bisexual experimentation that his wife stoutly encouraged. (The people in Tennessee Williams's circle could never be accused of following bourgeois convention.) But poor Reeves was uncomfortable in this group, and despite the interesting visitors at a Fourth of July party (designer Oliver Smith, actress Rita Gam and choreographer Jerome Robbins) he soon fled back to Nyack, to the comparative calm of his mother-in-law.

Late in July, Carson left with the first draft of the dramatized version of her novel. Acquaintances of both writers then and later were aware not only of their mutual affection and respect, but also of a strange and unfounded rivalry that sprang up between them. For her part, she quietly resented his increasing success. But Williams, always lavish in his praise, could afford to be generous: even after her play won the New York Drama Critics Circle Award in 1950, her frail health, her infrequent publications and her gradually debilitating strokes and decline into a private world of unreason prevented her from reaching anything like a full flowering of her always fragile talent. That did not always, however, prevent him from wondering if *his* fiction were as good. . . .

"From that summer," according to Paul Bigelow, "despite his kindness and warmth and coming forward to help her in her career, Tenn was very realistic about her. He recognized an iron determination underneath all that Southern guff."

The friendship with McCullers has, however, another aspect, which should perhaps be considered in light of a gift he made to her that summer: a small jade ring that had belonged to his sister Rose. In his collegial support of her — especially as her physical and mental health declined in a series of strokes and alcohol dependence while she was still in her early thirties — he saw an opportunity to do for McCullers what he could not have done for Rose, to help keep her demons at bay, to sustain her unpredictable moods and her almost pathological selfishness. Even he was horrified at her callous indifference to her husband's neurotic dependence on her (Reeves eventually committed suicide while alone in Paris), and he endured her moods and pretenses and emotional demands that he would never have endured from any man. The play he worked on that summer (with an epigraph he took from Rilke) was dedicated to Carson McCullers in memory of the weeks they shared. But half the royalties from it were assigned for the care and benefit of his sister Rose, to insure her more frequent holidays from the state hospital in Farmington, to buy her clothes and treats. Forever in his mind and memory, the ornery and ill and finally pathetic Carson McCullers — until her death at fifty in 1967 — was associated for him with Rose, from whom he was still separated by time and distance.

Before the summer's end, Williams gave a reading from his one-act plays to the summer residents of Nantucket. Thornton Wilder and actress Patricia Collinge were among those in the audience who especially liked *The Unsatisfactory Supper* (one of the bases for what would later be the controversial film *Baby Doll*), and on September first and third there were staged performances of *Moony's Kid Don't Cry* and *The Long Good-bye* at the Nantucket Straight Wharf Theatre. Two weeks later, with Williams suddenly and gruesomely ill, he and Pancho departed the island for New York, and for almost a month they were detained in the city; after an array of gastrointestinal tests, it was discovered that he had somehow become the unwilling host to a monstrous tapeworm, which took several weeks to be coaxed from his system. Quite irrationally, he insisted it was another indication of terminal cancer.

By the time he was discharged, Williams had arranged — through Pancho, who again preceded him and who was working hard to satisfy Williams's caprices — to rent a new apartment in New Orleans. From the end of October through the winter, they remained in quarters beautifully furnished with antiques collected by the owner, Richard Orme, at 632½ St. Peter Street. There he completed the first revision of *Chart of*

Anatomy and sent it along to Audrey with the suggestion that someone like the English star Celia Johnson would be right for the role, or the American actress Josephine Hutchinson. There was no immediate reply from Audrey, but there was from friends to whom he read it one evening, and their negative comments were enough for him to put it away and to return to the still only half-understood figure of Blanche DuBois, the lady of *The Poker Night*.

"I live," he wrote in an essay that autumn, "near the main street of the Quarter. Down this street, running on the same tracks, are two streetcars, one named 'Desire' and the other named 'Cemeteries.' Their indiscourageable progress up and down Royal Street struck me as having some symbolic bearing of a broad nature on the life in the Vieux Carré — and everywhere else, for that matter." *The Poker Night,* indeed, was taking shape as a treatment of the clash between desire and death; its two major characters — a faded belle (Blanche DuBois) caught in the web of her own illusions and hypocrisies, and her crude brother-in-law (Stanley Kowalski) determined to shatter those illusions at any price — were on an ineluctably tragic course. He completed revisions within days of learning of another death — this time, Laurette Taylor's. She died in New York of cancer at the age of sixty-two, four months after the final performance of *The Glass Menagerie;* her courage and her art had had a large part in validating his own, and her death moved him deeply.

"She was neither a well nor a strong person at any time during the run of the play," he wrote in a tribute that December. "Even when throat trouble made it painful for her to speak she continued in her demanding part and I have never seen her physical suffering affect the unfailing wonder of her performance." Comparing her favorably with Eleanora Duse and Sarah Bernhardt, he saw in Taylor "hints of something that lie outside the flesh and its mortality. I suppose these intuitions come to many people in their religious vocations, but I have sensed them more clearly in the work of artists and most clearly of all in the art of Laurette Taylor." Her death also confirmed his intuition about his own imminent death from what he insisted was pancreatic cancer. But *The Poker Night* must be produced first, and to that end he devoted what he thought were his last energies.

The arrival in New Orleans of Reverend Dakin, who had begged to visit his grandson as a refuge from the unpleasantness of Arundel Place, was a happy interval. On January 9, 1947, Williams wrote to Audrey Wood that Grandfather was no longer able to read, but was quite content to sit quietly with the radio. At this time, a noticeable change occurs in the tone of the correspondence between Williams and Wood; his letters are more open, more self-revealing, less guarded. They are signed "with love" or "devotedly," and betoken an exchange between son and mother more than between client and agent. And she often wrote only about family matters. To be sure, Audrey's services on his behalf now included her complete management of his financial life and the preparation of his income taxes. But her personal discretion about his private life was equally important to him; she understood without archness of condescension the complexity of the relationship with Pancho Rodriguez, she was willing to run interference with members of his family, and she spoke out clearly when his self-confidence failed.

On his side, there was no detail of his life that was not submitted for Audrey's approval. He was, he wrote in January, paying $150 each month for the St. Peter Street apartment; he was spending the same amount weekly for food and medicine; he had bought another new car for $1400, and that cost $20 a month to keep in a local garage; he was paying Pancho $200 each month (which he insisted was a bargain) — everything was sent to New York for Audrey's scrutiny, and nothing escaped her judicious comment.

The visit of Reverend Dakin improved not only the old gentleman's mood; Williams and Pancho had a new peace between themselves, too, after a month of acrimony and sometimes open fistfights because of Williams's extracurricular romances. The obligations connected with the care and comfort of a ninety-year-old forced them to temper the eruption of domestic melodramas to the more tender concern for another.

"Whenever I'm disturbed or discouraged with my work," Williams said at the time, "I just go and sit near [Grandfather]. Sometimes we don't speak at all, but even as we sit in silence I seem to get a great spiritual solace from him." Part of the comfort was undoubtedly due to the fact that the Reverend was, in his grandson's words, "an extremely liberal man. . . . He didn't disapprove of indulgences of the flesh. He played bridge and enjoyed his cocktail," and he never raised a disapproving eyebrow about his grandson's private life; in fact, the bonding of homosexual men always seemed to him rather an elite and stylish manner of living. No one enjoyed the gay bohemianism of New Orleans more than the Reverend; no one was more welcome to its colorful conceits than this quiet Southern cleric.

Which at least partly explains why Williams felt free, in mid-January, to take his grandfather from the drizzly chill of New Orleans on a motor trip southeast, to the warmth of Key West. They took several rooms at La Concha Hotel, with a wide view over the Gulf of Mexico. Miriam Hopkins, newly remarried, celebrated their arrival with a lavish party, but for most of the time Williams remained in his room, working on a final draft of *The Poker Night* while Pancho escorted the Reverend for walks in the sunshine.

The major problem Williams was battling seemed to be the ending for his play: would the distraught and crushed Blanche, robbed of her illusions and of any chance for happiness and social acceptance, simply leave her sister Stella and brother-in-law Stanley for more wandering, with no destination? Would she, like Anna Karenina, throw herself in front of a train? Or would she be removed to a lunatic asylum? During a short visit to New York in late February he was still unsure, and Audrey prudently withheld her opinion; she knew how deeply the tragic nature of the play was working itself within him, and she would not intrude on the natural term of his creativity. She heartily approved, however, his decision not to attend the revival of *Stairs to the Roof* in Pasadena, which Gilmor Brown presented at the end of February for a disappointed press and public.

At the end of March, when Grandfather and Pancho and Williams had been back in New Orleans for several weeks, *The Poker Night* was sent to Audrey for forwarding to prospective producers. Simultaneously, Margo Jones was ready to proceed with a summer production of *Chart of Anatomy* at her theatre-in-the-round in Dallas — but not until Williams insisted (and not until he had Audrey's favorable reaction) on a change of title — to the poetically more apt *Summer and Smoke*.

In April, when it became clear that the details and preparations for theatre productions would take Williams north for much of the year, Reverend Dakin decided to move on to Memphis, where he could be tended by friends and cousins without the necessity to move constantly. This freed Williams to accept Audrey's suggestion that he come halfway north to meet the producer she had interested in *The Poker Night* — Irene Mayer Selznick, the daughter of one legendary movie producer and the wife of another. She had come to New York to pursue an independent career as a theatrical producer, and Audrey felt, quite rightly, that her sensibility and her good taste (not to say her first-rate creative and financial connections) would make her the proper one to lead the play to success. To keep the meetings and negotiations quiet, Audrey suggested they meet away from New York, and she chose Charleston, South Carolina, a town of happy memories connected to her late friend and client DuBose Heyward (whose first novel, *Porgy,* became the basis for a play, an opera and a motion picture).

Williams and Selznick (whom he would often refer to, with ironic deference, as "Dame Selznick"), after a cautious and unsure meeting, were convinced of one another's seriousness. There was no doubt she loved the play and was moved by its tragic grandeur and its sharply etched portraits of men and women in conflict; and she agreed with Williams that the ideal man to direct was Elia Kazan, who with his wife Molly Day Thacher had been following Williams's career with great interest. Williams, Selznick and Wood had been equally perceptive in following Kazan's, for he was by then regarded as one of the most important talents in American theatre and film, and so he would remain. He had acted in the 1930s, made his directing debut in 1935, and within recent years had been highly praised for his direction of *The Skin of Our Teeth, Harriet, Jacobowsky and the Colonel* and *Deep Are the Roots,* among other plays. In addition, he had just directed Arthur Miller's first successful play, *All My Sons,* which had opened in January to great acclaim (and he would soon be awarded the first "Tony" for best direction).

But from Hollywood, where Kazan had had equal success directing the film of *A Tree Grows in Brooklyn,* and where he was completing direction of *Gentleman's Agreement,* word came that Kazan's first reaction was lukewarm — not indeed to the play, but to his directing it. Williams told Selznick that his second choice was John Huston. But by early May, Williams had changed his title to *A Streetcar Named Desire* — which his associates loved — and after being guaranteed major credit and twenty percent of the play's profits, Kazan agreed to direct.

Until Kazan arrived in New York, however, and while Selznick set to the producer's array of duties, Williams decided to break away from the dither of New York. He and Pancho drove to Provincetown, where he made still more changes on *Summer and Smoke.* On June 16, he wrote to Audrey that he had a summons from Margo, who wanted him in Dallas at once for pre-production. She was planning a July 8 opening at the Gulf Oil Playhouse, a theatre without proscenium. This invitation he flatly rejected, reminding Audrey (who, after witnessing several unpleasant scenes with Pancho in New York restaurants, hotel lobbies and suites, was hardly uninformed about such matters) that what he euphemistically called his unconventional private life would be unappreciated in Dallas.

With both plays ready for production, he was content, for the month of June, to enjoy Provincetown; decisions about casting would depend on Kazan's schedule in any case, and the leading ladies whose names were mentioned for the role of Blanche did not appeal to him — Margaret Sullavan, Bette Davis, Pauline Lord, Fay Bainter and — he laughed when he told Pancho — Mary Martin. As for Stanley Kowalski, the quintessential semi-Simian representative of undiluted virility, there was talk of John Garfield or Burt Lancaster.

But there was different talk in Provincetown that month; in the ongoing script of his own domestic disharmony a new name was now introduced. Frank Merlo was a twenty-five-year-old, New Jersey–born navy veteran, a self-educated, second-generation Sicilian. Short, muscular and strikingly handsome, Merlo was that summer at the end of an affair with lyricist John LaTouche; Williams felt that he, too, was near the end of an affair. He and Merlo spent a night together on the Provincetown dunes, but since Merlo was disinclined to a ménage or to the uncertainty of Williams's months ahead, they parted with intense mutual regrets and longing. The parting, however, would be only for a time.

By early July, two things were clear. First, the situation with Pancho was becoming intolerable. Jealous rages followed long nights of drinking by one or the other of them, or by both; outbursts of frightful, tearful hysterics followed the jealous rages; a day's disappearance followed the hysterics. In a letter to Donald Windham, Williams said he understood the reasons for Pancho's emotional immaturity: the young man had known no security as a youth, and now he was afraid of losing his only link with respectability, permanence and glamour. But there was also the report, carried through mutual friends from that summer, that Frank Merlo had returned to New York complaining how he missed Tennessee Williams. Pancho Rodriguez's days in Tennessee Williams's life were thenceforth numbered.

But because he still considered himself a dying man, Williams was cool to the idea of traveling alone on an imminent trip to California, which was necessary to consider an actress for the role of Blanche; accordingly, he postponed plans to send Pancho away with a cash settlement and a letter of employment recommendation.

The previous January, Hume Cronyn had produced a quartet of one-act plays for the Actors' Lab, a small professional company in Los Angeles. Three of the four plays were by Williams and one of them, *Portrait of a Madonna,* was directed by Cronyn. In it, his wife, Jessica Tandy, had

starred as the tortured, deranged Miss Collins, living in a world of romantic illusions and finally carted off to an institution. Cronyn had
hoped to have Williams travel out to see the play that previous winter; it
took until July, with the urgency of a scheduled opening for *Streetcar* in
New York before year's end, for Williams to agree to the trip. But he
would not travel without Pancho's companionship, he required guarantee of a hotel pool or nearby beach, and he demanded that the stay be
short.

The generous Irene Selznick had arranged for him to have his choice of
residences — at her house on Summit Drive, at a beach-house, or at a
small bungalow in Malibu. Over the period of a month, Williams —
sometimes with and sometimes without Pancho — stayed in all three.
And his companion, thrilled to near delirium with the movie capital,
maintained socially exemplary behavior, so that Williams felt easy about
prolonging the stay, while Cronyn restaged *Portrait of a Madonna* for his
especial benefit. A single performance, at which Williams was joined by
Selznick and Kazan (who had just finished editorial supervision on the
film *Gentleman's Agreement*), was enough to settle the matter of who
would play Blanche DuBois. There was no argument that it must be Jessica Tandy, who had acted in her native England and in America for almost twenty years, and whose career now had seemed tediously mired in
unexceptional films. Cronyn's early faith in Williams and his appreciation of his wife's great gift were at once vindicated and rewarded.

The first of August, tanned and overfed, Williams and Pancho left for
Dallas and Margo Jones, who swept round them with *passionate* an-
nouncements about the reactions to *Summer and Smoke,* and how *clearly*
she understood Williams's vision, and how *glad* she was that Kazan had
been engaged for the new play, but that she thought, *really,* she would be
thrilled to come back to New York to direct *Summer and Smoke* there, and
other Williams plays thereafter.*

"Margo Jones wanted desperately to be Tennessee's producer and
director after her work as codirector of *The Glass Menagerie*," according
to Randy Echols. "All she had to do was say to him, 'Your new play is
magic, Tenn, it's sheer magic,' and she had him eating out of her hand.
But of course when she finally directed *Summer and Smoke* it was an absolute disaster."

---

* On May 3, 1947, Margo Jones had presented the first offering of her new repertory company
"Theatre 47": it had been, at Williams's urging, William Inge's *Farther Off from Heaven,*
which Williams had referred to Audrey. *Summer and Smoke* followed.

And so it was, with her curiously imprecise direction. Brooks Atkinson, however — who made the trip from New York, where he was drama critic for the *Times* — recognized it, in spite of production flaws, as a deeply affecting play. He suggested that there be major changes before they come to New York.

Margo piled suitcases, and her friend and assistant Joanna Albus, into the car with Williams and Pancho and drove with them back to Cape Cod, chattering about the casting for *Streetcar* and making her usual bold suggestions — now mostly about the role of Stanley Kowalski. When he arrived in Provincetown, Williams found a letter informing him that excessive demands were being made by their first choice, John Garfield, who wanted a guarantee for a subsequent film of the play as well as the right to withdraw from the play if a good movie offer arose. These and other stipulations seemed even to the novice Mrs. Selznick as unconscionable, and Garfield was left out of subsequent negotiations.* This infuriated Williams. "A play is my life's blood!" he shouted over the telephone to Audrey. "What is Dame Selznick up to? I have more reverence for Miss Margo, who is here with me now. . . . I am more interested in getting Garfield back than in talking about another actor. . . ." And so on it went, for several nights at the end of August.

At this point Bill Liebling made a suggestion to Audrey; she thought it was inspired, and she wired Kazan and telephoned Irene and Williams at once. A twenty-three-year-old former New School student in Erwin Piscator's Drama Workshop had impressed Liebling with just four Broadway appearances — as the son in *I Remember Mama*, in 1944; in Maxwell Anderson's *Truckline Café*, directed by Harold Clurman (and co-produced by Clurman and Elia Kazan) in 1946; in Ben Hecht's salute to Israel, *A Flag Is Born*, with Paul Muni, also in 1946; and in a revival of Shaw's *Candida* with Katharine Cornell. His name was Marlon Brando. The last week of August, Brando was persuaded to travel to Provincetown to read for Williams.

"I never saw such raw talent in an individual," Williams recalled. "Brando was a gentle, lovely guy, a man of extraordinary beauty when I first met him. He was very natural and helpful. He repaired the plumbing that had gone on the whack, and he repaired the lights that had gone off. And then he just sat calmly down and began to read [the role of Stanley in *A Streetcar Named Desire*]."

* Audrey and Irene had sent Williams a list of names for consideration, some of them more amusing possibilities than others: Van Heflin, Edmund O'Brien, John Lund, Gregory Peck, etc.

The effect on everyone in the room — Williams, Margo, Joanna, Pancho — was instantaneous enthusiasm. "Get Kazan on the phone!" Margo shouted, leaping around the room. "This is the greatest reading I have ever heard — even in *Texas!*" As it happened, Kazan had already known and worked with Brando — but he had reservations about the actor's detached style, his frequently uncooperative moods, his unique but unpredictable acting method. Williams insisted that Kazan hear Brando read, in New York. "He is a God-sent Stanley," Williams told Audrey; he felt Brando's reading caught the humanity of the character, and the character of *A Streetcar Named Desire* as a play of misperceptions, of the callousness and insensitivity of youth. Brando's sensuality, Williams added, and his immediate physical appeal, would enable audiences to react with more appropriate complexity to the tragic ironies and shifting identifications he wanted them to feel.

By September, Jessica Tandy and Marlon Brando had, with some mutual wariness, met at a first reading under Kazan's confident, quiet guidance; Kim Hunter and Karl Malden were signed for the roles of Stella and Stanley's buddy Harold Mitchell (whose name and character were based on Williams's Missouri classmate). Irene Selznick fixed a December 3 opening at the Ethel Barrymore Theatre in New York, after previews in New Haven, Boston and Philadelphia.

"Tennessee was quite shy during our early rehearsals," Elia Kazan remembered, "but he became less so as time went on. He never interfered, but he was always there for us, always available if there were a question about the text." As the first performances drew near, rehearsal time increased — and by mid-October there were eight hours of work at night, at the New Amsterdam Theatre roof rehearsal hall, in addition to two hours of work each morning. At Williams's insistence (and with Kazan's quick approval), the script was frozen — as much because there was no need of alteration as because the author said this was his last play, that he was dying, and that he had no energy for any more work. But he looked quite well, and he ate heartily and kept late hours. The cast knew not what to think.

Two decisions by Tennessee Williams during the pre-Broadway tour suggested that he would not be so quickly departing this world. First, the dissension with Pancho had reached a critical stage when he tossed Tennessee's typewriter from a hotel window and then tore up the curtains. That was impossible to forgive. Williams gave Pancho a train ticket to New Orleans. To this he added two months' pay to assist him in a new

life; there could be no question, however, of a resumption of their relationship. Williams was on the verge of an important moment of his
career, he said. This was the first indication in months that he did not,
after all, expect to be buried just before (or after) opening night in New
York. The second was that he booked passage on a ship to depart
America on December 30 for a long holiday with friends in Europe.

"At the end of his affair with Pancho," Fritz Bultman said, "I saw
something I didn't like — something opportunistic and abusive in Tennessee. I must say that I thought he mismanaged things with Pancho,
and I didn't trust him after that. Later, my wife and I met him in Paris,
but he was more callous than I'd imagined anyone could be. After Kip
and Pancho, something seemed to go sour in him, to harden. And I felt
he was beginning to lose his friends. There were plenty of hangers-on,
but Oliver Evans [the poet and teacher] was probably the only deep
friend from the old days he saw regularly in the years after."

In New Haven Williams offered a spirited defense of the play and its
characters to his colleague, the venerable Thornton Wilder, who came to
a rehearsal and objected to Williams that the situation of Stella DuBois
Kowalski was incredible: a genteel Southern girl like her, he objected,
would never link herself with the scornful, proud, violent physicality of
Stanley.

"This man," Williams said to the bystanders when Wilder had stepped
away, "has never had a good lay!" Quite apart from presumptions about
Wilder's private life, Williams's intention was, of course, to indicate the
nature of Stella's perseverance with her husband. No one appreciated the
comment more than its speaker, whose piercing cackle could be heard in
every corner of the Shubert Theatre. He expected Wilder not to join
them in New York for the Broadway premiere, and he was right.

But an enormous crowd did — the audience at the Barrymore on December 3 applauded for a full half-hour, Williams was called to the stage,
and the critics rushed off to their typewriters to hail a brilliant new
American drama. From his subleased apartment on East 36th Street,
Williams hosted an after-theatre party, and the guests awaited anxiously
the first newspaper reviews. They need not have worried, then or for the
next several weeks, for the theatre had not only a solid commercial success but a play almost universally proclaimed great. Brooks Atkinson in
the *Times* called *A Streetcar Named Desire* "a quietly woven study of in-
tangibles. . . . [Williams's] knowledge of people is honest and thorough

and [his] sympathy is profoundly human. . . . Out of poetic imagination and ordinary compassion he has spun a poignant and luminous story." Howard Barnes, in the *New York Herald-Tribune,* described it as a play of "heroic dimensions. . . . Williams is certainly the Eugene O'Neill of the present period. . . . [*Streetcar*] is a savagely arresting tragedy . . . a work of rare discernment and craftsmanship." John Chapman, critic for the *New York Daily News,* wrote that it was "compassionate, heart-wrenchingly human. It has the tragic overtones of grand opera." For George Freedley of the *Morning Telegraph,* the play was "a drama of great and compelling honesty, [and the author] a dramatist of stature." And *The New Yorker*'s critic, Wolcott Gibbs, called it "deeply disturbing . . . a brilliant, implacable play about the disintegration of a woman, or, if you like, of a society."

The story of *A Streetcar Named Desire* is simple; its themes are complex. Blanche DuBois, a sad, thirty-year-old Southern belle who has suffered the loss of her ancestral home, arrives in New Orleans to visit her sister Stella, who has married a crudely forceful man, an archetype of machismo named Stanley Kowalski. Blanche's airs, her affectations and illusions about herself and others, her lies about a tragic and sordid past, are ruthlessly exposed by Stanley. It is revealed that — far from being a respectable schoolteacher who would only consider a chaste courtship prior to an old-fashioned wedding — Blanche has a reputation for seducing teenage boys, and has been the scandal of her home territory. Prior to her wanderings (and perhaps precipitated by guilt), she had been briefly married to a young man whose homosexuality she accidentally discovered and then deliberately and cruelly exposed publicly; as a result of this, he at once took his own life.

In a desperate attempt to salvage her sanity and the last vestiges of self-respect, Blanche hopes that Harold Mitchell, a crony of Stanley but bound to his own mother, will rescue her and provide some kind of emotional refuge. Stanley discloses her sordid past and then rapes Blanche, and this is the last act of retributive cruelty that seals her doom. At the end, the complexities of life and death are italicized: Stella has given birth to Stanley's baby and (contrary to what her sister had hoped) remains with him. Blanche suffers a complete breakdown and is led away to an asylum, now dependent in a new way — as before in a promiscuous way — on what she calls "the kindness of strangers."

The connection several critics pointed out — between the forlorn, tainted Blanche DuBois and the dying culture of the old American

South — Williams himself admitted: "I write out of love for the South.... [It] once had a way of life that I am just old enough to re-member — a culture that had grace, elegance, an inbred culture, not a society based on money. I write out of regret for that.... I write about the South because I think the war between romanticism and the hostility to it is very sharp there." He had treated the passing traditions of that culture before, to be sure — in Charlie Colton's diatribes of *The Last of My Solid Gold Watches,* for example.

But the social-cultural framework of *A Streetcar Named Desire* is just that — a framework, not a schematically proposed thesis. The loss of Blanche's homestead is more than a cultural consideration. For Williams, it is the play's first narrative marker of its major concern — that the hal-lowed things of the sensitive are cheapened and destroyed by contact with the brave new world whose brutish instinct can neither understand nor sustain what is fragile. (In this regard, *A Streetcar Named Desire* has a certain nostalgia that testifies to its author's veneration of Chekhov and his tragic seagull.)

But after all the critical and scholarly appreciations have been set down, we are left with the fact that Tennessee Williams brought from himself a play he was convinced was to be his last — that he would never have the energy for another long play — a work whose conflict (of desire and sensitivity against brutality) he associated with death. In his creative struggles with himself and in his domestic struggles with Pancho, in his desire for security and in his inclination for multiple and casual sexual partners, he met both the protective and the destructive Stanley, and the gentle, needy, spiritual but manipulative sensualist Blanche. And he was convinced that death was the term of his struggle.

"I draw all my characters from myself," he said later. "I can't draw a character unless I know it within myself." And as Elia Kazan well under-stood, "Blanche DuBois, the woman, *is* Williams. Blanche comes into a house where someone is going to murder her. The interesting part of it is that Blanche DuBois–Williams is *attracted* to the person who's going to murder her.... I saw Blanche as Williams, an ambivalent figure who is attracted to the harshness and vulgarity around him at the same time that he fears it, because it threatens his life."

In fact it was Kazan's unspoken understanding of the deeply personal complex of feelings in Williams's life at this time that made the staging of the play possible. "Kazan," Williams said, "has always given me con-fidence and always brought out the best of me." Instead of confounding his inner anxiety with explosions of guilt and with a paralytic remorse, Williams dealt with his conflicts the only way he knew — creatively.

The acuteness of perception and the truth of those shifting associations between Stanley and Blanche could be set down for audiences because Tennessee Williams first knew the battle and the shifting identifications within himself. He looked to Pancho Rodriguez for strength and protection against passersby and against the harsher tradesmen of the theatre; he needed him for traveling companion and he came to him for comfort and for tenderness when he was exhausted from work. Like Stanley toward Stella, he also needed someone to comfort and to protect, and in Pancho's insecurity he found the perfect recipient — perhaps too perfect, which is why he could finally no longer sustain the blunt demands that the younger man made, and that made him paradoxically so dependent that it was suffocating to Williams.

"Tennessee liked Pancho," Kazan reflected years later, "for the same qualities he saw in Kowalski — that he'd break up the joint if he didn't like what was going on." An admirer of brute strength and its often impolite, ungenteel manifestations, Williams nevertheless took more often the part of Blanche: he learned to yield to the temporary soothing of alcohol and to the comfort of strangers' arms.

But just as Williams was donor and receiver of the protectiveness, the encircling strength of Stanley, so was he prey to the crazy, ungentle animal instincts of both Stanley and Blanche. As he wrote to Donald Windham in March 1947, and to others throughout the year, he felt the need to supplement intimacy with Pancho with other sexual contacts — as he had during the time with Kip; he felt like the Blanche who went from bed to bed, and whose encounter with a newspaper-boy is the mirror image of Williams in those critical years, eager, like Blanche, to be affirmed by strangers.

But at last, he believed, this conflict between Stanley and Blanche leads to death — thus his conviction, even while he was depending on Pancho and driving Pancho away, while he was giving to and receiving from Pancho — that desire, unreined, leads to death: "They told me to take a streetcar named Desire, then transfer to one called Cemeteries," is Blanche's first line in the play.* He was himself convinced that the clash of desires in him was leading him to a literal death; and although time proved him wrong, there was a deeper awareness that with unchecked

---

* He has, with poetic license, modified the direct streetcar route of the French Quarter to suit his own purposes.

desires something always dies. He was, he felt in 1946 and 1947, Blanche herself — at the end of the line; and death, and maybe Elysian Fields, lay ahead. This inevitability, he felt, was due to the free play that desire had had, up to this time, in his life.

The part of him that was Stanley rebelled, and protected Stella, the sister who saw the necessity of compromise; the part that was Stanley wanted to tear away the mask of illusion and the drab phoniness that Blanche brought into his life. And there lay the heart of the battle, for although the part that was Blanche lied, wore a deceiving garb, clung irrationally to a dead past that could not be revived, yearned for a style that had already gone to rot, she still wore the mantle of a tragic dignity; she was still aware that "there has been some progress ... art, poetry, music ... such kinds of new light have come into the world ... some tenderer feelings have had some little beginning."* She was still aware, finally, that although she had not pursued those tenderer feelings as she might, and had squandered and falsified her emotions, there were still rations available to her — and if too late for her, available to Stella, and to others.

Viewers and readers of the play (and the audiences of the brilliant film of it directed by Kazan in 1951) sense that *A Streetcar Named Desire* dramatizes the eternal clash within everyone. Williams knew it most deeply in himself: his sister had been broken by conflict, he was always being *almost* broken by it. In the play that many still consider his masterpiece, he revealed not what all life is like, but what some of life is like, and what all life is in constant danger of becoming — a willing ritual sacrifice of humanity at its gentlest to the fierce demands of carnality. An empty immolation, it leads only to death, or to madness.

Accepting and mistrusting the praise for his play, he left for Europe by steamship at the end of 1947. He was exhausted and nervous but alone, and for once he was pleased with the solitude of a single room.

* In *The Glass Menagerie*, Amanda Wingfield praises "Superior things! Things of the mind and the spirit! Only animals have to satisfy instincts! Surely your aims are somewhat higher than theirs!"

Chapter Five

FIDELITIES
(1948–1952)

I always say that life is such a mysteriously complicated thing that no one should really presume to judge and condemn the behavior of anyone else.

— Alma Winemiller, in *Summer and Smoke*

H E HAD EXPECTED Paris in 1948 to be glamorous, happy, open, daring and full of international artists, as it had been in 1928. But from a damp and chilly room at the Hotel Lutetia, on the Boulevard Raspail, Williams wrote to Audrey Wood, Donald Windham and others that the city had on the contrary depressed him, and he had a bad cold and a sick stomach. Could Audrey send cans of condensed milk? She did. Would she write to Dr. Emmet Hoctor at the state hospital in Farmington, to arrange for a paid companion for Rose, so his sister could have more frequent outings? Audrey at once took the matter to the Missouri authorities. Could she send instant coffee, which would be less strong on his excitable heart? Audrey wrapped several jars and forwarded them by air mail.

By the end of January, Williams's Paris excursions had taken him to a few required tourist attractions and to the gathering places of the homosexual population there. At least once, he was robbed by a companion he had brought back for the night. Windham and Wood urged caution, and she added that walks in Montmartre at night were unlikely to be safer than those in Central Park (which, she knew, had already been disastrous for him). Audrey was also concerned at his report that his cold had turned to hepatitis and mononucleosis, and that he was confined to the American hospital in Neuilly, a suburb of Paris. But by the time she had sent a cable asking if she should go to him, he had been discharged with a prescription for cough syrup and was back at his hotel; as usual, he interpreted his symptoms as signs of grave illness.

In February, he began to retrace the journey he had taken twenty years earlier with his grandfather, traveling by train along the Riviera; then, without stopping, he proceeded through Italy to Naples and Reggio di Calabria, and went over for a brief visit to Sicily. Alone and unable to speak Italian, he at once returned to Rome, where he spent two weeks in a small apartment, completing revisions on *Summer and Smoke* for a Broadway production later that year.* It was the last attempt at serious work for many months, and it began the first protracted hiatus in his writing since adolescence. The outcome of such uncreative indolence was unfortunate.

In his new apartment at 45 via Aurora, his life was all play and no work. "His trip," according to Paul Bigelow, "recalled the earlier vacation with his grandfather. But now he could find more sexual freedom than he had found anywhere else — and a social and creative freedom when he wanted that, too."

The social and creative freedom of postwar Rome came as a surprise, both to the American colony and to the somewhat bewildered, struggling Romans. "In 1946 and 1947 Europe was still out-of-bounds for foreigners," as Gore Vidal remarked. "Rome was strange to all of us. For one thing, Italy had been sealed off not only by war but by Fascism. Since the early thirties few English or American artists knew Italy well." Very quickly, however, things changed, as an influx of artists — and the welcome American dollar — altered the pattern of Roman day and night life.

The invasion was chronicled by, among others, Harold Acton, who came from his house in Florence in March 1948 to observe what he called "a bohemian annexe to the American Academy [in Rome]," and where he met Williams ("a pudgy, taciturn, moustached little man without any obvious distinction"), composer Samuel Barber, Vidal (whose *The City and the Pillar,* the first serious novel of homosexuality by an American, was soon to be published), the poet-novelist Frederic Prokosch, and even the occasional heterosexual, like Orson Welles. Acton was not the only historian-observer to be struck by the Americans' creative zest and by their boldness in pursuing unconventional sexual mores. And pursuing is what they did with a vengeance; Williams, for one, wrote letter after letter to Donald Windham boasting of what he admitted was an excess of sensuality. Part of this was because a little money went a long way, and Roman boys and young men would, for the price of a meal or a coat, be available.

Typically, however, it was not long before Williams felt less calloused, warmer feelings. By the end of March, when he hosted a reception at his

* At the same time, he quickly drafted the short story "Rubio y Morena," a heterosexualized (and much sentimentalized) account of his travels with Pancho. The story concerns the lonely writer Kamrowski and his doomed affair with the Mexican girl Amada.

apartment, he had taken a young Italian lover named Salvatore (who was called Raffaello in Williams's *Memoirs* and letters). Williams at once found himself full of tender affection — a sentiment, he told Windham, he had very much hoped to avoid after the Pancho era.

Vidal — alert, serious but gifted with a keen, patrician humor — later recalled that in 1948 Williams had an "indifference to place, art, history. [He] seldom reads a book and the only history he knows is his own; he depends, finally, on a romantic genius to get him through life. Above all, he is a survivor. . . ." And surviving was what Williams intended during his remarkably sensual life that year; he discovered that he was not in imminent danger of death, and that the busy, affable crowd of Americans in Rome would not tolerate such ridiculous protestations to the contrary. With the Roman spring he caught the spirit of *dolce far niente,* of sweet indolence; a short story or two was occasionally attempted, but most waking hours were otherwise given over to wandering. He planned to stay as long as he could, at least until it was necessary to return to New York for *Summer and Smoke.*

In the midst of what he still often insisted was only a temporary escape from his death sentence, the good news came from Audrey: *A Streetcar Named Desire,* on March 31, received the award for best play of the year from the Drama Critics Circle, and on May 3 the Pulitzer Prize was added to its honors. Audrey wrote that his income was spiraling, and she recommended serious investments. In 1948, as international companies produced his plays and *Streetcar* continued to sell out in New York, his revenue was so great that he had to pay more than $100,000 in taxes.

From the end of April to early June, Donald Windham and his friend and companion Sandy Campbell came to Rome and joined Williams and Salvatore all day every day. They could see his restlessness, however, for a fierce promiscuity — in spite of Salvatore — was manifested that season: he was getting an appetite (Williams's word) for blonds, and said he might go north. (Sebastian Venable, in the later *Suddenly Last Summer,* becomes "fed up with the dark ones and was famished for blonds . . . that's how he talked about people, as if they were items on a menu. . . .") In a letter to Audrey Wood on April 19, he quoted at length from the Episcopalian act of contrition and added his own awareness of the sins of his life. Perhaps because he had almost completely stopped working that spring, the pull of the flesh was more strongly felt than ever.

Audrey replied to his letter, but changed the subject: in May, Jerry Wald, at Warner Brothers Studios, was hastening negotiations by reporting that Samuel Goldwyn was simultaneously trying to buy the rights to *The Glass Menagerie,* in which he hoped to star Teresa Wright and Dana Andrews, who had been so popular in his production of *The Best Years of Our Lives.* Warners, at Wald's behest, acted quickly and Goldwyn lost the rights.

Glad of the visit of his American friends and for the most part content with the longest vacation he had known, Williams was, precisely because of the gnawing sexual tension within him, glad of the news of Margo Jones's imminent arrival. A visitor he might otherwise have tried to avoid, she was due in Naples in early June to discuss the final revisions and production plans for *Summer and Smoke.* The consistency of feeling, the congruence between his own struggle and that of Alma Winemiller, the play's heroine, could not have been more exact if he had written literally about himself instead of about his surrogate, the minister's daughter. The complexities of his life with Pancho had been transformed into *A Streetcar Named Desire;* the conflict continued, unexpectedly, with the Italian boy Salvatore. And the last draft of *Summer and Smoke* — prepared for Margo's arrival that spring — reveals the shift in feeling, the deepening of the conflict far beyond what the play had dramatized in its earlier version, for now Miss Alma's conflict had a knife-edge poignancy, her Puritan guilt a breathless urgency.

By June 8 he and Salvatore had met Margo and traveled briefly to Capri and Ischia; the islands in the Bay of Naples would, Williams said, be relaxing for them all while necessary work was done on production plans. But Margo was uncharmed by Mediterranean beauties geographic or human, and so, after depositing Salvatore in Rome, he went with her to London. Margo returned to New York shortly thereafter, and in his suite at the Savoy Hotel Williams — energized by the contagious enthusiasm of "the Texas tornado" — resumed daily writing and met with the producer (Hugh Beaumont) and the director (John Gielgud) who were preparing the London version of *The Glass Menagerie,* in which Helen Hayes had agreed to star as Amanda. Also at this time he met the young Russo-English aspiring actress Maria Britneva, whom he often visited in London and whom he often entertained in America. A woman of strong loyalty and vitality, she was appointed by Williams as a cotrustee of a trust created by the terms of his will.

But the essential loneliness of London, which he detailed in letters to Audrey, was sharpened by the sudden awareness of how deep was his feeling for young Salvatore, whom he had at first tried to keep distant and who broke the unwelcome news that he might soon realize his dream of emigrating to America — in the company of an American woman he intended to marry. It seemed to Williams like the repetition of his relationship with Kip Kiernan, the Canadian dancer. But from the calm — almost stoic — observance of this, he shaped the final scenes of *Summer and Smoke:*

"Yes, it had begun that early, this affliction of love," Alma says to John Buchanan, the doctor she has loved, spurned and then after changing her mind and heart must at last lose, "and never let go of me since, but kept on growing. I've lived next door to you all the days of my life, a weak and divided person who stood in adoring awe of your singleness, of your strength. And that is my story! Now I wish you would tell me — why didn't it happen between us? Why did I fail? Why did you come almost close enough — and no closer?" As he knew, it was with the doctor as it was with himself — the distance, and the loss, were really due to the nature of Alma, and the nature of Tennessee Williams.

It was at this time that he met someone who suggested that he supplement the chemical effect of liquor with mood-altering pills. By the end of June, he admitted to Audrey, this dangerous combination had become a frequent indulgence. It was perhaps the next step in a life of increasing abandonment to sensual experience, even at the risk of health.

This experience was sufficiently frightening to him that he departed London and returned to Paris, where he took two rooms at the Hotel de l'Université, renewed his friendship with Gore Vidal and Frederick Prokosch, and his acquaintance with Truman Capote. Then a twenty-four-year-old whose first novel, *Other Voices, Other Rooms,* had caused some literary excitement, Capote regaled Williams with anecdotes about his birthplace, New Orleans. Williams found that Capote's boyish looks and fey humor took some time to appreciate. There was more substantial distraction at a luncheon given for Williams, Vidal and Prokosch by Jean Cocteau, who wanted the French rights to *A Streetcar Named Desire* for Jean Marais to act in.

"I came along as translator," Vidal recalled. "Marais looked beautiful but sleepy. Cocteau was characteristically brilliant.... Tennessee knew no French. He also had no clear idea just who Cocteau was, while Cocteau knew nothing about Tennessee except that he had written a popular American play with a splendid part in it for his lover Marais. Between Tennessee's solemn analyses of the play and Cocteau's rhetoric about theater ... no one made any sense at all except Marais who broke his long silence to ask, apropos the character Stanley Kowalski, 'Will I have to use a Polish accent?' "

Meanwhile, the London premiere of *The Glass Menagerie* was set for July 28. Edwina and Dakin arrived, and Audrey Wood hosted them at the Savoy. Then they — with Gielgud and the cast — awaited the scheduled arrival of the playwright. The afternoon of the premiere came, but no Williams; the first performance and a lavish reception followed, but still no Williams. Then Edwina was handed a telegram from her son, dated from Paris: "Take a bow for me." She was furious, Audrey was embarrassed, and Helen Hayes was perplexed. In a letter the actress received three days later, Williams begged pardon for his childish behavior, and explained his rudeness by detailing a condition of exhaustion, overwork, frayed nerves, emotional paralysis and — Alma Winemiller's complaint — constant heart palpitations. His failure to arrive, he wrote, was due to an accidental overdose of the sedative barbital he had taken to quiet a nerve crisis; he then fell unconscious for five hours and missed his train. He deeply regretted his gaucherie and felt that the patient and understanding Miss Hayes would forgive what his own mother would not. She tried, as did Audrey, to ignore the event, and with their good humor they kept Edwina off his track.

On August 4, Williams departed from Genoa for New York, having delayed as long as he could his return for the rehearsals of *Summer and Smoke*. It is not known whether there was a final meeting with Salvatore.

Back in New York, his friends Tony and Jane Smith had been on the alert for an apartment he might sublease, and they had arranged for him to move to 235 East 58th Street, which Tony had recently redesigned for its tenant, the artist Buffie Johnson. The Smiths welcomed him warmly, as did Paul Bigelow. But at once Williams began to complain that he was dying of heart disease — shades of Miss Alma yet again.

"I got tired of all this talk from Tenn about his imminent death from one malady or another," Bigelow remembered. "This time he insisted it was a heart condition, so I took him to a friend of mine who was a distinguished cardiac man. After several consultations, the doctor said to me, 'I think it would be better if you didn't disabuse Mr. Williams of this illusion about a serious illness — it would make him very unhappy to think he was in perfect health, and it might even bring about a heart attack!' We both smiled over that, and of course I never told Tenn what the doctor said. After a few days with his friends, however — all of whom took little notice of his hypochondria — he was for the most part his old self, full of fun and deviltry."

On October 6, *Summer and Smoke* opened at the Music Box Theatre, and most of the critics gave it a chilly reception: "a pretentious and amateurish bore" and "a juvenile and sadly delinquent effort" and "almost unendurably lengthy" were the kinder remarks, and even his mentor John Gassner thought the play represented "the weaknesses I have suspected in its author for a long time — an insufficient exertion of intellect." Among the few who praised it was Brooks Atkinson, in the *Times:* "It's tremulous with beauty . . . a work of art . . . the gift of a poetic and creative writer." Only Atkinson felt that the failure of *Summer and Smoke* was due to Margo Jones's unfortunate direction, and not indeed to any deficiencies in what he felt was an important play.

In fact, *Summer and Smoke* is one of Tennessee Williams's masterworks for the stage, a play of the eternal conflict between flesh and spirit — although these are often schematically represented by the heroine, Alma Winemiller and the man she has known from childhood, John Buchanan. She is the soul, or smoke, of the title — the exponent of something "immaterial — as thin as smoke," as John says of her — while he is represented by everything that refers to the body, to summer's heat, and to the plain, flat acceptance of physicality which he recommends to her and which he literalizes in his profession as a doctor. The story is straightforward: from his youth as a hell-raiser and womanizer, John is transformed into a serious and devoted physician, a change which occurs partly as a result of Alma's example and partly because his irresponsibility causes the death of his own father. By the time of his transfer of energies, however, Alma, too, has changed: she has come to know that an exaggerated, hermetically sealed angelism is inhuman. But when she is ready for a healthy life of the body, it is too late: John — who alone, over the years, has been her real heart's desire — is ready to marry a sturdy, uncomplicated girl from the town. "The tables have turned with a vengeance," Alma observes, in Tennessee Williams's most poignant assertion that balanced unions between the right mates are very rare indeed.

The objection that Alma and John are created as characters so extreme as to be incredible is perhaps not a fair one. It is in fact precisely because they are extreme people (like the two aspects, wild and sensitive, of their creator) that they are doomed to estrangement. Everything about Alma

Winemiller is too removed from the things of earth and body; every-thing about John is too involved with the things of earth and body. They should complement one another, but complementarity is rare — which is why not even the passionate Rosa Gonzales can win John, either: she is as sensual as he, and cannot balance him. And it is Alma's years of extreme living that lead her to a single dramatic gesture at the final curtain: she meets a young man in the park, by the statue of the stone angel, and agrees to go off with him for a night at the Moon Lake Casino. There is nothing to suggest entrance into a life of promiscuity (as some have presumptuously believed); it is simply a single gesture of reversal and defiance, a single attempt to correct a habit of an unbalanced nature.

At the opening (which, according to those present, brought tears of emotion from many in the audience) were two people who were becom-ing increasingly important to Tennessee Williams, and each for a differ-ent reason. He had invited, for a center seat and a place of honor at the party following, the woman to whom the play was dedicated — Carson McCullers. Earlier that year, from Italy, Williams had written to Paul Bigelow that he hoped he could do something concrete to help the frail, unstable Carson — something, he said, that would atone for the selfish-ness that marked his life in Rome. But he added that he knew he could not give up the "irregularities" of his life and nature, and that he feared this would add to Carson's unhappiness. Now, back in America, he was about to make a bolder suggestion: that he and she take Rose from the hospital to live with them in a kind of family situation.

This was, of course, an impossible (if poignant) fantasy. For a time, however, Carson and Williams spoke as if it were no more unlikely than a winter picnic. Privately, however, she told friends that she was nervous about Williams's nerves; and privately he told friends that he was ner-vous about her nerves. They were both, on the other hand, romantically attracted to the other's fragility.

But if Williams was disappointed with Margo's handling of *Summer and Smoke,* and unsure how to establish the little family of Williams, Williams and McCullers, he was buoyant and rock-sure about the other friend at opening night. Walking along East 58th Street, he had met Frank Merlo. Before the end of October, Merlo had moved to Williams's apartment, and so began the longest and the deepest intimacy of his life.

On the fineness of Frank Merlo's character there is simply no dispute, nor on the devotion and dutifulness with which he gave over his life to Tennessee Williams's. "Frank was the best person Tom ever lived with," according to Dakin. "My brother left every practical detail of his life to Frank, and he discharged everything wonderfully well. He cared for Grandfather equally well. Frank was a unique man."

"We were all very pleased when Frank moved in with Tenn," Bigelow remembered. "Frank was a warm, decent man with a strong native intelligence and a sense of honor. Those of us who cared about Tenn realized that Frank wanted to care for him and to provide some order in his chaotic life. Tenn had what I call 'artist's order,' which is something else — but he needed someone to look after the ordinary logical structure of everyday life. And with great love, this is what Frank did."

Christopher Isherwood agreed: "Everyone who ever met Frank Merlo found him a marvelous man. He was a support to Tennessee; he made everything work for him. He ran the house, he looked after him in a way that was uncanny. He was no goody-goody. He was just plain good. And he wasn't just some kind of faithful servitor. He was a lovable man with a strong will. We have a saying in Britain — 'He kept his wig on' — that is, he was a man who kept cool, even when he and Tennessee were exposed to the most appalling pressures of social and professional life."

Williams and Merlo had no sooner settled his belongings into the apartment than the playwright set out for a brief visit to St. Louis. Dakin — who was now acting on his brother's behalf in legal matters relative to the family — drew up the terms of a trust that his brother wanted for Rose. In addition to half the royalties from *Summer and Smoke,* he arranged for regular deliveries of gifts and clothing to her. And then, for the first time in over ten years, Tennessee went to see her at Farmington — on her birthday in November. The remainder of his short visit to St. Louis passed quietly. Only Edwina and her father were now at Arundel Place, Cornelius having moved first to live with his sister in Knoxville, and then to an apartment hotel nearby. Several afternoons in St. Louis, Williams worked on a tentative first draft — not more than very rough scenes, in fact — for a play called *The Big Time Operators;* it would form, after much time and development, the thematic and narrative basis for *Sweet Bird of Youth.*

Back in New York with Frank, Williams realized how fortunate he was to have so attentive, efficient and loving a companion. Frank had rearranged the furniture in the apartment so that Williams had uncluttered and private work-space, and he had assumed innumerable small du-ties designed to free him from daily concerns and smooth his writing and social schedule. This he did with easy grace and unselfconsciousness, and Williams was so touched and appreciative that he suggested they leave almost immediately for a long trip together, a kind of celebration of their new, shared life. The only place to go, of course, would be to Italy and Sicily, since Williams had loved the island on first sight earlier that year, and because Merlo's family had emigrated from Sicily. Before their de-parture, he wrote to Audrey, telling her he could be reached simply "in care of American Express, Rome," and assuring her that the important part of himself coveted not Broadway and fame, but a deepening of his creative life without concession to the demands of celebrity. Audrey and Dakin were seeing to the professional, legal and financial aspects of his life; now he could add to this pragmatic dependency the devoted atten-tion of Frankie. Neither before nor after this was Tennessee Williams ever surrounded with so much protection and support.

And so in early December they boarded the *Vulcania* from New York, and a week later were met in Tangier by Jane and Paul Bowles. It was the first meeting since 1940 between Williams and the hapless Mrs. Bowles, who resembled no one so much as Carson McCullers — she was exactly the same age, with the same delicate talent, the same complexity and am-biguity and unusual personality, the same scratchy persona.

"In appearance she was a lovely girl," Williams wrote, "small, piquant, darting between humor, anxiety, love and distraction. I had met nervous girls before, but her quicksilver animation, her continual cries, to me and herself: 'Shall we do this or shall we do that? What shall we do?' showed such an extreme kind of excited indecision that I was skeptical of its real-ity — intrigued, certainly, but still somewhat incredulous.

"Used to it as Paul [Bowles] must have been, he stood there, simply smiling in a bemused sort of way. It seems to me that Frank Merlo took command of the chaotic situation, much to the relief of us all. . . . All the indecision was a true and dreadful concern that she might suggest a wrong move in a world she had correctly surmised to be so inclined to turn wrongly."

In the company of one or both Bowleses, Williams and Merlo spent three weeks touring the charming and the seedy corners of Tangier, Fez and Casablanca. With the new year they crossed to Marseilles, retrieved a car they had shipped ahead, and drove across the Riviera and down to Rome, arriving January 7 at the via Aurora apartment which they made their base until mid-April. Almost immediately, as if the prospect of another long holiday were more nerve-racking than refreshing, he set in motion a series of anxious letters to Audrey and Dakin regarding Rose. Before departing America, he had sent money to Edwina through Audrey, to help arrange the final details for Rose's transfer from Farmington to a private sanatorium — with luck, permanently; but at least, he hoped, for several days weekly.

Fortunately, an assistant in Audrey Wood's office named Elizabeth Schauffler was the daughter of a Missouri physician, and he corresponded with Dr. Hoctor at Farmington; the exchange clarifies the patient's status but not the plans for removal. Rose Williams, Dr. Hoctor replied to Dr. Schauffler, had been diagnosed as suffering from dementia praecox, had insulin and electroshock therapy regularly since her lobotomy, and although her condition had shown some improvement, the prognosis was considered poor. He added that she remained a sweet and gentle patient, grateful for the help she had received. The irony of the final remark did not escape Williams's notice. Not long after, he had Rose moved to a clinic in Connecticut, and soon thereafter to a more expensive, more attractive institution in Ossining, New York.

Instead of setting up a regular writing schedule in Rome, Williams inquired about the possibility of collaborating on a screenplay with Italian director Vittorio De Sica; this would, he hoped, provide an immediate and substantial cash income to support himself and Merlo through the term of their European stay, and to support Rose at home. But an Italian deal did not materialize.*

In addition, Williams hoped to be able to send money to several needy friends in America — Donald Windham among them, whose literary fortunes were uneven and for whom Williams still had an amiable concern. In fact, he had an unselfish attitude about money even when he was worried about his own income, and friends of Tennessee Williams knew that as long as he had anything at all to spare they could turn to him for several hundred dollars in time of emergency. This was such a time for several of them, and he responded quickly.

He might have suspected, of course, that very good times were imminent for himself: very soon, contracts were negotiated providing hand-

* In a letter to Audrey Wood dated March 1, 1949, Williams listed his four favorite films: Visconti's *La Terra Trema,* Eisenstein's *Alexander Nevsky,* and De Sica's *Shoeshine* and *The Bicycle Thief.* In 1952, Williams was asked to improve an English translation of Visconti's script for *Senso,* for the English-speaking players. On this he worked with Paul Bowles; only the original Italian version has ever been released, however.

some compensation to him for the screen rights to both *The Glass Menagerie* and *A Streetcar Named Desire*. From these and from the foreign royalties of his plays came Williams's fortune, the bulk of which was established before 1965. And from this fortune came Rose's permanent care and his assistance to indigent actors, friends in need of surgery and anonymous young writers who applied for his help through the Dramatists Guild. Not ignored were the needs and requests of Frank Merlo and, in later years, more demanding companions.*

But much of this was still to come in early 1949. In February, Frank went ahead to visit relatives in Sicily and to arrange details for Williams's arrival in late spring, and for their motor trip across the island. Williams wrote several poems (which later found a place in his collection *In the Winter of Cities*), but most of them were unsatisfying and he turned instead to the outline of his first novel.

The image-basis for the novel's opening was a poem, "The Interior of the Pocket," which he wrote one drizzly morning in London the previous summer and which he now revised. The novel was at last called *The Roman Spring of Mrs. Stone,* a lightly veiled autobiography in which a middle-aged American actress is at once frightened of and attracted to the faintly cruel machismo of Italian gigolos. She ends an affair with a particularly handsome and particularly exploitive one and turns to another, a stranger who has been following her, and who is invited into her apartment where "the nothingness would be interrupted, the awful vacancy would be entered by something."

At about this time, his old friend from Santa Monica, David Greggory, arrived on holiday in Rome, and Williams told him, "I'm writing a novel — but I don't know why!" On reflection, however, he might have guessed. It was not only to pass time creatively while waiting for Merlo either to return or to send for him; it was also because, as soon as Merlo had left for Sicily, Williams had resumed his affair with Salvatore, and an obsessive pursuit of casual sex — much of it furtive, some of it dangerous. *The Roman Spring of Mrs. Stone* was virtually a journal of this time, although Karen Stone's adventures at fifty were considerably less frantic than Tennessee Williams's that year, when he was thirty-eight.

But his attitude about this interlude was neither cavalier nor callous;

---

* Williams's continuing concern for the situation of his friend Donald Windham is revealed in a letter dated June 21, in which he asked Audrey to speak to producer Charles Feldman about Windham being engaged as the screenwriter for *The Glass Menagerie*. That this did not happen was not the result of any lack of effort on Williams's part, or Audrey's.

what is notable, however, is that he *thought* his attitude was cavalier and callous. In a letter to Donald Windham dated February 20, he praised Frank Merlo for his remarkable qualities, but admitted that he himself had not altered his own personal habits much, and had continued to pick up sailors even while his most regular companion during Merlo's absence was Salvatore. Mrs. Stone's Roman spring was not much happier than his; he felt that he, too, was just "drifting," the word repeated no less than twenty-three times in the novel's last four pages.

By early March, Frank returned, after recovering from an intestinal illness that kept him housebound in Sicily for several weeks. They accepted an offer to drive south with Truman Capote and his friend Jack Dunphy, and from the Excelsior Hotel in Naples the four planned a visit to the island of Ischia. A spa for the wealthy international set had set up headquarters in the section known as Forio. Ischia again pleased Williams, but he quickly became bored with the company. There were unpleasant scenes with Capote, which, Williams admitted in letters to Audrey Wood and Donald Windham, were largely the result of his own foul mood. At the end of the month he had not only succeeded in alienating his travel-mates, but had also (by writing several hours each night) counteracted the boredom by completing a number of scenes for three plays in progress. But this work was not going well, and his increasing depression was exacerbated by his suspicion, expressed in a letter to Windham dated March 23, that the relationship with Frank would probably end in grief and tears. Already Merlo had mentioned to Williams that he resented Williams's "dependence" on him. There had been more than one loud shouting match.

The emotional scenes with Merlo and with his friends, set in splendid spas and great cities, the confession of soap opera sentiments, the dramatized illnesses and the attacks of palpitations, the periodic fabrication of domestic vendettas more typical of nineteenth-century melodrama — all these characterized Tennessee Williams's life from the late 1940s. Some of this is easy enough to understand: the dramatist who draws directly from his personal history must first keep his responses sharp, his controls clear; and nothing ensures that so well as casting his companions in the roles of characters in a real-life pre-Broadway tryout.

In April a visit to London was necessitated by the imminent production there of *A Streetcar Named Desire;* Irene Selznick had arranged for meetings with Laurence Olivier (who would direct) and his wife Vivien

Leigh (who would star), and there was already discussion about the film version. Williams took to London theatre folk the way he had the previous year — which is to say that, in spite of Merlo's company, he was not at ease with politeness and what he thought was affectation. But he loved the Oliviers' home, a former abbey, and he appreciated the special attention Vivien gave Frank.

Even before a journey to Hollywood later that year, the unpleasant memories of his time at M-G-M were already having a strange reprisal. Returning to Rome, he received the first draft of a screenplay for *The Glass Menagerie* which Warner Brothers had submitted, requesting his comments. He was outraged at the gross transformations, and in a letter to Audrey on May 13 he complained that Amanda Wingfield had been robbed of all dignity, poetry and pathos; that she had become a cheap and brassy caricature. Worse, he found unconscionable the reversal of the play's conclusion, entirely shaped to accommodate Hollywood's insistence on a happy ending. How different had been his recent meeting with Vittorio De Sica, he wrote, who thought that *The Roman Spring of Mrs. Stone* deserved a faithful, bold transformation to the cinema, and that it might be the right vehicle to tempt Greta Garbo from retirement.

Very soon after, Irving Rapper, who was contracted to direct the film, arrived in Rome for meetings with Williams. "I found him terribly shy and withdrawn," Rapper recalled, "partly because I think he felt great pressure about the film and about the Hollywood considerations of casting and treatment — but also because it was his nature to withdraw socially. In our conversations I always had the feeling that he wasn't really listening, that he became lost in another world, a more interesting inner world somewhere. He was not anti-social or unpleasant — far from it, he was a sweet, patient gentleman. And in spite of his concern for what might happen to his *Glass Menagerie,* I think he really preferred to continue relaxing in Italy, swimming, socializing with his Italians. His personal happiness and contentment were, I think, more important to him than any consideration of Hollywood movie success."

By mid-June, a larger concern than the fate of the film had settled into Williams's life. He was nearing forty, and he was feeling the pangs of creative, social and sexual anxiety that he projected onto Karen Stone at fifty. His poems, he thought, were awkward and selfconscious (not a harsh judgment); his stories he considered unimaginative (a shallow assessment in many cases); and the early drafts of his new plays, he was sure, were hopelessly unfeeling (in this, he was dead wrong). While working on screenplay revisions with Rapper (which he alternated with improvements on a new comedy tentatively called *The Eclipse of May 29, 1919*), he resumed an indiscriminate use of pills; he wrote to Audrey asking to have a New York physician send, via air mail express, tranquilizer tablets, which were then unavailable in Rome. Within the week, a month's supply arrived; within two weeks, the pills were consumed, and Frank cabled New York for a refill. No one suspected that this might be the beginning of a dangerous habit.

On the first of September Williams and Merlo returned on the *Saturnia*. In New York, Audrey greeted them with the good news that Feldman and Warners were agreeing to her terms for a second contract; for a half-million dollars, they would have the rights to *A Streetcar Named Desire*. This somewhat sweetened the prospect of an imminent trip to Los Angeles, where, everyone felt, the final script for *The Glass Menagerie* would benefit from Williams's contributions. Williams was especially glad to hear that Elia Kazan would almost certainly direct the film of *Streetcar*.

"By the time he and Frankie got to the studio," according to Irving Rapper, "it seemed to us that he really didn't want to have much to do with the picture. He said he didn't want to come on the soundstage — 'You people have all the experience, you've been doing pictures for years,' he said. 'If you want me or need me for anything, I'll help out.' And then we didn't see much of him."

They did, however, begin to hear from him when the first photographed scenes were screened in October — not because he disapproved of Rapper's direction, but because the script was so much Hollywood and so little Williams, moving along a predictably romantic course to the upbeat finale. The studio executives sensed his displeasure — and they feared it, since they would need his cheerful presence to publicize the film on release. In a memorandum from Warner Brothers executive Jerry Wald to producer Charles Feldman, it was admitted that writer Peter Berneis was, at their demand, adding an ending about which Williams knew nothing (regardless of what he suspected). At the same time, Williams was complaining to Audrey about the movie's Tom being shown on a ship, with the story told in a romanticized flashback; he wondered if Gertrude Lawrence, woefully miscast as mother to Jane Wyman and Arthur Kennedy, would appear on skates.

The situation was not helped when Williams read letters from Joseph I.

Breen, vice-president and director of the production code administration of the Motion Picture Association of America, who tended to see mud where there was hardly dust. He was demanding an irrational sanitizing of the film: "The room in which Laura seeks refuge should not be labeled 'LADIES,' nor should there be any toilet fixtures evident in the set. We think it would be better to establish this as a lounge, rather than as a lavatory."

Bored and disgusted with Hollywood, Williams took Merlo and left for St. Louis, collected Reverend Dakin and his suitcases, and headed for Key West, where they spent the winter. On November 25, they took a six-month rental on a house at 1431 Duncan Street, a modest three-bedroom cottage. Now virtually blind, Reverend Dakin learned his way about the house easily, for there was no clutter of furnishings such as Edwina had accumulated on Arundel Place. Frank set the rooms in neat order, prepared the meals, drove playwright and parson out to dinner, over to acquaintances, down to the beach. "Tom is so good to me," the Reverend wrote to Audrey Wood. "I love him."

According to Paul Bigelow, "They stayed the winter not only because they liked Key West life. The most compelling reason was that his grandfather loved it there. It was his refuge from St. Louis, and Frank saw to it that he was treated with deference by one and all and that no comfort was lacking. There was a homey atmosphere in Key West. Tenn wrote each day at one end of the dining room table, Frank cooked and ran the house, the Reverend was a respectable addition to the household — it was all very much a family."

The following year, when Williams finally bought the Duncan Street property, it was really for the sake of his grandfather. Never inclined to assume the material responsibilities connected with ownership, he felt that with Frank's management it was a worthwhile purchase. In September 1950 he bought the house from Lee and Katherine Huyck Elmore of New York, and over the years there were added a patio and swimming pool surrounded by palm trees and privacy-insuring shrubbery, and a small studio and guest cottage at the opposite end of the property. Also added eventually was a small gazebo to the left front of the house — "The Jane Bowles Summer House," he called it — to which he later attached small brass plates with the names of friends. The memorial plaques bore the first names of Marion (Vaccaro), Maria (Britneva), Bette (Reitz, the passionate coed at Iowa), Hazel (Kramer), Andrew (Gunn, a former sentimental attachment from the Macon summer of

1942), Kip (Kiernan) and Little Horse (his affectionate nickname for Frank Merlo). By the time of his death the once modest cottage was part of a tract valued at nearly $100,000, which was ten times what he paid.

As Christmas approached, so did a period of depression. Frank planned to visit relatives in New Jersey, and this gave Williams the chance (as he wrote to Donald Windham) to dip into his little book of names for casual sex partners. (Once, as he wrote to Paul Bowles, some Key West sailors became frisky with cutlery and had to be turned out. The Reverend's reaction has not been documented.)

He was also, that season, writing to Audrey, asking for fresh supplies of Seconal (a brand of secobarbital) and Syntropan (a brand of phenobarbital) — both central nervous system depressants, which he was by now taking regularly to counteract tension and insomnia. But he also often took them with gin-spiked grape juice. The effect was a predictable lethargy he offset with strong coffee. And the depressants, in 1949 and 1950, were almost as freely available as coffee — and were not thought to be any more harmful.

He continued, nevertheless, to devote the morning hours to his writing, and although he was angry with the quality of his work, he had finished by Christmas a first revised draft of *The Eclipse of May 29, 1919,* which he had for a short time called *Stornella* and then, after considering more possibilities, *The Rose Tattoo.** Audrey knew he would be cheered by the end-of-the-year report on the Broadway version of *A Streetcar Named Desire* (which had closed on December 17, 1949, after two years and 855 performances): it had won both the Pulitzer Prize and Drama Critics Circle award; it was doing brisk business on tour across America; and there were foreign companies presenting the play in London, Paris, Rome, Brussels, Stockholm, Zurich, Mexico City and Buenos Aires. *The Glass Menagerie* was before the cameras in Hollywood, the contract for Kazan to direct the film of *Streetcar* was signed — in short, Tennessee Williams was the richest and most famous playwright in America, and he was not yet forty years old.

But still he was not happy. Before Christmas he wrote to Donald Windham that ordinarily his life was fifty percent work and worry about

---

* Among other temporary titles: *The Vigil Light, Novena to a Rose, A Candle to a Rose, A Rose for Our Lady, The Grace of Our Lady, A Rose from the Hand of Our Lady, Perpetual Novena to a Rose.* There was not so much a religious obsession gripping him that season as there was a cultural interest in Sicily and a growing concern for Rose.

it, thirty-five percent a struggle against madness, and fifteen percent devoted to friends and lovers. But that season he felt eighty-nine percent of his energy went to worry about his work, ten percent to the fight against madness, and a scant one percent to love.

The New Year 1950 arrived without celebration, and after bringing in a companion for his grandfather, Williams went north to see Carson McCullers's play *The Member of the Wedding* and William Inge's *Come Back, Little Sheba,* of which he had been a champion for some time. Everyone was calling Inge a protégé of Williams, who had furthered with Margo Jones the cause of Inge's first play and who had recommended him to Audrey Wood. Williams accepted the designation, for he was indeed personally proud of Inge's rising star — but only for the present.

He and Frank returned to Key West, resuming a more settled household routine without (as Williams complained to Donald Windham) the variety of sexual contacts he had enjoyed in Frank's absence. In this regard, one of the few matters over which Williams and Merlo continued to argue was that of exclusivity: Merlo was willing to offer a companionship that was stable, committed and sexually monandrous — without other partners — and he hoped for the same in return; Williams thought that was a quaint Old World convention, but not realistic, and even dreary as a serious goal.

In February, *Flair* magazine published one of Williams's most autobiographical stories, "The Resemblance Between a Violin Case and a Coffin," which lightly fictionalizes the stages of Rose's illness. She is not named (although the brother-narrator is, as Tom), "Grand" and the Reverend are represented, as are the nursemaid Ozzie and a traveling father. There is an elegiac wistfulness (but not a sententious sweetness) to the story. It interweaves the author's inchoate homosexuality without disturbing the balance between a Chekhovian gentleness and a socially dreadful "secret" worthy of Ibsen. "The Resemblance Between a Violin Case and a Coffin" — with "Portrait of a Girl in Glass" and "Completed" — forms a trilogy-tribute to Rose Isabel Williams.*

A number of other stories are also based on direct personal history: "Grand"; "Two on a Party" (a celebration of wild weeks on the road, sharing liquor and men with Marion Black Vaccaro); "The Important

* Two late, unproduced screenplays — *The Loss of a Teardrop Diamond* and *Stopped Rocking* — were inspired, respectively, by Rose's awkward social life in her youth, and her confinement in institutions. But the characters are less closely modeled on Rose herself than those in the above trilogy.

Thing" and "The Field of Blue Children" (memories of school times and delicate friendships); and "The Angel in the Alcove" (an account of New Orleans life in 1939). But others of his stories are more overtly grotesque, more blunt in their narratives about sex, the emotional (or literal) cannibals or the erotically (sometimes pathologically) repressed personality. In this last category must be included "One Arm," "Chronicle of a Demise," "Desire and the Black Masseur," "Hard Candy" and "The Mysteries of the Joy Rio." The last two are variations on the theme of furtive sex in a movie theatre.

Most often, however, Williams used the form of short fiction as a sketchboard for his longer plays: "The Night of the Iguana" prepares for the play of the same title; "The Yellow Bird" for *Summer and Smoke;* "Three Players of a Summer Game" for *Cat on a Hot Tin Roof;* "Man Bring This Up Road" for *The Milk Train Doesn't Stop Here Anymore;* "Kingdom of Earth" for its later namesake. The best of his efforts in the short story reflect not merely an intensity of poetic diction, but also the intuition that human struggle is mysterious but surely not absurd nor without final significance.

This awareness is found especially in the extraordinary story "Three Players of a Summer Game." Unique among Williams's efforts at fiction, it comes very close to being mystical, and it joins the carefully interlocked style of Henry James with an almost religious sensibility. Compassionate but calm in its wonder about the mystery of spiritual anguish and emotional impotence, it suggests that there was a latent capacity for almost philosophical reverie that in Tennessee Williams did not flourish.

"The Resemblance Between a Violin Case and a Coffin," however, elicited a surprised and surprising response: Cornelius Williams wrote to Audrey Wood, objecting to the story's "very detrimental remarks about me."

"It was a very poor story," he continued, "and most of it is untrue. . . . I started to bring suit against these people [the publisher] including Tom. . . . I don't know his address — if he ever refers to me in any of his writing I will make him regret it as long as he lives. During the depression the last two years he was at the University of Missouri in Columbia I borrowed $1000 each year so he could go back. As far as I know I have never done him an unkind act and to me he has proven himself the most detestable of all persons — a liar and an ingrate. I want nothing further to do with him. I would appreciate your conveying this message to him, and he will also find there has been no insane people [*sic*] in the Williams family, but more than one on the immediate Dakin side."

There is no record of a reply from Audrey or her client. Cornelius's rage may in the final analysis not have been evoked by any particularly unflattering portrait of himself; the worst allusion to him in the story is that "my father . . . was a devilish man, possibly not understood but certainly hard to live with." The deeper anger may, on the other hand, have been because of his son's outspoken admission, in the story, of homosexual preference: Tennessee calls himself a "monster of sensuality" and a "devout little mystic of carnality" as he describes with great detail and appreciation the chest and arms of another schoolboy. This, for the likes of Cornelius Coffin Williams, must have been more dreadful than any detached observations about the Williams side of the family, in whose tradition of rowdiness his father always gloried.

Not two weeks after he had received word of this letter, Williams must have been amused by the ironic contrast of another letter from his family. Dakin wrote with the announcement that they were all descended — also on father's side! — from St. Francis Xavier. For the sake of his brother, Tennessee replied that he was simply delighted with the Xavier-Sevier connection. He may not have known that it was distant and doubtful; but the accumulating ironies of his family and their supposed traditions must have touched him as wonderfully funny.

There was other family correspondence gracing the Williams–Dakin postboxes that season. The Reverend dictated a letter (written by Frank) to his daughter, saying he had never been happier in his life, that the social whirl of Key West — he gave as an example dinner at Martha Hemingway's — he found delightful, and that Tom and Frank were the best companions.

"Apart from Rose," David Greggory said, "the Reverend was the only one Tennessee mentioned regularly. He was totally devoted to his grandfather, who was a man who offered him love and asked nothing in return, was not critical of him and really knew what Tennessee was all about. He wasn't just a nice grandfather being nice to some image of a nice grandson. He really understood Tenn, and his work. He was such a liberal spirit, and it was rather strange to all of us that his daughter should be so different."*

---

* "All his plays have a poetic foundation," Reverend Dakin said of his grandson to an interviewer that year, "and he is more interested in developing his characters than he is in the stories" (*cf.* the *Nashville Banner*, July 19, 1950).

At the beginning of May, Williams and Merlo deposited Grandfather at the Hotel Gayoso, Memphis, after assuring that he would be cared for by a companion and the amiable staff he had come to know on a regular basis over twenty years in that city. They then proceeded to New York, where they took a suite at the Sherry-Netherland and went to several receptions, private parties and news conferences announcing that Cheryl Crawford would produce *The Rose Tattoo*. They also went to the City Center where, two months after the final tour performance of *Streetcar,* the play reopened for a limited run with Uta Hagen and Anthony Quinn. At the end of the month, they boarded the *Ile de France.* Jane Smith traveled with them, for she was en route to furthering her career as an opera singer in Europe. She recalled hilarious nights aboard ship, with Tennessee and Frank as her two dancing and singing partners.

By early June Williams and Merlo were dining in Paris with Anna Magnani (on whom and for whom Williams based the image and the role of Serafina delle Rose, the leading character of *The Rose Tattoo*) and with Carson McCullers (who had taken a house in the French countryside). The formidable Magnani they at once adored, and she relished the adoration and returned it with a raucous affection that was both sisterly and maternal. As for accepting a Broadway role, she promised to discuss it further with them in Rome later that month: she liked the play, but was frightened at the prospect of English. McCullers — by this time significantly called his "Sister-Woman" by Williams — was not nearly so much fun to be with, for she was becoming more frail and ornery with the years and, although only thirty-three, looked much older after her first debilitating strokes.

By the second week in June, the two men had made the first of two summer excursions to Sicily. From the balcony of their room at the Belvedere Hotel, Taormina, they overlooked the Ionian Sea and the tourists and natives on the streets below the nearby plaza. Williams wanted authentic Sicilian dialect in *The Rose Tattoo,* but in true Chekhovian fashion he learned more than he used. Frank prudently convinced him that excessive foreign language in a play would only annoy the audience.

But the scenery, people and heritage — a colorful mixture of Greek, Norman, north African, French and southern Italian traditions — found a permanence in Williams's affection. He loved not only the elegance of Taormina, but the crowded, poorer streets of Catania and Palermo, too; not only the climate and palm trees and general "Southernness" of towns like Giardini di Naxos (which he found very like the rural villages along the Gulf of Mexico), but also the wildness of the hill country, the grandeur of Mount Etna, with its almost perpetual thread of white volcanic smoke, and the mysterious, ancient atmosphere of Cefalù, with its blend of Greek, Byzantine and Norman influences. Never had he felt so embraced by a land and its people; he would have preferred a Sicilian relative to a Sevier, a Williams or even a somewhat intimidating sixteenth-century Spanish missionary-saint.

On June 26 they moved to an apartment on via Firenze, Rome, after planning for a return to Sicily later that summer. That same day, he wrote to Cheryl Crawford that he felt restless, incomplete, dissatisfied even after the delights of Sicily, and he could not understand those feelings. Nevertheless, he added, he was working well on the revisions of *The Rose Tattoo*, tightening its classical allusions and unities and giving it more compactness. His producer had no doubt, after reading a second draft, that the play would fulfill its promise of being a serious comedy.

"I had been really rather upset about not having *Streetcar* submitted to me several years earlier," Cheryl Crawford said years later. "So I was delighted to have *The Rose Tattoo,* even though I learned that in fact Irene Selznick had a first look at it and turned it down. I never thought badly about Audrey for this, since she was, as always, thinking first of Tennessee, and she felt Irene should have it for first consideration."

The Rose Tattoo would be but the first of a quartet of plays by Tennessee Williams to be produced by Cheryl Crawford. From her earliest experience with the Theatre Guild in the 1920s, she became one of the founders of the Group Theatre, where she directed a number of plays in the next decade. Since 1938 she had also built a reputation as one of the theatre's most respected producers: by the time Audrey negotiated with her on *The Rose Tattoo,* she had produced *One Touch of Venus* (with Mary Martin in the leading role), *The Tempest* (starring Vera Zorina), two revivals of *Porgy and Bess,* and with Eva LeGallienne and Margaret Webster she had founded the American Repertory Theatre. She was also, with Elia Kazan and Robert Lewis, a founding director of the Actors Studio.

By the middle of July, advance copies of *The Roman Spring of Mrs. Stone* were available, and the intolerable heat of Rome was matched by the angry fire of critical and collegial resentment over his first novel. To escape the Italian capital and a platoon of inquiring journalists and photographers, Williams departed for Vienna. Defending himself against his critics, he wrote to Cheryl Crawford that his goal in chronicling the decline of Karen Stone was to arouse compassion for a sensitive nature, and how the awful obsession with power and fame change a once fine person into a caricature. If once you examine any honest nature, he concluded, only the distortions necessary to survive a mad world — or dullness incarnate — will be revealed.

But intentions do not structure a novel, nor do they invest its characters with credibility. *The Roman Spring of Mrs. Stone* is a book full of its author's emotional and spiritual fears, and it represents the battle being waged, in 1948 and 1949, in the corners of Tennessee Williams's soul.

The story could not have been simpler: following the death of her husband, the American actress Karen Stone settles in Rome, where after some hesitation she yields to the blandishments of an adoring but abusive gigolo. When her affair with him ends, she seems on the verge of an endless cycle of similar liaisons.

Williams knew that an irreversible decline into decadence was possible to him; he could identify with the insecurities of a celebrity who questions the reality of her talent and the rapid advance of time. The prevalent motif of the novel (which has a tripartite dramatic form) is artistic and sexual prostitution, and it is an amalgam of prostitutions that spells the final doom of the hard-hearted Mrs. Stone: "She looked at sick people with the hard eyes of a bird and her sympathetic tones [with the sick] were produced from her throat.... Everything that she did to court the favor of her professional associates, to create the legend of Mr. Stone [her late husband] as a paragon of loyalty and goodness, was directed by the head as distinguished from the heart. The result was that a great many people said *Mrs. Stone is a wonderful woman* in almost the same perfunctory tone with which she inquired of her secretary, 'Who died today, or Whose birthday is it?' "

Karen Stone's Italy is, for Williams, his own Italy: "I have fallen back on a great deal.... This country, these people," she says; and he had known what it was to be, like her, "crazily infatuated with a pretty young boy, in fact with a succession of pretty young boys of the pimp or gigolo class...." At the inevitably sad conclusion, Karen Stone yields to what Williams knew all too well: she throws her keys down from her balcony — like a grotesque Juliet or a decadent Rapunzel — so that a stranger may come to stop the drift of meaninglessness with a diversion of the flesh. For his friend Donald Windham, *The Roman Spring of Mrs. Stone* was Tennessee Williams's "first fictionalized self-portrait after his success — and it displays a hair-raising degree of self-knowledge."

* * *

The highlight of the summer, however, was the second meeting with Magnani, among the crowd at Doney's own via Veneto. There she said finally that she was committed to stage plays through 1951; but the real reason was her fear of English. She did agree, however, to appear in a later film verson, since the English dialogue could be rehearsed and recorded in small pieces.

"Magnani first said she would only sign on for a four-month run because of Italian commitments," according to Cheryl Crawford. "This, in addition to her nervousness about English, made it impossible for us to put her in the role of Serafina."

This news led to the advancement of two other major careers, continuing a hallmark of the Williams plays, which seemed to rejuvenate a major talent (Laurette Taylor) or to deepen a talent already established but not yet fully realized (Julie Haydon, Jessica Tandy, Marlon Brando). In the fall of 1950, those favored were the young actors Maureen Stapleton and Eli Wallach.

"Tenn had written it for Magnani," Stapleton recalled, "but when she couldn't do it, I was asked to read. Up to that time, Eli and I hadn't done so much in the theatre, so everyone was a little cautious about us — which is I guess why there were so many readings before casting was settled."

The season had other events for Williams besides agreeing on a cast and on the director, Daniel Mann (who that year had with such distinction directed *Come Back, Little Sheba*). Williams gave a party for the English poet Edith Sitwell, who was on a lecture tour in America, and he came to the Museum of Modern Art on November 16 with Carson McCullers and poet Marianne Moore for a bizarre presentation of *Macbeth,* with Sitwell improbably reading Lady Macbeth and the novelist and poet Glenway Wescott in the title role. Williams and Sitwell had met before in New York, at a famous photography session at Frances Steloff's Gotham Book Mart on West 47th Street. In the fall of 1948, Steloff had arranged for a *Life* magazine photographer to attend a reception at her shop for Edith and her brother Osbert Sitwell. In attendance were Williams, Stephen Spender, William Rose Benét, W. H. Auden, Horace Gregory, Richard Eberhart, Gore Vidal, José Garcia Villa, Elizabeth Bishop, Marianne Moore, Randall Jarrell, Delmore Schwartz and Charles Henri Ford. It was, as Sitwell biographer John Pearson wrote, "something of a classic exercise in elegantly engineered publicity.... The resulting photograph has something of Aquinas's Vision of the Heavenly

Host, with poetry's angels and archangels grouped around their virgin queen [Edith]."

There were other New York parties that autumn, and they helped to distract him from some especially unpleasant news. Bill Cannastra, the brilliant but disturbed Harvard student Williams had been attracted to several years earlier, had come to New York to pursue both his career as lawyer and his strange sexual habits. In a grotesque accident, he leaned through the open window of a moving subway car, apparently to follow the glance of a smiling stranger. A steel pillar neatly decapitated him.

By November, Williams and Frank had gone to Memphis to meet Grandfather, and the trio arrived in Key West for Thanksgiving. It was not a happy day, since Reverend Dakin was atypically withdrawn and depressed — he had submitted to radiation treatment for minor skin cancers, and although there was no doubt of his complete cure, he was a proud man and his blindness did not help him believe that he looked quite fine.

On Christmas Day, the company of *The Rose Tattoo* left New York for a Chicago premiere four days later. Williams did not intend to go to Chicago (his brother cheerfully represented the family at the first night at the Erlanger Theatre). He did, however, send several pages of script revisions. "We were performing every night and working on new business all day, every day," Maureen Stapleton recalled. "Everyone was weary, but the play had so much life, and put so much life into us, that we were revived by it every night."

There were, however, structural problems with *The Rose Tattoo;* the local critics (the faithful Claudia Cassidy among them) were quietly warning the producer and director, while the roving reviewer for *Variety* openly reported trouble in Chicago. Williams was finally summoned, and for several nights the ending of *The Rose Tattoo* was played with variations of the script at each performance.

But this is precisely the purpose of an out-of-town preview, after all: to see how a play plays, to hear how an audience reacts, to see what knots in dialogue or staging need to be untied. By the time they were ready to open in New York, according to Donald Windham, "Tennessee was counting the laughs in each scene and, when there were not enough to make him feel 'box-office secure,' [he suggested] the insertion of gags." Windham and his friend Sandy Campbell recalled sadly that, beginning about this time, "encounters with [Williams], although unlikely to be dull, were unlikely to be pleasant." He was not, it seems, coping well with what he had called "the catastrophe of success," and the single-minded devotion of Frank Merlo did not satisfy him.

"Frankie gave his entire life — without any reservation, without hesitation, and God knows without very much compensation — to the life of Tennessee," according to their friend Johnny Nicholson. When *The Rose Tattoo* opened in New York at the Martin Beck Theatre on February 3, 1950, Nicholson was in the audience; he was the proprietor of a popular café directly across from the East 58th Street apartment and had befriended his new neighbors from the start. In time, he found them another New York residence, and his good-humored support became particularly precious to Frank in later years.

From the time of the Chicago run of this play to his death, Frank Merlo had no closer friend than Maureen Stapleton; and as in the case of Johnny Nicholson, Williams did not always appreciate the kind of loyalty Frank elicited from others when he, sometimes, could not. "Frank Merlo was a man everyone adored," according to Stapleton. "It's really as simple as that — everyone loved him. I became a friend to Tenn by being a friend of Frankie. He was the liaison officer between Tenn and the rest of the world. He was at home with everyone, easy to be with, uncomplicated and understanding. And he loved and protected Tenn and did everything for him."

Although there were serious reservations about *The Rose Tattoo,* it was an instant commercial success. Some critics objected to the heavy-handed, profuse symbolism of the rose and the simplistic psychology of a Sicilian-American widow, irrationally (and unjustifiably) devoted to the idealized image of her late husband, but quickly restored to vitality (after a long period of mourning) by a slightly dim but sexy truck driver.

The Rose Tattoo is strong on charm and humor, but weak in understanding adult fears and emotions. Taking seriously the charge that he could portray only tragic scenes in the lives of repressed Southern belles, Williams gave his critics comedy. But since he was a searching poet at the same time, and not really intimate with the inner life of an immigrant woman, the comedy was instead smothered beneath a blanket of ubiquitous rose imagery, and the seriousness of a bereaved woman's predicament is diminished by the play's insistence that sexual response is the answer to life's problems.

In his correlative symbol of the rose, there are rather academic allusions to the mystic rose of religious literature, to the rose window of the medieval cathedral, to the cycle of death and rebirth: "*The Rose Tattoo* is the Dionysian element in human life," Williams wrote at the time, "the lyric as well as the Bacchantic impulse . . . the transcendence of life over the instruments it uses . . . a celebration of the inebriate god."

As it happened, *The Rose Tattoo* fared well with critics and audiences, and in a season that also featured *South Pacific, Darkness at Noon, Guys and Dolls, The Country Girl, Call Me Madam* and *Bell, Book and Candle,* the relatively uninhibited and joyous paean to the erotic in life was apparently another indication that Williams was the playwright attempting bolder themes. *The Rose Tattoo* was awarded the "Tony" for best play, Maureen Stapleton and Eli Wallach were honored for their performances, and Boris Aronson received the prize for stage design.

To the opening night came Edwina, who was embarrassed by the play's explicit talk of sex and lovemaking. Her father, also present, was blind but not deaf, and he thoroughly enjoyed it. "He was," Cheryl Crawford recalled, "quite an old eccentric — a little on the fey side, in fact." He also charmed everyone who met him, and some — like Maureen Stapleton — appreciated another element in the Reverend's personality:

"He was a crotchety old man, but Tennessee adored him. The old man was really a father to him, but what a demanding one! Tennessee took him wherever he could, and he was with us all the time in New York. He loved a good evening out, this old man in his nineties. And he didn't have one bit of trouble with the relationship between Tenn and Frankie, which is saying something, for he was an old-fashioned minister, or so his daughter described him."

As the critics continued a public debate over the merits of the play, however, they could not have known precisely how personal a work it was — and how the life-context of Tennessee Williams endowed it with both liabilities and assets. For it is really not so much the valentine to the world — nor even to "the inebriate god" of the senses that he insisted — it is rather a valentine to two loves, and that is why the rose imagery cannot overwhelm its aroma of death nor make wholly credible the swift and facile happy ending, in which Serafina is freed from her repressions and illusions by yielding to a new man in her life who has acquired a rose tattoo on his chest in imitation of her dead husband. The two loves for Williams in 1950 and 1951 were the spiritual and physical models for the play, and they were, of course, his sister Rose and his lover Frank. And there was a deep sadness in his life about both of them.

By 1951, Williams had arranged for his sister's permanent transfer to a special hospital-residence, Stony Lodge in Ossining, New York, and he was visiting her there often, usually in the company of friends like Johnny Nicholson or Cheryl Crawford.

"I made several trips with Tennessee to visit his sister," Cheryl Crawford remembered. "I always felt he had an enormous guilt about Rose — that he'd done nothing to stop the lobotomy years earlier, and that he felt responsible for the emptiness of her life. There was no question about his concern for her, and of his devotion to her. It was very touching to see them together." Johnny Nicholson remembered that the meetings were not gloomy or sad; Tennessee's sense of humor did not fail him, and alongside any guilt there coexisted an appreciation of her distance from life, and the good humor that distance gave his sister. "He found her special brand of logic very amusing," Nicholson said, "and he catered to her whims when she wanted to shop for an entire case of soap or a dozen bottles of perfume."

His sister in fact haunted his consciousness more than ever at this time, and the play reflects this — not only in its profusion of roses and rose names and rose allusions, but in its plain references to his sister. "Rosa had a very strict mother and wasn't allowed to go on dates with boys," says the sailor Jack Hunter of Serafina's daughter in *The Rose Tattoo,* summarizing the early adolescence of the playwright's sister; and Rosa makes her first appearance (in the play's first minute) as a girl of twelve with a jar of lightning bugs she has captured — a summer evening pastime of Rose and Tom that he had long ago mentioned in a poem whose title was inspired by Ozzie. That poem, "The Couple," fuses all loves into the love of a brother for his sister, whose captured fireflies taught them both death.

But the play really confuses the allusions to the virginal mother of Jesus with those to his own virginal sister. And finally all the jumbled rose imagery is patently sexual — as a universal symbol of sexual ecstasy, or at least sexual capacity. This connection is nowhere clearer than in another Williams poem, also called "A Liturgy of Roses" (which had been the working title of *The Rose Tattoo* for some months), which concludes with a deliberately blasphemous transformation of the Christian doxology, or hymn of praise, into an idolatrous celebration of male and female genitals. The "inebriate god," Dionysus, was never far from his soul.

The further connection he made between his writing of *The Rose Tattoo* and his sister was revealed by his more frequent visits, at this same time, to Carson McCullers, who from their first meeting in 1946 (and his giving of Rose's ring) became a kind of surrogate sister to whom he could offer a creative compassion.

"I spent several occasions with Carson and Tennessee," Cheryl Crawford recalled. "This was a unique friendship, and I think her special qualities of craziness appealed to him. It isn't going too far to say that he really liked and appreciated and understood and was amused by a crew of eccentrics throughout his life!"

Carson's instability was analogous to his sister's, and to his own; Carson's uncertain, constantly shifting sexuality and her self-absorbed, zany retreat into the refuge of alcohol both amused and frightened him. In the imprecise, variegated folds of *The Rose Tattoo,* he expressed his love for his sister, for Carson and for the unfettered freedom all three of them sought. On at least two occasions that winter, Williams brought Rose across the river from Ossining to Carson's home in Nyack. The meeting between the sister and the "Sister-Woman" could not have been more touching and funny. "Kiss me, Miss Rose!" cried Carson, her arms thrown open. "No, thank you," Rose replied politely, "I have halitosis." And when liquor was served before, during and after lunch, Rose — perhaps glimpsing a deep reservoir of St. Louis life-images — stood in a corner, "praying," as Johnny Nicholson remembered, "for drinking sinners."

But *The Rose Tattoo* was also a celebration of Frank Merlo. Thus far, since 1948, Frank Merlo seemed to be his salvation. And it was Merlo's unselfconscious love, his unfettered generosity, his deep attachment and his Sicilian lust for life that Williams so admired, tried to emulate, and celebrated in this play. (*The Rose Tattoo* bears the dedication "To Frank in Return for Sicily.")*

Tennessee Williams saw himself as the emotionally cloistered Serafina delle Rose, caring for a young girl named Rosa, transformed by the passion of a truck driver. Just before he met Williams, Frank Merlo had also been driving a truck (in New Jersey). From the first months of their first trip to Europe, Williams had called Frank — because of his passionate energy and his handsome, equine features — his "Little Horse." And it was in their beloved Sicily that Frank suggested to Williams the inevita-

---

* Frank, in return for himself and Sicily, received not only the dedication of the play that chronicled the psychological renewal of its author. He also received (in addition to a weekly salary of one hundred dollars) ten percent of all the profits from *The Rose Tattoo* and from the two plays that followed.

ble name for the Sicilian reviver of life in the play: the truck driver must of course be known as Alvaro Mangiacavallo, Alvaro Eat-a-Horse.

At the beginning of March, Williams took Frank, the Reverend, Edwina and Dakin to Key West. All of them promptly fell ill with a winter influenza. Frank nursed them all, but Tennessee decided that his mother and brother must return to St. Louis as soon as possible. The day after, he celebrated their departure by getting very drunk and taking his car on the main street of Key West. He had forgotten his license in New York, however, and was at once arrested for drunk driving.

At the end of the month, as if to impose some social order and responsibility on his life, he brought his sister and a nurse to Duncan Street for several weeks. Once again, Frank responded to the needs of the guests. And it was shortly after this that Williams knew a cook-housekeeper was needed. Almost daily when they were in Key West, and for the next thirty years, meals were prepared by Leoncia McGee, a calm, unshockable and devoted housekeeper. In one way, of course, Frank was pleased; but on the other hand he saw this as a first indication that perhaps in some concrete, practical matters he was a dispensable presence — that money would purchase for Tennessee any of the services Frank loved to provide.

In early May Williams was ready to depart again for an extended trip to Europe. By now, Merlo expected but was not entirely accustomed to the impermanence of their life; he would have been content to remain in the relative quiet of Key West. "He loved the stable home-life that they could have in Key West, with the house and the cook and Grandfather to care for," according to Johnny Nicholson. "And everyone in Key West was crazy about Frank and missed him. He was often referred to as 'The Mayor of Key West,' and this didn't always please Tennessee. He sometimes resented Frank's great popularity because he didn't have it."

They stopped briefly in New York, where Williams talked with Maureen Stapleton about a matter to which he had written her in March: he was then hard at work on revising *Battle of Angels,* a play for which he still had great affection. He was unsure of a new title but he thought (logically, after her triumph in *The Rose Tattoo*) that she might play Myra, the lusty wife of a dying man, or even Vee, the repressed, fanatical artist. That same week, he completed a poem that bore the eventual title of the revised play — "Orpheus Descending," a plangent lyric in which he yearned for a perfect art and a perfect mate, things "marked by their nature to be not completed / but only longed for and sought for a while and abandoned."

Before the end of May, Tennessee and Frank were at the Cavendish Hotel, London — the place from which, Williams wrote to Stapleton, Oscar Wilde was arrested. As usual, he complained about his failing health, perhaps because the news they received from America was for several weeks a series of medical bulletins: Audrey had an emergency appendectomy (soon to be followed by more serious surgery from which she needed a longer recovery period); Oliver Evans had an operation on his ear; and Paul Bigelow required surgery to correct a chronic jaw ailment. Both these latter two old friends were helped by checks from the sympathetic Williams, who responded to their need at once.

In mid-June they were in Rome, at 45 via Aurora. His bohemianism, Williams wrote to Brooks Atkinson, once again took a strong hold on his life; he still felt as if he were trying to escape the shackles of an intensely puritanical background.*

The correspondence between Williams and Atkinson that began in 1951 is a curious one. The two men were never very close friends, nor did they meet in person very often or share confidences. But when he sat at his typewriter and sent letters to this admiring critic, Williams became someone like a character in one of his own plays. His descriptions of his life are colored by all the melodramatic exaggerations he perhaps thought Atkinson would appreciate. As time passed, however, his letters have the unmistakable flavor of publicity. In a sense, Tennessee Williams wanted to be considered as controversial as his work, and perhaps even more enduring.

In early July, Williams visited Saint Tropez — while Frank traveled alone to Venice. When he eventually joined Frank in Venice, he completed the first draft of the short story "Three Players of a Summer Game" — about a once-powerful athlete-as-artist named Brick Pollitt, who has become an alcoholic. He has an affair with the widow of his doctor and at the end is abandoned by her and is dependent on the care of his wife, who drives him around in their car "exactly the way that some ancient conqueror ... might have led in chains through a capital

---

* Often, in interviews, essays, and letters to those with whom he was not on very personal terms, Williams dramatized his "puritanical background" — perhaps as a means of fashionable justification for his promiscuity: "What I do I'm not responsible for, it's all the result of my childhood repressions," etc.

city the prince of a state newly conquered." He did not finish the story for ten months; over the next two years it changed form and he added characters, and it became *Cat on a Hot Tin Roof.*

Williams could write that summer about the debilitating effects of alcohol on a middle-aged artist because so much of his own time was spent under its influence. On July 22, he was speeding north from Rome, drunk, when he lost control of the Jaguar. Had he never believed in miracles before, his mind might have been changed: the car was completely destroyed, but he walked away with a slight cut on his forehead.

Not for the first or last time, Frank came to the rescue. He drove them in a rented car to Göteborg, for the Swedish premiere of *The Rose Tattoo.* By the end of August, disagreeing over friends and travel plans, Tennessee and Frank agreed to separate — the latter went back to Rome and the former went on to London. Soon after, he was invited to luncheon at the Garrick Club by his publisher, James Laughlin, who was visiting T. S. Eliot. The American expatriate poet, playwright and essayist had won the Nobel Prize for literature in 1948 (an honor that somehow always eluded Williams, and whose omission in his life he greatly resented). The meeting between Eliot and Williams was very cordial, and not nearly as difficult as one with Carson McCullers, who was in London at the same time, more ill, more psychoneurotic and more demanding than ever. On August 29, Williams wrote to Frank that she was drinking heavily, apparently out of unrequited love for the sister of her British publisher.

By September 8 he was at the Hotel d'Angleterre, Copenhagen, for another premier of *Tattoo;* the trip, he wrote to Cheryl Crawford, was part of a sustained effort to avoid confronting himself, his responsibilities, his work and his relationship with Frank. He hoped to return to London for a November opening of *Summer and Smoke.**

The rest of the autumn was a fevered series of steamer bookings, short flights, long hours on trains, parties with strangers and virtually no productive work. He was by now smoking more than two packages of cigarettes daily, and, because of constant travel, he was not exercising regularly. After additional brief visits to London, Stockholm, Paris, Barcelona, Amsterdam and Rome — never for very long, and never with much interest in the art or tourist attractions — he and Frank returned to

---

* He had prepared, he said later, a major revision of that play, but he arrived when the original was already in rehearsal. More than twenty years later, the second version was finally produced — as *The Eccentricities of a Nightingale;* the critics and public received it even less warmly than the original Broadway version of *Summer and Smoke. Cf.* note below, on p. 317.

New York aboard the *Queen Elizabeth,* on November 7. They took Reverend Dakin to Key West for Thanksgiving, and at Christmas were in New Orleans.

"When I saw him in New Orleans that year," David Greggory recalled, "he was really depressed. He was drinking much more, and more heavily. I think he felt terrific pressure after his first few successes. His periods of depression didn't last long, but they were formidable when they did occur."

Somehow, work was resumed in New Orleans, and in spite of his increasing use of alcohol and various pills for sedation and alertness, a revised draft of the lengthened *Camino Real* was ready by the end of January. More than ever a wild, hallucinatory fantasy, combining characters from history and fiction as well as incidents from his own experiences in Mexico, Rome and New Orleans, the play had been structured as if it were modeled on Thornton Wilder's *Skin of Our Teeth:* the narrative stretched time and place arbitrarily; the emotional truth of the play was the truth of dream and fantasy, of memory and longing and hope — the truth of poetry, not the truth of verisimilitude.

From the start Williams hoped that Elia Kazan would direct *Camino Real;* this hope, in fact, seems to have influenced the construction of the play, for it was with *The Skin of Our Teeth* that Kazan's directorial career had been firmly established. (*Camino Real* was dedicated to Kazan.) His play, he wrote to Cheryl on February 10, was an extended poem on the romantic attitude to life, and everything that he had drawn from *Camille* and from the memoirs of Casanova had been reshaped according to that poetic ideal. She replied that of course she was interested in it, and before the summer Audrey had negotiated for both Kazan and Crawford to undertake this very delicate play.

At the same time another play was being prepared, and no one could have anticipated the results.

In 1951, a repertory company called the Circle in the Square (so named for its circular playing space in Greenwich Village's Sheridan Square) had staged a production of Lorca's *Yerma.* A young actress named Geraldine Page, who had acted in Chicago and New York and had worked at various odd jobs round the country, had impressed Theodore Mann, the Circle's producing cofounder, and José Quintero, who had directed her in *Yerma* in the role of the pagan crone.

"We were looking for a play that would be just right for her," Mann remembered, "and that would be within our limited range of financial and material resources. We hadn't had a real success in our first year. But then one day José came rushing in, shouting, 'I found it! I found it!' and he showed us *Summer and Smoke*. It had of course been a failure in 1948, and the rights were readily available. So we set to work. We required a fierce ardor from everyone in the company. They worked on props, costumes; they took out the garbage, stoked the furnace, worked at the box office — and for not very much money. But as soon as we were into rehearsals on *Summer and Smoke,* there was excitement among us."

Geraldine Page added that the play was their final choice by a process of elimination. "When we finished *Yerma,* everyone wanted to do a dramatization of Sherwood Anderson's *Winesburg, Ohio,* but we had to get the rights directly from Mrs. Anderson. She was doing a lot of traveling that year, and it was hard to locate her. Then there was talk of a revival of Lillian Hellman's *The Children's Hour,* but she said there was a Broadway version scheduled. And so at last the decision was made to do *Summer and Smoke.*"

Rehearsals proceeded in Sheridan Square. Meantime, Williams was unaware of the extraordinary historic night that was about to occur — not only for the cast and for him, but for what would be known as off-Broadway theatre.

In Key West, he was completing a 120-page screen treatment based on four of his one-act plays (*The Last of My Solid Gold Watches, 27 Wagons Full of Cotton, The Unsatisfactory Supper* and *This Property Is Condemned*). The story — sprawling, funny, bawdy — was something of a tangle, he wrote to Audrey, but he was sure it had promise. In time it became the single most controversial work of Tennessee Williams's career when, more than three years later, it reached the screen as *Baby Doll.*

Audrey, at the same time, was busy in her corner. The imminent revival of *Summer and Smoke* encouraged her to go to Hal Wallis at Paramount with the offer of its film rights, and within the year they were sold, as the rights to *The Rose Tattoo* had been, for $100,000.

March and April were busy in different ways for all those whose lives touched Williams's. Frank supervised construction workers who were building a studio and swimming pool in back of the Duncan Street house. At the same time, Williams flew to Los Angeles for the Academy Awards ceremony. *A Streetcar Named Desire* won Oscars for best actress (Vivien Leigh), best supporting actor (Karl Malden), best supporting actress (Kim Hunter) and best art and set decoration (Richard Day and George James Hopkins). It had also been nominated for best picture, best direction and best screenplay, but Williams himself received no award. He wrote to Cheryl Crawford that he resented his own resentment, that he wanted to be a winner of prizes like this, but he wondered if he would ever develop real humility and a solid sense of values. The letter, dated April 5, 1952, reveals a poignant self-awareness and honesty — until the final paragraph, where (in all seriousness) he expresses his anger over Frank's sexual infidelity. This would perhaps be pathetic if it were not ironic, since in fact it was Williams himself who so actively pursued other partners, and Merlo who kept himself free of such involvements.

"Merlo was a wonderful man for Tennessee," according to José Quintero. "Number one for his devotion to Tennessee, a real devotion. . . . He was enormously sensitive and one of the people that told Tennessee the truth without being afraid of 'Tennessee Williams,' in quotes. In 1952, Tennessee was really being loved and taken care of by Frank, and he needed that a great deal."

Opening night of the revival of *Summer and Smoke* (April 24, 1952) was a glorious event and a resounding success, but it came as something of a surprise to outsiders, and neither Williams nor his friends attended. The next day's reviews changed everything.

"Nothing has happened in the theatre in a long time as admirable as this production," began the review by Brooks Atkinson in the *New York Times*. "You might fairly argue that [*Summer and Smoke*] is a finer piece of literature [than *Streetcar*]. The analysis of character is subtler and more compassionate. The contrasts are less brutal. . . . From every point of view [it is] a beautifully wrought drama."

Atkinson and the other reviewers who came to the performances were right to compare the play to *Streetcar*, for in some senses it anticipated in the character of Alma Winemiller the forces in Blanche DuBois's background. The clash between emotional yearnings and repressions are more delicately explored in *Summer and Smoke;* the overrefined sensibility in conflict with the needs of the body receives a more compassionate treatment. But as with *Streetcar*, the drama derives its force from the depth of feeling that prevailed in the heart of the playwright; the theme of unreasonable idealism, broken open and humanized, was certainly plain in *Streetcar* and *Tattoo*.

"Everything in his life is in his plays, and everything in his plays is in his life," Elia Kazan reflected years later. "He was so naked in his plays, and *Summer and Smoke* is one of the best of them."

Williams admitted that Alma had a close connection to himself: "I think the character I like most is Miss Alma. . . . She is my favorite because I came out so late and so did Alma. . . . Miss Alma grew up in the shadow of the rectory, and so did I."

Summer and Smoke was, first of all, part of a tetralogy about the psychological imbalance in a woman caught between fantasy and reality. In *The Glass Menagerie,* Amanda Wingfield, bound to the traditions of her parish church, has a kind of daffy nobility in spite of her illusions and her envelope of memories. In *Summer and Smoke,* set in the early years of the century, Alma Winemiller — who has the same initials* — is a kind of early version of Amanda Wingfield. As with Amanda, the young Blanche and the older Serafina, so with Alma Winemiller: there is an exaggerated spirituality that must confront her counterpart — Dr. John Buchanan (as Blanche with Stanley Kowalski, and Serafina with Alvaro Mangiacavallo). In the final scene of *Summer and Smoke,* the genteel and the passionate unite as the rejected Alma seeks in the arms of a stranger the love she could not find with John Buchanan. In *The Rose Tattoo,* Serafina learns to accept the new man in her life, and to abandon the idolization of her dead husband. And Blanche DuBois is perhaps one possible term of this — the last route of the habit of sexual confusion and spiritual self-delusion in which the *alma,* or soul, is finally the tragic victim. (In his one-act play *The Dark Room,* first published in 1948, Williams comically explored the theme of repression and its final state in the [unseen] pregnant daughter and the sexually repressed social worker.)

Everywhere the text of *Summer and Smoke* reveals the personality of its author: Alma's "mental afflictions [have] to be brought under control"; and she speaks from Williams's level of personal anguish — "I wonder if they stop to think that I had had certain difficulties and disadvantages to cope with — which may be partly the cause of these peculiarities of mine — which they find so offensive!" And Alma speaks Williams's own final acceptance of life: "I know I'm not dying, that it isn't going to turn out to be that simple."

As soon as Audrey cabled Williams that *Summer and Smoke* was the surprise hit of the New York theatre season, he made a trip north. "I met him in the lobby after the show," José Quintero recalled, "and he rushed at me, put his arms around me, and gave me a terrific hug. I was of course petrified. He was carrying an umbrella with a very sharp point, and because we were standing so close together, when he put it down it

---

* It is perhaps only a curious coincidence that Amanda Wingfield and Alma Winemiller also share the initials of Tennessee's surrogate mother, Audrey Wood.

landed on my foot. Then he leaned on it. Right between my toes. Here was this great playwright full of admiration for the work we had done. How could I tell him he was puncturing my foot?"

For his part, Williams made sure the cast knew of his admiration and gratitude — a trait that became typical, and that of course always delighted the various companies. Later, he went on record in praise of Geraldine Page as "a talented and beautiful actress.... She is the most disciplined and dedicated."

The next month continued his good fortune. On May 28, he and Carson McCullers, Newton Arvin, Eudora Welty, Louise Bogan and Jacques Barzun were among a group elected to lifetime membership in the National Institute of Arts and Letters. And with this honor capping the success accorded *Summer and Smoke* (which played to capacity audiences for a year), he departed on June 11 with Merlo for a summer in Europe.

But Carson was departing at the same time, and she would not accept his initial refusal to visit the country house she and Reeves had taken at Bachvillers, a tiny village an hour's drive north of Paris in the Oise valley. To avoid spending time at the house, Williams brought Carson and Reeves back to Paris for several evenings.

Also in Paris he met Anna Magnani for discussions about the film of *Tattoo.* Being with Carson and Reeves was too draining, too depressing for him; they expected too much, while Magnani gave.

By early July he and Frank had arrived in Rome, and meetings both social and business-based continued with Magnani. She suggested that Vittorio De Sica or Luchino Visconti direct the film of *Tattoo.* Williams thought this inspired, but neither of them had any clear idea of international filmmaking union regulations about such things. (Daniel Mann eventually directed the film as he had the play.)

Until the end of September, Williams and Merlo remained in Rome, except for a brief excursion to visit Elia Kazan, who was directing the film *Man On a Tightrope* in Germany. They discussed the script for *Camino Real,* which was far from finalized and was presenting terrific problems in design and construction.

After a week in London at the end of September, Williams and Merlo returned to New York on the *Queen Mary.* They attended a Halloween party at Jane Bowles's rented townhouse on West 10th Street, where she was the only woman among a wild group of men who finally left her very much alone with the music and the food while they all crept, in groups of two or more, to intimate corners of the house. She seemed not to mind at all.

At Christmas, Tennessee Williams and Frank Merlo were in Key West, with only Reverend Dakin and his daughter to join them for a quiet holiday.

Chapter Six

THE NOON-DAY DEVIL

(1953–1957)

You know we live in light and shadow —
that's what we live in, a world of light and
shadow — and it's confusing.

— Vee, in *Orpheus Descending*

CAMINO REAL was scheduled for a mid-March 1953 opening in New York after previews in New Haven and Philadelphia. Williams insisted that the play was "my conception of the time and world that I live in, and its people are mostly archetypes of certain basic attitudes and qualities" he found in that world. In fact, for all its wild and idiosyncratic texture, its experimental and dreamlike progression of scenes, its fierce and funny series of almost kinetic images, *Camino Real* was not only an expression of the time and place Williams believed he inhabited; it was also his first and last frankly political play to open in New York.

The action is introduced as Don Quixote's reverie. In a mythical, vaguely Latin American town are gathered the lonely and disaffected, and those whose lives are synonymous for love, its loss, its pursuit and its varieties — Camille, Casanova, Byron — and the archetypical American, Kilroy. Very little happens in *Camino Real:* the play contrasts repression with freedom, violence with tenderness, despair with hope in alternating scenes of reflective dialogue and boisterous parades. The energy of the characters' struggles builds as the heroes and antiheroes — and finally Kilroy — pass through symbolic cycles of death and rebirth.

There were frantic, late meetings between Williams and Cheryl Crawford, between Crawford and Elia Kazan, and between Kazan and Williams — about sets, costumes and even script revisions — as late as March 1. "He was a more tense man than he had been when I'd worked with him on *Streetcar*," Kazan recalled. "A good bit of that I attributed to the nature of *Camino Real*, however. It was a risky thing. He knew that, and we all knew it."

Happily, the casting was easy. Since so much of the budget was allotted for Lemuel Ayres's sweeping set and for the colorful period costumes for over fifty actors, the producers avoided engaging major "name" stars;

in any case, Eli Wallach was ideal for the tough, naïve hero Kilroy, and Barbara Baxley, who had taken over major roles in long Broadway runs and touring companies, was Williams's first and only choice for the wacky, ingenuous, confused Gypsy daughter Esmeralda. He and Kazan heard her read at an audition, and when she protested that she loved the role — and especially its haunting, lyrical prayer near the finale — but that she was not quite certain she understood it completely, Williams replied, "Honey, you don't need to understand it — you just go do it!"

In New Haven and Philadelphia, the playwright's agitated state and his terror of a critical and popular failure after a series of successes were justified. The production was chaotic, and the audiences found the lack of a traditional narrative disconcerting: many of those who came slammed out of the theatre angry, confused and disgusted. For the sake of his cast and crew, however, Williams affected a detached composure, and he frequently explained his calm by quoting the narrator of his short story "The Angel in the Alcove," who reflects, "I had already learned to make a religion of endurance and a secret of my desperation."

"I was also in Philadelphia, with another show," José Quintero recalled. "I stood in the back of the theatre with Tennessee and watched the people walking out. The play had gotten very bad notices, and that's when I began to sense the enormous strength in this man who was so tender and so sensitive and so gentle. I thought, 'Oh my God. This stampede is going to destroy him.' But I had not counted on his steel." The uncanny, courageous Williams humor was never more evident than at the time of *Camino Real,* whose Broadway failure was almost a foregone conclusion. With a rueful smile, Williams remarked quietly to Quintero as they watched the audience leave in midact, "Well, I don't think they are really taking the play to their hearts, would you say?"

"He was a man who didn't reveal his disappointment," Quintero added. "I knew inside he was bleeding, just like anyone would in his position. But he believed in his creation. He may have found parts that were faulty, but he'd never waver or disown any of his work just because other people didn't like it." And his Southern gentlemanliness never failed him.

For all his public bravery, however, Williams's anguish over the play was clear to his intimates. Merlo coped with his black moods at home, and conveyed his intentions to the cast as the New York opening approached. "Frankie was the communicating line for all of us," according to Barbara Baxley. "He was so perfect about everything — he sensed everything Tenn needed, everything we needed. He was the one who brought everybody back to the reality of life before us every day. He was firm, he gave us all balance. They were both lucky men — Tenn was lucky to have Frank, and Frank was fortunate to be with this great poet."

In spite of later revivals of this experimental, poetic but not obscure play, American audiences would never in fact "take the play to their hearts," as its author suspected. From the typical heroes and heroines desiring freedom ("All of us have a desperate bird in our heart") to the sense of captivity ("Caged birds accept each other but flight is what they long for"), the play leaps to open expressions of Williams's own fears as a middle-aged poet, whose "vocation . . . is to influence the heart. . . . He ought to purify it and lift it above its ordinary level." But at the same time there is the fear that his vocation has been lost in the frenzy of celebrity, lost, like Byron, "among gondolas and palazzos, masked balls, glittering salons, huge shadowy courts and torch-lit entrances, baroque facades, canopies and carpets, candelabra and gold plate among snowy damask." The social subterfuges, the escape routes Tennessee Williams himself attempted in 1951 and 1952, haunted the part of him that was serious craftsman and sensitive chronicler of the human heart. In *Camino Real,* the royal road of glamour yields to the real road of life's demands — thus his insistence that the title be accented on the first syllable of each word, to stress the reality, not the royalty, of the road of life; the hardness of decisions, not the affect of sublimity.

It may be, however, that audiences in 1953 rejected the play not in fact because it was vague, but because it was all too clear in its denunciation of the fascist demagoguery then spreading over the country in the voice, especially loud, of Senator Joseph McCarthy.

"Walter Winchell and Ed Sullivan attacked the play as anti-American," according to Barbara Baxley. "They accused it of being a leftist manifesto. The earlier version of the play — what we performed in Philadelphia, not what was finally printed as the New York version — was an unwaveringly anti-imperialist play. It certainly wasn't anti-American, however — it was anti-fascist. But all references in the play to fascism in America, and to brotherhood and love were cut, since they were thought to be ringing cries of Communist sympathy."

Remnants of this concern appear in the printed version, nevertheless, as Casanova decries the situation in which "the individual becomes an undistinguished member of a collectivist state [under the control of] the maintenance of the military police. . . . Nothing wild or honest is tolerated here! It has to be extinguished."

In spite of lusty humor and a poise between politics and poetics, the play did not succeed even with the most sensitive and admiring among Williams's supporters. Walter Kerr, who was second to none in his respect for Williams as America's premiere playwright, wrote in the *New York Herald-Tribune* that *Camino Real* was "the worst play yet written by the best playwright of his generation." More than a disappointed critic, Kerr was a loyal admirer, and in a long letter the following month he offered Williams extended constructive criticism: the failure of the play, he wrote, was not because people were appalled at what was said, "but that people are simply not able to get through it to your intention at all. Actually, I think they are really outraged by a blank wall, by the play's defiant lack of esthetic clarity. . . . Surely you must acknowledge that your intention is not getting over; and that therefore the play *isn't* clear. . . . What terrifies me about *Camino Real* is not what you want to say but the direction in which you, as an artist, are moving. You're heading toward the cerebral; don't do it. What makes you an artist of the first rank is your intuitive gift for penetrating reality, without junking reality in the process; an intuitive artist starts with the recognizable surface of things and burrows *in*. Don't swap this for the conscious, rational processes of the analyst, the symbolist, the abstract thinker."

To this extended comment the director, Elia Kazan, later added a simple diagnosis of what he thought was the play's problem: "It doesn't have a third act — it doesn't seem to go anywhere at the end. We worked on it, over and over, but we never got it, we were never satisfied. The poetry of it is wonderful, though, the imagery is beautiful and the humor is terrific, as with all Tennessee's plays."

Opening night was a particularly difficult experience for Williams. In a letter to Brooks Atkinson two weeks later — perhaps because Atkinson, almost alone among critics, wrote favorably about the play — Williams admitted that he survived the first night on Nembutal and Seconal, that he was experiencing life like the motley, confused crew of pilgrims in his play, and that he was living among desperate outcasts in Key West, men of passion and endurance and tenderness — and as an artist, he concluded, he was honor-bound to speak for that world since it was what he knew best. The letters of Hart Crane, he told Atkinson, were always by his side; Crane's life was his support and his encouragement.

* * *

Within days of the opening, Williams and Merlo in fact returned to Key West, to the "desperate outcasts" with whom they felt more at ease. For several weeks Williams withdrew to his workroom and grappled with depression by working feverishly on revisons of *Camino Real* — not because he hoped that they could be incorporated into the Broadway production and reverse its anticipated demise, but because James Laughlin at New Directions was eager to publish it before year's end, and Williams wanted an improved text to represent him in print. On March 31 he wrote to Cheryl that some of the material he was adding restored the cuts demanded by Walter Winchell's political objections. Posterity could be the judge of his politics — which, he felt, were humanitarian impulses and not partisan prejudices.

There was another reason for his seclusion in the Key West studio in March and April, however. He had agreed to direct Margaret Phillips in Donald Windham's play *The Starless Air* for Joanna Albus's Playhouse Theatre in Houston, and before the premiere on May 13 he was working on staging and corresponding with Windham on structural changes.

"He wanted to try to direct at this point in his life," according to Paul Bigelow, who was then at the Theatre Guild, which intended to sponsor *The Starless Air* in New York after the Houston run. "But he wanted to direct a play far enough away from New York so the critics couldn't have a go at him if he failed. He knew he couldn't stage one of his own, because the press would swoop down on him from everywhere. So he went to Houston to direct a play by Donald Windham. Lawrence [Langner, at the Theatre Guild] said we would wait to see what happened with it there; if it became successful, the Guild would consider producing it in New York. But after a few days in Texas, Tenn called me and begged me to come down. 'Donald is being miserable to me,' he complained. 'He's not allowing me any directorial control.' When I arrived in Houston I saw they were at loggerheads, and the cooperation between them virtually ended then and there." Windham admitted that there were "morbidly sensitive" feelings, from the beginning, although he later wrote that Williams was "an inspired director." Windham, however, felt that he was not being given the consideration due a playwright: "The first thing [Williams] did was to bar me from rehearsals." Soon after, Windham found that Williams was "writing and inserting speeches" into the play.*

* *The Starless Air* never did come to New York — a fact due more to Williams's protracted European journey and his lack of strong support for Windham in negotiations with the Theatre Guild concerning script revisions than to the earnest efforts of Audrey Wood and of

Immediately before the opening, in fact, Williams left Houston and drove north, stopping in Memphis to visit his grandfather, who was planning to spend the year at the Hotel Gayoso. By the end of the month he was in New York, and Frank arrived by train two days before their departure for Europe on June 5; he now knew to expect the sudden announcement that they would pass each summer abroad.

The crossing did not ease Williams's tension, and by the time they docked in Le Havre Merlo was spending more time with their bulldog, Mr. Moon, then he could with Williams, whose nervous condition, constant physical complaints and moodiness were all but intolerable. "I wouldn't be a good person for anyone to latch on to," he had told an interviewer a few years earlier. Of the first month of the 1953 voyage in Europe, only Merlo knew the tension, and only he invented distractions to dispel it.

As soon as they arrived in Rome on June 22, Williams wrote to Paul Bowles in Tangier. They had come to their fourth-floor walkup, he said, right at the start of a suffocating Roman summer. No breezes stirred on either of the two terraces.

They left almost at once for Spain, but on arrival Williams was confined to bed with food poisoning for over a week and he became so restless that when he could eat he insisted on returning to Rome — which they did, only to depart for the southern coast. Then they went on to Vienna, Venice, Zurich, back to Spain, then down to the southern towns of Italy. Over two months — from August to October — Williams and Merlo (and sometimes Paul Bowles) moved from hotel to guest-house to inn, from scenic resorts (at Positano, for example) to cramped fishing villages. At one point, fearful that he had contracted a deadly fever, he drafted a short story that was a kind of last will and last confession in fiction form: "Man Bring This Up Road" is the account of a rich widow in Amalfi who takes in a talented but freeloading young poet. She teases him — with food and with an absurd offer of sex — but her exploitation leads to his weeping, and she dismisses him from her house.

A curiously cold story, related in its confessional motif to the later *Suddenly Last Summer* and anticipating also *The Milk Train Doesn't Stop Here Anymore* in its interweaving of life-force and death wish, "Man Bring This Up Road" reflects the malaise of summer 1953. It was a time

---

Phyllis Anderson (Windham's agent). On the entire sad issue, *cf.* Donald Windham, ed., *Tennessee Williams' Letters to Donald Windham 1940-1965* (New York: Holt, Rinehart and Winston, 1977), pp. 273-289.

he summarized in words he had recently put on the lips of D. H. Lawrence, in a revised version of *I Rise in Flame, Cried the Phoenix:* "All that I ever do is go packing around the world with women and manuscripts and a vile disposition. I pretend to be waging a war with bourgeois conceptions of morality.... What I'm fighting with really's the little old maid in myself." *Camino Real* had certainly been the pretense of a war with bourgeois morality: Kilroy, the archetypal American with a "heart as big as a baby," the wanderer with no sure harbor, was nothing so much as a stand-in for Williams himself. Now, in the summer following, he sought out the usual places in Italy where he might deal with the "little old maid" in himself. By the trick of a certain profligacy of the flesh, the old maid might be put to rest — or at least stung to a savage new vitality.

The result of the wandering — and this he admitted for the first time in his life — was a creative stasis, a writer's block such as he had never before experienced. By early autumn he had gone to Tangier with Bowles, and from the Hotel Rembrandt he wrote on October 14 to Audrey Wood complaining of a mysterious weakness, a fatigue that gripped him a half-hour into his morning work. He was prodding himself with morning liquor, he wrote, but he found that the writing was so forced and artificial he ended even more depressed than the previous unproductive day. He insisted in the same letter that there must have been something physical, something with the body that kept him from working successfully. With the patient and cheerful Bowles, Williams could work or not, wander at will or stay at the hotel, keep his private assignations with familiar or anonymous north Africans, or write letters at the bar. After meeting a small crew of international eccentrics of a particularly gruesome sort, he sailed back to New York on October 27, aboard the *Andrea Doria.**

Meantime, Johnny Nicholson had been alert for a furnished apartment to replace Buffie Johnson's subleased quarters, and he found one for them — at 323 East 58th Street, on the second floor of a house Nicholson simultaneously bought, and to which was annexed his relocated café. He had it beautifully furnished in oriental antiques for his new tenants, and it was ready for their return.

Typically, however, they did not remain long. Williams was eager for a

---

* The odd crew he met that summer inspired the weird assortment in his story "It Happened the Day the Sun Rose," which was published privately in 1981. The story features variations on those he had known in north Africa — exhibitionists, voyeurs, sadomasochistic prostitutes, etc.

warm climate, and they went South, collected Grandfather, and proceeded to New Orleans.

The trip to this city was motivated by neither nostalgia nor because they preferred it to Key West. This time, there was indeed a medical reason; it turned out, however, to be neither dangerous nor incapacitating. In Europe that summer, he had begun suffering with hemorrhoids, and his friend Oliver Evans recommended a New Orleans proctologist who could treat him. He was to be admitted for surgery at the Ochsner Clinic, and within a week he could be discharged.

But he did not undergo the operation at Ochsner. Thomas K. Griffin, for many years a leading New Orleans journalist, cultural historian and archivist, received a call from Williams asking that Griffin arrange for him to be removed to the Touro Infirmary for "emergency surgery."

"But the real reason," according to Griffin, "was that at Ochsner they were very strict about alcoholic drinks, and he wouldn't do without. I didn't know that until I had taken extraordinary measures to have him transferred to Touro. So they did this relatively minor operation there, and he had his liquor."

By mid-January 1954, Williams, Merlo and the Reverend left New Orleans for Key West. To Brooks Atkinson, Williams wrote that the bad time of last summer still prevailed, and that his discomfort was deeper than the lingering surgical discomfort; he had no vitality, no interest. At the same time he wrote to Donald Windham that he was a wreck, fit only for the movies or the beach. Prior to his operation, he had worked with some enthusiasm on the screenplay now based only on two one-act plays;* it was then called *Hide and Seek* — and, briefly, *The Whip Master* and *Mississippi Woman* — and it would soon be called *Baby Doll*. But now it lay untouched on the studio desk in Key West.

His letters to Cheryl Crawford were somewhat more explicit. He and Frank, he wrote, were trying to avoid the transient sailors at the Key West bars. For her part, the loyal Cheryl found Williams in the mid-1950s "courageous and fearful, suspicious and trusting, generous and acquisitive, sanguine and despairing, impulsive and cautious"; she always listened uncritically, patiently, like a prudent sister.

At this time, Key West's bohemianism began to peak. Margaret Foresman, then and for many years later the managing editor of the *Key West*

---

* *The Last of My Solid Gold Watches* and *This Property Is Condemned* did not figure in the last stages of working on the screenplay.

Citizen, recalled that in the 1950s, "although illegal, there was gambling in Key West, and even a brothel on Stock Island nearby, which was eventually closed. There was no open advertising of preferences, but it was certainly a relaxed place to be a nonconformist. Tennessee was honored there by virtue of his successes, and he often showed up at the Casa Marina or the Officers Club. In the 1950s there was no indication of anything like drugs — liquor and sex seemed to be the usual recreations. Tennessee might not have been invited to the blue-haired ladies' parties, but people were certainly respectful of him — if a little distant. For the gay population, young men were always available in Key West. And when the authorities got around to closing the brothel on Stock Island, well, there was always the house on Duncan Street for any sailors passing through. But in spite of his often wild living, and the groups of people tumbling in and out of his house, he was up early in the morning, and he worked until noon."

By early spring, Williams had resumed daily work on the play that would transform, expand and alter the mysterious short story "Three Players of a Summer Game." In the 1954 drafts of this new long play, Brick, the alcoholic ex-athlete married to a woman who keeps him in benevolent subordination, was becoming an enigmatically distant man, still alcoholic but now also impotent, refusing to take any interest in his sex-starved wife or in the machinations of his brother, who is maneuvering to take over the great estate and the wealth of their terminally ill father. The play was becoming *Cat on a Hot Tin Roof:* the wife Maggie was the anxious cat, and Williams saw with greater clarity the characters of Big Daddy and Big Mama, the humorous-pathetic scions to a family steeped in greed, mendacity and self-delusion.

A strange shift was occurring in Williams's writing in early 1954. Whereas *Camino Real* was loud with action, delirious with crowds and vague regarding time, place and purpose, the new play in its earliest development was observing classical unities of place, time and theme, and it entirely subordinated action to a series of very nearly philosophical dialogues. Perhaps because *Cat on a Hot Tin Roof* was dense with a network of personal references and personal fears, he was calling it a comedy of manners. In this play, everything that *happened* had happened before the curtain rose — or it *might* happen afterward. During the summer evening of the play's time, only the characters' reactions filled the stage, only these representative critical moments were held up for the audience.

By April, Williams had had enough of Key West; the doctors at

Ochsner, after he returned for a postoperative evaluation, pronounced him ready for travel. That meant Europe, and so Frank repacked their luggage and arranged for Reverend Dakin to go to St. Louis, either to live with Edwina again or to enter a nursing home. Then ninety-seven, the old gentleman was at last weary and suffering an array of geriatric ailments.

As they prepared to depart, Williams heard that playwright Arthur Miller had recently been refused a passport to attend the premiere of one of his plays in Brussels. On his colleague's behalf, Williams prepared a letter to the Department of State (dated April 1, 1954), in which he stated that he himself had spent the last several summers in Europe and could attest that Miller was highly respected there. Refusing him permission to travel outside America, he continued, could only strengthen Communist propaganda about the lack of artistic freedom in the West; if our country was not persecuting its finest artists, as Russia claimed, then Miller should be granted freedom to travel.

A noble and courageous defense, to be sure — but one of which Williams quickly repented. He admitted later (from Sicily, to Brooks Atkinson, in a letter dated September 4) that he never mailed the statement to the government. Just as he was about to do so, he realized that his own passport — then due for renewal — might be delayed or denied if he were an outspoken supporter of Miller. He decided that prudence was the better part of valor, and, so as not to irritate the Department of State and jeopardize his own freedom, the letter remained in his file.

In early May, Williams was in New York, and Carson McCullers invited him to share a stage with her for an evening. She had been invited to speak on "Twenty Years of Writing" at the Poetry Center of the 92nd Street YMHA, and she thought that Williams — much the stronger and the better reader — should accompany her. He agreed, on condition that a pitcher of martinis be set at his elbow. His intolerance for any substantial quantity of alcohol, and her generous refilling of her own glass, resulted in a strange event. Two of America's most famous writers sat for the evening, interrupting one another, stumbling and slurring over their words, perversely relishing one another's boozy humor as much as they were oblivious to the uncomfortable audience.

At the beginning of June, Williams and Merlo arrived in Rome and at once contacted Anna Magnani, who had promised to return to America with them later that year to film *The Rose Tattoo* for Hal Wallis at Paramount Pictures. She realized that Williams was depressed to a dangerous point, but neither she nor Merlo could convince him to seek help or to return earlier to New York for treatment. Instead, he wrote to Cheryl Crawford that he was passing through the worst nervous crisis of his life, trying to avoid total mental collapse with an almost round-the-clock reliance on liquor, an increased dependence on sedatives and barbiturates, and an incessant round of social distractions that gave him no pleasure.

He was, he told Cheryl, being helped by nothing — not even the affectionate attention he got from the new bulldog, Boffo, that had replaced Mr. Moon, who had recently died. He admitted that he was taking pills and drinking before noon and not stopping before dinner; he could not walk a Roman street unless there was a bar or wineshop. Cheryl would understand him, and how deep was the mental crisis of which, he was sure, this was but a physical expression. For the first time, Williams was admitting that the source of his unhappiness and of his addictions was not disease, but rather a wasting of the spirit. He agreed with Alma Winemiller: "I don't see how I'm going to get through the summer."

This letter was explicit: he was too shy with Audrey Wood, he admitted to Cheryl, to share these secrets. But he was at such an impasse that he must have treatment when he returned to the United States; he had avoided acknowledging this under pretext of the press of work, but now even the work was failing him, and the obsessive travel was no relief. He quoted D. H. Lawrence: "Face the facts and live beyond them"; he would, he promised, return to New York in August to face the facts.

Could Cheryl recommend a psychiatrist for him? he asked. Could Dr. Alfred Kinsey recommend someone, since he and Williams had once met, five years earlier, to discuss the relationship between art and neurosis? He said he did not want the same doctor as William Inge, since Inge — especially since his recent success with *Picnic* — seemed to him complacent and pompous. There was some ray of hope, Williams concluded: he had revised *Battle of Angels,* now called *Orpheus Descending.* It reflected the deeper spiritual crisis of the 1950s, rather than the simple sexual repressions of the 1930s. If he had not been so tormented, he told Cheryl, the play would not have had the ring of authenticity. He looked forward to being with her in New York that autumn.

But for several months he delayed his return, and apparently for no other reason than the distraction of travel across Europe with Frank. At last, on September 22, Williams, Merlo and Magnani left Rome, arriving a week later in New York. The following month, filming of *The Rose*

Tattoo began in Key West (which was to pass for a Mississippi Gulf town), next door to Williams's house. Locals appeared as extras, adoring Magnani, who was at first hesitant about her English and then relaxed among the townspeople. Her screen performance as Serafina would soon be considered the highlight of her career. Hal Wallis, the producer, appeared briefly in a bar scene with Williams, the two watching the furious Magnani stride into the shot. And the short, handsome man who tried to stop the ensuing fight is none other than Frank Merlo. Busy with filming, busy with writing, busy with his social life, Williams seemed to have abandoned the idea of psychotherapy.

By New Year's Day 1955, Audrey Wood had negotiated with the Playwrights Company to produce Williams's next Broadway play, *Cat on a Hot Tin Roof.* (Cheryl Crawford read and admired it, but she thought that there was "no one to root for.") The Playwrights — Elmer Rice, Robert E. Sherwood, Maxwell Anderson, John Wharton and Roger Stevens — had added to their number Robert Anderson, whose *Tea and Sympathy* had opened in September 1953 (directed by Kazan) and had played for over seven hundred performances.

"Audrey may well have been impressed with the Playwrights' handling of *Tea and Sympathy*," Robert Anderson said, "and since I had joined that group she considered it natural to submit *Cat* to them when Cheryl declined to produce it. It had been Elia Kazan and Roger Stevens on my play, and so it was to be Kazan and Stevens again on *Cat*. There was a certain logic to all this, and of course everyone involved was someone with whom Audrey felt confident."

The play is structured as a series of confrontations between members of the Pollitt family: Brick, a former athletic star and current alcoholic; his wife, Maggie, the "cat," who is sexually frustrated because of Brick's mysterious distance from her following the suicide of his friend Skipper; Big Daddy, Brick's father, whose imminent death means the transfer of a vast estate; his confused, loyal, long-suffering wife, Big Mama; and Brick's venal brother and sister-in-law.

Williams came to New York in January to approve the cast and to meet with Kazan, who had a number of important recommendations about the text. Although Williams later felt that the stuctural and character changes Kazan wanted were drastic alterations of his original intentions, he wisely followed the advice: he wanted a success, and an audience for his melodrama about truth and falsehood, about greed and sexual confusion, and he respected Kazan's perceptions.

Specifically, Kazan believed that the character of Big Daddy was too important to vanish after act two; he also thought that as a result of the confrontation between him and Brick some change should be evident in, the son; and finally he felt that Maggie should be a more sympathetic person at the end. Williams in some way acceded to all these counsels. "I do think my ending is better," Kazan said years later. "And Tennessee agreed. I gave him every opportunity to override my objections — the Dramatists Guild has rules about such things, after all — but he agreed." For a 1974 revival, Williams kept Kazan's structural changes (in spite of his insistence to the contrary for years before and after). He restored only a risqué joke told by Big Daddy and the ambiguous sarcasm of the last line of the play.

To work on the revisions of the third act, Williams left New York — and he had another reason to do so, for Tulane University in New Orleans had prepared productions of his one-act play 27 *Wagons Full of Cotton* and an opera by Raffaello de Banfield for which *Lord Byron's Love Letter* had provided the libretto. For the premiere of 27 *Wagons,* Williams chose Maureen Stapleton to play Flora, the slightly dim farmwife whose husband, Jake, destroys a neighbor's cotton gin. The neighbor, Silva Vicarro,* subsequently brutalizes Flora in a grim fable of revenge, greed and sadomasochism that Williams called "a Mississippi Delta comedy."

"Tennessee was very brave about this production at Tulane," Maureen Stapleton remembered. "The set they had built was so massive and heavy and awkward that it was impossible to act on or in or around it. And when Tenn and Frank arrived on January 15, Tenn just sat down with the man in charge of the set. He flattered, he cajoled, he offered to pay out of his own pocket for construction changes. Nothing would convince the man. So we finally put a swing downstage, and Tenn directed rehearsals in which I could act on and around the swing, in front of that impossible set, which we just pretended wasn't there." And that is how the swing, and the dialogue that occurs in the famous "swing scene," found its way into the film *Baby Doll* the following year; Williams made a virtue of necessity — a prop became a brilliant symbolic device, the perfect correlative for the reversed fortunes of the two men, and for the gradual erotic awakening of the "baby doll" wife. Quite coincidentally, Tennessee Williams was soon awarded the "Show Business" award for artistry and merit in dramatic construction. (27 *Wagons* came to New

---

* In 27 *Wagons Full of Cotton,* the name of the character is Vicarro; in the film script *Baby Doll,* which combined this play and *The Unsatisfactory Supper,* he has become Vacarro.

York for a six-week run in April, as part of an evening of various entertainments.)

After a brief visit to Los Angeles to see the first cut of *The Rose Tattoo*, Williams and Merlo flew back to New York, for on February 7 rehearsals began for *Cat* — with the revisions Kazan had suggested. Ben Gazzara and Barbara Bel Geddes were to play Brick and Maggie, the couple whose marriage is threatened by untruth, denial, jealousy and Brick's guilt for failing a needy friend who took his life.

"My father had a great gift for phrases," Williams said later. "The title 'Cat on a Hot Tin Roof' comes from him. 'Edwina,' he used to say, 'you're making me as nervous as a cat on a hot tin roof!' "

Burl Ives (who had played the tough-gentle sheriff in Kazan's film of John Steinbeck's *East of Eden*) at once impressed Williams during casting. Previously best known as a folksinger and archivist of the American ballad, Ives played Big Daddy Pollitt, the dying master of the Delta plantation whose combination of raw vulgarity and curious appeal was partly the figure of Cornelius Coffin Williams. "Tennessee told me," Ives recalled years later, "that he had written this part after his own father, and that on opening night he sat in the fourteenth row and saw Cornelius Williams."

The role of Big Mama required an actress who could suggest a combination of fidelity, silliness and a special kind of simple nobility. The choice was Mildred Dunnock, whom Kazan had directed in Arthur Miller's *Death of a Salesman*. She later said that "Williams was a dreamer and Kazan a realist, and they complemented one another perfectly. Williams was really a very shy man and he had to avoid anything that inhibited his creative writing. Kazan helped him to do this, for he had an extraordinary capacity of leadership and the ability to draw from the players what we didn't know was there inside us. He led us in a way that an orchestra conductor leads." (Ives used the same metaphor in recalling rehearsals: "Ben Gazzara and I were directed by Kazan as if the play were an orchestra piece, a fugue — building, building, building in the confrontation between father and son.")

The Pollitt parents indeed are modeled on the Williams parents — but with great freedom, since of all his plays of the 1950s *Cat on a Hot Tin Roof* most subjects characters to a system of ideas. There is great subtlety in the playwright's construction of Brick, the guilt-ridden son with his foot in a plaster cast and his hand on a liquor bottle; and in Maggie, the sex-starved, determined wife who stands outside the lies and sees patterns of weakness and a need for truth.

"I think Maggie is more himself than anyone else he may have pointed to, or who claimed to be the model for this woman," according to Kazan. And Williams himself expressed his admiration for this passionate sensualist, both in the notes to his play and in comments to the press. "Maggie was the only aristocrat," he said. "She was the only one free of greed.... I sympathized with her and liked her myself, and [she] had become steadily more charming to me as I worked on her characterization."

During rehearsals in February and March, Kazan denied Williams access to the cast. "Kazan didn't want us talking about the play with the playwright," Mildred Dunnock remembered. "We were all in awe of Tennessee, of course, because his talent surpassed that of other writers. But we had the sense that these characters were not written realistically, and that to discuss them as if we were dissecting neighbors would have been untrue to them and to the play. Tennessee wrote from the inside to the outside of the characters and he did not muddle them by analyzing them to us."

That the characters in *Cat on a Hot Tin Roof* are indeed "not written realistically" is a key to the play's nature and importance. Never before was Williams so clearly in debt to August Strindberg; never before was the machinery of family strife the symbolic canvas on which he painted something like a mysterious sense of the universe. And never before did he so deliberately refuse to explain the dark, tantalizing corners of characters' souls.

"The bird that I hope to catch in the net of this play is not the solution of one man's psychological problem," he wrote in the text. "I'm trying to catch the true quality of experience in a group of people, that cloudy, flickering, evanescent — fiercely charged! — interplay of live human beings in the thundercloud of a common crisis."

More elusive and richer than *Camino Real, Cat on a Hot Tin Roof* is not merely a stinging play about greed, the inheritance of guilt, and the refusal to acknowledge the possible homosexuality of a college friend. The play has the tragedian's sense of the mysterious nature of personality, for Brick's paralyzing guilt is due to his deeper refusal to be true — precisely by open understanding — to a friendship for which he claimed total devotion. Additionally remarkable is that there is finally no villain in this play about moral darkness: there is understanding, compassion and allowance for every conundrum of every character. They are all recognizably human, funny and unforgettable.

That Williams's concerns in this play go beyond one family (his own or the Pollitts) to a consideration of the nature of common guilt is further indicated by his insistence on a nonrealistic set, sparsely furnished — "far less realistic than I have implied ... the walls below the ceiling should dissolve mysteriously into air; the set should be roofed by the sky; stars and moon suggested by traces of milky pallor, as if they were observed through a telescope lens out of focus. . . ."

Brick Pollitt as idealist, unable to accept the fall of himself or others — the broken foot being the result of a literal and the sign of a symbolic fall — is in some sense a psychological self-portrait of Williams as idealist. But as impassive voyeur, unable to act, to choose or to enter without being led, Brick depends on the stronger Maggie — "more himself," as Kazan has suggested, the one eager to turn lies into truth, and to take the weak-willed by the hand and conduct him, with love.

As if the agony over this play were not poignant enough for him during that rehearsal period, he was told on February 14 that his beloved grandfather had died at Barnes Hospital, St. Louis, at the age of ninety-seven. Generous and uncritical, proud and grateful for his grandson's companionship in the last decade, Walter Edwin Dakin left an emptiness in Williams's life that would never be filled. "He left two small bequests," Paul Bigelow remembered, "one hundred dollars for Frankie Merlo, and one hundred dollars for me. It was all the old gentleman had in the world." Within the year, Williams donated one thousand dollars to the University of the South at Sewanee in his grandfather's memory.

On March 24, *Cat* opened at the Morosco Theatre, and although not all critics agreed about the value of Williams's deliberate ambiguities, there was no lack of praise for the cast or the seriousness of the play's content. And the salty language, an off-color joke about a tumescent elephant told by Big Daddy in the revised third act (and excised on April 4 at the request of the New York City license commissioner) and the psychosexual turmoil sent shock waves through the 1955 audience.

"The postwar theatre was extraordinary," as Robert Anderson said, "but in the galaxy of playwrights Tennessee Williams and Arthur Miller were in a sense the most exciting — not only because they were new, but because their material was different and was presented in a fresh way." With *Cat on a Hot Tin Roof* Williams showed that if he could not experiment with structure for his "fresh way" (as he had tried with *Camino Real*), then he would portray characters in recognizable but unconventional situations. For an audience he considered emotionally hard of hearing, he wanted to shout; for those blind in their smugness, he drew large and startling figures. His enemy was complaisance, and he fought it with shock tactics.

For three weeks in April, Williams took Carson McCullers to Key West. Mornings, they worked on their manuscripts; afternoons, they drank, sat on the beach, welcomed neighbors. French author Françoise Sagan visited, to Carson's special delight, and later Williams announced that they would go to Havana to meet Ernest Hemingway. But after two days of waiting on the island, they returned to Key West: Hemingway had never received the advance telegram, and was not there.

They returned to Key West to receive the news that *Cat* had won the Pulitzer Prize for drama; Williams at once announced that the five hundred dollars would be turned back to the Columbia University Graduate School of Journalism. By mid-June, Carson had departed, and Williams left for his summer holiday in Europe. As Audrey Wood soon wrote to an executive at Warner Brothers, Williams moved from one European capital to another that year with a rapidity and lack of motivation that she found frightening. She was also concerned (as were his other friends) that he was traveling without Frank Merlo, who explained quite openly when she telephoned to Key West. There had been growing tension between the two men, and they both thought a summer's separation would improve the relationship.

Meantime, Williams's arrivals and departures in the great hotels were so capricious and unannounced that it was several weeks before the telegram finally reached him that Margo Jones had died on July 25. The victim of an accident in her home, Margo was only two years younger than Williams — forty-two that year. She had not served his career well in the 1948 production of *Summer and Smoke,* but of her devotion there was never any question. With this news, he felt inconsolable for days and guilty for his neglect of her in the last several years. The remainder of the summer was, as he wrote to critic Kenneth Tynan, a period nearly blacked out by drugs and drink: he admitted to the habit of washing down Seconal tablets with double gin martinis.

In midsummer, he flew from Rome to Stockholm for the Swedish premiere of *Cat on a Hot Tin Roof,* as the guest of Lilla van Saher. She was a Hungarian immigrant to America, and the sister of the psychiatrist Dr. Franz Alexander. Lilla had been a casual visitor to Key West from her New York home since she and her husband saw *Camino Real.* By 1955, Lilla — whom Williams called "the last of the crêpe-de-Chine gypsies" — was a charter member of the curious entourage that surrounded Williams at home and abroad. She somehow managed to turn up wherever Tennessee Williams turned up. A thickset woman of modest wealth but generous eccentricity, she single-handedly took it on herself that September to ensure that Williams would be awarded the Nobel Prize in literature. She installed him in the Castle Hotel and proceeded to announce a series of lavish parties and press receptions to introduce him to Swedish society and those highly connected with both the court and the Nobel committee.

"She had all the press there," according to Williams, who thought that her publicity overkill had alienated the Swedish critics and Nobel executors. "She was like a field marshal! 'You over that way! You over there! You do not approach Mr. Williams until I give you the signal!' Barking out orders. Oh, it was just terrifying. The next morning the newspapers all came out saying Mr. Williams arrived in Stockholm preceded by a very powerful press agent!" And so ended his chances for the Nobel Prize, in his assessment — but not his friendship with the formidable, loyal and colorfully zany Lilla van Saher.

When he returned to New York in the fall of 1955, Williams took advantage of a quiet time at East 58th Street to complete revisions of his screenplay, now firmly titled *Baby Doll*. (Merlo remained in Key West.) He and Kazan exchanged an eager correspondence about it, but Kazan soon noticed that Williams had done all he intended and turned it over to the director. Kazan had worked with the one-act play *27 Wagons Full of Cotton* at the Actors Studio with the young Carroll Baker, and with Karl Malden. There was no doubt in his mind that they were just right for Baby Doll Meighan (the Flora of *27 Wagons*) and her husband (now called Archie Lee), and that Eli Wallach would be right for Silva Vaccaro, and Mildred Dunnock for Aunt Rose Comfort.*

"Then I began working on the movie, a little bit here and a little bit there," Kazan recalled, "and I kept facing the problem of structure. . . . I threw out [the other one-act plays], but I used *The Unsatisfactory Supper* [along with *27 Wagons*]. . . . Here again I was working as a writer in disguise, behind the scenes; when I showed the thing to Williams, he liked it. I said, 'You must work on it, though, you're really a great writer, and

---

* The subplot about Aunt Rose in *Baby Doll* derives from *The Unsatisfactory Supper,* a short play in which Aunt Rose fails to please Archie Lee with her cooking. Archie Lee and Baby Doll, in *The Unsatisfactory Supper,* are called the Bowmans.

I'm just a constructionist — or trying to be.' And he said he would but he never did much. He was writing another play at the time [*Sweet Bird of Youth*], and he would suddenly write a few scenes and send them to me with a note, 'Insert somewhere.' Some I used and some I didn't; he didn't seem to care. Finally, I was desperate, because I had no ending to it. I had got Warner Brothers to finance it, everything was set up, and I said: 'Tennessee, we have no ending!' He said: 'Well, I promise you I'll work on it.' So I said: 'Well, I haven't got much time now, you'll have to come South with us [for the filming in Benoit, Mississippi].' "

Kazan and his cast and crew were to arrive in Mississippi in December, and to be in a Brooklyn studio for interior filming in early February. Before that, however, Williams said he had to be in Miami, at the Coconut Grove Playhouse. Tallulah Bankhead — for whom he had originally written Myra in *Battle of Angels* and Blanche in *Streetcar* — was at last going to play the latter for three weeks before moving north for a two-week run in New York at the City Center.

At once, an electric tension crackled among Williams's loyal friends. Maria Britneva was visiting from England, and Bankhead, unaccountably, resented her. Donald Windham's friend Sandy Campbell noted at the time, "Tenn is licking his lips with the prospect of an encounter between Bankhead and her." There might well be seeds of a play here, after all; he did what he could to encourage the animosity — one way being to add still more women to his coterie.

Soon Marion Vaccaro arrived — "a sad, lost lady" by this time, as Bigelow described her — a friendly soul whose surname Williams had borrowed for the vengeful neighbor in *Baby Doll*. Next day, Lilla van Saher swept in. Euripides himself, in *The Trojan Women,* or Shakespeare at the opening of *Macbeth,* or Goethe describing a *Walpurgisnacht,* could not have assembled a team more ready for what Jane Bowles called an exercise in feminine wiles. What was crucial for Williams's purpose, as he relished the social tension from the sidelines, was that all these ladies adored him, but none of them liked each other. Physical combat was just barely avoided; mutually hurt feelings, tears, inebriate rages, were not. Only Williams escaped unscathed as this grotesque gavotte was danced around him. "I don't know what Tennessee gets from the Monster Women," Gore Vidal wrote later, "but if they give him solace nothing else matters. Certainly he has a huge appetite for the grotesque not only in art but in life." Jane Smith agreed: "He would allow and slightly gear things to a little drama offstage and then sit back and watch it, [but] his taste was not always reliable — about a number of things, and surprisingly enough, not always about people."

The finale of this brief winter scenario occurred, appropriately, backstage, late in January in Coconut Grove: "After the show last night," Sandy Campbell wrote in a memoir, "Tenn went in to B[ankhead]'s dressing room, got down on his knees, put his head in her lap and said, 'Tallulah, this is the way I imagined the part when I wrote the play.'" But at a party later that evening he told Jean Dalrymple, producer for the imminent move to New York, that if Bankhead "continued to give such an appalling performance he would not allow the play to open in New York. She was 'playing it for vaudeville and ruining my play.'" A reporter from a national magazine was nearby, his remark was published the following week, and a great classical repentance scene had to be enacted in New York (also for the benefit of the press) to soothe the burnt ego of Bankhead and to restore Williams to her favor. The revival of *A Streetcar Named Desire,* alas, was not well received, for Bankhead's fans disrupted her performance with atrocious displays of ill manners. There is no record of the reaction to this theatrical failure by the other ladies in Williams's social circle, but one may perhaps imagine.

While these intrigues continued, Kazan had more important concerns for Williams: he needed him on location for *Baby Doll.*

"He had a dread of going to [Mississippi]," Kazan recalled. "He said: 'Those people chased me out of there. I left the South because of their attitude towards me. They don't approve of homosexuals, and I don't want to be insulted. I don't want my feelings hurt.'" Finally Williams agreed to come, but after several days he announced that he was leaving: "'I can't find a swimming pool.' So I [Kazan] said: 'God damn it, I need an ending to this film! You can't use the excuse of a swimming pool to leave, Tennessee. You're leaving me in the lurch!' ... The next thing that happened was typical of him — after he's done something bad like that, he does something brilliant. In a couple of days he sent me an ending, which I thought was wonderful."

But his swift departure was not only to escape an unpleasant memory of social ostracism (real or imagined), or the sudden snap of subfreezing weather in Mississippi. Early in January, George Keathley, founding director of a theatre in Coral Gables called the Studio M Playhouse, had asked Williams if there were a new play available for him to produce and direct. Williams sent a very short one-act play, *The Enemy: Time,* about

With Tallulah Bankhead and Herbert Machiz,
before 1956 revival of *A Streetcar Named Desire*

In Key West, about 1960

With Maureen Stapleton, after a revival
of *The Glass Menagerie*, 1965

With Bill Glavin, 1968

With Edwina, 1969

In Key West, 1972

Before appearing at the YMHA, New York, 1972

In *Small Craft Warnings*, 1972

During rehearsals for
Out Cry (The Two-Character Play), 1973

the young gigolo to a retired movie queen. He returns to his hometown, only to learn from his former girlfriend that she had to be sterilized after she contracted venereal disease from him. He is savagely beaten by her brother at the end. Williams returned to Coral Gables from Benoit to meet with Keathley about an April production for what was becoming the first extended draft of (and was now titled) *Sweet Bird of Youth*.

"I found Tennessee Williams in good form in February," Keathley recalled years later. "He was very shy, and he seemed to be drinking too much, but he was full of brilliant ideas and charm. We cast the play and set an opening date without any trouble. He took a room at a hotel in Miami, and he came with new or revised scenes daily. Then we went to the house in Key West, where he continued to work before rehearsals were scheduled."

In Key West, however, Keathley saw that the relationship between Williams and Merlo was indeed — as Merlo had told Audrey — passing through some kind of crisis. "They were having troubles. Once, Tennessee turned to Frank after reading a new scene aloud and asked, 'Do you like it, Frankie?' — 'No, I don't!' — 'Why not?' — 'I don't know, I just don't!' — 'But why *not*? What's wrong with it?' — 'Don't ask me, I'm not your goddamned yes-man!' And with that Frank ran into another room, packed his bags and took off for a few days. There must have been some prelude to all this that I never saw. But after this they separated more and more."

Several days later, about the first of March 1956, Williams suggested to Keathley that they move back to Miami. From this point, Williams in fact spent less time in Key West, "and Merlo held the fort during his absence, entertaining a wide circle of friends," as one of them wrote. In his room at The Towers Hotel, Williams revised his lyric "A Separate Poem," which expressed the sadness over what he clearly recognized as an unbreachable distance that had finally come between himself and Frank:

> Oh, yes, we've lost our island . . .
> Our travels ranged wide of our island but nowhere nearly so far
> as our silence now enters the bare and mountainous country
> of what cannot be spoken.
> When we speak to each other
> we speak of things that mean nothing of what we meant
> to each other . . . a storm of things unspoken . . .

None of their friends was entirely surprised by the gradual separation between the two men. Williams's life had become increasingly affluent, increasingly restless, increasingly full of demands, while at the same time Merlo longed for permanence, for the quiet life. Now money made possible the quick, worldwide acquisition of anything Williams wanted: servants were available at home and abroad; various diversions could be arranged, and various means of pleasure, both chemical and human. The plain fact was that Merlo's usefulness had become obsolete — an unpleasant truth, but a truth Williams admitted to himself and to a few friends. It was one of the reasons he had traveled more. But an easy separation was not ahead for them; a decade of devotion could not be quickly reduced to insignificance. They were both sad, but they could not discuss that sadness. So when they went south they parted, and pretended it was more convenient, while in New York Merlo ordinarily accompanied Williams and socialized with the same crowd. All who knew Williams loved and respected Merlo, now as before.

"During rehearsals for *Sweet Bird of Youth* in March," according to Keathley, "Williams joined us every afternoon following his work and swim. He often spoke of his sister Rose — 'Once she was violent, but now she's just tranquil.' " There was good reason for Rose to be especially in his mind that season. First, the character of the sterilized, abandoned girl in *The Enemy: Time* was originally named Rose (not Heavenly, as in the final script). Also, he had completed arrangements for her to return to Ossining after she had been living on a small farm, cared for by a Missouri couple, and after an interval at a private sanatorium in St. Louis.

The play opened at Studio M on April 16, with Margrit Wyler and Alan Mixon in the leading roles. Calling it a "work in progress," Williams told a reporter from the *New York Times* that it was "an examination of what is really corrupt in life." He apparently thought it was not too strong even for his mother, for Edwina accepted an invitation to attend. "She was a nonstop, talking Amanda," Keathley recalled, "just as he'd led me to expect." Two weeks later, Kazan and Audrey Wood and Cheryl Crawford made the trip, too, with Paul Bigelow and Maria Britneva.

At the same time, *Baby Doll* was ready for the months of editing prior to a winter premiere across the country.

The first version of *Sweet Bird of Youth* set a number of people on edge, with its story of a middle-aged woman who fills up empty hours with young lovers, vodka and a variety of drugs; the emphasis was squarely on the charm of a young lover. Proudest among Williams's coterie of women friends was the unshy Lilla van Saher, who claimed after opening night, "Curtain rises, and I am there, in bed with my trade! Is very clear a play about me!" Lilla's fantasy life was far more active than her rather conventional morals, in fact, but her vivid imagination endeared her all the more to Williams.

The truth is that the inspiration for the leading character was Tallulah Bankhead. The revisions Williams offered Keathley in February and March reflected what Williams learned from Bankhead herself, from her servants and from the press. In 1951, for example, Bankhead had charged her former secretary Evyleen R. Cronyn (then fifty-eight) with stealing more than four thousand dollars from her by forging checks. Cronyn claimed that on the contrary she was ordered to buy drugs, liquor and male prostitutes for Bankhead, but that the actress was in such a drunken condition that she could not sign her own checks and in all innocence Cronyn did. "Of course I drink," countered Bankhead, "but nobody has to forge my checks to buy liquor. And if I had been getting dope, do you think I'd pay for it by *check?* And Gods knows I never had to *buy* sex!"

To this Williams could add a real empathy, for these habits were quite plain in his own life; it is this congruence that gives the character of the "Princess" (as she calls herself) a special poignance. The gigolo remains an empty beauty.

Throughout the late spring and summer of 1956, Williams's emotional crisis deepened. "The Williamses have suffered from nerves for generations," he told Sandy Campbell. "My father was an alcoholic, and I am a semi-one. I drink more lately." He admitted the same in a letter to Cheryl Crawford in May: he was drinking far too much, as an escape mechanism due to a diffuse anxiety attack. Did she think he should stay in New York to confront the problem once and for all — at last — in medical and psychological treatment? He did not wait for a reply, but passed quickly through New York and left alone for Rome, where he pursued the usual summer wanderings — for some of which he was joined by Marion Vaccaro. Merlo again remained in Key West.

On August 3 he wrote to Cheryl, complaining that he could sleep only an hour or two each night and was on the verge of a complete breakdown. His only ray of light was Anna Magnani's agreement to come to

Broadway at last for the revised *Battle of Angels, Orpheus Descending*. Merlo, he concluded, did not care about him any longer, and he had asked friends to find him a separate apartment — something he would never do on his own. He and Merlo would be separated more often now, he wrote, until they had a clear sense of the pain they were causing each other.

What he did not mention in the letter to Cheryl — but which other friends saw — was that Williams's reliance on alcohol and pills only exacerbated his paranoia, which was centered in the conviction that no one cared for him, that everyone wanted him dead, and that everyone else was addicted to drugs.*

"I had heard about a paranoid personality," Maureen Stapleton reflected sympathetically years later, "but I never really knew what it meant until I saw it in Tennessee in the 1950s. He would accuse Frank of something — in Frank's presence and mine — and Frank would prove Tenn wrong. But even then Tenn, while laughing at himself over it, wouldn't believe him. Once Tenn found a used hypodermic in Florida. Now Frank was not in the remotest way a drug-user. But Tenn got it into his mind that Frank was self-injecting drugs. Frank reminded him that some time earlier a doctor had come to give him an antibiotic, and had arranged for vitamin shots to be given later. One of the needles had fallen under the bed. Tenn was not taking drugs intravenously [yet]. It was a simple mistake. But he got it into his head, and the accusation [against Frank] stuck."

In September, Williams was back in New York. All his business he conducted from a subleased apartment high above East 36th Street, since Frank was staying at East 58th. Soon the playwright met with his agent and learned that Magnani refused to appear in *Orpheus Descending* for more than two months because of her fear of English; the producers, logically, turned again to Maureen Stapleton as a replacement. (Ironically, the play ran exactly two months.)

On November 17, *Cat on a Hot Tin Roof* ended a twenty-month run after its six hundred and ninety-fourth performance. National and international companies opened very soon after, and a filmscript was in progress.

But four days after *Cat* closed, an important revival began at the City

* In the original typescript of *Memoirs*, Williams wrote that from the summer of 1955, in fact, he wrote only under the influence of artificial stimulants.

Center, one much more favorably received than the *Streetcar* that brought Bankhead there earlier. Helen Hayes charmed audiences and critics in a limited run of *The Glass Menagerie,* and a curious development occurred with the praise that attended this production. The prevalent critical opinion was that this was the kind of play that Williams should continue to write, and that the grotesqueries of *Camino Real* and *Cat on a Hot Tin Roof* — and the rumors about *Baby Doll, Sweet Bird of Youth* and *Orpheus Descending* — were not nearly so satisfying as the values of *The Glass Menagerie.* This assessment was put forth most plainly by none other than Brooks Atkinson, who wrote in the *New York Times,* "Although Mr. Williams has written some overwhelming dramas since 1945, he has not written anything so delicate and perceptive. . . . To see it again is to see how much he has changed." He was joined by other influential colleagues, among them John Chapman, who called *The Glass Menagerie* "Tennessee Williams's finest play . . . [an] affectionate, compassionate and poetic nocturne."

This praise might have worked only in the play's favor, and in Williams's, had not the newspapers been at the same time beginning to report the imminent release of *Baby Doll* — and the emotion-charged meetings among Warner Brothers, the director, theatre owners, reviewers and self-appointed arbiters of public taste and morality.

For the final print of the film, Kazan had agreed to a number of excisions demanded by the Motion Picture Code, which finally approved the film for national and international release. Clear implications of sadomasochism, of madness, and of the awakening eroticism of a young virginal bride were considerably modulated. Code administrator Joseph Breen's requests were satisfied — including the alteration of a scene in which Karl Malden angrily breaks into the bathroom while Carroll Baker languished in the tub. Also tempered was Malden's general appearance as the husband who waits none too patiently for the day his wife has promised to consummate their marriage, as well as a scene in which Eli Wallach pets Baker's legs as she rides a swing and gazes at him with a look that Breen called "orgiastic."

The premiere of the suggestive but essentially comic film was scheduled for the evening of December 18. Two artists had been commissioned to paint Carroll Baker's picture on a block-long billboard over Times Square — an outsize, characterisically 1956 advertisement with eighty-foot limbs and ten-foot eyebrows. Although both the Code and the New York State Board of Censors approved the film, most family and organized religious groups did not. Typical of the thousands of letters sent to Warner Brothers within a month was one from California — "Clean up your productions or cross a family of five off your list of moviegoers!" Warners' archives remain full of similar letters — and those from more confused patrons, like a New York woman who wrote condemning the new film and simultaneously converting it into an Irish epic: "No decent Catholic boy or girl would want to see *Baby Doyle,* a picture underlying Christian morals!"

It was, unfortunately, the ecclesiastical voice of New York that gave the film a national importance: the Legion of Decency, a New York–based group of moral vigilantes, on November 27 gave the film a "C" rating, condemning it and de facto refusing most Roman Catholics permission to see the film. With that, Francis Cardinal Spellman stepped to the pulpit of St. Patrick's Cathedral and (without, of course, having seen the film for himself) condemned it as "revolting . . . a contemptuous defiance of the natural law . . . immoral and corrupting . . . evil in concept. I exhort Catholic people from patronizing this film under pain of sin. . . . Since these degrading and immoral pictures stimulate immorality and crime they must be condemned. It has been suggested that this action on my part will induce many people to view this picture and thus make it a material success. If this be the case, it will be an indictment of those who defy God's law and contribute to corruption in America."*

"I disagree that *Baby Doll* is immoral," Kazan calmly replied when the press appeared at his door, "and I am outraged by the charge that it is unpatriotic. . . . Tennessee Williams and I have tried to see four small pitiable people with honesty and charity. . . . In this country judgments on matters of thought and taste are not handed down ironclad from an unchallengeable authority. People see for themselves and finally judge for themselves. That's as it should be. It's our tradition and our practice. In the court of public opinion I'll take my chances." And Williams told a reporter: "I can't believe that an ancient and august branch of the Christian faith is not larger in heart and mind than those who set themselves up as censors."

Just as Cardinal Spellman expected, the condemnation helped business. But two things are noteworthy about this holiday frenzy. First, the vast majority of critics in the secular press were equally outraged by what they considered the degrading, overt sexuality of the film, and its array of char-

* Cardinal Spellman had, to be sure, his secular brothers: *Time* magazine termed *Baby Doll* "possibly the dirtiest American-made motion picture."

acters so very different indeed from those of *The Glass Menagerie*. From every major newspaper and magazine in America came expressions of disgust and dismay. Williams was compared to himself, and they did not like his new style.

It should also be pointed out that Catholics, as well as many other moviegoers, generally made up their own minds, and most who defied a parochial edict found that *Baby Doll* might have been sensual in its implications, but was certainly nothing like pornography. In fact, it is quite an old-fashioned morality piece, in which violent sex (never presented in the film) and greed and opportunism are solidly denounced. The film is played for humanizing comedy — gentle, bawdy, and sad. "There is a sense in which I've always preferred *Baby Doll* to the film of *A Streetcar Named Desire*," Eliza Kazan said later. "It's more ambiguous. It combines passion with farce and tragedy and comedy, and I think it has a real humanity to it. It's not a large canvas, it's a miniature. To this day, it's hard to understand all that furor."

As the snow and the condemnations accumulated in New York, Williams remained in Key West, where he brought Edwina — apparently, as he implied in letters to friends, so that he would not have to confront alone his deteriorating relationship with Merlo. But if Merlo's presence made him uneasy, Edwina gave him a sick stomach, as he wrote to Cheryl Crawford: everything his mother said and every time she looked at him was a cause of guilt. He insisted that he still loved her, but he pitied her too, and she was driving him quite mad.

The "madness," of course, had quite another basis, and by January 5, 1957, he was able to admit (in a letter to Donald Windham) that he needed professional help, since he was tired of living with himself as he had so long been. "I am increasingly restless as I grow older," he told an interviewer at that time. "That's just the opposite of what it should be, isn't it?" But he summoned the courage to write final revisions for *Orpheus Descending*, drawing on his depressed spirit for the insertion of passages about frustration and a hope of purification. "I am an anxious, troubled person," he said that winter. "I can't write about anything I don't feel. . . . I wrote from my own tensions. For me, this is a form of therapy."

This form of therapy continued as he returned to New York for rehearsals. Harold Clurman had been chosen to direct, a choice difficult to understand since he was no avid partisan of Williams's method or vision.

(He had, for example, called *Camino Real* "a fallible minor work of a young artist of important talent.")

"Tenn and Clurman should've got along better than they did," according to Maureen Stapleton. "They hadn't worked together before, and there was just something in Harold's personality that didn't mix well with Tenn's." This polite tension did not help Williams's mood, and for a time Frank Merlo appeared on the scene, to help in any way that seemed appropriate. But not even he could change the fact that the play was in serious trouble.

"When we were rehearsing," Stapleton said, "everyone — producer, director, cast — knew the prologue was not working. I was delegated to tell this to Tennessee! So I went and told him that the whole thing had to be cut — not just part of it, as he thought. By this time we knew each other well enough that I could get away with this, or I neither could have nor would have tried! Tenn seemed a little set back by this news, but he just went away quietly, and next day he came to rehearsal and said, 'Maw [his invariable nickname for Stapleton, who in turned called him "Paw"] seems to think the prologue isn't working, and so I think we should cut it.' " This sort of authorial humility is — as Rebecca West wrote about male chastity — not ordinarily found in vulgar profusion. But Tennessee Williams ordinarily responded to suggestions from colleagues by rethinking and reworking his material. (It should be noted, however, that he reinstated the prologue for the published version of the play.)

On March 21, *Orpheus Descending* — with a program-epigraph from Hart Crane — opened at the Martin Beck Theatre, where once before Maureen Stapleton had brought so much to the success of a Williams play.* But not even her energy and talent were enough to please critics and audiences. With memories of Helen Hayes and *The Glass Menagerie,* and of the *Baby Doll* scandal, fresh in critics' and audiences' minds, the play's sharpened motifs of sexual frustration and spiritual search were not readily palatable. The reviews were only lukewarm when they were not plainly denunciatory. The play closed, after sixty-eight performances, on May 18.

Precisely at this time, Williams began to speak openly about his fear of failure. "My writing has followed a declining line since [*A Streetcar*

---

* Williams had hoped to have Brando in the role of Val Xavier. Brando did play the role in the film, but Cliff Robertson (replacing Robert Loggia in the Philadelphia previews) took the part to Broadway. Lois Smith, who had been Laura in the Helen Hayes *Glass Menagerie,* played the Cassandra figure, now called Carol in *Orpheus Descending.*

Named Desire]," he told the New York Herald-Tribune in a woefully inaccurate self-description. "With Orpheus Descending I felt I was no longer acceptable to the theatre public. Maybe, I thought, they'd had too much of a certain dish, and maybe they don't want to eat any more." The "dish" of course, was violence, derailed sexuality, and the submission of mythology — in this case Orphic mythology — to his own dramatic purpose.

Orpheus Descending's title suggests that classical resonance and intention. All the Orphic symbolism that was so diffuse in Battle of Angels was intensified here, and this made the play more structurally satisfying but not clearer, since Williams could not seem to decide whether he wanted the play to be a story of concrete humans in a concrete situation, or a set of modern constructs in a universe of archetypes. The play subjects religious to mythic motifs, too: Val's speech about the bird that never settles on earth equates that bird with spiritual incorruptibility as well as wandering — and thus gives the wanderer almost a pilgrim sensibility. Lady (renamed from Battle's Myra) agrees that if there is a bird in perpetual flight, then "God's made one perfect creature." (The image recalls The Roman Spring of Mrs. Stone, when Karen asks Paolo, "Speaking of birds . . . is it true that the rondini don't have legs and that is the reason they stay in the air all the time?")

Also from the Orphic myth Williams drew the compelling image of the wheel on which souls spin, entering alternately the light and the darkness, death and life, until purified forever for a final transmigration of souls: "You know," says Vee, the artist, one of the three women whose sexual frustration at once focuses and destroys Val Xavier's life, "we live in light and shadow — that's what we live in, a world of light and shadow — and it's confusing." In 1957, no one found the world more confusing than Tennessee Williams.

On Wednesday afternoon, March 27, still smarting from the barrage of negative reviews, Williams was staying with Frank at 58th Street. A thoughtless friend had left him a copy of that week's issue of The New Yorker, so he could read the review of his play. "The people in it aren't really terribly interesting," began Wolcott Gibbs. "I could see nothing but purposeless ruin. . . . I don't believe that he has turned out a coherent play, or that he was quite sure of what was on his own mind."

As if on theatrical cue, the telephone rang and Dakin Williams told his brother that their father had suddenly died in Knoxville, at the age of seventy-seven.

"He always told me over the years that for him his father had long been dead," according to Paul Bigelow. "There was nothing between them." But as so often in such cases of long-term estrangement, the emotions and reactions were more complicated at the time of death. Father and son had met only once or twice, and then by accident, in the last decade. By 1946, Edwina had been able to change her life with her husband, "and cut him out she did," as her son wrote long afterward:

"He had been in a hospital for recovery from a drunken spree. When he returned to the house, she refused to see him. My brother had returned from the latest war, and he would go back and forth between them, arranging a legal separation. I suspect it was not at all a thing my father wanted. But once more he exhibited a gallantry in his nature that I had not expected. He gave my mother the house and half of his stock in the International Shoe Company, although she was already well set up by my gift to her of half my earnings from *The Glass Menagerie*. He acquiesced without protest to the terms of the separation, and then he went back to Knoxville . . . to live with his spinster sister, our Aunt Ella. [But she] wasn't able to live with him, either, so after a while he moved into a hotel at a resort . . . and somehow or other he became involved with a widow from Toledo, Ohio, who became his late autumn love which lasted till the end of his life."

Frequently in his later years, Cornelius and the widow — who, according to Dakin, was a faithful drinking companion but very much a companion, too — flew down to Gulfport or Biloxi, where Cornelius and Edwina had once been happy. He died soon after one such visit.

In Knoxville, the elder Williams's family gathered for the services, and Dakin and Tom sat together for the first time in years. Edwina, unmoved and unmovable, remained in St. Louis.

Almost at once, Tennessee Williams's attitude and statements about his father shifted. "I have changed my feeling about him," he said soon after. "My father was a totally honest man. . . . He had a strong character and a sense of honor. He lived on his own terms which were hard terms for his family but he should not be judged as long as he remains the mystery that he is to us who lived in his shadow. Maybe I hated him, once, but I certainly don't anymore." Twenty years later he still bore the burden of that missed relationship: "In retrospect, I don't think he was that bad. I think he wanted to talk, too. . . . I feel a great affection for him now. He had a tragic life."

If ever people doubted that Tennessee Williams's expressions of compassion, forgiveness and understanding were authentic, they had only to consider his response to the death of his severe, enigmatic father, a man with whom such unhappy, frustrating memories were always associated, and with whom he never had any real communion.

Not long before his own death, he told of a moment after his father's funeral that may have begun the healing of memories that is forgiveness. "Aunt Ella ... showed me a newspaper photograph of him outside a movie house where a film of mine, *Baby Doll,* was being shown. Along with the photograph of my father was his comment on the picture. What he said was: 'I think it's a very fine picture and I'm proud of my son.'"

His father's death caused him so much unexpected pain that all the usual ailments — hypochondria and a persecution complex — rushed over him with a new ferocity. "Tenn became a terrific hypochondriac that spring," according to Maureen Stapleton. "He thought he had every disease possible, and that he was always on the verge of death. If he'd ever been one-fifth as sick as he thought, he wouldn't have survived any single year of the 1950s. He tried to act very bravely with us during the short run of *Orpheus* — he was always trying to cheer us up, make us laugh when it was hard to laugh. He took us to dinner and was very generous with his time when it was clear to all who were close to him that he was going through a hell of a bad time. His paranoia could surface at the most unexpected times. More than once, we sat at a restaurant table and he would overhear someone nearby say something uncomplimentary — and invariably Tenn thought it was about him. And he'd be ready for a fistfight to defend an imaginary insult! He wasn't the subject of the remark — and he wasn't drunk or disoriented when he imagined all this, it was just his paranoia!"

By June 1957 he could no longer avoid his need for serious professional help, and on the advice of several colleagues he began intense psychotherapy — an hour daily, five times a week — with Dr. Lawrence S. Kubie, a strict Freudian analyst and author of the book *Neurotic Distortion of the Creative Process.* Kubie did not merely listen to Williams's outpourings, he tried to help with constructive advice on how to reassemble his fragmented life. In July the playwright mentioned that he had begun work on an original screenplay, *The Loss of a Teardrop Diamond,* but (according to Williams's description in *Memoirs* and elsewhere) Kubie urged him to put his writing aside for a time. Williams wrote that he was even more shocked when Kubie told him to consider a break with Merlo and to attempt a heterosexual life.

Whether Williams's memory can be relied on here is an open question. But according to Paul Bigelow, "At this point he could no longer take Kubie very seriously, and later, when he moved to another part of town, he changed analysts quite easily. He thought it was very chic to say, 'I'm going to see my shrink!' "

For the first summer since 1949, Williams sacrificed Europe and contented himself with visits to friends in and around New York. He made several trips to Ossining to visit Rose, and frequently he brought her to Manhattan for lunch and a movie or a day of sightseeing and shopping. His own crisis made him even more sensitive to the tragedy of his sister, and he redoubled his efforts to bring her some pleasure.

One day early that autumn, Lilla van Saher went with him to Ossining and, after their visit with Rose, she went back to the car so that he might have a few moments alone with his sister and with a nurse-companion. Williams returned to the car clutching a crumpled ten-dollar bill. Rose had given him the money as he was leaving.

"Tom," she had whispered, "I know how hard you are working at the shoe warehouse. I know you want to be a poet, and I believe in you. I have been saving some change for you, and I hope this will help things to be a little easier. If you will just be patient, I know good things will be ahead. Always remember I believe in you."

He looked at the bill in his hand, and then at Lilla. She started the engine and drove away from Stony Lodge, allowing her friend the privacy of his tears.

Chapter Seven

THE HEALING
OF MEMORIES
(1958–1962)

I know it's a hideous story but it's a true
story of our time and the world we live in.

—Catharine Holly, in *Suddenly Last Summer*

F OR OVER A YEAR beginning in mid-1957, Tennessee Williams underwent intense psychotherapy. And during the summer and autumn of that same year he visited his sister Rose with a frequency that astonished even the administrators of Stony Lodge. The connection between these two activities would not become evident to others until he had completed the play that, in spite of Dr. Kubie's advice, he drew from himself that season — his painfully autobiographical *Suddenly Last Summer.* "I think if this analysis works," he said as the year drew to a close, "it will open some doors for me. If I am no longer disturbed myself, I will deal less with disturbed people and with violent material. . . . It would be good if I could write with serenity."

The doors were indeed opened, but the resulting material was more violent than ever. Williams could not write "with serenity" — not only because his inner life was in turmoil, and undergoing severe scrutiny, but because had he then imposed a blanket of calmness over his writing, he would have been untrue to himself and to precisely what he had to bring to the American theatre. As Harold Clurman wrote that year, some of the greatest literature in the history of the world, "Sophocles, Euripides, Shakespeare, Strindberg, Dostoevsky, etc. — has been far more violent [than Williams]. . . . If critics cannot tolerate unpleasant subjects in contemporary plays, they should disqualify themselves as critics; and if an author feels obliged constantly to apologize . . . he must despair of maturing."

Williams had hoped, at the beginning of his therapy, to conform to the prevailing theatrical and cultural coziness of 1958; but the play that came from him was neither safe nor easy, nor would it be for his audience.

Suddenly Last Summer, written quickly, in something like a confused trance of guilt and remorse, was the most creative result of his psychoanalysis. With his doctor he felt confined and restricted; in the study at the new apartment on East 65th Street, he produced a confessional drama that dealt with his demons not by avoiding them, not by reducing that guilt to insignificance or by denying it, but by *asserting* that guilt and working through it: confession to begin the healing process. His doctor apparently disapproved; audiences, ever since the premiere that winter, were unable to avoid the seriousness of what Williams insisted was a moral fable for our time, drawn from his own history.

In its final version, all the dialogue of *Suddenly Last Summer* prepares for Catharine Holly's final speech. Violet Venable, the mother of her dead cousin Sebastian, attempts to bribe Catharine's mother and brother into having the girl lobotomized. She wants this operation performed because of Catharine's monstrous claims, about which we are fully told at the conclusion: last summer, Sebastian was devoured by urchins in Spain who had (it is implied) sexually prostituted themselves for him.

When he brought his mother to New York late that autumn, rehearsals for the play were in progress. In *Suddenly Last Summer* the formidable Mrs. Violet Venable (surely the most malignant archetype of the Terrible Mother in the Williams canon) seeks to silence her niece by brain surgery, if need be; seeks to "cut that horrible story out of her brain" — just, Williams felt, as Edwina Williams wanted the awful ravings of her daughter Rose cut from her brain in 1937. But Edwina was forever oblivious: "Why don't you write a lovely, long play again, Tom?" she asked repeatedly during her visit. "Like you did before — a lovely, lovely, long play," referring no doubt to *The Glass Menagerie,* of which she always saw herself as the indomitable heroine. What premiered in January 1958 was a profoundly unlovely short play, with the accidents of his life and of Rose's at its center.

By November the play was complete, and Audrey Wood suggested that it be performed on a double bill with a shorter work. He selected *Something Unspoken* as the other one-act play to be staged with it — a work written several years before, an ambiguous dialogue between two women who may or may not be (or have been) lovers but who are certainly bound to one another by a strange psychological dependence. The two works, under the collective title *Garden District* that described their New Orleans setting, would be presented in an off-Broadway theatre. As rehearsals began, Williams grew more and more uneasy: if the sex and violence in both *Baby Doll* and *Orpheus Descending* were rejected by critics and audiences, how would they respond to a play that contained two monologues about devouring flesh, two about seduction, one about lobotomy and a detailed description of sexual exploitation?

"Tennessee was absolutely terrified of this play," according to the actress Anne Meacham, who had several times played the first dramatic representation of Rose Williams, Laura in *The Glass Menagerie*. She was chosen to play Catharine Holly in the new play by the director Herbert Machiz, who had staged one of those early productions, and who knew her deftness at projecting fragility and strength.

"The play was so close to him that he wouldn't allow Audrey [Wood] to be at the casting or rehearsals, and he took a long time before he could show her the play," Meacham recalled. "Audrey was a mother to him in a way that Edwina never could be," and this may account for a hesitation that would otherwise seem inexplicable. In this play he accused himself of "devouring" others by buying sex and by paying for counterfeit emotion; just as he was the model for Sebastian Venable, so was Edwina the model for Sebastian's mother Violet.* Williams's emotional and psychological association with the maternal Audrey, therefore, caused him to delay submitting the text to her as long as possible. "He was so protective of it and frightened by it," Meacham said, "although I think he knew it was one of his best plays, and that in Catharine Holly he created one of the greatest roles ever written for an actress."

Throughout November and December there were daily meetings with the cast, with composer Ned Rorem and with set designer Robert Soule, who had to realize what Williams described in the published stage directions as "a fantastic garden which is more like a tropical jungle, or forest, in the prehistoric age of giant fern-forests when living creatures had flippers turning to limbs and scales to skin. The colors of this jungle-garden are violent. . . . There are massive tree-flowers that suggest organs of a body, torn out [the reference is to both Melville's devoured sea-turtles, described by Mrs. Venable, and to Sebastian's death, described by Catharine] . . . there are harsh cries and sibilant hissings and thrashing sounds in the garden as if it were inhabited by beasts, serpents and birds, all of savage nature." The effect of the setting, Williams insisted, should mediate the core of the play, which postulates that within the genteel arti

---

* "Venable" is an old form of the word "venal," and as late as the last century it meant both able to buy and able to corrupt, capable of being bribed, of unprincipled character, and associated with sordid and corrupt influences (*cf. Oxford English Dictionary*). And are Violet and Sebastian grotesque revisions of the twins Viola and Sebastian in *Twelfth Night?* Some have thought so: see Mary Lynn Johnson, "Williams' 'Suddenly Last Summer,' Scene One," *Explicator* 21 (April 1963), item 66.

fice of an apparently advanced civilization lie savagery and destruction: we live in a garden of our tending, a garden far from paradise in which we feed living things to living things, fruit-flies to Venus flytrap and one another to one another. Doctors can be bought, relatives bribed, attorneys compromised. The situations of the play are almost mythic. (The model for this grotesque garden was of course Muriel Bultman Francis's fantastic "Green Room" in the Garden District of New Orleans, which years before had so impressed him, and which he waited for years to recreate in this cathartic play.)

The network of autobiographical references is everywhere evident in *Suddenly Last Summer,* and the few friends and associates who knew of his and his family's private lives saw at once how clear the parallels were — most of all between Catharine's threatened operation and Rose's surgery, a connection suggested to him by his own sorry life in the 1950s: Sebastian Venable's pattern of exploitation was the pattern of his own: "Yes," says Catharine, "we all use each other and that's what we think of as love," and for Sebastian/Williams sexual exploitation had masqueraded as love, and had become a kind of human devouring. The final horror of "Desire and the Black Masseur" was at last narrated in the extreme: "We were going to blonds, blonds were next on the menu," Catharine says. "He was famished for blonds, he was fed up with the dark ones and was famished for blonds . . . that's how he talked about people, as if they were items on a menu. 'That one's delicious-looking, that one is appetizing,' or 'that one is *not* appetizing' — I think because he was really nearly half-starved from living on pills and salads."*

Williams made the connection between himself and Sebastian even clearer: they both had the habit of "popping little white pills" because of a "bad time with his heart . . . he had rheumatic fever and it affected a heart-valve . . . and [he] was frightened about it." And although Violet claims that Sebastian, like the author, "dreaded, abhorred false values that come from being publicly known, from fame, from personal exploitation," she admitted: "Time after time my son would let people go, dismiss them."

There is a brutal paradox that must be faced in coming to terms with the life and work of Tennessee Williams. On the one hand, of all American dramatists he is the one most deeply sensitive to the inequities, illu-

---

* On April 10, 1948, Williams had written to Donald Windham that after two months in Italy he was getting an appetite for northern blonds, since he was tired of the Romans who were mostly dark. See above, p. 147.

sions and potential exploitations in intimate relationships. In his plays he went deeply to the truth of love and its absence. Yet from his late twenties to the end of his life he pursued sex — for its own sake, as a quick, anonymous diversion — with a vigor recalling Casanova or a Byronic figure. Later, in *Small Craft Warnings,* he put a summary of this on the lips of Quentin, the aging homosexual writer: "The experiences are quick, and hard, and brutal, and the pattern of them is practically unchanging . . . like the jabbing of a hypodermic needle . . . more and more empty of real interest and surprise."

"The remarkable aspect of Tennessee Williams," Robert Anderson said, "is how he transmuted his anguished life into great plays. Wasn't it Faulkner who said that a writer needs experience, observation and imagination? Williams had them in abundance, and these qualities enabled him to turn his private pains into public art."

Nowhere was the art more confessional than in *Suddenly Last Summer,* in which Tennessee Williams gave as clear a perception of derailed creative energies and the abuse of love as any moralist could ever proclaim. Obsessed with what the play calls "the trails of debris" that he believed had characterized so much of his life in the 1940s and 1950s, he wrote a play that wept for the waste — most of all because he felt that he had abused the freedom of the creative life, and of life itself. He had squandered what had been denied to his sister. He always knew that the only thing that kept him from sharing Rose's fate was the hair's breadth of accident; they had, after all, both endured breakdown. According to the artist Vassilis Voglis, who had by this time known Williams socially for several years and would see him frequently to the end of his life, "He was devoted to Rose, but in a way she was an extension of himself. *He* could have had the lobotomy. *He* felt the outsider, marred in some way. He really cared for her, and perhaps he never really cared for anyone else in this life, ever. And I think he knew it."

Sebastian Venable's exploitation of others, his empty, decreative life, and his abuse of his cousin Catharine were for Williams the clearest portrait he could draw of his own remorse. The play is, then, both confession and act of penance. He perhaps misjudged his own best gifts and the healing effects of those gifts when he told the interviewer that he hoped to have done with violence, and to write with serenity. "*Suddenly Last Summer* is a play he would have liked to have back — as if he regretted writing it," said Joseph L. Mankiewicz, who directed a brilliant film of it the following year. "There is something not only of confession in the play, but of wish-fulfillment, too. Tennessee might have liked to have a garden with statues like Sebastian's, a study with paintings like Sebastian's. If he had a distaste for anything, it was for his own aging and his own humble background and circumstances. *Suddenly Last Summer* enabled him to have what he despised, in a way. And Mrs. Venable is certainly a composite of the women who defended and accompanied him all over the world."

Garden District opened in New York on Tuesday, January 7, 1958, at the off-Broadway York Playhouse on First Avenue. In the unpredictable nature of such things, the most influential critics surprised Williams (who later said he expected to be run out of town when *Suddenly Last Summer* was performed). Atkinson wrote that no other American playwright used "ordinary words with so much grace, allusiveness, sorcery and power. . . . *Suddenly Last Summer* is further evidence of Mr. Williams's genius." Walter Kerr agreed, calling it "a serious and accomplished work."

But even as favorable reviews were appearing, Williams prepared to leave New York. Although he had just moved to East 65th Street and was due daily at Dr. Kubie's office near by, he arranged for the rent and the doctor to be paid. Very likely in an effort to disconnect himself from the current of pain and tension which this play caused (right up to opening night, according to Anne Meacham, whom the reviewers all hailed), he went to Key West. Meantime, Audrey was concluding negotiations for a screen sale of *Orpheus Descending,* and she was trying to locate as collaborator for the screenplay a young writer who had impressed her and her client. Williams, for his part, was eager for sun and water in midwinter. By late March he was back in New York, calmer and apparently not so indulgent with alcohol and little white pills, and he told Audrey that a revision of *Sweet Bird of Youth* would be ready for Cheryl Crawford to consider. Before he departed for Europe, he formally ended his visits with Dr. Kubie.

At the same time, Random House published the text of William Inge's recent play, *The Dark at the Top of the Stairs,* which had opened on December 5, 1957. This was a revision of Inge's *Farther Off from Heaven,* which Williams had recommended to Margo Jones and to Audrey Wood; Inge and Wood now suggested that Williams write an introduction to the published version, since it was dedicated to him. He was lukewarm to this idea, however, since he said that he was entirely too occupied with his own plays and screenplay treatments. "Audrey," he told her, "it is one thing to type three words — 'For Tennessee Williams' — on a dedication page. It's quite another thing to write several pages of introduction."

But Audrey prevailed, and the text was submitted. It is one of the strangest pieces Williams ever wrote, best described as praising Inge with faint damns. He implies that Inge's life was a better drama than Inge would ever write.

The sudden emergence of a jealous, hostile streak toward Inge must be seen against the background of their respective fortunes in the 1950s. After *Farther Off from Heaven* in Dallas in 1947, Inge had his first New York success with *Come Back, Little Sheba,* which in 1950 ran for six months. But then in 1953, *Picnic* opened, ran for 477 performances, and won for Inge the Pulitzer Prize and New York Drama Critics Circle Award. The following month, *Camino Real* opened and failed, after only sixty performances.

At that time, Inge had invited his former champion to lunch. "Tennessee," he asked gently, "do you think you're blocked?" That was all Williams had to hear from a writer he still considered an apprentice. He replied that he would break through the block, as always; but later, in a classic transference, he wrote that his friendship with Inge began to cool at this time because "Bill's problem was one of pathological egocentricity: he could not take a spell of failures after his run of smash hits: so eventually he was cared for by two male nurses." But the fact is that in the 1950s Inge had an uninterrupted series of successes. On March 2, 1955 (three weeks before the premiere of *Cat on a Hot Tin Roof*), Inge's *Bus Stop* opened, directed by Harold Clurman. It ran for 478 performances. Although Williams's play won the Pulitzer and Drama Critics Circle Award, the quiet contest continued. Then virtually all friendly exchange between them was severed (until Inge's illness years later) when in 1957 *Orpheus Descending* (directed by Clurman) opened in March and ran eight weeks, while later that year *The Dark at the Top of the Stairs* (directed by Kazan) ran for 468 performances. In January 1958, in Key West, Williams said he hoped Inge would not win any awards for that play; in fact he did not.

"Williams was very jealous of Inge's success," according to Meade Roberts, who worked with Williams later that year on a screenplay. "He was, after all, Audrey's client, and Tennessee himself had introduced Inge to Audrey. Also, he thought that Inge wrote better dialogue than he did, that Inge had a true ear for American regional speech. He proudly said in public one day that 'Inge may be Audrey's gentleman playwright, but I prefer to remain her degenerate playwright.' " It may well have been this jealous attitude of which Williams was thinking when he told the press in 1958 that fame was agreeable, but that "it has poisoned my life."

From Rome that spring he heard of Cheryl Crawford's negotiation to produce *Sweet Bird of Youth;* this was facilitated by an advance sale of film rights to M-G-M, which amused Williams for years, since his former employer was buying the rights to his play even before it was played on Broadway. The letters to Cheryl continued throughout the summer, ending on September 14 with his reminder to her that he needed Kazan for director since this was certainly his last play. She must have smiled: *Cat on a Hot Tin Roof* and *Orpheus Descending* and *Suddenly Last Summer* were his "last plays" too.

During a brief stop in New York on his way to work in Key West, Williams was told how solid his financial condition was. The film of *Cat* had opened in August and was already the fifth largest grossing film in M-G-M's history. *Suddenly Last Summer* was a success in New York and London and a lucrative deal was struck with film producer Sam Spiegel. *Sweet Bird of Youth* had been sold in advance to M-G-M, and work was proceeding on a film of *Orpheus.* Williams was at the peak of his income and his fame. In the four-year period beginning in August 1958, Hollywood would buy seven of his plays, thus adding over four million dollars to his income. (Of the fifteen films based on plays by Tennessee Williams, he involved himself in the adaptation and script revisions of only seven — *The Glass Menagerie, A Streetcar Named Desire, The Rose Tattoo, Baby Doll, The Fugitive Kind, Suddenly Last Summer,* and *Boom!* He repeated, over the years, his keen dislike of all the films based on his work — with one exception, *The Roman Spring of Mrs. Stone.*)

The task that was to occupy him for at least the next several months of 1958 was the screenplay for one of them, *Orpheus Descending,* on which the collaborator was to be the young playwright Meade Roberts. Lilla van Saher, who had been introduced to Roberts through Gore Vidal, had brought Williams to a preview of Roberts's play *A Palm Tree in a Rose Garden* late in 1957. By June, Roberts had been hired to write the film treatment of *Orpheus,* and after working on this in Hollywood while Williams was in Europe, it was decided that they should collaborate in Miami that autumn.

Roberts returned briefly to New York before their reunion in Florida and by chance met Frank Merlo at a party given by mutual friends. "Tennessee doesn't believe how much I love him," Merlo said sadly. "He goes around saying I want him to die, that I only want his money." To this Roberts replied, "Frank, you know that's only Tenn's paranoia." Merlo repeated, "But he'll never believe I love him, never again."

During October, Roberts and Williams worked and the two kept Williams's coterie entertained.

"We didn't really discuss the collaboration very much," Roberts recalled. "I had written part of it in Hollywood and part in New York, and Tennessee wrote some scenes which we exchanged in the mail. Finally in October, because he did not want to go to Key West while Frank was there, he told me to meet him at the Towers Hotel in Miami, near his friend Marion Black Vaccaro.

"The Towers was the only hotel in southern Florida without air-conditioning," Roberts continued, "without a pool and without an address, which made it interesting for people to find us. The hotel simply listed itself as 'The Towers Hotel, Facing the Miami River.' But there is no Miami River — it was just a dried-up creek. There we were, in this huge establishment, which was quite empty. I had one wing all to myself, and Tennessee had another. When I asked why we were alone in this sprawling hotel when we could have stayed at the Robert Clay Hotel next door, where they had a pool and air-conditioning and an address, he said, 'Because the management is never astonished. . . .'"

The two worked separately each morning and then met at the Robert Clay pool, had lunch, and planned the afternoon and evening. "Late in the day or in the evening after dinner we read aloud to one another what we had written or rewritten. But we were not alone. The scenes were also heard by an audience of what can only be called extraordinary people — Lilla, Marion, a body-builder we knew only as Jack the Judo, and a mysterious, silent girl no one knew but who always joined us. We called her The Catatonic."

Often in the afternoons there would be excursions with this crew of admirers, to the Florida Seaquarium, to the Parrot Jungle — "and to the movies," as Roberts vividly remembered. "Tennessee loved the movies. Not only serious film artists Antonioni and Fellini and Visconti [whose work he had seen in Italy]. He loved old movies like *Hollywood Canteen* and *The Maltese Falcon*. One evening we all trotted off to see *Gigi* at Loew's Coral Gables. Fortunately, I had seen the movie earlier, because with Tennessee it was something of a riotous scene. First, he supplied himself and everyone else with popcorn, Goober's candy, Good-and-Plenty — whatever anyone wanted. He was in great humor. Then we'd settle into our balcony seats, and as soon as the film began Tennessee began a running satirical commentary. When [Louis] Jourdan made his first appearance in the film, Tennessee jumped up and shouted, 'I met you last year in Paris with Charles Boyer!' Then later, he decided that the movie was going on too long. He stopped munching popcorn, stood up and shook his fist at the screen — 'Actors! Actors! Pick up your cues!' We got hysterical of course, although the other patrons weren't so thrilled with our hysteria. And once, when he heard that the film of *Cat on a Hot Tin Roof* was playing — which he hated — he went downtown and said to the people on line for tickets, 'This movie will set the industry back fifty years! Go home!'

"We had many good times during those weeks," according to Roberts, "but Tennessee could be very paranoid too. He had just begun taking a combination of amphetamines and barbiturates [which produced alternating shifts in mood], and during the last days of our work together he had a strange attitude about himself, which was very divided. On the one hand he knew how important he and his work were, and he was angry and hurt that he had never received the Nobel Prize. And then within hours he would be convinced he was a terrible writer and a poor craftsman, and he was very insecure. At times like this, he would tell me that of course Inge was the better dialogue-writer, an opinion not widely shared."

In late November, Roberts returned to Hollywood to complete the script. (Eventually, after arguments with the producers, Williams settled on the title for this screen version of *Battle of Angels/Orpheus Descending:* he went back to his 1937 play and called it *The Fugitive Kind.*)

At the same time, in a rush of activity partly induced by drugs, he completed another draft of *Sweet Bird of Youth,* with greater emphasis in the opening scenes on the actress's use of hashish, marijuana, vodka, pills and sex; he also drafted the first version of a strangely ambiguous marital comedy, *Period of Adjustment.* By the end of December he was assisting with rehearsals on the latter at the Coconut Grove Theatre. In a letter to Cheryl Crawford, he wrote that it was not his best work by any standard, but that it was an honest appraisal of how he saw intimate relations; he added that his motive was to earn money for Rose's care.* He may also have had his mother in mind, for at Christmas he brought her to Miami, where he noticed a sudden deterioration in her mental state that sug-

---

* Once again — and beyond any link with reality — Williams gave the impression that his financial situation was precarious. Meade Roberts recalled that once, in a Miami bookshop, Williams had decided to purchase a limited edition of Van Gogh's letters to his brother. But when he was told that the book cost fifty dollars, Williams reneged, saying, "I can't afford it."

gested incipient senility, and that would demand her transfer to a senior citizen center where she could receive care and attention. She complained to him that season that a rocket from Cape Canaveral had fallen in the yard, and that she had to comb radioactive fallout from her hair. This first amused, then annoyed, finally upset him. For the most part, Edwina was lucid — and as sweetly tyrannical as ever — but there were occasional lapses into unreality. In St. Louis, Dakin continued to be devoted and attentive to her.

Barbara Baxley, who rejoined Williams to play in *Period of Adjustment,* remembered that during the opening night celebration on December 29, Edwina "couldn't stop telling Tennessee to stand up to greet a lady, to straighten his tie, to fix his coat, to use his napkin — as if he were five years old. She was, you might say, a very strong lady."

During the one-week run of the play (billed, like *Sweet Bird of Youth* in 1956, as "a work in progress"), Baxley recalled that Williams was a great help to actors. "In talking about [her character] Isabel, he could say a small thing that would illuminate the whole woman for me — and because he was a great actor as well as writer, he could play a bit of business for me, or for any of us, and any problem was solved. He and Bill Inge were the only playwrights I ever knew who could do that. They could act out the line for an actor, and then the whole sense of it became clear. But as solid as he was in this, he could be terribly insecure. Bill Inge visited us during that week, and he said to me, 'Barbara, Tenn is so insecure about his work and about actors. If he volunteers something, fine. But if you have a question, don't ask him outright — ask his assistant [i.e., the assistant director, Owen Phillips].' " But in spite of this counsel, Williams — who was directing the play himself for the early part of rehearsals — dealt smoothly with his cast.

With the new year 1959, Elia Kazan sent Williams a letter detailing those elements of the script of *Sweet Bird of Youth* which he thought needed special attention. "The relationship between Kazan and Williams," said Joseph L. Mankiewicz, who knew them both, "was a rare symbiotic relationship in the theatre. Williams's drafts were so rough as submitted, they had to be turned into workable, playable dramas for the stage. They had to be adjusted to specific dramatic requirements. Kazan did this. Tennessee gave him the softness, the malleable material of the work, and Kazan, like a truffle-dog, sniffed out the violence and brought it into the open. He peppered the work — sometimes, I think, over Tennessee's objections."

By early February, a cast had been selected. Kazan had recently seen

Geraldine Page perform the role of the faded model in *Separate Tables,* and he recommended her for the role of Alexandra del Lago (the "Princess Kosmonopolis," as she calls herself when traveling incognito); for her gigolo, the aptly named Chance Wayne, they chose Paul Newman, who had first appeared in *Picnic* and later in *The Desperate Hours.*

Rehearsals were full of strain and tension, as Williams wrote to Donald Windham. Williams was again convinced that this was his last play, that he was now — for certain — a dying man. "But he was always going to die the following week," Kazan remembered. "He was always very fair to me during rehearsals, however, whatever his personal complaints. He was as fine to work with as he had been on the other plays. He was never difficult, never falsely critical, always generous. He worked every day, he brought in new material for rehearsals every afternoon. He was really an adorable man to work with, and I loved and respected him enormously." The cast recognized that the respect was mutual: "Kazan was a wonderful influence on Williams," according to Geradine Page. "He worked so hard with him."

After a preview-run in Philadelphia, the play opened on March 10, 1959 at the Martin Beck Theatre in New York. (Williams was paid $400,000 for the film rights, plus a percentage of profits to come, and at once the box office drew almost $15,000 daily in ticket sales — of which he received ten percent.) Audiences found that the play contained Williams's strongest material: drug addiction, alcoholism and male prostitution, venereal disease, racism and castration.

A few critics responded favorably. Atkinson called the material "acrid," but felt that Williams was "in a relaxed mood as a writer." But the majority unleashed a storm of negative comments. Robert Brustein called it "disturbingly bad — aimless, dishonest and crudely melodramatic, [full of] hazy notions about Sex, Youth, Time, Corruption. . . . [It] contains the author's most disappointing writing since *Battle of Angels.*" Contrasting him with Strindberg, Brustein added that the Williams nightmare "does not penetrate to a deeper subjective reality [and is full of] fraudulent conflict." And Harold Clurman felt that Williams had "become immobilized in his ideology." He was joined by John Chapman, who emphasized Williams's strength but feared that he was essentially a "dirty minded dramatist who has been losing hope for the human race [and] has written of moral and physical decadence as shockingly as he can." *Time* magazine damned it and the few favorable reviews, calling the play "very close to parody," and three Williams partisans issued alarms:

Walter Kerr felt that Williams was capable of writing real tragic drama "but [was] not yet ready to reach for it"; Kenneth Tynan said everything about *Sweet Bird* "dismayed and alarmed" him; and even John Gassner lamented the sense of tragic isolation and a "sensational expression of his most nihilistic mood. . . . Williams ought to become more serious about the convention of tragedy itself." But audiences responded to its boldness in portraying the fading movie queen Alexandra del Lago; her young gigolo Chance Wayne; his former sweetheart Heavenly Finley; and her father, the hypocrite Boss Finley — all caught in a sordid net of corruption. The play ran almost a year, for 383 performances.

Considered later, as part of Williams's complex late development, *Sweet Bird of Youth* might be regarded as the best example of an earnestness of continued confession (drug-abuse, paying for sex, the fear of professional decline) unharnessed by a sufficiency of esthetic control. Kazan and Williams admitted that the play is essentially two separate works: out of the original Florida production came acts one and three, with the insertion of the Chance Wayne episodes in act two. Too often the characters are the author's mouthpieces, speaking not from their own inner logic and wholeness, but out of the author's own anger and frustration, with an inappropriately poetic reflectiveness. The Heckler, for example, present in one scene only to cause a political stir, suddenly says: "I believe that the silence of God, the absolute speechlessness of Him, is a long, long and awful thing that the whole world is lost because of. I think it's yet to be broken to any man. . . ."

This intrusion of the authorial voice into a character continues right through to the awkward curtain line, in which Chance Wayne addresses the audience: "I don't ask for your pity, but just for your understanding — not even that, no. Just for your recognition of me in you, and the enemy, time, in us all."* This is surely the single most jarring interruption of dramatic structure in Williams's work. As a rather presumptuous coda (permissible in a Mozart opera, but difficult to sustain in a modern-dress play), it suggests that in fact Williams may well have had in mind Billy Wilder's classic story of Hollywood madness, *Sunset Boulevard. Sweet Bird* has astonishing parallels with that motion picture, which Williams had seen in a preview screening in 1950, later telling friends like Meade Roberts that he found it shattering and "wonderfully awful."

---

* Cf. *The Roman Spring of Mrs. Stone:* "The opposite force had been time, time the imponderable, not moving amicably with her but treacherously against her, and finally meeting her and arresting her in mid-flight with a shattering crash."

Within the year, even the academic critics were joining the reviewers in a growing weariness against what they considered his shock tactics. In an important essay published in the *Tulane Drama Review,* Henry Popkin wrote: "Williams now seems to be in a sort of race with himself, surpassing homosexuality with cannibalism, cannibalism with castration, devising new and greater shocks in each succeeding play. It is as if he is trying to see how far he can push the Gothic mode of playwriting."

On opening night, the audience cheered wildly, there were many curtain calls, and Williams went to the stage. Clearly the public was fascinated by the latest of Williams's fading, fierce women and her dangerously appealing man. Alexandra del Lago and Chance Wayne joined their dramatic antecedents — Blanche and Stanley; Myra/Lady and Val; Serafina and Alvaro; Mrs. Stone and Paolo.

Later in the evening, however, Williams was terribly depressed. "He was wretchedly nervous and much changed," Kazan remembered, "and after the opening he wouldn't let John Steinbeck or me into his house. Despite the wonderful performances and some important good notices, he felt he and the play were a failure, and so he went into hiding — he didn't want any social intercourse. He wouldn't see Steinbeck, who had been a real admirer for years and wanted to let Tennessee know that."

Williams left at once for Miami and the Towers Hotel, and took Marion Vaccaro with him to Key West. From there, they went to Havana, for since Fidel Castro had come down from his retreat in the Sierra Maestre Mountains and had taken power on January 1, 1959, Tennessee had wanted to meet him. "He told me during several telephone conversations we had, from Miami to Hollywood, that he had a great crush on Castro," Meade Roberts remembered. "He invited me to come along with him, but I said, '*You* go! If *you're* kidnapped, MCA [the agency with which Audrey Wood was then associated] will ransom you — you're Tennessee Williams. *I'm* Meade Roberts: Ashley-Steiner [his agents] won't ransom *me!*'" Williams's desire to meet Castro was more than fervent, Roberts remembered: "In fact he wanted to be *kidnapped* by Castro and Ché Guevara even while the two were still outlawed and hiding in the Sierra Maestre, kidnapping Americans for ransom. Tennessee thought very seriously about getting himself into a situation like that — *anything* to meet Castro."

And so Williams and Marion Vaccaro, whom Roberts remembered as a "wonderfully warm, supportive and tragic woman, the prototype of

Cora in his story 'Two on a Party' " — made their second trip to Havana; they had gone briefly for Marion's fifty-third birthday on January 17, just after Castro's victory. Castro, as it turned out, had once entertained theatrical ambitions, and even took a nonspeaking part in a Mexican film; he was pleased to meet the playwright he called "that cat" (presumably identifying author and play). There is no record of his reaction to Marion Vaccaro, and it is likely that neither she nor Williams informed Castro about her husband: Regis Vaccaro had been a major executive with an American fruit company long accused of monopolozing the Latin American banana industry.

Williams and Castro — an intelligent, well-read, reflective host — talked of the theatre and movies, and Williams mentioned that Jerry Wald, the independent producer for Twentieth Century–Fox, was considering a film about Castro's life that would star Marlon Brando. "I was in Jerry Wald's office some time later," according to Meade Roberts, "and he phoned Castro, who was on a brief American tour. 'I'm here with the fella who's written Marlon's next movie,' Jerry said to Castro about me, 'and we can get Brando right after that to play *you!*' Politics intervened, however, and of course the project never got very far."

For years Williams praised Castro's gentlemanliness and charm, though he seems to have known about the capture and execution of political enemies. According to several friends, Williams even attended public political executions in Havana during one of his visits that year. To no one's surprise, Williams never admitted this publicly. For such a gentle soul to have endured this spectacle, he would perhaps have had to be in an atypical condition — under the influence of drugs, for example. Since pills were a regular part of his life at this time, it would explain conduct at variance with his normally gentle, nonviolent character. (He did, however, like bullfights and frequently dragged Marion Vaccaro to them in Spain, where he chided her for getting sick at the sight.)

But meetings with Castro were not the only activity of the Cuban excursion. Williams and Marion also went to a male brothel, where (Williams later told Roberts) they took adjoining rooms and later compared the avidity of their exploits.

By the end of May, Williams and Vaccaro had passed several weeks with Merlo in Key West; then they returned to Miami, flew to London for the British premiere of *Orpheus Descending*, and visited friends. By the time Williams returned to New York, in early June, Frank had reopened the apartment on East 65th Street, where he was needed — he was, after all, still on salary for practical duties — while Williams attended rehearsals of *The Fugitive Kind*.

"An odd situation prevailed by this time," according to Meade Roberts. "My play *Maidens and Mistresses* had opened off-Broadway, and Tennessee's attitude began to change. I think he thought of me as a competitor, the way he spoke of Bill Inge. One day he said to Sidney Lumet [the film's director], 'We can't have two writers sharing the limelight on this production.' He seemed to resent me being at the rehearsals, even though both he and Sidney had specifically wanted some on-the-spot rewrites."

But the rehearsals — held in the Palladium Ballroom on Broadway — were a tense time for everyone. During the first two weeks of June, Anna Magnani (who agreed to play in the film version of the play written for her), eager to work with Marlon Brando, now found herself in a strained relationship with him.

"There we were, in this dance hall," recalled Maureen Stapleton, who had played Magnani's role on the stage and had, with her typical breadth of spirit, agreed to take the lesser, supporting role of Vee Talbot in the film. "Marlon and Anna were there, and Joanne Woodward, Tennessee and Frankie, Sidney Lumet and Meade Roberts. The first week, Marlon and Anna and Joanne rehearsed alone. The second week, the rest of us were called in. Marlon sat there, mumbling his lines in a barely audible whisper. Anna refused to reply. Joanne was unsure what was going on. I had known Marlon ever since our days in the Drama Workshop at the New School, in 1945, so I wasn't afraid to say something to him.

"Finally, after we read our first scene and I couldn't hear anything being said, I said, 'I think I'm going deaf! You guys may be geniuses, but I have to hear what you're saying!' I was surprised Tenn didn't speak up and tell *them* to speak up. That night he and Frankie came over to my house, and I said, 'Tenn, you've got the muscle and the clout! Tell them what has to happen for this thing to work!' But he said, 'Oh, I'm just an old faggot to them.' "

This was, of course, far from the truth. Everyone on *The Fugitive Kind* had enormous respect for Williams and showed it, and Magnani, Brando, Woodward, Stapleton and Roberts were especially close to him and warmly supportive — and in spite of private differences, Merlo was ready to help Williams and certainly never wavered in his loyalty. But Williams had to hear what he wanted to hear — perhaps because of paranoia, but also to support his belief that he was an artistic and social outcast. He

wrote of marginal people, after all — those with whom he could emotionally identify, whose pain and loneliness and spiritual isolation he had
first known himself. Tennessee Williams had the energy, the vision, the
pride and the tenacity that mark the life of every artist, and he perhaps
unconsciously coveted the sense of being an outsider in order to see
clearly what is the grotesquerie of so much on the inside.

"If artists are snobs," he wrote in the introduction to the second edition of Carson McCullers's *Reflections in a Golden Eye,* "it is much in the
same humble way that lunatics are: not because they wish to be different
and hope and believe that they are, but because they are forever painfully
struck in the face with the inescapable fact of their difference which
makes them hurt and lonely enough to want to undertake the vocation
of artists ... [with] a sense, an intuition, of an underlying dreadfulness
in modern experience."

Rightly, he never believed in the enduring value of his wealth or of his
celebrity or of a position as the controversial man of modern theatre over
whom critics and academics argued. But he also realized that in the per-
verse nature of such things in our time, it was precisely his dramatic insistence on being different that made him newsworthy and that
guaranteed him an audience for the deeper values his work sought to af-
firm. Like Sebastian Venable, "he dreaded, abhorred false values that
come from being publicly known," but he always knew how to exploit
the media, how and when to shock onstage and off. "He created his own
dramatic world around him," as Meade Roberts said, "and he dealt with
it when he could."

It was perhaps from this point in his life, when his importance as a
dramatist was no longer unchallenged, when both he and America were
on the verge of new, louder questions and a new violence, that Williams
moved further into a distrust of colleagues, friends and self. And his concomitant reliance on drugs made him less appealing both to himself and
others. What he might have meant was not "I'm just an old faggot to
them," for in the matter of his sex life no one really cared very much;
what was of truer consequence was that he might be, at forty-eight, so
established in his visibility, so evident, so open and public about his art,
his life, his loves and his antipathies, that his newsworthiness itself would
soon be eclipsed by others. Less familiar, younger faces, and voices with
new vocabularies would soon be heard — on television, most of all, but
also in the theatre, where Harold Pinter and Edward Albee were about to
be proclaimed prince regents.

Among those willing to take a longer view in 1959, there was no doubt that Tennessee Williams had given the world a collection of enduring and important stageworks — *The Glass Menagerie, A Streetcar Named Desire, Summer and Smoke, Cat on a Hot Tin Roof* and *Suddenly Last Summer.* But it was an age of anxiety eager for constant and instant diversion, a time of the sudden eruption of the cult of bigness as excellence. Spectacle and size were everything — in automobiles, in the size of television and movie screens, and in household and national budgets.

In such a culture, Williams had won his two Pulitzer Prizes. He worked at his craft, and often enough he jolted his audience. But he was a known presence — too well known — by 1959. Celebrity had made him a commodity, and the culture was entering a time of such worship of novelty that no one person could satisfy for long. He had been for fifteen years in the vanguard of his craft, and he was now considered by the arbiters of changing taste — a few critics, a few academics, a new generation of young, flashy producers — to have fallen behind, simply by virtue of having survived so long. "Not new, therefore not interesting" was becoming the standard. And perhaps most significant of all, there was an accumulation of alcohol and drugs in his mind and body that contributed to a physical, emotional and mental confusion and decline that would eventually take a dreadful toll, and that would forever deaden something rich and essential in his creative powers.

In early July, while the filming of *The Fugitive Kind* proceeded in a Bronx studio and in the town of Milton, New York, Williams attended the Chicago production of *Suddenly Last Summer.* The role of Catharine was taken by Diana Barrymore, then thirty-eight; she had, after a series of roles almost twenty years earlier, made six films, but then led a wandering, unhappy life controlled by alcohol. She had also desperately hoped, after a period in an asylum and after playing in a road-company production of *Cat on a Hot Tin Roof,* to make a Broadway comeback in *Sweet Bird of Youth.* Williams, however, correctly judged that her life was too close to the role, and that her fragile mental condition would not be right for the role of Alexandra. Why he approved the not less intense part of Catharine is not clear, but she was determined and he was sympathetic. Socially, they had spent a good deal of time together during the previous year in New York, and he arranged for her to meet the Chicago director. But unfortunately by this time Diana Barrymore had augmented her theatrical aspirations with the desire to become Mrs. Tennessee Williams.

In New York, 1975

Cheryl Crawford

With Edwin Sherin, Bill Barnes and Anthony Quinn,
during rehearsals for *The Red Devil Battery Sign,* 1975

With Rose Williams, at the National Arts Club, 1975

With Mitch Douglas in Chicago, 1980

With Vassilis Voglis and Jane Smith
at Williams's seventieth birthday celebration in Chicago, 1981

Tennessee Williams

"Poor, sad Diana," Paul Bigelow said. "She was another in Tenn's group of lost ladies. She saw in him a savior for herself, and she hoped to marry him. Like others, Diana imposed on him, but she was really invited to do so because Tenn saw her as a defeated soul in every way, very like himself [and in some ways like Rose]. And so he took her on, as a project. This of course turned out very badly, very savagely, with a good deal of mutual abuse."

The relationship between Williams and Barrymore was indeed unfortunate — "one of the oddest and sickest," according to the director George Keathley, who saw them together that summer. Barrymore not only kept pace with Williams's drinking and drug-taking; she also quietly procured for him, helped him to dress in drag for private parties and — as contrary as all these were to her stated hopes of marriage — she agreed with Dr. Kubie's earlier assertion that Williams might not be permanently homosexual, and to his conversion to heterosexuality she was passionately dedicated. How she thought she could effect this even as she played offstage Catharine Holly to his Sebastian Venable is difficult to understand.

For a week following the run of *Suddenly Last Summer,* she joined Williams and Marion Vaccaro for a trip to Havana, and shortly thereafter began a series of desperate telephone calls to Dakin Williams, telling him how she hoped to be his sister-in-law.

"She had become part of Tom's social life," Dakin recalled, "and had partied with him and Frank and Magnani and the others. She had followed him to Havana, and by late 1959 she was terribly unhappy over him. It was all very sad, for she was a warm and likable person." And Dakin's wife Joyce agreed: "She had a childlike appeal, and a real sweetness. But there had been so many disappointments in her life, and by this time she was ill and confused." Within a year, Diana Barrymore was found dead in her New York apartment at the age of thirty-nine, in strange and violent circumstances that were at the time reported as suicide.* (Whether she was in fact murdered is still an open question, however, among some who knew her and her friends, and who have studied the ambiguous police reports.)

On August 20, Williams and Merlo departed for a three-month vacation around the world. From Japan, Williams wrote a sad letter to

* At the time of Barrymore's death, Williams was in fact writing a new play especially for her. Called *Poem for Two,* its (undeveloped) narrative had a vaguely political thesis and was set in a penthouse suite at a Houston hotel. The manuscript probably does not exist; the material resurfaced, years later, in *The Red Devil Battery Sign.*

Brooks Atkinson, admitting that both *The Roman Spring of Mrs. Stone* and *Sweet Bird of Youth* dealt with his own artistic and moral dilemmas. He said his low creative energies during the last several years were due to a screaming cry for love and forgiveness, and that, far from being helped by either doctors or success, he was more deeply troubled than he had been when he wrote *A Streetcar Named Desire*. As he was writing, however, he was risking an international scandal by carrying with him illicit drugs, which, he wrongly hoped, would help him through the period of deep trouble. "I am," he said that year, "poisoned by success."

By Thanksgiving they were back in New York, where a preview of *The Fugitive Kind* was scheduled at the RKO 58th Street Theatre. The Sunday of the holiday weekend was, as Meade Roberts remembered, one of the more newsworthy days in Williams's life, and it had some of the flavor of Federico Fellini's 1959 film, *La Dolce Vita*.

"The production of dramatic television shows was beginning the move to Hollywood that year, and actors in the East were out of work in greater and greater numbers. The audience that night, and the crowds of bystanders outside the theatre, included organized numbers of unemployed actors, resentful of just about everyone who had anything to do with this film. There were harsh words for Sidney Lumet, who had been a television director, and for Anna Magnani, who was a foreigner working here. Finally, Tennessee arrived, very drunk, with an equally unsteady Diana Barrymore. There was an unfavorable response from the enemy camp at the end of the film, and a small gang of hoodlums recognized Williams leaving the theatre. They spat at him, he spat right back, and he went off with Diana to watch a first print of *Suddenly Last Summer* at [the film's producer] Sam Spiegel's apartment on Park Avenue." And there, as Speigel later told Joseph L. Mankiewicz, Williams covered his nervousness at the film's powerful rendering of his play by giggling into his drinks all evening. (It is worth mentioning that Williams was not giggling when *The Fugitive Kind* opened to the public in April 1960; Bosley Crowther, in the New York *Times,* expressed a typical reaction when he wrote that it was the best film rendering of a Williams work since *Streetcar.*)

At the beginning of 1960, Williams and Merlo were living quietly in Key West. Although he was exhausted from the long trip and the month in New York, there was a sudden resurgence of purpose and energy, rather as if he were fulfilling a New Year's resolution. With an acute sense of self-criticism and an attitude that can reasonably be called valorous, he devoted himself to an expansion of what would, in the opinion of many, be his last great play — *The Night of the Iguana.*

Based only remotely on the short story of the same name he had written long before, *Iguana* was first performed as a one-act play at the Spoleto Festival in Italy, on July 2, 1959. For the director of this production Williams had great admiration — and well he could, for Frank Corsaro had staged *A Hatful of Rain* in New York, as well as the opera *Susannah.* Sensitive and imaginative, patient and energetic, Corsaro realized in 1959 that the manuscript of *Iguana* was (at a mere twenty-one pages) a full-length work in progress, and that the first production in Italy would have a successor.

"He was totally charming at first meeting," Corsaro remembered, "and he continued to work during that summer and winter until it was eighty-one pages, a kind of long one-act play. In the fall of 1959 we came to New York and I directed that longer version at the Actors Studio."

In Key West that winter, Williams continued work on the play. Inspired by his 1940 summer on the Mexican coast, it was becoming an important, poetic play about art and religion, about the nature of the poet's vocation (a subject introduced in *Suddenly Last Summer*), and about the necessity of self-forgiveness. The role of a wandering poet nearing one hundred years of age combined Williams and his grandfather; the grandfather's spinster granddaughter, the sketch artist Hannah, was a kind of half-achieved, half wish-fulfillment of what Williams would have liked to be; and the defrocked, alcoholic, sex-crazed minister "at the end of his rope" (like the captured iguana) was a self-portrait of the playwright. As it evolved into full-length form in 1960 and 1961, the personal models became more nuanced. For perhaps the first time since *Streetcar*, the lineaments of his inner life were transcended into something universal, and an overt concern for spiritual health gives this play at once a human warmth and a tragic serenity absent from his work in the previous several years.

Corsaro saw that depth emerging, however, and he joined Williams and Merlo in Key West in early 1960. "Frank [Merlo] was the best part of Tennessee's life. He took no nonsense from him — and Tennessee could ladle out nonsense — and he was a man of sense and good taste. He was a street kid who had grown up and become a real, literate gentleman. As Tennessee's general factotum, he was his right arm and I think the bright side of his life."

Merlo kept pace with Williams's daily work on *Iguana,* reading portions of the script as they came from the typewriter, realizing that a major work was in progress, and making their visitor Corsaro welcome. But Tennessee was unsure of the quality of the play. "He felt that his star was in decline by this time," Corsaro said, "and he wasn't at all sure he could pull off *Iguana.* He was always complaining about critics, and about the future, but on the level of daily work and conferences on the script he was extraordinary — just extraordinary. The problems with his life, and the interruptions in his production of first-rate work, were due to those who formed his social circle at the time — people like Marion Vaccaro and Lilla van Saher." Corsaro was right: for in 1960 it was clear to him, to Merlo, to Paul Bigelow, to Audrey Wood, and to a number of New York friends that Williams's creative life was in a period of sudden, mysterious enrichment, and that he required quiet encouragement, not distraction; as so often, he was not the best judge of who offered what.

"When he was working or reworking at this play," Corsaro continued, "he was a genius, and he was inspiring to be with. You could see his understanding of people's pain, his compassion, his gentleness, his modesty in the face of the universe. But outside the work, he was becoming a travesty of himself. Those he chose to be with were such a sorry crew. There was Carson McCullers, twitching her way through an alcoholic evening, and William Inge, who had such a bad problem with drink, too, and whom Tennessee did not like — he played on Inge's weakness for drink and was obviously jealous of his success in the 1950s. And Lilla van Saher — what a fantastic creature! — they were all like rejects from a road company of *Streetcar.*"

Occasionally, Williams interrupted work on *Iguana* to revise portions of *Period of Adjustment,* the bittersweet marital comedy Cheryl Crawford was producing for a fall Broadway premiere. There was considerable talk in the press that season about Tennessee Williams writing a comedy, and to the *New York Times* he replied to the objection that his tragic (and, some said, sordid) vision indeed needed correction. To the surprise of none of his friends, he chose the metaphor of illness and diagnosis:

"We [playwrights of darkness and violence] have done no worse a deed than the X-ray machine or the needle that makes the blood test. And, though these are clinical devices, I think we have tried our best to indicate which are the healthy blood cells and which is the normal tissue in the world of our time, through exposing clearly the dark spots and the viruses on the plates and in the blood cultures."

* * *

By late April, it was necessary to find a director for *Period of Adjust-ment,* and the offer finally went to George Roy Hill, whose first Broadway direction (for *Look Homeward, Angel*) won the Pulitizer and Drama Critics Circle Award for the play. Reporters eager for gossip ran from Williams to Kazan and back again, hoping to prey on Williams's para-noia by suggesting that Kazan had stormed away from the play in dis-appointment over its quality, had aligned himself instead with Inge's work, and had terminated the friendship. This made for imaginative writing, but an egregious lack of truth. The simple fact was that Kazan was scheduled to direct a film of Inge's original screenplay *Splendor in the Grass,* but that he was also developing other interests in his own career:

"After *Sweet Bird of Youth,* he offered me his plays all the time, but by then I was directing more films. It was hard for me to keep turning him down, to keep telling him that my interests were elsewhere. [Kazan directed only three plays in New York after 1959 — all in 1964, at the ANTA Washington Square theatre.] It was hard for him to understand why I wouldn't do any more plays, that I was increasingly involved in my own writing and filmmaking. The affection between us persisted, and he was always very interested and generous toward my novels and films. We didn't drift apart emotionally — that never happened — but we did drift apart professionally."

In early June, Williams invited his mother and his brother and sister-in-law to join him for a vacation in Los Angeles, where they took a bun-galow at the Beverly Hills Hotel. They visited William Inge, film stars and directors, and industry people Williams had known over the years — Miss Edwina took a particular delight in meeting Elvis Pres-ley — and at one party they were introduced to the legendary Mae West. Williams volunteered — with the hyperbole he reserved for ladies of stage and screen — that she was one of the three great movie talents in history, the other two being W. C. Fields and Charlie Chaplin. "Well," she replied slowly, "I don't know about Fields."

As usual, especially when he could not work on manuscripts, he kept up a lively correspondence from California. To Brooks Atkinson he wrote from the hotel that he had that spring supervised the construction of a patio at the poolside of his Key West house, and that life there was his only refreshment. He then outlined the contours of his life for At-kinson. The ugliness, blackness and violence of his late work, he wrote, as if still defending himself before the press, was not an expression of cynicism or nihilism. He dealt with evil obsessively because he hated it. Sensationalism was never, the letter concluded, his true aim: in spite of compromises and lapses of taste he now regretted, his purposes had always been humanistic.

By the end of June he had returned alone to Key West, where Merlo awaited with a copy of *Newsweek,* in which Williams had admitted that he took barbiturates regularly. As for drugs, it seemed to the playwright that Merlo himself needed some — but not for psychological or diversionary reasons. He looked pale and nervous, and he was smoking excessively. Silence prevailed between them, visitors detected an emotional vacuum, and Williams spent more time with other men (at bars and on the beach) and with his adoring women. There seemed to be a quiet *diminuendo* to what had once been the lively, tender duet of Tennessee Williams and Frank Merlo.

"The years in which Tenn was willing to have the scheme of order placed on his life by another, especially a lover," according to Paul Bigelow, "were coming to an end. Now there was enough money for hotels and servants and cooks. A great deal of what Frank had offered over the years became available with Tenn's fame and wealth, which had grown enormously, and which — his protests aside — he was entirely aware of. He knew just what he was worth, and what his considerable wealth was. As his material life changed so dramatically, Frank could not adjust to it. He grew more and more bitter as his usefulness diminished. He had put up, all those years, with Tenn's promiscuity and with certain of his acquaintances who were less than helpful and in fact contemptuous. There was never a dramatic, final break, or a grand scene, packing the bags and so forth. It just ended gradually, and more or less calmly.

"But there was another element in this, and it had to do with Williams's increasing distrust of others, and his essential inability to accept the fact that he was the object of someone's commitment. Friendship he could accept; but sex he distrusted, in spite of all the celebration of it in his plays — perhaps because he ordinarily disconnected it from affection in his own life. He never accepted that he was sexually loved — it wasn't that he didn't accept love itself. Physical intimacy he tended to distrust, even as he needed it constantly."

Not long after 1960, Williams himself admitted this in even broader terms: "I have an unfortunate inability to believe in people's admiration," he told a reporter, "or even their acceptance ... that's awful. I know it is." Meade Roberts saw this, too: "I don't think he could accept deep commitments, and I think that after a dozen years that's what really made Frankie so unhappy, for he too realized that Tennessee would never believe how much he *could* be loved, and not just in spite of any human failings, but because he had so much to offer."

In the years to follow, in some ways he had less to offer because he believed less in himself. The potential for great feeling would always be there and would occasionally manifest itself from his breadth of human understanding. But the ability for emotional commitment (apart, of course, from his devotion to Rose) began to be foreclosed as his belief in himself, as artist, friend and lover, diminished.

In August 1960 the evolution of *The Night of the Iguana* continued, as the Actors Studio cast came to Coconut Grove for another production. Williams arrived, unstable but full of praise for his cast and director, and sensitive toward a crew-member whose family was in trouble. Fragile and dependent himself, he was still in touch with others' pain and able to respond, warmly and directly, in word and, if necessary, with cash.

Ironically, his comedy *Period of Adjustment,* when it opened in November in New York, was what everyone had been demanding — a gentle, funny-sad treatment of heterosexual domestic life. (Two couples confront a time of psychological, sexual and social crisis — and all ends happily.) The reviews, however, emphasized its conversations about sexual performance and technique, although some correctly deduced that the play could be considered a comedy only because it was not clearly a tragedy.

"The real problem with *Period of Adjustment,*" according to Cheryl Crawford, "was not in the play, which I still think is delightful and has never been properly appreciated. The problem was, to put it bluntly, that the original cast was too old. The audience didn't really care very much about the problems and the arguments of couples who, because they weren't young onstage, couldn't make credible the cries and complaints and nervousness natural for young married couples." The play closed in March, after 132 performances; only a film sale made it profitable, and this did not help Williams's recessive confidence.

At the beginning of 1961, Williams was in virtual seclusion in Key West, working with sullen intensity on *The Night of the Iguana* — which, he assured Cheryl Crawford in a letter dated January 8, would be his last play; he understood (incorrectly) that she did not want to produce it, and this saddened him since the play was, he said, a dramatic poem of great personal value and one of his clearest autobiographical statements. (The play was produced by Charles Bowden.) What he did not say was that he had recently been rereading the poems of Rainer Maria Rilke, and whether he was aware of it or not, this new play drew on the poet who had so deeply affected him three decades before. *Iguana* was becoming a journal of Williams's soul, passed through the prism of his poetic-dramatic art. With Rilke the play shares an idolization and idealization of women: Hannah Jelkes is described as "a Gothic cathedral image of a medieval saint," and she is certainly the most spiritual woman in the Williams canon, the clearest exponent of Wisdom. But he was also writing *Iguana* in highly religious, not merely archetypal terms: the God sought by Williams, as by Rilke, was not the God of organized religion, but "an incomplete sentence," a tendency of the heart.

Cheryl Crawford — who held the record as producer of a quartet of Williams's plays — was disappointed in his unexplained decision to move to another producer, but she accepted this with her customary good grace. She was among the first whom he gradually separated from his life.

"After *Period of Adjustment* I saw very little of him, and when I did he was very cool and distant. I found this hard to accept at first, since we were so close for ten years [and considering how intimately he had disclosed himself in letters]. It had been a period during which I had produced four of his plays and spent so much time with him. But later I found that he was changing a good deal in his life, and that a number of other people were treated somewhat differently too." And according to Jane Smith, "He was unsure about who liked him for what reasons, and even his oldest friends were suddenly suspect. It was a difficult thing for him to be in the limelight. He dropped everybody at some point, and then he'd come back again into one's life — in and out — with everyone it was the same way."

But while there were changes in his professional associations, Williams preferred to keep the same comfortable traveling companions; they did not challenge him, they simply accompanied him uncritically. In late January he left for Europe with Marion Vaccaro, and from London he wrote a final letter to Cheryl in which he expressed concern for Frank's health. At this time, Williams believed that Merlo was taking drugs, and that this was responsible for his withdrawal from their Key West social life; in fact, Merlo took no drug more potent than an occasional bit of marijuana. But he was smoking several packs of cigarettes daily, and with Williams absent and no Reverend Dakin to cook for, he was eating irregularly and poorly.

In April, Williams and Marion were in Rome, where they met Donald Windham and Sandy Campbell. "We sat together on Via Veneto," Windham recalled; "it was fun to see him surrounded by the paparazzi; but it was a little unreal, as though we were on the set of a Fellini movie." Within days, however, Williams and Vaccaro had departed for Taormina, Sicily, where they took rooms at the splendid San Domenico Palace Hotel, a sprawling Renaissance monastery more luxurious in its refurbished state than it had ever been in the days of Sicilian friars. On the terrace of his suite he set up his typewriter, and when he and Marion were not at the bar or strolling the beach in Taormina or Giardini di Naxos, he continued to write mostly disconnected scenes for *Iguana*. The Reverend Shannon of the play, by early that summer when Williams had returned to New York, had become a surrogate for the author himself — a man haunted by "blue devils" (as he called them in the play and in letters to Donald Windham) who takes refuge in the oblivion of drink and the quick affirmations of sex with young people. Audrey Wood, a champion of this difficult play from the start, saw the connections at once between the aged Nonno (the Italian word for grandfather, and the term Frank Merlo had used for Reverend Dakin) and Hannah (the sketch artist who insists that "Nothing human disgusts me unless it's unkind, violent") and Shannon (the sensual renegade).*

Enthusiastic as Audrey was, she soon joined Cheryl in the discovery of a subtle transformation in Williams's attitude. *Esquire* magazine had asked him to compose an article detailing the client-agent relationship. This took a year, and when it was at last ready it was full of praise for her — but in a coolly professional tone, and with a subtext of resentment that she was his "mother-image . . . and this is bound to create an ambivalent relationship when the filial image has arrived, as I have, at an age in his life and profession as an artist when he feels humiliated by the acceptance of what he thinks is too much domination, too many decisions for him not made by himself."

With characteristic dignified calm, Audrey confided her reactions to

---

* Up to this point, all the full-length plays of Tennessee Williams (except *Camino Real*) were set in the South — including *The Glass Menagerie*, for its St. Louis, Missouri, was very much an extension of the urban South; and he would return to that setting for three full-length plays later. The action in most of the one-act plays is similarly located.

no one (at least not publicly); she might have thought that if she had not indeed assumed responsiblities, his life would have been more chaotic, less artistically fertile. Also, nowhere in the piece does Williams address the strange situation of an internationally famous writer of mature years who has supposedly allowed himself to be "humiliated by . . . domination." Strange words, an ungrateful tone and an imaginative transference of his feelings about Edwina to Audrey: if his agent had felt this, she would not have been sharing his paranoia. In any case, she must have been surprised to read the final sentence: "I know that if someday our professional relationship should come to a close, it is she who would close it, not I. . . ." That closure would occur in time, but even then, in 1961, Williams was putting distance between himself and a woman who had devoted her energies to his career for over twenty years.

By early autumn he had returned to Key West where, as he wrote to Donald Windham, Merlo's presence at least saved him from the results of his inability to function alone. Merlo found him more than ever addicted to liquor and pills. "That's the only thing [that keeps me going]: liquor and swimming — Miltowns [a popular tranquilizer then widely prescribed], liquor, swimming," he told an interviewer at the time. At least part of his unhappiness was due to the growing conviction that his creative life had desiccated: "My kind of literary or pseudo-literary style of writing for the theatre is on its way out," he said. Harold Pinter was the writer of the future, and Pinter "drives me crazy with jealousy." With that admission, Pinter joined Inge; soon, Edward Albee would join Pinter. The list would grow in the 1960s. His insistence that each long play was his last, or that his best work was behind him, eventually became a self-fulfilling prophecy.

The out-of-town previews for *The Night of the Iguana* were as violent, as tense and as suspenseful as the first uneven drafts of the play itself. In October, after cordial introductions of the cast (Bette Davis, Margaret Leighton, Patrick O'Neal, Alan Webb), rehearsals began.

"It was a very difficult time," according to Frank Corsaro, "for him, for me, for the performers. He was rewriting furiously and delivering new script every day, which was hard on the actors, and he had a strange lack of perspective about how the play might gather focus and momentum. His working habits were not helped by his reliance on pills and shots from a quack doctor, and his resulting nervousness didn't help the cast."

The last week of rehearsals in New York City, before the company's departure for a week in Rochester, Williams told an interviewer, "I create imaginary worlds into which I can retreat from the real world because I've never made any kind of adjustment to the real world." But the retreat was given a harder edge and an urgency by his increasing reliance on drugs. For an artist seeking deeper contact with reality through the forms of art and fiction and drama, a lack of adjustment to much of what passes for social intercourse can be helpful, and is in fact necessary. But if the inner realm where reflection occurs is influenced by chemicals, it becomes hard for an artist to gauge the depth or truth of his feeling, and harder still for him to evaluate the results realistically.

From Rochester, they moved to a two-week engagement in Detroit. Revisions descended from Williams's hotel room daily — brought to director and cast by Frank Merlo, who usually reported that the playwright had been awake most of the night and so was sleeping until afternoon. It was in Detroit that an unfortunate accident severed any hope of a reconciliation with Merlo.

"As if it weren't bad enough that the cast was hardly on speaking terms," Corsaro recalled, "we were told that Williams's dog had bit him on the ankle, and that an infection had set in. He had to be hospitalized." He also had to be calmed with increased sedation, for he was not only in acute pain from the wound but he was virtually irrational with rage and fear. The dog, given to him by Anna Magnani (and aptly named Satan), had been set on him by Merlo, he raved: Frank wanted him dead, all Frank wanted was his money, the dog always loved Frank more — it was a first major explosion of unreason. Only Merlo knew what was responsible, and he was powerless now to prevent Williams's pattern of self-destruction.

But somehow, with his remarkable recuperative and resilient powers, Williams returned to work on the production, bandaged ankles and unstable nerves notwithstanding. For the five-week run in Chicago he lived quite soberly and sensibly — but without Merlo, who took the dreaded dog and returned to Key West. Merlo was himself strangely weak and livid from a constant hacking cough; and neither he nor Williams had the emotional or physical energy for dialogue. This was the major moment of rupture in the declining relationship.

"I was shocked when I heard that they had really split," Maureen Stapleton said. "And it was Tennessee who brought it on. He was paranoid about everything — his health, the opinion others had of him, Frankie's intentions. And it was one of the things Frankie had dealt with so well, that paranoia. I was stunned by their separation, and although I never stopped loving Tenn — who could? — I think it was the craziest thing he ever did. And the craziness began with those awful crazy pills he was getting."

Finally, on December 28, *The Night of the Iguana* arrived at the Royale Theatre in New York. In the first night audience were Edwina, Dakin, Joyce and her father, but the author made no appearance inside the theatre: he paced outside before, during and after the performance. A bracelet of celebrities surrounded Edwina, who chatted gaily with Donald Windham, Judy Garland, Helen Hayes, Lillian Gish and Eleanor Roosevelt. The only one to speak with Williams that night was Carson McCullers. The two writers tried to cheer one another, but without success: he was convinced of his total decline, she of hers. He had remained attentive to Carson, visiting her on her birthday whenever he could make the trip to Nyack, recommending her for Guggenheim Foundation grants, reading manuscripts of her stories and of her new novel, *Clock Without Hands* (whose considerable flaws he saw at once, and which he urged her to withhold from publication — a counsel, unfortunately, that she did not follow).

The second night, Edwina dined with her son and Frank Corsaro at Sardi's. "There was Edwina," Corsaro said, "looking and acting like a grand duchess — and suddenly, to her son's dismay, she asked if she and I could exchange plates. She said my food looked better. When Tennessee scolded her, she just said, 'Well, honey, we do it down home.' This was certainly inconsistent with her famous manners. She was the archetypically mad Southern woman by this time."

The response to *The Night of the Iguana* was uneven; its overt yearning and discussion of matters transcendent seemed to confuse reviewers ready for a sequel to *Sweet Bird of Youth,* or expecting an addition to Williams's range of shocking topics. *Time* magazine was perhaps closest to the truth when the reviewer suggested that it was "the wisest play he has ever written."

The Night of the Iguana is set on the verandah of a rustic hotel on the coast of Mexico, in the summer of 1940. To this torrid, primitive way station come the Reverend T. Lawrence Shannon, a defrocked Episcopal priest leading a group of American women on a tour; Hannah Jelkes, a Nantucket spinster and artist; her aged grandfather, Jonathan Coffin (Nonno), "the world's oldest living and practicing poet"; a group of Germans, exultant over Hitler's early war victories — all of them guests of the hotel's proprietor, the formidably crude Maxine Faulk. Over one steamy day and a stormy night, Shannon confronts the demons of frantic sexuality, religious guilt and emotional confusion, and he learns from both the earthy simplicity of Maxine and the cool serenity of Hannah. At the end of the play, the old poet dies after completing a poem about the quiet acceptance of life's cycles of death and rebirth, and Shannon — with the help of the wise Hannah — accepts the possibility of a changed, healed life with Maxine.

No one could have foreseen then — although several may have suspected — that this would be considered Williams's last great work for the theatre. Certainly it has a poetic depth of compassion, and it allows hope even while it proclaims the author's love for Nonno and for the natural saintliness of Hannah and for the tortured but still searching Shannon. These three characters were closest to the playwright's heart, and they had the greatest value for him as poet, as artist, as struggling believer. Their names were changed late in his revisions, very likely to show — in the similarity of Shannon-Hannah-Nonno — how spiritually linked they are.

In an important way, this is the work that corrects the morbidity of *Sweet Bird of Youth*. In these two plays, Williams dealt with the attraction to youth and beauty (Alexandra's for Chance; Shannon's for Charlotte and other nymphets) — not only for the satisfaction of the flesh, but because each character identified with the ambitions of the young, whose energy was dramatized in terms of erotic power. And because the two characters identify with those young, they also (as Williams well knew) could overidentify with the less appealing aspects of that energy — with youth's unawareness of the passage of time, of the value of sacrifice; with its preoccupation with self and with the demon of fashion. In *Sweet Bird of Youth*, the refuge is the accident of a temporary restoration to work; but in *Iguana*, Williams suggested, there may not even be refuge anywhere in this world (although on this the play is indecisive). What is very clear, however, is that to be redeemed for meaning is to find a way through the jungle, and this we can do only in the company of one another. The terrifying, tangled, primitive garden of *Suddenly Last Summer* has become in *Iguana* full of promise for the future.

His compassion never wavered in this play, as it never did for his family and for his friends — and even as he knew the break with Frank Merlo was irreversible, he could not accept it with cold equanimity. "He was one of the few people I ever knew," according to Paul Bigelow, "who felt he had no basis for making judgments in human affairs. The power of his work is testament to that. There is no character anywhere for whom he expressed contempt. It's the breadth of his compassion and his understanding that gives his plays such power. At the same time, it's not that he offers approval to some of the worst excesses of a character — it's just quite simply the most unselfish compassion. And it was the same in life — he never expressed a severe judgment about anyone. A momentary remark, a sarcastic comment, certainly. But never a moral judgment."

Colleagues recognized the connection between the work and the man too. "His theme," Arthur Miller reflected years later, "is perhaps the most pervasive in American literature, where people lose greatly in the very shadow of the mountain from whose peak they might have had a clear view of God. It is the romance of the lost yet sacred misfits, who exist in order to remind us of our trampled instincts, our forsaken tenderness, the holiness of the spirit of man."

On March 9, 1962, *Time* magazine put Tennessee Williams on its cover and devoted six pages to an appreciative survey of his life's struggles and achievements. "*The Night of the Iguana* . . . is a box-office sellout and much the best new American play of the season. The fact is that Tennessee Williams . . . is a consummate master of theatre." The New York Drama Critics Circle agreed: on April 10 the play was chosen best of the year, a week after Bette Davis, unhappy with the production and her role, was succeeded by Shelley Winters as the boisterous hotel proprietor. To his surprise (but not his agent's) Williams received another accolade that season, a lifetime fellowship in the American Academy of Arts and Letters.

Immediately after the *Time* story, an editor at G. P. Putnam's in New York saw the possibility for an interesting book: the life and career of Tennessee Williams as seen from the viewpoint of the legendary Edwina. Author Lucy Freeman was sent to St. Louis, Edwina liked her at once, and a contract was prepared for her story to be told with Freeman's collaboration. "She simply *was* Amanda," Lucy Freeman said, "there in her cozy house full of Tennessee's awards and photos. She was a perky little lady, a nonstop talker, with a great veil of privacy she could lower whenever she wanted." To the author's credit, however, it must be said that she sustained Edwina's rambling memory, corrected several important lapses in accuracy, and produced a readable memoir, selective because of Edwina's own limitations.

While Edwina opened her scrapbooks and ransacked her memory for anecdotes, her famous son was once again in Europe, fleeing, like Shannon and Hannah, his "spooks and blue devils." Since 1958 he had worked intermittently on a series of reflective dialogues based on "Man Bring This Up Road," the 1953 story about the selfish Flora Goforth and the hapless young man who wanders quickly in and out of her villa.

In July 1962 a short version of *The Milk Train Doesn't Stop Here Anymore* (as he uneconomically called it) was presented — appropriately, in Spoleto, Italy, at the Festival of Two Worlds. Hermione Baddeley and Paul Roebling played Flora and Chris, and Mildred Dunnock the enigmatic Witch of Capri. Unfocused and undramatic, it was like a page of diary jottings, and it is in fact on her notebooks that Flora works (even in the earliest version of this much-transformed play): "I'm more interested in producing literature this summer than in having it read to me," Flora reflects. Like her, Williams had gone away to escape — in his case, the crowds then flocking into Key West: "they're pleasure-seekers, frantic choosers of silly little distractions."

The Spoleto audience was polite, the cast earnest, but the roles lacked what Kazan elsewhere called "spines" — controlling images, characteristics or centers from which the actors could develop and with which an audience could associate.

For the trip to Spoleto, Williams brought as companion (as he did for several other journeys in 1961 and 1962) the young poet Frederick Nicklaus. A graduate of Ohio State University who had moved to New York in the 1950s, Nicklaus had met Williams casually several years before the playwright invited the poet to live with him — and Frank — in Key West. At first, Nicklaus's relationship with Williams was pleasant and positive; their intimacy was sustained by a mutual professional respect. Then, as Nicklaus recalled years later, the domestic situation of a trio became intolerable — especially because of Tennessee's increased consumption of alcohol.

But there was, of course, something deeply hurtful to Merlo about this arrangement. And by tragic circumstance everything in the lives of all three men was very soon altered. In London, where Williams stopped to visit, a telegram arrived from Audrey Wood. Friends of Frank in Key West had called her with the news that he was desperately ill. For once, it was Frank who needed attention and care. Williams was in Key West the next afternoon.

Chapter Eight

DANGEROUS ELEMENTS

(1963–1969)

I feel this chapter ought to begin with a serious comment on the meaning of life, because ... sooner or later, a person's obliged to face it.

— Flora Goforth, in
The Milk Train Doesn't Stop Here Anymore

THE CALL to London, informing him of Merlo's illness, frightened Tennessee Williams. "There were a few people close to Tennessee who loved him over the years," said his old friend David Greggory, "not because he was a great and famous writer, not on a professional basis, but on a human level. Frank Merlo was certainly at the top of the list."

In agreement was Paul Bigelow, another who had known Williams long before, during and after the years with Merlo: "Tenn behaved with a great deal of generosity toward many people, and when Frank needed him he was there."

During the autumn of 1962, a situation had arisen that called for Tennessee Williams's generosity, and his response to almost fifteen years of companionship. In Key West, the tentative diagnosis was at first encouraging: Frank probably had bronchial pneumonia; or he was suffering from mononucleosis, or anemia; or — more alarming — he was to be tested for tuberculosis. All they could be sure of, as late as October, was that he was constantly exhausted, he had a hacking cough, he ate very little, and he and Williams found conversation difficult. Audrey Wood, at the same time, had arranged for Roger L. Stevens to produce *The Milk Train Doesn't Stop Here Anymore* on Broadway in January, and Williams and Merlo parted for a time. Frank would in any case be more comfortable in the warmth of Key West, where his physician could monitor him. Williams, meantime, would work on the script and attend rehearsals with the Spoleto cast in New York.

In January 1963, Frank came north to see Williams and a New York doctor. He stayed several evenings with friends like Johnny Nicholson, visited relatives in New Jersey, and then moved briefly to a hotel. A week later he called and asked to see Williams, and they met at an East Side bar. Frank, with astonishing calmness, told what he had just learned. His illness was inoperable lung cancer.

In fact, Williams had surmised as much: he had remembered his grand-mother's appearance and symptoms from twenty years earlier, and his sus-picions were confirmed by a call to Frank's doctor before they met. At once, he offered every practical and emotional support, but both of them suspected there was little to be done.

The cast of *Milk Train* had noticed Williams's anxiety during the last rehearsals in December and early January. "When he complained about anything," according to Mildred Dunnock, "it seemed to us that he was suffering over something other than the play, and one was fearful of in-truding on a man who was living such an intense level of creativity as well as enduring some personal anguish at the same time. I thought then that the character I was playing, Vera Ridgeway Condotti, was meant to bring out something in [the Hermione Baddeley character] Mrs. Go-forth — she represented the nastiness people thought was in Mrs. Go-forth but was not. And I sometimes thought that in this way the two women represented something about the public and the private Wil-liams, too."

The new year thus began unhappily for both the public and the private Williams. *Milk Train* opened in January during a newspaper strike, but even before the critics could publish their mostly negative opinions, audi-ences were making their decisions. "The opening night crowd," accord-ing to David Greggory, who attended with Cheryl Crawford, "was composed of those who wanted a great success for him, and those who didn't want it to be a big thing at all — it was a very uncomfortable feel-ing for those of us who really cared. At Sardi's afterward it was like being on a roller-coaster, and people who were expecting *Menagerie* or *Streetcar* were totally confused."

When the professional opinions were added to the public's, the roller-coaster ride was over, but only after an upsetting finale: Stevens kept the play running as long as he could, but business was so poor that the clos-ing notice was posted after sixty-nine performances. By that time critics like Richard Gilman had been in the vanguard of a new sourness in the business of reviewing. He wrote in *Commonweal* of Williams's "creative suicide," in an article superciliously and cruelly titled "Mistuh Williams, He Dead," and he expanded his anger for the *Tulane Drama Review* later that year: "The American drama is itself almost mindless; we weep for the intellectual deficiencies of [Arthur] Miller and Williams." A lacerat-ing tone was beginning to infect the writing of a few critics — a callous indifference not only to an artist's past achievements, but also to his present feelings. Apparently Miller and Williams were not acceptable to some academics; that they were intellectual deficients creating "mindless drama" was itself a mindless exaggeration.

"He just didn't have an armor for the criticism offered to his plays in the 1960s," according to Maureen Stapleton. "There was no life for him but his writing, and when he thought his writing failed, he thought it was the beginning of the end."

But not only his writing failed him that season. Very quickly, it became clear that Frank Merlo was not responding to any therapies. To his credit, Williams at once insisted on taking Frank to the warmth of Key West, which Merlo always preferred to New York in any season. Frederick Nicklaus was still in residence there.

"As Frank became more and more ill," Meade Roberts remembered, "Tennessee certainly realized how wrong he'd been about his life with Frank, how unfair and how selfish and ungiving to Frank he'd been in the last few years." He tried to devote equal time daily to his writing and to caring for Frank, who was not yet bedridden nor in need of hospital attention. But Frank felt himself an intruder in Williams's life, and kept to his room.

"It was so depressing to visit," according to Frank Corsaro, whom Williams invited to read new scenes of *Milk Train* he was preparing for a revival out of town that autumn and, it was hoped, a Broadway restaging later. "With Frank ill, Tennessee just couldn't cope for himself with the details of real life. Of course he told me, 'Baby, it's my last play,' and then he told me long, mournful stories about Frank's illness. I felt very badly for both of them, and when I sat with Frank he gave me vague hints about Tennessee's tendency to suicide. By this time, Tennessee had come to believe in his failures even more than his successes. The failures, after all, were tangible and provable, and the successes he tended to think of as unreal or accidents that could never be repeated. He was incapable of relying on himself or his own strengths, and I think this is why he turned to those bereft souls who provided him with easy distractions and no challenges."

In April, Merlo came to New York with Williams and Nicklaus and tried to keep a semblance of social life in New York, and although weakened by simple daily tasks, he insisted on going to see their friend Barbara Baxley in the new Broadway show *She Loves Me.*

"They took me out for a drink afterward," she recalled, "and when Tennessee left us alone for a moment Frank turned to me and said, 'I have cancer and I'll be dead in less than a year.' Just like that. No emotion, nothing. He said it with complete coldness, and from that evening I saw him gradually withdraw. I've always thought he did that to make his dying easier — for himself and for me as his friend, but most of all for Tennessee. Frank was a strong, good man, and I think his illness made him feel ashamed of being so useless to Tenn and so helpless for himself."

The revisions for the planned revival of *Milk Train* were becoming more and more clearly a dialogue with Death, approaching inexorably as the inevitable reality of a woman's age. The reality that had obsessed the playwright since before his fortieth birthday, since the months in Rome that had inspired Karen Stone, had now come into the parlor. "I think Tenn felt a strange guilt about Frank's final illness," Paul Bigelow said, "as if, just like with Rose, there was something he could have done to prevent it from happening."

But there was nothing to do except wait — and try to work, which is what Williams did. He also tried to invent distractions and comforts for Frank, at least one of which was imprudent. He took Merlo and Nicklaus to a rented house in Nantucket for several weeks in July — a period that Nicklaus remembered as emotionally trying for all three, especially since Frank's condition was deteriorating rapidly. By early August, it was clear to everyone that Frank would have to be hospitalized. His roommate at Memorial Hospital, in New York, was a man named Samuel Posnock, who was also from Elizabeth, New Jersey; Frank was at first quite talkative and outgoing with Posnock and with his family.

"Tennessee Williams came to visit Frank Merlo every day during August," according to Sheldon Posnock, who was also there daily, visiting his ill father. "Both Williams and Merlo were very friendly to us, but as the weeks passed and Frank's status deteriorated, it was clear that Williams was very upset, very drained by the ordeal. His attention to Merlo and his caring were certainly very intense and affectionate, and he was clearly upset by his friend's pain." Of those last weeks, Williams later said, "Frankie had an honest dignity. He gave his life to me, arranged everything and never lost a fraction of his pride in the face of the most awful death a person can have."

Cheryl Crawford was an attentive friend at this difficult time. "The breakup with Frankie, which Tenn really brought about, was a crazy thing. Frankie was the only one who really understood him, really knew how to deal with him and help him. When Frankie was dying, there was a new form of grief, and maybe a new form of guilt, for Tennessee to deal with, and I think it just broke him."

As so often in the last weeks of a lingering illness, the doctors could not predict the length of the final agony, and Williams was advised to proceed with his own professional plans. In this case, he was to attend a production of *Milk Train* in Abingdon, Virginia, before the new Broadway staging that coming winter. In early September, Williams went to the Carter Theatre, returning the third week of that month, the night after a dubious premiere.

Next afternoon, Williams went to Memorial Hospital.

Merlo removed his oxygen mask, and with a sudden rush of energy climbed from his bed to a nearby chair. Then he needed oxygen again, and had to be helped back to bed. Williams urged him to conserve his strength, saying that he already looked better — which they both knew was a pathetic lie. The two sat in silence, and when Williams offered to leave so that his friend could sleep, Frank asked him to remain, and not to admit other visitors: "I'm used to you," he said quietly.

Finally Merlo slept, and visiting hours ended. Williams was met downstairs by friends, who took him for drinks at a local pub. When he arrived back at his apartment after midnight, there was a message that Frank had died at eleven o'clock.

There had already been keen losses in his life, and for the first two days a haze of confusion blunted his grief. His beloved grandparents had died in 1944 and 1955, and even the death of his father in 1957 affected him in a deeper way than he had anticipated. Margo Jones had died suddenly in 1955, and before that people whose talents had been so important — Laurette Taylor first among them. But with the death of Frank, there was a wound in his life that never healed, and whose pain was comparable to what he felt about Rose.

Merlo had loved everything in Williams's work except what he considered the occasional lapses of sentimentality, and when he died Williams knew that anything he wrote would perhaps betray that quality. Risking it to deal openly with his sorrow, he wrote a letter to Frank in death, telling him how grateful he was that Frankie had never lied while he — Williams himself — was a person too sick to know the truth. The rooms of Key West, the rooms of East 65th Street, he wrote, seemed roofless and without walls; places no longer had names, and his sleep was now full of dreams of suffocation. He could go nowhere they had been together, he wrote, and nowhere they had never been, for Frank had always been the first to go with him to the new — and therefore terrifying — places, and to make them warm with memories.

As he resumed work on *Milk Train,* he wrote new words for the angel of death to speak to the agonizing widow Flora Goforth, words that described Williams when Frank was buried that September: like her, he would "go from room to room for no reason, and then go back from room to room for no reason, and then go *out* for no reason and come back *in* for no reason." Like Mrs. Goforth, he was mourning for having left a beloved "alone with his death."

Within a week of Frank's funeral, Williams and Frederick Nicklaus flew to Mexico, where John Huston was directing the film of *The Night of the Iguana.* By the end of October they were back in New York, where Williams pitched himself into meetings with the new director for the revised *Milk Train,* Tony Richardson, and with his new leading lady, Tallulah Bankhead. But the results were disastrous, for when the play finally opened she was in bad health and bad voice and could not be heard beyond the fourth row.

"I draw every character out of my very multiple split personality," Williams said later. "My heroines always express the climate of my interior world at the time in which those characters were created."

Just so, for Flora Goforth, whose name combines both his beloved flower-image and his cry — "En avant!" — "Go forth!" or, more fashionably, "Right on!" She expresses his "interior world" more directly than any character in his work, and the play, rewritten for the 1964 production after the death of Frank, became a conversation between himself and Death. Not a mystical or religious tract, as some have claimed, the last version of *The Milk Train Doesn't Stop Here Anymore* is an attempt by Tennessee Williams to come to terms with his relationship to Merlo, to articulate in death what was unspoken in life.

The identification between himself and Mrs. Goforth exists in every scene of the play, a work so intimate that it was virtually impossible for it to reach an anonymous public:

MRS. GOFORTH: My outside is public, but my insides are private. . . .
Blackie [the secretary-companion], the boss is sorry she took her nerves out on you. It's those night injections I take for my neuralgia, neuritis, bursitis. The pick-up pills and the quiet-down pills:

nerves shot ... I'm scared! You know what I'm scared of? Possibly, maybe, dying this summer!

BLACKIE (later): She eats nothing but pills: around the clock. And at night she has nightmares in spite of morphine injections. ... Insists she's only suffering from neuralgia, neuritis, allergies and bursitis. ... Morning doesn't begin on Mrs. Goforth's mountain till she sleeps off her drugs ... when people are very ill and taking drugs for it, they get confused, their memories are confused, they get delusions.

MRS. GOFORTH (later still): Why is it considered ridiculous ... to seriously consider and discuss the possible meaning of life? ... I've often wondered, but I've wondered more lately. ... Sometimes I think that everything that we do is a way of not thinking about it. Meaning of life, and meaning of death, too ... *What in hell are we doing?* Just going from one goddam frantic distraction to another, till finally one too many goddam frantic distractions lead to disaster and blackout?

More painful than *Suddenly Last Summer* because it derived from an actual death (and because it refers to all the antecedent deaths in Williams's experience, including that of Kip Kiernan), *The Milk Train Doesn't Stop Here Anymore* left Williams dry and breathless, naked and wounded. Revised — but as formless as before — it opened the first day of 1964 and closed three nights later. By January 13 the Brooks Atkinson Theatre was dark, the sets were dismantled and he had flown to Jamaica to recover (as he wrote to Donald Windham) from the latest professional disaster of his life — one made even more poignant because it was really a long poem of regret, of tribute, of gratitude and of guilt, for fifteen years with Frank Philip Merlo.

"When he died," Williams said later, "I went to pieces. I retreated into a shell. For nine months, I wouldn't speak to a living soul. I just clammed up. I wouldn't answer the telephone and I wouldn't leave the house." By March, even Williams's visits to Key West were so withdrawn, and frighteningly sunk in drink and drugs, that Frederick Nicklaus moved out. Soon after that, Williams flew back to New York, moved from East 65th Street and subleased a penthouse at 145 West 55th Street. In the spring and summer of 1964 he was virtually a recluse, although he did resume daily visits with a new psychoanalyst with whom he felt more comfortable. "I like [the new one] very much. The old one [Kubie] scared me. He reminded me too much of my father who scared me all my life."

Helpful as he found the new doctor to be, there was such complete withdrawal from people that in fact the writing began to suffer too; there were no longer springs from which to draw, no sources in which his feelings were nourished. At the same time, his fame reached its greatest peak. By 1964, twelve films based on his works had been made, to his great fortune. Three more would follow, in 1966, 1968 and 1969; for screen rights alone, he was paid in excess of five million dollars for these. But beginning in 1964, the celebrity which surrounded him for twenty years was no longer welcome; it became a terrible threat with a terrible toll. He was withdrawing from work to the solace of drugs, and from people to the darkness of solitude. And with this unfortunate shift in the personal and professional bases of his life, a cycle of misery and despair and decreativity enveloped him through the end of the decade.

"I had suffered a great loss in my life," he told an interviewer later, "and I sought oblivion through drugs. I lived from 1963 to 1969 under various drugs, and while I continued to write every morning, through the use of 'speed' injections, amphetamines intramuscularly, I was not in a very real world and unconsciously I might have been seeking death. . . . I went on speed, and my mind started going too fast for the typewriter."

The drugs were then easily obtained through the notorious Dr. Max Jacobson, who became widely known in artistic, political and social circles in the 1960s as "Dr. Feel Good," a provider of substances that were in those days neither strictly controlled nor difficult to obtain. Williams was first taken to Jacobson (so he claimed in a 1981 interview) by Robert MacGregor, his editor at New Directions: "He'd been a patient of Dr. Max Jacobson. He took only little pills that Jacobson gave him. I was in a state of such profound depression that he thought anything was worth trying, so he took me to Jacobson. . . . I had those three years of Jacobson shots that he mailed to me in the various parts of the country." According to Williams (who was in Jacobson's care considerably longer than three years), his error was not only in uncritically accepting the regimen of pills and injections, amphetamines and vitamins and barbiturates ("Nembutal, Doriden, Luminal, Seconal, phenobarbital — the same drugs we all took right through the 1960s"), but he continued to drink alcohol as well.

It must be remembered, however, apart from the grief and the creative pressures that may have motivated his initial visits to this doctor, that Tennessee Williams already had a well-established hypochondriacal personality. Since he was always, as he believed, suffering from cardiac arrhythmia, chronic indigestion, headaches and a wide variety of muscular, ocular and joint aches and pains and disabilities, he had for years been seeking from physicians all over the world treatments for ailments real and imagined. Many of these medications interacted badly, and most should have been taken only under specified conditions. Williams, however, used them liberally — not only for whatever pleasure or comfort they might induce, but because he felt he could not function as a writer if he were at all physically ill. "I have a sort of witch doctor," he said, "a very benign one. How I manage to stay alive I don't know. . . . It's not very comfortable to be a hypochondriac."

It was this unfortunate but fairly common trait that made him easy prey to the more dangerous results of drugs that added psychological to physical dependency. He never pursued the shabby-chic ritual of drug-taking as a bogus mysticism. For him, hypochondria, an obsession for constant work and his essentially Dionysian personality made alcohol and drugs perhaps inevitable. It was the ultimate phase of a frenzied pursuit both to celebrate and to deaden the senses.

By September 1964 he was seeing his new analyst seven days a week, he wrote to Paul Bowles from the penthouse on West 55th Street. He was taking little yellow pills for depression and said they worked for him like magic; to those he added the injections he had been taught to self-administer. With Frank's death from lung cancer he had stopped smoking cigarettes. "I now rely mainly," he said, "on drink and pills. My intake of liquor is about a fifth a day — half Bourbon, half vodka. . . . To pep up, I take half a Dexamyl, and when I find it's necessary to smooth things over I take one and a half Seconals. And when I suffer from acute insomnia, which is also often, I take up to four sleeping pills."

Energized and sedated by drugs, he simultaneously entered a fevered new inner world. The first writing to come from this was a pair of one-act plays which were, to no one's surprise, of violent and uneven quality — *The Gnädiges Fräulein* and *The Mutilated,* which were to be produced in early 1965, but for which sufficient funds could not be procured, and the performance dates were canceled. When this production failed to materialize, he wrote to Donald Windham that he was on the verge of collapse. At this point he realized that it was increasingly dangerous for him to be alone.

"I can't bear to be alone," he told a London critic. "I've got to have someone near me." And so he invited as a paid companion a man he had met through a mutual friend. William Glavin — tall, handsome, alert and long an admirer of Williams's art — moved into the penthouse within weeks of their meeting.

"He never saw much of his friends in the 1960s," Glavin recalled. "He always called it his falling-down period, his 'Stoned Age,' and he knew it was hard for people to be with him."* When a group of friends wanted to attend his reception of a Brandeis University award that season, he decided not to go rather than risk embarrassing others because of his unsteadiness and slurred speech. Even at the worst of times, he never lost a sense of manners or a respect for the feelings of others. At the same time, however, he had begun to classify those he knew: " 'Bigelow is on my side, he always was,' Tennessee told me one day," said David Greggory, "and that made me feel that he was dividing people into camps, those in favor and those against him. It was understood that those who were on his side were very few, a gallant band. And he became very suspicious."

Nothing offered him comfort in early 1965, neither awards nor a twentieth-anniversary production of *The Glass Menagerie,* starring his friend Maureen Stapleton as Amanda, nor yet another revival of *Milk Train* (in San Francisco; ironically, it ran over a month and was well received). "By this time," Stapleton recalled, "the pill situation was so bad that we'd enter a restaurant and before Tenn had had even one drink, he'd fall down. After a while he was always falling down, and it wasn't alcohol — it was the pills and the shots. I wasn't the only one who tried to convince him that Max Jacobson was an exploitive quack, but Tennessee defended Jacobson and insisted that he was doing just fine by him."

Very soon Bill Glavin learned about Williams's gypsy life: before the end of July 1965 they had moved to a thirty-third-floor apartment at 15 West 72nd Street. "I don't remember three mornings that summer that he didn't work," Glavin said. "He might tear it all up and say it was rotten, but he worked every day. Behind all the nonsense and all the sickness there was the courage of the writer. He really wanted to go on writing."

His misery was not helped by the news that his mother, too, was frequently disoriented; in her case, however, the reason was age. She turned eighty-one that summer.

* "I'm a built-in definition of hysteria," Williams told a reporter on his fifty-fourth birthday. "I hate myself. I feel I bore people — and that I'm too physically repulsive."

He went to St. Louis to see what could be done to help her, and he found his mother obsessed with the nation's space program, which she confused with the effects of the atomic bomb. He came back with the tragicomic tale of finding her in the yard, "combing radioactive fallout from her hair and crouching under a tree, like some ancient Ophelia in a mad world of her own." This somewhat grotesque visit found its way into an equally grotesque novella he was then completing. *The Knightly Quest* — with its double-edged title referring also to the protagonist's obsessive sexual searching for nighttime partners — begins as political antiwar satire in the style of *Dr. Strangelove,* but is blurred by muddled characterization and an incoherent narrative whose tone contradicts its theme.

In January 1966, *Slapstick Tragedy* — the combination of the one-act plays *The Mutilated* and *The Gnädiges Fräulein* — was at last in rehearsal with Margaret Leighton, Kate Reid and Zoe Caldwell. Although he was for much of the time unstable and in need of Glavin's constant attention, he had moments of sudden clarity and even of social concern. In a statement prepared for insertion in the play's program, he termed the Vietnam war "incomprehensible evil ... incredibly cruel, and believe me, nothing that will be won out of this war will be worth the life of a single man that died in it." To counteract the fear of the war's extension and also a growing fear of madness, he kept a Russian icon by his bedside, a gift from a friend. "I don't suppose I would keep it there if I did not have some religious feeling.... It isn't associated with any particular church. It is just a general feeling of one's dependence upon [a] superior being."

At rehearsals, Williams tried to encourage his valiant cast. "He laughed so hard at the rehearsals," Glavin recalled. "He loved giving actresses great moments on the stage — giving them fun so the audience could have fun. That cast really loved him, and it wasn't just pity." And to a woman who warned him that even his last-minute rewrites would not save *Slapstick Tragedy* from a critical attack, he replied, "I must continue to dare to fail. That is my life."

The cast was uncertain about the plays' contents, but audiences and critics were even more perturbed, and the double bill closed four nights after it opened at the end of February. Seen as a series of fantastic autobiographical vignettes from his "stoned age," the plays continue the author's anguished self-appraisal.

The Mutilated contrasts one woman's mastectomy with another's ample bosom, and the theme of the play is expressed in the claim that "we all have our mutilations, some from birth, some from long before birth, and some from later in life, and some stay with us forever." A funny-sad crew of outcasts is assembled, around the central figure of the tortured, maimed artist trying to persevere — an image of himself Williams would amplify in the later play *In the Bar of a Tokyo Hotel*.

In *The Gnädiges Fräulein,* a one-eyed performer past her prime has fallen into a wretched state and has become a demented resident of a fantastically rearranged Key West; the cottage-porch setting is his own house on Duncan Street. Written, as he admitted, under amphetamines, this play is unlike any other he wrote. But it has a strangely touching quality as the playwright identified with the battered, forlorn performer, and there is something heroic about the woman who gives everything for a vague chance to be loved. Her dignity, Williams perhaps tried to say, derives precisely from the fact of her endurance in the face of a hopeless situation. In February 1966 Tennessee Williams considered his own artistic, physical and emotional condition hopeless; his plays acknowledged that, even as their creation was a brave bid to prevent his total collapse.*

"Mr. Williams," wrote a critic in a typical reaction to these plays, "is turning old ground and re-working old characters [and] stealing from himself." But apart from any consideration of the merit of the double bill, the charge of self-plagiarism is not sufficient to demerit the plays.

"When critics accused Williams of repeating certain themes in his plays," Robert Anderson said, "they were being unfair. Artists are allowed to go back over the same material. Think of how many variations of water lilies Monet gave us! But perhaps because of the time and attention span demanded by a play, there has been the idea that playwrights especially cannot return to previously covered dramatic ground; they have to provide constantly new ideas. This is an unfair demand."

Perhaps the strangest aspect of the critical charge of repetition that was sounded against Williams in 1966 is how inconsistent it was with the prevailing state of theatre: that season, more than one-third of the sixty-nine new productions on Broadway were revivals, and to considerable critical acclaim.

Audrey Wood, meanwhile, was still working constantly on her client's behalf, placing short stories and poems and negotiating with film studios

* Edwina, who had been brought to New York for the premiere, suggested to her son after the abrupt closing, "Well, Tom, you can always teach!" He was not amused.

and book publishers. As for his private life and dangerous habits, he kept evidence of these from her — which was easy to do by simply avoiding personal contact. She was not unaware of his crises, but because he did not ask for help she rightly refused to interfere.

By spring 1966 Williams had completed a sprawling treatment for a film of *Milk Train,* and Audrey arranged for a contract by which he would be paid $50,000 for film rights, an additional $100,000 to write the screenplay, $20,000 as coproducer's fee, and a percent of any profit.

"I wanted to make a visually lyrical film about the welcome and the terror a person can give to death," said Joseph Losey, who was to be the film's director. "This is what I felt Tennessee's major feeling was in *Milk Train.*" In March and again in November 1966, Williams and producer Lester Persky and Glavin flew to London to meet with Losey. The remainder of the spring and summer Williams and Glavin went to a hotel high above the sea at Positano, where Williams's cousin visited; from there they went to Barcelona and Taormina. Somehow, even after late nights and continued chemical intake, Williams managed to work on the script of *Milk Train* — then called *Goforth!* — as well as on a dramatic treatment of his short story "Kingdom of Earth," and on a strange dialogue for two characters that suggested to his friends an imitation of Pirandello or Pinter.

"When he lost contact with his roots, he turned to others' roots and to their work for inspiration," as Vassilis Voglis put it. "He turned to Beckett's *Godot* for his *Two-Character Play,* and to other plays by other writers later." Humorless and lacking both focus and coherence, that title described this new play — *The Two-Character Play.* It was written, Williams wrote on the first-draft title page, "from the state of lunacy. . . . It is the story of the last six to seven years of the 1960s. The play is about disorientation — these people are lost as I am. They are two sides of one person."

The remainder of 1966 was crucial in the life of Tennessee Williams; it established a pattern of tragic drug dependence that would lead to a nearly fatal collapse almost three years later, and it marred his psychological and physical health for the rest of his life. That it began innocently — with nothing like an overt death wish or a desire to act either irresponsibly or rebelliously — made the results even more heartbreaking.

The central nervous system stimulants that he was obtaining from the misguided and finally criminal generosity of Max Jacobson were beginning, first of all, to have toxic effects. Intravenous amphetamines, commonly known as "speed," caused typical reactions in him: a sense of markedly enhanced mental capacity with little need for sleep, and frequent states of euphoria. But by 1966, tolerance had developed, and he had to have higher doses for similar results — with the concomitant side-effects: compulsive grinding of the teeth, extreme suspiciousness and a feeling of being watched (what his friends and associates called his "paranoia") and the alternation of periods of deep and prolonged sleep.

But in addition to the multiple daily doses of amphetamines, which he injected into his own veins, Williams had over the last ten years been taking, more and more often and in greater and greater doses, a drug called glutethimide, under the brand name Doriden. Introduced in 1954, Doriden was within a year the sixth most prescribed hypnotic drug in America. It was recommended for sedation or insomnia by many physicians, who naïvely believed that, because it was not a barbiturate, it would not be abused and could even be widely beneficial. By 1964 it was clear to pharmacologists that the potential for addiction and the severity of withdrawal symptoms were as dangerous as those of the barbiturates. In addition, treatment for overdose was found to be even more difficult.

Ordinarily taken for only a week before careful monitoring or substitution, glutethimide is usually taken in doses of 250 milligrams (a quarter-gram), no more than once or twice daily. If a person takes two and a half grams daily over a prolonged period of time he is certainly addicted; by 1966, Williams was taking four to five grams daily. (Lethal overdoses have occurred at five grams.) Passersby and acquaintances judged him drunk from this drug, since the effects of glutethimide intoxication resemble those of alcohol: a sluggishness, unsteady gait, slurred speech, hallucinations and a conviction of being plotted against or watched, faulty judgment, sudden and unprovoked laughter or crying, irritability, quarrelsomeness, moroseness, frequent tremors and a chronically dry mouth which the sufferer seeks to remedy by lip- and tongue-smacking and licking.

By 1966, Williams had unfortunately built up resistance to this drug which he regularly took to sleep well at night so he could work refreshed in the morning; or, alternately, to calm himself after a period of intense work. But simultaneous with his need for sleep and relaxation was the desire to be alert and energetic for daily work at the trying task of writing plays, which caused the vicious cycle of amphetamines, and then sedatives. These prescriptions were much easier to obtain and to have limit-lessly refilled in the 1960s. Besides Jacobson, Williams knew doctors in Key West, New Orleans, San Francisco and New York, and few house doctors at hotels would refuse a request from Tennessee Williams for a sleeping tablet. The round of "highs" and "lows" continued, as well as the chemically caused alertness and sedation — artificial stimulation and a state sometimes mimicking coma.

It is important to emphasize that the tyranny of both the ampheta-mines and the hypnotics was almost accidental. In the 1950s and 1960s, the chemical and medical dangers of regular drug ingestions were not considered with the alarm that such abuse has since caused through ex-panded medical knowledge and sad public experience. Just as it was for a long time believed that prolonged psychotherapy was indicated for every small confusion and minor crisis in the life of the average American, so the taking of tranquilizers such as Miltowns was a sign of sensitivity, of a busy and demanding (and therefore glamorous) life in the 1950s and 1960s. (A popular song called "Tranquillizers" lightly and amusingly de-scribed the chemical becalming available to anyone in the slightest dis-tress; in 1960, people were urged to reach for pills the way their grandmothers had urged fresh vegetables.)

With the widespread demand for counseling and for various prescrip-tions to deal with modern living, it was perhaps inevitable that there would be a few exploitative therapists and unscrupulous physicians, ready to keep a crowded list of regular patients by catering to their demands and even creating dependencies. Max Jacobson's name became synony-mous with this abuse; as "Dr. Feel Good," he was the open secret of New York.

In early 1967, Williams and Glavin were in the Virgin Islands, where work continued on both *Goforth!* and *Kingdom of Earth* — without vials of amphetamines when he could, but ordinarily with them in ready sup-ply. In New York, friends became more and more concerned, and when they expressed this to Williams he insisted that there was no danger, that he was simply tired, or that he was going to have a complete neurological examination because he thought there might be a nervous disease. About this time, Audrey Wood and her husband Bill Liebling pleaded with Williams to break with Dr. Jacobson. "No, Bill," Audrey reported Wil-liams replying with slurred speech. "He is a *lovely* man . . . a *lovely* man." This, as Audrey wrote, "was all he would say, over and over again, until the repetition made it obvious he was far from rational."

"I visited him occasionally at West 72nd Street," Elia Kazan remembered, "and he seemed to me less well than he'd ever been in his life — less in control of himself." By midyear even Williams could not avoid acknowledging that his mind was very confused after he had taken (or not taken) his now increased doses. To Oliver Evans in Florida he wrote in early summer that he was going on with his work although he felt wretched. Shortly thereafter, he was told by Audrey that David Merrick would produce *Kingdom of Earth* as a full-length play early the following year; it was based on the earlier short story and a one-act play published in *Esquire* in February 1967. Instead of taking encouragement from this news, however, Williams panicked. It was sure to be his last play, but he was unsure he had the strength to complete it.

In July, he and Glavin were in Spain, and then, because Williams wrongly suspected that Glavin was either hiding or stealing his drugs, they returned hurriedly to New York to have the supplies refilled and the hypodermic needles replaced. By this time, the chemical and psychological effects of the drugs greatly alarmed Glavin. He knew nothing about them and, because he suffered a series of illnesses which in fact required gastrointestinal surgery, never even considered sharing this part of Williams's life. At the end of July, they went to Rome and then to Sardinia, where the filming of *Goforth!* — now unhappily called *Boom!* — would proceed, with Richard Burton, Elizabeth Taylor and Noël Coward in leading roles.

"Swimming, drinking and sleeping — that's all he was capable of in Rome," according to Joseph Losey. "Williams was not much help to us there or in Sardinia. He stayed only three days on the island, and he was clearly in no condition to do any rewriting for us. He left me to cut the script as best I could."

In late August and early September they were back in New York, but then Glavin's need for surgery and a recurrence of Williams's hemorrhoids and his depression over the massive stroke and imminent death of Carson McCullers conspired to bring them South. From Key West they heard of the death of McCullers on September 29. He also heard from Lilla van Saher, and at first he thought he got a wrong message. No, she insisted, it was true: although she was over sixty years of age, she was pregnant! The crib and the infant clothes had been purchased, and he must come to visit her in New York. When he returned North later that year, he learned that poor Lilla had abdominal cancer, the news of which had deranged her.

In early December, "totally addicted and very depressed," as Audrey Wood described him, he went to London for the premiere of *The Two-Character Play*. She accompanied him and later wrote: "When we got to his hotel, he began to say, over and over again, 'I want to die. I want to die. . . .' Nothing but this, over and over." To this Audrey replied: "Well, I'm terribly sorry, you may want to die, my friend, but God is not ready for you. God is not strong enough to take you, it's impossible. You cannot die yet." And with this, she "broke through the spell of his self-pity. Miraculously, he began to laugh. The litany, at least for the moment, was ended." So was the brief run of the play, which the London critics found at best confusing, and at worst pretentious.

Kingdom of Earth opened in Philadelphia in February 1968, with Harry Guardino, Estelle Parsons and Brian Bedford. José Quintero, who directed, recalled that Williams was "very nervous, and his nerves would provoke this laugh that was like a hyena's — sometimes at the worst possible moments. He would be riding the action of the play, and would become more and more nervous as it developed. When the action neared the crisis he would let out one of his laughs, and, of course, it was most disconcerting." The sudden, unmotivated laughter was symptomatic of glutethimide intoxication.

Kingdom of Earth shows Tennessee Williams at a desperate time in his life and career, reaching back to a story and a simple one-act, three-character play in an attempt to wrest a full-length play from it. In spite of its obvious homage to D. H. Lawrence, with the connection between repressed sexuality, an imminent flood and the nature of proprietorship (all contained in Lawrence's *Virgin and the Gypsy*), and despite flashes of humor and poetry, the play never developed into a compelling drama. The characters — the dying Lot, his wife Myrtle and his brother Chicken — are ciphers in an incomplete parable of religious inversion (which was in fact clearer in the story). A static, spiritless work of terror written at a time of spiritual dissolution, it italicizes the playwright's suspicion that he might soon die, and that his estate would pass to unworthy others. The final scene, with a grotesque self-parody in a moment of gratuitous "drag show" as a last crazy joke, crudely parodies everything preceding.

Before the New York opening on March 27, everyone was almost as nervous as Williams. He suggested a change of title to help the play's commercial appeal, and soon the marquee announced the premiere of *The*

Seven Descents of Myrtle, but in spite of that and other last-minute changes the play opened and closed within a month. (At once, Williams blamed David Merrick for the change of title and the subsequent failure of the play. That account unfortunately became taken as fact but the reality — as Audrey Wood, her contracts and those in the Merrick office attest — is that the second title was ordered by the playwright.)

"The cast came over to Sardi's after the final curtain," according to David Greggory, "and they were as marvelous offstage as on. But nobody knew what to expect, because the play itself was far from marvelous. Tennessee finally came in, assisted by several people, but he was stumbling so badly and was so unhappy that the bad reviews didn't seem to touch him at all." His withdrawal continued into May, and although the notices on the release of *Boom!* were as disappointing, Williams sent a letter to Joseph Losey thanking him for his efforts. Once again, his illness and his apparent indifference had not deadened his thoughtfulness. Losey had seen to the final version of his beloved *Milk Train,* and Williams was quick to acknowledge that whatever failures it offered were not the fault of the director, but that its merits were to his credit.

Abruptly, Williams announced to Glavin that in June they must move from West 72nd Street. Quickly and quietly, Glavin did as he was bidden, moving their luggage to the St. Moritz Hotel on Central Park South. Days of city wandering followed — of half-eaten restaurant meals, of half-viewed movies at local theatres, of Williams's long blackouts in his separate suite. Then, in an outburst of irrational, suspicious rage directed at Glavin in public — at a Third Avenue restaurant on June 22 — he accused his companion of indifference, disloyalty and theft. Glavin, hurt and embarrassed, simply left the table, to wait outside. What he did not know for several days was that while he waited Williams summoned a waiter, asked for a piece of paper and scrawled a letter:

> Dear Dakin:
> If anything of a violent nature happens to me, ending my life abruptly, it will not be a case of suicide, as it would be made to appear. I am not happy, it is true, in a net of con men, but I am hard at work, which is my love, you know.
>
> Devotedly,
> Tom

The effect of the glutethimide was becoming more and more bizarre.

* * *

The following week, Dakin received the letter at his home in Collins-ville, Illinois. Unable to locate his brother at West 72nd Street and fear-ing for his life, he notified the police. Four days later, Tennessee (in virtual seclusion at the St. Moritz) had not yet been traced, and when Glavin read this in the *New York Times,* he all but ordered Williams to call Dakin at once, to reassure his family. On Sunday, June 30, the *Times* reported that Williams had indeed been depressed over the failure of *Seven Descents* and of the recent film, but that he was "alive and well."

That was only half true, and when several days later he learned of the death of Lilla van Saher after three more operations for cancer, he said that he, too, was near death.

During the summer of 1968 two deliberately autobiographical plays .occupied his uneven attention — revisions on *The Two-Character Play* and the first draft of *In the Bar of a Tokyo Hotel.* In spite of Audrey's sug-gestion that he consider revising the former for an experimental produc-tion in an off-Broadway house, he insisted that it was his masterpiece. To the end of his life it remained so important to him that he personally su-pervised several productions; invariably they were more highly regarded by him and his friends than by critics or public.

The Two-Character Play (later sometimes called *Out Cry*) has a brother and sister, Felice and Clare, trapped in a theatre during the run of some-thing called *The Two-Character Play.* In the "performance" part of this play-within-a-play, autobiographical elements from the childhoods of Rose and Tom Williams are introduced (parental fights, the Southern setting, the name-callings, the accusations that they are both insane). But in his now fragile state — as he was writing this play — Williams used those elements to establish most plainly the psychospiritual kinship with his sister that had been his obsession in *The Purification, The Glass Me-nagerie, The Rose Tattoo, Suddenly Last Summer* and elsewhere. Although the two characters are parts of Williams himself (as he always insisted), he had always seen Rose as part of himself, and the lost and confined characters-as-single-character in this play is as much Rose as her brother. Obsessed throughout his life with her illness and operation, and with his own life of (he thought) abused freedom, he was aware that from 1966 he too was destined for breakdown. The part of himself that he felt he had lost was the part of himself that was Rose — the virginal, the un-tainted, the Lady of the Roses. The play was a method of establishing in-tegration.

His precarious sense of sanity that year in fact strengthened the identification with his sister even more closely. Imprisoned in the theatre, Clare and Felice are surrogates for Rose and Tom, enclosed within the refuge of a shared asylum. They can neither escape from this nor, as they try, can they kill one another. They are doomed to a cold and endless grief, and to an inarticulate, misperceived love. *The Two-Character Play* represents what for Tennessee Williams was the greatest damnation — the possibility that he had lost, and perhaps never had, even the solace of spiritual intimacy with his own sister. The revisions and restagings of the play were not a repeated antiphon of therapy over the next several years; it was the constantly echoed cry of despair. And it was then, as Bill Glavin recalled, that Williams began to speak of admitting himself to Stony Lodge, to live with his sister forever in the asylum.

At the same time, he created two variants on these characters — the failed, dying artist Mark and his shrewish wife Miriam of *In the Bar of a Tokyo Hotel*. More brother and sister than spouses, this demonic inversion of Felice and Clare admit in the alternating, spastic dialogue that concludes part one:

MIRIAM: Are we two people, Mark, or are we
MARK: Stop there!
MIRIAM: Two sides of
MARK: Stop!
MIRIAM: One! An artist inhabiting the body of a compulsive
MARK: Bitch!
MIRIAM: Call me that, but remember that you're denouncing a side of
    yourself denied by you!

By the end of 1968, Williams and Glavin had returned to Key West, since there was no point in his remaining at a New York hotel: the walk along the corridor to an elevator, or from an elevator to a restaurant, was becoming a dangerous and embarrassing ordeal: "I was writing my plays under speed," he said later, "and I was falling down a lot." Those who spent time with him — Bill Glavin, Maureen Stapleton, Audrey Wood, actors, producers — could not recall a day that was not filled with the fear that he would suffer a fatal fall in public, or alone in his room.

Dakin arrived in Key West with the new year, after a call from Audrey that his brother was in a dangerous state. He found the man unable to complete a coherent sentence, unable to negotiate five steps without stumbling. His eyes were unfocused (and usually hidden behind dark glasses), he alternated long periods of erratic activity wih periods of twenty-four hours of nearly comatose sleep.

A convert to Roman Catholicism when he was in the military service, and a religious man ever since, Dakin Williams asked his brother if he did not think a visit from a local priest might be helpful, or at least comforting and encouraging as a first step toward health. Williams at once agreed, and during the first days of January, Father Joseph LeRoy, a Jesuit priest stationed at the Church of St. Mary Star of the Sea in Key West, visited Duncan Street regularly. From the time Dakin suggested his brother consider entrance into the Roman Church, very little of what transpired was clear to the drugged Tennessee: "My conversion was rather a joke. I couldn't learn anything."

"This is how it happened," according to Father LeRoy. "On Sunday, January 5, I was approached after Mass at the church by a gentleman who asked if he could speak with me. In my office, he introduced himself as Dakin Williams, brother of the famous playwright. He had come to tell me that Tennessee wished to be received into the Catholic Church as soon as possible." Later that afternoon, the priest accompanied Dakin to Duncan Street, where Tennessee provided a cordial if numbed welcome and in reply to Father LeRoy's questions said that he was indeed in despair, that he wanted to have his goodness restored, that he wanted to find God. "He wished to have now what as a child he said he had missed," Father Leroy said, "an understanding of the meaning of his baptism. I found Tenn an eager listener."

And so he remained for the next several days — an eager listener who unfortunately heard very little. Of the goodwill and concern of both Dakin and the priest there can be no doubt: since Tennessee refused to acknowledge that he needed hospitalization, or that chemicals were responsible for his deterioration, he submited with the casual carelessness of the drugged to the spiritual ministrations offered to him. Neither his brother nor the clergyman could assume anything other than his willingness to find consolation and challenge from the life of faith; they later learned, along with everyone else, that for Tennessee it was simply something of the moment. He was never, by even the widest of definitions, a churchgoer; much less did he subscribe to the creed or doctrines of organized Christianity. "I loved the beauty of the ritual," he said later, "but the tenets of the Church are ridiculous." He never had sufficient interest to consider the connection between the two.

On Friday, January 10, Margaret Foresman (managing editor of the

Key West Citizen) and Leoncia McGee (Williams's housekeeper) met with them in the small white church. "It had concerned him terribly that he'd had no success with his plays since Frank's death," Foresman recalled. "Frank's Catholicism was often a topic of discussion with him, and that might have had an influence on his decision to become a Catholic — and of course the guilt preyed on him too. That afternoon he told me that he thought a change might occur in his life because of his baptism."

The event, alas, ignited a minor ecumenical controversy; in the life of Tennessee Williams, not even a quiet religious ceremony could, it seems, pass without drama. It is irregular to rebaptize a Christian: the Roman Church has always recognized the validity of Christian baptism within a non-Catholic (Protestant) denomination, and after Vatican Council II (1962–1965) strict guidelines were issued on the matter to prevent offense to other Christian communions. If one of their members wished to enter the Roman Church, a simple rite of acceptance — without a repetition of baptism — was prescribed. Father LeRoy, not quite sure of those guidelines and wishing to accede to the Williams brothers' requests for a fully ritualized afternoon, was the unfortunate object of an ecclesiastical scandal. "It was [Tennessee Williams's] wish that the rite be repeated," Father LeRoy said later. "Neither he nor I intended to convey the appearance of any doubt regarding the validity of his baptism in the Episcopalian communion. Nor did we intend any other offense." As it happened, the event of Williams's baptism made worldwide headlines — as did every later, irreverent remark that he never took any of it seriously, or that it was done to please his brother.

Before the end of January, Williams had flown to Rome, where he met with Father LeRoy's superior general, the Reverend Pedro Arrupe, the Spaniard who headed the Society of Jesus at that time, an office commonly thought to be so powerful that the holder is called "the black pope" — i.e., he wears not white but black. On his return to Key West, Williams told Leoncia that he had met the black pope. She was delighted and replied that it marked a great step forward when one of her people headed the Catholic Church.

Never hypocritical with Father Leroy, Williams took his "religious period" as an extension of what he called his "stoned age." Rather like the bored Catholic convert in Evelyn Waugh's *Brideshead Revisited,* for whom religion is unimportant if not downright boring, Williams accepted the occasional practices of that winter as unharmful and perhaps even beneficial. But in a number of interviews later, he was inclined to refer to the whole event as "boring."

Exhausted after his visit to Rome, and with almost no resistance to infection, Williams was easy prey to the unpleasant strain of Hong Kong influenza that year, and for almost a week in February he was confined to Mercy Hospital in Miami. On his release, because rehearsals would soon begin for *In the Bar of a Tokyo Hotel,* he insisted that Glavin arrange for them to depart.

After meetings with Herbert Machiz (who had directed *Suddenly Last Summer*), Anne Meacham (who had starred in it) and Donald Madden (who would play opposite Meacham, as the dying artist Mark), Williams managed to accept an invitation to an evening at the home of Maureen Stapleton.

"It was a birthday party for Robert Whitehead [who had produced *Orpheus Descending*]," she recalled. "When Tenn arrived I met him at the door and he just stared at me and said, 'Maw, I've just overdosed.' So I pushed him into the bathroom and gave him two large beakers of warm water laced with mustard, to force him to throw up the overdose. Well, it took me quite a while to clean up — he was violently sick with all those pills. He rejoined the party, however, and he thought that everybody *else* was crazy."

What cannot be explained is how Williams in fact survived 1969, or how he saw to the revisions and rehearsals of his new play. "He stumbled a lot that April during rehearsals," Anne Meacham said, "even when he took over after Herbert Machiz was dismissed. But somehow he was mostly lucid with us."

Daily, Glavin walked him to the theatre, the Eastside Playhouse on 74th Street, "and if he could barely walk on the way, something miraculous happened when he arrived. He sat in the orchestra and directed Anne and Donald, and he was so sensitive and beautiful and encouraging with them. We were all amazed at how he could do this."

After several postponements, the doomed play opened on May 11, after an extended series of twenty-two previews. Critics and audiences were angry and disappointed, although there were almost universal expressions of hope and respect. "One must never forget that, despite his present esthetic humiliation, Tennessee Williams is a thoroughbred," *Time* magazine reminded. "I hope," Harold Clurman wrote plaintively, "that it's not Williams's last testament." Clive Barnes, in the *New York Times,* considered the play "almost too personal, and as a result too painful"; and Henry Hewes and Richard Watts, Jr., who for so long had been among the playwright's most fervent supporters, wrote essays expressing personal concern for him, affirming their affection and respect and their hope (as Watts put it) "that he will soon return to the high estate that has made him the foremost of our playwrights."

The play, as Williams told his cast, was about the humiliation of the artist who, when he loses confidence in himself, his body and his lovers, "hasn't the comfort of feeling with any conviction that any of his work has had any essential value." The eventual fate of the play neither surprised nor shocked him, it seemed; his generally detached state was a kind of emotional bulletproof vest.

But on May 21 there was some redress: he received the gold medal for drama from the National Institute of Arts and Letters, and his acceptance speech has probably not yet been equaled for brevity, wit and boldness:

"I think I'm essentially a humorist, you know, so I'm going to try to tell you something that will make you laugh," he said after Lillian Hellman had presented the award. "One time, Maureen Stapleton received a phone call from a friend who said that so-and-so was getting married, and the caller said, 'Why she is marrying that man, you know he is a homosexual,' and Maureen said, 'Well, what about the bride?' And the caller said, 'Well, of course we know she's a lesbian. And you know they're not even being married by a real minister, but by one who's been defrocked!' And Maureen said, 'Will you do me one favor? Will you please invite Tennessee Williams? Because he'll say "Oh, they're just plain folks!" ' "

Another award was to be presented to him that spring, and unenthusiastic as he was by this time, he had earlier agreed to visit the University of Missouri at Columbia to accept an honorary doctorate from his alma mater. On May 31, he and Glavin flew to St. Louis, where Dakin took them to Edwina's home on Wydown Boulevard. Then in her eighties and still an incessant chatterer, she seemed overwhelming to her visiting son, who withdrew to the basement with a portable typewriter. It was, Glavin felt, perhaps not so different from the situation at home forty years earlier. For three days, Williams was hardly seen except at meals. Glavin cared for Gigi, the bulldog Williams had insisted on bringing with them, and he sustained with good humor the role of substitute son Edwina imposed on him. On the third day of their visit, she suddenly burst into tears, telling him that Tom always blamed her for what had been done to Rose, but that a team of doctors had advised her about the lobotomy — two in favor and one opposed — and that she had been given six weeks to make a decision in which her husband took no part.

On Tuesday, June 3, the Williams brothers, Glavin and the dog went out to Columbia, where the playwright was given the honorary degree and escorted to the Alpha Tau Omega fraternity house where he had lived from 1929 to 1932.

"He was not in good shape at all," according to their host, Dr. Larry D. Clark of the university faculty. "Dakin had to be by his side constantly, and it was clear to us that he was ill when he announced that the journalism department should be shut down: 'You can't teach people to write!' he told us." Moody, withdrawn, uncongenial and suspicious of everyone around him, Williams had never been unhappier.

Before their departure from New York, Williams had told Glavin that they might proceed to Taos from St. Louis — or to San Francisco, and then on to Japan, where the famed Bungakuza Theatre was preparing *A Streetcar Named Desire.* "Poor Tom," Glavin remembered thinking to himself, "he has no idea where to go, or what to do now." One fact was clear, however: he could not much longer remain in St. Louis, for his mother was a torture to him, and her openly anti-Semitic and anti-black sentiments were an embarrassment. "You know," she confided to Glavin with complete seriousness, "the Negro parents don't feed their children so they can all get right thin and their parents can slip them through the mail chute and rob your home!"

On Saturday, June 7, Williams had finally made a decision. Glavin was to reserve seats for a flight to San Francisco. At the Fairmont Hotel there, he joined Williams in his room at odd hours for a meal or a drink — whenever he was summoned — or Williams would suddenly decide to leave the hotel for dinner across the bay, in Sausalito. With his amphetamine injections, he managed to sit at his typewriter a few hours each morning; the rest of the day and night he withdrew into a drugged sleep. The staff at the Fairmont catered to his requests, but within a week they were as nervous as Glavin.

As if Williams were not miserable enough, he had the ill fortune to read *Life* magazine's review of *In the Bar of a Tokyo Hotel,* which appeared that week. Not content with detailing his negative comments on the play, critic Stefan Kanfer also indulged in a vicious *ad hominem* attack against Williams, calling him a "White Dwarf," the label given by astronomers to stars that shrink and fade in space: "Tennessee Williams appears to be a White Dwarf. We are still receiving his messages, but it is now obvious that they come from a cinder.... Gone are his sustained flights of rhetoric — which always bordered on hysteria. Gone, too, are his poetic tendencies, which always risked ridicule.... Other playwrights have progressed: Williams has suffered an infantile regression from which there seems no exit."

Even in his emotional isolation, Williams was devastated by Kanfer's article. He wept — just once — and then kept to his hotel room, refusing to leave the floor for three days; his pain and his terror were mirrored yet again in manuscript pages, this time of a short play he called *The Frosted Glass Coffin,* with its references to heart failure, the problems of old age, the horror of senility and breakdown.

But he was not the only one ill, although he could not recognize that another might require care too. Glavin, who had already required several intestinal operations, needed still another. When Williams insisted that Japan was to be his next stop but that Glavin should return to New York for surgery if he preferred, it was then necessary to find a replacement companion. Anne Meacham, who had stood by Williams during the difficult experiences surrounding the play, agreed to fly to San Francisco and then attend him in Japan. She was to arrive June 19.

During the several days before this, Glavin tried to discourage Williams from a voyage that could only be disastrous. Unable to walk or to perform the simple task of feeding himself, Williams was close to toxic coma; when he knocked over a liquor glass, he accused others of doing it to embarrass him; a plate of pancakes required more than an hour to be eaten; Seconal tablets were still washed down with gin. Equally unfamiliar with the intricacies of drug protocols, and equally concerned, Dakin flew to San Francisco on June 16 and found his brother in a desperate condition. Two days later, Glavin — relieved to depart to the relative comfort of a hospital room — flew to New York; the next day, Dakin, unable to convince his brother to enter a hospital, returned to St. Louis. Meacham arrived at the same time, and the final arrangements were completed for their departure for Japan.

"We arrived in Tokyo on Saturday, June 21," she recalled, "and from the start it was exhausting and difficult. First, the necessary papers had not been cleared for the admission to Japan of his dog Gigi, so the animal had to be quarantined at Haneda Airport, which upset Tennessee terribly. Then, when we arrived at the Hotel New Otani, he was so weak and tired that he just wanted to sit in the lounge for a while. He didn't want a drink, but he hadn't the strength to go to his room." And there, in a bizarre congruence of art and life, the drained, sick artist and his leading lady sat in the bar of a Tokyo hotel. This did not escape the attention of the press, who reported a drunk and disorderly Williams.

The next day, novelist and playwright Yukio Mishima came to pay his respects, and he took them to — of all places — a local Italian restaurant where Mishima's quiet, gentle manner temporarily soothed Williams. But just as Glavin had predicted, the situation was soon too burdensome even for Anne Meacham's patience. Williams's regimen was unchanged — self-injected amphetamines by day, along with Seconal and Doriden — and she was anxious not only for his health but also for his freedom: Japanese drug laws (especially regarding drugs imported by foreigners) were known to be much more severe at the time than America's. She sought help from Mishima, and from Raymond Purls and Walter Nichols.

Purls was an executive of Union Carbide, and he and his wife were living in a Tokyo suburb; Nichols was on the staff of the American embassy. By June 28 they had moved Williams from the hotel to a rented house, the better to insure freedom from public scrutiny. Within days, however, Williams was accusing Meacham the way he had accused Glavin and others: she was stealing his pills and syringes. She telephoned her friend and co-star Donald Madden in New York, asking him to call Audrey Wood and Dakin Williams. She knew the limits of her ability, and Tennessee would have to return to America for treatment — that would be the best thing she could do for him.

At once Dakin made a reservation for Tokyo, but then a call came that Williams had insisted on flying alone from there to San Francisco, and his brother need come only that far. Meacham remained to close the house and settle final details with friends, officials and the solicitous people at the Bungakuza. Williams, as it turned out, had seen only the first act of *Streetcar;* illness forced him to leave.

By July 13 he was in New York and Glavin, released after surgery, resumed the attentive care he, too, might have appreciated. Unable for several days to decide on their next destination, Williams at last chose Key West. For ten days there, Williams slept, ate little, rarely left the house, and wrote the draft of an absurdist political nightmare-drama, *The Demolition Downtown*. One evening, obviously aware of the trouble he was causing others, he apologized to Glavin and offered to read aloud to him — an evening pastime they had once enjoyed together. In a strained and touching effort, he opened a biography of Hart Crane and read the account of the poet's suicide.

Since they had left West 72nd Street in June 1968, Tennessee Williams and Bill Glavin had never been a month in any one place. The restlessness was symptomatic of the sedative's overdosage; for Glavin the constant moving was simply exhausting. On Monday, July 28, they were back in San Francisco at the Fairmont, where Williams continued his self-imposed isolation. In one of his rare conversations with Glavin during a dreadful three-week stay, he again told his companion that he would move to Stony Lodge to live with his sister Rose — after all, he said, he wrote only for her.

He added that the cause of his unsteadiness was a brain tumor, and that the people in the room adjacent to his were plotting his death. Glavin, trying to ignore these irrational suspicions, was keeping account of the Doriden tablets: Williams was then taking more than five grams daily, and it was entirely possible, if not likely, that he might not awaken one morning. Once again, Dakin received an emergency call, and once again he responded by coming to San Francisco, only to be dismissed by his brother five days later. When Williams badgered the hotel staff with constant complaints that the people in the hotel were shouting at him, laughing at him, planning to kill him, Williams and Glavin were politely but firmly asked to quit the hotel.

On August 17 they flew to New York, Williams obtained a bottle of one hundred Doriden tablets, and another black week passed. (Audrey Wood, in spite of her efforts, could not locate him, and he never contacted her.) The following Saturday, they were driven to Stony Lodge, where Williams visited his sister and took her for dinner at a local restaurant. "Rose never took her eyes off her brother," Glavin remembered. A sad, inarticulate connection existed between them; it was a scene from *The Two-Character Play* poignantly sprung to life.

For the first week of September, Glavin attended Williams in New Orleans, where the playwright wanted to visit with Pancho Rodriguez. They met for dinner, and with an irony worthy of the character-reversals in *Summer and Smoke,* Pancho was now leading a professionally stable, quiet life radically different from the one he had known with Williams more than twenty years before. And it was the older man who now seemed childish and unpredictable and destined for grief.

On September 7 they returned to Key West, where Margaret Foresman met them. "I was ready to help my genius friend," she recalled, "but he was in a paranoid state. He insisted someone was going to break in the house and kill him. After he sent Glavin away for a week, he'd call me to come over and check around the house — he was convinced there were prowlers and murderers. He wouldn't call the police himself, he had me do it — he was used to having people do things like this — and when the deputy sheriff arrived, Williams insisted that someone guard the house all night. All that week he became worse and worse."

Foresman called Audrey Wood, who recommended calling Dakin. But he was understandably hesitant to respond when his help was never accepted.

Finally the inevitable crisis occurred. In mid-September, Williams was preparing a pot of coffee in his newly rebuilt kitchen and, as Margaret Foresman remembered, "he fell and spilled some, burning his shoulder. It was not such a terrible burn, but since he dramatized everything he was convinced he was dying. He told me to call Dakin, who came at once. Dakin took advantage of the situation to convince his brother that he had to go to a hospital. And thank God, Tennessee was willing. I think he knew he needed to get off the drugs. This was the most painful moment for all of us. A lot of eccentricity went along with his genius, but now he was really dangerously ill. And because of what happened in the next week, he cut me and Dakin dead for the rest of his life."

What happened saved the life of Tennessee Williams. When Dakin arrived in Key West, he urged his brother to come back with him to St. Louis, where he could enter Barnes Hospital, a first-rate medical center near the family. When Williams agreed, it was the first indication that a seed of life-affirming energy still lay beneath the self-destruction of the last years. There was a brief hesitation, when he stopped to see his mother and gather personal items: he had changed his mind, he said, and would recuperate nicely at her home. Rightly, Dakin forced the issue and drove his brother to Barnes where, the record shows, he admitted himself voluntarily. Physicians determined that his violent, destructive and possibly suicidal behavior warranted the constant supervision and confinement in the psychiatric division, and he was placed (as "Thomas L. Williams") in Room 9126 of the Renard Psychiatric Division; he was denied telephone, mail or visitors for the first several days, and immediately evaluated for total withdrawal from all drugs.

"I was so demented," he admitted later, "that even the television programs in the psychiatric ward seemed to be personally directed at me. Even Shirley Booth's little program, *Hazel*. I thought Shirley was making veiled innuendoes about me."

And then it happened. The total withdrawal of all drugs — especially the strong doses of Doriden — took a toll on the third day, in a way that could not have been foreseen in 1969. He had three *grand mal* seizures in one morning, suffered a violent upset of normal body chemistries, and had two heart attacks within the next two days. These reactions, it is now known, are typical of sudden withdrawal from prolonged megadoses of glutethimide; why Williams was in fact put on the "cold turkey" treatment is unclear, but it is important to stress that the effects of such withdrawal were not always foreseen. As of October 1, no one was quite certain he would survive.

Gradually, however, he responded to treatment; slowly, awareness, lucidity and normal speech returned. His mother and brother were at last permitted brief visits, but the greetings were not what they expected. With his remarkable resiliency there was a new articulateness, and it was neither quiet, humble nor grateful. He had always been terrified of hospitals and confinement, he told his brother: Dakin knew what a terrible thing it was to put him there, and that was just why he did it; Dakin hated him, he wanted him dead, he wanted only his money. Shortly afterward, Dakin Williams was permanently excised from any mention in his brother's will.

For the rest of his life, Tennessee Williams could never admit that he needed in 1969 the sort of drastic treatment for an illness that afflicted celebrities from Judy Garland (that same year) to, later, his friend Elizabeth Taylor, the singer Johnny Cash, even a First Lady, Betty Ford. These people admitted their problems, sought help, and (except for the doomed Garland) recovered and have tried to help others similarly afflicted. Perhaps it was only guilt that led him to consider the experience as reprehensible; his open admission of it later should not be mistaken for anything other than shame.

But there is another element too. All his life, Williams had been somehow able to avoid the extreme to which Rose (and Blanche DuBois, Catharine Holly and others in his plays) had been subjected — unwilling confinement in an asylum. Now what he had always feared had become a reality, and, unable to see how his life had been saved, he instead accused his brother of making real the terrible event which hitherto had been dealt with, as if by sympathetic magic, in his art. What must never happen, happened. "It's true," Elia Kazan said later, "he was absolutely terrified of confinement and of breakdown. And of course there was the example of Rose."

As Maureen Stapleton reflected, "Tennessee could never accept that what Dakin did for him saved his life. He would have been dead in no time. Dakin stepped right in and saved his life. It's that plain. I called Tennessee later and told him he should be grateful to his brother, but he never forgave him for what he did, and when I said that, he turned on me for a time, too. He made up his mind that Dakin was the enemy, that Dakin had done this awful thing to him. A blind goat could see that Dakin acted unselfishly, but Tennessee could never see that point. And he remained unconvinced for the rest of his life."

His return to health, the doctors had to admit, was nothing less than astonishing. By early December he was back in Key West, playing with Gigi, telling Bill Glavin the horrors of institutional life, inviting friends for drinks and inspecting the completed patio garden and new kitchen appliances.

"He looked better than I had ever seen him," according to Father LeRoy. "He said he was limiting himself to one drink a day, and only limited pills."

Chapter Nine

ENDURANCE

(1970–1976)

Sometimes you work on a play by inventing situations in life that correspond to those in the play. . . .

— Clare, in *The Two-Character Play*

Chapter Nine

FROM 1970 to the end of his life, Tennessee Williams continued to work at his craft with his habitual, insistent energy — daily, and sometimes on more than one play, story and poem simultaneously. Only rarely, however, was the result satisfactory to him, to audiences or to critics. Tennessee Williams was mentioned as the great American playwright whose creative powers went into decline after 1969, and in an important way that much was true. The extreme partisans — friends and colleagues with varying accuracy of judgment — were indeed more enthusiastic than he about his writing. But no artist's powers remain at the most fervent creative peak, none of the gifts retain their sharpness and brightness undimmed. In fact, few artists in our time worked so long and with such brilliantly fruitful results as he: from 1944 to 1960, there was no doubt that he was the most consistently serious, the most poetic (and not merely the most controversial) playwright in America.

As cultural fashions shifted, so did his own fortunes, however, and he endured inner exhaustion and outer confusion, the effects of physical dependencies and psychological depletion. His body was wounded, his mind was ravaged, his spirit had been shattered — by the death of Frank Merlo, to be sure, but just as violently by chemicals. It would be naïve to pretend that this confluence did not affect his art. With great courage and simplicity and hope he kept on, and he was always grateful — sometimes even desperate — for the interests of producers and actors and directors.

But as the writer Louis Auchincloss suggested in a perceptive tribute, Williams after 1969 "never recaptured his old stature. Why? [There was] a lack of coherent thinking that wrought havoc with Williams's later theatre, [and a] sentimentality that ultimately broke through walls unsupported by any basic moral fabric."

That may seem a harsh assessment, but in fact it defines the enduring value of Williams's great early achievements as much as it laments what came after; it describes the contours of the works in which Tennessee Williams gave an accurate diagnosis on the condition of an era, and of what Rilke called a tendency of the heart. What happened in American culture in the 1960s and after has eluded the understanding of very many statesmen, teachers and parents — as well as men and women, young and old, everywhere. To expect that the upheavals in contemporary life would not also leave behind some great artists like Tennessee Williams would also be naïve — especially if, as was the case with him, there were the concomitant problems of poor health, emotional instability and psychological frailty.

Somehow, Williams summoned the old Dionysus in himself, to go on working, to go on seeking for a resting-place with someone, somewhere; the romantic voyager continued to travel, even if he often seemed as doomed as the Flying Dutchman. Somehow, for the unaccountably long period of thirteen years after his worst collapse, he found the courage to go on going.

But as Auchincloss added, "Dionysianism, undiluted, is, in the last analysis, only chaos," and chaos was always the predominant motif of Tennessee Williams's life.

In his golden period, however, his gift shone as a spectacular blessing on the development of art, and his late decline cannot diminish the splendor of those early accomplishments. *The Glass Menagerie, Summer and Smoke, A Streetcar Named Desire, Cat on a Hot Tin Roof, Suddenly Last Summer, The Night of the Iguana* — these remain among the great literary and dramatic works of our time, and at least a few of the short stories ("One Arm," "Three Players of a Summer Game") will perhaps be recognized as masterpieces of that genre.

"I hope I can continue," he told a reporter from the *New York Times* at the beginning of January 1970. "I hope I can escape. I think I can. I've been through a great catharsis ... I've been abusing myself for at least seven years. Although I continued to work, God knows I didn't work well."

There was a great hope of newness with the new year, and clearly a desire for change. The press, which had not missed a nod of his head during the last two years, reappeared, pens and cameras and tape recorders at the ready, as soon as he emerged into public view. He wanted to give the impression that much had altered; indeed, he no longer seemed dependent on drugs and alcohol, and he had a new companion. But there was an uncharacteristic bitterness in his voice. His brother Dakin was mentioned in angry phrases, and the staff at Barnes Hospital was denounced. He was glad to be returning to work, but his judgment was at least questionable.

"The young men who attended him in the early 1970s," David Gregory believed, "were very pretty and not very bright, but I don't think he really cared very much one way or the other. Merlo had been the one person for whom he felt a really deep personal attachment. Unfortunately, the feeling that replaced deep attachment, the situation with later companions, had the tone of employer-employee. Still later, when he was drinking heavily again, I think he accepted people into his life that he would not have accepted earlier. Some of them seemed to me like people who were in it for what they could get out of it."

With this new era, Williams paradoxically lost another type of steadiness in his life, that of companionship. In the last months together with Glavin, during 1970, the suspiciousness caused by drug intoxication had become ingrained. He left a two-page note for Glavin one day, requiring them both to read what he said was one of his three favorite modern plays, Strindberg's *Dance of Death*. He was living, he reminded Glavin, for his work — and since he believed that Glavin was destroying him, he accused him of the worse sin of destroying that work.

The choice of *The Dance of Death* for required reading is indicative of how Williams saw his life in 1970, for Strindberg in that play depicted a long-term marriage as a strange symbiosis of love and hatred. The story of Alice and Edgar is that of a dying man who attempts to continue his dominance of his wife after years of emotional imprisonment. Finally she attempts to retaliate, and their relationship becomes like the medieval *Totentanz*, in which Death personified triumphs over all mortals. But Williams also knew that the couple in Strindberg were self-parodies; they dispense with maniacal delight a mixture of cruelty and pain. That this grotesque black comedy should occur to Williams as he considered the end of his companionship with Glavin tells us how consistently theatrical he saw his own life. But it also tells us that he was capable of a self-fulfilling prophecy. The drama of his illness required an epilogue if not a sequel; the dismissal of Glavin would do nicely.

When he spoke to the reporter from the *Times,* Williams had come to New York to promote the revival at Lincoln Center of *Camino Real.* He appeared on David Frost's live television program, and before Maureen Stapleton, Jessica Tandy and Eli Wallach joined him onstage, he submitted to the usual inquiries about his family and his past life. Guarded in most of his replies, he then answered Frost's question about homosexuality in his work with the first public statement on the matter as it related to himself: "I don't want to be involved in some sort of a scandal, but I've covered the waterfront."

In this and other interviews that winter, his ingenuousness about his collapse and his hospitalization was remarkable; for the present, however, he chose not to elaborate on what had slipped out to Frost before a commercial interruption. His willingness to discuss his "stoned age," however, was to his advantage as a celebrity, for in the late 1960s began a time when the public fed on "sincerity" and "honesty" and "letting it all hang out," especially if the news was sordid or at least intimate. Williams at fifty-nine was taking all the laundry from the baggage, hanging it out for public scrutiny. But in the curious nature of such things, the more horrific his admissions were, the more people gasped in admiration. It was consistent with a new pattern: murderers, assassins, terrorists, irresponsible celebrities and cheap crooks in government office were being paid enormous sums, and appearing on television talk shows, to describe their stories to a public famished for trash. Tennessee Williams was not at all like them, but for a while many were confused about his attitude to himself.

It is odd, therefore, that when reporter Tom Buckley spent several days with Williams in Key West with a tape recorder that spring, Williams later resented the appearance in print of the details of his home life and social intercourse, which he had offered with casual abandon. Perhaps he wanted to be controversial — the hard-drinking, openly homosexual writer with nothing to hide — and at the same time, a man of *his own time,* a Southern gentleman from a politer era who would never abandon propriety and privacy. In any case, he was not always so alert or so guarded that he was able to pre-edit his own remarks.

The day after the television appearance, he flew back to Key West. Other reporters and some university students wanted to discuss a strange story published that month in *Esquire,* "A Recluse and His Guest." His sudden retreat was in fact a clue: *he* had been the recluse in his own period of confusion. He had not much interest in the story, however, and he preferred to resume work on what he thought would be the greatest plays of his career. He could not admit to himself that he was barely strong enough or disciplined enough yet to produce any serious piece of work.

"I work so hard," he told David Greggory at that time, "because I know it [success] will happen again."

Greggory was not so sure: "I wasn't at all convinced it would happen again, however. If you live at the top of fame and material success, of course, it's hard to live anywhere else. At this time he began to group people in terms of those who believed it would happen again and those who didn't. There were times when he felt he might prefer becoming the unofficial dean of American theatre, and the mentor to younger play-wrights, or a much sought-after writer in residence at a prestigious uni-versity, but that feeling didn't last. He had to feel he could do it again — hit the jackpot."

But during the last dozen years of his life, Tennessee Williams was clearly of divided heart about this matter. He would sustain with good grace the changing patterns of Broadway, and the changing taste of the theatregoing public; he would often agree to the first productions of new plays in modest circumstances, and he would be grateful for these pro-ductions. What mattered was that he continued to work in the theatre.

If serious work was indeed his major goal in 1970, he apparently ap-proached it with some diffidence, for in Key West he celebrated his re-turn by hosting a number of parties, often for as many as forty guests. Liquor flowed, guests brought uninvited friends, and factions and cliques quickly formed round him: *This* one must not be trusted, since he tells everything to Tennessee.... *That* one is a friend of so-and-so, and he passes information on to such-and-such a crowd, so be careful of *him*.... *This* one is an aspiring actor and wants to be Tennessee's houseboy but he also wants money for drugs.... *That* one sleeps with *this* one in order to ingratiate himself with *those over there* ... And so it went, with all the charm of typical social carnivores. Key West, once a quiet retreat where he could work well, live a reasonably ordered life with Frank and Grand-father, was now really no longer suitable for him.

"The crowd there really did not help him to live well or to work well at all in the last years," according to Edwin Sherin, a director who collaborated with Williams in the 1970s. "They gave him nothing but a phoney admiration, and took whatever they could get."

The social life he had known changed, too, as his friends died. There were no longer women like Lilla van Saher to shield him with her warm, crazy humor, and to hold forth with a crowd nearer his own age. Then, in April 1970, his loyal, tortured friend Marion Black Vaccaro died. "He took care of everything," according to Father LeRoy, who looked in reg-ularly on Williams. "He made the funeral arrangements at St. Paul's, he invited their friends, he gave a reception."

At the same time, Williams was trying to improve his image in the community. For the benefit of the local library's expansion fund, he agreed to read from his own work at the Waterfront Playhouse on May 2. A vision in white — he was, after all, a risen soul — he arrived in a white suit, a white lace shirt, and white buckskin loafers. With a decanter of red wine at his elbow, he stood in a pale blue light, rather like a movie ghost, and read from *The Frosted Glass Coffin* and *A Perfect Analysis Given by a Parrot.* The two hundred guests attended politely, but there was some shuffling when he read certain sexually explicit paragraphs from *The Knightly Quest,* and then some coughing when he read the text of an angry dialogue he had had with a Barnes Hospital doctor, and then a series of homosexual love poems, most of which were later published in his collection *Androgyne, Mon Amour.* Williams was back, and Key West — like it or not — had him.

In the audience was Audrey Wood, who had come to visit. Her husband had died the previous December, just as Williams was returning to Key West, and she had looked forward to the trip south. She helped in the preparations for the evening, obtaining the rose design he wanted for the program leaflet, meeting with local press people, and generally straightening difficult turns in the social road. For her arrival, Williams arranged a pleasant ceremony, a public ground-breaking for the small garden and gazebo to be added to his property. Just to the left front of the yard, he had planned the Jane Bowles Summer House, named for his friend and Audrey's client, and for her 1953 play (*In the Summer House*) about a tyrannical mother. The earth was turned by Williams and Wood on Saturday afternoon of that same weekend, and by June the little wooden structure was complete. The Monroe County Library Association, grateful for his public reading in May, presented him with what he had requested — Key West rock roses that were at once planted by his gardener, Frank Fontis.

When Audrey returned to New York, she took a sheaf of poems, short plays and one short story she placed immediately, called "Happy August the Tenth," the story of two lesbian lovers who live in an East 61st Street brownstone. The two are plainly modeled on Tennessee Williams and Frank Merlo, and the story is a gentle tribute to what was and what might have been. Elphinstone (as in "elf in stone") is the variant stand-in for the author himself: she has become hard and somewhat bitter, is in psychoanalysis, was born under the sign of Aries at the end of March, and regularly visits her aged and confined mother in an upstate institution called Shadow Glade. Her mate, Horne, has a different group of friends and has grown emotionally distant.

His real-life August was followed by a three-month cruise to Asia, on which he was accompanied by his old friend, the poet and teacher Oliver Evans. After a brief visit to the retired streetcar named Desire in New Orleans, they departed from Los Angeles for Honolulu, where they visited Christine Jorgensen (one of the first to undergo sex-change surgery), and then they continued to Yokohama. There, on October 1, Yukio Mishima dined with them and warned Williams about his drinking. After Hong Kong, they finally arrived at their destination — Bangkok — and there Williams learned that Mishima, before a great crowd, had committed ritual hara-kiri and was then beheaded, a death that did not surprise Williams: the suicide, he later wrote, was "because [Mishima] felt that . . . he had completed his major work as an artist." Oliver Evans's interpretation of the death was even more curious than Williams's, however: in an article for *Esquire* he maintained that Mishima's death was an inevitable decision resulting from his having achieved a perfect physique — there was no bodily ideal left to pursue.

In Bangkok, Williams submitted to minor surgery to remove a fatty tumor from his breast, a simple procedure he was told could be treated in any large city. In California and Yokohama, however, he told the press he was dying of breast cancer; that report was spread around the world at once, and Williams was able, when he finally returned to America at year's end, to hold forth on his brave insouciance in the face of what might have been terminal disease.

By early 1971 he had revised and retitled *The Two-Character Play* as *Out Cry;* its second production, later that year, caused an event of such emotional and professional significance that there are almost as many versions about it as there were productions and versions of *The Two-Character Play/Out Cry.*

Responding to a request for a play, Williams gave George Keathley, the director of the first version of *Sweet Bird of Youth,* the revised manuscript called *Out Cry.* By this time, Keathley was manager of the Ivanhoe Theatre in Chicago, and he at once saw fascinating possibilities in the play. He suggested a summer revival, with Donald Madden and Eileen Herlie as players. "I knew it bore the stamp of illness and confusion," Keathley said, "but he was very devoted to it and I thought we could make it work."

From the start, however, the project was doomed. Instead of working with Keathley and the cast, Williams withdrew to a Chicago hotel room where — perhaps because the bases and resonance of that play were simply too frightening and depressing — he resumed a round-the-clock dependence on drugs. He no longer self-injected amphetamines, but he was able to find a doctor who agreed to supply him with shots of methylphenidate hydrochloride, sold under the brand name Ritalin, which was then available by injection. A nonamphetamine stimulant, Ritalin must be given cautiously to unstable patients — especially those with a history of drug dependence or alcoholism. At the same time, Williams needed something to counteract the effects of the Ritalin, and to sleep, and since he was afraid of returning to Doriden, he requested a generous supply of Nembutal, a barbiturate brand of pentobarbital sodium he always called "yellow jackets." These he obtained in the highest dosage, one hundred milligrams. A short-acting sedative, Nembutal takes effect in ten to fifteen minutes and lasts for about four hours — enough for him to sleep between long bouts of revising the play.

Pre-production for *Out Cry* was, therefore, difficult for the players and director. By the time of the preview performances in early July, Williams's anxiety had been caught by everyone else. The entire time in Chicago was frantic, as he wrote to producer William Hunt, who at the same time was staging his short play *Confessional* at a Maine summer theatre.

Audrey Wood had sprung to Williams's defense by firing an indignant publicized letter to *Life* magazine when the devastating attack by Stefan Kanfer appeared, and when the *New York Times* republished it as an advertisement for *Life*. Now, she knew that this play — with its intimate importance for Williams — would encounter difficulties even if Williams were in the best health. At once she went to Chicago for the last rehearsals and previews, intending to remain through the opening and assist in any way possible; her presence alone, she might have suspected, could benefit her client in dealing with the press.

"Audrey wanted to protect him until the play was ready," according to Anne Meacham, who was in Chicago at the time. "Tennessee was terrified about *Out Cry* and he never should have asked for a fully staged production of it. When it encountered troubles he had to blame them on someone. Audrey was closest. She was a mother to him in the way his own mother had never been, and he turned on her the way one can turn on a parent."

In *Memoirs,* Williams told his account. In one of his hysterical mad scenes, he turned on her after the second preview performance and quietly said, "You must have been pleased by the [cool] audience reaction tonight. You've wanted me dead for ten years. But I'm not going to die." He admitted that this was a terrible thing to say, but that he was convinced she had neglected him for a decade — especially during his years of drug abuse — and that he felt like a lost child.

But Audrey offered a somewhat different account: after the preview, she was met backstage by Williams, who — in the cast's presence — "swiveled about to stare at me, and with the vigor only he possessed, shouted at me, 'And as for you, you have wished I was dead for the last ten years!' . . . As I exited, I heard him say, 'That bitch! I'm glad I'm through with her!' "

George Keathley, who was present, confirmed Audrey's version, with this nuance: "We were all in Eileen Herlie's dressing room after the performance, and I suggested to Tennessee an idea about altering a line of dialogue. This set him off in a rage — 'How dare you make such a suggestion to me,' and so forth. Audrey, trying to smooth the situation, said quietly, 'Tenn, it may be a good idea — just listen to George for a moment.' And with that he turned on her and shouted, 'And you! You've wanted me finished and dead for years!' Audrey was devasted, Tennessee remained furious, and that was the end of their relationship. Still in a very bad state, he left Chicago immediately after opening night, July 8."

This unfortunate incident — over which both Williams and Audrey grieved for the rest of their lives — could never be healed. Because he felt she no longer gave him total dedication and because, as he told his next agent, he felt she was simply too old, he had even before that night decided to seek another representative: "I want my work in younger hands and she is seven years my senior."

"This was another shocking episode in Tennessee's late life," Cheryl Crawford said, "and none of us could make much sense of it. He had turned Frankie away, he had turned against his brother after the breakdown, and now he turned against Audrey."

Unfortunately, the final severance of the relationship was, ironically, due to Audrey's near-sightedness. At a New York hotel restaurant later that year, Williams went to greet her, but when she reached out she was momentarily unsure it was he, and she withdrew her hand. Misunderstanding her and just as vulnerable, he walked away, angry and (he thought) rejected again.

"Audrey was a great lady," according to Robert Anderson, her client for over thirty years, "and she could act very much the grande dame.

Whether the split between her and Tennessee was precipitated by his rudeness or by his earlier decision to leave her, we'll never know for sure. But Audrey had a way of speaking somewhat imperiously to men by beginning, 'Now, young man —' and this may have, at one bad moment, rubbed Tennessee the wrong way. As for his statement that he wanted a younger agent, well, that's the remark of an aging writer who's afraid that his powers may be declining and who hopes that a change of agent may bring about a change of his fortunes or a deepening of his talent."

Wisely, however, Audrey — who never lost her concern or devotion for the writer she had represented since 1939 — saw to it that he remained within the agency of which she was then a senior member. By the autumn of 1971, she had effected a meeting between Williams and Bill Barnes, and for the next seven years Barnes gave his new client as much loyal devotion and attention and personal sacrifice as any agent could. At their first luncheon, Williams announced, "I want my name back up in bright lights, Bill!" And to that end Barnes devoted himself, as Anne Meacham and others said, "twenty-five hours a day." In time, he, too, would be followed by a thoroughly dedicated professional.

In October, Williams was back in Key West. He kept an active correspondence with Barnes, asking that he not be dismissed as a working playwright. He added that he lived to write, to swim, to love. By November, Barnes, inspired by the Maine production of *Confessional,* had interested a trio of New York producers in the play, and he wrote to Williams about expanding it for off-Broadway as a full-length drama. Williams in turn wrote to Hunt in the poignant tone of a man unsure of his current worth, claiming that he felt only half-alive when he was not at work in the theatre.

By November's end, Williams had determined once again that a change of locale would improve his spirits, and he and his companion had moved to a New Orleans hotel while he sought an apartment. Almost immediately, they went on to Houston, where Nina Vance was reviving *Camino Real* at her Alley Theatre. Actor Ray Stricklyn, who had met Williams in New York twenty years earlier, was cast as Lord Byron, and he recalled Williams's presence on opening night in November 1971 as "a very sad occasion. . . . Tennessee's condition had degenerated — he was on pills and arrived intoxicated. He was completely out of it. He was practically carried backstage, presumably to pay his respects to the cast. But he could have been in any city in the world that night."

It seems clear that the situations which triggered Williams's return to drug dependence were invariably connected with the theatre, or with theatre people. In many social situations, when he entertained a few neighbors, or when engaged in other important activities, he could be quite sober and alert. One of those occasions was his attendance, in December, at an anti–Vietnam war rally at the Cathedral of St. John the Divine in New York. He spoke against the war and was greeted with some bewilderment by young activists who were not quite sure what era he represented.

While in New York, he met often with Bill Barnes: he intended to be involved in every aspect of the forthcoming production of the extended *Confessional,* now called *Small Craft Warnings.* He reminded Barnes that when his play was staged, the playwright himself would be the real subject of the reviews; too much was at stake for a risk, and he intended a major revival not of a play, but of himself.

Until rehearsals brought him to New York in the spring of 1972, Williams shuttled uneasily between New Orleans, Key West and New York, anxious, as he wrote in notes for the published version of the play later, that a "remnant of life . . . redeem and save me . . . from a sinking into shadow and eclipse of so much of everything that has made my life meaningful to me." He wrote to William Hunt, who agreed to direct the play in New York, that he hoped desperately for the restoration of his destroyed reputation. His last play (as he said it would be) had a humanistic purpose that the corrupt press and public of New York must be made to appreciate.

In 1972 Williams made his second house purchase, this time in New Orleans, at 1014 Dumaine Street. He lived in modest quarters on the second floor and rented out several smaller units, which were managed by a resident housekeeper-superintendent. Later, he added a landscaped patio and a small kidney-shaped pool — so small, in fact, that he often walked to the nearby New Orleans Athletic Club, where he had retained membership over the years. At the same time, he continued revisions on *Small Craft Warnings,* for which Hunt and the new producers had set an April 2 opening date at the Truck and Warehouse Theatre on East 4th Street.

The final weeks of rehearsal for that play, however, were a stormy period. Personal differences between Williams, Hunt and the cast led to Hunt's withdrawal from direction, and for several days Williams himself led the cast; Richard Altman was then engaged to undertake that task. In vain, the playwright sought to have the April opening postponed. He felt the play was "inviting disaster" with the cast "groping after lines [and] mugging.... [We] have been warned by two [preview] audiences that the sea is very rough."

But his anxiety about the critics' reactions was not entirely warranted. Although most thought that the evening was more a series of character revelations in the tradition of Eugene O'Neill's *The Iceman Cometh* (with which it shared the barroom setting), there were none of the personal attacks that he expected. The collection of reviews was mixed, but there was no personal vituperation, nor even the veiled attacks that had hurt him before. His frailty that season was well known in New York, and there was apparently an unspoken agreement not to discourage a man who told everyone he had been broken by the theatre to which he had given his life.

With the play open (and, as it happened, showing a profit quite soon), Williams departed for Purdue University, in Lafayette, Indiana, where he accepted an honorary degree and introduced the actors Olive Deering and her brother Alfred Ryder, who performed *The Two-Character Play.*

"In spite of a certain timidity and uncertainty that he'd had all his life," recalled Ryder, "he showed a compulsion to charm everyone." Olive Deering was an especially welcome guest at Purdue, for she had been a good friend to Williams for years, and she had succeeded Anne Meacham in *Suddenly Last Summer* in New York; she played the same role to equally great acclaim in Los Angeles later, and would appear in *Vieux Carré* in 1977. "Tennessee was very gracious," according to Deering, "but it was getting harder and harder for him to camouflage his tragic life, his deeply tormented life." Williams loved their readings at Purdue, and several years later he asked them to act in the same play off-Broadway in New York.

He returned to New York at the request of the publicist for *Small Craft Warnings,* and submitted to dozens of interviews and promotional ideas that became embarrassing and sometimes bizarre. Williams himself was turning into the attraction, the barker who would perhaps be more interesting than the play, but he would bring them in. When the play moved uptown in June, he went into it in the role of the alcoholic doctor. But there was too close a resemblance between art and life, as he had once said of Diana Barrymore's desire to play Alexandra del Lago. Onstage frequently that summer — only to improve business off-season — he stumbled over his lines and others' and ad-libbed outrageously, addressing the audience (and thus disorienting the cast) and generally advertising the very condition for which he dreaded condemnation. "It's a successful little play," he said later, "but it's not a major work. It's badly constructed, with one monologue after another. I enjoyed acting in it very much, but the other actors hated it because they didn't know what I was going to say — I ad-libbed so much!"

Bill Barnes, always ready with professional support, had advised Williams against this kind of showmanship, but to no avail. Williams went on with this, and with an appearance on a television newscast in which he warned small crafts about an impending summer storm. His manner for these increasingly hammy tactics was that of a man under the influence of Ritalin injections, which, as he openly admitted, he was obtaining all that year.

"He liked people to pay a lot of attention to him, even when it was somewhat embarrassing," according to Paul Morrissey. A member of Andy Warhol's film production crew, Morrissey had become a director, and had met Williams at this time through the curious Candy Darling, a transvestite actor who (as Cherry Davis) was appearing in *Small Craft Warnings* as the indomitable, oversexed Violet.

In his suite at the Elysée Hotel — the very one formerly leased by Tallulah Bankhead — Williams drafted in July the short story "The Inventory at Fontana Bella."* This grotesque tale concerns a century-old Italian principessa who lives in a wild, hallucinatory world of memories of past lovers. She forces her household of servants and a doctor to take her to Fontana Bella, her estate across the Bay of Naples. En route, her entourage exchange (*à la* Boccaccio's *Decameron*) tales of sexual exploits, and they engage in appropriate illustrative actions; after one such, the principessa dies. The story is noteworthy insofar as it fuses images of uncontrollable sexual urges with the fact of death: Williams was exploring sex from its first to last experiences in this (as in all the stories he wrote that year and the vast majority thereafter). There is a link between the habit of insatiable sexual arousal, guilt and death. And the need for penance is regarded wistfully, but it is invariably overwhelmed with a lunatic lewdness.

That autumn, he also completed "Miss Coynte of Greene," in which the same theme is emphasized: the erotic life of a thirty-year-old spinster

---

* The story seems based on Mrs. Goforth's remark in *The Milk Train Doesn't Stop Here Anymore:* "I had an intuition that things were disappearing ... fabulous china, my Sèvres, Limoges, Lowestoff. . . . Half of it gone, decimated! And my Medici silver . . . gone! That's what the inventory disclosed!"

(like Alma Winemiller) is awakened after the death of her mother, and she leads a life of frenzied promiscuity. Years later, visiting the grave of her first lover, Miss Coynte — now sixty-one (as Williams was when he wrote the story) — is on the verge of a new, interior revelation. But Williams draws back, afraid: "In her prone position among the roses . . . the clouds divided above her and, oh, my God, what she saw. . . . Knowledge of . . . Well, the first man or woman to know anything finally has yet to be born. . . . It's time to let it go, now, with this burning inscription: *En avant!* or 'Right on!' "

And onward he moved. He was invited to be an honorary juror at the Venice Film Festival in August, and he gladly attended with Barnes, Morrissey, Warhol and actors Sylvia Miles and Joe Dallesandro. At the Cipriani Hotel, Venice, activities took on an atmosphere vaguely reminiscent of the glamorous literary-social set popularly connected with the Riviera in the 1920s — fashionable, attractive, monumentally self-indulgent. Williams was disappointed by all the films screened except Morrissey's *Heat,* which starred Miles and Dallesandro; he spent an entire night talking about his story "Two on a Party," which he thought would be the perfect vehicle for them. For years, his friend the producer Lester Persky hoped to realize that project.

But at the end of August, Williams returned alone to New York while the others remained in Italy: he had been notified by the company of *Small Craft Warnings* that box-office business had decreased, and he resumed acting in it. He also resumed an inchoate companionship with a young Vietnam war veteran named Robert Carroll, whose writing and person he very much admired. This relationship deepened intensely over the years, and even after they eventually lived apart, Williams maintained a profound affection for Carroll, and an unshakable belief in his talent. Only Carroll and Rose Williams were mentioned as personal beneficiaries in the last will and testament of Tennessee Williams.

When Morrissey returned to New York in September, he invited Williams to rest in Montauk after the closing of *Small Craft Warnings*. There Williams stayed in a sparsely furnished cabin at Deep Hollow Ranch, where he revised *Out Cry* for a projected Broadway revival the following year. A picture of English actor Michael York was set up over the typewriter — "my inspiration," Williams told Morrissey, who recalled Williams's "enormous vitality, in spite of about thirty bottles of pills and several bottles of liquor that were strewn around his rooms." His work, his swimming, his medications — these provided buffers against loneliness for several weeks that autumn, his companion having for the time traveled elsewhere. In *The Night of the Iguana,* the defrocked Reverend Shannon observes that "people need human contact." Just so with Williams: "I need to be touched and held and embraced," he said that year. "I need human contact. . . . Age bothers me only in this area; at my age, one never knows whether one is being used as an easy mark or if there is a true response."

"He had a sometimes disastrous need for companionship," according to Paul Morrissey. "He simply could not be left alone for any period of time that summer or in the fall, back in New York. He depended entirely on others for advice — not only about his plays, but about all the practical details of everyday life."

The desire to see *Out Cry* succeed on Broadway became an obsession in 1972, and on revisions of this play he worked with an almost manic frenzy in Key West, New York and New Orleans throughout the rest of the year. But when it finally opened on March 1, 1973, at the Lyceum Theatre, *Out Cry* disappointed and confused both audiences and critics. About this time, speaking of this play, Williams described more and more openly the link between himself and his sister:

"I've had a great deal of experience with madness; I have been locked up. My sister was institutionalized for most of her adult life. Both my sister and I need a lot of taking care of. . . . I'm a lonely person, lonelier than most people. I have a touch of schizophrenia in me and in order to avoid madness I have to work."

As he worked and reworked the elliptical dialogue between Clare and Felice ("This is me," he told Bill Barnes that year, "and it's my most personal work"), Williams inserted stage and character descriptions: the exterior setting, he insisted, "must not only suggest the disordered images of a mind approaching collapse but also, correspondingly, the phantasmagoria of the nightmarish world that all of us live in at present. . . . [Felice] is a playwright, as well as player, but you would be likely to take him for a poet with sensibilities perhaps a little deranged."

It is in the work patterns and the comparisons of manuscript revisions of this tortured play that the inner world of Tennessee Williams is most clearly revealed, for *Out Cry* was not merely the revised text of a play that documented an earlier breakdown: it was also a description of a continuing state of decline. At every stage of reentering this play, of re-presenting it, it became the artistic canvas on which he drew the harsh and disjointed lines of his own illness. "I consider myself scattered," he said at the time of another revival of this play. "Very scattered. Psychoanalysis didn't put me together at all. I'm about as together as Humpty Dumpty after the fall."

Audiences, critics and admirers of Tennessee Williams's art could not have been expected to know that the image he tried so valiantly to offer in the 1970s — that of a healed survivor — was simply that, an image. On closer examination it could be seen, however, to have shattered, as he said. The public, whom he continued to address in his work and in interviews and all the glittery tawdriness that publicity and celebrity demanded, could not have known that he was only apparently a well man — and often enough he did not even seem very well.

Whenever he said he was ill and confused and frightened, friends and colleagues too often contradicted him: he looked fine, they said; he was working hard; all was well. But he was more honest. As an artist of the first rank, Tennessee Williams felt the tragedy of the modern world — of its alienation, of its loneliness, of its loss of a sense of the transcendent. He heard its echoes of pain and despair earlier and louder, within himself, and in his great plays he told us what was wrong. But at the same time, he lived — by his own ready admission — on an alarmingly grim course of self-destruction.

Out Cry closed on March 10, after twelve performances. The critics were as disappointed as the New York public, sensing the energies Williams had put into it but feeling left outside of it. Each of the critical reactions lamented the burial of authentic feeling in a morass of verbal and dramatic confusion, and it was Harold Clurman who came closest to the mark when he expressed a hope that Williams would abandon his confessional, turn his attention away from himself, and reach out to an affective, dramatic consideration of others — for that, after all, was his great strength. Williams needed to change the topic of his personal and professional meditation, but no one was willing to suggest this to him.

Within days, he was in Los Angeles, where he introduced the film of *A Streetcar Named Desire* at the Los Angeles County Museum and, on Sunday, March 18, spoke to a luncheon gathering at the University of Southern California, where he accepted praise from its president, the local press and several actors. He also went to Grauman's famous movie palace, looking for Vivien Leigh's footprints, and he visited William Inge, who was even more ill and withdrawn than Williams had been in the last year. Williams's birthday was celebrated after he attended a new production of *Streetcar*, with Faye Dunaway and Jon Voight.

"His companion called me and invited me to the party," David Gregory recalled, "and most of the cast was there. To be frank, I don't think Tennessee really cared about this or any other revival. The great performances were past, the play was finished, and no one was really going to add very much. He retained cast approval over the years, but I heard him say many times that if the actor was nice enough, what the hell, it didn't make any difference." (For the next three years, there was every month, somewhere, an important American revival of a Tennessee Williams play: *The Glass Menagerie, Summer and Smoke, A Streetcar Named Desire, Cat on a Hot Tin Roof, Sweet Bird of Youth, The Night of the Iguana* — even *Kingdom of Earth* — were staged by major companies with star casts.)

During his Los Angeles visit, Williams welcomed Harry Rasky, the Canadian filmmaker who had had his cooperation in producing a filmed documentary celebrating Williams's life and career. Rasky brought a completed print of it for a birthday celebration. At the same time, Williams's magazine and television interviews altered significantly once again. Perhaps because his plays were no longer shocking people, he was trying to do just that with his life (in April 1973 *Playboy*, for example). Now he was speaking more intimately, more crudely in fact, about his sexual history. This new bluntness, of course, was just what journalists and interviewers wanted, and just what "sold" in the 1970s, as was described above; the more personal, even the more imprudent a public figure became, the more the statements were valued as newsworthy. When Tennessee Williams himself replaced his characters, detailing the private corners of his life, it was the new showmanship replacing art.

That spring he was working on an original play (for televison, he said, since his theatrical experience had recently been so unhappy). Titled *A Second Epiphany* (and later, less felicitously, *Stopped Rocking*), it was a story of madness and confinement, of breakdown, of infidelity, despair and self-destruction. Written for and dedicated to his friend Maureen Stapleton, it was presented to her that year. Later, as she recalled, "a number of meetings were held with producers and network people and public broadcasting executives. Then they asked for more revisions, so he rewrote. Then we had more meetings, but we just couldn't arouse sufficient interest, and it was abandoned."

Also in progress that spring was a short story he called "Sabbatha and

Solitude," about a writer full of sexual energy who keeps her Italian lover in a Maine cottage and tries to sort out her failing professional life and her fierce sex drive. "I detest confinement, you know," Sabbatha says, and the omniscient narrator comments: "Going mad can have a certain elation to it if you don't fight it, if you just pull out all the stops, heedless of consequence . . . there is slight difference between the noun 'decade' and the adjective 'decayed,' just an accent." The story stops abruptly with a further link between profligacy and death; even her crippled state does not deter Sabbatha from paying for sex.

The story was completed during a sea voyage that brought him the news of two deaths. On May 4, Jane Bowles died; then, in Rome, he read of the death (on June 10) of William Inge, who had also been for some time in the grip of alcohol and drug dependence.

"Near the end of Bill's life," according to his close friend Barbara Baxley, "when he was in great trouble, I turned to Tennessee. He gave detailed instructions on what to do. He said, 'Don't let them put Bill where they put me,' and he asked hard questions so I could try to help Bill's sister decide what to do. 'What has he taken?' he asked. 'How much of this and how much of that?' He advised me how to go about getting Bill the proper help."

But nothing availed, for all their concerted efforts, and on June 10, Inge succeeded in a last suicide attempt. Although his feelings about Inge had passed from romantic attachment to mentorship, then from collegial support to a deep resentment and jealousy, Williams had recently felt a real concern for Inge's suffering, which in so many ways was like his own. He was deeply upset by Inge's death, and soon after he said quietly to the grieving Barbara Baxley, "Don't you think that our whole lives, yours and mine and Bill's, have been one long nervous breakdown?"

He wanted also to be with Paul Bowles, and now, on his journey, that was possible. For two weeks in July he visited Tangier where, according to a companion, "he was not at his most buoyant. . . . He was preoccupied with finishing a play, *The Red Devil Battery Sign*. He was exceptionally restless, having cut short a stay in Italy, as he would cut short the stay in Tangier."

The visit was difficult for everyone, not least of all because Williams's restlessness was exacerbated by drugs: "I take Nembutal myself," he said. "But only one, to fall alseep." The other drugs were taken at other times, along with alcohol.

From Tangier he proceeded to London — before returning to New York and the Elysée Hotel. Once again in a scattered state, he visited several physicians and obtained, as he wrote in a letter to Sylvia Miles in August, medications for high blood pressure, high cholesterol, for heart palpitations, for anxiety. He was also revising *The Milk Train Doesn't Stop Here Anymore,* and he thought it would be a good vehicle for her and for Michael York, perhaps in London. But he was in no condition to make any serious decisions until he had rested in Key West. There, in September, he was deeply affected by the death of Anna Magnani, who succumbed to cancer, in Rome, at the age of sixty-five. For her coffin he sent twenty dozen roses.

The return to Key West resulted in another story in the "Rose cycle," written at exactly the time he was considering bringing his sister to live with him. Titled "Completed," it was about twenty-year-old Rosemary who endures a painful social debut. She has a grandfather named Cornelius and, because of her mother's selfish manipulation, takes refuge with her Aunt Ella in a timeless world of confinement and seclusion. Her life is "completed" before it begins.

The story threw him, for several days, into a blank depression from which he emerged to return to New York in December to receive the first centennial medal — as "the foremost dramatist of our day" — from the Cathedral of St. John the Divine. He also met with Kate Medina, the editor at Doubleday with whom Bill Barnes had contracted the previous year for Williams to write his memoirs. Tennessee had originally hoped to call this project *Flee, Flee This Sad Hotel,* from a poem by Anne Sexton, who had also documented her mental breakdowns in her writing. But when she took her life the following year he settled on the simpler *Memoirs.*

This collection of random thoughts and impressions of his life (a first, 650-page draft was completed in October 1972) could not have come at a less auspicious time for Williams, and to her credit his editor worked bravely for two years to give shape to the palette of impressions. In the revised version of *Milk Train* he was writing at the same time, Williams inserted extended comments about the enterprise of publishing these reminiscences: "My memoirs, my memoirs, night and day," says Mrs. Goforth. "The pressure has brought on a sort of nervous breakdown, and I'm enjoying every minute of it because it has taken the form of making me absolutely frank and honest with people."

Although the original intention of his own memoirs was to attempt a

new form for the autobiographical genre — images and impressions
floating to the surface of his mind while he was performing in *Small
Craft Warnings* — *Memoirs* suffered from the chaos, inner and outer, that
marked his life ever more acutely in the 1970s. As in his interviews and
press appearances, he wrote frankly about sex — more frankly, in fact
than he could in any other medium. But such frankness must not be
confused with real psychological intimacy or spiritual self-disclosure, and
in fact *Memoirs* conceals more than it shares, misrepresents more than
it documents, omits major events, confuses dates and, as every critic
lamented, tells virtually nothing about the playwright's career. For a
writer who insisted that his life was his writing and that to write was the
core of his being, this was a curious treatment of the life indeed: the
craft is mentioned casually here and there as if it were an avocation.
This is not beguiling humility, it was partly deliberate obfuscation
and partly the incoherence of the 1970s. Kate Medina stitched and rearranged, and Barnes encouraged them both. The book that resulted was
often spicy, sometimes witty, never self-approving and always madden-
ingly disorganized. Near the conclusion of the first draft, Williams had
written — on October 1, 1972 — that he had just completed a task
for which he had been duly engaged but which he was incompetent to
discharge.

For his friend Anne Meacham, Williams created in early 1974 another
role, actually a revision of *The Gnädiges Fräulein*. But after various problems before and during production, the play — into which both director
and star had put considerable emotional energy — fared even less well
than in 1966. As *The Latter Days of a Celebrated Soubrette,* it was seen for
only one performance in the spring at a church hall in New York. Another revival — of *Out Cry,* in Greenwich Village that June — contained
excessive cuts, as would the numerous productions to follow across the
country in the next several years. Few found it more coherent.

Interviews continued throughout the year, and work on three new
full-length plays in which he made valiant attempts to inject an easier,
gentler style and a more traditional structure. But he took advantage of
opportunities offered to travel to Puerto Rico and California, in addition
to the normal, sudden jaunts to New York and New Orleans to approve
revival casts, to meet with his agent or editor, to accept an award, to
grant an interview, to do a campus reading. Restless travel was the single
constant characteristic of his life, then as always.

But he also paid regular visits to Rose in Ossining. No matter the weather, his mood or his level of energy, his sister was never neglected. Often he brought her to New York for a few days, and they strolled, shopped for clothes, saw a movie, lunched at the Plaza. Rose chain-smoked in private and public — which, because of Frank Merlo's death from lung cancer, disturbed Tennessee more than Rose. But she was in all respects a lady of great dignity, and she very often greeted passersby with a Windsor wave of her right hand, whispering that it was her duty as queen of England to greet all her children. At dinner, she invariably ordered a soft drink, but when it was served she would not touch it until her brother had sipped it first and assured her it contained no gin. At such moments, he was convinced there were vague memories of Edwina's tirades against liquor. Harry Rasky recalled watching his film about Williams in New York with Rose and her brother present. "The entire time she listened to the voice on the television set, but she stared at her brother in the room."

About the same time, Williams seemed to be considering the place of religion in his life. "I never defined it precisely to myself. In times of great distress I pray ... the act of prayer is consoling. And back of existence there has to be a creative force ... otherwise we wouldn't exist!" His spiritual life was indistinguishable from his artistic quest, however, and the formalities of Christianity did not interest him; it would be difficult to imagine him feeling at ease in a crowded church. If asked by a prodding interviewer to detail his pattern of worship, he parried: "I love to receive Communion, but I'm usually working on Sunday morning, so I take Communion at funerals."

But back of the humor and the vagueness, it was clear there was also concern. Working on *The Red Devil Battery Sign* in late 1974, he inserted a telling line beginning with a prayer: "God, in whom my heart fervently believes ..." — and the play describes, among other less clear concerns, the crisis of faith in both God and man.

In early 1975 he moved freely between cities and manuscripts, interrupting work on *Red Devil* to polish a scene on a seriocomic fantasy titled selfconsciously *This Is (An Entertainment)*. In New York, the National Arts Club presented him with a gold medal for literature on February 20, and the dinner was attended by Elia Kazan and Maureen Stapleton, among others whose confidence was dear to him. "My obligation is for me to endure," he said, and often repeated this over the next several years.

The endurance was manifest that spring in his work in Key West, mostly on *The Red Devil Battery Sign*. To direct, Edwin Sherin was engaged; he had in 1974 staged a revival of *A Streetcar Named Desire* in London with Claire Bloom as Blanche, and Williams had very much admired it.

"In Key West that spring, I found Tennessee lonely and worried about his health, but pushing on," Sherin remembered. "A typical day began with his rising at five in the morning, and setting to work at once in his small studio. He finished by eight or nine, and then we had breakfast by his pool. Scene by scene, we went through the typescript, making changes. Then he swam, and after lunch he'd sleep. In the evenings we always went into town."

But by this time there was a group in Key West who took advantage of Williams, according to Sherin: "There was a loud and boisterous crew who weren't really worthy of him, and when he was in his cups he was especially vulnerable. At times like this he seemed helpless. He was very protective of me, since he knew I wasn't quite at home with them — and I thought, well, he wasn't either. He had so much more to offer. With those hangers-on, he lost some of his focus and identity."

Also that spring, Edwina arrived for a visit. Now in her ninetieth year and sometimes disoriented, "She was a hard lady to reach," Sherin said. "But Tennessee catered to her every whim, although it was clear — and he said it — that he neither liked her nor felt comfortable with her. I don't think he was very clear really what he felt about his family deeply. But when it came to the play, and why and how he wrote what he wrote, he had enormously keen perceptions. Apart from the writing, I found him terribly shy and rejected, as if hesitant about reaching out to any director. Alone with his work, he had more confidence."

In May, Williams returned to New York, to congratulate others and to promote his own work. Paul Newman and Joanne Woodward were honored by the Lincoln Center Film Society, and Williams, in a bright red dinner jacket, came onstage to introduce a selection of film clips. "This country has served its time with moral decay," he said somewhat enigmatically, in tones of doubtful sobriety, "and the redemptive power is in the country's culture."

The promotion and publicity that month surrounded the publication of his second novel, *Moise and the World of Reason*. What the editors at Simon and Schuster had hoped would be a major literary event turned into a major disaster; readers agreed with critics that the incoherence and lack of sustained tone or theme destroyed the work.

Essentially a partial autobiography linking his Greenwich Village life in the early 1940s with his difficult time during *Small Craft Warnings,* the novel is a lightly veiled counterpart to *Memoirs,* without which it can scarcely be comprehended. The narrator is a failed, thirty-year-old writer with an unconventional, sex-crazed friend named Moise who shares her art the way she shares her bed — prodigally. Interwoven are Williams's real-life and openly named friends, Christopher Isherwood and Don Bachardy, Jane and Tony Smith and a host of others; these private connections did not help the general reader through a tangle of times and feelings and cross-purposes.

There, too, were Frank Merlo's hospitalization and death, travels with Marion Vaccaro, childhood scenes, constant journeys — all bearing the veil of fiction. The novel is a conversation piece among three aspects of its author: the young man he remembers being — talented and idealistic but expert only at sexual athletics; the mature playwright he has become, now in decline, "a has-been attempting a comeback at the Truck and Warehouse [where *Small Craft Warnings* opened]"; and the alter ego Moise (based on his artist-friend Olive Leonard), the sexually voracious artist in whom the Smiths — most loyal of all friends — persistently believed. (Among his fraternity brothers pictured in the 1932 yearbook for the University of Missouri was the handsome Matt H. Moise, whose name was borrowed for the title character.)

A grimy novel about the terror of failing powers in sex, art and faith, *Moise and the World of Reason* depends for its effect on many incomplete sentences (which even the characters wonderingly appraise). It is Williams's most overt homosexual statement (before *Memoirs,* published later that year), but it celebrates no self-understanding, no liberation to adult living — only a gray accommodation to the ravages of time. The novel was dedicated to Robert Carroll.

The unpleasant reaction to this unpleasant book could be diluted only with the hasty business of the next production, for as *The Red Devil Battery Sign* approached a June opening in Boston, there were script revisions and design problems; producer David Merrick still hoped, however, to bring the play to New York later that year.

Anthony Quinn and Katy Jurado joined Claire Bloom in the cast, but their energy and dedication, with Sherin's, could not save the play, a disjointed, unclear story of political terrorism and social enmity. With a pervasive fear as its major emotion — fear of being followed, of being drugged, beaten, overheard, misjudged, confined — *Red Devil* is not at all a political manifesto, as some have claimed, in spite of its allusions to the assassination of President Kennedy. In fact it is a treatment of Williams's drug-induced paranoia, which he believed was mirrored by a national paranoia. The title itself is the clue, for a "red devil" is the popular jargon for secobarbital, a short-acting barbiturate which, under the brand name Seconal, he used liberally right up to the time of his death. That drug, like all others, was dangerous for him, and that it warned like the flashing neon sign advertising an identically named brand of battery appealed to him all the more; thus it reinforced desire with danger, the personal with the public. But again, as with *Out Cry,* his personal anguish was related to the "cutting through the skull" that was performed on his sister, and which is mentioned here along with the second act's numerous other references to the details of Rose's earlier years.

Confessional and private or not, the response from audiences was at first polite, then impatient; the critics, however, were furious: "Dreadful," wrote Kevin Kelly in the *Boston Globe.* He found a "lurking pomposity in [Williams's] ever-darkening vision.... It is all utterly raucous." And Elliot Norton, who had for more than thirty-five years admired Williams's plays, found it "unfocused.... It needs to be rewritten." And so it was, but subsequent European and British productions managed only minimally to improve its wild admixtures of sense and nonsense.

"Part of what made him really sick," according to David Greggory, "was the realization that his level of creativity didn't remain the same. Nothing else remains, why should that? But Tennessee didn't want to acknowledge that. The realization that just working hard and constantly doesn't necessarily 'do it' was hard for him to see. After the failure of *The Red Devil Battery Sign,* I thought, 'What will happen to Tennessee?' He always bounced back, and publicly at least he said he had ideas for reworking failures. But by the mid-1970s, he was unable to accept that he wasn't going to do what he once did."

Before the play closed after ten days in Boston, on June 28, Williams fled to Rome; before his departure, however, he approved Sherin as director of a planned revival of *Sweet Bird of Youth,* which would star Irene Worth and Christopher Walken. It opened in Washington that autumn, and continued a healthy run in New York through early 1976; if anything, it showed that even the lesser but earlier works by Tennessee Williams could be successfully revived. These productions brought money and attention and a new generation of admirers; they also revealed the sharp decline in his ability to structure a drama, or even, apparently, to select a consistently sustained narrative idea.

Throughout the autumn, he was back in New York: for a revival of *Summer and Smoke,* for multiple interviews and media appearances surrounding the publication of *Memoirs,* and for rehearsals for another revival of *The Glass Menagerie,* again with Maureen Stapleton as Amanda. (Her performance as Serafina in a New York revival of *The Rose Tattoo* in 1966 had been also greatly praised.)

"By this time he was a *cause célèbre* of the season," she said. "A lot of *Memoirs* seemed designed to shock for its own sake, and Tennessee was becoming that way in some social situations too. He would talk of various details of his sex life to embarrass or to shock, or for whatever reasons I couldn't figure out. At the same time he was a wonderful person to be with most of the time. He saw everything with a blinding clarity."

Theodore Mann, whose association with Williams went back to *Summer and Smoke* in 1952, produced and directed *Menagerie* for Circle in the Square's new uptown theatre. "Tennessee came to the first rehearsal in November and he frequently interrupted to say, 'Let's change that word or phrase,' which made the time very exciting for all of us — it made *Managerie* like a new play. He told us quite openly how it was based on his family — himself, his mother, and especially his sister. He was totally devoted to her."

Before that revival opened in December, Williams had already begun work — and play — for several weeks in and around San Francisco. The American Conservatory Theatre there, under William Ball, had engaged Gene Persson as producer-in-residence; through Bill Barnes, negotiations had been concluded for ACT to stage the work in progress, *This Is (An Entertainment)*.

"There was a lot of talk about Tennessee when he arrived in San Francisco, because of the recent publication of *Memoirs,*" according to Persson. "He was offered a suite free of charge at the Clift Hotel, but he preferred the less formal El Cortez nearby, and there he settled in for rewrites and rehearsals."

The form and tone of *This Is* resembled *Camino Real:* the play is a dreamlike, hallucinatory, kaleidoscopic jumble of scenes in which a Count and Countess try to withstand the attack of an alien, unseen enemy from their base in a European hotel. Crude and disjointed, it lacks the poetry of the fantastic *Camino Real,* and even as a work in progress its subordinate theme — the same as *Red Devil,* that American society is on the brink of collapse — is lost in fragmented diction, unclear characterization and dizzy narrative. Little was clarified by rapid-fire alternation of slapstick, farce, songs, multiple scene changes, the apparently gratuitous introduction and disappearance of half-understood characters, and the interruption of dialogue by coy asides to the audience. One of them allows a rare mention of the playwright's brother, alluding to Dakin's current political aspirations: "Go Dake! He carried Peoria, too, in the last primary. Who needs Chicago?"

This is demanded extraordinary energies from cast, crew, technical staff and director Alan Fletcher. While they plotted the action, costume and set changes and timings of music and special effects, Williams and Robert Carroll drove daily to Kentfield, in Marin County, to swim. Back in San Francisco, his life was very active in the evenings. He was also very generous to several young writers: Williams read their work, offered criticism and financial assistance, and sometimes retired with them to their hotel rooms or his. He frequently came to the ACT offices, where he met with students and apprentice actors. "During rehearsals in December and January," Persson recalled, "he rewrote vast amounts of material and was in quite good spirits. Some of the dialogue, however, was very blunt sexually, and that eventually cost us some subscriptions."

During rehearsals, Williams rushed off to Vienna, for an end-of-the-year revival of *The Red Devil Battery Sign* at the English Theatre. That city was not, however, appropriate for a play of such pessimism and sordidness with its bestial gangs and multiple onstage deaths, its barbarous language and muddled pieties. Like so much in his late work (and so little in his masterworks) sexual motifs were prominent, and psychological aberrations were gratuitous rather than markers of deeper turmoils. Accidents of life masqueraded as its deepest level. It is difficult to say whether this continued decline infected the revised version because he thought it was what the audience wanted, or because he thought it was all an audience would be capable of receiving. In any case, he returned to San Francisco full of unrealistic expectations that *Red Devil* could be further reworked and presented, perhaps in London, the following year.

Prior to the opening of *This Is,* friends of the ACT presented, at the Geary Theatre, "An Evening with Tennessee Williams," at which he read poems, scenes from plays and a short story. Because of his easy humor and unassuming attitude with his audience, the evening was in fact more warmly received than the play two nights later. One San Francisco critic found *This Is* "a sadly, even sorely deficient work"; the visitor from *Variety* thought it "terribly depressing." Even after the dust had settled backstage, a Williams scholar had to admit that the fault was not in Williams's desire to experiment, but in the uncritical acceptance of an unformed, sloppy work: Ruby Cohn wrote in the *Educational Theatre Journal,* "He is such a grand old man that I suppose no one will tell him when a play simply stinks." Crude but true (and a quote from the play), her bluntness might indeed have been appreciated by Williams, to whom everyone deferred, but to whom criticisms were rarely offered.

If anyone in the cast needed encouragement after the reviews appeared, they had only to approach Williams himself. Grateful for their efforts, he appeared the morning after opening — even as the unhappy reviews were being circulated — and distributed twenty-one pages of rewrites.

Before the mid-February closing, however, at least one San Francisco theatregoer was sufficiently impressed to contact Williams's agent. Lyle Leverich, leaseholder and managing producer of the 99-seat Showcase Theatre, asked Bill Barnes if there might be a new play to offer later that year. Barnes, knowing how close *The Two-Character Play/Out Cry* was to Williams's heart, and how much he wanted a production of the latest version, suggested that playwright and producer meet. They did, and thus began a friendship that lasted until Williams's death.

Then Williams was off to New York and Key West, working still — on scenes for unlikely plays and screenplays, on revisions of works current and past, and on first drafts of a series of plays that would cast the net of his memory back over his entire history. "At my age," he told an interviewer, "you know you're approaching death and air becomes very clear, very refined. . . . You cease to feel the little things that weren't worthy of such big things as life and death. Although I feel well physically, I know that I am approaching the end of my life and thank God I'm not scared."

This remark, spoken while en route to the Cannes Film Festival that May — where he was an honorary jury president — was the first recorded example of a shift in his discussions about mortality. Up to this time, his tune had been the standard one of hypochondria, "my last play . . . I'm a dying man," and so forth, as usual. But there was a difference now, an acceptance and a quiet conviction of approaching death. There was, several interviewers recalled, a lightness about it, as if their replies did not much matter. They wondered, years later, if his survival to 1983 did not in some way disappoint him.

In August of that same year, 1976, he returned to San Francisco for conferences with Leverich and with the director of *The Two-Character Play,* Jay Leo Colt. (After 1974, subsequent stagings of *Out Cry* were always billed with the original title.) Colt recalled Williams as endlessly patient with the two actors, polishing their Southern accents and cutting and rearranging lines until he felt it was as good a play as he could make it.

Concomitant with his concern for the play, however, was a new strain of loneliness in his life. A protracted separation from Robert Carroll evoked a cry from him, which he poured into a poem about the last solitary moments of a typical day and evening:

> Turning out the bedside lamp . . .
> taking an extra wine-glass of Dry Sack sherry, placing
> the sleeping capsule where I can locate it easily
> in the dark, should the preliminary tablet of Valium not suffice,
> Because you see, at sixty-five
> abdicating your consciousness to sleep
> involves, usually, a touch of nervous apprehension
> that it may not ever revive. However
> I suspect that there's
> a certain luxury submerged in this: a touch of
> concealed fascination in the surrender as well.

His fascination with the possible effects of his dependence, as well as an endless loneliness — with or without company — plagued him from this time forward. To most people he showed a thoughtful cheerfulness (he knew that nothing alienates so quickly as gloom). But there were some who knew he was whistling in the dark.

"Tennessee knew so much about loneliness," José Quintero recalled later. "He learned the pain of loneliness, [but he] was probably one of the funniest men I've ever known. I adored his wit. It was like a needle that pierces bubbles — goes right through the masquerade. . . . And he was a very kind man."

One of the objects of his kindness was a young aspiring playwright Williams engaged as secretary-companion for several months in 1976. "My first assignment," Dan Turner remembered, "was to walk Madame Sophia, [his] asthmatic English bulldog. My last effort was to type the first draft of *A Lovely Sunday for Creve Coeur.*" From San Francisco, Williams and Turner departed later that summer for New Orleans.

"It was there that I was introduced to his routine of rising every day before dawn to write. I prepared a thermos of coffee the night before. . . . He took a nap before we went out for brunch. After an afternoon walk, or nap, he took me to the Athletic Club, where we swam."

At this time, Williams's old friend Oliver Evans was suffering a long, gradually paralyzing battle with a malignant brain tumor. Williams not only stopped in a local church to pray for his friend; he also offered Evans the use of his Dumaine Street apartment, since the nursing home seemed so uncongenial; he would, in addition, pay for a nurse-companion if Evans wanted to make the move. But more care was needed, and to insure that, he sent checks — channeled through Muriel Bultman Francis — for Evans's nursing home maintenance.

By early October he was back in San Francisco at the El Cortez Hotel. But not for long: the management, he wrote to Gene Persson, would not allow his dog. But the hotel staff recalled another reason for his transfer to another residence:

"We simply couldn't have Mr. Williams as a guest in our hotel a second time," according to Chuck Ingebritsen, the assistant manager. "He made a most unpleasant scene in the lobby, and it was clear to everybody that he was drugged — not just drunk and a little disorderly, but worse. And there was a dreadful commotion, because even though he was a Pulitzer Prize playwright, we just couldn't allow him to remain. It was very embarrassing for us, and he was very upset."

Immediately after the opening of *The Two-Character Play* at the Showcase Theatre, he returned alone to Key West, and then he left almost at once for New York with Robert Carroll. The reason for the sudden travel was that finally, after years of effort, *The Eccentricities of a Nightingale* (a reworking of *Summer and Smoke**) was finally to be staged. For the opening at the Arena Theatre, Buffalo, Edwin Sherin had assembled a cast headed by Betsy Palmer as a more aggressive, determined character than the Alma of the earlier play. Bill Barnes arranged to have a New York producer, Gloria Hope Sher, attend a performance in Buffalo and then meet Williams in New York.

---

* After the 1948 Broadway failure of *Summer and Smoke,* Williams revised the play drastically. The new version lay unproduced for years — and no wonder, for it is a vastly inferior work in which the protagonists lack subtlety and sensitivity, and the writing lacks coherence. Alma Winemiller, for example, is merely an aggressive flirt intent on the seduction of John Buchanan. Donald Windham has put forth the fascinating hypothesis that in fact *Eccentricities of a Nightingale* may not, as Williams said, be a revision — rather, it may be a first draft of *Summer and Smoke.*

THE KINDNESS OF STRANGERS

"At our first meeting," she recalled, "Tennessee was quite charming and during rehearsals in New York at the end of November he was wonderful. He loved everyone in the play and everything connected with it, and his laugh filled the theatre. I remembered that he got to the stage to speak to the cast only once. He simply said, 'Look, *I'm* Alma,' and he acted out a long scene for Betsy Palmer. He then added that Alma was his favorite character."

Williams was well tended at this time: Gloria Hope Sher and her colleagues, Edwin Sherin (again the director) and the entire cast brought him an alert respect and attention to every detail they knew he wanted for the play. "But he didn't seem to be eating much," according to Sher. "He only picked at food. The wine saw him through any social occasion. And the minute he had one sip of red wine, his personality changed completely. He became very aggressive, caustic to waiters, unpleasant to be with. A maître d' once had to ask him to calm down." What Sher perhaps did not know was that wine interacted badly with the pills he had taken for sedation or alertness.

The play fared poorly. *Summer and Smoke* did not benefit from wholesale revisions that made its sensibilities broader, duller and cruder. "When the bad reviews came out after our opening on November 23, Tennessee was shocked," according to the producer. "The night before our closing in December, we held an onstage symposium after final curtain. Henry Hewes [a critic and admirer of Williams for many years] was moderator, and Tennessee and I and the cast were onstage. He charmed everyone until someone asked about the critics, and then he really lashed out. He went on for two hours about the rotten critics, how serious work wasn't appreciated anymore, and how playwrights were at the mercy of a few reviewers and one newspaper. And he didn't mince words."

One event during the run of the play, however, escaped Williams's notice. To a performance at the Morosco Theatre came Audrey Wood, who went quietly to Sher, with tears in her eyes, and thanked her for the production.

Because the play opened at Thanksgiving, the producer invited the cast and crew to a festive dinner at Sardi's after the holiday matinee. Williams, to her surprise, arrived too. "He was so lonely, so forlorn. People drained him. He was so vulnerable at this time in his life. He was frightened to be alone, and anyone who extended a helping hand would be confided in. He seemed such a lost soul, so alone, that anyone could touch him and get a warm response. In my playbill for our show, he wrote, 'Stay in my life, Gloria, to keep me alive.' So many people were taking advantage of him — in the theatre and in his personal life — everyone wanted his life and his blood. He was responsive even to the crazy autograph hounds on the street. He never denied anyone, even with that custom. He always stopped to smile and to sign. But what I remember most of all is that he really thought he was Alma Winemiller — he was writing himself, playing himself in the rehearsal. He was enchanted with Alma, and with her density and her dilemma. That much was clear to me, and I think to everyone in the cast too."

That same season, Williams taped an interview for publication in *Gay Sunshine,* a review dedicated to serious exploration of issues of special relevance to the homosexual population and its more open and active participation in the cultural and political mainstream of American life. Williams spoke with playwright-novelist George Whitmore at the Elysée Hotel.

"We met at two in the afternoon," Whitmore said, "and without any difficulty Mr. Williams drank a full bottle of red wine, ate a large roast beef sandwich and took several cups of strong coffee. He looked perfectly dreadful, ruddy and puffy-faced and incoherent. But when I played back the tapes and then read the transcript, much of what he said was articulate. It was the long pauses that had confused me."

It was the playwright himself who requested the interview with this publication, to counter the statements issued by some activists in gay circles who claimed he could never deal openly with the theme of homosexuality in his plays. After admitting that the politics of gay liberation did not much interest him, he continued: "People so wish to latch onto something didactic; I do not deal with the didactic, ever. . . . You still want to know why I don't write a gay play? I don't find it necessary. I could express what I wanted to express through other means. . . . I would be narrowing my audience a great deal [if I wrote for a gay audience alone]. I wish to have a broad audience because the major thrust of my work is not sexual orientation, it's social. I'm not about to limit myself to writing about gay people."

Williams also revealed that day that he was at work on a play called *The Wild Horses of the Camargue,* which had "a great deal to do with a relationship between a tyrannical older man and a very beautiful younger man who's not really a homosexual but who is enslaved by the older man." It is not likely that his remark, or the projected play, would have found favor with those in the gay political movement, nor with many homosexuals in general — like much in his plays (and in this Whitmore was on the mark) there was a negative quality, and an underlying resentment, to Williams's attitude to homosexuality in his work. And Christopher Isherwood, Paul Bigelow and Meade Roberts are among many who had the distinct feeling that Tennessee Williams in fact hated homosexuality, hated being homosexual, and could never accept those who could come to peaceful terms with being one of a sexual minority. (To Gene Persson, Williams had written on July 1 of that year that *The Wild Horses of the Camargue* was shaping up as an obscene and decadent play, with a simple and terrifying narrative line. The play remained incomplete at the time of Williams's death.)

Meantime, Persson had gone ahead to London to prepare for the third production of *The Red Devil Battery Sign*, which was to open in the middle of 1977. "Tennessee kept saying he'd never be alive when the time came," according to Persson. "He complained constantly toward the end of 1976 about his health, but that's one of the things you put up with in genius."

Before Williams left to join the company in London, he attended rehearsals for the revival of *The Night of the Iguana*, which had been imported from Los Angeles to the Circle in the Square. "He made extensive comments for us about the lighting and the backdrop," Theodore Mann said, "and he was very precise in his feelings about the production." But his good cheer was an effort to hide a return of a deep depression as 1976 ended. He wanted *Iguana* to succeed; his friend Sylvia Miles was playing Maxine in it, and he still hoped to rewrite for her the dying Flora Goforth, now closer than ever to his heart (and in his correspondence) as an alter ego. Before departing for London he accepted life membership in the American Academy of Arts and Letters.

When he arrived in London, however, he gave Gene Persson cause for alarm. "He was staggering, he was unable to arrange the practical details of everyday life, money appeared and disappeared strangely. There was a lot of vagueness at this time."

Chapter Ten

THE KINDNESS
OF STRANGERS

(1977–1983)

Whoever you are — I have always depended
on the kindness of strangers.

> — Blanche DuBois, in
> *A Streetcar Named Desire*

THE LAST six years of Tennessee Williams's life were a restless quadrille into which he drew various professional and personal partners. Scenes from old plays were revised, restructured, updated and shuffled with odd bits of new material written in hotel rooms or on the Concorde. Acts of new plays were rewritten late at night in Key West, or after dinner with a new producer. Major changes were incorporated at dizzy rehearsals. Always on the jump, eager to have his remarkable survival extend to his art, Williams at sixty-five was in one way as energetic as he had been at twenty-five. That was the year of *The Magic Tower* and of the constant flow of lyric poetry. He had the same zeal at thirty-five, when he completed *Summer and Smoke* and drafted short stories and scenes for what would very soon be *A Streetcar Named Desire.* At forty-five, he divided his time between *Sweet Bird of Youth* and *Orpheus Descending,* and new stories and poems. And now, in 1976, he demonstrated a vigor that exhausted some who worked with him and astonished all who knew him. At this time, he began to call his studio "the Madhouse."

"He seemed to have no great personal needs except to write," Gene Persson said, referring to the time Williams spent in London in late 1976 and early 1977. "He made a number of trips back and forth from Key West — someone said he held the record number of trips on the Concorde."

In mid-January 1977, he wrote to Persson in London that he was en route to New Orleans; he was at work on a new play that would be set there, and which joined parts of earlier plays and short stories and finally became *Vieux Carré.* He added that his traveling companion was a young, handsome Frenchman he had met in a New York restaurant, whose only asset was that he was trying to teach Williams French, and whom he intended to discard in New Orleans.

Once the young man was paid and dismissed, Williams settled for several weeks into the Dumaine Street apartment, where his resident manager saw to practical details. Since Robert Carroll was off on a Mexican holiday, Williams often. ate alone at the Quarter Scene, at the corner of Dauphine and Dumaine, or took his laundry, alone, to the machines at Dumaine and Burgundy. Neighbors found him at Marti's Restaurant and at the Café Lafitte in Exile, a famous bar that never locks its doors. "*Garden District* is about one side of Canal Street, which is the fashionable world of New Orleans," Williams explained, "and *Vieux Carré* is about the Bohemian world, which is much more interesting."

After shuttling a half-dozen times in ten weeks between Key West and New Orleans, he was back in New York at the end of winter for rehearsals with director Arthur Alan Seidelman on *Vieux Carré*. Some of the problems with it were foreseen by actress Sylvia Sidney, but having worked with Seidelman when she played Amanda Wingfield in *The Glass Menagerie,* she was eager and hopeful about a new play by Tennessee Williams.

"When I first read the play," she said, "I was very enthusiastic but disappointed. I said I'd love to do it if it were a *play,* but as it was there were terrific problems. That was late in 1976. Several months later, Seidelman called me and said, 'Now it's a play, we're ready to go.' "

At the rehearsals, however, the cast and director were left very much on their own; promised rewrites were delivered by Williams's friends, who made notes, reported decisions, conveyed requests to and from the playwright. "None of us saw Tennessee for a long time," according to Sylvia Sidney, "until we had major problems with several scenes. When he finally arrived, his excuse was, 'I need to see it on its feet!' By then it was almost too late." But when she insisted on a rewrite for a certain phrase, or on a good exit line or a revision of some action, he could accommodate himself magnificently — "almost on demand," she recalled.

But she and others also noticed that the reasons for Williams's absences at this crucial time were a way of avoiding one disaster by courting another: Williams was wandering around New York, mostly at night and often in unsavory quarters, and at rehearsals he was too often incoherent. And there was a coterie of young men, of dubious value to him, who clung to him constantly.

"We were nervous, and he was sad," Sidney said. "He was frightened of getting old, terrified that he was no longer attractive, that his figure wasn't good anymore, that he couldn't attract young men except with his money. Meanwhile, we were in trouble. The set was impossible, clumsily built, and the production was misconceived.... After the last preview [in early May], he came backstage, and he was crying with gratitude. I don't know what I'd done, but it must have been good, because he said he was going to rewrite the whole play and no one would ever play Mrs. Wire [the New Orleans landlady] but me. Of course the following year it reopened in London with Sylvia Miles, but I knew that he gave dozens of actresses this line about 'You're the greatest actress who's ever done my plays.' "

At this time, it seemed as if Williams himself was beginning to sabotage his name and reputation before columnists or critics could. Richard Alfieri, who played the young writer in *Vieux Carré,* recalled that a few weeks before opening, Williams sat for a newspaper interview and "individually attacked all the major theatre critics in New York, charging them with everything from incompetence to hypocrisy.... The cast groaned almost in unison upon reading the interview. We knew it would jeopardize the play's chances — and perhaps Tennessee did, too."

As for the public self, his conduct often did not help in that regard, either. On March 10, he appeared onstage at the Winter Garden Theatre to address over eight hundred New York high school students. But he brought a bottle of vermouth along, and the event, to the dismay of everyone present, turned into a "hard-to-hear question and answer session, with the students trying to outshout each other for Mr. Williams's attention," as one eyewitness reported.

As opening night approached, Williams affected an unjustified if generous optimism, dancing late into the night at the opening of a new discothèque and laughing for society photographers — but he was, as Alfieri recalled, "very nervous about what the critics would have to say." His nervousness was unfortunately manifest with his cast, just before the opening, as Alfieri and Sidney remembered; he stormed away after delivering an angry tirade about what a disservice he had done to himself by being too kind with them all. "We knew he didn't mean all of it, and we loved him when he came backstage after the first performance," according to Alfieri, but the damage had been done.

"He was so passionate about everything going well with regard to his work," as Bill Barnes said of that time, "that he was in absolute despair when there was not a successful outcome. His life was full of trauma, turmoil and pain — and this paradoxically made his life and work possible."

Just before opening night, Williams fled New York in panic. "I don't think I chose the right place. It's so desolate here," he said of Atlantic City in early May. "But I simply have to travel, even if it's to Atlantic City. I have a fear of confinement, of claustrophobia."

"The day after opening," Sylvia Sidney added, "a small group of us lunched at the Stanhope. He had made a surprise return to New York just before opening night, and at the Stanhope he told me that he knew he had to be surrounded by a few respectable-looking people in order to be accepted for luncheon at better places. He had a bad reputation in New York by this time — or so he said. I don't think he was helped much by the group of hangers-on and sycophants that surrounded him then, either." At a reception in his suite at the Elysée Hotel, a few days after the opening of *Vieux Carré,* that group begged him to read his poetry; he complied, and then said everyone had to read Shakespeare aloud. Most of the cast, embarrassed and angry at the coterie who seemed to be taking advantage of Williams, quietly departed.

The poetry reading was prompted by the publication that spring of a second collection by Williams, *Androgyne, Mon Amour.* The book did not demonstrate anything even his greatest admirers did not already know: that Williams's poetic genius was invariably passed through the prism of dialogue into prose, and that on the contrary the selfconsciousness, the coyness of most of his poems — unmoored by character or conflict — were hollow and inauthentic. His best plays were characterized by an astonishing inevitability of narrative line, by a fluid and poetic diction that belied countless revisions; the poems, on the other hand, sounded artificial — or, like the worst moments of his last plays, designed to shock rather than to illuminate.

Vieux Carré was a crashing failure. But those who had followed his career felt that he was entitled to minor exercises at this point. "Tennessee Williams's voice," Walter Kerr wrote in a warm appreciation that week, "is the most distinctively poetic, the most idiosyncratically moving, and at the same time the most firmly dramatic to have come the American theatre's way — ever. No point in calling the man our best living playwright. He is our best playwright, and let qualifications go hang. In fact, he has already given us such a substantial body of successful work that there is really no need to continue demanding that he live up to himself, that he produce more, more, more, and all masterpieces. We could take some casuals and just tuck them into the portfolio, gratefully, as small dividends."

That generous comment, however, was part of a longer piece in which Kerr — like all the critics — regretted that *Vieux Carré* was simply a pastiche, not a play; a series of dream-images, not a coherent and focused drama. Box-office business was poor, and the play closed after five performances. Pointed and cogent remarks like Kerr's did not encourage Williams; he needed critical approval, reinforcement, constant commendation.

Vieux Carré is, however, remarkable in retrospect for what it reveals about the mood and temperament of the playwright at the time of writing, for it is as much a play of *tableaux vivants* as *The Glass Menagerie*, and the first in a series of late plays in which he created scenes that were really leaves from a personal album, without the transmutation found in earlier plays of the great period, 1944 to 1961. Narrated by a young writer who is clearly the young Williams, the play animates real-life events at 722 Toulouse Street in the winter of 1938–1939, between his graduation from Iowa and the trip with Jim Parrott — the season when he lived in penury but as a practicing poet and writer, the season in which he became actively homosexual.

But the other characters incarnate aspects of Williams, too: the older sick and haunted artist, desperate for sexual intimacy and even more desperate for friendship, and the young couple, Jane and Tye, caught in a brutal duel for sexual and emotional dominance. Offstage voices call "Edwina, Edwina, come see this dream of a little courtyard," as the young writer speaks of a home where "the storm of my father's blood obliterated the tenderness of Grand's," whose spirit comes to comfort him in the alcove of his cramped room. Scene images tumble haphazardly in *Vieux Carré;* it is a series of free-associations, drawn on a poeticized past, and its deepest value was for its author, as he reentered in memory the closed house on Toulouse Street, and as he forgave and dismissed some of its ghosts and begged an embrace from others.

Before the end of May, Williams had jetted to London for more work with Gene Persson and the new director of *Red Devil*, Keith Hack. In an effort to raise needed funds, Persson invited an English publisher to meet with Williams for luncheon at the Berkeley Hotel, the playwright's preferred stopping-place because of its swimming pool. "But Tennessee put the man through such a relentless grilling — 'Are you going to kick in some money or aren't you?' — that the man of course backed out." Exhausted, nervous and unwilling to rest, Williams had resumed taking

megadoses of Ritalin tablets, alternating them with Nembutal for sedation. The producer and his staff had to be alert to prevent him from
stumbling and falling in offices, on the street, and in the theatre.

After preliminary performances in June, the third version of *Red Devil*
opened at London's Phoenix Theatre at an hour they thought might
bring them luck: seven o'clock on the seventh day of the seventh month
of 1977. But no occult force guided the critics' reactions or the audience's response. Another closing quickly followed.

Back in Key West, Williams revised the teleplay *A Second Epiphany*,
now called *Stopped Rocking*, for his friends Maureen Stapleton and Anne
Meacham, in hopes of a television sale. A story of despair, lunacy and attempted suicide in and around an asylum, it carries to an extreme the
dual personalities trapped in the theatre in *The Two-Character Play/Out
Cry*. The teleplay also dramatized the association between playwright and
sister, as the man who in this case visits his demented wife feels that his
affair with another woman has been a selfish betrayal. Fraternal and con-
jugal feelings meld in a series of ever more violent scenes, and the specifi-
cations of St. Louis, of St. Vincent's asylum, of the needlework done by
both wife and sister reveal a concern for the linked lives. ("I have been
punished by her punishment," Williams said of his sister, "and by difficulties of my own.")

As he wrote each day, Williams was also erecting a little shrine to Rose
at his Key West home — a crude altar modeled on Serafina's shrine to
her late husband in *The Rose Tattoo*. Here, he set pictures of his sister and
of St. Jude, patron of hopeless cases — which, as he said in private and in
this teleplay, he considered her and himself: "Such cases exist; we know
that, so what can we do but pray?"

The failure of *The Two-Character Play*, after numerous reproductions,
may have necessitated *Stopped Rocking*. Its brutality, its confession of guilt
and its longing for forgiveness recall the earlier play, and it advances the
motif of a man's freedom and a woman's confinement. His work was becoming more and more a folio of memories, indistinguishable from what
private journals might have been. But since his private heart was often
worn on a public sleeve, he described the feelings, the guilt and the
longings in plays that were by this time of his life perhaps never really
meant to be staged, in images he never really wanted to share much of
the time. And this may explain why his producers and casts and directors
felt, from 1977 to the end of his life, that Tennessee Williams himself
wanted to sabotage and subvert the work — and his own name — before

anyone else could. *The Glass Menagerie* had, long ago, been as personal. But it had been gentler, devoid of the overt madness, the grotesque breakdown, the storm of sexual confusion; it was, as Tom said in the opening scene, "truth in the pleasant disguise of illusion." There were few pleasant disguises in 1977.

During the last weeks of that year, Williams accepted an offer from the Alliance Theatre in Atlanta to present a new play. What he gave them was a rescaled version of the film *Baby Doll,* adapted to the limitations of the stage and called *Tiger Tail.* In appreciation for the documentary film, he arranged for Harry Rasky to direct. At the same time, a new twist of pain entered his life. The circle of attractive young men ever in attendance now more than ever, and more boldly than ever, sought the glamour of association, some too willing to exchange sexual for professional favors, and a number who simply filled idle hours drinking his liquor and draining his energies. They had manuscripts for him to read, stories for him to hear. If they were at all talented, he listened and supported and helped financially. If they were at all attractive to him, they were guaranteed even more attention. He was, unfortunately, an easy prey for the unscrupulous, and his best instincts — a generous concern for fledgling writers, a desire to protect and to embrace — often clashed with an acute vulnerability.

Meantime, another project was being developed. A year earlier, José Quintero had told theatrical producer Elliot Martin that Williams was at work on a long play, called *Clothes for a Summer Hotel,* about Scott and Zelda Fitzgerald. From the start, Quintero and Williams thought of Geraldine Page for Zelda. Now, Quintero again contacted Martin (who had produced *More Stately Mansions* and *A Moon for the Misbegotten* as well as a revival of *Camino Real* and a series of major Broadway successes). The three met in Key West, Martin recommended some cuts, Tennessee agreed. "He was bright and articulate and cheerful in January 1978," according to the producer, who also remembered Quintero's belief that the play had all the ingredients of a hit. If Williams could be surrounded with the loving support he needed, they could all repeat the miracle of 1952 (when Quintero, Williams and Page made history with *Summer and Smoke*).

Tiger Tail was staged, and *Clothes for a Summer Hotel* now received daily cutting. Williams met with Bill Barnes and Maureen Stapleton about still another project, a one-act play he had written in San Francisco in 1976. Titled *Creve Coeur,* after a park not far from central St. Louis, it was a simple play, set in the 1930s, about lonely women seeking love and security. A key role, they thought, was tailor-made for Stapleton. They read the play for Craig Anderson, founding director of the Hudson Theatre Guild in Manhattan, who would produce the play; Keith Hack was brought from London to direct.

"Tennessee was cool and somewhat distant at our first meeting," Anderson recalled. "But we were deeply interested in a new play by him, of course, and he seemed to need the public life the play would give him. He needed to have something in the works, something that could guarantee him a production and soon." Anderson's wife, Elena Azuola, found Williams in March 1978 "a fairly fragile man, but with an ability to lash out suddenly if a tender spot were touched."

The reworking and expansion of *Creve Coeur* (literally, "heartbreak") continued through the spring of 1978, when they all moved to Charleston, South Carolina, where the play was to be in the Spoleto Festival scheduled for late May and early June. (By this time, there had been inaugurated an American counterpart to this Italian gala.) Barnes attended Williams, and frequently the playwright withdrew to Kiawah Island, twenty miles offshore, to enjoy its secluded beaches and ten thousand acres of maritime forest.

For the first week in Charleston, the Andersons recalled, Williams rose each morning and was at his typewriter by five o'clock (this Elena knew since his motel room adjoined hers). He swam midmorning, before the sun was at its zenith, then worked again until lunch.

But before the preview performance on June 1, "the pills and the drinking really played havoc with him," as Anderson said. "We didn't know how to take care of all the needs he had, but we felt that as producers we had to demand better writing. We knew one thing clearly: he had to be protected from the press, and from the nagging of those around him who wanted to pick at him and bother him. As it was, he had an adoring entourage entirely too much and too close." On June 2, there was some uneasiness when he read from his work and fielded questions for students at a local college in Charleston; the pills he was taking, in injudicious combinations, reacted badly with wine. Three nights later, at the play's formal opening, as Anderson recalled, "He became something of an amusing outrage. He arrived at a formal reception in a safari suit with short trousers, sneakers and a Panama hat. He got away with playing the eccentric — after all, he was Tennessee Williams, the playwright."

To everyone's relief and surprise, visiting critics from New York newspapers joined local reviewers in praising the play, expressing the hope that it would move to New York. At once, the Andersons met with Bill Barnes and offered to do everything to bring about that move.

In Charleston, some of Williams's paintings were exhibited, and this greatly pleased him. What had begun as a hobby in the 1950s was now a public curiosity, and his celebrity guaranteed fancy prices for the essentially simple, unsubtle work he could sell.

"He made us feel very welcome when we came to discuss *Clothes for a Summer Hotel* that June," Elliot Martin said. "He invited us to a party, and we discussed casting. I felt by this time that we had what we were going to get from him. The play was still much too long, but I felt he had reached his limits. 'I want to warn you, Elliot,' he said to me, 'the critics are out to get me. You'll see how vicious they are. They make comparisons with my earlier work, but I'm writing differently now.'" This was especially curious in light of the recent favor toward *Creve Coeur*.

The enterprise of raising money for a Broadway production of *Creve Coeur,* however, was a difficult one. "After the unfortunate reception of *Vieux Carré* in 1977," Anderson said, "everybody distrusted his abilities. No one would come across with money for a production. During this period, death was very much on his mind — he spoke of it frequently — as he spoke of his sister Rose, even more than usually. We strolled around Charleston and he remarked that a lace gown or a parasol or this or that item would please his sister. It was very touching and a little sad."

During the summer, Williams flew to London for the revival of *Vieux Carré*. Generous and supportive with his cast, he especially appreciated the robust humor and enthusiastic attitude of his leading lady, Sylvia Miles, with whom he still talked about Flora Goforth. "We spent a lot of time together," she said, "and he was full of ideas for plays and stories. His humor seemed quicker than ever. One day we were walking through Piccadilly and I saw a terribly thin young girl. I whispered to him, 'Oh, Tennessee, look — anorexia nervosa,' and without the slightest hesitation he shot back, 'Oh, Sylvia, you know everybody!'" (He appreciated his own joke, for it found its way later into the final version of *Clothes for a Summer Hotel.*)

Vieux Carré opened in London in August — to poor reviews for everything about it except Sylvia Miles, whose performance as the crusty Mrs. Wire was edged with humor, brittleness and an unsentimental poignancy of madness at the end.

In September there were at least two more trips to and from London from New York and Key West — necessary, it seems, only as distractions from the pressures of *Clothes for a Summer Hotel,* which he did not want to refine further, and *Creve Coeur,* which he did. Just after Labor Day he wrote to Craig Anderson that he had substantial revisions and expansions for what they now called *A Lovely Sunday for Creve Coeur;* he added, however, that he felt that sustained praise would elude him as long as he was alive. This play, he hoped, would mark the return to his rightful place during his lifetime: he did not believe, he added, that there was any reward coming in the hereafter.

He also mentioned, in the same letter (dated September 7) that it was now clear that Bill Barnes would sever his ties with International Creative Management to pursue an independent career, and that there would be a new agent representing him by winter. The tone of the letter has more than a hint of desperation: Williams also hoped that Anderson would consider reopening *Vieux Carré* on Broadway, and that together they could show an anonymous "them" that Tennessee Williams could inject real power into the theatre.

The carousel of activity continued to revolve, and he continued to reach for an elusive gold ring. "He seemed more fragile than ever when he returned from another trip to London," Elena Azuola said. "He needed constant encouragement and protection. But for all the care he needed, he was also seeing to the needs of others. He was supporting a number of actresses who had fallen on hard times." Her husband agreed: "He was very generous as well to a number of young writers who needed cash. There was a generous streak in him, and he seemed to want to protect as much as he asked for protection."

After quick journeys to San Francisco, New Orleans and Key West that autumn — travel again for its own sake — he returned to New York and signed a lease for an apartment at Manhattan Plaza, a complex on West 42nd and 43rd Streets especially designated for those in the arts. Although he took the residence for the privacy and the swimming pool and at first spent a good deal of time there, the noise and crowded atmosphere finally displeased him and he relinquished the lease after three years, having spent most of the time at the Elysée Hotel in any case. "He hated the sheer size of Manhattan Plaza," according to Vassilis Voglis, "and the fact that everyone there recognized him. He much preferred to live at the Elysée, and even sometimes to stay with me and John Cromwell [the writer] at our apartment on East 72nd Street."

From San Francisco Williams invited Jay Leo Colt, who had directed *The Two-Character Play,* to become a temporary secretary and assistant throughout that autumn and winter. "I helped him furnish the Manhattan Plaza apartment and helped him keep the script of *Creve Coeur* up-to-date, which wasn't easy with all his rewrites. Tennessee didn't like to give orders, so I had to be very persistent with him to determine just what he wanted me to do." Eventually, Tennessee's irrational suspicions, certainly exacerbated by his mixed regimen of tablets and capsules, were turned on Colt, whom he accused of stealing the manuscript of *The Wild Horses of the Camargue;* it later turned up in the Key West studio, where Williams had forgotten it in a hurried departure.

In the thick of professional and personal problems for the playwright, he accepted as his new agent Mitch Douglas, a literary agent at ICM whom their actors' agent, Williams's old friend Milton Goldman, recommended. "The real trouble, I remember thinking in 1978, was the people around him," Douglas said. "Everyone wanted a piece of him, and sometimes he seemed to thrive on those who were the worst for him. He was forever getting himself in some sort of entanglement or other, either with his professional or his intimate life, and after a while he really seemed to trust nobody. He believed he was constantly being cheated, and no convincing changed his mind." The paranoia, as his friends called it, had a strange basis in truth at that time (as Douglas and a few others realized), for Williams was surrounded by a pack of glamour-hungry jackals who used sex like a fly-swatter. But his suspicions were diffuse, and eventually he turned against those like Jay Leo Colt and Mitch Douglas.

"As the rehearsals for *A Lovely Sunday for Creve Coeur* began in New York," Craig Anderson remembered, "we had the impression that Tennessee would have preferred not to have it presented. He enjoyed working on it, but once he realized that audiences and critics would be there in January, with their possible disapproval, he began to withdraw."

The holiday season Williams spent with his sister, whom he brought from Stony Lodge to New York. "So much love passed between them," Anderson said. "He brought her to dinner, and there she sat, this quiet little lady, almost seventy years old, and Tennessee gently mothered her — he cut her meat, responded to her every whim and need. She seemed in all innocence to bring out something very sweet in him."

As the reopening of the play drew near, Williams tried to defuse his anxiety by writing an open letter to the cast. As never before, he begged plainly for their attention to every word of the script, every nuance of every line, each cadence of the language; he asked them to review the play with intensest care. Creating a play, he concluded, was an act of love. He added that he was writing to them at four in the morning, before his coffee and even before his first glass of wine. He begged for their attention and their love and their patience.

"By the time we opened [in January 1979]," Anderson said, "he was in a terrified, suspicious state. The failure of the play [which closed after thirty-six performances] he seemed to blame on me, and that was the end of our relationship."

The reviews, however mixed (and less favorable by far than what had been written about the Charleston premiere), were nowhere near the disaster Williams believed; several critics in fact praised the gentleness and humor of the play, and welcomed his return, after other wilder experiments, to the traditional form of *A Lovely Sunday for Creve Coeur*. Like *Vieux Carré*, it has a desperate tone, and the lonely women are very like the confused quartet of *The Glass Menagerie*. *A Lovely Sunday for Creve Coeur* presents four emotionally unfulfilled women, each terrified of being abandoned: one (Sophie) cannot go back to her apartment alone after the death of her mother, and so remains with neighbors; another (Bodey) fears losing her brother to marriage, and fears losing her roommate (Dorothea) to anyone at all, so she encourages a match between them in order to keep them in her life. Another (Helena) desires a companionship that may be spinsterish, but may be something else. This is a play of heartbreak indeed, and of a sad accommodation to the realities of adult life. With the character of Dotty, Williams felt at the time that "we must pull ourselves together and go on. Go on, we must just go on, that's all that life seems to offer and demand." Spiced with literally two dozen references to his own life in St. Louis in the 1920s and 1930s, *A Lovely Sunday for Creve Coeur* is another page in Williams's personal album, for the four driven, lonely women each speak from a part of the author's life in the days of his attendance at the Ben Blewett school and University High, the days at International Shoe, the front porch in Memphis, and the final acceptance of life's compromises. But Williams offered only the accidents of his past, without the shape of emotionally compelling characters or dramatic structure.

Before the play had completed a brief run, Williams had left the New York winter for the warmth of New Orleans and Key West, meeting before his departure with Elliot Martin and José Quintero about *Clothes*

for a Summer Hotel. In New Orleans he was told that his Key West home
had been burglarized — twice, in fact, on January 8 and 14 — and he was
furious and puzzled that the reports on this should have taken more than
three weeks to reach him. But the second burglary was accompanied by a
crime even more bizarre. Williams's forty-nine-year-old gardener, Frank
Fontis, who also tended the house during Williams's absences, was found
murdered in his own home. When police searched Fontis's house for
clues, a pile of manuscripts was discovered — all by Tennessee Williams.

Williams affected detachment when he returned to Key West at the
end of the month. "Fontis was a very eccentric but harmless man, I
thought, but it now appears he really wasn't my friend, and it took his
murder to reveal this to me. The things he confiscated over the years,
found in his safe, included personal letters, pictures, one of my earliest
journals, written when I was very young, and an only copy of a manuscript, which I value very much. I don't know how many times I'll have
to be taught the lesson that even friends aren't always what they seem."

Until the end of February, Williams remained in Key West, coping
once or twice with a sudden burst of antihomosexual prejudice in the
neighborhood. Once he was involved in late-night street scuffles, although the altercation was caused by a sailor's angry rebuff of Williams's
gentle proposition — not, as was claimed, by a gratituitous attack on
Williams and a companion. Strollers on Duval Street at two in the
morning in 1979 were not surprised by this incident: young wanderers,
sailors or not, heterosexual or not, had long been amused, tolerant or
even flattered by an occasional invitation from Williams. But in this case,
a fight broke out. Within days, at least two groups of young drifters had
stopped their cars in front of Williams's house, tossed empty beer cans
and dirty names, and roared off in a cloud of smug vulgarity. "Maybe,"
Williams told guests, "they weren't punks at all, but New York critics."
But he told a visitor, with sudden ominous anger several weeks later, "I
suspect I'll live only another two years. I've been working like a son of a
bitch since 1969 to make an artistic comeback . . . there's no release short
of death."

For a revival of *The Eccentricities of a Nightingale,* Williams flew to
Long Beach, California, in late March. He was welcomed by Gloria Hope
Sher, who introduced him to Sandy Dennis and the rest of the cast, but
according to Sher "he became very abusive and insulted a lot of people
after he'd had a few sips of red wine. That was all it took to change his
attitude for the evening. He was very polite up to that point." Mitch

Douglas agreed: "Unfortunately, by this time he had no tolerance for alcohol at all — one glass of red wine went straight to him." And the reason was that he had preceded the wine with pills.

In April Williams was back in Key West, working with Keith Hack on yet a further revision of *Goforth,* but delaying further toil on *Clothes,* which he insisted must be staged before he would make any further cuts. To Sylvia Miles he wrote on April 11 that he was negotiating the purchase price of a second house in Key West, fully furnished and suitable for several guests, complete with sun deck, swimming pool, television. He invited her to join them for work on *Goforth,* which he hoped to stage in Vienna and London. He also mentioned that a screenplay was almost finished, and that he hoped she would play in it under Paul Morrissey's direction. (Morrissey thought later that this must be the film of "Two on a Party," which Lester Persky had so long hoped to produce.)

Miles did visit Williams several times from that summer through the following year, and the planned production of *Goforth* went as far as meetings in Vienna with the managers of the English Theatre, Franz Schafranek and his wife Ruth Brinkman. Williams, however, thought the facilities there not lavish enough, and he at last withdrew, in September 1980, what he had so long developed. This was perhaps another act of fear, although one more reasonably founded: no version of *The Milk Train Doesn't Stop Here Anymore* had ever pleased more than a small San Francisco audience.

In May, Williams accepted invitations from two universities to address their students; neither appearance did much to increase the respect of a younger generation for an older playwright. At New York University's Loeb Student Center, on May 10, he read several poems and two grotesque pieces — the one-act play *Lifeboat Drill* and the short story "Tent Worms."

Throughout the 1970s, Williams's stories and short plays were invariably about sexual exploitation, madness, disease, death and the ultimate triumph of catastrophe. So much was true of the play he read that day, and of stories like "Mother Yaws" (which *Esquire* published in 1977) and "The Killer Chicken and the Closet Queen" (which appeared in *Christopher Street* the following year). His writings, except for two long plays in progress, were replete with images of disfigurement and addiction and with a merciless absence of any human warmth. The reaction of New York University students that day was neither serious nor respectful, since unfortunately they had difficulty understanding his slurred speech. At the University of Pennsylvania commencement the following week, the situation was scarcely improved.

When he was in the company of old and trusted friends, however, he fared better. With several he attended the opening production of a festival at the Williamstown Theatre; opening night, June 28, was a production of *Camino Real* devised by Nikos Psacharopoulos, a staging highly praised and much appreciated by audiences, critics and playwright. He remained through a long weekend at Williams College, meeting visitors and students, giving readings of poems, and enjoying himself more than he had in months.

The Williamstown journey was sufficiently heartening to send him back to New Orleans in a rush of optimism. He ransacked the files of old manuscripts kept there, and found, among other neglected items, a teleplay that had later been used as the basis for *Creve Coeur*. It was titled *All Gaul Is Divided,* and he submitted it to Mitch Douglas with a note that it, like *The Loss of a Teardrop Diamond* (a screenplay inspired by his sister's social debut), were his offerings to a theatre which had given him life despite what he called his transgressions.

But in addition to scripts devised for television, there was one short play that could never be offered to anything but an experimental, intimate theatre company that thrived on risk as much as talent. A bizarre mixture of softcore pornography, hallucinatory comedy and poorly considered social comment, it was titled *Kirche, Kutchen und Kinder: An Outrage for the Stage.** In the summer of 1979 he tried to find a home for this "doodle of a play," as the director eventually described it.

Because Williams was so eager to see it in production, Mitch Douglas suggested one of New York's off-off-Broadway companies, one with an intelligent appreciation of American theatre and the requisite willingness to take a risk. A German television company had once come to the Jean Cocteau Repertory Theatre on the Bowery to film Williams reading. In addition, the Cocteau's artistic director Eve Adamson had presented *In the Bar of a Tokyo Hotel,* and because Williams still had an affection for that failed work, Douglas asked Adamson to stage it for Williams's especial benefit.

"Mitch cared deeply about Tennessee's work and wanted the best for him every time," Adamson said. "They came to a revival of *Bar,* and I found poor Tennessee so besieged by people that we were functioning as

* On all versions of the script, Williams mistakenly wrote "Kutchen" for what should have been "Küchen." His title will be used here.

much like bodyguards as producer and agent. He seemed like such a bewildered little man, as if he always needed to be headed in the right direction, which is probably why there was always someone living with him who saw to the practical details of his life.

"The summer of 1979, Mitch said only that it [*Kirche, Kutchen und Kinder*] was an eccentric play about a male hustler who finally returns to work after retirement. I read it, and we agreed to present it as a work in progress in repertory during the 1979–1980 season."

During late summer and autumn of 1979, Williams divided his time between the Elysée Hotel, his apartment at Manhattan Plaza, meetings with Elliot Martin and José Quintero about the increasing difficulties of *Clothes for a Summer Hotel,* and irregular work on *Kirche, Kutchen und Kinder.*

"Tennessee had great faith in how Eve Adamson was handling his material," Douglas said, "and although his first choice for *Clothes* was certainly José, he wanted Eve to stand by as second choice. Because he was having trouble in his personal life at the time, and because he couldn't keep a secretary very long in such chaos, he wanted me to assume various personal and domestic duties. I insisted I could serve him best as his literary agent, period, and to that he replied, 'I like you, Mitch, you're funny.' I never quite figured out what he meant by that."

Attempts to make theatrical sense out of the bizarre *Kirche* continued, however. "He revised it on little scraps of paper that were always turning up," Adamson recalled. "As a play it was as badly structured as a later full-length play we did was much better structured [Williams's *Something Cloudy Something Clear*]. He was full of paranoia about both plays, about the productions and everyone in his life at the time, but there was a certain nobility and courage in him. And I do feel that the paranoia was partly caused by and was capitalized on by the coterie around him."

Kirche, Kutchen und Kinder is nevertheless remarkable for two diametrically opposed elements: it reveals, on the one hand, Williams (as Mitch Douglas put it) "trying to shock an unshockable society and an unshockable audience. There was a strong masochistic streak in Tennessee which sometimes made him want to undermine a work before the critics or audience disliked it. This was not a good play, but he insisted it be done. And Eve and her company gave it the best they had."

The best was in fact extremely ingenious for a play about a male hustler in New York's SoHo. "We designed it like a Fellini movie, and Tennessee loved the concept," Adamson said. "When we ran it in repertory during our ninth season, beginning in September, we found it was smart to bill it as a work in progress. We all knew the press would roast him on this, so we had a way of keeping them out."*

But beneath the vulgarity and a text resulting from unstable health, there is a character named Miss Rose who wanders through the lunacy, offering gentle encouragement and calming the craziness by playing hymns at the organ. "Miss Rose," says the retired hustler whose voice is Williams's own as both try for a comeback, "you've given me all the poetry that's in my soul."

His sister was not only in his mind and on paper, as it turned out. The second house in Key West was at last his, and he decided that it was time to move Rose from Stony Lodge to a more private residence, and one near himself. Late that autumn he brought her to 915 Van Phister Street, a two-story gray clapboard where he arranged for their cousin, Stell Adams, to be a companion. The arrangement lasted just over a year, when it became clear that more specialized care was still indicated. Rose returned to Ossining at New Year's 1980, far less disappointed than her brother.

As the plans to bring Rose to Key West were realized, he completed a bitter satire on the famous painting idealizing the American dream; *This Is the Peaceable Kingdom* describes total personal and social breakdown, and is set in a nursing home during the 1978 New York strike against those facilities. The play presents images of war, senility, disease, hatred and death, and ends in a staged battle between blacks and whites, Jews and Christians, patients and families.

Also by autumn 1979, Elliot Martin and José Quintero were ready to complete casting for *Clothes for a Summer Hotel,* a play which, in its first three extended drafts, reveals its clear purpose: the visits by Scott to Zelda Fitzgerald in the mental asylum are representations of the visits by Tom to Rose Williams. For the leading man, Williams was eager to sign Donald Madden, and when Madden declined the role, "Tennessee just backed off," as Elliot Martin recalled. "He didn't concern himself with casting after that." Kenneth Haigh played Scott Fitzgerald.

With that, Williams and Mitch Douglas left, at the end of October, for Gainesville, Florida, where a revival of *Tiger Tail* was to be staged at the University of Florida, in the Hippodrome Theatre. From his arrival

* Ironically, a review did appear in, of all publications, *The Tennessee Williams Newsletter* (which later became *The Tennessee Williams Review*). "Call it 'The Katzenjammer Kids Meet the Boys in the Band,'" wrote Richard Wray Hornak.

on October 31 to his departure November 3, there was a crowded schedule of theatrical, academic and social events that left him drained and irritable. At a reading of his poems he took his revenge for what he considered wretched personal exploitation by reading several of his more blatantly sexual poems and "chuckling wickedly throughout," as an eyewitness noted. Then, at the performance of *Tiger Tail*, as director Marshall New observed, Williams was in "the worst case of opening night paranoia known to man," which was not alleviated by "three bottles of white wine [drunk] during the day since breakfast . . . the formal dinner that evening ended with only a brief stop-in by the playwright, who had coffee and carried away three doggie-bags full of beef Wellington." And a professor from the University of Florida, Winifred Frazer, sadly reported — in the *Tennessee Williams Review* — "his paranoia, his irritability, his fear of death, his frustration at not producing any new successes."

On December 2, Williams, Henry Fonda, Martha Graham, Ella Fitzgerald and Aaron Copland were honored at the Kennedy Center, Washington, for their contributions to the arts. No one appreciated his best work better than Elia Kazan, who that evening reminded the audience that "One comes out of his plays feeling that particular mixture: sadness transmuted into joy, the two together or the one unexpectedly following the other. Also this: that despite ourselves we may have a chance after all. One feels — gratitude. . . . His concern is humanity and what can be found there to sing about and respect. Still he is anything but bland: his words have sharp teeth."

The White House dinner and the Kennedy Center honors buoyed him for a time. Close friends accompanied him, the press observed the formalities and asked no intimate questions, and with his medal in his pocket he returned to New York determined to apply his "sharp teeth" to the problems brewing over *Clothes for a Summer Hotel*. As trying as those problems would be, however, they were equaled by the ugly sexual sparring that now intensified around him, and that would become even more brutal until his death. A number of those in Williams's social entourage — several of whom tried to remain as "personal assistants" — were interested only in the social and sexual contacts that can always be made through a celebrity; and several were all too willing to offer themselves in the hope of some sort of compensation. Terrified as he was of being abandoned, of being thought unattractive, of aging and death, he was just as fearful of the loss of all creative instincts and powers. And since he was already aware of the severe diminution of those powers with the dependence on pills, he did not intend to complicate his life with risk of venereal disease — a condition familiar to him from several earlier escapades. In early 1980, he pitched himself out of a sexual frenzy that had plagued him since the early years. He announced that he would live a chaste and celibate life. As he and others may have suspected, however, this would not be long sustained.

"He was absolutely terrified of going back to Broadway for *Clothes for a Summer Hotel,*" Eve Adamson remembered. "At the same time as his minor doodle of a play, *Kirche, Kutchen und Kinder,* was in our repertory season, he was getting ready to confront the hassle again. He was as full of fear and insecurity as he was of dramatic insight, but those of us who cared for him seemed more often to be catching him from falling."

Work with the cast on *Clothes* began in early January 1980 with a mood of high expectations, deriving mostly from a deep nostalgia: the team of Williams–Quintero–Page was thought unbeatable, after all.

But at once things were, as Quintero said, "very, very painful. The play touched on his own terrifying experience in the hospital. There were still some vestiges of his paranoia that clung to his psyche in that play. He knew that there were lapses in the play, parts that didn't quite connect, and he didn't know how to make them connect. He didn't blame anybody, but he wouldn't come out of his [hotel] room. I would have to go and say, 'Come on, Tom. It's alright.' There were sad moments, very sad moments."

The New York rehearsal period was, as Elliot Martin remembered, a nightmare for everyone. There were personal problems among director and cast, there were winter illness and budget problems. And the script was at least an hour too long. "We got to the point that Williams was so defensive that I couldn't even mention the possibility of a cut to him, and there was very little editing, although some rearranging. When we opened in Washington at the end of January, I begged him, saying that we could have a fine show by Chicago or New York if he would just cut the play. But we never really got very far on this."

As first rehearsals began, in fact, Williams absented himself from the Cort Theatre in New York. He not only withdrew from rehearsals, he also failed to keep publicity appointments, failed to meet the press to publicize or discuss the play.

"Williams refused," according to journalist Stephen Silverman, "to

show up for a press conference. The press agent told the barrage of photographers and newsmen we could catch up with him at his Manhattan
Plaza apartment. I led the parade. Williams answered the door half-naked
and very coquettish. 'I didn't think there'd be any ladies,' he told the
woman from one magazine. The apartment was a pigpen. Unflushed toi-
lets. Broken glass on the kitchen floor. The photographer had to fix a
coffee machine so Williams could stop and have a cup — even though he
was obviously enjoying the chase and leading everyone on. The one time
he snapped was when the young lady asked if his plays were autobiographical.

" 'Where did *you* come from?' he replied, dismissing her. My only personal question was, 'Are you going to leave your apartment in this condition?' — 'When I arrive in Key West,' he drawled, 'I'll call back here
and get an actor to come in and clean it up. For twenty-five dollars, you
can get an actor to do anything.' "

The very next morning, in fact, Williams quit New York for Key
West — with an excuse more legitimate than nervousness over Broadway. Florida Keys Community College was about to open its new Tennessee Williams Performing Arts Center with a production of his 1969
play *Will Mr. Merriwether Return from Memphis?* Written when he was on
the verge of collapse, it was then packed away with no hope of production. When the administrators of the college and the social leaders of
Key West asked him in 1979 for a play with which to christen the center,
he offered them the yellowing manuscript.

"He came to rehearsals and to campus several times [in January]," according to William Seeker, the college president. "He was complaining
of insomnia and bursitis, and we all knew his health, like his local
friendships, blew hot and cold. At the same time, his beard was growing
one week, shaved off the next, back and forth. There were constant
changes in his appearance: he was healthy and cheerful, then sickly and
depressed. The alternate moods were startling. All the same, he could not
have been more cordial to the campus community. He signed a notarized
document giving the college the right to use his name at the Fine Arts
Center. On the second night of the play [January 25] a number of private gala parties had been planned for him, but when he heard that the
students and campus employees were to see his play that night, he
showed up — in tennis shoes and an informal shirt — to meet them. He
signed programs, chatted with people and did everything his normally

shy nature shrank from. He took time to walk around with me and meet the audience. This was the other side of the man, the gentler soul who was so much the reverse of the paranoid man of tantrums and unpredictability."

The events of that week in late January were a success for the college and for the town. The play, however, was dismal, obviously the product of a confused mind. Apparitions of historic characters (Rimbaud, van Gogh) appear to a woman and her neighbor, lonely souls each, one of them awaiting the return of the romantic Mr. Merriwether. The daughter of one initiates a young man to the mysteries of sex. Finally, Merriwether returns — in terms and dialogue recalling Williams's return from Memphis to St. Louis in 1934, and the apparition of the other woman's late, drunkard husband Cornelius returns to admit his infidelity.

There was a desperation in his trying, in an earlier drugged state, to come to terms with the ghosts of what he and his father were in the 1930s. And the event of his 1969 entrance into the Catholic Church — however briefly before he made an exit — was reflected in the character's seriocomic confessions. Nightmare rather than dream, distortion rather than clear memory, *Mr. Merriwether* is a virtually unperformable play. It does, however, anticipate the same stream of memories with which he would deal somewhat more successfully in 1981 and 1982.

Williams prolonged his Key West interval for a long weekend — not only for the round of social events, but also to draft scenes for an idea suggested to him when he saw this play staged. The history of his own family life was foremost in his mind, and he began a strange household melodrama, *Some Problems for the Moose Lodge;* the title referred to his father's attempts to be accepted by the Elks in St. Louis.

At the end of January, *Clothes for a Summer Hotel* opened at the Eisenhower Theatre, Washington. The response was so loudly negative that Williams rushed at last to make cuts and meet with his director. He then returned to Key West, locked the door of his room (telling a new young companion that he feared burglars and muggers), slept for two days, and emerged to work in his studio.

Calls continued to come from his agent in New York and from his producer in Washington, but as messages accumulated he departed again, for a festival of his plays in Atlanta, at the Alliance Theatre. His next association with *Clothes* was in Chicago, where the company moved in February. "He seemed in better form there," Martin recalled. "His brother Dakin came to opening night with a big crowd of well-wishers, and Tennessee agreed to make more cuts. He worked closely with the cast, we had a good notice from Claudia Cassidy, and by the time we were ready to move to Broadway we all had a false sense of security."

Quintero recalled a poignant moment in Chicago. "The morning after the [press] notices, which in general were not very good, it was windy, cold and snowing. I saw Tennessee leave the hotel, so I put on my coat and caught up with him in front of the Art Institute. He was sitting on the steps, in the snow, like some half-demented creature. I said, 'What are you doing, Tom?' He said, 'I'm waiting for them to open because I know they will have a swimming pool, because this is a place for artists where I can catch my breath to go on living.' " It was apparently an episode of complete withdrawal from reality. After a day's rest, he was more lucid.

Back in New York, Williams met with Elliot Martin. "We discussed the fate of the show," Martin said, "and of course I said we still had a fighting chance. But then the blizzard of 1980 came, and on top of that a transit strike. The play had been budgeted at $400,000 — one-fourth came from Columbia Pictures, one-fourth from the Shubert Organization, and I raised the remainder privately." (Mitch Douglas added that in fact Elliot Martin gave substantially and generously of his own funds to try to keep the show running when funds were depleted.)

"Tennessee also agreed readily to defer his monies until some of our costs could be made up," Martin continued. "We opened on March 26 — his sixty-ninth birthday — and the audience was really ecstatic about the play. But the critics were not, and the weather and the transit strike finalized the decision. We had to close the show on April 16. All plays did badly that season, but especially plays like ours, which had every problem well documented in the press during rehearsals and the out-of-town run. Tennessee was eager to keep it going, but when that was impossible, he said, 'What did I tell you? They were all out to get me.' The *Times* had asked him for the usual Sunday prior-to-opening essay, but he gave them a bitter, anti-press piece, which of course wasn't published."*

---

* Some who attended opening night and performances afterward were not quite as ecstatic as Martin recalled. Part of the problem was that some of the players simply could not be heard, even in the first rows.

With the failure of *Clothes for a Summer Hotel,* Tennessee Williams never returned to the Broadway theatre, although he did bring a play back to the Jean Cocteau the following year. He harbored a deep bitterness toward the New York critics, an attitude more justified by what had happened a decade earlier than by the tone of the press in 1980. When Walter Kerr was asked about Williams's allegation later that year, that the critics all hated him and wanted his work to fail, Kerr replied, "That's so silly, of course. If anything, we were overeager to see the play do well. . . . I think he's the finest American playwright. But the talent isn't always there every time you turn on the faucet."

Producer Martin was convinced that almost everyone, however, misread and misheard the play — an easy thing to do, one might add. "It's not about the Fitzgeralds, it's about a brother and sister, about Tennessee and his sister, with the image of the asylum looming over all. And it's a play with a certain transferred paranoia — from the situation of Rose to that of Williams himself who [exactly like the tortured and alcoholic F. Scott Fitzgerald] was blaming the critics and the media for his own failures."

As a studied text, the play indeed has that sensibility, and it continues the personal meditation he began with *The Two-Character Play.* From the 1960s, his sister had been the source and inspiration of everything he wrote, either directly — with a surrogate character representing her — or indirectly, in the situation of romanticized mental illness or angrily unvarnished verisimilitude. Fitzgerald was clearly modeled, in this play, on Williams's experience, and the claims of heart trouble and heavy drinking linked them: "At one point I went through a deep depression and heavy drinking," Williams said. "And I, too, have gone through a period of eclipse in public favor. . . . [The Fitzgeralds] embody concerns of my own, the tortures of the creative artist in a materialist society. . . . They were so close to the edge. I understood the schizophrenia and the thwarted ambition."

He could perhaps most of all understand those experiences because he had spent many years confronting the fate of his sister, who is the real character behind Zelda Fitzgerald in this play. As a reminder of their shared covenant with the past, Scott gives her a ring — just as Williams had given a ring to Rose (which, after its return to him, he had given to Carson McCullers). "Between the first wail of an infant and the last gasp of the dying," Zelda says, "it's all an arranged pattern of submission to what's been prescribed for us unless we escape into madness or acts of creation. . . . I'm not your book anymore! I can't be your book anymore! Write yourself a new book!" After this play, he would.

A final cry about lunacy and institutionalization, about alcoholism and the fear of waning creative power, about the confusion that had always linked Williams to his sister, *Clothes for a Summer Hotel* could, as Martin rightly suggested, be easily misperceived. That it was not a dramatically compelling work made it even more disappointing for Williams. The confession to and about Rose in this play pleased almost no one. His last two works, yet to come, would be confessions to others.

With this fresh disappointment, friends in New York gave him refuge whenever he was willing to stop shuttling from city to city, from apartment to apartment, hotel to hotel.

In the last years his visits to his mother had been infrequent; his own instability was the main reason for this, but his mother's condition was another. From the early 1970s, she had grown increasingly disoriented, and finally Edwina Dakin Williams had to be removed from a condominium apartment to a nursing home. She failed distressingly in mind and body from 1975, and on June 1, 1980, at the age of ninety-five, she died.

"Tennessee was a guest at my summer home on Long Island," Vassilis Voglis said. "At three in the morning a call came for him. I awakened him and said his brother was on the telephone, but he simply said, 'It's probably the news that my mother has died,' and rolled over in his bed. 'Tell them to call me in the morning.'"

This reaction should not be regarded as merely callous.

"I was spending as much time with Tennessee as anyone," Mitch Douglas said, "and I can say that he was very upset about his mother's death — more deeply than he wanted people to know."

There was no question, however, that his feelings, as expressed and recorded, were mixed. "I can stand my mother for only fifteen minutes at a time," he said once to Lucy Freeman. "Then I have to flee." And Freeman understood why: "Edwina infantilized everyone. It was clear that there was a terrible rage in Tennessee against her and what she had done to turn her children against their father, and what she had done to Rose. Edwina was a great woman and a courageous woman and a terrifying woman, and every woman she saw was in competition for her in the lives of her children. She was ever the dominant Southern belle."

Shortly before his mother's death, the playwright admitted: "I cannot feel anything about my mother. I dream about her, but I can't feel anything.... She was always on the verge of hysteria. She was called a nightingale. She had nice legs and kicked up her legs very high for a minister's daughter."

He had remembered her telling him, years earlier, that she had been so impressed at learning that the violets she had so admired in the state of Tennessee were imported by English settlers. For the funeral in St. Louis, he imported a blanket of two thousand English violets which covered her coffin with a simple lettered ribbon — "Love from Tom."

"I think there was a great relief and a great release for him when his mother died," Maureen Stapleton said. "He was attentive and supportive and generous with her — and the portrait of her in *The Glass Menagerie* is extremely generous — but how much deep love there was, or how much resentment, is hard to gauge."

Within a week of the funeral, Williams was at the White House again, this time receiving from President Carter the Medal of Freedom. (More than a dozen others were similarly honored at the same time.) Friends accompanied him; he was glad there were no critics. "When he wanted to," according to Mitch Douglas, who was present, "he could be the gentleman of the world, as he was at the White House. He behaved very well there."

From mid-June to late July, Williams and the Southern artist Henry Faulkner, then fifty-six, traveled in Europe. In Taormina, Carlo and Mirella Panarello welcomed them to their home for luncheon, as they had often welcomed Williams in the past. They recalled that he was relaxed and in good spirits that June, but when the reporter arrived from *La Sicilia,* Williams was outspoken about his resentment of critics, the academic establishment and the theatregoing public. "They gave me the Medal of Freedom, sure," he told journalist Giuseppe Di Bernardo. "It's as if they wanted to say to me, 'Here's your award, now take it and get out!' " His anger was short-lived, however, and by early August he had returned to Key West, gathered various manuscript drafts and departed for Chicago to meet with Gregory Mosher, artistic director of the Goodman Theatre.

Williams was eager to give them three one-act plays, as Mosher had requested. At first he offered *The Chalky White Substance, The Traveling Companion* and *Some Problems for the Moose Lodge.* These were to be directed by Gary Tucker, who had directed a Williams one-act play, *The Frosted Glass Coffin,* in Atlanta.

"Gary introduced me to Tennessee at the Ambassador Hotel," Mosher recalled. "He said he was working on a new one-act play, *Some Problems for the Moose Lodge,* a comedy about insanity and a release from an asylum, and death — serious in its concerns, but definitely comic in treatment." At the same time, Williams was writing to Anne Meacham that he felt utterly rudderless, without direction for his future. All the more reason, Mosher thought, to give Williams the opportunity to have professional activity.

In spite of the Goodman's interest, Williams's personal insecurities were unalleviated. Quite simply, his life had no basis of really adult emotional reinforcement. He was traveling so obsessively that he was unable to spend sufficient time with his older friends; the only constant companionship was provided by men young enough to be his children, which is how most of them acted.

Nevertheless, personal anguish notwithstanding, Williams spent the first part of autumn in Chicago, supervising rehearsals of *A Perfect Analysis Given by a Parrot, The Frosted Glass Coffin* and *Some Problems for the Moose Lodge,* the trilogy on which they had finally agreed to compose an evening called *Tennessee Laughs.* "He was staying in an apartment hotel," Mosher said, "working very hard and very seriously on the new short play, and we were all very impressed."

But Williams was also anxious about other markets for his work — especially for the full-length plays of the 1970s. "By this time," Mitch Douglas said, "he was out of vogue and he knew it. His plays had lost money and he was hard to sell. There was no new market for him, and naturally this upset him." There seemed, however, to be a cheerful answer when an offer came from Vancouver, where the University of British Columbia offered him the post of Distinguished Writer in Residence. "But I wanted also to make things happen for his plays," Douglas added, "which I knew he wanted. So I suggested to Vancouver that they do one he liked — *The Red Devil Battery Sign.*" And so he went to Canada that autumn.

Life in British Columbia began very well, and Williams was at ease in the social life. "The theatre people there called a press conference with the local Gay Activists League," Douglas said, "and they threw him a party with a band of worshipful admirers. Tennessee was in his element.

"But when rehearsals were underway for *Red Devil,* Tennessee got very nervous, and suddenly he mysteriously vanished! Finally he turned up, in San Francisco, some time later, living quietly. He was soon on his way back to New York, and then to Chicago. It was, frankly, getting harder and harder to deal with his professional life at this time. Since he wouldn't open his mail, you couldn't send him checks, and everything was forwarded from here to there. Finally, mail had to be sent to his accountant. And Tennessee forgot so many practical details that more and more often he would accuse someone else of stealing money from him, forging his checks, not sending statements of his account, and so on. If he had only opened his mail, every problem would have been solved."

Some Problems for the Moose Lodge, the only play of the evening trilogy to be a world premiere, raised sufficient interest at the Goodman Theatre, meanwhile, that Mosher and Tucker approached Williams to suggest that it be expanded to a full-length play for spring 1981. He promised to work on it in Key West, in New York and back in Vancouver. Almost at once, the name of the play was changed — at the suggestion of an assistant on the production — to *A House Not Meant to Stand.*

For the Christmas–New Year holiday, he returned to Key West, where it was now necessary to arrange for Rose's return to Ossining. Then, ignoring his own dismay at her departure, he pushed forward on the new play, which suddenly took quite a different turn. He wrote on the new title page that it was his kind of "Southern Gothic spook sonata," pointing literally and deliberately to Strindberg's play *The Spook Sonata* (sometimes also called in translation *The Ghost Sonata*).

The dilapidation of the house of Cornelius McCorkle in *A House Not Meant to Stand,* he wrote to Mosher, was a metaphor for the state of society; the characters of the play, however, were obviously emblematic of the Williams family — especially with the alienating, heavy drinker Cornelius, his aging and confused wife Bella (named for Cornelius Williams's sister, their Aunt Belle) and the vague dreams of political stardom that refer to both Williams's paternal grandfather and to his brother, Dakin. There is also a pointed reference to his own use of drugs: "When a man's got to live off pills in the quantity and at the price, with only temporary relief at best, why I say it's time to quit hangin' on, it's time for a man to let go." *Clothes for a Summer Hotel* had been a last cry of pain and apology for Rose; *A House Not Meant to Stand* was an attempt at another exorcism of family ghosts, and each page of the new and expanded script contained references to him and to his bitterness about his family.

The action concerns the McCorkles, whose advanced age, selfishness and illusions about the past conspire to estrange them from one another, their children and their neighbors. A struggle for a hidden family fortune is complicated by the visit of their negligent son and his pregnant fiancée. At the end, Bella sinks into irreversible madness.

But the writing did not have a cathartic effect on Williams. Instead, he lost confidence as he spread out his personal pains, and this frightened him. He wrote again, early in 1981, to the patient and supporting Mosher, reflecting that it might be nice to be dead without having to endure the business of dying. And in another letter shortly after, he referred to a speech in his one-act play *I Can't Imagine Tomorrow* which, he said, perfectly described his life since the death of Frank Merlo almost twenty years earlier:

"A small man came to the house of Death and the uniformed guard at the gate asked him what he wanted. He said that he wanted Death. The guard said that's a very large order for a small man like you. The small man said yes, he knew it was a large order, but that's what he wanted. The guard asked him for his documents. The only document he had was his birth certificate. The guard looked at the date on the birth certificate and said: Too early, you've come too early, go back down the mountain and don't come up here again for twenty years. The small man started to cry. He said: If you won't let me in for twenty years, I'll wait twenty years at the gate, I can't go back down the mountain. I have no place down there. I have no one to visit in the evening, I have no one to talk to, no one to play cards with, I have no one, no one. But the guard walked away, and the small man, who was afraid to talk, began to shout. For a small man he shouted loudly, and Death heard him and came out himself to see what the disturbance was all about. The guard said the small man at the gates had come twenty years too early, and wouldn't go back down the mountain, and Death said: Yes, I understand, but under some circumstances, especially when they shout their heads off at the gates, they can be let in early, so let him in, anything to stop the disturbance."

Mosher at once set in motion, in early February 1981, plans for a gala celebration of Williams's seventieth birthday. Invitations were sent to dozens of friends and colleagues. This was also, Mosher thought, an excellent way of getting Williams back to Chicago, for he feared that the playwright's spirits had fallen so low that he might not arrive with the revisions for production. A turnout of friends, a display of loving support, might enable him to go forward with his work.

Williams did indeed return to Chicago, but his mood was erratic, his health fragile. "After Tennessee emerged from his breakdown," Mosher said, "theatre had changed so much, had altered so radically. Nonprofit theatres had proliferated, old-fashioned producers were no longer producing, long and expensive road tryouts were no longer possible, and not-for-profit productions were numerous: 15 of them quickly became 250. Tennessee never really understood the changes in American theatre, yet in a way he may have felt responsible for them. He often spoke of his agony at not being taken seriously, of being old and washed-up. His expectations weren't unreasonable. He expected serious writing to be attended seriously. He was also a man coming to grips in his plays with what he was coming to grips with in his life — the price of fame, the value of true relationships, the approach of death."

Rehearsals proceeded with considerable delicacy, for it was clear to everyone that feelings all around were vulnerable — not only Williams's, but those of his friends, and those of Gary Tucker. "It was hard to know who to please," recalled Bonnie Sue Arp, a member of the 1981 cast; another, Marji Bank, remembered that Williams could be "a blessed man when we needed him during rehearsal, but he was unpredictable. I remember him coming to lunch with us at the Art Institute cafeteria, in his fur coat, his arms loaded with manuscript pages and all his paraphernalia. Most of the time he seemed a little vague — it was as if there were a wall around him. But he wrote me a dear note when my husband died, and suddenly he could clarify a line of dialogue with a single rewritten line. When we were ready to open, there was still much to be reworked, but it just seemed to elude him."

Other problems were even more sensitive. "When [Gary] Tucker [the director] had me wear jockey shorts for one scene," according to Scott Jaeck, who played the indolent son Charlie, "Tennessee heard about it, came to the rehearsal and was furious — he didn't want his play to be a burlesque." Instead, as another player, Rachel Stephens, recalled, Williams wanted the emphasis on the fact of aging and death — not the attraction of youth: "He became enamored of what the character Jessie could tell us all, and he made revisions to stress that. He gave a character profile to each of us for the role we played, and he often gently evaluated our performances — in fact he rewrote the role for me as we went along. This was not always diplomatic as far as the director was concerned, and there was some tension." And Les Podewell recalled that Williams was always involved with his cast, "and he never showed whatever unhappiness was plaguing his private life. His only concern was, would he be remembered?"

Because of his concern for them, the 1981 cast of *A House Not Meant to*

Stand had great affection for Williams in spite of the bumpy road of re-hearsals. "From what we saw of his rewriting," Scott Jaeck said, "he was obviously concentrating on his own family and its destruction. But he simply couldn't solve the creative problems of the play. He worked hard, but his energies faded quickly, and he came to rehearsals only in the morning."

The seventieth-birthday dinner at the Goodman was attended by none of the invited theatre luminaries and actors (who sent various excuses with their messages of congratulations) and only a few close friends of Williams — Vassilis Voglis and Jane Smith, whose husband Tony had recently died.

"His mood changed sharply," Mosher recalled. "The night before the party, Tennessee ordered to his hotel room a print of [Alfred] Hitch-cock's movie *Lifeboat,* and a group of us sat and watched while he pro-vided a hilarious running commentary about the star, Tallulah Bankhead. But hours before the party next day, he was so upset about the revisions of the play that he said, 'Let's cancel!' Well, he wasn't the first playwright to feel that way when it comes down to the wire, but in his case it took some hard convincing. By that evening, he was in good form, and he danced the night away with just about every woman among the two hundred guests."

After the toasts at dinner, Williams took the microphone. "Chicago was the first place I had a success, and perhaps it will be the last." As it would happen, he was correct — but it was not the last in 1981; that would happen in 1982. *A House Not Meant to Stand* opened in previews the following evening, and Williams remained to make several textual emendations. Again, his manner changed sharply, and again it was an imprudent mixing of mood-altering pills that was the cause.

"There was a short period of time during which he made no sense at all," said Mitch Douglas, who may have guessed the reason but never mentioned it to anyone then or later. "He came up with the notion that I had been dealing with the airlines to put him on a depressurized air-plane to cause him to die of a heart attack. His paranoia was becoming more and more bizarre. And he threatened to make this publicly known. He said we'd have to get a hit-man to silence him, he was going to pub-licize everyone's crimes.* Finally, I said, 'Tennessee, I'll do anything for

---

* This imagined murder-method suggests that Williams was living out the fear of the deranged Mark (*In the Bar of a Tokyo Hotel*), who "kept complaining that the plane cabins were not pressurized enough, and they were pressurized perfectly."

you, but *I* won't have a heart attack.' I always insisted that he deliver his work on time, that he show up for appointments. He owed that to himself. Whenever he failed to keep appointments with the press, I knew he'd be criticized for it. But he just said he didn't want to be an Olympic high jumper for the press."

Then, even more irrationally, Williams began to accuse Douglas of stealing mail and money again, and claimed that his agent was diverting cash due to him. Even when the records and canceled checks were produced, he would never take the proof.

"He listened to everyone but those he should have," Douglas added, "and many of the people around him were concerned only for themselves. When he accused those who didn't deserve the accusation, he could have a nasty side, and a few like myself found that we were always defending ourselves. I, for one, was more and more unwilling to be a doormat for him."*

On April 30, 1981, Audrey Wood suffered a massive stroke that kept her comatose for years. Williams said nothing, but he was then at work on a gruesome one-act play called *Now the Cats with Jewelled Claws*. Set in hell (or its anteroom), it is a tale of madness, depravity and death, and a single revision paid tribute to what must have been his sorrow at the news of Audrey's incapacitation: "What dreadful news about Susie," one woman says, "a massive brain hemorrhage but may linger indefinitely in a coma." Six weeks later, when asked to make a formal statement on her behalf, he admitted: "I was a difficult client for Audrey Wood from the beginning."

For the summer, he divided his time between New York, Key West and Vancouver, where he worked on an adaptation of *The Sea Gull* in which he hoped to star Anne Meacham and Donald Madden, and perhaps Kate Reid. He also drafted scenes for a bizzare tale of venality and seduction which he then called *Gideon's Point*.

In August he was in New York discussing a third memory play he had written, and one with the same evident intention of reconciliation, apology and healing that he had attempted in *Clothes for a Summer Hotel* and

* Williams was still convinced that people were becoming rich at his expense. Years before, he had sent Audrey Wood to Bergdorf Goodman to buy a fur coat for his mother. When it arrived at the hotel where he was entertaining Edwina, he ordered the coat returned, since he suddenly had the idea that Audrey was receiving a percentage of the store's profit. Audrey loved to tell this account of his absurd suspicion. By 1980, his fears included not only agents, but attorneys, actors and accountants as well, and a good number of loyal old friends.

A House Not Meant to Stand. It was from the start titled *Something Cloudy Something Clear,* and it was, he said, "one of the most personal plays I've ever written — it released for me some of the emotional content of my life during the pivotal summer when I took a sort of crash course in growing up. . . . It's wrecked my nerves, but I felt I had to complete certain things because I felt time was limited. . . . I'm very conscious of my decline in popularity, but I don't permit it to stop me because I have the strength of so many playwrights before me. I know the dreadful notices Ibsen got. And O'Neill — he had to die to make *A Moon for the Misbegotten* successful. And to me it has been providential to be an artist, a great act of providence that I was able to turn my psychosis into creativity — my sister Rose did not manage this. So I keep on writing."

For what would be his last New York play, he once again turned to Eve Adamson. There was a professionalism she could offer, a sympathetic hearing and a sensitive interpretation of his play. She was no sycophantic yea-sayer; instead, she combined a sharp eye and a clear voice with her respect. She became, at the end, the last woman who offered the support other women had earlier: Margaret Webster, who surely could have given more had she herself been given a better play to work with; Margo Jones, who adored him and his work, but had limited gifts; Irene Selznick, who had given him all the support and creative freedom he needed to write a masterwork in 1947; the patient, generous and understanding Cheryl Crawford, who had produced a quartet of his plays; and of course the great Audrey Wood, who perhaps gave him more attentive devotion, certainly for a longer time, than any woman in his life.

Something Cloudy Something Clear was a remarkable play late in Williams's creative life. He had spoken of it to virtually no one. This in itself would not have been unusual, except that it was possibly the best work of his last twenty years, and he must have known it. Set on the Provincetown dunes late in the summer of 1940, it is a memory play in which the writer August (the only name changed from real life, and the play's surrogate Tennessee Williams — possibly from his spiritual association with August Strindberg) meets Kip, Frank Merlo and Tallulah Bankhead — to sift and sort the memories, the long buried feelings of love and friendship, and to say farewell. Blatantly autobiographical, the play interweaves the beginning of Williams's affair with Kip with the refractions of later time, granting August the ability to interject latter-day observations from the perspective of Williams's later life. Frank, dying of cancer, makes a brief entrance, and Bankhead is brought out for a brief dialogue. More than any play in his life, it was a simple, tender elegy to three he had loved and lost; it is a poetic and apologetic farewell, an act of forgiveness of himself for the love he had not had the time to acknowledge. His life, as he then felt, was an alternating perception of "something cloudy and something clear," and the condition of his eyes, which those words described, fit his inner perceptions perfectly. Most of all, however, the play is an acceptance of the death which had already embraced them all, and that he knew must soon come to him — thus the final dance to the music of Ravel's funereal "Pavane."

It was indeed so personal a play that Williams considered withdrawing it during rehearsal. "Tennessee was so frightened," Eve Adamson said, "that the closer we came to opening the more convinced he was that we shouldn't. He could be very difficult at times like this, when his fears overwhelmed him, and as much as he rewrote, it never seemed to bolster his confidence. At one point he was really trying to sabotage his own play, to harm himself before the critics got a chance to harm him. This was a very sad part of his nature, and I must say I went through absolute hell on this production. But even when the worst did happen, and the critics savaged what I and the audiences knew was a very fine play, he called to ask if I was feeling all right. As depressed as he was, he was concerned for me."

In September, Williams returned from the distant retreat of Vancouver and attended, with friends, several performances of his last New York production. All who saw it loved it, and the Jean Cocteau Repertory sold out its performances then and again the following February and March. The play was an unexpected surprise, a minor miracle.

"I saw Tennessee for the last time at a performance of *Something Cloudy Something Clear,*" Meade Roberts remembered. "I felt that the play — had it been prepared away from New York in a 'lab' kind of atmosphere — would have had the time to be improved. Even as it was, it was very, very fine, both beautifully written and played. Tenn looked wonderful that night. He was very warm, and we embraced, and he wanted to know all about my life, what I'd been writing and so forth. He talked about his adaptation of Chekhov, and ideas he had for new work. He seemed so young, as if the whole world lay before him that night.

"After that evening's performance, a symposium was held, and he was articulate and witty. Ruth Gordon and Garson Kanin were in the audience — God bless them, they were the only members of the uptown,

Broadway crowd who cared enough to come. Kanin rose from his seat and said he wished it to be made clear that Tennessee Williams was unquestionably the greatest dramatist America had brought forth and he wished the audience to acknowledge that fact. Everyone cheered, and it was all very genuine. Tennessee beamed, with tears in his eyes, and then he went out into the night, his shoulders squared, with a look on his face that seemed to say 'En avant!' "

That autumn, he was told about the deaths of the painter Henry Faulkner and the poet and teacher Oliver Evans, and this pitched him for days into despondency. Then he and Harold Pinter were selected as recipients of the third annual Common Wealth Award, a grant of $11,000 to each "for excellence and outstanding achievements in various fields of human endeavor." In his acceptance remarks at the Shubert Theatre, a withdrawn and unclear Williams said of the award money, "I'll have to think about using this for a tombstone," but then he recovered better manners and said he would like to dedicate the award "to my sister, Rose Isabel Williams," who was in fact in the audience that November day, celebrating her birthday with her brother.

Backstage, Pinter, who had just told the audience of his long admiration for "the greatest American playwright," was approached by him. "Harold," he said, "take care of your health. I could have done a lot more if I had taken care of my health." That day, according to Larry D. Clark, who was visiting from the University of Missouri at Columbia, "Tennessee was very ill, very frail."

The fact was that Williams had unfortunately resumed regular megadoses of pills for both sedation and alertness — mostly Nembutal and Ritalin and Seconal, although he was often able, with the help of those who called themselves friends, to obtain more potent, less legal substances. "He behaved very badly that day," as Eve Adamson recalled, "and he treated Mitch Douglas abominably."

Indeed, Douglas's days as Williams's agent were over: "The last time we really met for any period of time was the day of the award. Later I heard he was working and that he was sometimes even happy, and I was glad for him. And several times before the end of our relationship, he told people that I had had a real interest in his career and had kept him going — which I had, and which I was pleased to do — and that gratified me. He could be a terribly sweet man, childlike and grateful and the soul of sincerity. At the White House, for example, he was chipper and courtly. He pinned a flower in my lapel when I was wearing a dark suit.

At times like that his real gift for friendship shone out, and those are the times I like to remember."*

But those times were too rare, as Audrey Wood and Bill Barnes had known, too. Williams remained in New York until the end of the year, attending small dinner parties with friends like Vassilis Voglis and Jane Smith. "He was extremely reserved and quiet unless he had a drink," Voglis recalled, "but when I commissioned a portrait of him he gladly sat for it. That autumn we were at other gatherings — Milton Goldman honored Virgil Thomson, and Patricia Kennedy Lawford gave a party for him also. It was a pleasant enough season for him." (The party Mrs. Lawford offered was a polite and generous substitute for what was to have been a gala in Williams's honor at Lincoln Center on December 2. It had been canceled when virtually no tickets were sold.)

In January he was back in Key West, still revising *A House Not Meant to Stand,* which Mosher had promised to present at the larger main stage of the Goodman, after two productions in the smaller studio. New York friends, however, were concerned for Williams's health; Voglis flew down for a visit, but the coterie that still attended Williams annoyed the visitor — as it had a number of others, like Edwin Sherin — and a few days later, content that at least Williams was looked after and fed, he returned to New York.

By February 8, Williams, too, returned to New York. The mayor presented the city's medallion of honor on February 10, and the next evening there was a fashionable party for Williams, at which his former friend and sometime nemesis Truman Capote was present. Quietly, Williams asked when he thought they would meet again. "In Paradise," was Capote's response. For the moment, Williams was content with Key West.

On February 13, from Duncan Street, he telephoned a young film-maker named Peter Hoffman, who had been eager to transform two of Williams's short stories — "The Resemblance Between a Violin Case and a Coffin" and "Completed," both based on Rose's youth — into a full-length screenplay. Two days later, Hoffman was at the Pier House restaurant in Key West, dining with Williams and discussing a collaboration.

No work on this project was possible until June, however, for Williams was still hopeful about the Goodman Theatre. The play was now over one hundred pages, and he took it to Chicago for meetings with

* From the end of 1981, executives at ICM assigned Luis Sanjurjo to represent Tennessee Williams's literary interests.

Mosher and the new director who had been engaged after personal and creative differences led to the dismissal of Gary Tucker.

Of his meetings with Williams, director André Ernotte recalled that the playwright was "afflicted with self-doubt, [eager to] say something bad about himself so that he can say it first before anyone else ... he's often hard to deal with." Mosher agreed that at this time Williams was riddled with vulnerability and pain, and that still he kept on revising and rewriting, even when that work produced no substantial improvements.

"Tennessee confronted his weaknesses and faults for years in a way that few others ever did," Elia Kazan said later. "We all try to appear tougher and stronger than we are, but there was something in him that reached out and touched everyone who saw his plays or who knew him. You felt that your own faults and sins were understood and that he had compassion for them. He accepted his own weakness and sinfulness, and he went on courageously and bravely — always writing. He never backed off."

The insistence on writing even in the midst of depression, even when exhaustion nearly pitched him into total collapse, was certainly a courageous part of Williams's character. The habit of work was an ingrained one for decades, not simply the automatic response to boredom or the autonomic response to drugs. "A playwright writes," as Kazan added, "even if he is in decline. Gallant is the word to describe Tennessee at the end. He went on writing, even when he was told his plays weren't very good by comparison with what had preceded. On he went, always working at the craft, never ashamed. All people in the arts have special weaknesses, but all we can be judged on is what's been worthwhile. If people are judged for their failures, the balance is upset, and the successes are themselves diminished."

But there is, after all, a limit to human genius, as there is a limit to the genius's lifetime; it is only a truism, only a cliché to say that everything human is finite. No one must have been more aware of this than Tennessee Williams, who had so long admitted that his masterpieces were things of the past.

On another level, of course, he continued because that is precisely the way struggle is endured by writers: the gift is exercised, not short-circuited or dulled by neglect. The only way he could maintain some affirmation of value, the only route he knew to attempt meaning in his life was to write. It was his way of healing, of thanking, of forgiving, of making a final attempt at inner order out of the external muddle that he knew had marked so much of his life.

He must have known, contrary to his sometimes cantankerous attitude about critics, his reputation, his place in history, that over the last forty years — the longest and the most public and most highly compensated career in the history of American theatre — he had been neither unappreciated nor underappreciated. Because he was a true artist, this never left him merely content; that it did not, however, give him a greater inner calm, a quietness and an inner gathering in the final years, must have been his keenest penance. It would have been natural for him to think in penitential terms, for that is very much the tone of the last plays and the last stories.

In late April 1982, after a stormy rehearsal period of frayed nerves, raised voices and hurt feelings, *A House Not Meant to Stand* finally opened and did a respectable business until the end of May. "There was a strong impression all around," recalled Scott Jaeck, "that this was his last play, and that he just didn't have the strength to deal with it. He came to the opening night, and he came back to thank us all, but he was a weary man." A month later, *Time* magazine called the play the best Williams had written in a decade, a work "inhabited by a rich collection of scarred characters."

But by this time Williams was beyond encouragement. He wrote to his friend, the actors' agent Milton Goldman, whose professional counsel he so valued, that he had endured an agonizing solitude for twenty years, since Frank Merlo's death; he knew not how much longer he could endure. Small dinner parties by New York friends did not cheer him, nor did the acceptance of an honorary doctorate at Harvard University's June commencement. Weary and distracted, he appeared disheveled in an open sportshirt at the Cambridge ceremonies. Then, with his loyal and concerned friend Jane Smith, he went to a festival of his plays at Williamstown, where he said plaintively, "Give my goodbye to Broadway, my many, many goodbyes, for there is a rock there, and it is not one from which water nor violets nor roses spring."

At Williamstown, however, on the suggestion of friends, he agreed to meet with Peter Hoffman, who presented a prose treatment of the projected screenplay. Until the end of July, they worked erratically in Key West. The major interruption was provided by the goodwill and concern of Gregory Mosher, who agreed to hear Williams's idea for another series

of one-act plays to be called *Williams's Guignol*. There were also two un-
finished longer plays, *In Masks Outrageous and Austere* (the new title for
Gideon's Point) and *The Lingering Hour*. Williams, however, never resumed the contact.

Toward the end of July, he was again eager to travel, and he took Jane
Smith and Peter Hoffman with him first to London, and then, on July
24, they checked into suites at the San Domenico Palace Hotel, Taormina. He was glad to return to the quiet, sprawling monastery that had
become a regular hotel for kings and princes, for artists and writers and
actors and the less celebrated who appreciated its cloister of plants and
palm trees, and the clear, warm waters of the Ionian Sea below.

He continued to write every morning. And what he wrote was not the
screenplay for a collaboration with Hoffman, but *The Lingering Hour*, a
violent apocalypse of devastation and universal death.

"All the volcanoes of the world explode at more or less the same
time," he told a visiting reporter, "and there are earthquakes and destruction everywhere. Here [i.e., in Sicily], there is Etna and the action is set
in the main square at a cafe, with people talking. . . . The first earthquake
happens in California. Hollywood first disappears into the sea." The title
of his play is the usual translation of the Italian *prima sera* — the first
dusk he had described in *The Roman Spring of Mrs. Stone* as the moment
"before the lamps go on, when the atmosphere has that exciting blue
clarity of the noctural scenes in old silent films, a color of water that
holds a few drops of ink . . . the amethyst light of prima sera."

The three visitors to Taormina were welcomed to the home of the
Panarello family, who found their old friend, as Carlo said, "gentle and
quiet — he listened a lot rather than speaking as much as he usually did
with us. His family seemed to be the great sorrow in his life, and he understood them with great warmth and humanity. When he spoke of
them, his eyes would often fill with tears. This is perhaps why he understood so quickly and so deeply the family troubles of others, and people's
anguish in general."

After a week, however, Williams grew restless again. "He found traveling difficult," Jane Smith said, "so we did not go on to Russia, as he
had hoped.* And once the film people who had gathered in Sicily for a

---

* The plays of Tennessee Williams (invariably with some cutting and alterations) have been
perenially popular in Russia. He had by this time amassed more than one million dollars in
Russian royalties, which could not be taken from that country but would have had to be
spent there.

festival found that he was there, he was plagued constantly. Finally we fled because some people at the hotel complained that his typewriter made noise at odd hours of the night."

On August 13, after stopping in Rome, they arrived in New York, where he met a last time with Gregory Mosher, who remembered being present after Williams had brought Rose to New York for a day. "He had bought a ring for her, and he was worried that she might not like it. But she loved it, and he was very relieved." *Clothes for a Summer Hotel* had reached its final closure. Rose (like Zelda in the play) again had a ring; this time it would not be removed, not given to any other.

During the first week in September, Williams ate little, slept much, and wandered around the house in Key West. His housekeeper, Leoncia McGee, was alarmed, and very nearly panicked when he vanished from the house early one morning and did not reappear all day.

There was an explanation. Williams had boarded a bus, heading north for an unknown destination. He got as far as Key Largo, where he waved the driver on and sat alone in a bar that rarely hosted more than drifters or desperate tourists who had stopped at the filling station outside.

A young couple were seated nearby. "As we were having coffee," the man recalled, "we noticed a man seated alone at another table." After a few moments of casual conversation across the aisle, they invited the man to join them. "We figured he was just a local hanging out by himself, but an intelligent man, because he was impressed with the fact that I said I am a writer." The conversation continued, and the strangers introduced themselves as Mr. and Mrs. Steven Kunes; their companion said he was Tennessee Williams, but that they should call him Tom.

"He was waiting for a bus, God only knows why, but soon we were driving him back toward Key West." They took him to Duncan Street, talking en route about writers and writing. Something in the young couple's optimism had opened him up, and made him for a while more expansive. They had just moved from New York, were taking a short holiday, and planned to move to California. Williams invited them into his house, and over coffee and a table piled with scattered manuscript pages, he asked about Kunes's novel in progress.

"And that's when it happened," he said. "Williams went into another room and emerged with a square black case, telling me to look inside. It was an Underwood typewriter from the 1940s. 'I write very rarely on this anymore,' he said. 'But I used it for *Summer and Smoke* and *Cat on a Hot Tin Roof*. It needs a new ribbon, and perhaps some oil. I didn't know I'd be finding a place for it so soon.' " He looked at Steven Kunes. "Write a play, Steven," he said. "Just write a play. I know you can hit the core. I know it like I know a good wine. Don't be flattered when I say this. You can flatter me by using this old machine here to do the job." They thanked one another for the kindnesses they shared that evening, and the couple left. Four months later, as a courtesy, Kunes sent Williams the first draft of the novel he wrote on the typewriter, but there was no reply.

In mid-September, Williams flew for a week to New York, went four days to Vassilis Voglis's summer house on Long Island, then returned to Key West. He was beyond encouragement. At Duncan Street, the petty sexual intrigues of a small group depressed him further; when his house should have been serene, he opened it to acquaintances who could not have been less helpful. At the end of the month, he invited Peter Hoffman for a few days' work on the screenplay, but he was so morose and withdrawn, living now only on wine and Seconal and coffee, that no work was possible. He was losing weight and also all interest in continuing with anything. By 1982 the life of travel that had been both diversion and search took him nowhere but to a deeper point of loneliness, and his Key West social circle enclosed nothing. On October 1, he told Hoffman that they would leave at once for New York, and then proceed to Asia, but once in Manhattan he abandoned further travel for the moment, and Hoffman was dismissed.

He then returned to Key West, only to find that his dog and cat had abandoned the house in his absence. Soon he was back in New Jersey, where he visited briefly with Jane Smith at her suburban home; he selected from her library the letters of Chekhov for them to read over the next several days.

In November, Williams was invited to read from his work at the 92nd Street YMHA. The reading at Kaufman Hall turned out to be his last public appearance. Richard Kennedy, an English teacher who regularly attended the readings by writers and dramatists, recalled that Williams received a most enthusiastic welcome from the audience. "His speech was occasionally slurred," according to Kennedy, "and his opening remark was that he almost forgot to show up. He seemed very uncomfortable." Williams read excerpts from unpublished poems and from a short story-in-progress, and after only a half-hour with his audience "abruptly stood up and said, 'That's the end of the performance.' " And according to Jane Smith, "When he came out onstage, I was shocked — I thought something was missing, I was so used to that vigorous man, and the energy seemed to have left him. Later, I learned from another friend that he became depressed in New Orleans and Key West."

In December, back again in Key West, he added a codicil to his will, transferring the joint administration of one special trust fund to the sole custody of Harvard University, which would also in time become for writers the repository of certain remaining papers. Within days, neighbors who were alerted to his frail condition were alarmed when they received no reply to persistent calls. Finally, on Christmas Eve, two of them found him comatose and rushed him to a hospital. Next day, Leoncia McGee telephoned Dakin: "She called to tell me that Kate Moldawer [a neighbor in Key West] and Gary Tucker had taken him to the hospital the night before, that he hadn't been eating and had locked himself in his room for three days. He was found totally dehydrated, and they had to flush the drugs out of his system."

Jane Smith went to Key West at once, suggesting that he come back north to rest, to stay with her and to see several New York physicians she knew.

After a week's recuperation at Jane Smith's home, however, Williams insisted on resuming his travels. He went south, to visit Robert Carroll, then he was in Key West again, then back in New Orleans, where he concluded the sale of the Dumaine Street house, and then he returned to Key West. It was as if he were animating the last lines of *The Glass Menagerie,* when Tom described how he had "followed, from then on, in my father's footsteps, attempting to find in motion what was lost in space. I traveled around a great deal. The cities swept about me like dead leaves, leaves that were brightly colored but torn away from the branches. I would have stopped, but I was pursued by something."

On Friday, January 21, 1983, Anne Meacham telephoned to report that their friend Donald Madden was desperately ill. At once Williams wrote to him that he, too, had recently been confined to a hospital. He praised Madden's decision to remain at home, among loved ones, rather than submit to the care of strangers; his own complaint, he added, was a serious one — he had had a sufficiency of life, and was in irreversible depression. The letter concluded with the hope that when he came to New York he hoped to find Madden restored; if he was not, Williams wrote, then life was surely the black joke he had mostly accused it of being.

In New York in early February, he announced to Jane Smith, and to his occasional secretary and companion John Uecker, that he would soon leave for Taormina — alone. When Uecker, who had a professional commitment that month, suggested engaging another traveling companion, Williams said simply, "It's too late for a stranger."

And so he made his way to Taormina; it was the first time he had traveled alone in years. The staff at the San Domenico Palace Hotel welcomed him on February 11, but as the concierge noted, "He was so sad and exhausted and withdrawn, and we could not encourage him to eat at all." Carlo and Mirella Panarello were surprised to learn, months later, that he had been to Sicily in February; it was the first time in more than thirty years that he had neither visited nor telephoned from the few blocks' distance.

Instead, he went alone and for the last time to the piazza where he and Frank Merlo had so often sipped wine or coffee, had dined together, watched the crowds go by, and walked arm in arm for the evening *passeggiata,* the traditional stroll, along the Corso Umberto. But there was no one in the empty piazza that February; there was only what he once called "a cold wind around my heart that wraps me in despair."

After five nights he returned to New York, where he secluded himself in his suite at the Elysée, refusing food and almost all company.

"I don't want to wind up in an intensive care unit with all kinds of tubes stuck in me," he said earlier. "I wouldn't allow that, and I don't think that's going to happen. . . . But I go mad at night. I can't be alone, because I have this fear of dying alone." He asked John Uecker to remain nearby, although he neither requested nor would accept much contact or conversation.

For the last five years, he invariably included in public readings his poem "Old Men Go Mad at Night," which, he felt, conveyed himself directly to his audience:

> What's left is keeping hold of breath
> and for cover never now a lover
> rests them warm . . .
> Was that a board that creaked
> as he took leave of us,
> or did he speak —
> "I'm going to sleep, good night."

On the evening of February 24, 1983, he withdrew quietly to his bedroom with a bottle of wine. On his bedside table was the traditional array of prescriptions — capsules, tablets, eyedrops and nosedrops and all the paraphernalia associated with decades of hypochondria and chemical dependence. It was later reported by the New York medical examiner and the pathologist that during the night Tennessee Williams had ingested small quantities of a variety of drugs — cocaine among them — with the wine, and that a barbiturate overcap had somehow lodged in his throat: apparently he had used the cap like a spoon, to swallow two Seconal capsules. He had been, it seemed, unable or unwilling to summon help.

In the morning, friends entered the room. One of Tennessee Williams's hands was resting gently, palm upward. At last there was stillness.

Notes

Preface

p. xvii "Tennessee's life is" Elia Kazan to DS, Feb. 1, 1984.
xvii "a drama" TW, "If the Writing is Honest," *Where I Live* (New York: New Directions, 1978), p. 104. Originally published as a preface to William Inge, *The Dark at the Top of the Stairs* (New York: Random House, 1958).
xviii "I hope" TW, in a taped interview with Stephen Banker (1974) preserved in the *Tapes for Readers* series (Washington, D.C.).

Chapter One

5 "I was rarely" Edwina Dakin Williams, p. 162.
6 "I danced" Diary of Edwina Estelle Dakin, entry under year 1900–1901.
6 "Mr. Frederick" *Ibid.,* Oct. 8, 1901.
6 "secret ambition" Edwina Dakin Williams, p. 183.
6 "I remember" Melissa S. Whyte to TW, Dec. 7, 1948.
6–7 "Mr. Lide" Diary of Edwina Estelle Dakin, Aug. 18, 1905.
10 "She was" "The Life and Ideas of Tennessee Williams," *P.M.,* May 6, 1945, p. 7.
10 "I was" Washburn, p. 6-E.
10 "Other children" Edwina Dakin Williams, p. 15.
11 "diggin' to" *Ibid.,* pp. 13–14.
11 "It was" Rice, Apr. 24, 1958, p. M-2.
11 "She never" Lucy Freeman to DS, Sept. 1, 1983.
12 "I got" Davis, p. 12.
12 "Grandfather was" Dakin Williams to DS, Oct. 23, 1983.
13–14 "The changes" David Loth to DS, Oct. 9, 1983.
14–15 "At the boardinghouse" Dakin Williams to DS, Oct. 23, 1983.
15 "I preferred" Rice, Apr. 24, 1958, p. M-2.
15 "Her coming" "Grand," *The Knightly Quest: A Novella and Four Short Stories* (New York: New Directions, 1966), p. 172.
15–16 "Grand cared" Dakin Williams to DS, Oct. 23, 1983.
17 "The many moves" *Ibid.*
18 "He took no" Edwina Dakin Williams, pp. 35 and 39.
18 "I hated him" Rice, Apr. 24, 1958, p. M-2.
18–19 "Life at home" Dakin Williams to DS, Oct. 23, 1983.
19 "In her transition," Keith, sec. 3, p. 6.

19 "Rose was caught" Dakin Williams to DS, Oct. 23, 1983.
20 "She was doing" *Ibid.*
20 "It was just" *Ibid.*
20 "It immediately became" Rice, Apr. 24, 1958, p. M-2.
21 "Old Things" and "Nature's Thanksgiving" *The Ben Blewett* (junior high school newspaper), Oct. 1925.
22 "Mother became" Dakin Williams to DS, Oct. 23, 1983.
23 "Tommy Williams" Margaret Cowen, English teacher at University City High School, in Rice, Apr. 27, 1958, p. M-2.
23 "drinking, smoking" "Can a Good Wife Be a Good Sport?" *Smart Set,* vol. 80, no. 3 (May 1927), pp. 9, 13.
23 "Tom and Hazel" Dakin Williams to DS, Oct. 23, 1983.
23 "My mother did not" TW, *Memoirs* (New York: Doubleday, 1975), p. 15.
24 "She married another" Jennings, p. 74.
24 "Hushed were the" Thomas L. Williams, "The Vengeance of Nitocris," *Weird Tales,* vol. 12, no. 2 (Aug. 1928), p. 253.
24 "set the keynote" Rice, Apr. 24, 1958, p. M-2.
25 "His great affection" Paul Bigelow to DS, Feb. 3, 1984.
25 "the hospitalities were" *Clarksdale Daily Register,* July 6, 1928.

Chapter Two

31 "One had to go" David Loth to DS, Oct. 9, 1983.
31 "There were no" *Ibid.*
32 "Campus life was" *Ibid.*
33 "We went through" Donovan Rhynsburger to DS, Nov. 11, 1983.
33 "a play with" Unsigned review of *Beauty Is the Word,* in the *Daily Missourian* (student newspaper of University of Missouri at Columbia) 188 (Apr. 12, 1930): 2.
33 "I thought, when" Donovan Rhynsburger to DS, Nov. 11, 1983.
34 "The fact is" Lucy Freeman to DS, Sept. 1, 1983.
34–35 "There were forty" Elmer Lower to DS, Dec. 6, 1983.
36 "It's true that" Maxwell, p. 24.
36 "We used to drive" Brown, p. 276.
36–37 "one of the most amazing" Elmer Lower to DS, Dec. 6, 1983.
37 "I attacked my" Rice, Apr. 27, 1958, p. M-2.
37 "I was deeply" Jennings, p. 74.
37 "None of us" *Ibid.*
37–38 "It was so moving" *New York Post,* Dec. 12, 1947 (magazine), p. 1.
39 "those bound by" Sheaffer, p. 253.
40 "Father used the" Dakin Williams to DS, Oct. 23, 1983.
40 "There was absolutely" Elmer Lower to DS, Dec. 6, 1983.
40 "He had been" Donovan Rhynsburger to DS, Nov. 11, 1983.
42 "Mother was an" Dakin Williams to DS, Oct. 23, 1983.
43 "the very handsome" *Ibid.*
43 "Rose became" *Ibid.*
44–45 "It was a terrible" *Ibid.*
46 "the most moving" TW, in Harry Rasky's film, *Tennessee Williams's South.*

47 "By this time" Dakin Williams to DS, Oct. 23, 1983.
49 "Tom had fanatical" Clark Mills McBurney, in Rice, Apr. 28, 1958, p. M-2.
49 "the worship of" H. D. F. Kitto, "Dionysus," in Phyllis Hartnoll, ed., *The Oxford Companion to the Theatre,* 3rd. ed. (London: Oxford University Press, 1967), p. 242.
50 "She then became" Dakin Williams to DS, Oct. 23, 1983.
50 "[She] was rarely" William Jay Smith, p. 191.
51 "The amount of" DLB, p. 25.
51 "Even at parties" DLB, p. 26.
51 "We have been" Arleen Thyson, in *Washington University,* vol. 53, no. 3 (Summer 1983), p. 24.
51 "the model contributor" John M. Pickering, *ibid.*
51–52 "the shyest" William Jay Smith, p. 193.
52 "She never stopped" *Ibid.,* p. 190.
52 "I don't know" Thomas L. Williams, "27 Wagons Full of Cotton," *Manuscript,* vol. 3, no. 4 (Aug. 1936), p. 28.
52 "but Mother and" Edwina Dakin Williams, p. 83; see also DLB, p. 26.
53 "There was not" DLB, p. 26.
54 "a poignant little" Anne H. Jennings, "Review of Theatre Guild's Plays Presented Oct. 13," *Webster Groves Missouri Star-Times,* Oct. 16, 1936, pp. 1–2.
54 "I needed" Rice, Apr. 28, 1958, p. M-2.
55 "They were the" "Something Wild . . . ," *Where I Live: Selected Essays* (New York: New Directions, 1978), pp. 9–10.
55 "showed much more" Rice, Apr. 28, 1958, p. M-2.
55 "It was a" *Ibid.*
55 "very jealous of" Dakin Williams to DS, Oct. 23, 1983.
55–56 "He wore conservative" *Ibid.*
56 "very pitiful" Edwina Dakin Williams to Rose O. Dakin, letters dated Nov. 17 and 26, 1936
56 "She still says" *Ibid.,* letter dated Dec. 6, 1936.
56 "I can't take her" *Ibid.,* letter dated Jan. 26, 1937.
57 "It wasn't only" Dakin Williams to DS, Oct. 23, 1983.
57 "For all the" Davis, p. 13.
57 "that dreaded city" *Memoirs,* p. 28.
57 "It was a great" At Univ. of Southern California, Mar. 18, 1973.
58 "Well, I guess" Tischler, p. 56., e.g.
58 "Mr. Williams has" A report of the reading committee of the Mummers of St. Louis (HRC/Univ. of Texas, Austin).
58 "a vital and" Reed Hynds, "Mummers' Play Brilliantly Done, Though Unconclusive [sic]," *St. Louis Star-Times,* Dec. 1, 1937, p. 17.
58–59 "I was a terrible" Calendo, p. 31
59–60 "I was a freshman" Dakin Williams to DS, Oct. 23, 1983.
60 "She gave permission" Buckley, p. 98.
60 "My sister was" Berkvist, sec. 2, pp. 4–5.
60 "I don't think" Brown, p. 278.
60 "She was the" Maxwell, p. 256.

Chapter Three

65 "He had" Anthony Dexter to DS, Aug. 28, 1983.
65 "I have only" Elsworth P. Conkle to his wife Virginia, recalled in a letter to DS, Jan. 24, 1984.
65 "Tom Williams" Virginia Conkle, quoted in a letter from Ellis Conkle to DS, Jan. 24, 1984.
65 "The course also required" Elsworth P. Conkle to DS, Jan. 24, 1984.
67 "sounds like it" Press release, Liebeling-Wood Agency, 1948.
67 "the fellows in" *Memphis Commercial Appeal,* Nov. 24, 1940, p. 14.
68 "It was a period" *Tennessee Williams: Theater in Process,* an Encyclopedia Britannica Educational Corp. film, 1976.
68 "I found the" Rice, Apr. 39, 1958, p. M-2.
71 "I was desperately" Davis, p. 13.
72-73 "There's a wonderful" Elia Kazan to DS, Feb. 1, 1984.
74 "After all" Wood, p. 130.
74 "Tom's great god" William Jay Smith, p. 191.
76 "His primary need" Wood, p. 133.
76 "These plays were" Hume Cronyn to DS, Aug. 19, 1983.
76 "I was just" Steen, pp. 159-160; DLB, p. 80.
76 "That was truly" Wood, p. 133.
77 "Audrey came to" Robert Anderson to DS, Dec. 16, 1983.
78 "He put writing" Windham (a), p. 110.
78-79 "I had an" Paul Bigelow to DS, Feb. 3, 1984.
79 "He was a charming" Langner, p. 331.
79 "And so I put" Paul Bigelow to DS, Feb. 3, 1984.
81 "one of the irascibles" Fritz Bultman to DS, May 30, 1984.
81 "just like" Ruth Hiebert to DS, Oct. 15, 1983.
81 "My left eye" *Paris Review,* p. 169.
81 "Kip was" Fritz Bultman to DS, May 30, 1984.
81n "It was an intense" Paul Bigelow to DS, Feb. 3, 1984.
82 "a desperate period" "A Summer of Discovery," *New York Herald-Tribune,* Dec. 24, 1961.
82-83 "he had been" Webster, p. 66.
83 "Why they should" *Ibid.,* p. 66.
83-84 "a short, sturdy" *Ibid.,* p. 69.
84 "a mixture of" *Memoirs,* p. 62.
85 "astonishing" *The Boston Herald,* Dec. 31, 1940, p. 10.
85 "most interesting" Elliot Norton, " 'Battle of Angels' a Defeat, But No Disaster," *Boston Post,* Jan. 12, 1941, p. 25.
85 "sordid and amateurish" *Variety,* Jan. 1, 1941, p. 45.
85 "Then it was" "The History of a Play (With Parentheses," *Pharos* 1-2 (Spring 1945), p. 120.
85-86 "putrid.... This show" *Boston Post,* Jan. 7, 1941, p. 1.
86 "Tom asked me" Smith, in DLB, p. 29.
86 "Wherever he went" Wood, pp. 131, 138.

86 "although *Battle*" Windham (a), p. 110.

87 "just not being" Paul Bigelow to DS, Feb. 3, 1984.

87 "His eyesight" Webster, p. 71.

88 "I had a small" Fritz Bultman to DS, May 30, 1984.

90 "Then I must" "The Siege," *In the Winter of Cities* (New York: New Directions, 1964), p. 20.

91 "The Beggar's Bar" Fritz Bultman to DS, May 30, 1984.

91 "a pathetic lady" Paul Bigelow to DS, Feb. 3, 1984.

91 "our blood" "Iron is the Winter," *In the Winter of Cities,* p. 96.

92 "and just a few" Paul Bigelow to DS, Feb. 3, 1984.

92 "He was a real" *Ibid.*

93 "It was a" Anthony Dexter to DS, Aug. 28, 1983.

94 "He hated being" Paul Bigelow to DS, Feb. 3, 1984.

96 "I went to" David Greggory to DS, Aug. 12, 1983.

96 "We found" *Ibid.*

96 "I visited" *Ibid.*

97 "This is what" *Ibid.*

97 "This really hurt" *Ibid.*

97–98 "He just showed" Christopher Isherwood to DS, Oct. 7, 1983.

98 "sitting typing" Isherwood, pp. 135–136.

98 "It was wartime" David Greggory to DS, Aug. 12, 1983.

98 "In his private" Christopher Isherwood to DS, Oct. 7, 1983.

98 "He always had" Paul Bigelow to DS, Feb. 3, 1984.

100 "From the day" David Greggory to DS, Aug. 12, 1983.

101 "tidying up" *New York Times,* Oct. 17, 1943, sec. 2, p. 2.

101 "Tenn was in" Paul Bigelow to DS, Feb. 3, 1984.

101–102 "Son" Quoted by Dakin Williams to DS, Oct. 23, 1983.

102 "Tennessee was very" Burl Ives to DS, Aug. 26, 1983.

102 "a living poem" "Grand," pp. 169, 172.

Chapter Four

110 "Of course her" Eloise Sheldon Armen to DS, Sept. 1, 1983.

110 "a small flame" Courtney, p. 416.

110 "rather dull" Notation across the original ms. of *The Glass Menagerie,* deposited at Humanities Research Center, University of Texas/Austin.

111 "Mr. Dowling" Young, p. 33.

111 "the stamina" Claudia Cassidy, "Fragile Drama Holds Together in Tight Spell," *Chicago Daily Tribune,* Dec. 27, 1944, p. 11.

111 "has the courage" Ashton Stevens, "Great Actress Proves It In Fine Way," *Chicago Herald American,* Dec. 27, 1944, p. 11.

111 "Actually, she directed" Courtney, p. 396.

111 "It gripped players" Claudia Cassidy, "On the Aisle," *Chicago Sunday Tribune,* Jan. 7, 1945.

113 "the reluctant" Courtney, p. 411.

114 "The events of" Dakin Williams to DS, Oct. 23, 1983.

114 "We all knew" Randolph Echols to DS, Sept. 27, 1983.

114 "never understood" Blais, sec. 2, p. 2.

114 "All work is" Winakor, p. 4.

115 "It's human valor" "The Life and Ideas of Tennessee Williams," *P.M.* May 6, 1945, pp. 6–7.

115 "I may not" *New York Post,* Dec. 30, 1957.

116 "less a play" Nathan, pp. 326–327.

116 "pity for people" Nightingale, sec. 2, p. 3.

116–117 "It is usually" Miller, p. 30.

117 "and new problems" *Paris Review,* p. 154.

118 "During the" Randolph Echols to DS, Sept. 27, 1983.

119 "I never knew" Bosworth, p. 113.

120 "he was more" Steen, p. 151.

120 "a restless person" *Ibid.,* p. 101.

121 "If I can" Press release, Liebling-Wood Agency, 1948.

122 "Pancho was a" Fritz Bultman to DS, May 30, 1984.

122 "romantic pessimism" Joseph Wood Krutch, "Tennessee Williams," *The Nation* 162 (Mar. 2, 1946): 267–268.

123 "sentimental" Denham Sutcliffe, "Tennessee Williams," *New York Times Book Review,* Feb. 24, 1946, p. 8.

123 "Tennessee was such" Muriel Bultman Francis to DS, Dec. 17, 1983.

124 "Tennessee behaved very" Fritz Bultman to DS, May 30, 1984.

124 "It wasn't a" Ashley Pond, M.D. to DS, Oct. 10, 1983; see also *Albuquerque Tribune,* Feb. 29, 1983.

125 "hypochondriacal being" Maxwell, pp. 59–60.

125–126 "The meeting between" Paul Bigelow to DS, Feb. 3, 1984.

126 "a tall, slim" Carr, p. 272.

126 "Pancho was of course" Paul Bigelow to DS, Feb. 3, 1984.

126 "Carson went wild" *Ibid.,* p. 276.

127 "From that summer" Paul Bigelow to DS, Feb. 3, 1984.

129 "I live" Press release from Liebling-Wood (1947), e.g.

129 "She was neither" TW, "An Appreciation," *New York Times,* Dec. 15, 1946, sec. 2, p. 4.

130 "Whenever I'm disturbed" Maxwell, p. 132.

134 "Margo wanted desperately" Randolph Echols to DS, Sept. 27, 1983.

135 "I never saw" *Paris Review,* pp. 159–160.

136 "Tennessee was quite" Elia Kazan to DS, Feb. 1, 1984.

137 "At the end" Fritz Bultman to DS, May 30, 1984.

137 "This man has" TW at the University of Southern California, Mar. 18,1973.

137–138 "a quietly woven" Brooks Atkinson, "First Night at the Theatre," *New York Times,* Dec. 4, 1947, p. 42.

138 "heroic dimensions" Howard Barnes, "O'Neill Status Won by Author of 'Streetcar,'" *New York Herald-Tribune,* Dec. 14, 1947, sec. 5, p. 1.

138 "compassionate" John Chapman, "'A Streetcar Named Desire' Sets Season's High in Acting, Writing," *New York Daily News,* Dec. 4, 1947, p. 83.

138 "a drama of" George Freedley, "Williams Writes a Brilliant, Moving Play in 'Streetcar,'" *New York Morning Telegraph,* Dec. 5, 1947, p. 2.

138 "deeply disturbing" Wolcott Gibbs, *The New Yorker* 23 (Dec. 13, 1947): 50.
139 "I write out" Davis, p. 14.
139 "I draw all" Whitmore, p. 322.
139 "Blanche DuBois" Ciment, p. 71.
139 "Kazan has always" David Susskind's MetroMedia network program *Open End,* Nov. 13, 1960.
140 "Tennessee liked Pancho" Elia Kazan to DS, Feb. 1, 1984.

Chapter Five

146 "His trip recalled" Paul Bigelow to DS, Feb. 3, 1984.
146 "In 1946" Vidal, p. 130.
146 "a bohemian annexe" Acton, p. 213.
147 "indifference to place" Vidal, p. 132.
149-150 "I came along" *Ibid.,* p. 143.
150-151 "I got tired" Paul Bigelow to DS, Feb. 3, 1984.
151 "a pretentious and" Howard Barnes, *New York Herald-Tribune,* Oct. 7, 1948, p. 16.
151 "a juvenile and" John Chapman, *New York Daily News,* Oct. 7, 1948, p. 81.
151 "almost unendurably" Wolcott Gibbs, *The New Yorker* 24 (Oct. 16, 1948): 51-52.
151 "the weaknesses" John Gassner, *Forum* 110 (Dec. 1948): 351-353.
151 "It's tremulous with" Brooks Atkinson, *New York Times,* Oct. 17, 1948, p. 33. See also the *Times* for Oct. 17, 1948, sec. 2, p. 1.
153 "Frank was" Dakin Williams to DS, Oct. 23, 1983.
153 "We were all" Paul Bigelow to DS, Feb. 3, 1984.
153 "Everyone who ever" Christopher Isherwood to DS, Oct. 20, 1983.
154 "In appearance" Jane Bowles, *Feminine Wiles* (Santa Barbara: Black Sparrow Press, 1976), pp. 7-8.
158 "I found him" Irving Rapper to DS, Aug. 11, 1983.
159 "By the time" *Ibid.*
160 "They stayed" Paul Bigelow to DS, Feb. 3, 1984.
163-164 "very detrimental remarks" Cornelius Wiliams to Audrey Wood, Feb. 8, 1950.
164 "Apart from Rose" David Greggory to DS, Aug. 12, 1983.
166 "I had been" Cheryl Crawford to DS, Jan. 18, 1984.
167 "first fictionalized" Windham, p. 262.
168 "Magnani first said" Cheryl Crawford to DS, Jan. 18, 1984.
168 "Tenn had written" Maureen Stapleton to DS, Jan. 16, 1984.
168-169 "something of a" John Pearson, *The Sitwells: A Family's Biography* (New York: Harcourt Brace Jovanovich, 1978), p. 401.
169 "We were performing" Maureen Stapleton to DS, Jan. 16, 1984.
169 "Tennessee was counting" Windham (a), pp. 59-60.
170 "Frankie gave his" Johnny Nicholson to DS, Mar. 2, 1984.
170 "Frank Merlo was" Maureen Stapleton to DS, Jan. 16, 1984.
170-171 *"The Rose Tattoo* is" "The Meaning of *The Rose Tattoo,*" *Vogue* 117 (Mar. 15, 1951): 96.
171 "He was quite" Cheryl Crawford to DS, Jan. 18, 1984.

171 "He was a" Maureen Stapleton to DS, Jan. 16, 1985.

172 "I made several" Cheryl Crawford to DS, Jan. 18, 1984.

172 "He found her" Johnny Nicholson to DS, Mar. 2, 1984.

173 "I spent several" Cheryl Crawford to DS, Jan. 18, 1984.

173 "Kiss me" quoted by Johnny Nicholson to DS, Mar. 2, 1984.

173 "praying for" Johnny Nicholson to DS, Mar. 2, 1984.

174 "He loved the" *Ibid.*

177 "When I saw" David Greggory to DS, Aug. 12, 1983.

177–178 "We were looking" Theodore Mann to DS, Aug. 3, 1983.

178 "When we finished" Geraldine Page at a seminar at the New School for Social Research, New York, Dec. 6, 1982.

179 "Merlo was a" Galligan, p. 46.

179 "Nothing has happened" Brooks Atkinson, "At the Theatre," *New York Times,* Apr. 25, 1952, p. 19. See also the *Times,* May 4, 1952, sec. 2, p. 1.

179 "Everything in his" Elia Kazan to DS, Feb. 1, 1984.

179–180 "I think the" *Saturday Review of Literature,* Apr. 29, 1972, p. 27. See also Jennings, p. 72.

180–181 "I met him" Quintero (b), p. 4.

181 "a talented" "Five Fiery Ladies," *Life* 50 (Feb. 3, 1961): 88.

Chapter Six

185 "my conception of" "Foreword to Camino Real," *Where I Live: Selected Essays,* p. 63.

185 "He was" Elia Kazan to DS, Feb. 1, 1984.

186 "Honey, you don't" Barbara Baxley to DS, Aug. 31, 1983.

186 "I was also" Quintero (b), p. 4.

186–187 "Frankie was" Barbara Baxley to DS, Aug. 31, 1983.

187 "Walter Winchell" *Ibid.*

188 "the worst play" Walter Kerr, "Camino Real," *New York Herald-Tribune,* Mar. 20, 1953, p. 12.

188 "but that people" Walter Kerr, in a letter to TW dated Apr. 13, 1953.

188 "It doesn't have" Elia Kazan to DS, Feb. 1, 1984.

189 "He wanted to" Paul Bigelow to DS, Feb. 3, 1984.

190 "I wouldn't be" *New York Post* magazine, Dec. 12, 1947, p. 1.

192 "But the real" Thomas Griffin to DS, Dec. 16, 1983.

192 "courageous and fearful" Crawford, p. 184.

193 "although illegal" Margaret Foresman to DS, Nov. 14, 1983.

196 "Audrey may well" Robert Anderson to DS, Dec. 14, 1983.

197 "I do think" Elia Kazan to DS, Feb. 1, 1984.

197 "Tennessee was very" Maureen Stapleton to DS, Jan. 16, 1984.

198 "My father had" In Harry Rasky's film *Tennessee Williams's South.*

198 "Tennessee told me" Burl Ives to DS, Aug. 26, 1983.

198 "Williams was a dreamer" Mildred Dunnock to DS, Aug. 24, 1983.

198 "Ben Gazzara and I" Burl Ives to DS, Aug. 26, 1983.

199 "I think Maggie" Elia Kazan to DS, Feb. 1, 1984.

199 "Maggie was the" Davis, p. 13.

199 "Kazan didn't want" Mildred Dunnock to DS, Aug. 24, 1983.
199 "The bird that" *Cat on a Hot Tin Roof*, in *The Theatre of Tennessee Williams*, vol. 3, p. 114.
200 "He left two" Paul Bigelow to DS, Feb. 3, 1984.
200 "The postwar theatre" Robert Anderson to DS, Dec. 14, 1983.
202 "She had all" *Paris Review*, p. 181.
202-203 "Then I began" Ciment, p. 74.
203 "Tenn is licking" Campbell, pp. 31-32.
203 "a sad, lost" Paul Bigelow to DS, Feb. 3, 1984.
203 "I don't know" Vidal, p. 140.
203-204 "He would allow" Jane Smith to DS, June 13, 1984.
204 "After the show" Campbell, p. 32.
204 "He had a dread" Ciment, p. 75.
205 "I found Tennessee" George Keathley to DS, Sept. 6, 1983.
205 "and Merlo held" Leavitt, p. 93.
205 "Oh, yes" "A Separate Poem," *In the Winter of Cities*, pp. 126-129.
206 "During rehearsals" George Keathley to DS, Sept. 6, 1983.
206 "work in progress" *New York Times*, Apr. 17, 1956, p. 27.
206 "She was a nonstop" George Keathley to DS, Sept. 6, 1983.
207 "Curtain rises" quoted by Meade Roberts to DS, June 3, 1983.
207 "Of course" *Time* (anniversary edition), Oct. 5, 1983, pp. 159-160.
207 "The Williamses have" Campbell, p. 15.
208 "I had heard" Maureen Stapleton to DS, Jan. 16, 1984.
209 "Although Mr. Williams" Brooks Atkinson, "Theatre: Early Williams," *New York Times*, Nov. 22, 1956, p. 50.
209 "Tennessee Williams's finest" John Chapman, "*Glass Menagerie* is Still Aglow," *New York Daily News*, Nov. 23, 1956, p. 60.
210 "revolting . . . a contemptuous" *New York Herald-Tribune*, Dec. 17, 1956, pp. 1, 15; *Newsweek* 48 (Dec. 31, 1956): 59.
210 "I disagree that" Elia Kazan in the *New York Times*, Dec. 17, 1956, p. 28.
210 "I can't believe" *New York Times*, Dec. 17, 1956, p. 28.
210n "possibly the dirtiest" *Time* 68 (Dec. 25, 1956): 61.
211 "There is a" Elia Kazan to DS, Feb. 1, 1984.
211 "I am increasingly" Davis, p. 14.
211 "I am an" Rose (a), sec. 4, pp. 1-2.
212 "a fallible minor" Harold Clurman, in *The Nation* 176 (Apr. 4, 1953), pp. 293-294.
212 "Tenn and Clurman" Maureen Stapleton to DS, Jan. 16, 1984.
212-213 "My writing has" Ross (b), sec. 4, pp. 1, 7.
213 "The people in it" Wolcott Gibbs, "Well, Descending, Anyway," *The New Yorker* 33 (Mar. 30, 1957), pp. 85-86.
213-214 "He always told" Paul Bigelow to DS, Feb. 3, 1984.
214 "and cut him out" "The Man in the Overstuffed Chair," *Antaeus* 45/46 (Spring-Summer 1982): 289.
214 "I have changed" Rice, May 4, 1958, p. M-2.
214 "In retrospect" Brown, p. 176.
215 "Aunt Ella" "The Man in the Overstuffed Chair," 291.

215 "Tenn became" Maureen Stapleton to DS, Jan. 16, 1984.
216 "At this point" Paul Bigelow to DS, Feb. 3, 1984.
216 "Tom, I know" Quoted by Lilla van Saher to Meade Roberts; Roberts to DS, June 3, 1983.

Chapter Seven

219 "I think if" Ross (b), sec. 4, p. 1.
219 "Sophocles, Euripides" Harold Clurman, "Theatre," *The Nation* 86 (Jan. 25, 1958): 87.
220 "Why don't you" Quoted by Anne Meacham to DS, Feb. 4, 1984.
221 "Tennessee was absolutely" Anne Meacham to DS, Feb. 4, 1984.
223 "The remarkable aspect" Robert Anderson to DS, Dec. 14, 1983.
223 "He was devoted" Vassilis Voglis to DS, Sept. 22, 1983.
223-224 *Suddenly Last Summer"* Joseph L. Mankiewicz to DS, Feb. 24, 1984.
224 "ordinary words" Brooks Atkinson, *New York Times,* Jan. 9, 1958, sec. 2, p. 1.
224 "a serious and" Walter Kerr, *New York Herald-Tribune,* Jan. 8, 1958, p. 16.
224-225 "Audrey, it is" Quoted by Meade Roberts to DS, June 3, 1983.
225 "Bill's problem" *Memoirs,* p. 165.
225-226 "Williams was very" Meade Roberts to DS, June 3, 1983.
226 "it has poisoned" Rice, May 2, 1958, p. M-2.
226-228 "Tennessee doesn't believe" Quoted by Meade Roberts to DS, Apr. 15, 1983.
229 "couldn't stop telling" Barbara Baxley to DS, Sept. 1, 1983.
229 "The relationship between" Joseph L. Mankiewicz to DS, Feb. 24, 1984.
230 "But he was always" Elia Kazan to DS, Feb. 1, 1984.
230 "Kazan was a" Geraldine Page, at a seminar at the New School for Social Research, New York, Dec. 6, 1982.
230 "acrid" Brooks Atkinson, "The Theatre: Portrait of Corruption," *New York Times,* Mar. 11, 1959, p. 39.
230 "disturbingly bad" Robert Brustein, "Sweet Bird of Success," *Encounter* 12 (June 1959): 59-60. See also Brustein, "Williams' Nebulous Nightmare," *Hudson Review* 12 (Summer 1959): 255-260.
230 "become immobilized" Harold Clurman in *The Nation* 188 (Mar. 28, 1959): 281-283.
230 "dirty minded" John Chapman, *New York Daily News,* Mar. 11, 1959, p. 65.
230 "very close" *Time* 73 (Mar. 23, 1959): 58.
231 "but [was] not" Walter Kerr, in *New York Herald-Tribune,* May 17, 1959, sec. 4, p. 2.
231 "dismayed and alarmed" Kenneth Tynan, in *The New Yorker* 35 (Mar. 21, 1959): 98-100.
231 "a sensational expression" Gassner, pp. 228-231.
232 "Williams now seems" Popkin, p. 64.
232 "He was wretchedly" Elia Kazan to DS, Feb. 1, 1984.
232 "He told me" Meade Roberts to DS, July 29, 1983.
233 "I was in" *Ibid.*
234 "An odd situation" Meade Roberts to DS, Apr. 15, 1983.
234 "There we were" Maureen Stapleton to DS, Jan. 16, 1984.

235 "If artists are" Introd. to Carson McCullers, *Reflections in a Golden Eye* (New York: Bantam, 1950), pp. x–xi, ix.

235 "He created" Meade Roberts to DS, Mar. 15, 1983.

237 "Poor, sad Diana" Paul Bigelow to DS, Feb. 3, 1983.

237 "one of the oddest" George Keathley to DS, Sept. 6, 1983.

237 "She had become" Dakin Williams to DS, Oct. 23, 1983.

237 "She had a" Joyce Croft Williams to DS, Oct. 23, 1983.

238 "I am poisoned" Michelfelder, p. 17.

238 "The production of" Meade Roberts to DS, June 3, 1983.

239 "He was totally" Frank Corsaro to DS, Oct. 30, 1983.

239–240 "Frank [Merlo] was" *Ibid.*

240 "We [playwrights]" *New York Times Magazine*, June 12, 1960, p. 78.

241 "After *Sweet Bird*" Elia Kazan to DS, Feb. 1, 1984.

241 "Well, I don't" Jennings, p. 81.

242 "The years in" Paul Bigelow to DS, Feb. 3, 1984.

242–243 "I have an" Stang, sec. 2, pp. 1, 3.

243 "The real problem" Cheryl Crawford to DS, Jan. 18, 1984.

244 "After *Period*" *Ibid.*

244 "He was unsure" Jane Smith to DS, June 13, 1984.

245 "We sat together" Windham (b), p. 311.

245 "mother-image" TW, "The Agent as Catalyst," *Esquire* 58 (Dec. 1962): 216, 260.

246 "That's the only" Funke (b), pp. 72–73.

246 "My kind of" *Ibid.*

246 "It was a" Frank Corsaro to DS, Oct. 30, 1983.

246–247 "I create imaginary" Funke (b), p. 73.

247 "As if it" Frank Corsaro to DS, Oct. 30, 1983.

247–248 "I was shocked" Maureen Stapleton to DS, Jan. 16, 1984.

248 "There was Edwina" Frank Corsaro to DS, Oct. 30, 1983.

248 "the wisest play" *Time* 79 (Jan. 5, 1962): 53.

249–250 "He was one" Paul Bigelow to DS, Feb. 3, 1984.

250 "His theme" Miller, p. 30.

250 *"The Night of"* *Time* 79 (Mar. 9, 1962): 53.

250 "She simply *was*" Lucy Freeman to DS, Sept. 1, 1983

Chapter Eight

255 "There were a few" David Greggory to DS, Aug. 12, 1983.

255 "Tenn behaved" Paul Bigelow to DS, Feb. 3, 1984

256 "When he complained" Mildred Dunnock to DS, Aug. 24, 1983.

256 "The opening night" David Greggory to DS, Aug. 12, 1983.

256 "creative suicide" Richard Gilman, "Mistuh Williams, He Dead," *Commonweal* 77 (Feb. 8, 1963): 515–517.

257 "He just didn't" Maureen Stapleton to DS, Jan. 16, 1984.

257 "As Frank became" Meade Roberts to DS, June 3, 1983.

257 "It was so" Frank Corsaro to DS, Oct. 30, 1983.

257–258 "They took me" Barbara Baxley to DS, Sept. 1, 1983.

258 "I think Tenn" Paul Bigelow to DS, Feb. 3, 1984.

258 "Tennessee Williams came" Sheldon Posnock to DS, Feb. 23, 1984.

258 "Frankie had an" *People,* May 26, 1975, p. 37.

258-259 "The breakup with" Cheryl Crawford to DS, Jan. 18, 1984.

260 "I draw every" Calendo, p. 28.

261 "When he died" Hirshhorn, p. 22.

262 "I like" Margaret Laing, "T. L. Williams — All Play, Some Work," *Los Angeles Times,* Apr. 11, 1965.

262 "I had suffered" Taped interview with Stephen Banker in the *Tapes for Readers* series, 1974. *Cf.* also Kakutani, p. C17.

262 "He'd been a" *Paris Review,* p. 166.

262 "Nembutal, Doriden" Bosworth, p. 330.

263 "I have a sort" Laing.

263 "I now rely" Hirshhorn, p. 22.

263-264 "I can't bear" *Ibid.*

264 "He never saw" Bill Glavin to DS, Feb. 12, 1984.

264n "I'm a built-in" Hirshhorn, p. 22.

264 "Bigelow is on" David Greggory to DS, Aug. 12, 1983.

264 "By this time" Maureen Stapleton to DS, Jan. 16, 1984.

264 "I don't remember" Bill Glavin to DS, Feb. 12, 1984.

265 "incomprehensible evil" Wagner, p. 42.

265 "I don't suppose" *Ibid.,* p. 15.

265 "He laughed so" Bill Glavin to DS, Feb. 12, 1984.

265 "I must continue" Quoted by Lester Persky to DS, Feb. 12, 1983.

266n "Well, Tom" Quoted by Bill Glavin to DS, Feb. 12, 1984.

266 "Mr. Williams" Whitney Bolton, *New York Morning Telegraph,* Feb. 24, 1966, p. 3.

266 "When critics accused" Robert Anderson to DS, Dec. 14, 1983.

267 "I wanted to make" Joseph Losey to DS, Jan. 25, 1984.

267 "When he lost" Vassilis Voglis to DS, Sept. 22, 1983.

269 "No, Bill" Wood, p. 196.

270 "I visited him" Elia Kazan to DS, Feb. 1, 1984.

270 "Swimming, drinking" Joseph Losey to DS, Jan. 25, 1984.

271 "totally addicted" Wood, p. 192.

271 "very nervous" Quintero (a), p. 4.

272 "The cast came" David Greggory to DS, Aug. 12, 1983.

272 "Dear Dakin" Schumach, p. 19.

274 "I was writing" Christiansen (a), p. 41.

275 "My conversion was" *Paris Review,* p. 155.

275 "This is how" Rev. Joseph LeRoy, S.J. to DS, July 16, 1983.

275 "I loved the" *Paris Review,* p. 156.

276 "It had concerned" Margaret Foresman to DS, Nov. 12, 1983.

276 "It was" Rev. Joseph LeRoy, S. J. to DS, July 16, 1983.

277 "It was a birthday" Maureen Stapleton to DS, Jan. 16, 1984.

277 "He stumbled" Anne Meacham to DS, Feb. 4, 1984.

277 "and if he could" Bill Glavin to DS, Feb. 12, 1984.

277 "One must never" *Time* 93 (May 23, 1969), p. 75.

277 "I hope that" Harold Clurman, in *The Nation* 208 (June 2, 1969), p. 709.

278 "almost too personal" Clive Barnes, *New York Times,* May 12, 1969, p. 54.

278 "that he will" Richard Watts, Jr., *The New York Post,* May 31, 1969, p. 17.

278 "hasn't the comfort" TW, in a letter to the cast of *In the Bar of a Tokyo Motel,* in Leavitt, p. 146.

278 "I think I'm" Proceedings of the *National Institute of Arts and Letters and the American Academy of Arts and Letters,* second series, no. 20 (1970), pp. 27–28.

279 "He was not" Larry D. Clark to DS, Oct. 21, 1983.

279 "Poor Tom" Bill Glavin to DS, Feb. 12, 1984.

279 "You know" Quoted by Glavin to DS.

279–280 "Tennessee Williams appears" Stefan Kanfer, "White Dwarf's Tragic Fade-out," *Life* 66 (June 13, 1969), p. 10.,

280 "We arrived in" Anne Meacham to DS, Feb. 5, 1984.

282 "Rose never took" Bill Glavin to DS, Feb. 12, 1984.

282–283 "I was ready" Margaret Foresman to DS, Nov. 12, 1983.

283 "he fell" *Ibid.*

283 "I was so demented" Jennings, p. 78.

284 "It's true" Elia Kazan to DS, Feb. 1, 1984.

284–285 "Tennessee could never" Maureen Stapleton to DS, Jan. 16, 1984.

285 "He looked better" Rev. Joseph Leroy, S.J. to DS, July 1983.

Chapter Nine

289 "Never recaptured" Louis Auchincloss, "TW: The Last Puritan," *DLB,* p. 410.

290 "I hope I" Funke (a), p. 45.

291 "The young men" David Greggory to DS, Aug. 12, 1983.

292 "I don't want" TW, *The David Frost Show,* Jan. 21, 1970.

292 "I work so hard" Quoted by David Greggory to DS, Aug. 12, 1983.

293 "The crowd there" Edwin Sherin to DS, Sept. 17, 1983.

293 "He took care" Rev. Joseph LeRoy, S.J. to DS, July 16, 1983.

295 "because [Mishima]" *Memoirs,* p. 236.

295 "I knew it" George Keathley to DS, Sept. 6, 1983.

296 "Audrey wanted" Anne Meacham to DS, Feb. 4, 1984.

296–297 "You must have" *Memoirs,* p. 228.

297 "swiveled about" Wood, p. 200.

297 "We were all" George Keathley to DS, Sept. 6, 1983.

297 "This was another" Cheryl Crawford to DS, Jan. 18, 1984.

297–298 "Audrey was" Robert Anderson to DS, Dec. 14, 1983.

298 "I want my name" Quoted by Bill Barnes to DS, Nov. 4, 1983.

298 "a very sad" Ray Stricklyn, "Memories of Tennessee," *Drama-Logue,* June 9–15, 1983.

299 "remnant of life" *The Theatre of Tennessee Williams,* vol. 5, p. 228.

300 "inviting disaster" *Ibid.,* pp. 291–292.

300 "In spite of a" Alfred Ryder to DS, Apr. 17, 1984.

300 "Tennessee was very gracious" Olive Deering to DS, Apr. 17, 1984.

301 "He liked people" Paul Morrissey to DS, Sept. 20, 1983.

302–303 "my inspiration" Quoted by Paul Morrissey to DS, Sept. 20, 1983.

303 "I need to" Jennings, p. 74.

303 "He had a sometimes" Paul Morrissey to DS, Sept. 20, 1983.

303 "I've had a" Eugene B. Griesman, "Williams: A Rebellious Puritan," *Chicago Sun-Times*, Mar. 27, 1983, p. 4.

303 "This is me" Quoted by Bill Barnes to DS, Nov. 4, 1983.

303 "must not only" *The Theatre of Tennessee Williams*, vol. 5, pp. 308–309.

304 "I consider myself" Patrick O'Haire, "Tennessee's Dream," *New York Daily News*, June 3, 1975, p. 43.

305 "His companion called" David Greggory to DS, Aug. 12, 1983.

305 "a number of" Maureen Stapleton to DS, Jan. 16, 1984.

306 "Near the end" Barbara Baxley to DS, Sept. 1, 1983.

306 "Don't you think" Quoted by Barbara Baxley to DS, Sept. 1, 1983.

306 "he was not" Choukri, unpaged introd.

306 "I take Nembutal" *Ibid.*, p. 38.

309 "The entire time" Harry Rasky, *Nobody Swings on Sunday* (Don Mills, Ontario: Collier Macmillan, 1980), p. 211.

309 "I never defined" Harry Rasky's film *Tennessee Williams' South*.

309 "I love to" Jennings, p. 84.

309 "My obligation is" Encyclopedia Britannica film, *Theatre in Process*.

310 "In Key West" Edwin Sherin to DS, Sept. 17, 1983.

310 "This country has" *New York Times*, May 6, 1975, p. 48.

312 "Dreadful" Kevin Kelly, "New Williams Play Opens," *Boston Globe*, June 19, 1975, p. 25.

312 "unfocused" Elliot Norton, "Tennessee Williams's New 'Red Devil' Here," *Boston Herald American*, June 19, 1975, p. 14.

312 "Part of what" David Greggory to DS, Aug. 12, 1983.

313 "By this time" Maureen Stapleton to DS, Jan. 16, 1984.

313 "Tennessee came" Theodore Mann to DS, Oct. 3, 1983.

313 "There was a lot" Gene Persson to DS, Sept. 17, 1983.

314 "During rehearsals" *Ibid.*

315 "a sadly" Stanley Eichelbaum, *San Francisco Examiner*, Jan. 21, 1976; reprinted in *New York Times*, Jan. 25, 1976, sec. 2, p. 5.

315 "terribly depressing" *Variety*, Feb. 4, 1976.

315 "He is such" Ruby Cohn, *Educational Theatre Journal* 28 (Oct. 1976): 406–407.

315 "At my age" Robert Hayes and Christopher Makos, "Tennessee Sings for Madame Sophia," *Interview*, vol. 6, no. 6 (June 1976), p. 20.

316 "Turning out" "Turning out the Bedside Lamp," *Androgyne, Mon Amour*, p. 88.

316 "Tennessee knew so" Galligan, p. 45.

316–317 "My first assignment" Dan Turner, "A Tennessee Waltz," *The Advocate* 376 (Sept. 15, 1983), p. 47.

317 "We simply couldn't" Chuck Ingebritsen to DS, Sept. 2, 1983.

318–319 "At our first" Gloria Hope Sher to DS, Sept. 26, 1983.

319 "We met at" George Whitmore to DS, Sept. 16, 1983.

319 "People so wish" Whitmore, pp. 319, 320, 315.

319 "a great deal" *Ibid.*, p. 313.

320 "Tennessee kept saying" Gene Persson to DS, Sept. 17, 1983.

320 "He made extensive" Theodore Mann to DS, Oct. 3, 1983.

320 "He was staggering" Gene Persson to DS, Sept. 17, 1983.

Chapter Ten

323 "He seemed" Gene Persson to DS, Sept. 17, 1983.

324 *"Garden District* is" Arthur Alan Seidelman, "Tennessee Williams: Author and Director Discuss *Vieux Carré," Interview,* vol. 7, no. 4 (April 1977), p. 14.

324–325 "When I first" Sylvia Sidney to DS, July 30, 1983.

325 "individually attacked" Richard Alfieri, "Tennessee Williams: A Remembrance," *Mandate,* Sept. 1983, p. 38.

325 "hard-to-hear" Klemsrud, p. 51.

325 "very nervous" Richard Alfieri to DS, Oct. 7, 1983.

325 "He was so" Bill Barnes to DS, Nov. 4, 1983.

326 "I don't think" Bernard Carragher, "Born-Again Playwright: Tennessee," *New York Sunday News,* May 8, 1977, pp. L3 and L14.

326 "The day after" Sylvia Sidney to DS, July 30, 1983.

326 "Tennessee Williams's voice" Walter Kerr, "A Touch of the Poet Isn't Enough to Sustain Williams's Latest Play," *New York Times,* May 22, 1977, sec. 2, p. D5.

327 "But Tennessee put" Gene Persson to DS, Sept. 17, 1983.

328 "I have been" Blais.

329 "He was bright" Elliot Martin to DS, Oct. 19, 1983.

330 "Tennessee was cool" Craig Anderson to DS, Sept. 14, 1983.

330 "a fairly fragile" Elena Azuola to DS, Sept. 14, 1983.

330 "the pills and" Craig Anderson to DS, Sept. 14, 1983.

330 "He became something" *Ibid.*

331 "He made us feel" Elliot Martin to DS, Oct. 19, 1983.

331 "After the unfortunate" Craig Anderson to DS, Sept. 14, 1983.

331 "We spent a" Sylvia Miles to DS, Aug. 23, 1983.

332 "He seemed more" Elena Azuola to DS, Sept. 14, 1983.

332 "He was very" Craig Anderson to DS, Sept. 14, 1983.

332 "He hated the" Vassilis Voglis to DS, Sept. 22, 1983.

333 "I helped him" Jay Leo Colt to DS, Nov. 8, 1983.

333 "The real trouble" Mitch Douglas to DS, Oct. 11, 1983.

333 "As the rehearsals" Craig Anderson to DS, Sept. 14, 1983.

335 "Fontis was a" Blais.

335 "Maybe they weren't" *Ibid.*

335 "I suspect I'll" *People,* May 7, 1979, p. 34.

335 "he became very" Gloria Hope Sher to DS, Sept. 26, 1983.

336 "Unfortunately" Mitch Douglas to DS, Oct. 11, 1983.

337–338 "Mitch cared deeply" Eve Adamson to DS, Oct. 3, 1983.

338 "Tennessee had great faith" Mitch Douglas to DS, Oct. 11, 1983.

338 "He revised it" Eve Adamson to DS, Oct. 3, 1983.

338 "trying to shock" Mitch Douglas to DS, Oct. 11, 1983.

338–339 "We designed it" Eve Adamson to DS, Oct. 3, 1983.

339n "Call it" Hornack, p. 33.

339 "Tennessee just backed" Elliot Martin to DS, Oct. 19, 1983.

340 "chuckling wickedly" Frazer, p. 32.

340 "the worst case" Quoted in Frazer, p. 34.

340 "his paranoia" Frazer, p. 37.

340 "One comes out" Elia Kazan at the John F. Kennedy Center, Dec. 2, 1979.

341 "He was absolutely" Eve Adamson to DS, Oct. 3, 1983.

341 "very, very painful" Quintero (b), p. 5.

341 "We got to" Elliot Martin to DS, Nov. 2, 1983.

341-342 "Williams refused" Stephen Silverman, in a letter to DS, Nov. 25, 1983.

342 "He came to" William Seeker to DS, Nov. 11, 1983.

344 "He seemed in" Elliot Martin to DS, Nov. 2, 1983.

344 "The morning after" Galligan, p. 46.

344 "We discussed" Elliot Martin to DS, Nov. 2, 1983.

345 "That's so silly" Blum, p. 29.

345 "It's not about" Elliot Martin to DS, Nov. 2, 1983.

345 "At one point" Weatherby, p. 38.

346 "Tennessee was a" Vassilis Voglis to DS, Sept. 22, 1983.

346 "I was spending" Mitch Douglas to DS, Oct. 11, 1983.

346 "I can stand" Quoted by Lucy Freeman, Sept. 1, 1983.

346-347 "I cannot feel" Blais. See also *New York Post,* Dec. 3, 1976, p. 31.

347 "I think there" Maureen Stapleton to DS, Jan. 16, 1984.

347 "When he wanted" Mitch Douglas to DS, Oct. 11, 1983.

347 "They gave me" Giuseppe Di Bernardo (tran. DS), "Desiderio a Taormina," *La Sicilia,* July 9, 1980.

347-348 "Gary introduced me" Gregory Mosher to DS, Oct. 10, 1983.

348 "He was staying" *Ibid.*

348-349 "By this time" Mitch Douglas to DS, Oct. 11, 1983.

350-351 "After Tennessee emerged" Gregory Mosher to DS, Oct. 10, 1983.

351 "It was haid" Bonnie Sue Arp to DS, Oct. 28, 1983.

351 "a blessed man" Marji Bank to DS, Oct. 28, 1983.

351 "When [Gary] Tucker" Scott Jaeck to DS, Oct. 28, 1983.

351 "He became enamored" Rachel Stephens to DS, Oct. 28, 1983.

351 "and he never" Les Podewell to DS, Oct. 28, 1983.

352 "From what we" Scott Jaeck to DS, Oct. 28, 1983.

352 "His mood changed" Gregory Mosher to DS, Oct. 10, 1983.

352 "Chicago was the" At the Goodman Theatre, March 1981.

352-353 "There was a short" Mitch Douglas to DS, Oct. 11, 1983.

353 "I was a" Wood, p. 325.

354 "one of the most" Kakutani, p. C17.

355 "Tennessee was so" Eve Adamson to DS, Oct. 3, 1983.

355-356 "I saw Tennessee" Meade Roberts to DS, July 1, 1984.

356 "I'll have to think" *New York Times,* Nov. 20, 1981, p. 84.

356 "Harold, take care" Quoted by Larry D. Clark to DS, Oct. 21, 1983.

356 "He behaved very" Eve Adamson to DS, Oct. 3, 1984.

356-357 "The last time" Mitch Douglas to DS, Oct. 11, 1983.

357 "He was extremely" Vassilis Voglis to DS, Sept. 22, 1983.

357 "In Paradise" Quoted by Lester Persky to DS, Oct. 20, 1983.

358 "afflicted with" Christiansen (b), p. 6.

358 "Tennessee confronted" Elia Kazan to DS, Feb. 1, 1984.

359 "There was a strong" Scott Jaeck to DS, Oct. 28, 1983.

359 "inhabited by a rich" *Time,* June 28, 1982, p. 69.

359 "Give my goodbye" Hughes, p. 232.

360 "All the volcanoes" Andrews, p. 12.

360 "gentle and quiet" Carlo Panarello to DS, Dec. 30, 1983.

360–361 "He found traveling" Jane Smith to DS, June 13, 1984.

361 "He had bought" Gregory Mosher to DS, Oct. 10, 1983.

361–362 "As we were having" Steven Kunes, in letters to DS, Nov. 17, 1983 and Jan. 18, 1984.

362 "His speech was" Richard L. Kennedy, in a letter to DS, Mar. 12, 1984.

362–363 "When he came out" Jane Smith to DS, June 13, 1984.

363 "She called" Dakin Williams to DS, Oct. 23, 1983.

364 "It's too late" Quoted by Jane Smith to DS, June 13, 1984.

364 "He was so sad" Antonio Savoca to DS, Dec. 30, 1983.

364 "a cold wind" Quoted by Bill Barnes to DS, Nov. 4, 1983.

364 "I don't want" Gaines, p. 28.

364 "But I go mad" Jennings, p. 74.

364 "Old men go mad" *Androgyne, Mon Amour,* pp. 9–10.

Selective Bibliography

EACH of the following entries is preceded by the abbreviated form used in the Notes. Many sources, particularly newspaper and magazine articles, are not listed below but are cited only in the Notes.

Acton. Acton, Harold. *Memoirs of an Aesthete 1939–1969,* vol. 2. New York: Viking, 1970.

Andrews. Andrews, Nigel. "The Key to Tennessee," *Financial Times* (London), Aug. 7, 1982.

Barnett. Barnett, Lincoln. "Tennessee Williams," *Life,* Feb. 16, 1948; reprinted in Lincoln Barnett, *Writings on Life: Sixteen Close-Ups.* New York: William Sloane, 1951.

Bentley (a). Bentley, Eric. *The Dramatic Event: An American Chronicle.* New York: Horizon, 1954.

Bentley (b). ———. *In Search of Theatre.* New York: Knopf, 1953.

Berkvist. Berkvist, Robert. "Broadway Discovers Tennessee Williams," *New York Times,* Dec. 21, 1975.

Blais. Blais, Madeleine H. "Tennessee Williams Gracefully Survives, in Violent Key West," *Chicago Tribune,* Apr. 9, 1979.

Blum. Blum, David J. "The Art and Anger of Tennessee Williams," *Wall Street Journal,* Nov. 21, 1980.

Bosworth. Bosworth, Patricia. *Montgomery Clift.* New York: Harcourt Brace Jovanovich, 1978.

Brown. Brown, Cecil. "Interview with Tennessee Williams," *Partisan Review,* 45 (1978).

Buckley. Buckley, Tom. "Tennessee Williams Survives," *Atlantic* 226 (Nov. 1970).

Calendo. Calendo, John. "Tennessee Talks to John Calendo," *Interview,* April 1973.

Campbell. Campbell, Sandy. *Twenty-nine Letters from Coconut Grove.* Verona: Stamperia Valdonega, 1974.

Carr. Carr, Virginia Spenser. *The Lonely Hunter: A Biography of Carson McCullers.* New York: Doubleday, 1975.

Choukri. Choukri, Mohamed. *Tennessee Williams in Tangier.* Santa Barbara: Cadmus Editions, 1979.

Christiansen (a). Christiansen, Richard. "At 70, Even Tennessee Williams is Impressed," *New York Daily News,* Apr. 23, 1981.

Christiansen (b). ———. "The Pain, Risk and Tumult of Staging Williams' New Play," *Chicago Tribune Arts and Books,* May 29, 1982.

Ciment. Ciment, Michel. *Kazan on Kazan.* London: Secker & Warburg, 1973.

Cogley. Cogley, John. "More on 'Baby Doll,'" *Commonweal* 65, Feb. 1, 1957.

Cole. Cole, Toby and Helen Krich Chinoy. *Directors on Directing* (rev. ed.). Indianapolis/New York: Bobbs-Merrill, 1963.

Courtney. Courtney, Marguerite. *Laurette.* New York: Rinehart, 1955.

Crawford. Crawford, Cheryl. *One Naked Individual: My Fifty Years in the Theatre.* Indianapolis/New York: Bobbs-Merrill, 1977.

Davis. Davis, Louise. "That Baby Doll Man," *Nashville Tennessean Magazine,* Mar. 3, 1957.

DLB. Dictionary of Literary Biography: Documentary Series, 4. Detroit: Gale Research, 1984.

Donahue. Donahue, Francis. *The Dramatic World of Tennessee Williams.* New York: Frederick Ungar, 1964.

Evans. Evans, Oliver. "A Pleasant Evening with Yukio Mishima," *Esquire* 77 (May 1972).

Falk. Falk, Signi. *Tennessee Williams.* Boston: Twayne/G. K. Hall, 1978.

Frazer. Frazer, Winifred L. "A Day in the Life of Tennessee Williams," *The Tennessee Williams Review,* vol. 3, no. 2 (1982).

Funke (a). Funke, Lewis. "Williams Revival? Ask the Playwright," *New York Times,* Jan. 8, 1970.

Funke (b). ———, and John E. Booth, "Williams on Williams," *Theatre Arts* 46 (Jan. 1962).

Gaines. Gaines, Jim. "A Talk about Life and Style with Tennessee Williams," *Saturday Review of Literature,* 44 (Apr. 29, 1972)

Galligan. Galligan, David. "Director José Quintero: Recollections of a Friendship," *The Advocate,* 376 (Sept. 15, 1983).

Gassner. Gassner, John. *Theatre at the Crossroads.* New York: Holt, Rinehart & Winston, 1960.

Gelb. Gelb, Arthur. "Williams and Kazan and the Big Walkout," *New York Times,* May 1, 1960.

Goodman. Goodman, L. S. and A. Gilman. *The Pharmacological Basis of Therapeutics.* New York: Macmillan, 1975.

Hewes. Hewes, Henry. "Broadway Postscript," *Saturday Review,* 35 (June 21, 1952).

Hirshhorn. Hirshhorn, Clive. "When I'm Alone It's Just Hell," *London Sunday Express,* Mar. 28, 1965.

Hornak. Hornak, Richard Wray. Review of *Kirche, Kutchen und Kinder, The Tennessee Williams Newsletter,* vol. 2, no. 1 (Spring 1980).

Hughes. Hughes, Catherine. "Tennessee Williams, Remembered." *America,* Mar. 26, 1983.

Ingersoll. Ingersoll, Louise. *Lanier: A Geneology of the family who came to Virginia and their French ancestors in London.* Springfield, Va.: Goetz Printing Co., 1981.

Isherwood. Isherwood, Christopher. *My Guru and His Disciple.* New York: Farrar, Straus & Giroux, 1980.

Jennings. Jennings, C. Robert. *"Playboy* Interview: Tennessee Williams," *Playboy* 20 (April 1973).

Kakutani. Kakutani, Michiko. "Tennessee Williams: 'I Keep Writing. Sometimes I Am Pleased,'" *New York Times,* Aug. 13, 1981.

Keith. Keith, Don Lee. "New Tennessee Williams Rises from 'Stoned Age,'" *New Orleans Times-Picayune,* Oct. 18, 1970.

Klemsrud. Klemsrud, Judy. "Tennessee Williams Is a Reluctant Performer for an Audience of High School Students," *New York Times,* Mar. 13, 1977.

Langner. Langner, Lawrence. *The Magic Curtain.* New York: Dutton, 1951.

Leavitt. Leavitt, Richard, ed. *The World of Tennessee Williams.* New York: G.P. Putnam's Sons, 1978.

Lewis. Lewis, R.C. "A Playwright Named Tennessee," *New York Times Magazine,* Dec. 7, 1947.

Londré. Londré, Felicia Hardison. *Tennessee Williams.* New York: Frederick Ungar, 1979.

Maxwell. Maxwell, Gilbert. *Tennessee Williams and Freinds.* Cleveland: World, 1965.

Michelfelder. Michelfelder, William F. "Tennessee Williams, Sensitive Poet, Still Searches for Serenity," *New York World-Telegram and Sun,* Mar. 11, 1959.

Miller. Miller, Arthur. "An Eloquence and Amplitude of Feeling," *TV Guide,* Mar. 3, 1984.

Nathan. Nathan, George Jean. *The Theatre Book of the Year 1944–1945.* New York: Knopf, 1945.

Nelson. Nelson, Benjamin. *Tennessee Williams: The Man and His Work.* New York: Obolensky, 1961.

Newlove. Newlove, Donald. "A Dream of Tennessee Williams," *Esquire* 72 (November 1969).

Nicklaus. Nicklaus, Frederick. *The Man Who Bit the Sun: Poems.* New York: New Directions, 1964.

Nightingale. Nightingale, Benedict. "This 'Menagerie' Is Much Too Cozy," *New York Times,* Dec. 11, 1983.

Popkin. Popkin, Henry. "The Plays of Tennessee Williams," *Tulane Drama Review,* 4 (Mar. 1960).

Quintero (a). Quintero, José. *If You Don't Dance They Beat You.* Boston: Little, Brown, 1974.

Quintero (b). ———. "The Imprint He Left," *Performing Arts,* vol. 17, no. 8 (Aug. 1983).

Reed. Reed, Rex. "Tennessee Williams Turns Sixty," *Esquire,* 76 (Sept. 1971).

Rice. Rice, Robert. "A Man Named Tennessee." *New York Post,* Apr. 21 through May 4, 1958.

Ross (a). Ross, Don. "Williams on Art and Morals," *New York Herald-Tribune,* Mar. 3, 1957.

Ross (b). ———. "Williams on a Hot Tin Roof," *New York Herald-Tribune,* Jan. 5, 1958.

Schumach. Schumach, Murray. "Tennessee Williams Expresses Fear for Life in Note to Brother," *New York Times,* June 29, 1969.

Selznick. Selznick, Irene Mayer. *A Private View.* New York: Knopf, 1983.

Sheaffer. Sheaffer, Louis. *O'Neill: Son and Playwright.* Boston: Little, Brown, 1968.

Smith, Helen C. Smith, Helen C. "Williams's Atlanta Visit Proof 'I'm Hanging In There, Baby,'" *Atlanta Constitution,* Feb. 12, 1980.

Smith, William Jay. Smith, William Jay. *Army Brat.* New York: Penguin, 1982.

Stang. Stang, Joanne. "Williams: 20 Years After 'Glass Managerie.' " *New York Times,* Mar. 28, 1965.

Stanton. Stanton, Stephen S., ed. *Tennessee Williams: A Collection of Critical Essays.* Englewood Cliffs: Prentice-Hall, 1977.

Steen. Steen, Mike. *A Look at Tennessee Williams.* New York: Hawthorn, 1969.

Stein. Stein, Harry. "A Day in the Life: Tennessee Williams," *Esquire,* 91 (June 5, 1979).

Tharpe. Tharpe, Jac, ed. *Tennessee Williams: 13 Essays.* Jackson: University Press of Mississippi, 1980.

Tischler. Tischler, Nancy M. *Rebellious Puritan.* New York: Citadel, 1961.

Vidal. Vidal, Gore. "Selected Memories of the Glorious Bird and an Earlier Self," *Matters of Fact and Fiction (Essays 1973–1976).* New York: Vintage, 1978.

Wagner. Wagner, Walter. "Playwright as Individual: A Conversation with Tennessee Williams," *Playbill,* 3 (Mar. 1966).

Wallace. Wallace, Mike *Mike Wallace Asks: Highlights from 46 Controversial Interviews* New York: Simon & Schuster, 1958.

Washburn. Washburn, Beatrice. "Tennessee Williams," *Miami Herald,* Jan. 22, 1956.

Weatherby. Weatherby, W.J. "Scott and Zelda Relive the Jazz Age," *London Sunday Times,* Mar. 29, 1980.

Webster. Webster, Margaret. *Don't Put Your Daughter on the Stage.* New York: Knopf, 1972.

Whitmore. Whitmore, George. "Interview: Tennessee Williams," *Gay Sunshine Interviews,* vol. 1. San Francisco: Gay Sunshine Press, 1978.

Williams, Dakin. Williams, Dakin, and Shepherd Mead. *Tennessee Williams: An Intimate Biography.* New York: Arbor House, 1983.

Williams, Edwina Dakin. Williams, Edwina Dakin, as told to Lucy Freeman. *Remember Me To Tom.* New York: G.P. Putnam's Sons, 1963.

Winakor. Winakor, Bess. "Tennessee's 'Out Cry,' " *Woman's Wear Daily,* June 28, 1971.

Windham (a). Windham, Donald. *Footnote to a Friendship.* Verona: Stamperia Valdonega, 1983.

Windham (b). ———, ed. *Tennessee Williams' Letters to Donald Windham 1940–1965.* New York: Holt, Rinehart and Winston, 1977.

Wood. Wood, Audrey, with Max Wilk. *Represented by Audrey Wood.* New York: Doubleday, 1981.

Young. Young, Michael C. "The Play of Memory," *The Tennessee Williams Newsletter,* vol. 2, no. 2 (Fall 1980).

Index

Ford, Charles Henri, 168
Ford, Ruth, 101
Foresman, Margaret, 192–193, 275–276, 282–283
Fox, The (D. H. Lawrence), 100
Francis, Muriel Bultman, 123, 222, 317
Frazer, Winifred, 340
Freedley, George: on *Glass Menagerie,* 116; on *Streetcar,* 138
Freeman, Lucy, 11, 250, 346
Friedland, Louis, 45
Frost, David, 291–292
Frost, Robert, 78
Frosted Glass Coffin, The (Williams), 280, 347, 348; TW reads from, 294
Fugitive Kind (Williams play), 58, 60, 70
Fugitive Kind, The (Williams film), 228, 234, 236, 238; *Battle of Angels/Orpheus Descending* as basis of, 58n, 228; TW's work on, 226
Furies, The, 109

Galloway, Marion, 75
Galsworthy, John, *Strife,* 55
Gam, Rita, 127
Garbo, Greta, 158
Garcia Villa, José, 168
Garden District (collective title of *Suddenly Last Summer* and *Something Unspoken*), 123, 220, 324
Garfield, John: and Group Theatre, 71; and *Streetcar,* 133, 135
Garland, Judy, 248, 284
Garnett, Constance, 45
Gassner, John: TW in seminar of, 77; and Theatre Guild, 77, 78, 87; and *Battle of Angels,* 79; and *You Touched Me!,* 93; on *Summer and Smoke,* 151; on *Sweet Bird of Youth,* 231
Gazzara, Ben, in *Cat,* 198
Gentleman caller(s): of Edwina's youth, 5–6, 7; Paul Jameson as, 17; for Rose, 22, 43; in *Glass Menagerie,* 43, 113–114
Gentleman Caller, The (early title of *The Glass Menagerie*), 94, 96–97, 109
Gentleman Caller, The (unproduced screenplay), 97
Gentleman's Agreement (film), 132, 134
Gert, Valesca, 91
Ghosts (Ibsen), 37–38
Gibbs, Wolcott: on *Streetcar,* 138; on *Orpheus Descending,* 213
Gideon's Point (later titled *In Masks Outrageous and Austere*), 353, 360
Gielgud, John, directs London *Glass Menagerie,* 148, 150

Gigi (film), 227–228
Gilman, Richard, on TW's "creative suicide," 256
Gish, Lillian, 248
Glass Menagerie, The (previously titled *The Gentleman Caller*), xv, xviii, 97, 110–112, 113–117; Edwina Williams portrayed in, 42, 114, 220, 250, 347; gentleman caller of, 43, 113–114; and Rose Williams, 94, 97, 113, 114–115, 273; "Portrait of a Girl in Glass" as basis of, 96–97; and Laurette Taylor, 109–111, 112, 113, 116, 129; and Margo Jones, 110, 134; Edwina's income from, 112, 121, 214; and TW's life, 114–115, 116; critical acclaim for, 116–117; and *You Touched Me!,* 119; Nantucket performance of, 125; as McCullers model, 126; in London, 148, 150; psychological imbalance theme in, 180; revivals of, 208–209, 313; and *Orpheus Descending* reception, 212; Meacham in, 221; as major work, 236, 290; and *Milk Train* expectations, 256; twentieth-anniversary production of, 264; and TW revivals, 305; Sylvia Sidney in, 324; as *tableaux vivants,* 327; and *Stopped Rocking,* 329; and *Creve Coeur,* 334; and TW's travels, 363
Glass Menagerie, The (film), 147–148, 155–156, 158, 159–160, 161, 226
Glavin, William, 264; TW's need for, 265; on *Slapstick Tragedy* rehearsals, 265; with TW, 267, 269, 270, 277, 278, 279, 281–282, 285; and drugs, 270; illness of, 270, 280, 281; TW's public outburst at, 272; and TW's death scare, 273; and TW's falling down, 274; and TW on self-institutionalization, 274; Japan trip disadvised by, 280, 281; TW's suspicion toward, 291
Gnädiges Fräulein, The (Williams), 263, 265, 266; as *The Latter Days of a Celebrated Soubrette,* 308
Goforth! (revised version of *The Milk Train Doesn't Stop Here Anymore*), 267, 269, 270, 336
Gogh, Vincent van: TW play about, 66; as character in *Mr. Merriwether,* 343
Golden Boy (Odets), 71
Goldman, Milton, 333, 357, 359
Goldwyn, Samuel, and *Glass Menagerie,* 148
Gone With the Wind (film), 97
Goodman Theatre, Chicago: TW staged at, 347, 349, 357; TW seventieth-birthday party at, 352
Gordon, Ruth, 93, 355–356